Shoot Down

Mark A. Hewitt

BLACK ROSE writing™

First printing

ISBN: 978-1-61296-431-7

PUBLISHED BY BLACK ROSE WRITING

www.blackrosewriting.com

Printed in the United States of America

Suggested retail price $22.95

Shoot Down is printed in Adobe Caslon Pro

In memory of my brother, Paul.

ACKNOWLEDGEMENTS

Several people helped with this book. First, the indomitable Mike O'Toole; I will always be in your debt. To Shelby Stricklen; many thanks for the amazing artwork. To my wife Barbara, George Fennimore, and Rosemary Harris. Thank you. Your keen eyes and insightful comments made this a better book and me a better writer. Any errors found in Shoot Down are solely my responsibility.

Shoot Down

PROLOGUE

1200 July 15, 1995
U.S. Embassy
Algiers, Algeria

He could see it now. The lad, all of six years, raced over cobblestones toward the gate and guard shack, his pantaloons flapping with every step. One hand held secure the blue-braided *kufi* on his head, the other a cream-colored invitation envelope.

At the huge, ornate entry gate, he decelerated to a walk and stopped, wide-eyed, at the six-foot-tall, fifteen-foot-wide bronze plaque bolted to the wall. Though he couldn't read, he knew he was at the correct place—the embassy of the United States of America. It was much more beautiful and impressive than he imagined.

The U.S. Marine Corps security guard behind the two-inch bulletproof glass watched the youngster intently. He wasn't like the other kids who wandered along the stretch of road filled with embassies. This kid was clean, his clothes white and bright, and his sandals and dark-blue *kufi* were of high quality, maybe even new.

Security cameras recorded the boy's walk to the guard shack, holding high the envelope with both hands. The Marine pushed the lever to send the heavy-duty pass-through toward the boy, who was startled when the brass device unfolded from the wall.

When the pass-through was fully extended and the cover flipped down, the boy looked at the envelope, then at the metal maw. He stepped forward and gently placed the packet into the mechanical box and stepped back.

As the pass-through retracted and folded back into the wall, the boy waved, turned, and ran away. The Marine guard carefully extracted the envelope, checked its weight, and turned it over in his fingertips to read the inscription.

To the
U.S. Ambassador Extraordinary
and Plenipotentiary
Extremely Urgent

Within minutes of the Ambassador receiving the envelope, FLASH precedence and encrypted cables were sent to the U.S. State Department and the Central Intelligence Agency. The dispatch mentioned how a letter had just been received demanding the release of three men held in an American jail. The ultimatum read:

Failure to release my brothers and transport them to Algiers within 48 hours will result in one American airliner shot down every 48 hours.

Ten hours after the embassy cable was received in Washington DC, the National Security Council convened to assess the threat. The State Department reported no further communications from Algeria. The CIA and the National Security Agency reported no intelligence chatter. Three Muslim men mentioned in the dispatch were secretly held as accomplices for bombing a federal building in a Midwestern state.

During an hour's discussion, the President and most of his Cabinet took the long-standing policy position that the U.S. didn't negotiate with terrorists. The Vice President took the position that the administration needed to conduct a poll on whether the U.S. should negotiate with them.

The Secretary of Defense, the only dissenter, asked, "How do we *not* negotiate with terrorists when we don't know who sent this letter? Are we really prepared to ignore and dismiss this threat as more Islamic extremist hyperbole? This threat is subtle, but it's not *that* subtle. It's a business offer. We'd better have an answer more substantial than we don't negotiate with terrorists or take a poll if a jet falls out of the sky in, what, thirty-six hours?"

The President wasn't amused with the SECDEF's comments. "It's a bluff, a game of Chicken. Nothing will happen. Go home."

Thirty-six hours after the NSC meeting, a Trans World Airlines 747 disappeared off radar scopes east of Long Island, New York. Several people claimed they saw a rocket or missile launch in the night, followed by an explosion of light in the distance.

Sixty hours after the NSC meeting adjourned, three Middle-Eastern men stepped off a nondescript Gulfstream jet and onto the tarmac of the Houari Boumediene International Airport in Algiers. They kneeled on the concrete ramp and kissed the ground. When the three men stood, they shouted, "Allahu Akbar!"

CHAPTER ONE

1930 August 1, 2012
Murtala Muhammed International Airport
Lagos, Federal Republic of Nigeria

Duncan Hunter stepped from the taxi and waited for the driver to retrieve his roll aboard from the trunk. After exchanging fare for his luggage, Hunter extended the handle and proceeded inside the terminal pulling the ballistic nylon bag and queued in the first class line for British Airways. He placed a black Zero Halliburton briefcase on top of the rollerbag and removed his travel documents from inside his coat pocket.

While he waited for passenger check-in, he dabbed sweat from his forehead and cheeks, and reflected on the past twelve hours. Shuttling between Abuja and Lagos, meeting the Nigerian President, Chief of Air Staff, and the Minister of Immigration, Hunter presented his case that the solution to Nigeria's problems of billion-dollar oil pipeline losses and hundreds of illegal aliens pouring across the borders could begin to be resolved with scores of low-noise profile aircraft patrolling the pipelines and borders. The fact that he sold six powered glider aircraft with options for six more brought a thin smile to his face and a stifled laugh. He never saw himself as a salesman.

Passport control was unimpressed with the quiet American with the displaced smile and asked him several questions. The only white man in a sea of Africans, Hunter knew the pointed questions were part of the security program and counterterrorist profiling. He took no offense. The uniformed woman behind the counter was all business. He smiled at her and thanked her for returning his blue-covered tourist passport. After receiving a visa stamp and his boarding pass, Hunter walked to the security checkpoint.

As he approached the expansive screening facility, he pulled his roll aboard to the side and quietly observed the screening process. In a previous life, Hunter had been the general manager of a contracted airport security firm at the Cleveland Hopkins International Airport. When traveling alone, he usually took a few minutes to watch the screening personnel—the X-ray screeners, magnetometer guards, and supervisors. He knew how easy it was to smuggle a weapon aboard an airplane, if someone had help.

Just over ten years earlier, as some of the 9/11 hijackers were still airborne, Hunter called his friend and mentor, Greg Lynche, the former CIA Chief of Air Branch, and immediately identified the method the terrorists had used to get their weapons aboard the planes; the screener operating the X-ray machine ignored the weapons in the terrorists' carry-on bags as they passed through the X-ray machine. The screeners had all looked away from their monitors to see who was in line during a very narrow window of time.

Hunter also identified the group behind the infiltration of the airport screening process. A dedicated group of Muslims manned the X-ray machines at each of the airports where hijacked aircraft originated. At the Boston and New York airports, where four hijacked aircraft departed, every one of the Middle Eastern screeners had been relieved from their assignment, and disappeared immediately after the hijackers passed through to the screened, or sterile, side of the concourse.

Within hours of the World Trade Center collapsing, FBI agents had fanned out across dozens of American airports and were stunned to see videotapes of weapons being passed through the X-ray machines without being stopped by the screener. Six airports were noteworthy; at each airport Middle Eastern-looking men and women, who performed pre-boarding screening, failed to intercept knives and box cutters in the luggage of other Middle Eastern-looking men. Once those men retrieved their luggage and were past the security checkpoint, those screeners left their posts and disappeared from the airport.

Satisfied that the screening process in Lagos was unremarkably average, Hunter retrieved his bag and briefcase and stepped into the rat's maze disguised as passenger control. Minutes later, on the other side of the X-ray machines and metal detectors, Duncan continued down the concourse toward his departure gate.

Five minutes after Duncan Hunter had passed through the airport security checkpoint, a woman at one of the X-ray machines checked her watch repeatedly and surreptitiously glanced up from her monitor and screened faces in the passenger-control lanes, where people stood before placing their luggage on the X-ray conveyor belt. Once she identified the men in the queue, she focused intently on her monitor screen. She never looked up until well after all the men passed through the magnetometer and retrieved their bags at the far end of the X-ray machine.

After twenty other passengers had worked their way through the metal detector and baggage screening, the x-ray machine operator suddenly turned to her supervisor and asked to be relieved.

The tall man snapped his fingers, motioning a young uniformed man to replace her. The woman adjusted her head scarf and held her tummy, and slid from her chair. Turning toward the supervisor, she thanked him and nodded her appreciation. She stole a glance down the concourse, turned toward the ticketing area, and left the checkpoint.

Boarding an international flight is rarely troublesome for first class passengers. They go to the head of the line, board first, and are welcomed aboard with attentive personal service and luxury amenities. Duncan Hunter was first out of his seat in the waiting area and was first through the cabin door. More than a few passengers noticed the arrogant white man who positioned himself to board the plane quickly.

Extracting a thin book from his briefcase, Hunter tossed it onto his seat and stowed his luggage in the overhead compartment. Before he slipped into his seat at the front of the Boeing 747, an attractive flight attendant offered to take his jacket, while another rushed up to offer champagne, water, or juice. Hunter gave up his jacket and took one of each drink from the tray. After kicking off his shoes he walked toward the lavatory. He was about to enter the toilet when movement from the corner of his eye made him stop and reassess.

He glanced up momentarily at two men who had just entered the jet. Something about them triggered deep concern. Hunter stood behind the lavatory door, watching the duo progress down the aisle. They noted the jet's layout and meandered before taking the rearmost seats in business class.

Hunter's brows narrowed, and he frowned. He tried to dismiss the feeling of uneasiness about the men. As they settled into aisle seats across from each other, Hunter stepped into the lavatory, closed and locked the door, and relieved himself. Staring at the silver flap at the bottom of the commode, he said, "Those two are bad news."

He zipped his fly and washed his hands and face. As he left the lavatory, he glanced back at the men, but this time he felt no bad vibrations. *Maybe they had never been on a jet before.* He settled into his seat to read and soon the cabin door closed.

After reading a few pages from *The New Left: The Anti-Industrial Revolution,* Hunter yawned, unable to focus. He stuffed the boring book into a side pocket on his wide seat and closed his eyes as a disembodied voice spoke from a loudspeaker.

"…your seatbelt has been designed for easy fastening and release. To fasten, insert the metal fitting into the buckle, adjust to fit snugly with the loose end of the strap, and simply lift the buckle release to unfasten. Your seatbelt should always be worn low and tight across your lap…."

The first time Hunter awoke during the flight was during the meal service. The second time was when a flight attendant had raised her voice and scolded a passenger, quietly telling a man he wasn't allowed in the first class cabin. Hunter lifted a lazy eye toward the disturbance and half-recognized the man as one of the two who gave him a bad feeling when they boarded.

The first class cabin was darkened. The subdued lighting and fog of waking after deep sleep contributed to Hunter's gradual awareness that the man was a threat. He remained still to observe.

When the flight attendant tried gently to urge the man to leave the cabin, he drew a gun from his pants and pressed it against her neck.

The sight of a pistol shocked Hunter fully awake; noticing the weapon wasn't cocked and wasn't an immediate threat forced him to think more aggressively. Adrenaline surged through every capillary as he formed a plan. From under his blanket, he unbuckled his Rolex chronograph and slipped it into his seat, and then he reached across his body to lift the buckle release with one hand while feeling for the webbing of the seat belt. He ran his hand down the material toward the seam of the seat and back, locating the clip holding it to the seat. He unhooked the clip and wrapped the webbing around his hand, testing the weight of the buckle at the end of the material. Hunter didn't have much time.

The man with the pistol had his back to the front of the jet as he terrorized the flight attendant, whispering into her face; threatening her as he pushed her toward the galley. Hunter slid from his seat and ran in a crouch down the aisle. As he closed the distance between his seat and the kitchen, the man with the gun sensed movement and turned his head just as Hunter viciously swung the seat belt, slamming the buckle hard into the man's face.

Hunter judged the distance and windup perfectly, as if he were swinging his favorite racquetball racquet to crush a little blue ball. The armed man didn't have time to react. The buckle tore into his eye and nose, crushing the eyeball and breaking his nose. The man tried to scream and protect himself, throwing up his arms in a late response. The shock and ferocity of the attack loosened his grip on the pistol.

Hunter drove his free fist into the man's throat, cutting off any sound. He snatched the gun from the man's hand and redirected the butt at the man's temple; the sound of crushed skin and bone reverberated within the galley. The African dropped to his knees unconscious and rolled forward onto his face. Dark blood oozed from his head onto the carpet.

"You aren't allowed in the first class cabin," Hunter whispered; then he became serious. His heart was pounding and mouthed, "There's probably at least one other gun with the other man."

He looked up and saw the flight attendant in shock, trembling with fear and hyperventilating. He slipped the pistol into the small of his back and grabbed the woman's arms, gently shaking her to get her attention.

"Listen to me," he hissed. "Listen! This is serious. There's at least one other passenger traveling with this guy. We have to believe they want to take over the jet. Can you call the pilot and tell him there are passengers with guns in the cabin and not to let anyone into the cockpit?"

Though dazed, she slowly understood the severity of the situation and nodded. Her eyelids fluttered, as she fought back fear and anxiety. She struggled to move toward the side of the jet to the cabin door and the cabin's communication system.

Hunter eased toward the gap between the curtain dividing the aisle and the corner of the galley, trying to locate the downed man's companion. He didn't expect to see two men walking up and down the two aisles of the darkened business class section. The man who came in with the downed man wasn't visible.

Hunter stepped back into the kitchen to retrieve the gun at his back. It was a 9mm Russian Makarov. He depressed the magazine release and verified the magazine was full. The pistol's hammer wasn't cocked, nor was there a round in the chamber.

Hunter pulled back the slide to chamber a round. With the gun loaded, locked, and cocked, he depressed the safety and slipped it back into the small of his back. He was about to step into business class when he had an idea.

The flight attendant was barely coherent when Hunter moved across the aisle to snatch the handset from her. "Are you talking to the pilot?" he asked softly.

She nodded.

"Sir, this is Duncan Hunter, in seat 2A. I subdued one man with a weapon and believe there are at least three more aboard. I see two walking in the business class aisles with pistols. I can't locate the third man. I think he may be upstairs heading your way. Do you copy?"

The stunned pilot responded with a mild Scottish accent. "Aye, copy."

The copilot looked at the pilot with great concern.

"I think I can subdue the other two if you give me a couple seconds to get into position, then put the jet into a little negative G for ten seconds. Then give me five seconds of positive G and ten more seconds of negative G. If I'm successful, I'll get back on the interphone. How's that?"

The captain was still in shock at the idea of his jet being commandeered, and hearing a crazy plan from an unknown voice didn't convince him. "I don't know…."

"OK. Try this. Somehow, these guys got weapons aboard. They could have explosives, too. I don't think there's much time for discussion. The other guy could be trying to get into your cockpit as we speak. These guys are on a schedule. Sir, I submit we need to do something fast to interrupt them."

The pilot sighed. "OK, Mate. In five seconds, zero G, for ten, then repeat." He clicked off the microphone and tightened his lap and shoulder belts while barking at the copilot to do the same.

The pilot disengaged the autopilot, spun the IFF control knobs to read 7500, and hit IDENT. Pulling the yoke toward himself, he sent the jet suddenly up before he pushed the nose over.

Hunter warned the flight attendant, "Strap in now!" and moved quickly into the business class cabin. Three steps after passing through the curtain, he heard the big jet's engines reduce power as it nosed over. Instantly, anything unsecured—blankets, pillows, shoes, glasses, magazines—remained momentarily suspended in midair as the aircrew programmed the flight controls for negative G flight. Some passengers awoke and gasped as Hunter threw himself airborne at one of the armed men several paces ahead, both of whom had crashed into the jet's ceiling.

The men with the pistols released them when they tried to stop their quick ascent to the ceiling, but at negative G, the thin Africans were firmly plastered between the overhead storage compartments over the aisles. The man Hunter had targeted was unable to move or think.

Hunter reached the weapon stuck against the ceiling before the terrorist could understand his predicament. The confused, frightened man was spread-eagled, trying to make sense of what just happened. The last thing he saw was his gun's butt slamming into the side of his face. Pinned on the jet's ceiling, Hunter thought once wasn't enough, so he hit him again a couple more times just as the captain pulled back on the yoke.

Anticipating the change in G force, Hunter pushed himself off to the center and tried to land across several seats. Everything that was pinned to the ceiling during the negative G maneuver fell onto the floor and seats, as the aircraft momentarily returned to straight, level, one-G flight.

The unconscious terrorist fell heavily to the floor between the seats. Hunter's trajectory was slightly off, and he fell on top of a large black woman with bulging eyes, hitting her nearly nose-to-nose. She tried to scream, but he covered her mouth with his free hand, apologized for landing on her, rolled off her bulk, and slid to the floor.

On his knees, Hunter tried to locate the other man over several fully reclined seats. Just as the man stood with his gun ready, the aircraft dived again, catching everyone by surprise. Amid the screaming and another round of unsecured items—beverages, books, dirt, shoes, and assorted trash—flying to the ceiling, the other terrorist again flew upwards into the ceiling just as Hunter launched himself across four rows of seats to slam into him, and rabbit punched his face. As the man tried to protect himself, Hunter wrested away the pistol.

Every passenger in all three classes of cabins was now awake and terrified, many screamed as the jet raced toward Earth in a parabolic arc. Two seconds later, the big jet slowly returned to level flight and one G flight. With a firm grip on the man's pistol, Hunter backhanded the terrorist viciously across the face.

He stood there for a moment, pistol ready, watching the man to see if he tried to move. When it was clear he'd been knocked out, Hunter popped his head over the seats. Breathing hard, waving the pistol in one hand, he said, "These guys are terrorists. Someone tie them up. There may be more aboard."

Hunter was surprised that no one moved. The huge woman he nearly shared an intimate moment with started screaming, which joined a cacophony of other shrieking women and wailing children.

From behind Hunter a voice said, "Drop it!"

Hunter instantly dropped to the floor between the seats and spun to take cover behind a row. He thought the voice could've been an air marshal or the missing man. He bet it was the other terrorist, who'd probably been upstairs on the 747's upper deck level.

Before he could take action, he heard a body fall to the floor. A few seconds later came the unmistakable clicking of metal handcuffs ratcheting closed. Hunter got on his hands and knees to work his way forward along the aisle, scooting four rows to see what transpired.

As he tried to peek around the end seat, he saw a man down, but then a gun barrel pressed against the side of his face. From behind the legendary Walther PPK came a voice with a Cambridge accent.

"Scotland Yard. Drop the weapon."

Hunter froze, knowing American Federal Air Marshals were armed with such weapons filled with low-velocity bullets that would knock down a terrorist but wouldn't pierce the aircraft's hull. He had little knowledge of what a British aviation security man would be carrying.

Shocked and relieved, Hunter said, "I've subdued three. I don't know if there are any more. There may be others in coach." He tossed two Russian pistols into an empty seat, feeling the barrel press harder against his face with every movement.

"Get up."

Hunter stood. It was a long time since anyone held him at gunpoint.

After a moment of assessment, the short, stocky man with the elegant Walther looked left and right at the downed men in the aisles, he then returned his gaze to Hunter. Amid the mayhem of business class passengers trying to understand what happened, he asked, "Who are you?" Scotland Yard took the two pistols off the seat and stuffed them into the pockets of his tweed sport coat.

He leaned to speak into the man's ear. "Duncan Hunter, U.S.A."

Two of the downed men began moving and some passengers crawled over their seats to reach the terrorists. Before Scotland Yard and Hunter could exchange any pleasantries, those passengers began beating and kicking the downed men in the aisles.

Scotland Yard raised thick eyebrows and wriggled his mustache. With a sigh, he said, "If I let them kill them, there'll be even more paperwork for me. As it is, I'll be stuck in the office for a week, thanks to you." He lowered his PPK slightly. "Nice work, Mr. Hunter."

"I don't know if there are any more, Sir. I thought I identified two. I was shocked to find three. I suppose he was upstairs."

Scotland Yard nodded and reset his shoulders, admiring the American's handiwork. "Do ye think there are any more?"

He said it so fast and with such a thick accent, Hunter almost asked him to repeat it. Delayed comprehension struck, and Hunter blurted, "It seems prudent to clear the whole airplane. It might be wise to tie up these three before someone kills them."

Hunter was astonished at the passengers' hate and fury toward the terrorists on the floor. More and more people crawled over each other to hit or kick the men. He was briefly reminded of a video clip of a turkey hunt where three huge toms walked into a road. When the lead one was shot, the other two jumped on it. With the terrorists down and disarmed, the passengers wanted revenge. Hunter had damaged the two in the business class cabin, but passengers came from other aisles to finish them.

"Let's clear the other cabin first," Scotland Yard said. "You take that side."

The two men had to step on seats to get around the bodies, where flailing fists and flying feet were aimed at the terrorists' heads. As Hunter and Scotland Yard peered around the curtains separating the cabins, they found another pair of men trying to defend themselves from dozens of men and women beating them.

Scotland Yard rushed up the aisle, relieving one African man of a pistol. Hunter took his cue and found a woman holding another Makarov while several men beat someone hidden under the pile of bodies.

"I'll take that," Hunter said. "Thank you, Ma'am."

Scotland Yard took charge of the situation, as the cabin lights came up to full brightness. The two negative G maneuvers left the cabin a disaster area, though the only injured people seemed to be the battered terrorists. Those passengers not pummeling the men in the aisles were searching for their belongings.

Hunter left the flight attendants and Scotland Yard to sort through the extracurricular activities in the coach cabin. Returning to the front of the plane, he passed the flight attendant who previously had the gun jammed under her chin. She was still strapped into her seat, curled up and sobbing. Duncan went to his knees, taking her hands in his.

Reading her nametag, he said, "It's all over now. You did a great job, Ashley. You don't know how much of a help you were. We probably need to tell the captain that the situation down here is secure. Can you ring him and tell him, or would you like me to call him?"

First Class Flight Attendant Ashley Chavers composed herself, reached for the panel, and pressed a series of buttons before handing the receiver to Hunter. She unbuckled her straps as the pilot answered the intercom.

"Captain Montgomery."

"Captain, this is Duncan Hunter. Sir, I think the situation is secure. It looks as if we had six men with pistols. All have been disarmed and are in various states of…incapacitation. A man from Scotland Yard and your flight attendants are working to restore the cabins to normal. Your negative G maneuvers did the trick, Sir. Thank you."

"That's glorious news, Mr. Hunter," the captain said in obvious relief. "Thank you for your help." Several seconds elapsed. "May I speak with the security chief or the flight attendant?"

"You're welcome, Sir. Here's Ashley." He offered the receiver to the quickly composed flight attendant.

Duncan moved toward his seat when he realized the first terrorist he encountered was still on the floor in the first class galley. He stepped toward him and bent to check his pulse. When he didn't find one, he wandered toward his seat. He felt no remorse for the dead man and wasn't interested in events in the other cabins. Though he just killed a man, his only thought was how to get off the airplane without major intervention by police and investigators asking what he did and how he got the pilot to defy regulations, flying the jumbo jet like a porpoise and bouncing terrorists off the ceiling.

The aircraft continued toward Heathrow. Half an hour passed before the man from Scotland Yard came up to Hunter's seat. Duncan looked up to see the unsmiling face of the law, he reached into his side pocket and handed the man two old Russian Makarovs, pistol grips first. "I think you'll want these."

"Aye. That would be the appropriate thing to do." He added the weapons to the collection in his suit coat pockets, which bulged from other machine pistols. "Do you have any idea how they got these on the plane? Catering?"

Hunter shook his head. "Catering is too difficult; too risky. I'm sure the X-ray machine operator ignored them as they came through screenings. I remember her wearing a head scarf. The airport will have a video of what went through the X-ray; there are cameras and that's just standard policy. She probably expected them to come through at a prescribed time, so she must've been part of it. I've seen it before."

"I never considered that. Thank you." He looked around the cabin to make sure they weren't overheard. He leaned down and said, "There's reports of a man flying through the cabin, walking along the ceiling, and disarming those suspects. Do you know who that might be or how someone could do something like that?"

Duncan resigned himself to his fate. He acted on instinct, but was careless with his name; there were too many witnesses. With very few Caucasian men aboard, he stood out like a white race car on freshly poured asphalt. He told the captain and Scotland Yard his real name, which meant there was no way out of his predicament. Soon, his name would be splashed across news print and on TVs worldwide. His cover would be blown, and there was no one to blame but himself.

"No, Sir. I never saw a thing. I found those two weapons in a seat. I don't know who they belonged to. I guess their owners didn't need them anymore."

Scotland Yard stood and took a deep breath; he scanned across the first class cabin before squatting back down until he was eyeball-to-eyeball with Hunter. His breath exuded Scotch. "Mate, you did a great thing back there. I take it you're Special Forces?"

Hunter sighed and stared straight ahead. The non-answer confused the security man momentarily. Whether it was the highballs he drank earlier in the flight that slowed his ability to discern subtleties or the benign, unresponsive body language from the man in the seat that finally clued him in, the man from Scotland Yard had an epiphany and he unconsciously jolted backward, his eyebrows shot up in mild surprise.

"You can't tell me," he said softly.

Hunter nodded a fraction. Scotland Yard glanced around the almost empty cabin.

"You're undercover?" he whispered. "You can't be exposed?"

Hunter looked forward, his lips mashed together before he spoke. "I need to get off the plane when we land. No cameras or interviews."

Scotland Yard was taken aback and became serious. "You need me to get you off the plane without cameras or interviews?"

"Yes, Sir. Whatever it takes."

"Aye. I don't know how to do it. Scotland Yard will be waiting to talk to everyone before they release them."

Duncan looked up at him. "I think I know a way."

The security man's eyes narrowed. He wasn't sure he'd like what the man had to say.

Once Hunter explained, the man from Scotland Yard responded with a nod and a wink. "Aye, I'll speak with the captain."

British Airways Flight 0074 arrived at Heathrow on time, very early in the morning. The main terminal had few travelers, and the shops on the concourse were closed, too early in the morning for them to open. One hundred police officers and detectives from Scotland Yard and the airport converged on a secluded gate to meet the aircraft that had somehow thwarted an in-flight terrorist takeover.

The man from Scotland Yard clipped his badge on his breast pocket; the gold shield flashed his absolute authority on the jet. He met the incoming company of detectives and police as the door opened, first directing them to the perished or bound terrorists. Police work began. Passengers and flight attendants waited.

After the main body of police and detectives rushed into the aircraft, the Scotland Yard Air Marshal directed the copilot to depart the airplane. A senior police supervisor, with a huge paunch and jowls, held up his hand at the cabin door to stop the crewman from leaving.

"He wasn't part of the situation and needs to catch his other flight," the man from Scotland Yard said, no longer emanating Scotch vapor.

The supervisor at the door was slightly embarrassed. "So sorry. Aircrew, aircrew; of course!" He pulled back against the wall to make way.

The man in the British Airways uniform, with three gold stripes on his sleeves, pulled down his cap slightly as he walked up the jetway, glad he was free to go. He pulled out the handle from his roll aboard with one hand and lifted a black Zero Halliburton briefcase with the other as he quickly deplaned. He braced himself against the counterflow of police racing down the air bridge and was quickly onto the concourse, hurrying to catch his next flight.

Later that morning, a pilot's jacket and cap were found at an empty British Airways ticket counter when the ticket agent arrived on duty. No one claimed the black Brooks Brothers sport coat left in first class of the British Airways flight from Nigeria.

CHAPTER TWO

0900 August 5, 2012
CIA Headquarters
McLean, Virginia

Nazy Cunningham guided her red Mercedes SL up to the security checkpoint as heavily armed men in black uniforms and black body armor gave the hand signal to stop.

Nazy and her passenger had their badges ready for inspection. Turning her head to the left, she completed the screening process by looking into the fisheye lens for a retina scan. Green lights approved her entry into the compound. The new Deputy Director for Counter Terrorism proceeded through the heavily fortified gate toward the Old Headquarters Building and steered into the underground parking lot.

Duncan Hunter slid his fingers teasingly inside her stockinged thigh. She anticipated the move. He was incorrigible, predictable, and not wholly serious. The early morning crowded parking lot of the CIA wasn't the place to engage in frivolous play with one of the agency's rising senior intelligence service executives.

She didn't remove his hand as she spoke with precise Queen's English. "You will be late for your meeting with the President, Mr. Hunter. Do not start something you cannot finish."

Her cinnamon-scented perfume, which was dormant for most of the trip, filled his nostrils anew.

Nazy's voice, scent, and accent sent a rush of warmth through him, and he responded by leaning across the center console. "But Ms. Cunningham, I can't help myself. Whenever I'm near you, my persistent arousal disorder flares up."

Nazy moved toward him, turning her head to receive his kiss. Hunter slid his hand from her thigh to her face and kissed her passionately and thoroughly. She playfully bit his lower lip when he tried to release.

He caught his breath. "I think you're right. It wouldn't look good that I was summoned to the White House and then didn't show up."

"We will continue this later. I have to get to the office, and you have to leave. Do you know where you are going?"

"I need to be at the transportation center in fifteen minutes. It's at the other end of the property. I can walk."

"Nonsense. You're late. Take the car." She handed him the keys. "I really must leave. I have a meeting. You should be back well before I am done. Then we can finish what you clumsily tried to start." She lowered her eyes and shot him a sultry look, which made him take a deep breath.

They simultaneously opened their doors, and Hunter came around to her side of the car. He admired the view as he took her hand. Knees together, she spun in the saddle-leather seat and lifted her legs over the door sill. Hunter gently pulled her to her feet. He stared deeply into the platinum-green eyes of the raven-haired beauty who won his heart nearly a decade earlier.

As she turned toward the elevator, her magnificent long, black hair cascaded across her shoulders in waves, always moving. Then there were her legs—Hunter was again convinced she had the best legs in Virginia. She thrilled him whenever they were together, and it saddened him when she walked away. The view was always spectacular, but duty called.

The daughter of an Iranian royal and the head of the Royal Jordanian court had been sent to spy on him. He frequently recalled the day he first saw her in a skin-tight white leotard and dark eye makeup, watching him play racquetball in Newport, Rhode Island. Her face should have been the subject of several fashion magazines, and he had difficulty concentrating on anything other than the woman watching him play. After she sat in rapt attention for over an hour, watching old guys smack little blue racquetballs around the glass-walled court, it didn't immediately occur to him she might be a "swallow," a woman trained to seduce intelligence agents. He eventually saw through the deception.

All that was ancient history; Nazy Cunningham was her name now, and she had a new life as a senior intelligence officer in the CIA. She was also his fiancée.

Hunter drove from the underground garage and around the expansive parking area. He slowed to admire and appreciate the big, black A-12 as it came into view, in what was essentially the backyard of the CIA's Old Headquarters Building.

The former top-secret supersonic reconnaissance jet was built under the Oxcart program as the precursor to the Air Force's much-heralded SR-71 Blackbird. Every time Hunter saw the majestic aviation icon on concrete mounts, he sighed and thought the jet should be lovingly cared for in a museum, not sitting outside in the weather.

"Whoever made the decision to put her outside should have his ass beat," he said. He repeated that line every time he saw the A-12 outside, "on a stick."

After negotiating his way past the matte black jet and endless rows of cars, he took a pair of lefts and ended up behind towering oaks that completely obscured the OHB and its huge parking lots. He entered the small parking spaces of the transportation center.

Once he stepped out of Nazy's car, he was surprised by the number of limousines, glossy black SUVs, SWAT-type vehicles, unmarked Crown Victorias, and trucks, vans, and cars which filled the compound. Sixty seconds after he closed the red Mercedes' door, he stood in the dispatch office awaiting transportation to the White House.

As he waited for the huge man without a neck behind the counter to respond, Hunter wondered, "What are the chances I'll get one of the limos to ride into Washington, DC?"

The balding chief of dispatch checked his computer monitor as Hunter sidled up to the four-foot-high counter.

When Hunter showed his green badge, the chief said, "I was beginning to think you wouldn't show. You're late. Fifteen minutes before departure. You need to get on the Dunhill truck. It's right outside, and it leaves in three minutes." The mountain of a man returned his attention to the monitor, moving and clicking a mouse.

"Dunhill truck?" Hunter was crestfallen.

The glabrous man, who dealt with prima`donnas daily and didn't have time for any of them, didn't bother to look up. "Ten-four. You're late. All aboard. Two minutes."

Duncan frowned to express his displeasure. To his disappointment, he was completely ignored. Feeling unsatisfied, he turned and dashed from the building.

The uninteresting-sounding transportation center was a huge operation that few knew about. While spies and intelligence community executives garnered the headlines, the transportation center made sure the executives had the right vehicle with the right security level to travel safely to their destinations in the Washington, DC area. Undercover or unmarked vehicles of all varieties were used to shuttle intelligence officers between locations. Someone somewhere, either at the CIA or the White House, planned or scheduled the special transportation accommodations for Duncan Hunter to reach the White House. His mode of travel was a nondescript catering van; Hunter sat among empty pastry shelves on a cheap lawn chair. His visit would never be recorded in the official visitor logs.

When he arrived at the White House, a Secret Service agent met the Ford Econoline, opened the rear door, and whisked Hunter from the cargo van. The two men walked side-by-side, silently passing a dozen overfilled garbage bags and several dumpsters before Hunter was ushered through the doors of a very empty, huge kitchen.

Another Secret Service agent took control of Hunter, lightly frisked him, and led him down a long hallway before showing him into a small, poorly lit room that was more a closet than an antechamber.

"Wait here," the agent said.

Hunter nodded, and the agent closed the door, leaving Hunter alone with his thoughts.

He stood at loose parade rest—arms behind his back, legs straight, head erect. Thinking he was probably under surveillance, he faced the door and quietly waited for it to open so he could get on with his meeting with the President.

Three minutes passed and no one came. There were no noises in the hall. Just as a fourth minute passed, he heard the mechanical sound of a latch unlocking behind him. Startled, he turned his head to look over his shoulder and saw the President of the United States wrestling with a panel Hunter had assumed was a wall. The "wall" opened into the washroom off of the Oval Office.

President Javier Hernandez appeared deeply embarrassed and apologetic. He offered his hand, and Hunter received a firm, long handshake. The President's dark-brown eyes were friendly under his salt-and-pepper hair. The former TV reporter for a San Antonio TV station ran for Congress and won the seat as the first Republican ever to represent the district. Congressman Javier Hernandez put an earmark in the budget for quiet airplanes for the U.S. Border Patrol, but it was the politicians in the opposition party who diverted the money and killed the program.

Not to be deterred, when Hunter secured the necessary funds for Schweizer quiet airplanes through the Drug Forfeiture Program, neither the Border Patrol leadership nor Congressman Hernandez advertised the acquisition of the three quiet surveillance aircraft. When special-purpose aircraft helped shut down the illegal alien traffic in the Del Rio Sector – a million illegal crossings a year – the success propelled Hernandez into the national spotlight. His telegenic presence, accomplishments on the border, and superb leadership skills gained him national prominence in the Republican Party and was elected as the Speaker of the House, the first Hispanic to hold the office. When the former President resigned, and the Vice President was found dead at the Naval Observatory, the 25th Amendment was enacted, installing the Speaker as the next President.

President Hernandez patted Hunter's shoulder with his free hand. "Duncan, I'm so sorry! I hope you weren't waiting long. Please, have a seat." He released his grip and closed the panel behind them, pointing to one end of the sofa, while he took the other.

"No factor, Mr. President," Duncan said, still smiling broadly. "It's good to see you again." *What's an old fighter pilot doing sitting on the sofa with the President of the United States?*

"The pleasure is mine, Duncan, all mine."

An awkward moment passed, as President Hernandez marshaled his thoughts through his wry smile. His words were directed at the cushion between them.

"So you're the guy who made all this possible. I suppose, a 'thank you' is in order." His eyes rose to meet Hunter's.

Duncan felt stunned. He gritted his teeth; his temples pulsed with every heartbeat. He couldn't speak for a moment. *I hadn't thought about it, but there's more than a little truth to that. The left called whoever released the file a traitor, but they had no idea who it was.*

"What you did was a true patriotic act," the President continued. "It had the desired effect when my predecessor stepped down, as did most of his cabinet. The timing was also propitious. The disclosure of that file interrupted several plans that we're just now beginning to comprehend."

His demeanor changed and the President became more serious. "You probably interrupted the overthrow of the government, or at least permanent one-party rule. It's apparent we didn't know what we were dealing with, but somehow, you did. I suppose you could have sat on that file."

"Mr. President, if I saw anything, it was how the press acted. When they chose to report only favorable news of the President that was the first clue something was up. It was more than just lapdog media at work. They had become Pravda. Yes, Sir, there was a sense of urgency to release it."

"He was able to bury his past with lawyers, and a totally compliant and enamored press wouldn't investigate anything about the man. It was obvious something wasn't right with him."

"A free press would've screamed at the top of their lungs," Duncan added, "from the top of the Washington Monument, irrespective of party affiliation, that the man was a fraud. It wasn't an issue of giving him the benefit of the doubt. Everyone knew something was wrong with him."

"They all knew it, Duncan. Few could see through that smokescreen."

"It could only mean Whittaker Chambers was right about the extent of the infiltration of communists in government and the press. The press assumed he was one of them, and he fostered that belief, but he was a different kind of socialist. It was as if the Fourth Reich was rising in plain sight in America, with Islam spearheading the effort, and the media was on vacation in Tahiti. That he was a Muslim was a revelation that shouldn't have surprised anyone."

"I can't disagree. We've come to learn those guys basically found themselves in charge of the government with a population expecting them to lead and govern. That was never their desire or their motivation. They wanted to overthrow the government, and they did, but when they found they owned the country, they didn't know what to do with it. I think, deep down, they wanted to rule like Lenin, Stalin, or Hitler, but they found out they couldn't. We still had the Bill of Rights. So when they went after Americans and tried to strip them of their First and Second Amendment rights, it wasn't just Republicans who heard the wakeup call. It was loyal Democrats, too."

"Yes, Sir." Hunter never would have believed he'd be sitting with the President and discussing politics.

"Those on the right knew something was wrong with my predecessor, but the media still protected him. They didn't want to vet him or paint him in a bad way."

"Sir, I believe it was the greatest scam ever perpetrated on the American people."

"It was, absolutely. One of these days, it might leak that he had several government agencies purchase and stockpile hundreds of millions of rounds of hollow-point ammunition. Why the Social Security Administration needed 500 million rounds of hollow-point ammunition is beyond my comprehension. All of that's being investigated."

Hunter recovered from the compliment and the outburst. "I had no idea, Sir."

President Hernandez nodded. "Then there's the matter of the Vice President. I doubt we'll ever get to the bottom of how he acquired a silenced pistol that was stolen in California, and used it to…shoot himself." He rubbed his chin and said slyly, "It was all very strange, but for the sake of this Republic, we will press ahead and put that sordid chapter of our history behind us."

"Yes, Sir. I'm surprised how corrupt the media was—is—and how they facilitated the charade for so long." Hunter smiled at the thought that a certain retired Navy SEAL may have had something to do with the former Vice President's "suicide."

"They certainly did. That won't change appreciably, I'm afraid. That's the nature of politics today." He looked down at the sofa, choosing his words carefully before raising his head. Another sly smile came to his lips. "So, Duncan, how was your trip to Nigeria?"

Hunter, realizing the President knew the truth about the British Airways hijacking, knew it wouldn't do him any good to sugarcoat the truth. "Sir, I saw a hijacking taking place, and I tried to stop it."

The President nodded, unsurprised. "The British government and British Airways send their gratitude. It seems 'congratulations' and 'well done' are in order. I also understand the chairman of the airline was very grateful. He thought your actions were so meritorious; he awarded you a pair of first-class tickets anywhere, anytime for life. That's a better deal than former Presidents get."

Hunter matched the President's broad smile and attempt at humor. He felt slightly distracted, though, because if the President knew, who else did? Would that impact his cover and clearances?

The President seemed to read his mind. "Once MI5 figured out you left the aircraft disguised as the copilot, I understand, and with some assistance from Scotland Yard, they squelched your involvement and sent their regards—and their deep admiration." He shook his head with pride.

Visibly embarrassed, Hunter took a deep breath. "That's very good news, Sir. The pilot made it possible. But I thank you." He recalled the final events of his escape from the British Airways terminal in Heathrow.

Once clear of the concourse, but before he left the terminal, he shed the copilot's uniform jacket at a British Airways ticket counter. Then he caught a taxi and jumped onto the Eurostar Chunnel train to France, where he chartered a private jet to the States.

The President's next words snapped Hunter from his reverie.

"Well, Duncan, you're probably wondering why I asked you to come and why all the subterfuge."

He nodded. "Yes, Sir."

The President stole a glance at his watch. "You and I have a little history. You've proven yourself unusually capable, whether it's helping to curtail illegal immigration, finding narcoterrorists, or fighting the global war on terrorism and against Islamic extremism. Contrary to my predecessor's bogus assertion that al-Qaeda is a shadow of its former self and doesn't pose any threat to America that requires thousands of troops fighting abroad, the near hijacking of that jet rammed it home again that freedom-loving people are still under attack. The attackers show no sign of easing off. They have an affinity for airplanes, it seems.

"The danger, as I see it, is that radical Islamists have become emboldened; more active in their efforts to infiltrate and destabilize Africa, mostly North Africa, and pose a growing threat to Europe and the U.S."

The President sighed. "We need to do more to prevent additional attacks against our great nation. It's been ten years, and the country has slipped back into pre-9/11 mentality. With the release of those documents and my predecessor's relationship with terrorists, I'm determined to reverse the notion that America is soft on terrorists. My goal is no longer to simply defend but to preempt and take the offensive. We have to do whatever it takes to keep those radicals and terrorists off balance and out of the country. I'm determined to protect America and prevent anything like that from happening again."

Hunter responded with pinched lips and subtle, approving nods.

"Your last mission convinced me, the Secretary of Defense, and the Joint Chiefs of the benefits of quiet aircraft over drones, er, unmanned planes. I understand you've been the lone voice touting quiet airplanes over drones."

"It seems like it, Mr. President. I love and value unmanned systems. Today's optical systems are amazing. UAVs have their place, but when you need discretion and precision, and you don't want to leave a trace that someone's been there, then there's nothing like a low-flying quiet airplane. I know there are projects coming out of our research labs that'll make even my old quiet airplane obsolete, but, for the moment, we have a unique capability.

"I know DOD and the Agency don't want to lose pilots on dangerous, challenging missions. The CIA doesn't want another Gary Powers incident, and the DOD is quickly getting to the point where they don't want to lose a pilot over unfriendly territory.

"Sometimes, a manned aircraft is a far superior platform for the missions, even though it comes with high risk. UAVs are mass manufactured for a reason. They're built "on the cheap" and have an appalling accident record. Some systems have a 50% attrition rate. Manned systems like the high-flying U-2 still can't be beat, and my YO-3 has been the perfect platform for high-risk, low-level work. Plus it's really the only game in town for the most-challenging and secretive work. Where satellites and unmanned systems with the latest cameras couldn't get any pictures of bin Laden, we could have looked right in his bedroom window. That's the difference the YO-3 makes."

"And you really have the only quiet airplane?"

"Yes, Sir. Well, me and NASA."

"That's amazing. Duncan, I read your Naval War College paper. What you did for the Border Patrol and CIA made me a believer. I don't have to tell you we can no longer use drones indiscriminately shooting Hellfire missiles at suspected al-Qaeda hideouts or safe houses. There's too much collateral damage. Too many innocent people are needlessly killed, and the political fallout is too great. That's why my predecessor used them as he did, to make America look bad.

"Our relationship with some of our Muslim allies is very tenuous after several spectacular failures which portrayed the U.S. killing hundreds of innocent women and children. I've suspended UAV operations in Afghanistan, Yemen, and the Sudan until the Pentagon can find a better solution. There's no mistaking this may leave us with a blind spot where DOD and the CIA might have anticipated the need for precision quiet aircraft."

"Mr. President, once upon a time the Agency embraced quiet airplanes, which were basically Schweizer motorgliders. My partner, Greg Lynche, started that program. He was the guy who put missiles on unmanned airplanes. He knew armed UAVs, like quiet airplanes, solved a discrete set of problems.

"Then everyone found UAVs, or at least, someone at the Agency jumped on the bandwagon and thought they were being left behind. That lasted until they started crashing in large numbers and required five times as many people to operate and maintain relative to comparable manned surveillance aircraft. They're expensive for a reason. Just taking the man out of the cockpit shouldn't be enough justification to embrace them totally."

"Isn't relying on a forty-year-old aircraft dangerous?"

Hunter grinned. "Sir, that forty-year-old airplane doesn't have that many miles on her and is in pristine condition. For the last fifteen years, we've improved her capabilities. Like the six-million dollar man, you'd never know she was that old or that lethal. I recently installed a long-range, high-caliber gun to see if I could hit a target out to three miles. She gives us a unique capability for a unique set of problems." He exchanged a smile with the President.

"The Secretary of Defense has expressed a desire to use you, but I talked with him. DOD can't have you. I have something else in mind."

"That's OK with me, Mr. President."

"I didn't think you'd mind that much." His mood changed from light and jovial to cold and serious. He easily telegraphed his next words. "Duncan, prior to 9/11 we looked at Islamist terrorism as isolated events, the actions of madmen, or as criminal activity. What

September 11 taught us was that we were witnessing the new normal. Moderate Muslims are losing on the defensive and radical Islam is winning, and they're changing the paradigm in the Middle East and Africa."

Hunter's demeanor changed, too, and he remained expressionless. His mind juggled options and anticipated possibilities. His curiosity stopped when the President spoke again.

"You're probably aware there's been a noticeable, palpable shift in Islamist extremism. I could say there's an even-more disturbing trend of our liberal friends having an unholy alliance with them, but that's a topic for another day.

"Duncan, if you look at photos of the graduating classes of Tehran, Baghdad, or Cairo Universities in the '40, '50s, '60s, and even the early '70s, you'd see men in suits and women in dresses. You'd be hard-pressed to tell if those photos were taken in the U.S. or Great Britain. Those countries were becoming Westernized, and they were producing smart, educated, dynamic world-class thinkers.

"If you study the photos of the late '70s, '80s, and '90s, you'll see a distinct transition. There are fewer and fewer women in dresses. If there are any women at all, they wear headscarves and *abayas.*

"Pictures from the late '90s show only men, and they wear *dishdashas* and beards. The de-Westernization and the radical Islamization of North Africa and the Middle East are in full swing, and the effect has been staggering."

"The rise of international terrorism and radical Islamists." Hunter stated his understanding of the President's line of reasoning and why he'd been summoned to the Oval Office. It sounded more like a lecture than a conversation. The President's tone became more serious and ominous by the minute.

"Correct," the President replied. "If the West can't reverse this trend, it will reach a tipping point. Strategically, we could lose them all —from Pakistan to Morocco—to radicals and face decades of conflict. Imagine a world of Irans from Casablanca to Istanbul with Islamists overpowering moderates." Shifting position, he moved to better face

Hunter.

"Terrorism is a many-headed hydra. You have to keep cutting off heads before they can grow back. We've seen what an unimpressive and unqualified yet charismatic community organizer can do to an unsuspecting nation. Key people—these charismatic leaders—provide the spark to galvanize people into action. Whether they get people to vote or overrun an embassy, those leaders are extraordinarily effective and very dangerous. You remember that cleric al-Sadr?"

"Of course. Mullah *Atari*, supposedly a direct descendant of the Prophet Muhammad. He was more preoccupied with video games than Islamic studies; he made life miserable for our troops in Iraq."

"Exactly. Al-Sadr is the perfect example of the kind of unimpressive and unqualified yet charismatic leader who can spin people up until they're out of control. We tried to contain him, yet those efforts were mixed at best. My point is, if we could have reduced his stature or eliminated him early; many American lives would have been saved. We don't know how many suicide attacks he was responsible for."

"Sir, I recall thinking several times that someone needed to take him out."

The President nodded. "Neutralize the spark and enervate the leaders. In essence, you cut off the heads of the hydra. If you do, at least in theory, the rest become disorganized, unable to fund or plan mischief and mayhem. While we must continue our antiterrorism vigilance, military strength, and speak honestly to the public while seeking alliances with sympathetic nations who share our views about radical Islam, I think we need to do more. Not regime change, but eliminate the rising stars or lifelong terrorists. We must redouble our efforts and go on the offensive."

"Sir, it seems the radicals are at war with us, and we're on the defensive—if not in flat out denial. I know the left believes terrorism isn't an existential threat to America and won't acknowledge Islamic terrorists are at war with us. I believe we're at war with a discrete part of Islam—those who are radical and extremist who distort their religious beliefs to maim, mutilate, and murder innocent people. It astonishes me when I see the level of Muslim-on-Muslim violence worldwide. There's one-point five billion Muslims in the world and I read where three hundred million are radicalized. The radicals are winning battles and are out of control. They marginalize, and repress, and rape and mutilate women whenever they get the chance, and they're at war with anything they perceive as American or Western.

"I think there are more of them than we realize, and we should do more, as you said, to neutralize them. Their radicalism makes a good case that they should be stopped before they become a greater threat."

President Hernandez nodded. "Agreed, Duncan. That's where I was going. One of the greatest failings of our intelligence community has been the quick identification of potential terrorists and then neutralizing them. My predecessor and his DCI cut the CIA budget to the bone. They set us back ten years, and those costly self-inflicted wounds have weakened our intelligence capacity for years to come. Someone at the CIA should've started a file on a young bin Laden or Zawahiri or Mullah Omar when they first heard of them, and they should've collected intelligence on them over a period of years. I'm convinced politically correct policies or hamfisted budget issues prevented us from taking any early action against them. We didn't declare war on them, and they were free to inflict absolute mayhem, terror, and hell on peace-loving people."

The President frowned as he marshaled his thoughts, "The problem, as I see it, is that while we collect information on these guys, your basic radical Islamists, there's a significant lag in quantity and quality of intelligence that comes through the different channels for a case officer to build a file on a person of interest—someone I'd call a world-class potential terrorist. I believe the gaps in collecting, analyzing, and acting on the intel on one of those budding terrorists is often significant and severe. Just when these guys start to become somebody and affect thought or fund mayhem, I'm convinced it's often a case, for us, of too little too late to do anything about him. Maybe we can't take action because the situation has already gotten out of control.

The crucial intelligence skill is the ability to spot a pattern and increase focus with the fewest possible indicators. We must have people who can see trends early and make that intuitive leap."

"I'm sorry, Sir; I believe we once had people like that. Things have changed, though, and our intel people have become stale and comfortable in their jobs. I've been dealing with them for the past fifteen years, kind of sitting on the fence, watching and observing. My view is that the Agency has hired more and more people on the basis of political correctness. As a consequence, it's become an extension of the egregiously liberal State Department—soft, squishy, and weak; completely misguided and ineffective.

"What we have today isn't the same CIA of Pierre Ortiz, Bill Donovan, and Allen Dulles. The last bastion of hope is the Clandestine Service. We need people who can see trends early and make the intuitive leap you mentioned. There aren't many today, but I know of one."

An image of Nazy Cunningham walking across the huge CIA emblem at the headquarters building came to Hunter's mind.

The President, grinning, glanced at his watch again. "The die has been cast. It's very difficult to interrupt the obvious chain of events that led radical Islamists to embrace, lead, or foment terror. I believe, more than not, that when these guys get to a certain point in their professional development as terrorists or bankrollers of terrorism, there's been a feeling that there's little we can do about it. But, I think that view is wrong; we can and should do better."

Hunter was momentarily confused. The President's scenario sounded like a job for an analyst, which made Hunter feel he was the wrong person sitting on the sofa. *Shouldn't some analyst turd be sitting here?*

The discussion of national strategy was enlightening and engaging, but Hunter had difficulty making sense of the topic and why he'd been called to the White House. His sense of being lost in thought showed. "Sir, if I may...."

"Duncan, the only way to protect ourselves is to go after these budding terrorists wherever they are. I think you and your quiet airplane are a perfect combination for the next step in the war against these extremists. I don't just want to identify these threats early before they can mature and fester; I want to eliminate them. As many as we can. I'm not going to send a missile to blow them back to the stone age because they surround themselves with women and children. There is a better way." Then the President pointed at Hunter.

Though Hunter was a smart man, he didn't understand the final twists of the conversation. After a few moments' thought, it finally came to him. He smiled and cocked his head in admiration.

"Sir, just so there's no ambiguity.... What I'm hearing is that we'd like to stop the next generation of terrorists, that when a potential terrorist *is* identified, either through an initial case file or some other assessment, we should take action to eliminate the threat before it becomes a problem. Basically, we should apply the model that if we developed a file on, ascertained the threat, performed a risk analysis, and killed bin Laden before he was thirty, we would've saved 3,000 Americans. We must interrupt and break the terrorist's kill chain."

The President nodded and said seriously, "Exactly. I'd also like to deny them their safe havens. I want to turn the tables on them. If we could eliminate a handful of potential terrorists with pinpoint accuracy, and if their friends and supporters have no idea how these people met their untimely ends, others would think twice. If they're continually on the run, worried about detection and possible termination, they'd have less incentive to plan attacks. Cut off the heads of the hydra...one at a time. You did a marvelous job of cutting off the head of one community organizer, and I'm not really sure how the other met his demise."

Hunter smiled and acknowledged the compliment, though he didn't offer the information that, by then, Osama bin Laden had been turned into a billion rat droppings.

"I think—no, I *know*—you're the right guy to do more of that work. I anticipate it'll be risky, but you've demonstrated that you do well in high-risk situations. I feel the time's right to expand the broader war against Islamic terrorists, wherever they may be hiding. If…you're willing."

Hunter smiled at the passing reference to his release of the file of the former President to the press. "Sir, I'm your guy." Then he realized he'd gotten a little too far ahead. "But, ah, I'll need a little help."

"Whatever you need, Duncan. You'll work directly with the new CIA Director. You won't have any problems with him. He's a good man. Like you, he came up from the ranks and made it to the top of the food chain. He's also the former Director of the National Clandestine Service. He *is* on board. Whatever you need, he'll provide." The President checked his watch again. His body language said it was time to go.

"Wilco. Sir, it's been an honor. Thank you, Mr. President. I'll do my best."

"I have complete confidence in you. You'll do just fine." He paused. "Of course, we never had this conversation."

His comment and body language may have suggested a joke. Hunter responded with a broad smile and opened his arms wide. "Sir, I've never ever been to the White House."

The President gave a discreet nod as he struggled to his feet, showing a sense of urgency. Hunter rose smoothly.

"Duncan Hunter, you're a great American. Good luck and Godspeed." He reached into his coat pocket. There was the muffled dull tinkle of metal on metal as the President withdrew a huge, intricately cut, enameled coin—a Presidential challenge coin. He flashed the three-inch gold disc, artfully sculpted and enameled, at Hunter, then offered his hand with the coin in his palm.

Hunter accepted the coin and handshake humbly. "Thank you, Mr. President."

The President patted his shoulder with his free hand. "My pleasure."

Extracting Hunter from the White House was quietly coordinated and on a time-sensitive schedule. After President Hernandez released Hunter's hand, he checked his watch one last time. Hunter followed the President to the Oval Office washroom. President Hernandez touched a hidden latch near the floor with his toe. The wall panel opened, revealing the small, dimly lit room on the other side. Hunter stepped past the President and took his position in the closet and said, "Thank you again, Sir." The President patted Hunter's back as he moved into position.

Immediately after the panel closed, the door at the opposite end of the room opened, and the same Secret Service agent who ushered Hunter into the space gave a hand signal and nod for Hunter to follow him back down the hall, through the kitchen, past the trash and dumpsters, and back into the catering truck. Hunter didn't see anyone else during the walk, and no words were spoken.

The thirty-minute drive back to the CIA was made in silence. Alone with his thoughts, Hunter felt the ride from Washington to McLean was one of the loneliest of his life. He reflected deeply on what he would do for the President. He would be a lone man fighting a secret war that had to be done solo, in the dark.

During the previous year, he would've relied on his business partner and mentor for help and guidance, but Greg, the "Grinch," was too old for flying, or so he indicated. There was no denying that his friend wouldn't be interested in the mission the President outlined.

Lynche's outlook and demeanor changed dramatically after using the laser on the YO-3A to disable a killer, saving Hunter's life. What Lynche's actions did, more than anything else, was show there was another application of the top-secret airborne laser system designed to eradicate poppy, coca, and cannabis plants. Lynche had committed the ultimate leap for a liberal—he used a environmentally-friendly "weapon" designed to kill plants and turned it on a human to maim him. Although Lynche was glad to have saved Hunter's life, the idea that he shredded the eyeballs of another human in the process bothered him greatly, as if he had tortured the man. If the Grinch didn't like killing, Greg Lynche was totally against torture in any form.

In retrospect, Hunter thought that losing his partner of fifteen years was more than Lynche growing old. Lynche's philosophy changed, too. He wasn't a closet liberal. It was more an issue that his level of effort and focus changed, and he wasn't as effective while in the air. Greg was fine flying missions that didn't draw blood—quiet ISR work, done in the dark where no one knew they were there.

When the missions changed to direct action, identifying and targeting terrorists, Lynche nearly balked. And when the Grinch put the red dot of the laser designator on a terrorist's forehead, he suddenly found reasons to get out of the business. Hunter came to understand that when Lynche laser-designated the al-Qaeda chief, it was an action made under significant duress. Four Hellfire missiles, from a pair of Predator drones, rode that beam down to the designated spot. When they slammed into their target and obliterated one of the masterminds of 9/11, Lynche realized he couldn't continue any more of the "direct action" missions. He hadn't taken Hunter's interrogation of Osama bin Laden very well, but targeting the head of al-Qaeda in Yemen was the final straw. Lynche had to tell Hunter it was over.

Hunter tried to turn away from thoughts of being abandoned during the incredibly risky missions to those focusing on their quiet airplane. He turned the Presidential coin over in his fingers, unable to make out the details. It was difficult to move away from thoughts of the man who first gave Hunter the opportunity to fly the super-quiet airplane on the special access program and who became his best friend and closest advisor. Hunter acknowledged he loved the former CIA Chief of Air Branch and his wife, and he knew they loved him. Greg Lynche was more father than brother and Connie Lynche was the big sister he never had. Despite their political differences, Duncan Hunter knew he would unquestionably follow the old spook to the ends of the Earth.

Lynche completely surprised Hunter when he announced, "007 is all yours," as if he no longer wanted anything to do with it. Perhaps targeting al-Zawahiri poisoned the aircraft for him.

The stealthy airplane had long since been Hunter's anyway. He realized he was obsessed with the YO-3A. He babied it in flight as if it were as fragile and rickety, yet as significant as Charles Lindbergh's

Spirit of St. Louis. He continually improved the unique little airplane between flights, between missions.

Over fifteen years of flying Lockheed's quiet low-level masterpiece, number seven off the assembly line, made 007 an extension of Hunter and his psyche. As the airplane's capabilities improved, so did Hunter's. The transformation from passive, silent, low-altitude sensor platform into an invisible harbinger of death and destruction was an unplanned, unexpected outgrowth of the special access program. It shouldn't have surprised anyone even the remarkable visionary Greg Lynche.

With Greg's departure from the black program called *Wraith,* its name more apropos than ever, Hunter found himself at a crossroads. *For this phase of Wraith, do I bring someone new onboard to operate the sensors, or do I modify the airplane and perform the missions solo?* He took a deep breath as his mind raced. *I could walk away from the intelligence community and continue to build my growing businesses. At some point this has to stop.*

"I'm not getting any younger," he said softly.

Hunter banished the diversion. He never considered any other alternative and wasn't about to begin. There wasn't another sufficiently capable quiet unmanned system available and there was work to be done. No one else had the means and clearances to do it. Taking the fight to the enemy under an executive special access program was a tremendous honor and privilege. And, what the President suggested triggered several desires in Hunter. The prime one was to be more active in the war against terrorists and turn his quiet little airplane into a strategic weapon; he would become the point man for an extraordinarily controversial plan. In retrospect, it was astonishing, much more than anything he had ever contemplated or envisioned just a few years earlier.

The airplane was ready. Hunter shook his head in wonder and admiration, at the change of the ultra-quiet sailplane's nature and character. 007 went from being a modern two-place cockpit to a fully multifunctional single-seat attack aircraft. With the aft seat removed, several retired Schweizer's engineers were able to install a retractable, interchangeable multi-sensor pallet and increase the electrical power output with more-powerful alternators for the expanded sensor suite of cameras, FLIR, laser designator, an experimental gun, and the *Weedbusters* drug crop eradication system.

Hunter placed his chin in his hand. His vision of immediately modifying the aircraft for single-seat operation when Lynche quit looked more like a stroke of genius than a petulant reaction to his friend's abandonment of him and the program.

I should be able to do this alone.

He told the President he was ready for the challenge. He was caught up in the moment, sitting on a couch in the Oval Office, and his other responsibilities were swept aside. Thoughts of chasing terrorists took precedence over losing his business. If he chased and killed budding terrorists, he had to delay the growth of his three small businesses.

Doing double duty on *Wraith* wasn't something he considered. Lynche did much with the support and logistics of the program as well as in the cockpit. Sharing the airborne workload, they divided the mission execution responsibilities equally.

I can do this myself. It's a matter of planning and scheduling. Performing the logistical requirements to ensure *Wraith* missions were executed flawlessly wasn't something he considered while sitting with the President. The unintended consequence of being caught up in the moment meant he let his emotions get the better of him, and he hadn't thought it through. He acknowledged he might have taken on more than he could physically handle. He considered the ramifications of not being able to manage his businesses adequately, and they might fall apart. Having so many employees counting on him—especially those men and women with special needs, maimed by war, dealing with Post-Traumatic Stress Disorder—and the stigma of failing them, troubled him greatly.

After Lynche stepped back, Hunter thought he responded appropriately. While 007 underwent modifications, he bought the plans and jigs for Schweizer's quiet airplanes. The famous glider company stopped making the powered motorgliders largely because the company that purchased them was interested in their small helicopter line; they were not in the business of building handcrafted reconnaissance airplanes.

Hunter transferred the jigs from New York to Texas, and began low-rate production of a modern version of the secret motorized sailplane in Texas. He sold six of the planes to his first customer, the Nigerian Air Force. He didn't want to think about where the new business would take him. He didn't want to walk away from the President's challenge. Killing terrorists from the air had more to do about *duty* than appeal, but without Lynche as his longtime backup in the back seat, he began to question himself and his abilities to do it alone.

I guess I'll find out.

Hunter leaned back in the lawn chair in the transport van while considering his options. He would take a tremendous risk getting into the firing position and pulling the trigger on an unproven weapon. Those risks were incrementally reduced as jihadis relaxed vigilance in their own territory. They wouldn't anticipate an air attack at night.

Attacking overseas terrorists worked in his favor. After fifteen years of flawless execution, he placed the utmost trust and confidence in his airplane's capability and effectiveness. Identifying the targets would be a challenge, but, with sufficient intelligence, it could be done. Getting into a firing solution could be time-consuming. Flying the YO-3A, windows of opportunity would be very short and narrow. Most of the really bad actors had been driven completely underground, during the day. Only recently were the handlers and supporters of terror operating in the open, at night, though even then, they were very well protected.

Hunter presumed the Agency had a special program to track certain high-profile, high-value targets. Such people operated only in the dark and were never or rarely seen operating in the open or during daylight. He had little confidence the CIA had sufficient files on the high-profile, up-and-coming jihadists and radicals, since the previous CIA Director eliminated several similar programs to identify and track the different categories of evil men. Given enough resources, though, anything was possible. The new Director of the CIA might be helpful...even if he was on Hunter's shit list. Apprehensive and conflicted, Hunter sucked all the air out of the van.

As the driver turned off the George Washington Parkway onto Route 123, Hunter leaned forward and placed his head in his hands. He had long thought communism was the great evil. Twenty years as a Marine solidified that view. Now he saw that radical Islamists were as bad if not worse. Both were pure evil with little degree of separation. Radicals and communists of all kinds killed hundreds of millions of men, women, and children, often violently, around the world. Islamists purged Christians and Jews from their lands for a millennium, and radical Islamists brutalized and killed their fellow Muslims as horribly as possible. Trying to take out upstarts before they could wreak violence would never be a noble job. It was dirty work, like a sniper on the battlefield trying to kill the bad guys before they killed your friends, or you. Someone had to do it. Hunter had the tools and skills. All he needed was permission, resources, and cover; and the President just provided all three.

He would need plenty of help, too. Maybe his favorite Navy SEAL might be interested in participating with some of the groundwork. *McGee must be pulling his hair out doing nothing but teaching students,* Hunter mused. *He might want to get back in the game. The problem was, once you dipped your toe in the sticky fluid of counterterrorism, it had a way sucking you in, pulling you under the surface, and rarely did it let you go. Few got out alive or with their mind intact.* Hunter paused and allowed a disturbing chain of thoughts to finally be confronted. *Maybe that is why Greg Lynche really left the program. We had played on the edge for so long...killing plants but not killing anyone. He knew. But once I decided we could be more proactive, the old guy somehow knew he couldn't go there. He knew there was a tipping point, that it would be eventually be too dangerous or even fatal. The old liberal was smarter than he looked. Now I know. I don't think I'll have problems killing terrorists. If I do, I'll say it's too much; it's someone else's turn to do it. When that happens, I'll see a shrink and lose my clearance. I did my part! I suppose at that point, I'll be able to focus on business and customers. If I need to go to the couch, I can use the psychiatrists I hired for my guys with PTSD.*

Hunter was in the middle of a grin when he was forced to return to the present as the van slowed. When it turned sharply to negotiate a bump or curb, he grabbed the shelving lest he be dashed to the floor. The driver stopped the vehicle, which left Hunter confused. He assumed the van would be stopped before entering the CIA compound, so it could be searched.

Concern filled him when he felt a weight shift, as the driver got out. A few moments later, the driver opened the rear door and said, "Follow me."

Hunter stepped from the van and squinted against the sunlight while the driver closed the van's door and walked toward a red-painted door labeled *Deliveries.* Though confused, Hunter followed the man through an empty commercial bakery.

Is this Dunhill's? He saw ovens and industrial mixers everywhere; hundreds of stainless steel cooking instruments hung from overhead racks and hooks. Hunter closed the gap with the driver when they passed through the kitchen into the storefront.

An older woman in a light-blue apron and paper chef's hat waved to the driver as he approached. She lifted a pastry box and gave it to him. *Dunhill Bakery* was printed on the box top.

No words were exchanged, but the driver nodded and smiled as he walked through the front door with the box in front of him as if it were a baby with a dirty diaper. He stepped directly to the curb into a waiting black Suburban. Hunter followed and closed the door behind him.

He saw the van driver, sitting in the front passenger's seat, lift the pink pastry box slightly as he spoke.

"These are for the dispatcher."

Hunter chuckled and settled into the deep leather seats.

By the time they arrived at the CIA transportation center compound, Hunter had resolved the operational imperatives of his new mission. He fought back the sense that he was totally alone. He'd be alone in the air, but there would be plenty of help on the ground.

He thanked the driver for the lift as he crawled out of the big, black vehicle. Setting his thoughts aside, he walked to Nazy's bright-red Mercedes, slid into the driver's seat, and contemplated his next phase in life as an airborne assassin. Of course, he couldn't tell Nazy what he was doing.

The last time she knew of his special access activities, she blew his cover. It may have been unintentional, but he wasn't about to let that happen again.

CHAPTER THREE

2200 August 8, 2012
CIA Headquarters
McLean, Virginia

Duncan Hunter and Nazy Cunningham arrived at the New Headquarters Building parking lot at eight o'clock. Ten minutes later, the two entered the NHB lobby entrance, side-by-side and strolled across the sixteen-foot inlaid seal of the Central Intelligence Agency. They walked as if they were strangers who just happened to share some space; Cunningham's high heels reverberated on the white and black granite, and throughout the lobby. A few heads turned to see who was announcing their arrival. Nazy veered left toward the banks of access control turnstiles and took a blue-coded badge from her purse. Hunter surreptitiously admired the leggy view of his fiancée as he flashed his contractor's green-coded badge to the security personnel.

He processed his briefcase through the X-ray machine before walking through the airport-style magnetometer. On the other side, he "assumed the position," his arms and legs spread as a heavily armed guard in black battle fatigues and a slung M-4 waved a metal detector wand front and back and side to side, and up and down his inseam. By the time Hunter finished the process, Nazy had passed through the turnstiles and was out of sight.

Hunter gathered his black Zero Halliburton off the conveyor belt, moved to access control, and swiped his green badge across the turnstile reader. Green lights flashed, small doors opened, and he proceeded through.

He ran another gauntlet of men in black uniforms, with black M-4s and electronic clipboards, to gain access to the seventh floor, the offices of the Director of Central Intelligence and his staff. Once cleared by name, he waited for a man in black to program the elevator for the top floor. When told to enter, he did.

Once lifted to the executive suite, Hunter stepped from the elevator and immediately recognized the DCI's secretary. He stopped in front of her busy, overflowing L-shaped desk and asked, "Is welcome back in order, Miss Mayo?"

For over twenty years, Penny Mayo was the personal secretary for the last dozen DCIs until the previous one ignominiously replaced her with his longtime male secretary. She was no Miss Moneypenny, but she was pleasant and efficient.

"Why, *Mr. Hunter*, so good to see you again," she cooed.

Hunter leaned forward slightly and smiled at the plain woman with oval, Coke-bottle glasses. Once she might have been attractive. Myopic brown eyes hid behind tiny, thick spectacles, and her mess of auburn hair probably discouraged potential suitors.

"Yes, it's good to be back," she continued. "I'll let the Director know you're here. Follow me."

She swiveled away from her computer monitor and escorted him down the hall to a small conference room to await the DCI.

Hunter stood when the new Director of Central Intelligence entered the remote conference room. Dr. Bruce Rothwell, a tall, thin man with penetrating eyes, a commanding chin, and a soft blue tie, greeted Hunter with a reserved handshake with one hand and Hunter's three-inch personal file in the other.

So this is the creep who keeps chasing Nazy?

The DCI took command of the meeting. In a low monotone, he outlined what he understood to be the President's vision and wishes, and what the Agency could do to provide support to Hunter. While the DCI's spoken lines were articulate, pithy bullet phrases, Hunter sensed stifled hostility and couldn't understand the source of the DCI's apparent angst. With over 100 missions flown for the CIA, every planning meeting with intelligence officers of various grades and levels was conducted with cooperation, collaboration, and *esprit de corps.* And, all of the previous DCIs were very supportive. But, apparently, not this one.

The current meeting was noteworthy and unique, because it appeared it was made under duress. Hunter wondered if the man knew he was engaged to Nazy. Rothwell had been after her for years as one of the deputies at the National Counter Terrorism Center, and she rebuffed him continuously. Since their engagement was a secret, the man couldn't possibly know. The animosity had to stem from something else.

With civil wars roiling in Libya and Egypt, DCI Rothwell was a busy man and hadn't reviewed Hunter's file thoroughly. Had he, the DCI would have learned that Hunter was fully trained in kinesics and reading micro-expressions. Hunter was stunned momentarily, realizing that the DCI's language and comments could be interpreted in only one way—he had little interest or energy to support the President's directive. Rothwell's nervousness and intonation conveyed he wasn't on board with the President's view and direction, and he also wasn't convinced the man sitting across from him was the right asset to conduct such sensitive missions.

Rothwell was especially troubled to learn that Duncan had never been an intelligence officer. That meant Hunter wasn't qualified to be briefed on or cleared to execute such a high-profile mission, one that was "inherently governmental." Hunter may have been awarded the Distinguished Intelligence Star, but to Rothwell, Hunter was "just a pilot" who'd been recruited by an old, retired senior intelligence service executive. Duncan wasn't one of the good ol' boys in the intelligence community, and never would be.

Hunter appeared not to have much of the specialized training intelligence officers typically received, and to Rothwell, that was a major problem. The DCI had told the President that what they needed for a mission of this import was a career intelligence officer, preferably several very seasoned, trusted officers from the National Clandestine Service. When he suggested that he had several officers at the NCS who were perfectly suited for such a project, the President vetoed the idea and offer. Instead, he indicated he had "someone in mind." The

DCI resented the President's prerogative to dictate key personnel over the DCI's superstars in the NCS.

Hunter sensed conflict in the DCI's body language. Seconds passed as the two men stared at each other. Finally, Hunter broke eye contact and said, "Director Rothwell, I sense this is a bad time."

"Mr. Hunter, timing isn't the issue. I have a problem with you on this program. I don't know you. You have been—no disrespect—a valued contractor. For this work, I have significant problems turning it over to a ... contractor. This is inherently governmental work, not contract support." He held a cheap plastic pen in his hand and unconsciously tapped the thick file, never breaking eye contact with Duncan.

Hunter heard from Lynche that the new DCI could be very direct and was a no-bullshit kind of guy, even if he shook hands like a wimp. He came up through the ranks of the NCS and made his name as a deputy at the National Counter Terrorism Center. Lynche heard Rothwell did whatever was required to complete and execute his missions, including an unsubstantiated rumor to infiltrate Islamic extremist organizations overseas, he converted to Islam. Some suspected such a move actually bolstered his career.

To know your Enemy, you must become your Enemy. Rothwell often quoted Sun Tzu in counterterrorism conferences. His close understanding of Islam and his fight against radical Islamists helped propel him through the CIA's ranks. Hunter read there was great concern in Congress with Rothwell's appointment to the top Agency position, but what those concerns were was anyone's guess. The press rarely divulged the whole story. Lynche emphasized he knew enough of the new DCI to know he was as proud of his NCS heritage and the NCS as Hunter was of being a Marine. As a deputy director in the NCS, Rothwell guarded the organization and his agents' assignments jealously. Any conversion to Islam had to be a nasty rumor.

For fifteen years, the previous DCIs Hunter and Lynche worked for were very accommodating, cooperative, and collaborative. Had there been any issues having a contractor, who had never attended the intelligence officer's course, on a sensitive special access program like *Wraith,* Greg would have intervened as one intelligence officer to another. Hunter knew the stratification within such cliques. Fighter pilots dismissed other pilots as inferior. Border Patrol agents dismissed non-agents as nonentities. In the intelligence community, if you weren't an intelligence officer, especially in the NCS, you weren't shit.

Hunter knew he had broken some of the rules during the run on their wildly successful special access program and had generally been accepted as one of the boys "in the IC" after 100 missions, but he was unaware of any previous conflicts or concerns regarding his qualifications or his leadership position on the program. When Greg Lynche was on active duty, he was a very Senior Intelligence Service officer, equivalent to a three-star general. Early on during the black program *Wraith,* Greg had been able to run interference for, and affirm Hunter's *bona fides* whenever there was a question about Hunter's qualifications or dedication to the Agency.

Hunter was currently on his own, facing a hostile DCI. If anyone had a reason to be pissed off, it was Hunter. "Director, Rothwell, Sir, I may understand some of your concerns and reluctance to embrace me to lead this project. Is the issue I'm not a government intelligence officer, or do you think I'm not the best resource for this work?"

Dr. Rothwell was surprised at the green-badged man's temerity. "Not being an intelligence officer is part of it. I really don't know you, Mr. Hunter. You have an outstanding file. Put your file aside for a moment. You have built a reputation. The book on you is that you're something of a maverick. My experience has been that mavericks get themselves or others killed. How many contracted personal security firms have been in the news because they hired a few mavericks that bent the rules or pulled the trigger when they should have stood down?

"I won't condone unprofessionalism. That's my main problem with you. From your file, I see you've performed flawlessly and meritoriously for over fifteen years. I know you received the Distinguished Intelligence Cross earlier this year. While that's impressive, what I need to know is, are you the maverick some suggest? Am I wasting my time with you, or is that assessment a complete mischaracterization?" Rothwell was very proud of himself and was nearly sneering. He waited for Hunter to respond.

Duncan took a deep breath, giving himself time to choose his words carefully. "Director Rothwell, I think there's a misunderstanding. I was once a government 'blue badge' employee. Several directors ago, it was suggested I become contracted help to maintain my cover, so I retired and worked as a contractor. Second, you're concerned I might be a maverick. It's true I've been called that many times in this building by my former partner. I believed it was a sign of respect.

"Thirty years ago, while in flight school, I earned the call sign Maverick, not because I was wild or a nonconformist, but because I came up through the enlisted ranks, got my commission, and became a pilot—much like how you came through the ranks of intelligence officers. While my peers and I got along, it was obvious I viewed life a little differently by having humble beginnings.

"I went to school at night. I didn't socialize much. I worked harder than my peers. I wanted to become a great pilot and worked at achieving that goal. Much like how I approached playing racquetball and competing at a national level, I applied the same level of energy and commitment to mastering high-performance fighters.

"My view was a little contrary to those of my peers and superiors. They were fighter pilots. Once they were at the top of their game, many put their careers on cruise control. If you asked them today, they would probably admit they took the easier road for whatever reason, and enjoyed the fruits of their labors.

"I took a much harder path, studying engineering and business. My goals were different. I *was* a maverick in the fighter-pilot community and was headed for test pilot school. A high-speed ejection interrupted those plans. I thought I was recruited by the CIA, because I was, like most everyone in this Agency, a maverick with certain special skills. During all that time on *Wraith,* I applied the same level of effort and dedication to every mission as I did to learning how to fly supersonic jets or playing at the U.S. Racquetball Open.

"Sir, Greg Lynche and *Maverick* practiced each one of those 100 missions thoroughly before deploying on them. The training always paid off. I have a long record of getting the mission done, quietly and professionally. I'm here, because the President thinks what I've done in the past, in my quiet little airplane, might be helpful in the war on terror; specifically against radical Islamists on this program. I don't think *Maverick* is wasting your time, Sir. I'm just looking for help to accomplish the President's goals."

The DCI glanced at the file again. He was livid that he'd just been upstaged and upbraided, and didn't appreciate it. When he looked up, he wore a tight smile to hide his embarrassment. "That was helpful, Duncan. That explains much."

He sat still, contemplating his next move, tapping the file with his pen. Hunter thought the cheap plastic might crumple under the pressure.

Hunter waited for the next barrage of questions. He didn't believe his spiel was enough to assuage the DCI's concerns and anticipated some backlash for challenging him in this manner. The longer the DCI remained silent, planning his next move, the more Hunter expected the worst. With a stroke of his throwaway pen, Director Rothwell had the power to pull Hunter's access to the classified world. Hunter's speech was a target-rich environment for getting himself kicked from the building, surrendering his green badge, and being frog-marched from the premises. He waited for the verdict.

Rothwell was furious and embarrassed that his deputies had unwittingly set him up. He didn't have time to review Hunter's file thoroughly and outsourced it to his deputies. Those who reviewed it knew Hunter was called a maverick but had blown the context. The DCI convinced himself he would disqualify Hunter for the project and install a hand-picked officer from the NCS to lead and execute the missions. He couldn't believe the missions required an obsolete airplane and an aging pilot just to kill some up and coming terrorists.

The DCI needed a face-saving way out. He settled on kicking the can down the road, he would not address the issue, and would pretend he and Hunter never had the conversation.

"Duncan, I apologize. We'll need to reschedule something for tomorrow. Get with Penny, my secretary, and get on my calendar tomorrow. I'm up to my ears in alligators with this Libya crap and need to head to Capitol Hill. Tomorrow will be better. I have an hour opening in the afternoon."

Hiding his shock well, Hunter said, "Wilco. Sir, I have a set of slides if you want to look through them before tomorrow. They outline our capabilities and a basic CONOPS, concept of operations."

Director Rothwell stood. "I'd appreciate that. It would be very helpful." He offered his best disarming smile. "Thank you for coming."

Hunter stood and opened his briefcase, extracted the material, and offered the DCI a thin binder, then extended his hand. The men shook firmly, which also surprised Hunter. Maybe there were no hard feelings.

As the two men left the conference room, Hunter walked toward the elevators buoyed by the meeting. He assumed the new DCI, prior to being confirmed by the Senate, was unaware of his and Lynche's activities on *Wraith.* His file told only so much of the story.

Hunter debated what to disclose. Only President Hernandez received a full brief, and Hunter was certain he hadn't shared all of Hunter's extracurricular activities with anyone. Nazy told the newly sworn-in President how Hunter released the former President's Agency file to Congress and the media, which expedited his resignation. She also informed him that Hunter took custody of a very alive Osama bin Laden from the Navy SEALs who snatched him from his bed in Pakistan, and the results of her and Hunter's interrogation of him. Knowing Hunter was almost killed while discovering the true nature of the former President was enough for President Hernandez to award him the CIA's highest honor, the Distinguished Intelligence Cross, and a Presidential pardon for any improprieties he may have committed—such as releasing top-secret CIA files concerning the former President.

The following day, Hunter and the DCI greeted each other as warmly as if they were longtime professional acquaintances. The DCI set the tone and pace of the discussion. The previous level of angst was replaced by cordiality.

Hunter briefed his CONOPS slides as he would have briefed a multi-aircraft air combat sortie, with brevity and specificity. He began with the situation—to kill potential terrorists before they could emerge into something more lethal. The DCI complimented him on proposing that the list of terrorists and their financiers be called a "disposition matrix" and not "the President's kill list."

Rothwell agreed that even the eunuchs of the mainstream press would string them up if such a term as "the President's kill list" ever came out. He was impressed by the briefing material. The mission was to leverage the capabilities of Quiet Aero Systems, Hunter's company, and the modified YO-3A to take direct action against those on the disposition matrix. The CIA, or more specifically, the DCI, would provide the targeting criteria and the execution order. He would identify which target was the priority and provide as much information as possible to ensure a successful mission. He would also be responsible for requesting presidential cross-border authorization. Only the President could authorize clandestine assets to cross the borders of another country. The President would sign a brief document authorizing a "covert action" program. Hunter would provide the basic concept of operations, from the administrative phase of moving aircraft and people into position, through the execution of the mission, and how to bring all assets out of the country later.

During their third meeting, the DCI immediately brought up the issue of compensation and what to call the special access program.

Hunter sat down to respond. "Are we going to use Agency assets for ingress and egress, or am I providing a full turnkey operation? If we use one of your cargo aircraft, the costs are lowered significantly. If I have to procure a C-130 and crew, the costs will be much higher. I can do either, but I would prefer to use your planes and crews. They're already cleared, but I know they're also on tight schedules, and you have limited assets. It's really up to you."

"Let me run some numbers and get back to you. What do we call the program? It needs to be differentiated from *Wraith.* It's a wholly different mission."

Hunter anticipated a naming scheme. All special access programs needed a program name. "What about *Noble Savage?*"

Director Rothwell smiled broadly and eased back in his chair. "I like that. Where'd that come from?" He seemed genuinely excited and impressed.

"I read somewhere that when some explorers moved farther west into North America, they were astounded to see Indians hunting any and all game. The right to hunt anything was a privilege France granted only to aristocrats, who took that right for granted. The Indians demonstrated the same carefree right to hunt as the French aristocracy.

"One of the explorers wrote a book when he returned to France, and one chapter had the title of *The Savages Are Truly Noble* or something like it, hence *Noble Savage.* The parallels to hunting and hunters and the privilege afforded to only those with a special clearance were too much to ignore."

"And you're a Hunter." Rothwell smiled at the irony. Pleased with himself, he continued, "*Noble Savage* it is. How about something like '*Happy Hunting*' for the program's emergency code words?"

"How about something simple like *Diablo? Happy Hunting* is too close to my name."

"Good point. Emergency code is *Diablo.*"

If Hunter had to abort the mission, uttering the emergency code across the classified radio frequency would bring Agency and DOD assets to the rescue—in theory.

By the end of the week, Hunter realized that Miss Mayo, the DCI's secretary, was working hard to make herself more attractive. She traded business suits and flats for dresses and heels. She cut her hair short and smooth. She was much more attentive than normal as she escorted him to the small working conference room at the end of the hall, clumsily trying to flirt, as they walked down the long corridor.

He complimented her new hair but didn't reciprocate or discourage her flirtations. Minutes after she left Hunter alone, the DCI entered, and the two men focused on the program. The DCI soon resigned himself to the notion that Hunter had everything thought out. It was clear the man was a thorough, professional mission planner. Hunter's personnel file was as thick as a ream of paper, and it wasn't easy to believe he was pushing fifty-five. The top or newest documents weaved a fifteen-year story of a no-nonsense, fearless pilot with 100 counterdrug or counterterrorism missions under his and his partner's belts.

It was clear there was something special about the man and his relationship with the President. Director Rothwell considered it was unique and very controversial for the President to take a personal interest in facilitating Hunter's new mission. That meant the two men had a history not mentioned in the file. He scribbled a note on from a sticky pad sheet and placed it on the folder.

The DCI acknowledged the President was probably on solid ground to limit a mission such as he proposed to an outside contractor. When the DCI expressed the idea that government agents should do clandestine work that was "inherently governmental," the President dismissed his concerns by asking, "Do you have those capabilities in-house?"

Even the newly installed DCI had enough knowledge of the capabilities of the Air Branch and Clandestine Service to know the Agency did not, nor did Special Operations Command. He lowered his eyes and silently shook his head.

Rothwell confirmed that several senior analysts had identified and been tracking terrorists or "persons of interest" for certain divisions or leaders in the intelligence community. Those programs were already in place. One analyst tracked the whereabouts of the top terrorist leaders around the world. It resembled the unclassified FBI's Most Wanted List with the exception of the red TOP SECRET stamps on the footer and header of each page.

Another program provided a listing of confirmed or suspected financiers of terror, outlining transactions, beneficiaries, and charities. Yet another program, managed by the public affairs office and called *Early Bird,* provided a daily accounting of excerpts of speeches or statements of terrorist leaders or sponsors. The Presidents of Russia, Iran, Syria, Egypt, Venezuela, Pakistan, Libya, and Cuba could always be counted on to provide incendiary statements or rhetoric. *Noble Savage* would target the lesser known activist terrorists.

There was no single program that identified persons of interest for elimination. Hunter didn't have the "need to know" to understand the mechanics of the process whereby the DCI culled names from disparate listings and turned them into a kill list. He did explain that the sole authority to "rack and stack" or prioritize those key "persons of interest" and migrate them onto the disposition matrix would be confined to him.

"From my list," Director Rothwell said, "I brief the President, who gives his concurrence. Each POI is individually briefed. The President either authorizes or disapproves the operation."

Hunter nodded when Rothwell announced he populated the first group of POIs onto the *Noble Savage* disposition matrix. The DCI tossed a thin binder across the table to him.

"I'd like to expedite this one."

CHAPTER FOUR

2200 August 14, 2012
Fredericksburg, Texas

On the north corner of East Main Street sits the National Museum of the Pacific War. Originally named after Fredericksburg's favorite son, Chester Nimitz, the Admiral Nimitz Museum provides displays of Allied and Japanese aircraft and other artifacts made famous during the Pacific War campaign. Hundreds of visitors tour the museum as well as the boulevard's small tourist traps, antique shops, and microbreweries which line both sides of Main Street. At the other end, where the street becomes West Main Street, sits a nondescript 1930s-era bank building. Tourists walking down West Main rarely gave the old bank any consideration. It's largely ignored and no one visits.

Originally erected to house the First National Bank of Texas, the building passed through several owners before becoming the corporate offices of Quiet Aero Systems. No signs mark the structure as anything but a well-maintained heritage facility, consistent in theme and style with the other restored buildings of old Fredericksburg. Some have tried the front door but no one answers.

Recently a front company for the CIA's Air Branch, the Quiet Unmanned Aircraft Research Laboratory outgrew its initial charter as an undercover government research facility to become the privately held company Quiet Aero Systems. Formerly the product of special access or black programs for ten years, the government-sponsored business boasted several world-class engineers and scientists who focused primarily on researching and developing quiet aviation technologies and related stealthy products. The front company's goal was to develop special-purpose aircraft for the government, never acknowledging the customer was the CIA.

Developing aircraft, big and small, manned and unmanned, which could fly at very low altitudes "as quiet as an owl" was a unique, high-priority capability, especially for special activities and operations. Other research was conducted in myriad fields unrelated to aircraft, noisy or quiet. When the research laboratory was transferred to private ownership, two aircraft assigned to the lab were stricken from the U.S. Government's inventory.

A white, red, and gold Gulfstream IVSP was the first airplane struck from the DOJ inventory. The jet was the property of a Colombian drug lord before it was seized by the Miami office of the Drug Enforcement Agency. Days after it was confiscated, the aircraft was transferred to the secretive Quiet Unmanned Aircraft Research Laboratory with a promise the jet would be modified with instruments and sensors to conduct classified quiet-aircraft research. The other airplane, though it was a relic, was the crown jewel of the bogus company.

During the mid-1960s, as American servicemen were being ambushed in the fields of Vietnam, the U.S. Army rushed a requirement to develop low-altitude, "quiet" surveillance aircraft for the war effort. A very small research-and-development program was created to solve the challenges of quiet, low-level powered flight. A few brilliant engineers and a dynamic U.S. Navy physicist, all with Top Secret clearances, were pressed into a research facility to develop and test an acoustically quiet aircraft—one that had an integrated aero-system of a quiet airframe, a quiet propeller, and a quiet engine. An owl was used to establish the aural benchmark and low-altitude threshold where a human could detect the sound of an owl's wing beats during flight and the goal was to be able to operate at an altitude where an owl could no longer be heard. During 1967-1968, several prototype "Quiet Thruster" aircraft were rapidly built and tested in response to the Army's request for a low-level nighttime surveillance and reconnaissance aircraft.

The initial QT designs would have given Rube Goldberg a coronary. Engineers modified a Schweizer glider and installed a heavily muffled engine behind the pilot's seat. A huge multi-blade propeller was mounted on a post on the front of the glider's nose. Propeller and engine were connected by a long, thick driveshaft which ran over the top of the canopy to the front of the plane. Radical designs and test beds validated the concept of low-altitude, virtually silent powered flight, and a contract was awarded to the Lockheed Aircraft Corporation for a short production run of more conventional-looking prototypes. Eleven prototype aircraft were built; a Y and an O indicated the type of aircraft—prototype observation—and were designated YO-3As. The airplanes were called "Yo-Yos."

In addition to the Gulfstream, Quiet Aero Systems possessed the sole remaining operational YO-3A. While NASA had a flying YO-3A, number 010, few people knew of the status or whereabouts of the other aircraft—number seven off Lockheed's assembly line. Many assumed the airplane was in flyable storage somewhere or was held by a warbird collector; no one knew where it was or how it was acquired. Only those with a need to know were told how number 007 was transferred from the FBI to the CIA's Air Branch where it was stricken from the unclassified listing of government aircraft. In the hands of Lynche and Hunter, 007 was upgraded and improved over fifteen years while it served primarily as a sensor platform for one of the CIA's most-secretive and longest-duration special access programs.

That aircraft number 007 was engaged in some of the Agency's most clandestine, dangerous counterdrug and counterterrorism work didn't escape notice of those on the black program. The highly modified spy plane was routinely referred to as "James Bond" or "Double-O Seven" as a tribute to Ian Fleming and his master spy.

After five days of meetings with the DCI, the Chief of Air Branch, and scientists from the Science and Technology Directorate, Duncan Hunter repaired downstairs and waited in the CIA cafeteria. He camped out at a window seat overlooking one of the outdoor courtyards where hundreds of tiny potted ponytail palms lined the long window sill. There he'd wait until she walked past, and then followed her at a discrete distance; around the wide hall and up the escalator to the lobby. Hunter rarely took his eyes off the shapely figure of Nazy Cunningham innocently ascending the moving stairs but when he did, he momentarily cast them high above the escalators, to the ceiling, to the one-sixth-scale black models of the CIA's most famous surveillance aircraft—the manned U-2 and A-12, and the unmanned D-21 reconnaissance drone. When he reached the end of the ride and stepped into the lobby, he continued his fixation on the moving target.

She knew she was being followed; it excited her to know they'd be together soon. Across the CIA emblem, out of the NHB she walked; Duncan followed several dozen paces behind. At the end of the long concrete walkway, Nazy stopped and acted like she had dropped or forgotten something. She looked at the ground, from side to side; confused, searching, questioning. When he caught up to her, he was confused by her antics and asked, "Excuse me miss, can I help you? Did you drop something?"

Nazy continued to scan to her left and right, her brows severely furrowed with concern. She spun to check from whence she came. She shook her head gently, assured no one could hear her, and whispered, "I've lost my panties, and I don't know where they could be." She teased him a bit more when he helped her into her car, not taking his eyes off of hers when she slowly sat down—knees together—and lifted her legs over the doorsill. When they arrived at her house, she led him upstairs to the bedroom, still playacting like they were strangers. She addressed him as Mister Hunter; he addressed her as Miss Cunningham; Miss Cunningham kicked off her shoes and turned to Mister Hunter and said, "I need a shower." Whenever Hunter was in town, their last night together always was a long, steamy, soapy, erotic and emotional affair, culminating with them exhausted and satiated, and falling asleep in each other's arms.

The following morning, after Hunter made and served Nazy

breakfast in bed, they showered together—this time expeditiously—and dressed. Nazy steadily powered the Mercedes 380SL along the beltway, favoring the left lane and sped up the Washington-Baltimore Parkway. Almost an hour after leaving her house, she dropped Hunter off at the General Aviation Terminal at the Baltimore Washington Airport and headed to her office at the CIA. Her intriguing Mona Lisa smile would turn mirthless when she entered the seventh floor of the New Headquarters Building.

After Duncan filed his flight plan and received a weather brief, he walked from the building into a sunny day and onto the Quiet Aero System's corporate jet. That he flew the aircraft solo shouldn't have surprised anyone except the bureaucrats at the Federal Aviation Administration, who would have been apoplectic had they known. The former Marine Corps fighter pilot had a way of getting around restrictive regulations by ignoring them altogether, something his former partner disapproved of and discouraged to little avail.

Forty-five minutes after takeoff, Hunter stepped off the big jet at the Newport State Airport. There he met a muscular black man in the terminal, and the two men embraced ecstatically. After thirty minutes of close, hushed conversation, the men stood, embraced again, shook hands, and departed in opposite directions.

Hunter returned to the jet, folding the air stairs behind him, and flew to Elmira, New York. He had a thirty-minute meeting with the former Schweizer Aircraft Company CEO before returning to his jet and flying directly to Gillespie County Airport in Texas.

After the special-purpose Gulfstream was hangared in its air-conditioned space, the chief executive officer of Quiet Aero Systems walked from the standalone hangar, as the folding door closed high overhead and behind. He slipped into the black Aston Martin DB9 and drove through old Fredericksburg to his office.

Duncan checked the time before hurrying downstairs to the operations laboratory, taking the stairs two at a time. As he entered the double garage-sized room, he met the triple-digit decibel, high-pitched hum of dozens of high-speed propeller blades. A moment later, the noise ceased.

A short, thin man with a heavy beard and glasses, his ears covered by red-and-black sound suppressors, stood over a computer terminal hammering the keyboard with bony fingers. Hunter didn't interrupt him while he took visual inventory of the lab.

Curtains of inch-square stainless steel netting hung from floor-to-ceiling, separating the computer work station from the rest of the room. Near and parallel to the ceiling, thin black rails resembling track lighting were attached to the walls. Each rail was bisected by a black, Coke-can-sized sensor which pointed downward into the center of the cage.

Behind the net, in the middle of the room, stood a square wood structure made up of two-by-fours. Two uprights terminated crosswise to form a two-foot-square opening. On the floor, covered by sheets, lay sixteen foot-square quadrotors in a "plus sign" formation. Groups of four tiny four-propeller helicopters aligned perpendicular to the others.

The bearded man looked up at his visitor, beaming with enthusiasm and pride, as he shouted over his suppressed ears, "You have to see this!"

Dr. Burt Aguirre leaned over the keyboard, typed a short string of letters, and pointed at the steel mesh before he hit the Enter key and shouted, "Watch!"

Hunter moved closer to the netting. One second later, the sixteen tiny quadrotors came to life. Sixty-four small propellers spun and lifted the micro-helicopters into a hover just above the white sheet before they stabilized in pitch and roll. Hunter jammed his fingers into his ears. The sound from the high-speed rotors was deafening and painful.

Every one of the quadrotors hovered at the same altitude without discernible drift. They were stable and steady, with no hint of drifting into the other tiny helicopters. After a brief delay, Dr. Aguirre typed another keyboard command. With a discernable change of pitch, all sixteen quadrotors uniformly shot up three feet above the floor while maintaining formation. The precision was stunning. They formed perfectly straight lines, perfect squares, and remained completely level, aligned, and stable.

The noise of the sixty-four high-speed propellers reverberated in the closed room. Hunter winced and repositioned his fingers, jamming them deeper into his ears. Dr. Aguirre looked up from the monitor to check the position of the quadrotors and entered another string of commands into the computer.

After a pause, the quadrotors slowly rearranged. One group of four flew through the center of the wooden structure's opening, followed by groups of four. After all four squares of quadrotors flew through the wooden square; they reassembled with uncanny exactitude into their original plus sign formation on the other side of the structure, still hovering three feet above the floor.

Hunter expressed astonishment at the precision of the battery-powered rotorcraft. Smiling, Dr. Aguirre entered more commands into the computer and shouted, "Look, no hands!"

Immediately the hovering four-block formation of quadrotors broke off, one-by-one, and flew through the wooden opening before arcing around and going back through the hole at a slightly lower altitude. In seconds, the sixteen tiny quadrotors moved continuously through space, carving a three-dimensional Figure 8 through the opening, flying higher on one side of the opening, then dipping marginally lower on the other. Each tiny helicopter remained perfectly spaced and avoided hitting the others.

A few more keystrokes, and the sixteen quadrotors finished their choreographed routine and flew to the side of the uprights; they reassembled in two uniform sets of eight, and landed in formation, all shutting off their rotors when they softly touched down on the sheet.

Hunter, astounded and excited, unplugged his ears and rushed to congratulate the man. "Burt, you're amazing! You did it! How?"

Pointing to the black sensors on the rails overhead, Dr. Aguirre peeled the sound suppressors off his ears. "Each one of those transmitters acts like a GPS satellite for the quadrotors, providing precision three-dimensional location information. With the ultrahigh frequency transmitters, we can make them do anything with total precision. Now we can make them autonomous, not just remote controlled."

"That's fantastic, Burt. I knew you'd break the code soon. Thanks for showing me. I can't get over how solid and steady they are. I want to talk to you later on the next setup. I'd like them able to carry a payload, nothing much. Maybe a pound."

"Can do easy, Duncan. How much time do I have? There shouldn't be any problems. If we can do that," he pointed at the caged quadrotors, "we can scale them so they can easily carry something."

"No hard timetable. I have some other ideas and modifications I'd like to see. Can we discuss it tomorrow afternoon? I need to be on the road in a bit."

Dr. Aguirre, smiling broadly, gave him two thumbs up. Hunter clapped his back and hurried from the ops lab to go upstairs.

As he turned toward the steps, Hunter was immediately struck by the view in the hallway. He froze, his eyes tried to make sense of what he saw. The wainscoting and walls moved slightly, as if a mirage filled the hallway. He saw a slight shift in coloring, like a thin, diaphanous membrane or lens stretched across the hall.

He blinked and squinted, trying to clear his vision from the distortion. He saw something else in the hall, like a tiny ripple distorting the walls and floor. The ceiling was clear and didn't move. It remained perfectly focused.

"What's ... *that*?" he whispered.

From a spot just a few feet ahead, right where the rippled view stood, a voice erupted, "Light-bending material. Welcome home, Duncan." An instant later, in a move reminiscent of someone taking off a "cloak of invisibility," one of the nanotechnology scientists, Dr. Brian LaBrake, stood and folded the material in front of him.

Hunter saw waves in the material, but it still resembled a flimsy membrane. He hadn't moved. *"What the hell is that?"* he demanded.

"We're calling it 'light-bending material' for now. It could be the next generation of camouflage; a couple of other companies are experimenting with the technology. I think ours is a better solution. It completely reflects what's behind it with little loss of clarity, although there is a slight shade differential, but at a distance, you can't tell. God, I love, nanotechnology! Gotcha!"

Hunter stepped forward and touched the material, which felt like tiny glass beads under his fingertips. Astonishment and concern showed in his face.

Dr. LaBrake, who had short brown hair and a square face, chuckled until he was nearly falling over with laughter.

Hunter was between livid and grateful. "LaBrake, you can't do that to me! I thought I was having a stroke."

"Is this some cool shit or what? That'll teach you to go away for a month. You know when the cat is away, the mice will play. You know what else? While we played with this, we stumbled on some combination of materials that block IR. There's absolutely no heat transfer. Right now, we can't combine the two technologies into one material, but even individually, both are radical leaps in camouflage."

Astonished, Hunter fought for words, as he rubbed the light-bending, glassy material between his fingers. LaBrake beamed, his laugh cackled like a banty rooster.

Relieved at not having a stroke, Hunter said, "Brian that's amazing. Nice work. You'll have to show me how it works. We'll discuss what we can do with it. Can we do that tomorrow? I'm late for an appointment."

LaBrake nodded. "Absolutely, boss. Go do your thing. We'll see you tomorrow."

The two men shook hands. Hunter patted the younger scientist's back, as LaBrake tossed the material over his head like a cape and walked down the hall of the old bank building. Hunter stared in amazement, seeing only the man's hips and legs moving.

The image played tricks with his mind, as LaBrake whistled the theme song from *The Good, the Bad, and the Ugly*. One-half of him took a right turn and disappeared. Again relieved he wasn't having a stroke; Hunter shook his head before racing upstairs.

After stopping at his office and the lavatory, Hunter ran from the rear of the building across the parking lot and into the garage. He bypassed the Aston Martin and entered the glossy black Hummer2 parked beside it. He loved the big Hummer, primarily because it irritated liberals and environmentalists who muttered openly, "No one needs a truck like that." Of course they were wrong. It was an operations night, and Hunter needed all the big black truck's capabilities.

The Hummer2 was modified to shield its occupants from mayhem and mischief. It carried 1,000 pounds of armor-piercing protection and state-of-the-art technologies to protect its passengers from a variety of weapons. Every window was replaced with 40mm bullet-resistant multilayer polycarbonate glass. Under the hood was a large, supercharged Corvette motor, armored and specially tuned to allow the big truck to escape trouble, on or off the road.

The tires were "run flats" that enabled the diver to continue at high speed over long distances even when punctured by multiple bullets. The 700-horsepower engine enabled the truck to do four-wheel burnouts. The fuel tank was reinforced with quarter-inch ballistic steel; a self-sealing bladder made the tank bullet resistant and blast proof. It was a brute, a tank on four chrome wheels and Hunter loved driving the gas-guzzling monster. He eased the Beast from the garage onto West Main Street.

The plan for the evening was to ops-check and field test the laser-designated .70 caliber gun in flight. The receiver, barrel, and ammunition were recent deliveries from a pair of top-secret programs from one of the CIA's Science and Technology laboratories. The initial goal of the program was to develop a very long-range sniper rifle using special-purpose ammunition, which would have a probability of kill ratio of 98% effective at three miles. Agency scientists were challenged to improve the reliability of the electronics and seeker head being subject to 1,000 Gs, when rounds were fired with conventional powder cartridges.

Researchers determined that a hybrid propellant source, a combination of black powder and a tiny solid rocket booster, significantly reduced the severity of the G-load on the electronics in the head of the bullet to under 500 Gs. Once the bullet left the rifle's muzzle, the solid rocket booster lit off and further accelerated the projectile to its target like a bottle rocket.

Instead of the twist of the barrel's rifling providing a spinning mass for the necessary stability during the ballistic flight, the new projectile was guided by tiny, fully-controllable, triangular fins that popped from the four-inch projectile once it cleared the muzzle. It was no longer a ballistic projectile but flew to the laser-designated aiming point. The weapon saw limited use in Afghanistan but was never tried on an aircraft. Hunter's engineers found a way to modify the weapon for in-flight use; at least that was the hope.

Hunter's longtime support crew, Bob and Bob—both Vietnam veterans who cared for the small fleet of U.S. Army YO-3As in combat—had the custom tractor-trailer ready for departure. One Bob was somewhat taller and had bushy, shoulder-length gray hair. The other was a bit heavier and sported a long, thick, ZZ Top beard. For the past fifteen years, the two septuagenarians had kept 007 in better than pristine condition. Bob and Bob worked whenever there was a mission and always under cover of darkness. For all that time together, 007 saw daylight only once.

In the days of the special access program *Wraith*, at least one of the two men escorted the aircraft in its shipping container, either over the road or on a container ship when overseas. As 007 and the aircrew proved the concept and began to respond to more immediate action missions, the quiet airplane jumped to the head of the line and rode first class in the belly of Air Force C-17s or C-130s. In rare cases, the YO-3A rode in one of the Agency's civilian L-100s.

The hot, summer evening's trip to the remote auxiliary field near the Mexican border would take a couple of hours. The two-vehicle train would pass through the small town of Uvalde, the home of FDR's Vice President, John Nance Garner, and the site of the National Soaring Championships. Long narrow trailers, obviously holding sailplanes, were common passing through town and were largely ignored. The U.S. Border Patrol rarely gave the long, thin custom rigs a second thought.

As the two vehicles left Uvalde on Highway 90, Hunter contacted Bob and Bob on their AN/PRQ-7 handheld radio on a discrete, secure frequency to brief them on the mission. Once Hunter gained entry to the field, Bob and Bob would extract 007 from its container, install the wings, and perform a functional check of the flight controls. They would double check that the gun master switch was off and ensured the weapon was safe before connecting the battery.

While they assembled the aircraft and made it ready for flight, Hunter would drive along one edge of the runway and drop infrared chem-lites every 200 feet. When he reached the end of the runway, he would set up a full-scale silhouette of a man for a target. On the return trip on the other side of the runway, he would drop more chem-lites. In less than three minutes, he should have dropped enough of the disposable chemical light sticks to mark the runway boundaries and target silhouette.

The moonless night helped Hunter calm his emotions. He pulled up to the side of the gate of the U.S. Air Force Auxiliary Field Spofford, jumped out, and hurried to the huge chain and multiple locks that secured the gate. It had been almost fifteen years since he last had access to the combination locks used by the Border Patrol to gain access to ranch properties when they chased illegal aliens across private property. The mission hinged on his being able to gain access to the remote airfield. Otherwise, they would abort.

Of the two large Master locks linked together, one was an antique with wheels and numbers on the bottom. Betting the Border Patrol hadn't changed the combinations on the thousands of locks that hung on ranch gates in the Del Rio sector, Hunter rotated the four thumbwheels to the old combination of 2-7-0-7, the same number of the old Boeing SST that was never built.

He pulled on the shackle, and to his smug relief, the lock unlatched. He swung the gate wide, allowing Bob and Bob to enter, then he jumped into his Hummer and drove onto the field before closing and locking the gate behind him.

By the time Hunter finished his chores, the highly modified YO-3A was rolled from its container. Working with the practiced choreography of a NASCAR pit crew, Bob and Bob attached the wings and connected the flight controls. Hunter bounded from the Hummer and raced up onto the wing to lean into the aft cockpit, where he loaded the gun with three rounds.

Each man hurried to finish his tasks. It wouldn't be a good idea to be caught using the Air Force's training field without permission.

After double-checking the charging system for the weapon, Hunter climbed into the seat and pulled on his helmet. He flipped the battery switch to ON and started the engine, just as Bob and Bob finished taping the aircraft's exposed seams. The big Continental 360 was quiet; its exhaust gases diffused through two large conformal mufflers and specially perforated piping that ran along the fuselage. For this mission, the Bobs had installed a small three-bladed wooden propeller. Also a top-secret design, with blades as wide and long as a child's desk, the propeller turned slowly because of the reduction gearbox mounted on the front of the engine.

Hunter lowered the canopy, flipped the ANVIS-9s night vision goggles over his eyes, checked the flight controls for the appropriate response, and taxied to the runway, brightly outlined by the chem-lites. He jammed the throttle to takeoff power and was airborne in moments. He energized the forward-looking infrared and scoured the area for vehicles, Border Patrol trucks, or an accidental illegal alien. The closest vehicles shone brightly in the FLIR miles away. It was a quiet night, with just two cars between Brackettville and Del Rio along Highway 90.

Hunter powered up, zoomed to 1,000 feet, turned toward the auxiliary field, and selected GUN on the multifunction display panel. The gun assembly rotated out from the lower confines of the fuselage and locked into place under the belly. One multifunction display panel showed the combined FLIR and targeting imagery.

Hunter twisted the Gun Master switch to ON and called, "Hot," into the microphone.

"Roger," the taller Bob replied into his handheld radio. Both men slid into the armored Hummer and closed the doors to protect themselves from possible ricochets.

Duncan flipped the night vision goggles up and out of the way, as he slewed the gun forward to aim at the target. In the FLIR, the silhouette stood out sharply. He selected the laser designator rangefinder to determine the range.

For the first run at 1,000 feet of altitude, the slant range would be one mile. Subsequent runs would be at one-and-a-half miles and two. The rangefinder indicated he was at 1.3 miles, with decreasing range. Hunter engaged the autopilot and took his hand off the control stick to re-illuminate the target with the laser designator, tagging it and allowing the computer software to compute the firing solution.

He squeezed the trigger on the gun-control joystick on the right side of the cockpit. The integrated, intelligent-tracking scope on the rifle, fed sighting information into the multifunction display, overlaying the FLIR image. A pair of large green circles constantly computed incrementally finer corrections, decreasing in size while increasing in intensity, as the firing point solution intersected with the tagged target and locked on. It was now a fire-and-forget weapon.

Once the tagged spot intersected the firing solution, the gun fired automatically. While the recoil and muzzle flash startled Hunter, he was mesmerized by the bullet's flight, as the FLIR traced the white-hot self-guided round with its tiny rocket motor into the target in a few seconds. It struck the silhouette slightly up and to the right, just a bit off center of the tagged aiming point. The laser was set on the tip of the nose and the round went through the left eye. Hunter shook his head in disbelief. The system was even more accurate than he envisioned.

He turned the YO-3A hard left, checked for vehicles in the FLIR, and turned left again. The runs at one-and-a-half and two miles brought similar results. The bullet struck the silhouette slightly high and right of the tagged aiming point, but both times, the impact point was within two inches of the laser-tagged spot. That was an insignificant deviation at two miles.

Hunter turned off the autopilot and turned hard toward the field. He flipped the gun master switch to OFF, selected STOW, and searched for any signs of life in the FLIR. Sweat ran down his face, and he realized he hadn't opened the outside vents while he focused his capabilities solely on the mission.

During his last run, a vehicle had turned off Highway 90 and headed down the access road. It would soon pass the entrance to the auxiliary field. At that late hour, Hunter surmised it could be a rancher or Border Patrol truck. He rotated the thumbwheel on the control stick and zoomed the FLIR to maximum with the vehicle centered on the screen.

It wasn't law enforcement but a private four-door car. Off in the distance, at the upper edge of the FLIR scope, he saw six very small white images emerging from the brush. He again slewed the FLIR toward the heat sources and zoomed in.

Hunter harrumphed. The thermal images were very-well hidden illegal aliens waiting in the brush. As he closed the distance to them, it was obvious the vehicle was slowing. He allowed a passing thought that he could target the people scrambling from the brush as they got into the vehicle, but their rapid movement toward the car would probably be enough to make the gun's intelligent targeting system fail. It was designed to tag a stationary target.

He made a mental note to laser-tag a moving target someday and see if the software could accommodate all the variables. A fixed target was easy, while a laterally moving target could prove impossible. As the thought drifted away, he scanned the surrounding area with the FLIR one last time, shut it down, and selected STOW.

He pulled the throttle to idle and headed to the field to land. Seven minutes after he shut down the engine, the wings were removed, the aircraft stowed in its container, the chem-lites and target silhouette were recovered, and the tractor-trailer left the airfield.

Hunter closed the gate, attached the shackle, spun the four wheels on the lock, and got back in his Hummer. After a right turn onto Highway 90, he floored the pedal, spinning all four wheels.

CHAPTER FIVE

2200 August 16, 2012
Laughlin Air Force Base
Del Rio, Texas

First Lieutenant Kelly Horne followed the crew chief's marshaling to turn into the parking space and the hand and arm signal to stop. She depressed the toe pedals of the gray T-38C and expertly brought the sleek jet to a halt, the nose wheel perfectly centered on its spot as the end of the yellow taxi line. When the crew chief swiped his fingers across his throat, Horne moved the throttles to OFF.

As the engines wound down, she unbuckled her lap belt and shoulder harness, and then removed her leg restraints, helmet, and skull cap. Pink foam plugs stuck out of her ears. She shook her short, sweat-drenched hair, but the movement didn't dislodge a single dark-red strand.

Lieutenant Horne stepped onto the seat and crawled from the cockpit, legs and backside first. She carefully climbed down the ladder with one hand, holding her helmet bag with the other. Once on the tarmac, she unzipped the form-fitting torso harness to relieve pressure on her back and walked around the aircraft. After completing some post-flight maintenance paperwork on the jet's wing, she strode toward the operations building, the long G-suit hose swaying out of synch with her steps. The crew chief stole a long, admiring glance as the pretty flight student strolled away.

Walking across the flight line in a damp flight suit chilled Horne. After almost 100 sorties and 100 hours of flight time, she no longer reflected that flying a jet was hard work. Even student pilots who were weight lifters were soaked after an hour in the cockpit of the venerable Northrop T-38. She left all recollections of flight planning and mission execution at the jet and thought about the package in her car. But as this was her last training flight as a student, she first had to go through "debrief."

Outside the massive operations building, named after Major Rudolph Anderson, the U-2 pilot shot down over Cuba, Lieutenant Horne entered the flight equipment room and shed her torso harness and G suit, hanging them on a peg. Anxiety prodded her to hurry. She inventoried her helmet bag for gloves, kneeboard, and helmet.

She took a brush and repositioned the curling, drying, itinerant hair with a couple of scrapes across her scalp. The helmet bag went into the large square cubbyhole over the peg.

During mission debrief, she was unfocused. It had been a good final flight, but she wanted to leave the building and reach her apartment to see if the contents in the package would finally lead to the end of her quest.

The debrief was uneventful. Horne's instructor gave her a pat on the back as she was released for the weekend. Horne raced from Anderson Hall toward her car. Before she hit a full stride, she placed dark wraparound sunglasses to hide her large hazel eyes from the bright sunshine. They also helped mask her sultry beauty from the testosterone-fueled males in flight suits. All heads turned when Kelly Horne walked by.

She stopped jogging short of a burgundy Pontiac Fiero, unlocked the door, and slipped inside. A shoebox-shaped package, wrapped in brown paper and tied with twine, rested on the passenger floorboard. Excitement filled her actions.

In minutes, she was out of one parking lot and entered another. With the package under her arm, she raced up the stairs to her third-floor apartment. Once inside the air-conditioned space, she placed the package on the computer table and debated whether to open it immediately. The still-damp flight suit against her skin was enough to make her step into the bedroom and remove her boots and flight suit. She emerged in dark-blue sweatpants and a sweatshirt with silver USAF letters across her chest.

"Let's see what we have," she whispered, cutting the cords and brown paper. Once the box was open, she paused to reflect on the small red diary bound with a heavy elastic band. She ignored the green Rolex box and other contents.

The executor of her grandparent's estate notified Kelly that during the reading of her grandmother's will, it became clear that she would receive the contents of a safety deposit box. She understood some of her mother's jewelry, bearer bonds, and other paperwork would be sent to her. She never expected her mother's diary to be part of her grandmother's belongings held in safekeeping. Katherine Horne lost her daughter to a rare form of breast cancer and gained an infant granddaughter. She promised her daughter, Kimberly, she would never reveal the baby's father's name and took that promise to the grave.

Kelly cut away the rubber band around the diary and returned the other papers to the box. She took a deep breath, not knowing what to expect of the thoughts of a mother she never knew. Would she be embarrassed or disappointed?

Not yet ready to open it, she set it in front of her and spun in her chair before padding to the fridge for a wine cooler. Taking a sip, she walked back for the diary and made herself comfortable on the sofa before skimming through the red book. She turned many pages before she suddenly stopped.

I met the most-amazing man last night. He and his friends walked into our club. I couldn't believe how beautiful he was. He looked at me, and there was instant electricity. I had a couple glasses of wine and was feeling pretty loose, so I walked right up to him and noticed he wore gold wings and a nametag that read *Maverick.*

He was Navy, I thought. I asked, "You a sailor?"

He looked hurt and said, "Marine."

I think I embarrassed him, and I felt embarrassed for my mistake. I said something stupid like, "Too bad. I have a thing for sailors."

I turned away and went back to my classmates, laughing at myself.

All night long, we kept eyeing each other. I think everyone in the club knew there was something going on between that Marine and me. I wanted to dance with him. I didn't dance with anyone else.

After two of his friends left, he finally walked over and asked me to dance. I think the DJ purposely chose something slow. *Unchained Melody?* It was perfect.

We danced slow and close. I swear my knees were knocking. I wanted to kiss him so bad! He told me he and his friends were passing through on their way to California. They would leave in the morning. He said he never expected to find a goddess in the middle of the desert. He said he was dancing with the most-beautiful woman he ever saw and had to be dreaming. He said he was luckiest guy he knew and thanked me for making every man in the club jealous of him.

When the music stopped, he thanked me for the dance and told me, "Good night." I didn't want him to go and thought he didn't want to leave, either. He asked for my address and phone number, and I knew he was serious. I had a thousand things going through my mind. I didn't want the night to end. Not like that.

Before turning to the next entry, Kelly reached for her drink and took a long pull. She felt gooseflesh on her arms as she anticipated the intimate details of her mother's infatuation with a Marine pilot. She was convinced she was on the path to knowing her father's name. Was he the one? Someone her mother picked up at a bar? Interest and excitement built, as she turned the page.

It may have been the alcohol, but I tingled all over. I asked him to walk me to my room. He didn't say a word, but he nodded.

He walked out of the club, and I told my classmates good night. I met him outside. Before we started walking, he asked me my full name. He called me, "Miss Horne." He took my hand, and we walked.

That is how I met Duncan Hunter.

Kelly sat bolt upright, staring at the name. She flipped through the remainder of the diary, looking for another man's name. As she turned the pages, she picked up enough pieces of information to know her mother fell in love with a Marine Corps pilot named Duncan Hunter. Page after page showed how hard it was for an Air Force pilot and a Marine pilot to stay in touch or get together, but, when they did, it seemed the Marinc pilot would move mountains to be with her. He drove a bright-yellow Corvette convertible. They drove all over the country, usually with the top down, and obviously enjoyed each other.

Page after page, her mother lamented how it became more difficult for them to meet and travel, but they didn't give up. Her notes became infrequent. Some months passed between entries. Another twenty pages covered a year of inconsistent writing.

Kelly was shocked when she read another entry.

One of the worst weeks ever!!

I cannot listen to my mother anymore, hearing her list all the people who called to tell her I should abort the baby. One even offered to drive me to Planned Parenthood. Disgusting bitch!! I'm having enough trouble keeping the baby secret. I don't want Duncan distracted with responsibility for the baby. If we ever get married, it has to be on our terms....not because I am pregnant.

I'm so worried about Mom. I thought she'd be happy and proud of me. I can't believe so many of her liberal friends and relatives have called her. Mom is so torn, but she seems to side with them at times and thinks it shouldn't even be an issue. Obviously, I'm single and pregnant—encumbered is the word they use—and so, I NEED to have an abortion. They NEED to mind their own business!!

I've come to learn that progressive women don't want or intend to have kids. They're afraid of children and the responsibility they bring. They get jobs in government and education. They look professional and intimidating. They're richer and more influential than the full-time moms they look down on—schleppy housewives driving minivans subservient to their "master husbands." Many of those arrogant witches are social workers who think it's their duty to drive vulnerable teenage girls to abortion clinics.

It's a damned sickness. It's absolutely EVIL!!

They don't just kill their own children—they want to kill everyone else's!!! And somehow that's OK????

BUT NOT MINE!!!! NO WAY!!!! They can't get me to kill my baby.

I can't imagine the grief and fear Mom is going through to protect me from her friends and my crazy relatives. I thought she was lying when she first told me. It's so bizarre.

For a modern liberal woman, it has to be very hard on Mom that her only unwed, professional, Air Force Captain daughter insists on keeping her baby. But I love Mom so much!!!! She accepts and respects my decision. She has raised me to be independent and to make my own decisions—that's the REAL modern woman she's raised me to be. Thank you Mom.

I'm having this baby. He or she will be a great baby. And I will be a great mom!!!

The next entry was several weeks later.

Please, God help me!!!! I don't know what we'll do. I found out today the lump in my right boob is malignant. I want to tell Duncan, but he's on a ship in the Pacific. I am soooo afraid. God, I don't know what to do!!!

Doc wants to run more tests soon, but she says it's very aggressive. Lord, I am so scared....

Doc says I have a ten percent chance of beating this cancer, but the treatment would kill the baby. I have to choose.

Kelly flipped through more pages before realizing that was the final entry. *I have to choose* echoed in her mind.

Kelly closed the diary with trembling hands. She hugged it to her chest, curled into a ball, and wept. She'd cried many times for many things. She was embarrassed that she yelled at her mother countless times for abandoning her.

This time Kelly cried for her mother and begged her forgiveness.

CHAPTER SIX

0130 August 21, 2012
Timbuktu, Mali

The line of heavy earthmoving equipment shook the ground as it crawled along the dirt road. Headlights piercing the blackness gently swayed up and down and from side-to-side, as the slow-moving vehicles negotiated the deeply rutted path. A cacophony of roaring diesel engines and dull metallic noises shattered the night and signaled intrigue was afoot.

Construction vehicles belching oily black exhaust were rarely seen anywhere in town and never in remote parts of the city. There was no reason for heavy machinery to move at night, especially near the ancient mosques. Those were sacred grounds.

After an hour of travel through the thin jungle, three clattering vehicles braked behind the dim taillights of a small dirty pickup. Emerging from clouds of dust kicked up by the old, tired bulldozer, Yambo Griot stepped out of the Toyota HiLux and scampered up into the truck bed. The leader of Anwar al-Islami, the Light of Islam, wasn't a happy man, but he was energized. The ancient tombs of Muslims saints towering before him were an affront to Islam and he was on a mission from Allah.

Yambo barked at the men on the bulldozer and backhoes, waving his arms to the sky. "My brothers! All Muslims are charged with applying the teachings of Islam to remove false idols. Our brothers removed false idols in Afghanistan when they destroyed the Buddha statue. Here, they venerate the holy saints as gods. This is blasphemy. There is no God but Allah! Only when there is no shrine to these false gods can good Muslims once again pray to Allah! Only to Allah! *Allahu Akbar!* God is great!"

Under the full moon, the suspended dust kicked up from the equipment enveloped the men as they responded, "God is great!"

Intermittently illuminated by shifting clouds, the centuries-old mud and brick walls posed no threat to the machines. Yambo slowly pointed at the huge mud structure behind the fortress wall, pausing for effect. His men stood on their machines, mesmerized by their leader and their goal.

Over the idling diesels, Yambo shouted, "We have a righteous wind at our backs! Take it down!"

The men roared their approval and leaped into action. Those not driving jumped off the heavy equipment and approached the small wrought-iron gate of the old fortress. They waited for an opening to attack the inside of the fortress with picks and shovels, the thought of finding riches and jewels foremost in their hearts and minds.

They waited for the bulldozer operator to slew the decrepit machine around and line up the blade to dislodge the gate. Once the wall was breached, those on foot would race into the fortress. The two backhoe operators raised their scoops and throttled the diesel engines, their eyes wide and teeth bared in anticipation. *Allah would approve!*

One month earlier, the Anwar al-Islami leader said to a bevy of reporters that while he and others were aware of the international outcry against the plan, he didn't care. *Allah is on my side! Allah would approve!*

It was Yambo's duty to impose the strictest-possible interpretation of Islamic law on the region. The newly formed al-Qaeda-affiliated group recently eliminated every member of a rival separatist movement. A dozen men with black and white Light of Islam headbands, brandishing long machetes, entered the homes to butcher their foes and their families as they slept.

Mali's government, having already lost the northern third of the country to rebels, called the attacks war crimes. Yambo Griot dismissed that assertion and was energized with his new power. He escalated his attacks on hamlets and villages in the central region of the country. The United Nations Secretary General spoke before the full UN general assembly. Without naming Anwar al-Islami, he decried the worsening humanitarian and security crisis in Mali. Reports of the planned destruction of the ancient mausoleums caused great concern. Such attacks against cultural heritage sites were unjustified and meant they would be considered crimes against humanity. The Secretary General appealed to the world and specifically those engaged in the conflict to exercise restraint and responsibility. For the sake of future generations, he asked them to spare the legacy of the past.

Yambo stepped from the bed of the Toyota HiLux. He was five-feet-six-inches tall, a thick, middle-aged man with a plain face, tiny ears, and a shiny bald head. He wore an off-color brown combat uniform; his trousers legs tucked into his heavy black boots. He grinned, flashing a mouth of yellow teeth. His followers barely had enough teeth among them to fill another mouth.

He laughed at the weakness of the UN. Nothing could stop him. Forced underground because of his radical beliefs, he found an all-too-willing supporter within a branch of the broader group known as al-Qaeda in Africa. Once he made contact and committed to join the fight for Allah and against the government, taking the blood oath and receiving monetary support and weapons, he quickly earned the nickname, "The Butcher of Mali."

The AK-47 was a wonderful assault rifle, but the machete was his weapon of choice. Griot converted many to Islam. Those who refused and couldn't run watched their women raped and sexually mutilated. Families were dismembered before the men were killed, slowly and barbarically. Fear motivated converts when he and his men moved into a village searching for recruits.

Griot quickly became a national figure who influenced the

government politic. He was about to put his stamp on the old burial crypts. He would dismember the saints as he dismembered others who didn't submit to Allah.

Dukoo, the bulldozer operator, lowered the big blade and engaged the clutch. The ancient Caterpillar turned toward the fortress, its diesel roaring. He looked over his left shoulder to smile at Yambo for more encouragement, but at that moment, the great man suddenly stiffened and fell lifelessly on his face.

Dukoo couldn't comprehend what he saw through the swirling dust and jammed his eyes shut. When he reopened them, he was surprised he hadn't imagined that the mighty Yambo was in the dirt, prostrate on his face.

Dukoo took a deep breath and shouted before moving toward the fallen man. He unconsciously depressed the clutch and shifted the big Caterpillar into neutral. He began climbing from his seat when he saw others on the ground had also witnessed the great Yambo fall. They did not move; they too were in shock.

He stood and turned to the men in their backhoes, each quietly questioning what happened. Time froze. The body was surreally illuminated by the headlights from the heavy equipment, with dust swirling over him.

Then, as if a giant unseen hand slapped them down, one-by-one, the men with picks and shovels jerked spasmodically and fell backward. Dukoo jumped. His adrenalin spiked, shocking his nervous system. He struggled to move, and he was barely able to turn his head.

Seeing one person fall was an incident. Several men cascading onto their faces overwhelmed him. He struggled to move, to shout to the backhoe operators on his right, as they came into view. He jerkily raised his hands to his mouth to call to them when the farthest man collapsed in a heap and fell off his backhoe.

Synapses fired commands to Dukoo to run, as the other backhoe operator's head burst open, spraying blood and debris across the machine, as he fell. The man's backhoe jumped forward, nearly stalling, as the dead man's foot released the clutch. The machine recovered and ambled toward the fortress wall.

Dukoo trembled at the power of a displeased Allah and lowered his head, only to be shocked again at the sight of a bright pink dot dancing around the tops of his sandals. Shuddering, he leaned over for a closer look.

The tiny neon spot stabilized and slowly moved up the front of his leg. Terrified, he struggled to brush away the glowing creature and stop its advance. Unable to erase it, he tried to run, but he was locked in place with fear.

Dukoo stopped breathing and watched helplessly as the dot relentlessly moved up his thigh and belly before stopping in the middle of his chest. His chin rested against his chest, mouth agape, as he shook with terror. His bladder emptied.

As he slowly raised his head to the sky, a star exploded in the dark distance. Seconds after the flash of light pierced Dukoo's eyes, Allah tore his heart from his chest.

CHAPTER SEVEN

0830 August 31, 2012
CIA Headquarters
McLean, Virginia

Duncan Hunter stepped from the private elevator into the view of the DCI's secretary. She jumped to her feet as Hunter warmly greeted her with a smile and a compliment about her hair, which was short and trim and helped make her less unattractive. Now she approached "interesting." Before she could respond, Dr. Bruce Rothwell appeared in the office doorway and motioned for Duncan to enter.

Walking into the Director's office, Hunter sat before the huge wood desk in the middle of the room. When he turned to greet DCI Rothwell, he saw the man stopped before his secretary. They exchanged a few words, and Mayo scurried about, searching through In and Out boxes stuffed with thick files and sealed packages. Whatever she sought was soon found. An energized DCI returned to his office with a file in one hand and closed the door behind him before marching to his desk without offering a greeting or verbal exchange.

"Nice job in Mali." The DCI scurried around his desk and plopped down in the overstuffed black chair outlined with brass rivets.

"Thank you, Sir." Hunter reached for his briefcase and extracted a file to hand over. "Our after-action report. The intel was spot on. They showed up at the designated place and time. It wasn't hard to determine who the lead dog was. Your guys were terrific."

Rothwell cautiously allowed a grin, as he accepted the double-wrapped smooth envelope. "Are you ready for another one?" He handed a file package across the desk to Hunter.

It seemed to Hunter that the DCI was in a hurry, talking more rapidly than he remembered. *The turmoil in Libya and the recent death of Muammar Gaddafi is probably a factor. He must be overwhelmed. This is probably a distraction.*

Before Hunter could offer to return at a better time, Rothwell said, "Islamist cleric, well-connected to several Saudi and Omani princes. He's been traveling between Yemen and Jordan every four weeks like clockwork. On one hand, he acts as if he's a simple message courier. On the other, whenever he comes to Amman, a veritable who's who of al-Qaeda and Muslim Brotherhood sympathizers materialize at the same location where he's staying."

"Sounds like any interdiction depends on a very narrow window of opportunity. Amman? I get a sense these guys are meeting at the Marriott and not in some tent outside Petra. Downtown is a bad environment for me to operate in—too much light and too congested. Maybe an intervention in Yemen?" His skepticism showed. He didn't open the file. He didn't need to. This one obviously wasn't safe and wouldn't be possible.

Rothwell, picking up on Hunter's body language, countered, "We were thinking Amman would send a message. We can reach out and touch you anywhere, anytime."

"What's his story?" Hunter placed his hands on the file in his lap. He tried not to stare at Rothwell, his mind weighing basic strategies and pitfalls of operating over downtown Amman in his quiet airplane. It wasn't just extremely high risk. It was crazy. As envisioned, he and the aircraft would be operating well past the edge of detection and discovery.

At night, Amman was congested and bright. A black airplane might well be easily silhouetted if there were any clouds. In his zeal to accommodate the President, Hunter didn't discuss rules of engagement for situations on the ragged edge of exposure. He wasn't convinced the DCI's concept of operations was sound or safe and was about to veto the mission.

The happenings in Libya must be affecting everyone's response and judgment, Hunter thought, *especially the DCI's.*

"This guy's a money man," Rothwell explained. "He bought tickets for most of the 9/11 hijackers and provided cash for them when they arrived in the U.S. That cash paid for their flight training. He's a former U.S. citizen, who converted to Islam and is now a cleric. He joined AQ on the Arabian Peninsula.

"He pops up in Amman every four weeks via private jet, usually in the company of a Saudi or Omani price. When the jet leaves, he's nowhere to be found. He disappears. It's pretty apparent he's in disguise when he leaves the hotel. We haven't been able to pick him up and surveil him. We do know he's based out of Yemen.

"Shortly after the jet leaves Jordan, we get reports of sightings of him, some in Aden but primarily in Sana'a. He's an escape artist who has dodged several Hellfires. His nine lives should be up. And he goes to the Sheraton, not the Marriott."

Hunter inhaled, opened the file, and looked through the pages. Any facilitator of 9/11 deserved another look.

"We've had eyes on him for years. He's very slick."

Hunter looked up and closed the file. "What does he do when he's in Amman?"

"Don't know. The whole floor is blocked with guards. We think meetings. They change floors every time he's in town. We can't bug every room."

"He probably has a girlfriend—or a boyfriend."

Director Rothwell nodded. "They all do."

Hunter paused to marshal his thoughts. "Director Rothwell, I don't think this is a good fit. I don't want to turn down work, but under these circumstances, this is in the too-hard-to-do category with my airplane. I'd think this is more suitable for ground intervention. This is more in line for someone in the NCS. He should be a sniper's target.

"If I had ground capability, we might be able to tag-team him. An attempted air intervention in Yemen isn't optimal but doable. It's nearly impossible if there's a questionable location. I've flown from Djibouti to Sana'a before. It's a long flight that provides very limited overhead time. I wouldn't have much time to look for him before it was time to RTB, return to base.

"It was truly fortuitous that we identified and popped Zawahiri when we did. We had a specific location in Sana'a. We patrolled a couple hours and were about to leave. I was deep into my fuel reserves when he showed himself at the last possible moment. We stayed on target and laser designated him knowing I'd probably run out of gas over the Red Sea.

"As soon as the first Hellfire hit the target, I headed for the coast. Sana'a is possible. Sir, I regret Amman is a no-go for now."

"It may be several months before we have another candidate." Rothwell's voice was tinged with disappointment.

"Sir, I know with all the things you're dealing with in Libya, please accept another candidate can wait. I want to convey…."

"Or a few weeks. I'm adding to the disposition matrix weekly." He raised his hands to make quotation marks with his fingers for *disposition matrix*. Hunter, mildly amused, smiled faintly in understanding.

Lifting the file from his lap to return it, Hunter asked, "Could we put this one aside until conditions for success are more favorable?"

Rothwell didn't answer immediately. The pause was palpable, as if Hunter's question threw cold water on the man across the desk. Breaking eye contact, he pushed away from the desk to show the meeting was over.

Both men stood simultaneously. Hunter was taken aback when the head spook said, "That will work for me. I have a plate full dealing with the aftermath of Gaddafi's reign of terror. He would've been a good candidate for this, but he was too high profile. The President said 'no regime change,' so that probably disqualified him.

"Anyway, Duncan, nice job in Mali. I wanted this one. If you say it's in the too hard to do category then he's not the right candidate and it's not the right time. I'm getting better at knowing what you can do and what's in the realm of the possible, and this is a bad fit."

"Thank you, Sir. I appreciate your understanding. Maybe another time in Yemen as intel develops on him." Hunter was pleased and surprised at the turn of events. It was a good meeting that ended without confrontation or animosity.

He felt encouraged. Had it been one of the other DCIs he and Greg Lynche had worked with, he would have contemplated offering an olive branch as a demonstration of good faith. He would have felt free to say, "It might be instructional to provide a flight demo or have you visit our labs in Texas." Lynche always offered but the DCIs were always too busy.

Despite his feelings about Rothwell's advances to Nazy, Hunter wanted an atmosphere of good will and teamwork. Nazy wasn't interested in the man, and worrying about it was unproductive. Always in the back of his mind, Hunter knew the DCI held all the cards.

One wrong word and Rothwell could find the slimmest reason to pull Hunter's clearance, and there wasn't a thing Hunter could do to reverse the decision. There were countless ways to lose ones clearance; only a handful of ways to get it back. In the intelligence community, there was no such thing as protesting or suing the government over the loss of one's clearance.

When Lynche was on the special access program *Wraith* and running interference, any animosity was squashed, and goodwill and teamwork prevailed. Although Rothwell and Hunter initially got off on the wrong foot, Hunter's strategy to remain professional and friendly even when the man across the table was hitting on his girl, seemed to be paying off.

Having kept up with the newspapers, Hunter allowed a passing thought that the DCI might not hold his position much longer. Sharing additional intelligence on his manufacturing and operational capabilities would probably be counterproductive, assuming the CIA didn't already know.

He knew Rothwell had largely stopped his sexual harassing comments to Nazy after his appointment to the DCI, but she still felt he was infatuated with her and wouldn't give up. She insisted he was simply waiting.

"He always gets what he wants," Nazy told Duncan after the two of them flew to Liberia to interrogate Osama bin Laden. "When he doesn't get what he wants, he looks for ways to gain an advantage to take the next step. He won't ever give up."

She felt that giving Rothwell an audio copy of her interrogation of the world's supposedly greatest dead terrorist, with the stipulation that Rothwell stop harassing her, would provide enough incentive for the then Deputy Director of the National Counter Terrorism Center to curtail his suggestive comments and advances lest he be reported and lose his job. That lasted all of one week.

Hunter and Nazy failed to anticipate one of the unintended consequences of Rothwell possessing and analyzing the top-secret bin Laden interrogation. He rocketed to the top of the list of contenders and was seriously considered for the Director of Central Intelligence.

Once he attained that position, he felt bulletproof. He began another kinder and gentler, more-subtler approach on Nazy, and involved her in more strategic planning sessions with senior intelligence executives. That required her to make more visits to the seventh-floor offices and conference rooms. He had her promoted into one of his old positions. As a member of the NCTC, she would be invited to the executive-level strategic planning sessions and top-level meetings.

When he traveled, he suggested she travel with him, but she demurred. When he wasn't trying to sit beside her during conference work, he sat directly across from her so he could continually make eye contact. Nazy wouldn't look at him and kept her feet under her chair, so Rothwell couldn't make inadvertent contact with her feet or legs under the table. His actions didn't constitute any of the seven levels of sexual harassment, but he kept pushing her boundaries, hoping to wear her down.

Hunter, returning to the present, struggled to control his emotions. He sought a distraction from thinking about the turd standing before him, who lusted after his future wife. A small article buried in the back of the most-recent edition of the *Washington Post* suggested Rothwell wasn't just infatuated with Nazy but at least one other woman. A mother of two was profiled, and the article suggested that she had *worked closely,* with Rothwell, and he reciprocated.

The other woman had once been inside the Agency but had since transferred. The key line in the article floored Hunter. She had unprecedented access to him and even wrote a biography about him. The story oozed details in wild directions. The CIA establishment immediately took notice, and so did a growing number of members of Congress.

Red flags went off at the CIA Publication Review Board when the woman submitted her manuscript for review. Historical biographies and books on CIA Directors were common enough, but a biographical manuscript on a deputy at the NCTC was unheard of. The slavish manner in which it was written telegraphed to members of the PRB that there must have been significant pillow talk between the author and deputy director.

Unpublished details with need to know specificity were tied to secret operations which the deputy director had led or had been a team member. The manuscript contained several dozen top-secret references to operations —wildly embellished to make the man more impressive —and named dozens of intelligence agents. The manuscript was initially classified at the top secret level.

Six months of PRB coordination with the author, striking unauthorized sections of classified material, were necessary before they would approve the manuscript. Only after fifty pages of redactions were made would it be considered unclassified and was released for publication.

However, rumors of impropriety, leaked by someone at the PRB, flew up the chain of command and stopped at the former DCI's office, just before he was nominated to become Vice President. No action was taken to advise or counsel the NCTC Deputy Director regarding the PRB's observations or the material in the woman's manuscript.

The suddenness of Rothwell's ascent as acting director, then DCI, meant there was no one at the agency to brief the President of the potential conflict of interest. The *Washington Post* article suggested after the biography hit the bookstores, another woman with close connections to Special Operations Command executives and leaders privately informed the FBI that she'd been receiving threatening email, warning her to stay away from Rothwell.

Only after the FBI opened a case file and analyzed the threatening email traffic did they determine the perpetrator was the author of the recently released biography of the newly installed CIA Director. The information was so explosive, someone with an axe to grind at the FBI leaked to a highly placed correspondent at the *Washington Post* that the FBI was investigating a bizarre *ménage a trois* between two women and the new DCI.

Since Hunter wanted to work, and the DCI authorized all of it, it would have been inappropriate to comment on the new director's name being mentioned in the paper, however ignominiously.

As the two men said their good-byes, Hunter allowed himself a moment of *schadenfreude*. Whatever was happening to Rothwell, it couldn't have happened to a nicer piece of shit.

He stopped at Miss Mayo's desk to say good-bye. But with a phone in her ear, her smile turned to a frown, and she was deflated as Duncan Hunter disappeared into the elevator.

CHAPTER EIGHT

1000 August 31, 2012
Near East Division
CIA Headquarters

CIA Headquarters is a giant Sensitive Compartmented Information Facility with several dozen smaller, special-purpose SCIFs scattered throughout the different divisions and directorates. Information contained within a SCIF is compartmented; all documents are marked with their classification level and either a code word or special access program code name. Access to a particular SCIF is restricted to those with need to know, a determination that an individual requires access to specific classified information in the performance of lawful, authorized government functions and duties.

The highest security level of a SCIF is Top Secret. If the compartmented information were publicly disclosed, it would cause "exceptionally serious damage" to national security. Occasionally, some information is considered so sensitive it exceeds that benchmark. Some Presidential decisions and authorizations are considered ultra-sensitive. If such information were publicly disclosed, it would cause "exceptionally grave damage to national security." Information in that category has always been stored, maintained, and discussed in the executive spaces of the CIA in a special executive SCIF on the seventh floor.

Nazy Cunningham entered the executive SCIF with three men. The DCI, Director of Security, and a man to whom she wasn't introduced but who was vaguely familiar took seats around the three eight-foot work tables. The Director of Security asked Nazy to sit in the middle of the room directly behind a projector. One sheet of paper was slid in front of her.

"Miss Cunningham, you're being read into an Executive Special Access Program. The nature and sensitivity of the compartmented information will be revealed once you affirm you're a willing officer of the United States government, and that you take this assignment freely without any mental reservation. Please stand and reaffirm your oath."

A very bewildered Nazy stood to face the three men. The security officer said, "Raise your right hand and repeat after me. I, Nazy Cunningham…."

"I, Navy Cunningham…."

"…do solemnly swear that I will support and defend the Constitution of the United States against all enemies, foreign and domestic; that I will bear true faith and allegiance to the same; that I take this obligation freely, without any mental reservation or purpose of evasion."

She repeated the sentence.

"That I will, well and faithfully, discharge the duties of the special access program on which I am about to enter. So help me God."

She repeated that as well.

"Thank you. Please have a seat and sign the nondisclosure agreement in front of you."

This is different, she thought. *What have I gotten myself into?* She became more concerned that she was being read into the program for something other than meritorious performance. She'd been asked earlier that week if she could fill in for another senior intelligence officer at a hardship post while the woman was pregnant. It was imperative the woman come home and have the baby.

Nazy wasn't impressed by the excuse but was a team player, and Duncan would probably be out of the country for a while, anyway. Most beneficial, it would take her away from the lecherous Director Rothwell.

She agreed. When the DCI informed her that she was to be read in on an executive SAP, Nazy didn't know what that was and had never heard of such a thing. She was suspicious that the DCI was trying to impress her, and she'd be sucked into some bogus intrigue or training program. Or it was probably just a way for the man to try to use a SAP to get closer to her.

Not probably, she told herself. *The man's a pig.*

She waited for him or the security officer to say, "You'll have to work very closely with the Director," but those words never came.

After collecting the NDA, the security officer began his spiel. "This brief is classified Top Secret, access code PD, Presidential Decision. It's NOFORN—distribution to non-U.S. citizens is absolutely prohibited, regardless of their clearance or access permissions. This program is coded 100X1, indicating information will remain classified for 100 years, since it pertains to intelligence activities, sources, or methods under Reason One of Section 3.3, paragraph b, of Executive Order 13526. You cannot divulge any of this information, ever. You'll be required to oversee certain work at your temporary duty station. Ready, Miss Cunningham?'

"I am." Curiosity replaced suspicion. Nazy placed her hands together and waited.

"Slide!" barked the unnamed man.

CHAPTER NINE

1830 August 31, 2012
JW Marriott Presidential Suite
Washington, DC

"I have to pee!" Nazy squealed, sweeping through the door past Hunter. Her long black hair streamed back as if she was in a wind tunnel, and she tore through the entrance, flinging her purse and small bag into a chair. She left a trail of heel prints on the carpet as Hunter's gaze naturally dropped to her ankles to admire her legs and callipygian figure in the tight skirt race through the suite and disappear into the bathroom. Nazy in heels and unpinned hair created a chemical reaction in Hunter. Warmth filled his chest. A broad leer crossed his face, and he cocked his head as he flicked the door shut behind him.

He realized that Nazy's assimilation was complete. The former Muslima sent to spy on him, who trembled and feared for her life, who worked like a galley slave as a CIA analyst for ten years, was now so comfortable in her American skin she could unabashedly exclaim that she needed to pee.

"I think I've ruined that girl." He chuckled as he walked through the huge suite to the bedroom and plopped onto the bed, waiting for her to emerge from the bathroom.

He was picking at his cuticles as the bathroom door opened, and black high heels were tossed into the room. He raised an eyebrow, then untied and slid off his Johnston Murphys and socks.

His head came up toward the bathroom door when he realized Nazy was singing, though he couldn't make out the distantly familiar tune. The hotel had installed high-pressure flush systems in its bathrooms, and the one-second eighty-decibel swoosh overtook her voice. He anticipated the sound of running water in the basin.

After a few seconds, the door flew open, and Nazy emerged with kohl-rimmed eyes, and a salacious, exuberant smile. "I so missed you!"

He stood, already firm with anticipation, held his arms wide, and she rushed to him. After several seconds of tongue play, she brushed hair away and gently broke free.

"I think you missed me, too," she said with a breathless whisper.

He nodded and brought his lips down on hers.

That was how it had been for almost eight years. He would fly into town on business, and, when Nazy was able to leave the CIA compound, they met at the Marriott or the Hilton, rarely her house in Bethesda. After several hours of lovemaking, talking, and napping, Hunter would call for room service.

Early in their relationship, they tried to talk about things other than work, but that was impossible. After renouncing her Muslim faith and becoming an intelligence officer, Nazy was like a wide-eyed kid in a toy store. The counterterrorism training was fascinating, exciting, tough, mentally challenging, and she wanted to share every new experience with him. Both knew they couldn't share certain information without violating their oaths. They didn't trust themselves not to spill a secret that might place them in the awkward position of withholding information during a polygraph.

After that morning, when she was read in on a unique executive special access program, she would have had an amazing secret to share, but she couldn't and didn't. She wanted to tell Duncan, because he would have found it fascinating.

In the beginning, he knew tangentially what she did. Greg Lynche filled him in on her training. Nazy, completely preoccupied with learning the art of espionage and running spies, analyzing or writing top-secret documents, didn't have a clue what he did other than being a contracted pilot for the Agency. It wouldn't have been good for them to be seen together…too often.

The two lovers agreed not to disclose what the other was doing until the time Duncan was almost killed by a sniper. Their self-imposed rules of secrecy changed immediately when Hunter announced he and Greg Lynche were going to retrieve the very-alive Osama bin Laden and do what the previous President didn't want to do under any circumstances—interrogate him.

Nazy and Hunter sealed their lifelong pact and became partners in a conspiracy. After taking custody of OBL from the Navy SEALs who spirited him out of his Pakistani compound, Hunter wasn't the main interrogator, but he played the bad cop.

Hunter quickly brought OBL to the edge of being exposed to what the press would have called "enhanced interrogation techniques." Nazy, the good cop in an *abaya,* counterbalanced Hunter's edgy aggressiveness and she easily interrogated the compliant, docile, cowardly prisoner for twelve hours. Hunter threatened to hook up bin Laden's testicles to a car battery and may have helped the master terrorist to be a little more talkative.

When Hunter and Nazy talked shop, they shared information in coded phrases in case the walls had ears, but not that evening.

After room service delivered a cart full of food, they sat at a table for two in their bathrobes, their legs touching and their calves gently stroking the other. The smell of braised beef overpowered the thick remnants of sex in the air. Hunter brought a full glass of water across the table to toast Nazy. Goblets chimed, as he said, "You cut a fine figure in that robe, Miss Cunningham."

Nazy gripped the collar. "But you can't see anything. This thing is huge. It swallows me." Her dark-red nails contrasted sharply with the bright-white bathrobe.

"Although I have to say you'd look better without all that terrycloth."

She looked at him with her unique smile, part bashful, part sensual, part wonder. The first time he saw that smile was in his room at the Naval War College.

"I want to go ice skating," she said. "I may never get another chance."

She offered that unique smile, full of wonder as she was unleashed and unburdened from Islam. Duncan had glanced out his suite's picture window. Over a foot of snow covered the war college ground and was still falling lightly, obscuring the lights of Newport Bridge in the distance.

The man at the outdoor rink had said they were still open. She had no clothes other than her dress. Duncan bundled her in layers of long-sleeved T-shirts and sweatshirts and sweat pants until she could barely move; she looked like the roly-poly Michelin Man. He fretted continually she'd be too cold.

She could barely move, but she insisted she'd be warm enough even in the subfreezing weather. Grateful for his four-wheel-drive truck, he drove for an hour to get through the Navy base and into town, often being stuck behind snowplows pushing tons of snow to the roadside. It was crazy.

"You're an amazing man, Duncan Hunter. You really would do anything for me." She held his hand as he drove, her incredible smile melting his heart once again.

Nazy smiled to herself as she worked fork and knife to cut long green beans into something more manageable. She looked up at him, platinum-green eyes flashing with an impish grin. *How am I going to tell him?*

"So, how was Mali?" She popped a piece of vegetable into her mouth, trying to look serious and banish thoughts of Algeria from her head.

Hunter's eyes narrowed and he looked at her with intrigue. She couldn't possibly know about his Mali mission. He hadn't said where he was going, and she wasn't read in on that executive special access program. Still, she knew something.

"Mali's nice this time of year, I suppose."

"Imagine my surprise when I was asked to help consolidate some listings for the boss, and a certain name appeared in the pages of the *New York Times* a couple days ago. The poor man died. I knew it had to be you. It had to be you and nobody else but you...." She returned to cutting her steak and deliberately teased him, wagging a bit of beef on her fork.

Hunter suddenly recognized the tune she sang in the bathroom. "Did you see where your boss is the subject of an FBI probe?"

"No fair changing subject. Couldn't happen to a nicer man. Mali, Mr. Hunter?"

"You're teasing me...."

"You're avoiding me."

He rubbed her leg a little higher. "How could I ever avoid you? I'm worse than Pavlov's dog, always wagging my tail, waiting to see or touch you. I missed you, Baby." He wasn't certain he liked the idea that she knew what he did. *It's one thing to be an assassin. It's entirely different when the love of your life knows, too.*

"The not-so-good doctor asked me to compile several lists into one master file. Of course, he thinks that since he's now the director and promoted me he can task me directly. He hopes that if I'm forced to work more closely with him, I'll eventually swoon and want him."

"He doesn't know you very well, does he?"

"At the top of the list was a bad guy in Mali. You have a meeting with the not-so-good doctor. You go away. You come home. Bad guy gets his name in the paper. You go see the not-so-good doctor. Yes, it had to be you...."

"You can't believe what's in the papers. I learned a few things at the war college, and one is that the press is self-serving; liberal, they have a hard time reporting the truth, and what they do report is obfuscations or great distortions. They can't help themselves. They're either commies or liberals. You have to read outside the press, get what they don't report, to get a sense of what's really going on."

When the last words escaped his lips, something triggered a thread of a long-suppressed memory—a thought or concept? Something from school? Was Nazy acting a little strange? *Something is going on.* He looked down at his plate, trying to reel in the jumbled string of pieces of a memory, forcing the fragments to jell.

Nazy slid her foot up his calf, stopping at his thigh. Hunter's head snapped up. Whatever was trying to creep into his consciousness was usurped by a well-placed, naked size-seven with toes.

Nazy, pleased she interrupted his thoughts, made him pay attention to her. "Nice try. I thought you might want to know who is next on the list." She wondered how she was going to say, *"I'm going to Algeria and your next target is in Algeria! I'm afraid!"*

"I don't know what list you're talking about, *Miss* Cunningham."

Becoming frustrated, her demeanor changed to concern. "You know what list. I know who's on it, because I'm the one compiling it. I consolidate names, review files, and prioritize them from low to high. There are some extremely dangerous people on that list. And. I'm. Concerned!"

Her teasing foot went to the floor, and her utensils crashed into her plate. She couldn't hold it in anymore and took a deep breath. With faraway, baleful and misty eyes, she said, "I'm afraid."

Her transition from carefree sexiness to despair was sudden, taking him by surprise. He stood and moved to her. Taking her hands, he brought her to her feet, where she buried her head in his chest. Their movement unleashed ripples of musk, hints of their lovemaking, back into the air.

Hunter held on tightly, knowing she was on the edge of hyperventilating. "Oh, Baby, there, there. What's going on? Talk to me."

Nazy, trying to compose herself, shifted positions and buried her head against his bicep. Hunter stroked her hair with one hand and wrapped his arm around her naked waist while bringing her closer.

Their movements dislodged the belts of their robes, which fell apart, and the robes opened. They stood toe-to-toe, their flesh pressed together.

Nazy wrapped her arms around his waist, and his went around her arms and shoulders. He felt her heart pounding, while she worked up the energy to say something.

"The men on that list are horrible. They take…take great sport in killing, especially infidels. If something were to happen to you, I'd… die."

"Oh, Baby." He held her close, burying his face against her hair.

"I can't help but worry about you. I know you're careful. You've been successful, but…the men…on that list…have a history of retaliation. They can…be brutal. They make Saddam and his sons and their torture and rape rooms look tame by comparison."

"Hey, hey, hey! I'll be OK, baby. I promise."

"There's more. There's no easy way to say this, but…I'm going away for a few months. I'm not sure I'll even be able to talk to you."

Hunter gently released Nazy to better look at her; her erect nipples barely touched his pectorals. "Whoa. I thought Rothwell wouldn't let you out of his sight. What's going on? Where are you going?"

Nazy lowered her head, unable to look into his eyes. "I'm supposed to take over for the Chief of Station in Algiers. She's having a baby. When she returns to work, I'll come home. I'll have an assignment while I'm there. I'll pick up some of her work that needs continuity of effort."

She was being deliberately obtuse. Hunter nodded at the coded suggestion that she would probably continue to run spies, while his mind raced down a different track.

"The Agency has a pregnant woman in Algeria? What moron let that happen?"

Nazy frowned. Hunter understood and held her tighter.

"That's crazy," he said. "Baby, I'll miss you. I'll worry about you, too. We can still send text messages and talk. Anytime! I'll have plenty to keep me busy. If Rothwell doesn't have work for me, I still have a class to teach. The business will keep me out of trouble until you're back. I'm still selling airplanes. Maybe I could fly to Algiers. I've never been there. When do you leave?"

Her eyes met his. "Sunday night."

Stunned, he held her closer. Shaking his head at the sudden change, he said, "So we have only forty-eight hours? What's the rush?"

"She's having a baby."

"Oh, yeah. Sending a pregnant woman to a Muslim outpost was on-the-order-of felony stupid."

Nazy nodded against his chest. "I don't want to leave you. You just came back to me."

"We can go do something, have some fun before you have to leave."

They held each other tightly, rocking back and forth with her toes against his. Their grip tightened in a redoubled show of compassion for each other.

Still embraced, Nazy took her time to say, "I don't want to leave the room. I want to stay here."

Pulling away, she let the bathrobe slither off her shoulders and fall to the floor in a heap. She looked like a finalist in the Miss Nude World contest. Hunter never broke eye contact with her, as his bathrobe slid to the floor, too, and he moved toward her.

"You're an animal, Nazy Cunningham." Scooping her into his arms, he carried her back to bed.

CHAPTER TEN

2130 September 7, 2012
Anderson Hall, Laughlin Air Force Base
Del Rio, Texas

The room was hot and acrid from twenty-five bodies moving about in the confined space. A faint foul smell, the musty stench of two dozen men and women in sweaty flight suits, was slowly dissipating and becoming the norm. For Duncan Hunter, the pungent scent of working pilots bit and watered his eyes, but he considered that he was in heaven, back among his kind. All were operational pilots—slim, trim, fighting machines—fresh off the flight line. No beer guts there. They flew all day, trained students with a high degree of care and professionalism, and then took classes at night. They might be Air Force pilots, but for the old Marine fighter pilot, they were solid patriots and his rock stars.

His eyes and nose became accustomed to the tainted air as he continued the lecture, moving from behind the lectern to lean against its side. He conducted class as a maestro; all eyes were on him. Whatever he did, his students watched; whatever he said, they listened.

Two weeks into his annual Aircraft Accident Investigation Course, his students, primarily seasoned U.S. Air Force instructor pilots, found themselves in another of Professor Hunter's courses that challenged the notion that graduate school was easy and boring, and they could do just enough to get by and earn their Master's degree.

Nothing was easy or boring in Hunter's classes. They were thought-provoking and challenging. If students didn't stay awake and keep up, they'd be dropped from the class and the school. Hunter taught with the same flourish he flew a jet fighter—with precision, an aggressive pace, and humor. The most-unusual aspect to his classes was that students never fell asleep. He didn't read from a textbook; he kept them engaged in discussion from start to finish.

Embry-Riddle Aeronautical University knew it had a winning instructor when students began signing up for Hunter's classes from other bases. Those who weren't stationed in Laughlin Air Force Base drove from bases in Texas, some traveling 150 miles, to come for one of his weekly five-hour classes. Class size was limited, and students enrolled as early as possible to get one of the two-dozen prized seats.

As an adjunct professor, Hunter didn't lecture for the money. Instructing former, current, and next-generation military pilots was challenging and intriguing. It kept him current in the aviation industry. The young bucks and does in flight suits kept him on his toes.

"Let me ask you, in the context of the 9/11 hijackings, are there any similarities that happened, logistically, operationally, or functionally, to Flights 434, 800, and 990. If so, what jumps out at you?"

Professor Duncan Hunter gazed over the students, searching for a brave soul to break the ice. Someone had to raise his hand and start the conversation.

"The not-so-obvious answer is the FBI, and often the CIA, became involved in each of those incidents. The 9/11 aircraft are a no-brainer, but what about Flight 434?"

A hand rose from the middle of the stadium classroom.

"Captain Kirk? I'm sorry, Nikki. I know you'll love making major and not having to hear all the chuckling when someone addresses you. I'm sorry. What do you think?"

A smile erupted on the petite, blonde, brown-eyed young lady in a flight suit. "No factor, Professor Hunter. Flight 434 was the basis for the Bo…Bo…."

"Bo-jink-a."

"The Bojinka plot. Terrorists wanted to destroy a dozen commercial airliners over the Pacific."

"That's good. Who were the principals? Anyone? Does the name Ramzi Yousef trigger anything?"

"The first World Trade Center bombing," several students replied. Several heads nodded in assent.

"What's his connection with Khalid Sheikh Mohammed, the architect of 9/11?" Hunter held his arms up and out, begging for an answer.

Twenty-four men and women in flight suits narrowed their eyes and tried to focus. Some raced their brains to find the answer; others looked in their textbook without success. But that line of discussion wasn't in the book. Hunter always strung out a line of trivia, hooked his students with a thread of the unknown, and reeled them in. He wouldn't let them jerk at the end of the line for long. His goal was getting their attention.

He moved behind the lectern, gripped the top, and leaned forward to press his point. "KSM is Ramzi Yousef's uncle. Aviation terrorism is a family affair, apparently."

Surprise registered on many of the faces. Hunter stepped to the center of the classroom and continued.

"KSM traveled to the Philippines in 1994 to work with Yousef on the Bojinka plot. The 9/11 Commission Report indicated that Bojinka marked the first time KSM took part in the actual planning of a terrorist operation where aircraft were involved."

He pivoted 180 degrees to the green board behind him, made up of three large 4x8 forest-green panels. He walked to the right panel and picked up a piece of chalk to write in the upper-left corner, *434*. Below it he wrote *1994*. Below that went *Bomb*, with the name *Yousef.* Beside *Yousef* he wrote *KSM*. Under *Yousef* he wrote *CIA/FBI*. He then wrote *800*, *990*, and *9/11*, filling the right third of the board.

When he turned to face his students, he gave them a curious smile. "Now let's take Flight 800. Who in this class thinks the TWA jet went down because of a fuel-cell explosion? We're going to look at the actual FBI and NTSB, National Transportation Safety Board, report on Flight 800. We're going to analyze their conclusions.

"I see no one here, collectively with several hundred years of flying large or high-performance jets, is brave enough to say, 'It was the fuel cell.' Why is that?"

He turned and wrote *1996* under *800,* then bent over and scribbled *CIA/FBI* adjacent to the same words in 434's column.

A female voice blurted, "There were reports of a missile from several witnesses!"

"Exactly. Good. Very good. Why is that important, and what role did the CIA play in this purely domestic event? Anyone?" He paused. "Most of you were probably still in high school, but the Agency provided a very detailed graphic simulation of what supposedly happened in the fuel cell. The Counterterrorism Office at the CIA. Isn't that a little weird; a little curious?

"Now the FBI gets involved in cases of domestic terrorism, and we see them here, after the NTSB said it's a fuel-cell problem. When some witnesses jumped up and down and said it was a missile, they got involved.

"You're correct. There were reports of a streak of light racing into the night, followed by an explosion in the sky. The NTSB proposed handing the investigation over to the FBI, as their initial evidence suggested a criminal act took place. But then they, the FBI, changed their mind."

Hunter crossed his arms and grunted, "Hmph. Imagine that. They changed their mind. Let's look at 990. What do we know about EgyptAir 990? Anyone? Yes, Ma'am." He pointed to a young woman with short red hair in the back who raised her hand.

"Didn't another pilot enter the cockpit and commandeer the aircraft?"

"Very good. Here's the thing that bothers me...."

Most of the students were engrossed, sitting perfectly still, waiting for the storyline to develop. Was it possible Duncan Hunter, trained aircraft accident investigator, was suggesting a conspiracy theory? For the students who attended several of Hunter's classes, there was palpable unease, as Hunter shifted into conjecture.

That was why they signed up for the class. It was never dull, and students always learned something. Hunter snap-checked his Rolex and returned to his place behind the lectern, held onto the edges and leaned forward.

"The Boeing 767 crash occurred in international waters, so the Egyptians did their investigation, and the NTSB did theirs. This was after the U.S. Navy retrieved the cockpit voice recorder, where it was clear and obvious what Relief First Officer Gameel Al-Batouti did. He entered the cockpit, took a seat behind the controls, and said, '*Tawkalt ala Allah*,' which I'm told translates roughly to, 'I rely on God,' about eleven times.

"However, two separate investigations came to very different conclusions. The NTSB found the crash was caused by the obvious, deliberate action of the First Officer. He's on tape pushing the jet toward the ocean. The aircrew fought him and tried to get the 767 back under control, while he's screaming, '*Tawkalt ala Allah.*'

"Then the Egyptian equivalent of the NTSB reported—surprise! —that the crash was caused by mechanical failure of the airplane's elevator-control system. Because the jet stopped at JFK, again the FBI was consulted, as the evidence the NTSB gathered suggested a criminal act took place, and the crash was intentional, not accidental. He's on tape doing his, '*Tawkalt ala Allah*,' routine, and the Egyptians say it was a mechanical problem.

"That's some weird *shisha* in whatever *hookah* they're smoking. Isn't that fascinating? Let's add to our little chart.

"The perpetrator was First Officer Gameel Al-Batouti." He wrote *1999* under *990,* and then added *Al-Batouti* under the year *1999.*

"Now, Al-Batouti was a member of the Muslim Brotherhood." He faced the class. "If that term isn't familiar to you, you need to make it so. The spawn of the Muslim Brotherhood is al-Qaeda. Ayman al-Zawahiri was bin Laden's number-two and right-hand man, as well as a Muslim Brotherhood member in bad standing. al-Zawahiri was tortured by them, reportedly.

"The Egyptian government, in the face of overwhelming evidence to the contrary, lied to the world and said it was an accident. That the elevator control system went hard over, pushed the jet over, and it sped into the water. The relief pilot was just trying to save the aircraft."

Hunter held imaginary flight controls, and pushed them forward and backward, left and right, saying, "*Tawkalt ala Allah,*" repeatedly. When he stopped acting, he said, "Not my fault, the airplane did it!"

Several students laughed. Hunter grinned and allowed that to sink in before launching another line of discussion.

"I'm sure that's what happened. Anyway, I used to think that 990 was a kind of dress rehearsal for 9/11, but after discovering there had been several more unexplained incidents involving air carriers from Muslim countries, I began to wonder if there was more to it. The Egyptian government said a Muslim man wouldn't do such a thing yet there are several similar and questionable incidents that were never reported in the U.S. press. You know how thorough and apolitical our media can be.... Anyway...." He rolled his eyes and spun to write on the board.

Students, sitting two at a table, turned to each other incredulously. Hands flew up to ask questions, but Hunter ignored them.

Brandishing the chalk in his hand, he waved it in the air, as he marshaled his thoughts. Hunter stabbed the chalk under the 9/11 heading and wrote *Atta + 19*. Below that he wrote *Box Cutter,* and then continuing his list, he wrote *KSM/OBL* and *CIA/FBI*.

The students retracted their hands and studied the chalkboard.

Hunter returned to the lectern. "What's this starting to look like? Anyone? I admit it's a little thin. OK. Let's see if we can add to the discussion. Let me expand the scope a bit."

He wrote on the chalkboards for several minutes, creating several tables of data about the flights. Pieces of chalk crumbled and flew as he aggressively attacked the middle board.

Hunter surveyed his work, stepped to the far right and stared at the board. "Airplanes, structures, airplanes. Interesting. Let's finish this by adding the departure airports for Flights 800, 990, and half of the 9/11 aircraft. In 2009, Northwest Airlines—if you recall, it was an Airbus A330, Flight 253—with Umar Farouk Abdulmutallab, the panty bomber."

The students chuckled loudly, as Hunter disparaged the explosive-laced underwear terrorist.

"And the 2010 cargo bombing attempt—one bomb on a UPS jet and one aboard a FedEx jet in Dubai—the so-called 'toner cartridge' bombs. Of course, they were al-Qaeda or affiliates. Now what does all this look like?"

He completed the chart on the far-right board, tossing the chalk in a long arc back to the tray, and returned to the lectern, raising white-chalked hands for an answer.

Half the students leaned back in shock and awe. All were silent. The only sound came from the air-conditioning unit rumbling overhead.

Finally, the redheaded officer said, "If that was a large corkboard, that's how police arrange pieces of evidence in space and time. It looks like how police officers connect the dots in a case, as if they were trying to find a serial killer."

Every student turned to look at the pilot in the back row.

"In the movies, they hang pictures and notes and things—whatever they have—on corkboards when they're looking for patterns and trends."

Several students nodded. All eyes returned to Hunter.

"That's outstanding." Hunter did a double-take at the intense, luculent lieutenant in the back row. Rapping his knuckles on the board, he scanned the room with squinted eyes. "What jumps out at you from this very basic analysis?"

The perspicacious female pilot again answered, "The missing information under Flight 800 and that several mishap aircraft flew out of New York City."

"Right. There's a little-known fact you won't read anywhere except in a classified document—and you'll never get access to that. From 1994 until the time the government federalized passenger screening, creating the Transportation Security Administration, TSA, a curious, unreported thing happened at airports nationwide. A certain group of people—let's call them Eastern-looking men and women—applied for jobs at the contracted airport security companies that provided baggage screening. Technically, they were called pre-board screeners. These companies primarily provided people to run the X-ray machines when you go through airport security.

"In addition to Kennedy and Boston Logan, Eastern-looking men and women also worked at the Dallas, Denver, and Chicago, Miami, Memphis, and LAX airports to provide airport security."

Several students looked shocked or pained. Hunter certainly had their attention.

"I have it on good authority," he continued, his voice becoming more husky and serious, "that when the FBI confiscated the concourse security tapes at those eight airports on 9/11, they were astonished to see several box cutters clearly visible on the X-ray tapes, with Eastern-looking men passing through the magnetometer at the same time as their carry-ons were being processed in the X-ray machines. And… no… one… stopped… them." Hunter made quote marks in the air every time he said, "Eastern-looking men."

Every student was subdued and incredulous.

"Yeah, those tapes showed something else. In every case, the tapes revealed there was another 'Eastern-looking' man or woman operating the X-ray machines. The women wore a *hijab*, or head scarf. From the security tapes, it was apparent the operators identified their buddies queued in the security line. Every one of them checked his or her watch shortly before the weapons appeared in the X-ray machine.

"When the operators identified the men in the line, each operator suddenly focused very intently on his or her X-ray machine. They never looked up until after four or five 'Eastern-looking' men passed through, picked up their bags from the X-ray machine, and walked down the concourse.

"Then the most-amazing thing happened. Within fifteen minutes of those 'Eastern-looking' men passing through and picking up their bags, every one of those 'Eastern-looking' X-ray machine operators asked to be relieved from their post. Some just up and left. In every case, none of them ever returned to work. They all disappeared.

"What the 9/11 report didn't provide was that after the FAA grounded all airborne aircraft, this scenario was repeated at eight U.S. airports—JFK, Logan, Dallas, Denver, Chicago, Miami, Memphis, and LAX."

Unconsciously, the students shook their heads.

"The FBI rolled in on those contracted airport security firms. Some little bird suggested they check the airports and the contractors providing the screening services—I wonder who that could have been—to discover that on 9/11, several employees suddenly quit or walked off the job. Nearly every airport reported airport security uniforms were found in trash cans in the airport's rest rooms. Over fifty employees nationwide went missing. Not only did they walk off the job, they completely disappeared! None were ever found. 'Eastern-looking' men. 'Eastern-looking' women."

He paused to let that sink in. "Now with that little bit of circumstantial evidence, do you think that might explain why the government rushed to federalize airport screening immediately after 9/11? What do you think? Maybe that had something to do with it? That there was a major breech in airport security?

"While you might think the TSA is bad, remember that those contracted firms were the weakest link in the security process. Those terrorists exploited the weakest link and had inside help. Those who clamor for a return to contract screeners are willfully ignorant. But maybe that's just me."

It was late in the evening, but he still had their attention. None of the students had ever heard about such people working at airport security. That politically incorrect thinking was possibly explosive.

"So in the case of Flight 800, do you think it was just a bad fuel cell?"

Two dozen heads shook slowly.

"Here's a little bit of additional information. Some of you know I worked airport security at the Cleveland Hopkins Airport after I retired. It was 1994, and I was there only a couple months when suddenly, out of nowhere, 'Eastern-looking' men and women began applying for pre-board screener jobs. I was flooded with applications from ... Muslims. Oh my!

"It was beyond strange and odd. I probably experienced the same feeling that something wasn't right just as those flight instructors felt when they had Muslim men sign up for flight school wanting to fly a Boeing but had no desire to learn how to land a Boeing. I didn't hire a single one, primarily because they couldn't pass the background check. Some came back and weren't happy when I refused to hire them. Let's just say that whole experience was odd."

"Were you the little bird who told the FBI?" asked a salty, quick-thinking student with *Captain Brian "Brutus" Haines* emblazoned on his nametag.

Several students chuckled.

Hunter wore a wry, conspiratorial grin. "On the advice of counsel, I respectfully invoke my constitutional rights under the Fifth Amendment. Anyway, one purpose of this exercise was to get you to look beyond the most-obvious answers and ignore the politically correct ones. You have a tried-and-true process. You have to work through it. Don't assume. During an accident investigation, you should be surprised at the end at what you find. When you're assigned to an accident investigation, you'll be investigating someone else's mishap. You'll never investigate your own air group or air wing."

He paused to let them take notes. When heads rose again, he said, "There may be extraneous factors that affect your investigation. EgyptAir demonstrated their government couldn't or wouldn't tell the truth for whatever reason, whether that was cultural, political, or economic. Our own government didn't, couldn't, or wouldn't provide the full truth of the scope of what happened on 9/11 for the same reasons. Obviously, we cannot handle the truth.

"TWA Flight 800 came at a time of significant political turmoil. There was amazing mischief occurring in the White House. In my estimation, what the NTSB and the press reported was beyond belief. When we look at that report in more detail in a couple weeks, you'll see what I mean. The report created an impression, an illusion, that the problem was the center fuel tank. That NTSB report was complete BS, and every aviator on the planet that's flown a big jet knows it.

"I'm sure one of these days we'll have an NTSB investigator come forth—after he or she has retired—or as an after-the-fact whistleblower and say something like, 'I was pressured to say it was a fuel leak, a frayed wire in the tank and not a missile.'"

Hunter chuckled, took a deep breath, and debated whether to say more. His students were still absorbing major revelations and were astonished, but they were alert and ready for more.

If any of them were perplexed, though, they were more so when Hunter said, "Here's a little something else. You can tell that crappy NTSB report was ... done by ... liberals."

Shock registered on every student's face. Sitting in the front row, the prematurely balding and chunky Major Cooper was stunned and visibly distressed. He chose his words carefully.

"Professor Hunter, what do you mean, done by liberals?" he asked.

The rest of the class shifted uneasily in their seats, as they recovered from the shocking statement and became intrigued. The twists and turns in Hunter's lecture were dizzying. He rarely drifted off script or discussed politics. It wasn't like any student to challenge him, just as it wasn't like him to inject political philosophy into their discussion.

Some in class might have thought his remark was uncalled for. Major Mike "Sleepy" Cooper threw down the gauntlet, and the others waited to see how Hunter would extricate himself from the situation.

Disarming the pilot by addressing him by his call sign, Hunter said, "OK, Sleepy. After six months of teaching studs, what's the one thing you can discern when you're given a nice, new, shiny student? Correct me if I'm wrong. You know within a few seconds into a brief if that student will be good or troubled. Can I get general agreement on that?"

Major Cooper and the other instructor pilots nodded. They watched Hunter move to the side wall of chalkboards and begin writing as he talked.

"You find good students are smart, study hard, and do their homework. The not-so-good students struggle with everything—emergency procedures, homework, following directions. Agreed? OK. Why is that? Come on. Someone be brave. No takers? OK. What do we have here?" He pointed at the words he wrote on the blackboard: *Abstract, Hypothesis, Review of Literature, Test and Analysis, Conclusions, Recommendations.*

"Master's thesis outline," several students said.

"Correct. That's the basic recipe for getting your thesis done." He swept his arm from left to right across the whole class. "Now like you, I know that after working closely with my superstar grad students for several months, I can tell within a very short period of meeting a new student whether that newbie will be good or have trouble. And when we get to the subject of writing their Master's thesis, I can tell who's conservative and who's liberal."

He banged his knuckles on the board. "After fifty theses, the most amazing thing I've noticed is that conservative students have no problem following these procedures. Remember, I work very closely with a student to develop a master's thesis package. I'm working with several of you now, correct?"

Several heads with frowns nodded in unison.

"My conservative students appear to work and think left to right. They develop an abstract and hypotheses. Then they research and review the available literature. They develop testing tools, so they can test and analyze what they tested. Then they report their findings and write the best conclusions and recommendations.

"All with me so far? OK. Now without fail, I find my liberal students appear to want to work backward. That is, they invariably want to start with the conclusion—they know what the outcome is before they have tested anything—and work from right to left. Without fail, they state their conclusions up front—they tell me what they'll find before they have researched anything—and then work to prove those conclusions.

"If they can come up with a topic or subject, they will have immediately formed conclusions and want to work backward to prove them. They struggle with the simple linear process of left to right. They find right to left is more natural. They strive to prove their conclusions, not be surprised by them. Somehow, that might be a learned reaction or hardwired into them.

"So I can say with certainty that all of my liberal students, when conducting the thesis process, started with a preconceived notion or conclusion. Then they researched the literature and cherry picked their findings to fit or support their conclusion. This may be done unconsciously, without malice. I don't think they know they're doing it. They even develop test instruments and hypotheses to support their conclusion.

"It's also obvious when reports are written by a conservative or a liberal. Put them side-by-side, and it's very clear, at least to me. Conservative students write reports that follow the left-to-right protocol. They have coherent arguments; go through a literature review, good and bad, pro and con. They read it all.

"Most of my liberal students' reports are ambiguous, anfractuous, and dissimulated. They're right-to-left, like Arabic writing. Their review of related literature is fractured, shoehorned piecemeal into the paper to support the obvious conclusion. If I don't force my liberal students into breaking down the process piece by piece—this week we work on developing the abstract, next week the hypotheses, and so on —then their papers read like a large newspaper article. I should make them pay more for the class."

All the students laughed.

"The only F I've ever given was to a lieutenant colonel. He didn't do his homework and refused to follow proper thesis procedures and research. He was obviously a liberal. His actions after receiving that F were pure liberalism. He blamed everyone but himself.

"Anyway, back to our topic. If you look at the political environment, then the NTSB report obviously had an agenda. The political climate at the time said Flight 800 couldn't have been brought down by terrorists. That went against the President's narrative and they constructed and manipulated their findings in the report to reflect their conclusion. Like EgyptAir, they didn't report what they found but told a bogus story. EgyptAir concluded at the start that a Muslim man would never take his life like that. He didn't disengage the autopilot and shove the nose down while saying, '*Takwalt ala Allah,*' repeatedly."

The class erupted in laughter.

"Therefore, it had to be something else. Roll the dice, spin the wheel, interpret the tea leaves, and holy moly! It was an elevator malfunction. We're going to study a bunch of NTSB reports to see how Flight 800 sticks out, as my grandmother said, like a sore thumb, like it appears here on the board.

"Before I let you go, there's one more data point we should consider regarding Flight 800."

Duncan jumped, as his BlackBerry vibrated and played *Pipeline* by the Ventures to announce an email. Embarrassed, he snatched the device from his belt, mashed buttons to squelch the sound and vibrate functions, and snap-checked the email subject line. He jutted his bottom lip as he returned the device to its holster.

Only momentarily distracted, he referred to the binder on the lectern, flipping through pages until he found what he sought and pulled out a newspaper clipping

"More interesting stuff. Immediately after Flight 800 fell from the sky, Congress held several closed-door hearings. A few Congresscritters leaked that they were discussing the 'latest threat.'" Again, he made quote marks with his fingers.

"The gist of the conversations those Congressmen had with some reporters, without clearing it with their leadership, was that the hearing was specifically focused on the Flight 800 tragedy. I quote, 'The threat terrorism presents to commercial aviation was the focus of the closed-door meetings.'"

Hunter held up the news clipping and said, "I quote. The latest threat was the risk of shoulder-fired missile attacks or MANPADS. There are over half a million MANPADS worldwide, and a good number of those weapons are available and obtainable on the black market. The number of MANPADS in the hands of non-state actors or terrorist group is unknown. Estimates state that dozens of non-state groups in Africa, Asia, Europe, and the Middle East have anywhere from several dozen to hundreds of MANPADS. The availability, portability, and concealable makeup of MANPADS all add to their appeal to terrorist groups.

"The outcome of the closed-door meeting was the Congress directed the DOD to conduct research and development of missile defense systems for commercial aircraft. The idea was to take military missile defense systems and install them into commercial jets to prevent another Flight 800."

He waited to let that conclusion settle in. "Let me say again, to prevent another Flight 800." He returned the clipping to his binder and scanned the stunned faces of his students. Whether it was fatigue or shock, most of his students were speechless. "If it wasn't a missile that knocked down Flight 800, why is the congress jumping through hoops to install military missile defense systems and install them on commercial aircraft? Hmmmmm!"

"That initiative was proposed by our current President, the former Speaker of the House, I might add. However, it came and went, primarily because DOD doesn't do research for commercial aviation. It wasn't until after the 9/11 commission that the antimissile defense systems initiative was raised again. In early 2003, in a mark-up session of the Senate Committee on Commerce, Science, and Transportation, Congress directed the Secretary of Homeland Security to conduct a ninety-day study of the threat and report to Congress on recommendations for protecting airliners against shoulder-fired missiles.

"The official version is that Flight 800 had a problem with its fuel tank. Yet after Flight 800, Congress went into overdrive to do something about MANPADS in the hands of terrorist groups. There was a sense of urgency to take military defense systems and install them into commercial jets—and I quote—to *prevent another Flight*

800. I find that fascinating. I'll let you think about that.

"And on that happy note, we're done for tonight. Thank you for a glorious evening. Class dismissed. See you next week."

Three-fourth of the students shook their heads in wonder, as they gathered their belongings and bolted for the door. For the life of an instructor pilot and graduate student, class was the culmination of a seventeen-hour workday. Most of the married students rocketed from the building and headed home to eat cold dinners or leftovers.

Several of the remaining students stood and formed a line to speak to Hunter. He engaged each of the stragglers, discussing homework assignments or arranging to make up work if the student would miss class the following week.

One wag in line asked if Hunter's powers of discernment were sufficient to tell who'd ultimately be a fighter pilot or if the person would fly a different aircraft.

Hunter smiled broadly. "When I was a flight instructor, it was a no-brainer. I just knew. I suspect you do, too. When I was your age, I was clueless, apolitical, and uninterested in politics. I never made the connection that fighter pilots and SEALs and those in Special Operations ever had strong political leanings. They were, by and large, strong conservatives. There are always a few closet liberals. I suppose Myers-Briggs can ID those preferences, too. It's not rocket science."

The last of the students received answers to their questions, retrieved their backpacks and books, said goodbye, and headed from the room—except one. One of the new students sitting in back was content to observe the horde surrounding the instructor.

When the last of them seemed done lobbing questions and banter at the professor, she gathered her materials and slid them into a black backpack. The young woman was stunning even in her unflattering straight-lined flight suit. Its olive green color accented her dark-red hair and hint of freckles.

As Hunter finished with the line of students, he noticed they surreptitiously sneaked peeks at the woman sitting in the rear as they left the classroom. She was definitely smart, poised, confident, and attractive—and vaguely familiar. Hunter placed his note binder and textbook into a tan Hartmann Gladstone and waited for her to leave.

He turned to erase the board behind him when she said, "That was an interesting discussion at the end...."

It was the first time Hunter came face-to-face with the lieutenant. She glanced at him as she walked toward him. When she came within a few feet, he stopped and waited. She seemed strangely nervous, which left Hunter feeling confused.

Like a bubble slowly escaping the bowels of a mud pit, the hint of a long-dead memory oozed from the depths of his subconscious and slowly popped. There was something even more familiar about the young woman, but Hunter couldn't resolve it. He couldn't exactly recall her name, but knew it was distantly familiar. He admonished himself, he should have known.

It took several weeks of class to get to know his students well enough to get a feel how they would do in class, and the class had several new ones. He taught almost 400 students. Over the course of the class, he came to know all their names, but he struggled to recall the young lady's when she stopped walking toward him.

She came close enough to read her nametag; his eyes rose to meet hers. Kelly Horne. He wondered if he offended her with his talk of conservatives and liberals. The kinder, gentler, apolitical Air Force wouldn't be happy that he mentioned politics in front of its officers, especially the young and impressionable Kelly Horne.

From her actions in class, though, he thought, *she can't be a liberal. They get their panties in a wad at the least provocation. That is just not her. So what does she want?*

He considered his response and decided to disarm the attacker with positives first. "That was a nice analysis about an evidence board. That's exactly what I hoped to accomplish. You're the first student to put it in the right context. Nice job, Kelly. You'll do well in class. I can see that."

"So am I a conservative or a liberal?" She smiled.

He returned the smile. It was the moment of truth. "Easy.

Conservative. You've very smart and prescient."

"Thank you." She swayed almost imperceptibly, like a proud little girl getting a word right at a spelling bee.

"I hope I haven't offended you or scared you off, have I? Old guys sometimes say things they later regret. I think this is a great course. For your first grad school class and being a new instructor pilot, it's not that bad. I don't think you'll have any issues."

She told herself it was a stupid idea. She hadn't thought it through. She should have picked up her things, left the room, and let the man live his life.

She shrugged her backpack off onto a table and held on. Why had she thought this was a good idea? She'd come so far. It seemed like there was no time like the present. "The course isn't what I wanted to talk to you about."

Hunter tried to inhale surreptitiously to hide his concern. Whatever she wanted, it couldn't be good. He hoisted his briefcase to another table and stepped behind it, unconsciously protecting himself. It wasn't just a mindless move to take up time while he faced her.

Hunter caught himself. He'd been too cute; trying to be funny and make a political point. *Be a man,* he told himself. *You said something stupid and improper. Apologize and move on.*

He came around the lectern, and they met in the aisle of the rows of two-man tables on either side. "OK. What's on your mind?"

There was something strangely familiar about her voice, a faint, distant timbre. His first thought was she was way too young for him to have known her in any way. He was certain they had never met. He checked her nametag again. *Kelly Horne.* He strained to answer his hidden question. *Who are you?*

Kelly felt she came too far to stop. She had researched Duncan Hunter's name on the internet and found the only one was a retired Marine Corps pilot living in Texas 100 miles away in Fredericksburg. He was the president of a small company and was an instructor for Embry-Riddle Aeronautical University. His online university biography showed that Professor Hunter was scheduled to teach a class at Laughlin Air Force Base.

Kelly enrolled, wanting to see him anonymously and find out what kind of man her father was. After the first class, she was very pleasantly surprised to see he was an impressive man, smart, articulate, and well-respected by his students. He even had a good sense of humor. From appearances, she would be proud to call him her father.

She thought she'd be nervous when she told him, but the remarkable calm that had steeled her seconds earlier was retreating, tugging at her as if she'd been caught in a tidal wave's outflow of fear and embarrassment.

I can tell him. I can tell him! I want him to know. It'll be OK.

She took two deep breaths. Hunter forced his eyes to remain on hers and not the nametag on her heaving bosom.

Her adrenalin spiked, sending her heart racing. She blurted out, "My mother was Kimberly Horne. I'm your daughter."

Hunter's eyes slammed shut. He weaved in place, struck dumb and mute. *Kimberly Horne* was a name from the distant past, long buried, and now it was suddenly alive again—released into the open to again rip his heart apart. His eyelids fluttered, and he lowered his jaw, as his mind refused to function. He never saw it coming.

Kelly Horne? Kimberly's…daughter?

Differential calculus wouldn't solve this problem. He didn't know what to do or say. Closing his eyes, he tried to hit the reset button in his mind. He didn't know how, but somehow, he saw Kimberly and himself in the sweet reality of the trembling young Kelly, and knew it was true. *That's why she looks familiar!*

He stopped wobbling on his heels, caught his breath, and tried to compose himself. Very slowly, he said, "You're… my… daughter. Wow. I had no idea. I don't know what else to say, other than I'm so very glad ... you favor your mother."

Another trembling wave of pent-up emotion rolled in, filled with turbulence, looking for an escape. Kelly hadn't thought she would cry, but twenty years of wondering why she didn't have parents suddenly ended. When her shaking stopped, she released a torrent of tears.

She tried to hide her embarrassment. Tears streamed from her eyes, and tears welled in Duncan's, as twenty-year-old memories of Kimberly erupted to saturate his senses. His thoughts oscillated between *What do I do?* and *What do I say?* After the initial stream of consciousness, the shock of finding an unknown daughter standing in front of him in his classroom left him unable to move or speak.

The only body function that responded to an unseen stimulus were his arms, which slowly raised in an offer of comfort and compassion. Kelly released her backpack and stepped in. Somehow, his arms were instinctively programmed to close around young, crying daughters. She buried her head against his chest and cried tears of joy. Hunter steadied himself, inhaled the sweaty scent of his daughter's hair and flight suit, pinched his tears that fell into her hair, and kissed the crown of her head.

After holding each other for two minutes, Hunter gingerly released his grip and said, "We have a lot to talk about. We need to get out of here before they lock us in."

Kelly nodded gently against his chest before fully releasing him. She looked up into his brown eyes. "Thank you."

Composing herself, she straightened her flight suit with a tug, tossed her backpack over her shoulder, and walked out the door, daubing tears on her sleeve with every step. *I told…my dad!*

Hunter dried his eyes with the back of his hands. He reached for his Gladstone and glanced at the incompletely wiped chalkboard with the Flight 800 information on it. Someone else would work on that. He turned off the lights as he left.

Kelly couldn't take her eyes off of him; she stopped and let him catch up. He smiled at her with red eyes, and she smiled back. His eyes were puffy, and he was still in shock. He was lightheaded enough that he had to force his feet to work. He hoped he wouldn't fall over.

I have…a daughter!

"I had no idea," Hunter whispered, his head oscillating gently in disbelief. He was still in shock as he turned the final pages of Kimberly Horne's diary. He closed the little book after reading the final entry and held it tightly in both hands, his head down for a long time.

When he looked up, tears rolled down his cheeks. "Your mother was a remarkable and brave woman. I loved her dearly. I really had no idea."

Kelly, still in her flight suit, sat in the opposite chair, quietly watching Hunter read. She sipped a wine color as she watched him and his body language, as he discovered her mother's most-intimate thoughts about the man named Duncan Hunter and why she gambled with her life to have the baby. He appeared pleased, even ecstatic, to learn he had a daughter, but it was obvious sadness filled him at the way Kimberly shut him from her life while she struggled to have the baby.

"I think you could say my mother was pro-life, probably a conservative," she said with a meek smile, trying to lighten the conversation.

"No doubt. She was a remarkable woman. That was a time before either of us were very political. She broke my heart, and I never knew why she stopped writing. It was a year after I returned from my cruise before I knew she'd passed away. Your grandmother wouldn't talk to me. I never knew you were born."

"I'm pretty sure she thought you'd take me away from her."

"I don't know what I would have done. I do know I'm very grateful you found me and told me. Jeez, I still cannot believe it, but I also feel like I just won the lottery. Thank you Kelly. What you did was incredibly brave. You're just like your mother."

They smiled at each other, their emotions trying to stabilize after the roller-coaster ride of the past half an hour. The jolt of the evening was wearing off for both of them, and it was late. Without looking at his watch, Hunter slid into an unknown father role.

"Kelly, it's getting late, and you need sleep if you're flying tomorrow."

Kelly pursed her lips and nodded. She wasn't sure she wanted him to leave just yet. They had a lot to talk about.

"I get the feeling you'd like to continue this conversation. I'd like that, too. I want to get to know you better."

"Yes. I'd like that, too." She nodded approvingly.

"OK. That's a start. How about this? I could come back to Del Rio this weekend? We could go to dinner or something."

Meekly, she offered, "I could also come to Fredericksburg ... tomorrow after work?"

Hunter was buoyed by the idea. "You could come to the ranch, maybe spend the weekend. I could show you what your old man does for a living."

The moment he said it, he winced. Maybe that wasn't a good idea; at least not yet. The trauma of the evening was still affecting him. He wasn't thinking clearly. He almost forgot he received an email from the DCI requesting his presence. Most likely, that meant he had a job.

Oh, Christ! What'll I tell Nazy? That question rattled in his head when he heard his daughter speak.

"That would be great. Let's do that." She let that decision hang in the air a moment. "What do I call you?"

Hunter, grateful to return to the present, grinned, but his voice was a bit anxious as he said, "Anything you like. I respond to several names." His attempt at humor was trumped by her answer.

She smiled and asked, "How about Dad?"

"I love the sound of that. If Dad's OK with you, that works for me."

"OK, *Dad.* Thank you."

CHAPTER ELEVEN

1800 September 8, 2012
Yellow Corvette Ranch
Fredericksburg, Texas

Kelly Horne raced through her apartment, flinging her flying boots off and shedding her flight suit like a snake wriggling out of its skin. She was in and out of the shower in a few minutes, then into jeans and a Polo shirt. She put on makeup in her Fiero.

Why am I putting on makeup? It's my dad! She laughed at herself. She was so happy; she couldn't focus and hadn't slept much the previous night.

Throughout the day, Kelly wore a smile or grin, her mind on something pleasant and exciting. The other instructor pilots recognized the change in her tone and demeanor immediately. Kelly bounced around the flight room like she had slammed back a dozen coffee espressos.

When the squadron commander addressed the new instructor pilot as "Kelly," she frowned. The commander, who thereafter always called her "Lieutenant Horne," was taken aback by the articulate, plain-speaking pilot of serious mien. Her economy of effort and surplus of confidence gave her a quality he hadn't seen in the rest of his IPs. He'd been around several Marine Corps officers when he was stationed at the Pentagon, and they were impressive with their spit shines, high and tight haircuts, and professional attitude; no fluff or hyperbole with that crowd.

It wasn't a stretch to think that Kelly Horne acted like those crazy

Marines. While his instructor pilots worked at teaching flight students, Lieutenant Horne also worked on being a consummate professional pilot and dedicated Air Force officer. She also took graduate courses. None of his junior officers would do that.

It was noteworthy and remarkable that Lieutenant Horne was suddenly acting like Kelly Horne, one of the guys. Something happened in her life, and it was obviously good. As the squadron commander shrugged and left the fight room, the other IPs talked.

"She must've gotten laid," a captain said who'd flown with her several times. Horne was known for being unusually quiet, reserved, and all business, but not that day.

"I think she's got a boyfriend, maybe a girlfriend," a senior lieutenant whispered to another IP. "Who knows? Something sure has her going."

The tall handsome lieutenant had been repeatedly rebuffed by Horne and wished he'd been able to get her excited about him. He felt crushed all over again at the thought she had her eyes and heart set for someone else.

Late in the day, after the first set of flights and recoveries, Horne was back in the flight room, and the lieutenant instructor noted she was still unusually cheerful. She bounced around like a kid at Disneyland, impatiently waiting for the next ride. He had to say something.

"I have to say, Lieutenant Horne, I haven't seen you this pumped up since you were assigned to the squadron. I'd almost say you have a man in your life."

Kelly hadn't noticed she was still affected by the events of the previous night and felt a little embarrassed. Then she laughed, and smiled, and burst out, "I *am* stoked. I'm going to have dinner with my *Dad,* and I hope to spend the weekend with him. It may sound boring, but I'm very excited."

Her comments stunned the other instructors in the briefing room. Who got excited about having dinner with her parents? The woman was definitely strange in a beautiful sort of way. The lieutenant was relieved and thought he may still have a chance.

She hadn't wanted her dad to leave. She stood on the walkway of her apartment and watched him drive off in his beautiful black sports car. She never saw a car like it before. It was obviously rare and expensive. She only heard of Aston Martins from old James Bond movies, but that car was unlike anything she remembered in the movies.

Dad's car was stunning, even sexy. It fit him. She googled Aston Martin before going to bed. If her father could afford a $200,000 car, he must be doing pretty well. *Why was he teaching Air Force IPs?* She had a thousand questions to ask him.

The drive to Fredericksburg was uneventful, as the sun quickly set. Hunter's directions past the town to the ranch were easy and straightforward, although before she turned off onto the access road, she paused at a simple sign, placed low where it could be easily missed. It read: *Yellow Corvette Ranch.*

She wondered why he drove a black Aston Martin and lived on the Yellow Corvette Ranch. Another question she would ask.

The one-lane blacktop wound up and down rolling hills. Huge palms, cacti, and mesquite trees lined the drive. Several groups of whitetail deer grazed along the road, undisturbed by the Fiero puttering by. She drove cautiously for a few minutes, thinking the house was near. Finally, she went up a small incline and took a hard left around a house-sized boulder very slowly when she saw the ranch house, lit by a pair of street lamps, a few hundred yards away.

She approached a circular driveway framed on one side by a sturdy barn on the left. In the center, a sprawling single-story log cabin house with a shallow, red-tin roof and a deep covered porch which seemed to wrap around the house. To her right was a spectacular view of wide-open Texas hill country.

Three people waited on the porch. Horne's heart pounded; she checked her makeup in the mirror and stopped.

Duncan Hunter bounded down from the porch and raced to greet her, but she had already killed the engine, opened the door, and swung her legs out of the low car. He offered to help her out. She took his hands and pulled.

He smiled, unsure if he was allowed to show affection, but he was so overcome with joy that he hugged her and was firmly hugged in return. They released and walked around the car, arms around the other's waist, to two stunned Native Americans. It wasn't like Captain Hunter to entertain ladies when Nazy was away.

"Kelly, let me introduce Theresa and Carlos Yazzie," Hunter said. "Theresa, Carlos; Kelly is my daughter."

The Yazzies had been promised a surprise but a daughter wasn't on the list. Theresa's knees buckled, and she nearly fainted. Carlos caught her before she tumbled off the porch. The Fiero clicked and clacked, as the engine cooled.

Hunter beamed broadly at Kelly, who felt emotional and couldn't even say, "Glad to meet you." The spectacle of the portly woman nearly falling changed the dynamics of the introductions.

Seeing that Theresa wasn't in danger of being hurt, he turned to look at his daughter. "I haven't seen Kelly in a long time," Hunter said. "What's it been, eighteen hours? I hope she can spend the weekend with us before she has to go back to Del Rio. She's an instructor pilot at the air base."

The rotund Theresa Yazzie finally recovered, though she swayed and looked hard at Duncan. She barked, "Are you trying to give me a heart attack?" She brushed aside her husband and Hunter, and hugged the lithe young woman. Horne was surprised at the outpouring of affection from Theresa.

Hunter smiled, thoroughly enjoying the moment.

After a hearty hug, Theresa gripped Kelly's hands. "You're so very beautiful, and…I don't know what else to say. Welcome home, Miss

Hunter."

Carlos, confused and dazed, remained silent. He knew Duncan while in uniform as an enlisted man and officer, and then his boss for almost ten years, but this was a real surprise. He knew Hunter had been a ladies' man for all that time, but there were no wives and no hint of children.

"Theresa, it's Kelly Horne," Hunter corrected. "She's been looking for me a long time. She found me, in all places, at my class last night. Apparently I was lost but now I'm found. We have much to talk about."

Theresa Yazzie, still shocked, mumbled and retired to the kitchen after Horne extracted an overnight bag, and Carlos drove the Fiero into the barn.

"Even out here," Hunter explained, "it's common to find illegal aliens crossing the property. I don't want them to find a target of opportunity. We lock all vehicles in the barn."

After entering the house, Hunter said, "Make yourself comfortable. Dinner's almost ready. I hope you like lasagna and have an appetite." He walked toward the kitchen, while Horne gave him a smile and thumbs-up to show her approval.

She wandered into the adjoining room, unconsciously rubbing her shoulder. She looked around the living area and was overcome by the space and rustic furnishings. The living room was framed by stacked blonde-colored logs rising into a warren of smaller beams, crisscrossing others to support the metal roof. The floor was natural dark flagstone of various shapes and sizes, punctuated by colorful Navaho rugs. A ten-foot-wide stone fireplace that rose to the ceiling dominated the center of the room. She judged her apartment was the size of the living room.

Decorations consisted of pottery from the Southwest, with two large sofas facing the fireplace. Overhead, centered between the couches, was the most-incredible glass chandelier Horne ever saw. The product of a local glassblower, the four-foot work of art consisted of hundreds of twisting red spires of varying lengths with bright lights in the center. The walls featured several watercolors by local artists, while wooden and bronze *Kachina* dolls lined the mantel.

Over the fireplace she vaguely recognized a brilliantly colored, expressionist painting in the style of LeRoy Neiman. Stepping closer, she saw it was an original. It showed Duncan and an old yellow Corvette racecar. A metal tab at the base of the frame suggested Hunter had the painting commissioned after he won a Vintage Grand Touring race in Monterey, California.

Suspended in the corner, opposite the Neiman, was a six-foot Apache war bonnet. The double rows of foot-long white-tipped eagle feathers descended in long red tails all the way to the floor. Worn only by chiefs and warriors, Carlos Yazzie presented it to Hunter after Yazzie came to work for him. Horne had never seen a real headdress up close and found the feathers, leather and ermine trim, and fancy beadwork a powerful emblem of history that was both beautifully stunning and elegant. Her father had eclectic tastes.

She wandered down the hall where the bathrooms and bedrooms were, occasionally massaging her shoulder. She poked her head into an open room filled with bookcases, airplane models, and pictures, and what looked like a huge slab of granite that served as a counter or desktop.

In the subdued light, her eyes noted a small black airplane model sitting at one end of the desktop. She didn't recognize the aircraft with its bulbous silver canopy, six-bladed propeller, and long, glider-like wings. She stared at it, trying to determine what kind of crazy airplane it was, when she heard her father calling. She raced down the hall toward the living room.

"Dinner is served!" Hunter shouted. "We'll eat on the deck unless the mosquitoes chase us back in, if that's OK."

Jogging around the corner to intercept where the voice came from, she was astonished by the size and furnishings in the kitchen. Huge ovens, refrigerators, and acres of red granite countertops became a blur, as she saw her father and Theresa heading out a door, and she hurried to follow.

"OK with me!" she said.

When Kelly emerged from the door, she saw Hunter standing behind a chair at a small table set for two. Dozens of round candles lined the railing on the deck, tossing a warm glow onto the patio. Two candles placed strategically on the table illuminated their meal.

As Hunter held her chair, he asked, "Will this work?"

"Wow. This is very nice."

"I saw you liked wine coolers. I have a little something of everything, whatever you want."

"Water's fine. This is quite a view." She rubbed her shoulder unconsciously,

"You get away from town, and on a clear day like today, you can see the Milky Way in all of her glory. It's very cool." Taking his seat, he drew a napkin across his lap.

"I can see that. The house is beautiful. Dinner looks scrumptious. It's a little overwhelming." She paused and asked, "Grace?"

Hunter, a little taken aback, smiled and nodded. Largely agnostic, he admired the great religions and was respectful of those who practiced, but he wasn't much of a believer. "Please."

Kelly quit massaging her shoulder and reached across the table with both hands, inviting Hunter to hold them. When he complied, she hung her head and said, "Bless us, Oh Lord, and these gifts which we are about to receive. We look at the food that has been prepared by loving hands; we look into the faces of those who love us and whom we love. We thank You as You bless this food and this time together. Amen."

"Amen. *I* am blessed for this time together."

They talked throughout dinner. Horne relayed her childhood, saying it was mostly good, but she learned early she was different. She didn't have a mother or father. Her grandmother and grandfather were her parents. She did well in school partly because she thought her mother would have wanted her to be smart, and worked hard to make her grandparents proud. She imagined having parents, a mother and father like other kids, but, as she grew older, she came to love her grandparents, so thoughts of real parents faded.

It wasn't until one day when she was fifteen that she asked her grandmother, "What was my mother like?"

She was surprised to learn her mother was an Air Force officer and pilot. Kelly was so impressed that her mother was one of the first women fighter pilots in the Air Force, she decided to follow in her mother's footsteps and attend the Air Force Academy and go to flight school.

"Kind of finish what Mother started," she told Hunter. "For my sixteenth birthday my grandfather took me to the airport to fly gliders. I wanted to be an Air Force pilot like mother while my folks wanted me to try to go to a university to get a degree."

"And you got to do both."

"I did."

Kelly's grandmother never spoke of her father. Early on, she was under the impression her grandmother didn't know him. Over time, she wondered if her grandmother didn't *want* to know him. There was something about her grandmother's demeanor and tone that suggested she believed Kelly might have a living father and her grandmother knew him, but she didn't want Kelly to know anything about him.

When her grandparents passed away within a couple of months of each other, Kelly believed she'd never learn who her father was. Then her world was thrown into a tailspin when she received a box from her grandmother's estate executor that contained her mother's diary and some jewelry.

"I've been flying high ever since," she finished. "That's really all there is to it."

"Was there a woman's Rolex in the box?" Hunter asked, reaching into old memories. It wasn't likely.

Stunned, Kelly nodded, and then she broke into a broad smile. "Yes. How'd you know?'

Duncan smiled. "I didn't really know. I guess I just kind of hoped. The rest of the story is I bought that watch while I was aboard ship. I sent it to your mother and was going to ask her to marry me when I returned stateside from my cruise. I also bought a ring when I was in

Hong Kong."

He hung his head. "Right after I sent the watch, Kim stopped writing. I always wondered what happened to her. I figured she knew where this was leading, got scared or fed up with the sea duty and me being gone all the time. It was a year before I found your grandmother's phone number, and she told me Kim had passed away from cancer. I was so devastated; heartbroken."

Long silence passed between them. Several times they looked at each other. Kelly dabbed her eyes with her napkin and said, "I don't think that watch has ever been out of the box."

"It's yours now." He held up his left arm, showing a two-tone Rolex Submariner around his wrist, the gold links sparkled in the candlelight. "I bought the two as a pair. Kim got the gold one. I liked the two-tone. They're pieces of art. It hasn't been off my wrist many times over the last twenty-plus years. I used to think of your mother every time I put it on. Now I'll think of you." He twisted his wrist to get a better view of the shiny stainless-and-gold chronograph with the blue dial.

"It's beautiful. I don't know about wearing mother's watch. What about you…Dad? What's your story?"

"Me? Not much to talk about." He was finally confronted with what to tell his long-lost daughter. He'd been grappling in his mind about what to say when the time came.

"That's hard to believe. This is quite a house. That's quite a car."

Hunter exhaled loudly and squirmed in his chair. Nodding, he realized he wasn't ready. "What's with your shoulder, Kelly?"

"The Air Force makes us take the anthrax vaccine, a series of immunizations. I just started the series, and my shoulder's sore."

"That might come in handy someday." He recalled how America was terrified of an anthrax attack so soon after 9/11, and no one knew who was behind the attack, though the press reported that the FBI got their man, a rogue U.S. Army scientist who recently passed away. Duncan remembered thinking the government's story was bullshit and too bizarre to be believed.

"I kind of doubt it," she replied. "How would a pilot get anthrax?"

"You may have a point. How about we move inside and clear the table?"

"OK."

They sat across from one another in front of the fireplace, and talked until two in the morning.

"Don't be surprised if you're awakened by Theresa in the kitchen. It doesn't do any good to ignore her. You just have to get up and have breakfast. She won't stop fussing over you until you say 'uncle.' I'm not kidding. She's absolutely wonderful and takes care of me."

"What's their story?"

Hunter chuckled and yawned. "I've known Carlos a long time. We were sergeants together in Okinawa. Once we were passing through Iwakuni, Japan, from Korea, and Yazzie and some of the other mechanics were on their way out of the barracks to go bar hopping. I knew he just received a big re-enlistment check, maybe two or three grand, which was big money in 1978. I told him before he went out to leave the check with me.

"While the rest of the aircrew went into town, I stayed on base to head for the racquetball courts. I knew Carlos a little. He had a little reputation as a drinker. Nothing was private in the sergeant's barracks. I didn't want him to piss away his check on firewater. That might be politically incorrect, but it's true. He argued with me a little, but he trusted me enough to leave his check with me.

"At three in the morning, he banged on my door and woke me up saying he needed the check to pay for all the drinks he bought. Someone had his ID card, and he couldn't get it back until the bar tab was paid. I told him to go to bed. He could get a new ID. I wasn't going to give him the check, and he wasn't going back out there. I kept telling him to go to bed, and it would be OK.

"He didn't get ugly or angry. Eventually, he headed for the rack and slept it off. In the morning we flew home to Okinawa; so it turned out OK. Theresa thought I saved Carlos from becoming a washed-up drunk and made sure he stayed in the Marines.

"When I started building this place, I needed someone I could trust to help me run it and be its caretaker. I needed a ranch foreman, because I was always gone or headed out someplace. I called Carlos and Theresa, and they agreed.

"They've been with me for ten years. Carlos has a nice blacksmith shop on the other side of the garage. He makes wonderful wrought-iron things for the ranch and for sale for craft shows when he's not being a foreman. Theresa does the cooking and cleans the ranch house and their place out back when she isn't making pottery or weaving rugs in the Apache way. They're wonderful. I take care of them, and they take care of me. I don't know if you saw the war bonnet in the living room. Carlos gave me his family's war bonnet. I consider it's just a loan."

The narrative nearly brought tears to her tired eyes. "That's a great story."

Hunter was tired and thought the evening had been a success. "How about after breakfast we go flying? I have a Super Cub. I need to do a few touch-and-goes. You might like flying the little beast. Then we'll go into town, and I'll show you my office and business. How's that?"

"That would be great. Thank you for a great evening. Good night, Dad." She stepped forward and kissed his cheek before turning toward her room. He reached up to touch the spot she kissed, breaking into a broad smile before walking down the hall to his bedroom.

CHAPTER TWELVE

1000 September 9, 2012
Fredericksburg, Texas

Kelly thought it was extremely odd that her father felt he needed to do several touch-and-goes in the Super Cub. Hunter didn't offer an explanation. Thrilled to be flying in the back of the little antique airplane, she soon banished those thoughts from her mind and enjoyed the ride.

When he turned the controls over to her, she concentrated on trying to hold altitude and land the airplane from the back seat. The big wing and thermals bounced the plane all over the sky, shaking her confidence. She frequently flew and landed her T-38 jet from the back seat when a student was in the front, but today she was the student and still didn't have a good sense of how to fly the scrappy little tail dragger. Visibility was nonexistent. She watched her father execute four wildly steep approaches culminating in smooth touch-and-goes. The Super Cub was a different airplane, slow and unsteady, and definitely did not handle like a jet.

Kelly was a fast learner, and she watched her dad coordinate throttle, rudder, and stick for incredibly smooth landings. In her jet, it was a vector aircraft and went wherever the turbojets were pointed. Most fighter pilots just rested their feet on the rudder pedals and moved them only when touching the brakes. That didn't work in a Super Cub. It was real, almost primitive flying, and it was exhilarating.

It's been a very long time since I last flew like this. I forgot how much fun little airplanes can be!

Once they had crawled into the tiny airplane, the first thing Kelly noticed was that Hunter didn't waste time starting the engine before he called the tower for takeoff. He was very fast and obviously had the checklist memorized. The Air Force frowned on such expediency.

"I need three or four touch-and-goes," he said, "then you can fly it, and I'll let you try to land it from the back seat. Then we'll bring her home."

"Sounds good."

She couldn't wait for her turn, but it was unnatural and unsettling for her to see her father race through the checklists and get airborne as fast as humanly possible. If he was trying to impress her, he was almost scaring her.

Hunter's approaches were very steep, and he cross-controlled the flight controls to encourage the little airplane to fall from the sky, as if he were clearing an imaginary obstacle. Right before flare, he centered the controls and progressively pulled back on the stick until the gear touched down.

At the end of his fourth touch-and-go, he said, "Your airplane."

They were still on the runway, and she couldn't see. Hunter leaned as far left as possible to give her a little windshield view, as he kept light pressure on the control stick.

"I'll get us to takeoff," he said. "You just slowly program the stick forward very gently to get the tail to come up. There you go. Now center it. You're basically flying it now. The mains will lift off in a few seconds by itself, or you can program the stick back. Yes, just like that. Good, good. Nice work."

"It happens fast."

"It does. OK, let's turn downwind and set up for a landing. We'll make this one nice and easy. I probably scared you with my approaches."

"*A-firmative!*" She grinned after she agreed with him. He *had* scared her a little, and she wondered why he felt he needed to do that.

Hunter leaned left and talked her around the pattern and into the landing flare, then he said, "OK. My airplane."

"Your airplane." She released all pressure on the flight controls and instinctively showed her hands just as he centered himself in his seat. The tires barely touched the ground and rolled out very smoothly. She felt there was nothing to it.

"That was very nice. You're a natural."

"I tried to watch and feel what you're doing."

Hunter couldn't tell her he would be leaving soon and would be flying another tail dragger at night, where he would take off and land as fast as he could. The whole process probably confused her, but he couldn't explain they were in his YO-3A landing simulator.

He couldn't say anything that might jeopardize the mission. He received several coded emails from the DCI that he was needed for a project. Most likely it was a *Wraith* event, because they were nearing a major coca harvest in Colombia and Peru. He'd find out when he met with the man in two days.

He was in his office before breakfast and Kelly was still in bed. He was transfixed by an email from Greg Lynche, announcing that a YO-3A was coming up for sale. A museum in Washington State was looking to make space in its collection, and their odd spy plane was sent packing and moved into outside storage. The bad news is that the airplane hadn't been protected from the elements and it resembled a dirty, abandoned waif.

The attached pictures showed a poorly maintained, shabby-looking airplane. The Grinch indicated Number Three would be sold at auction in several weeks to the highest bidder and asked, *Are you interested?*

"Hell, yeah, I'm interested, but I'll probably be in Africa or the Middle East," he said softly in exasperation.

Hunter sent a reply to his old mentor and best friend, and asked if Lynche could bid on it, because he would probably be out of the country. He still hadn't received a response when he heard Theresa banging around in the kitchen, which was her way of encouraging everyone to get up and shower before a big breakfast. Only an idiot missed Theresa's *huevos rancheros*.

After breakfast, Hunter and Horne walked across the roundabout to an open barn. He depressed a button on an electronic fob, unlocking the doors, and opened the driver's door of the Aston Martin to offer

Kelly the chance to drive.

Overwhelmed by thoughts of accidently destroying the car, she shook her head vigorously and refused the offer. *"Oh no, no, no! I'm afraid I'll wreck it!"*

"Nonsense. This is more up your alley. You fly fast jets. This is a fast car. You'll love it. I guarantee it."

It took a lot of coaxing to get her into the driver's seat. Once behind the wheel, she tried to take it all in. She'd never been in a car like it before. The leather seat formed to her frame; electric motors moved the pan forward and up for a perfect grip on the leather-wrapped steering wheel.

Compared to her Fiero, it was like parachuting into the cockpit of another generation of aircraft and be expected to fly it. She waited for Hunter to hand her the key.

"Clutch in," he said, "depress the brake, and press the start button."

Horne looked at him, bewildered. *Start button? You must be kidding.*

"Right here. Race cars have start buttons. Clutch in, foot on the brake, and press start."

Taking a deep breath, she depressed the button. The engine immediately turned over. In two seconds, the V-12 rumbled at idle. Horne looked at him wide-eyed and giggled. Any thoughts of a sore shoulder were replaced with the excitement of being behind the wheel of the luxury race car.

"Wow. Oh, my! I can't do this," she said shaking her head and grinning profusely.

"Yes, you can. I know; it's very cool."

After parking and securing the Super Cub in its T-hangar, daughter drove father into Fredericksburg, going slowly down Main Street and following his directions to the offices of Quiet Aero Systems. She was very careful with the car, and Hunter told her how to approach some road entrances to avoid scraping the low undercarriage.

He escorted her across the street to the old Chevrolet dealership, where twenty or thirty men worked on a variety of old cars in the service bays. Kelly noticed immediately that all the mechanics she saw were young men, most with missing limbs. Hunter didn't explain about their handicap, but he said one of his businesses was to restore old race cars. He raced a car occasionally.

"The one in the Neiman?" she asked.

She noticed, he thought, nodding. "Out at the other end of the airport, we do something similar, restoring antique aircraft as well as manufacture some planes. The plant's locked on weekends."

"I'd like to see that one of these days."

"We can do that." He turned toward the tall garage door at the end of the service bays where the motor coach was stored that he and Nazy took on road trips to see America.

Nazy! he thought. *I haven't mentioned Nazy!*

"Are these yours, too?" Kelly pointed at the old-time dealership showroom where yellow Corvettes from the '50s through the '90s, as well as a 1974 black Jaguar XKE, were displayed. "Yellow Corvette Ranch?"

"Busted." He grinned, thoughts of Nazy filling his mind. *How do I tell them about each other?*

"That Jag is beautiful."

"I'm sorry?"

"It's beautiful. I never saw one like it before." Kelly was so transfixed by the sleek, black convertible with red leather interior, she didn't realize there were other cars nearby.

"It's been recently restored. I'm not sure what I'll do with it. It took a long time to find one in the right condition. When I put it in the showroom, everybody and his brother wants it. I've received some crazy, crazy offers but I'm going to hold on to it for a while. It's a special kind of car."

He saw she wasn't listening. A *foudroyant* vehicle had that effect on people. Some machines were more than labor-saving devices. They were labors of love, created by unusually gifted people with a vision and an eye to construct the perfect blend of art and functionality. Many tried, but few succeeded on the scale of the 1974 XKE. That seeing a car could stop people in midstride and render them mute meant it was definitely something special.

Horne stared, relishing the *objet d'art* behind the glass. She thought her dad's Corvettes were interesting, the Aston Martin beautiful, but the old Jaguar was breathtaking.

Hunter noticed Kelly couldn't take her eyes off the XKE in the window. Her response was amusing but he wanted to tell her about Nazy, but that would have to wait for a better time and place. He ran through various scenarios of what he would say.

Kelly, I need to tell you something. I've been so preoccupied being with you that I failed to say that I'm engaged.

Letting thoughts of Nazy go, he focused on the present. Nazy could wait. It wasn't every day a daughter was thrilled about one of Dad's old cars.

After dinner, Horne asked, "Have you ever been married?"

It was time to tell her. He nursed a tumbler of orange juice to bolster his courage. Kelly sipped a wine cooler. They sat before a fire in the huge stone hearth, with Hunter on one sofa and Horne on the other, as he explained what happened to him after he learned Kimberly passed away. After draining his drink, he explained he became an empty shell, depressed and focused on work. He went to graduate school and got degrees and played dozens of racquetball tournaments; raced his car when he could. He tried to be the best pilot he could be —anything to shake the thought of Kimberly Horne from his mind and heart.

He had plenty of dates but none ever came close. It wasn't until he met a woman while attending the Naval War College that he was able to put his memories of Kimberly Horne to rest and focus on someone new.

He got up and went to his bedroom, returning with a framed photograph that he offered to Kelly. "Her name is Nazy Cunningham. She's of Iranian extraction. Nazy means 'cute' in Farsi. She's currently working at the U.S. Embassy in Algeria on temporary assignment."

"She's quite beautiful." The woman in the photo resembled an exotic model, with platinum-green eyes and silky black hair that fell across her face to accentuate her eyes. Kelly found Nazy striking yet there was another quality about her that was foreign, mysterious. "Is she a Muslim?" Horne surprised herself by asking such a direct question.

"Uh, no. Was. It's a long story. She renounced Islam many years ago. She's got a high-level government job, with security clearances and access out the wazoo. She's a remarkable woman and has been through a lot. She's seen me at my best and worst, and she still thinks I'm pretty special. We're engaged. One of these days, I'll marry her."

"What's stopping you?" Horne was convinced there was more to the woman than she was being told. She wanted to know more, but her father wasn't being very forthright. His guarded answers showed there was something he wasn't saying.

"Mainly it's our schedule and our jobs. She moved up the corporate ladder very quickly and is a rock star …." He paused to choose his words carefully. "She's a rock star in the intelligence community. That's probably as much as I can tell you about her."

That was intriguing. "I look forward to meeting her, Dad. She's a lucky woman."

"Thank you. I'm the lucky one. I have a great daughter, a great fiancée, and life looks pretty good right now. It doesn't get much better than this." He winked at her, and Kelly grinned back.

CHAPTER THIRTEEN

2330 September 11, 2012
CIA Annex
Benghazi, Libya

Most of America ignored the news that America was attacked again on 9/11, and more Americans were murdered. Most Americans had slipped into a pre-9/11 mindset and forgot the horrors surrounding the World Trade Center towers collapsing and the Pentagon being rammed by a Boeing. The events of the day, past and present, didn't resonate with many citizens.

The U.S. Consulate in Libya, normally considered sovereign soil under international law, came under assault in the evening, and the Ambassador was killed. At the first hint of the attack, every major news service in the Middle East and Europe dispatched journalists and film crews to eastern Libya to pick up the trail and investigate the event. It wasn't every day a U.S. Ambassador was captured and killed.

Several bored journalists covering the small but never-ending anti-U.S. government demonstrations in neighboring Egypt, Algeria, and Tunisia raced to Libya and were interviewing witnesses by daybreak. First reports painted a picture that the well-known consulate came under assault by groups of rebels with heavy machine guns mounted in the backs of trucks.

Thirty or more insurgents poured from vehicles carrying AK-47s and rocket-propelled grenades, and assaulted the consulate. The day after, hundreds of local Libyans emerged from their houses and wandered over to check out the compound that came under such a fierce attack.

Few Libyans were surprised that the main target was one of the American compounds. Some spoke among themselves, describing and gesturing how mortars rained down into the compound whilc dozens of armed men, on foot and in pickup trucks, assaulted the Americans. As journalists began to leak into the porous country and spread throughout the city, one correspondent stumbled upon a large group of onlookers and found a Libyan official who reported that the Ambassador had been killed and his body transferred to the local hospital. Unspoken at the time were the atrocities which had been done to the diplomat.

As news teams steadily arrived at Benghazi's airport, they easily located the consulate, because it was still smoldering. A column of smoke rose from the middle of the city like a stick pin jammed into a map. Correspondents hired men with vehicles to take them to the column of black smoke.

Journalists and film crews converging on the consulate found the cinderblock walls breached and blown apart. The gate was a crumpled mess, torn from its hinges and thrown into the dirt street. Film crews transmitted images of burning vehicles, their tires still aflame, contributing to the twisted oily black smoke rising into the azure sky.

As they investigated the remains of the consulate, some film crews elbowed-out other news services to televise the most-dramatic images, still fresh from battle. Smoke-charred rooms, burnt furniture and the smell of death hung in the still air. Thousands of spent AK-47 cartridges littered the grounds.

Wide-eyed cameramen culminated their reports with ten-second transmissions of bloody smears and bloody handprints on the white stucco columns of the Ambassador's quarters. The images of blood that shimmered and suggested it was still tacky, bounced between satellites, and soon seared into the American consciousness.

The sun sat on the horizon, as invading journalists and video crews fanned out across the city, seeking answers. Foremost was *where is the*

Ambassador? Some found the hospital in Benghazi willing to provide a range of replies and observations to the badgering media. When asked if any other Americans were injured, the emergency room doctor responded that several Americans had been treated, and the bodies of their dead had already been removed.

Bill McGee had no time to change the bandages on his arm and thigh. The airplane was landing, and they'd soon be aboard to leave the hellhole that was Benghazi. The bleeding from his leg had stopped but the bandage on his arm was soaked, with fresh red rivulets intermittently streaking out from under the gauze to run over his elbow and down to his thick wrist. He hadn't been shot in almost twenty years, and every time he moved, the wound stung like a bitch and reminded him he was getting too old for this shit.

Thirty minutes earlier, he had crawled off the roof of an outlying building and helped his men abandon the CIA facility, innocuously referred to as "the Annex." He struggled with six M-4s slung across his bad shoulder. His good hand carried an ammunition can of 5.56mm to an idling pickup. McGee ignored the pain and heaved the ammo into the truck, and then he allowed the carbines to slide off his shoulder into the bed. Stepping on the bumper, he crawled over the tailgate, falling between the M-4s and plastic tubs filled with U.S. dollars. Everything hurt like hell.

The sudden drop into the bed was more than he expected, and he fell heavily, momentarily taking away his breath. When the huge black man recovered enough to speak, he took a deep breath and shouted, "That's the last load! Let's go!"

The driver of the Toyota HiLux dropped the gear shift and mashed the pedal, and the retired SEALs in the last vehicle roared away from the Annex. McGee brought an M-4, with a foot-long, banana-shaped magazine, to his shoulder and was ready to engage any threatening target. The only sound and action were the engine exhaust and the HiLux racing from the ruined facility.

The order to evacuate the Annex required all hands on deck. Time was of the essence to pack up and get out. While the pretentious, embassy-run consulate appeared to be the primary target of the assault, the unpretentious and low-profile CIA-run Annex also came under heavy fire, and it was nearly compromised. McGee and four of his fellow retired Navy SEALs repelled several waves of thirty or more guerillas armed with Kalashnikovs, rocket-propelled grenades, and mortars.

The former SEALs picked off the belligerents one-by-one with precision fire and littered the Annex ground and access roads with bodies. As the old SEALs responded to the surprise attack with withering firepower, they couldn't respond to cries of help from the consulate. There were too few of them, and they were pinned under heavy attack. It was basic Clausewitz, divide and conquer. The SEALS assumed it was planned that way; that's what they would have done. Warfighting 101.

When there was a break in the fighting, a CIA officer and a former Delta Ranger raced to help the consulate, almost a mile away, through dusty, heavily-rutted streets, only to be told to return to base. The *jihadis* had already overrun the consulate and were probably reorganizing and headed toward the Annex.

With the consulate ransacked, the ecstatic insurgents consolidated their fighters and took up positions to augment the attackers at the Annex. The newcomers attacked fearlessly, as they had at the consulate. Despite the zealous re-attack, with bullets and mortars raining all over the area, the retired SEALs calmly held their positions atop the several structures in the multi-building facility and eliminated the guerillas. Night vision riflescopes enabled them to pick off their attackers with single shots—one shot, one kill.

When one budding terrorist peeked around the wall of a neighboring compound 300 yards away, a former SEAL sniper, call sign "Slash," placed the reticule of his sniper scope on the man's forehead and squeezed the trigger. The man's brains exploded out of the back of his head, and his corpse fell into a heap on two other *jihadis* who also tried to peek around the corner. Anyone who tried to dash across the road from the edge of one compound wall to another was stopped in midstride by a bullet from Slash's .300 Winchester Magnum sniper rifle.

During a lengthy lull in the action, one former Navy chief petty officer and twenty-year SEAL, Anthony Parker, a short but beefy man with the call sign "Tonka," climbed off the roof of a small building he used as a sniper hide and ran to the main operations building. He emerged a few minutes later with provisions to resupply his teammates with ammo, bottles of water, and information.

Talking with other members of the group, he provided the latest SITREP. The compound had one breach in the wall, but every time a rebel tried to shoot through the gap, a calm, former SEAL sniper and first class petty officer, Kyle Drumm, call sign "Spanky," popped a cap and sent a bullet into the brain of anyone trying to rush in. After a dozen bodies lay stacked across the threshold and plugged the hole, the onslaught at that location stopped.

When an RPG shook an adjacent wall, punching another hole, Spanky readjusted position and aimed and filled the breach with suicidal men dumb enough to try getting through. Gray matter and blood splattered all around the breach in the wall.

Surveillance cameras at the four corners of the facility suggested a lull in the fighting due to retreating insurgents. It was either that, or the SEALs were so effective in providing security there were no more guerillas left to kill. Tonka informed McGee that the lead CIA officer had ordered a bug-out. The U.S. Embassy ordered a NEO, noncombatant evacuation operation, for the remaining Annex personnel. McGee asked, in whispers, "*What if you're a combatant—*

don't we get evacuated too?" It was an old joke. The State Department would pull their diplomats out of harm's way and leave behind the guys with guns to fend for themselves. It was easy to loathe "State" when things got nasty.

The NEO airplane was en route from Tripoli, and the team needed to reach the airport within thirty minutes to make their escape. McGee was sure another crisis was brewing, and the skirmish was just an interlude. He knew it was 9/11 and expected an attack. Someone at the consulate should have expected an attack. If you're in a Muslim country on 9/11, you must expect an attack. For Al-Qaeda, 9/11 would always be a date to celebrate with an attack on a facility of the United States, somewhere; today it was Benghazi.

With no bullets flying at the moment, McGee took time to re-bandage his wounded arm. His men provided protective cover and security while Tonka returned to the main building and gathered all his friends' go bags. CIA officers loaded tubs of money into the back of a couple Toyota HiLux pickups. Other CIA officers worked furiously to shred documents and destroy or pack classified equipment before the bug out. The communications officer notified the senior CIA officer that the Ambassador's body had been delivered to the main hospital in Benghazi.

The CIA officer offered the only good news was that the hospital was on the way to the airport. He quietly prayed that the Ambassador's body was in one piece.

Dawn was still hours away when the plane touched down on the runway and taxied to the main terminal building. McGee and his men, first on the scene at the airport, continued to assume a defensive position. Two other vehicles soon joined the Toyota HiLux; they were loaded with former SEALs, money, and guns. Tonka shouted over the increasing din of turboprop engines, "What the hell is that?"

The gray-and-black Basler BT-67 stopped adjacent to the three trucks and feathered its port propeller. Twelve men, their arms full of weapons, bags, and tubs of money, approached the side of the aircraft, as the cargo door opened just forward of the empennage. Two men fireman-carried another and brought up the rear.

As the men neared the airplane, they didn't have time to marvel at their ride. The retrofitted Douglas DC-3 airframe sported dull gray paint and a pair of turboprop engines. In less than a minute after the cargo door closed, the Basler was filled with CIA officers, contractors, and dead diplomats, and was heading west to Tripoli.

Bill McGee, finding a seat facing aft, saw he was leaking blood again. It wasn't enough to worry about, but it dripped steadily onto the floor, soiling the carpet of the nicely refurbished interior of the antique aircraft. As he bounced around in the rear of the seventy-five-year-old airplane, he took inventory of the activities in the cabin. CIA officers repositioned plastic containers filled with hundred- and fifty-dollar bills toward the front of the old Douglas. The two former Delta men cared for the bodies of men McGee believed were the Ambassador and a Foreign Service Officer. Tonka and Spanky sat in back on the floor with an open ammo can, reloading one magazine after another. Slash cleaned his sniper rifle. The two remaining CIA men were in seats, their expressions showing exasperation, defeat, and concern. No one bothered to fasten his seat belt.

McGee relived the events of the previous ninety-six hours; from arrival to evacuation, it had been a goat rope. The initial flight into Tripoli and the security briefings and processing at the embassy were normal, standard operating procedure. He didn't know what to expect after Muammar Gaddafi fell, but he hadn't expected to find the embassy operating as if there wasn't a civil war raging just outside the gate. Something was wrong, though he couldn't put his finger on it right away.

His massive head swung from side-to-side, analyzing the facility. Where were the Marines? What about personal security details? Did these people have any security at all?

Feeling naked and unprotected, he expected something to explode at any moment; it was like jumping on a pogo stick to bounce through a minefield while wearing a blindfold.

The other SEALs sensed it, too. Something was wrong; the apparent security operation was atrocious and nonstandard. There were too few security personnel for the size of the operation, and the Libyan Embassy was a huge facility. Outside the walls were remnants of the old Gaddafi regime struggling against different interest groups. Each one vied for position to dominate and lead the country. Sporadic gunfire was the new normal and those in the embassy just ignored it.

Inside the embassy there was no sense of urgency, no concern that the occupants lived on borrowed time.

"Wait here." McGee turned from his charges and returned to the security office to glare at the security officer and ask some heated questions.

"I see something is bothering you, Mr. McGee," Cassie M, the security officer, said.

In a voice barely above a whisper, McGee spat, "What the hell's going on here? The only thing missing from Margaritaville here is a Landshark Lager and a beach ball."

Cassie unconsciously placed her hand on her holstered pistol, pinched her lips, and nodded toward the door. McGee, three times the size of the petite blonde security officer, followed her outside. Her story shook him to the core.

The Ambassador fully embraced the former liberal President's foreign policy and notions of how to improve Islamic relations. Security was deemed too oppressive and expensive. The Ambassador didn't want to have an incident like the one in Iraq where a huge personal security detail of former SEALs and Deltas engaged in a firefight with insurgents, killing Iraqi civilians. The sight of muscular former special operations personnel with their natural swagger and penchant for carrying lots of powerful weapons, as they walked in and out of the embassy, wasn't the picture the Ambassador wanted to portray as he tried to foster better relations with the new rulers of Libya. Instead of hard men providing hard security, the priority was low key and nonthreatening security—soft security.

The embassy drastically cut costs and hired inexpensive security personnel from Britain and Libya. Funds earmarked for security upgrades were reallocated for landscaping the embassy and consulate grounds in what were referred to as "green energy" initiatives. In a land awash with oil, the embassy purchased electric cars from America for use. Cassie M told McGee that the Ambassador was very vocal and proud of his Muslim outreach program and fleet of electric Chevy Volts. When McGee asked if the Libyans providing security were from the Muslim Brotherhood, Cassie M shrugged her shoulders. Her response said it all.

Sitting in the aircraft, McGee shook his head violently. The Ambassador had been insane. He studied the two long mounds covered with airline blankets at the rear of the plane.

The Ambassador traded sago palms and electric cars for security, and now the dumb ass is dead. Who knows how many others are dead? This is why you can't put liberals in charge of anything. It's so typical to downplay and ridicule personal security details. They completely ignore the obvious threats until their own stupidity kills them.

He recalled that the Ambassador's death could have been predicted just like the environmentalist who convinced himself he could live among grizzly bears in the wilds of Alaska. He lived with them peacefully until one day, *ursus arctos horribilis*, gave up berries and salmon for something more tasty, and turned the brain-dead tree hugger into steaming piles of bear scat.

The Ambassador was like an addlepated woman who wrote love letters to an imprisoned murderer, somehow believing her love would turn him around. *How could U.S. foreign policymakers believe and repeatedly act as if the power of their love and substantial taxpayer generosity could turn jihadi thugs into responsible democratic leaders?*

He leaned over and exchanged a dozen near-empty high-capacity magazines for full ones. Tonka grinned broadly, grateful to be alive to fight another day. McGee regretted taking a leave of absence from school. He felt he just had to get back into the fight one more time. He'd done it for more than a return to action.

"The money's incredible," he told his wife, "more than I'll make in a year of teaching school."

"So are the risks," Angela cautioned. "It's time for others to do their part."

She was right. He walked into a shit sandwich. For the first time in a long time, he thought the situation could only get a lot worse before it got better. If they didn't keep their wits, they wouldn't survive.

He overheard two of the survivors from the U.S. Consulate assault confirm to Slash that the "lowest cost, technically acceptable" Libyan security forces dropped their nightsticks and ran when the heavily armed *jihadis* rounded the corner of the block, leaving the Ambassador and the few embassy personnel at the Benghazi consulate virtually unprotected.

One CIA officer was livid. "Security should not have been contracted to the Muslim Brotherhood or the local chapter of al-Qaeda! Black al-Qaeda flags are flying everywhere, and we get locals with nightsticks? *The Ambassador had the Brotherhood inside the compound! No one is that stupid!*"

And it almost killed you, McGee thought. *The belly button to blame is dead with a blanket over his head.* It was unnatural for McGee to malign the dead. *That shot-up, immolated corpse was responsible for protecting the Americans serving both the State Department and the Agency in Libya, but due to his ignorant personal philosophy he and several Americans under his leadership were dead. It didn't have to be. Typical State liberals!*

Despite black al-Qaeda flags flying everywhere, which made McGee and the SEALs very nervous, some things went well. Immediately after the fall of Muammar Gaddafi, several intelligence officers swept into Tripoli ready to embark on a shopping spree. After months of trying to locate the most-recent arms dealers, those who could empty Gaddafi's armories while Muslims fought Muslims, a trio of CIA intel officers finally made contact with several weapons and intelligence sellers. High on the shopping list was the status and location of weapons of mass destruction programs, the location of caches of shoulder-launched surface-to-air missiles, and the whereabouts of certain terrorists.

CIA officers handled the negotiations and money, while their TS/SCI contractors did the grunt work and provided hard security and muscle to identify and transport the weapons out of the country. Known for his ability to do the nearly impossible with the lowest profile and logistical footprint, McGee, Special Operations Instructor at the Naval War College, was contacted.

Special Operations Instructor at the Naval War College wasn't supposed to be the capstone of his career. The capture of Osama bin Laden was. A gruff, take-charge man, William "Bullfrog" McGee was one of a few African Americans in the U.S. Navy SEALs, and the only African American officer ever to command the vaunted United States Naval Special Warfare Development Group, DEVGRU, SEAL Team Six; one of the U.S.' four secretive counterterrorism and Special Mission Units. The U.S. Navy's principal special operations force wasn't an affirmative action program for any group. SEALs performed.

Navy Captain Bill McGee rose through the ranks to become the commanding officer of SEAL Team Six. Acutely intelligent, muscular, poised, and confident, he was the best of the best—the most-accomplished, most-decorated, and most-successful SEAL in the history of the Naval Special Warfare Command. Few knew of him and that's how he wanted it.

When jets flew into the World Trade Center, the Joint Special Operations Commander called his 911 reaction force. Within weeks, McGee led the SEALs of Team Six into the mountains of Afghanistan to find and capture Osama bin Laden.

After chasing the master terrorist for five months under incredible hardship, McGee and his SEALs were evacuated and sent back to the U.S. empty-handed. The mission failed spectacularly when the CIA, which had long believed bin Laden was hiding in caves in the mountains of Tora Bora, refused to admit he was actually in Pakistan.

The CIA thought it was being smart to use radio telemetry to triangulate and pinpoint OBL's location, but the master terrorist was smarter. Bin Laden knew the CIA would try to locate him, so he had someone carry a radio and a recording of him giving directions as he wandered through the valley of the Tora Bora, keying the microphone while the tape recorder played.

The CIA didn't blame the quality of their intelligence. Instead, they blamed the SEALs for failing to find bin Laden. As the team commander, Bill McGee took the brunt of the blame. He was removed as commanding officer and sent packing to the Naval War College, first as a student, then as an instructor, where he was largely forgotten by Special Operations Command.

When the resident CIA officer at the NWC approached the retired but still amazingly fit man to see if he was interested in an adventure, McGee jumped at the chance to serve as an independent contractor to the Agency. Soon after arriving in Libya, he regretted leaving home, family, and job. The embassy and Annex in Benghazi were man-made disasters of epic proportions. McGee had doubts about success from the beginning, but their fortunes looked ready to change as quickly as the wind shifting during a frontal passage. When the lead CIA officer and Annex facility manager suddenly announced they made contact with "the sellers," and the team would meet them immediately, it looked like McGee might be able to salvage all or part of his mission.

Thirteen blocks away from the Benghazi consulate, in a five-acre compound with fifteen-foot walls, CIA officers and McGee met with three local men in traditional garb and white *keffiyehs.* No salutations or greetings were exchanged. McGee immediately recognized the quiet confidence, muscularity, and deliberateness of the three. He wasn't aware there were any such thing as Libyan Special Operations Forces soldiers, but he felt at that moment, if there were, then he was looking at three of them. If they were SOF, where'd they come from?

The Americans were quickly led through a gate and into an underground bunker. No one spoke as they crept down concrete stairs.

The footing was treacherous. Slick desert sand would quickly upend the impatient if someone hurried.

When they reached the bottom, the buyers and sellers labored against soft sand to push through into darkness. One of the Libyans who spoke very good English commanded the attention of the two CIA officers. The other men's flashlights threw sticks of light that didn't penetrate far, though they illuminated suspended dust in the stale, plastic-smelling air.

In the diffused light, McGee recognized the two-foot-wide, cylindrical building forms laid out in a 20 x 20 grid. He flipped his torch up and saw the ceiling was made of rough, uneven concrete, which he determined to be somewhat clever but very strange.

He inspected the underground room's ceiling, his flashlight beam moved back and forth, highlighting the unevenness and roughness of the concrete. It made no sense until he realized how the room had been made, and then he was stunned.

He walked to a column and slapped it. Someone above ground had drilled holes into the desert floor and inserted paper-wrapped tubes into the ground then filled them with cement. He envisioned someone had tossed heavy rebar, thick steel rods with ridges, onto the ground to reinforce the concrete as it was poured over the desert sand. After the concrete hardened, the sand underneath the concrete slab was sucked or trucked out, and probably tossed on top to leave a spacious underground warehouse below, to store and hide things. Once a layer of sand covered the concrete base, few would know what lay underneath.

It wouldn't have met building code in the U.S., but, for Libya, it was the perfect makeshift structure to store and hide things from satellites. No one would ever suspect what was down there.

McGee was stunned, then concerned. *I've never seen anything like this. It's huge. It might be the size of a football field, maybe two. How safe...how thick is that ceiling?*

The smell of paint and plastic became more intense in the thick, dusty air, as long, olive-green shipping cases came into view. Navy

SEALs are difficult to impress, but McGee was speechless with awe. Illuminated by their handheld lamps, he saw rows and stacks of shipping containers containing man-portable shoulder-launched anti-aircraft and antitank missiles, as far as the most powerful flashlight beam could reach. There were hundreds, maybe as many as a thousand missiles stacked in nice, neat columns and rows.

As the sellers and CIA men stopped walking and continued talking, McGee walked alongside a stack of Russian Strela-2 missile containers. The number of missile shipping crates would've made a six-foot-deep, six-foot-high, fifty-foot long wall.

"ST-7 Grails on this side," he said softly, "old British Blowpipes and Javelins and a few new Starstreaks."

Farther down in the dark, he crossed to another wall of weapons. An even-greater wall of shipping containers disappeared into the dark.

"Here are some French Mistrals and American Stingers."

When the State Department and CIA deployed contractors, primarily former SEALs, to go into Libya and track down shoulder-launched, surface-to-air missiles, none were found on the battlefield. No one was prepared for what was hidden underground. There were so many MANPADS; the CIA officers immediately realized they didn't bring enough money.

While McGee tried to estimate how many Stingers there were, he wondered how acquiring and storing such a cache was possible. Intelligence sources had long feared hundreds of MANPADS would be looted from Libyan military installations across the country. With the fall of the Soviet Union, hundreds of SA-7 Grails and SA-9 Grinches entered the black market. Like Libya, with the collapse of the regime, dozens of CIA officers and their contractors rushed to old Soviet bases to buy MANPADS, nuclear weapons, and classified information. Often they came home empty handed. Someone had beaten them to the punch.

Like the former Soviet Union, after the fall of Colonel Gaddafi, U.S. officials were concerned that MANPADS could fall into terrorist hands, creating a threat to military aircraft and commercial airliners.

With Gaddafi gone, the U.S. was in a race to find Libya's MANPADS, buy them, and destroy them before al-Qaeda and the Muslim Brotherhood started a bidding war or worse. The sellers could easily be al-Qaeda or Muslim Brotherhood sympathizers, and might turn over the MANPADS by the hundreds. The opportunity to purchase them was a unique opportunity to ensure they didn't fall in the hands of terrorists.

Generally, in a cash-and-carry post-apocalyptic economy, money talked. Neither al-Qaeda nor the Muslim Brotherhood could compete with the millions of dollars appropriated for the buyback program. The CIA's intel indicated there were no more than a couple hundred MANPADS in Libya, but that was grossly wrong. McGee estimated there were almost 1,000 containers.

The buyback operation was classified at the highest level. *Buyback* was one of the few black programs administration officials never revealed or leaked the details. Regular U.S. ground forces were insufficient for the job, because they didn't have the necessary clearances or training. A basic Marine Corps infantryman would be unfamiliar with Stinger anti-aircraft missiles. U.S. Special Operations Forces, with top-secret clearance and comprehensive training, were experts with all makes and models of weapons, from handguns to machine guns to RPGs to tactical nuclear weapons. That included a comprehensive knowledge of all international makes and models of shoulder-launched anti-aircraft missiles.

Active duty SOF from all branches of the U.S. military were overcommitted and stretched to the breaking point in Afghanistan, Yemen, the Middle East, and Western Africa. The most-pressing threats, al-Qaeda and Muslim Brotherhood, were growing at an exponential rate. They were global and transnational in scope. Terrorism, weapons proliferation, piracy, hostage taking, cybercrime, narcotics, and criminal gangs of all sizes were growing too fast for governments to deal with successfully.

Government contractors, those who held some of the highest security clearances granted to companies and individuals, bid on the dangerous, lucrative, and necessary contracts to try to stem the flow and growth of the multifaceted problem. Private contractors hired retired and former Navy SEALs, Army DELTA, and Marine RECON by the dozens to curtail hijacking and hostage taking, protecting ocean liners and tankers in shipping lanes and natural choke points like the Strait of Malacca. Special operations warriors were in high demand for security jobs all around the world. Many signed up for the excitement and the money. It was a seller's market, and former special operations personnel went to the highest bidder, except in Libya.

After Gaddafi's death, all of Libya was considered "injun country." Natives on both sides of the fighting were in a tug of war to the death. Gaddafi's backers had broken spirits and fought and ran for their lives. The opposition, with more warriors and whipped into a bloodlust frenzy, hunted down the dwindling number of Gaddafi's men and killed them savagely, mercilessly. When the dust settled, few in Libya wanted to talk about MANPADS except al-Qaeda and the Muslim Brotherhood.

Black al-Qaeda flags popped up all over the city, suggesting Benghazi was a growing al-Qaeda stronghold. The CIA, trying to operate in the shadows, was in a race with the terrorist organizations on who would be the first to control the supply of Gaddafi's MANPADS. Al-Qaeda and their affiliates in North Africa, and, to a lesser extent, the Muslim Brotherhood, sought the full range of leverage technologies, including MANPADS, but generally didn't have much money to purchase weapons. If they couldn't purchase them, they would steal them. Or they hoped some sympathizers would just give them away.

Terrorists didn't need many anti-aircraft missiles to be a major threat. For the CIA, it was a race against the clock to prevent terrorists from finding and acquiring some of the deadliest weapons a single person could use against military and civilian aircraft. The intel was wrong again, and the CIA didn't have enough money to ensure the weapons in the underground warehouse would be kept out of al-Qaeda or Muslim Brotherhood hands. The only good news was neither did al-Qaeda or the Muslim Brotherhood.

McGee recovered from the shock of seeing all the MANPADS before him. As briefed, he walked down several stacks of the weapons and pulled out at random, a hard-shell shipping container of a Stinger. It felt heavy enough, so it wasn't an empty case.

Wiping dust off the top, he twisted open the latches. He opened the container and unbuckled the restraints to extract a six-foot missile from its custom foam-cut packing. Even in the subdued light of tired flashlights, the missile launcher emanated death and destruction.

McGee flipped it over and checked the date of manufacture. It was less than four-years old. Cases of fresh battery coolant units sat nearby. All it would take to activate the Stinger was to insert a charged BCU into the hand guard. The BCU would shoot a stream of argon gas into the system and provide enough battery power to activate the acquisition indicators and the missile's firing circuits.

Point, shoot, hear the tone, knock down a jet, he thought, returning it to its case and replacing the shipping container in the stack. *There are probably more than enough BCUs to power all of these. Damn!*

Ten minutes later, the groups quietly left the compound and walked to their vehicles. Before separating, the sellers wanted to negotiate. The CIA wanted all the missiles and made an offer. McGee returned to the HiLux and sat in the truck to wait for the bargaining to finish. Feeling exposed, he wanted out of there. No deal was reached, but the sellers and CIA officers agreed to meet again soon. McGee and his crew returned to the Annex in silence.

One hour later, all hell broke loose.

When news flashed through the city that the Ambassador was killed, that also meant foreign correspondents were inbound. The bug-out and NEO occurred barely in time. Just as the Americans lifted off from the Benghazi airport, several aircraft called the tower for landing instructions. Some media might have already been on the ground. The CIA couldn't afford to have its people seen or photographed, blowing their cover.

McGee glanced at the two dead men. *What the hell were you doing there?*

The more he thought about it, the less he liked the answer. What *was* the Ambassador doing in Benghazi, and why then? He must have been briefed on the program to buy back the MANPADS, but he wouldn't have been involved in the CIA transaction. He must have arrived in Benghazi unexpectedly. Agency personnel at the Annex didn't know why the Ambassador was in town. Why had he come? That was just one of the many questions above McGee's pay grade.

Since the overthrow of Muammar Gaddafi the previous year, Benghazi evolved into a rebel stronghold. Rebel groups popped up everywhere. Libya's second-largest city became the temporary base of the alternative government during the peak of hostilities and remained restless and dangerous.

With all the AQ and Muslim Brotherhood flags in the area, the U.S. Ambassador waltzes into town with a security detail of Libyans with nightsticks and British Army rejects? Whiskey Tango Foxtrot, over?! Nothing makes sense. The original operation was going well, and then, out of nowhere, the rebels attack the consulate?

Was it a coincidence those shitheads attacked just as we were making our deal? The consulate looks more like a planned attack than a target of opportunity. What am I missing?

"Bullfrog!" Tonka shouted.

The interior of the plane was loud but not deafening. As Tonka shoved .223 Remingtons into the big banana magazines, he asked, "Who owned that compound?"

McGee, deep in thought, shook away the cobwebs and shook his head to answer the question. Maybe it was loss of blood that made him slow and unable to comprehend the obvious. The MANPAD compound was deliberately built and was heavily fortified. The walls were higher than those in the neighborhood, with guard towers in the corners. No other compound in the neighborhood was that expansive or had towers.

No one was there, either, McGee thought. *With hundreds of millions of dollars of MANPADS sitting under a foot of concrete and sand, there was no security. No one was home. There was more defense and offense than your typical affluent Libyan would care to display, but when we got there, no one was there. Then there's the issue that the sellers didn't act exactly like owners or caretakers. Were they SOF? Were they even Muslims? Whiskey Tango Foxtrot, over?*

At the embassy, during the CIA officer's in-country mission brief, he mentioned something about the heavily fortified compounds in Benghazi. There were several in the area, but intel on who owned them or their purpose was incomplete. After almost a year of rebel fighting and civil war, it was no surprise that the intelligence community didn't know who lived there or owned it.

When the old SEALs arrived at the Annex, that particular compound was mentioned as a "location of interest" in several dispatches to the Libya desk at the CIA. One of the case officers remembered the compound from overhead surveillance photos. The fact that it had guard posts at the four corners of the facility instantly made it unique, a high-value place of interest. He mentioned there was a file on an old, suspected terrorist or financier who lived on or near the compound.

"Tonka," McGee replied after thinking it over, "we may never know."

CHAPTER FOURTEEN

2100 September 11, 2012
Dallas-Ft. Worth International Airport

Under normal circumstances, the American Airlines concourse was loud, with hundreds of passengers passing through security, emplaning and deplaning, eating at restaurants, or hurrying to catch ground transportation. First reports of another attack on U.S. sovereignty on 9/11 were met with skepticism, and, if true, incredulity. For most networks, the reports from North Africa were fragmented and inconsistent, typical of foreign correspondents from foreign lands. The timing of the event, eleven years after al-Qaeda attacked America and killed 3,000 people, was a cautious reminder of the changing world view of a radical branch of Islam. On what was otherwise a news-quiet day, the news streaming from Libya caught the public's attention, especially for those about to board airliners. In retrospect, 9/11 would always be a bad day to fly.

The concourse and waiting areas were quiet and subdued. The first feeds from Libya flashed on the airport's overhead television monitors. Images of burning vehicles, a burned-out consulate, and blood-smeared walls transfixed passengers waiting to board. Those getting off airliners and learning of another 9/11 attack hurried to leave the airport. Islamists were still at war with America, but the country was off to catch a jet or shop at the mall.

Saul Ferrier, the former chief executive officer of the recently sold Schweizer Aircraft Company, peeled his eyes from the overhead monitor, re-gripped his rollerboard, and walked up the concourse for the American Airlines Admiral's Club. He hadn't gone far when he saw a tall, gray-haired man weaving and bobbing, and racing through the human traffic.

A flash of recognition made Ferrier stop and grin. It was common enough for businessmen and businesswomen to see other businesspeople *en passant* in an airport. Airports were business hubs, and airlines carried the mavens of industry to conduct and foster commerce in every corner of the planet. Seeing a familiar face in the airport, one that was well outside the business environment, wasn't all that unusual but usually fortuitous.

Ferrier watched with fascination as the man ran and flailed. He trailed a camouflaged rucksack in one hand and a Burberry field coat in the other as he jumped bags, dodged kids in strollers, and pirouetted around little old ladies and flight attendants without knocking anyone over. The sometimes correspondent for a cable news network was a man on a mission.

As the two men converged, Ferrier waved and shouted, "Colonel Eastwood!"

Recognition was instantaneous. The dashing man vectored directly toward the familiar face. "Saul!" shouted a nearly breathless Lieutenant Colonel Demetrius "Dory" Eastwood, U.S. Marine Corps, retired. As he closed the distance, Eastwood struggled to switch hands with his overfilled backpack and coat to shake the CEO's hand, or so Ferrier thought.

Once Eastwood stopped running and stopped in front of Ferrier, shedding his bag and coat in a pile, he asked, "Could you watch these for a second? I have to hit the head."

Without waiting for a reply, Eastwood raced toward the men's room.

Ferrier grinned and laughed. "Engineer, CEO, and now bag watcher for a news correspondent. I'm moving up in the world."

His eyes returned to the ubiquitous TV monitor overhead, as a muted newscaster read from a laptop. A banner crawling across the bottom of the picture announced *AMBASSADOR MURDERED IN LIBYA.*

After a minute, Lieutenant Colonel Eastwood ran from the facilities and back into the throng of passengers, nearly colliding with a male flight attendant. He recovered, apologized, and sped back to his bags and Ferrier. They shook hands and exchanged greetings. Ferrier realized the man hadn't aged a day since he saw him several years earlier at a political event.

"Saul, good to see you."

Eastwood was tall with broad shoulders, his full head of gray hair cut short. He wore tan, baggy cargo pants, what one might see on troops on a battlefield, and a white, long-sleeved denim shirt. For a man pushing seventy-five, he was supremely fit and seemed to have a nuclear power plant for a heart. Energy and excitement oozed from his pores.

The former infantry officer became very well-known and a household name, primarily as an unindicted coconspirator accused of trading weapons for hostages while working for another administration. After a stint in politics, he found a niche as an embedded correspondent in war zones reporting from battlefields, working alongside young Marines, Soldiers, Airmen, and Navy SEALs in Afghanistan and Iraq. He reported the news without spin, garnering the respect and professional love of men and women in uniform everywhere. Liberals hated him.

Eastwood pointed at the TV monitor. "Anything new on the Communist News Network?"

"An ambassador is dead. It's 9/11. Is it any surprise our consulate was attacked? I'm so angry ... but who knows what the real story is?" Ferrier took a deep exasperated breath and asked, "Dory, where are you heading?"

Eastwood loaded his bag onto his back. "Libya. Got a call from my producer. They want me in-country as soon as possible to report on the U.S. Ambassador and find out what happened. Pakistan, Afghanistan, Iraq, and now Libya—the garden spots of the Middle East and North Africa. I'm always headed somewhere interesting and crappy."

"I thought you were still in Afghanistan. I saw you reporting from there."

"I was. I was embedded with the Second Marine Division until a week ago. I'm just returning from shooting a show on unmanned systems and looking into the ethics of using them when almost without fail, they kill women and children when a missile is fired at a terrorist. What about you? I thought you'd be flying a private jet wherever you need to go."

"We're ... *we were* a small company, Dory. No jets for me. I'm on my way home to New York. I came from seeing one of my business partners in San Antonio, Duncan Hunter. He's also a retired Marine."

Eastwood snapped his fingers and stuck one meaty digit at Ferrier's chest. "I know Hunter! Captain, Marine F-4 pilot. Know of him very well. Really good shit. What's he doing nowadays?"

"You know how pilots are, always flying off somewhere."

"Aren't we all? Saul, I hate to say it, but I need to get going if I'm going to catch my jet. Safe travels, and if you see him, please tell Hunter I said hello and *Semper Fi*!"

As fast as he whirled in, Lieutenant Colonel Eastwood spun away and rocketed down the concourse, the straps on his rucksack snapping in the breeze, his soft-soled boots chirping with each pounding step. In seconds, he vanished into the sea of passengers.

Ferrier shook his head in admiration, grabbed the handle of his rolling bag and headed toward his gate, wondering how the former infantry officer Colonel Eastwood could possibly know the former fighter pilot, Duncan Hunter.

CHAPTER FIFTEEN

1600 September 17, 2012
U.S. Consulate
Benghazi, Libya

The only way to enter Libya was as a correspondent. Press credentials and several hundred dollars of entrance fees were the only way to expedite a visa and passage into the country and out of the airport. Post-Gaddafi Libya wasn't Eastwood's first rodeo into a war-torn country. Like other post-régime change or countries in the midst of civil war, electronic business was impossible.

Money still talked. Every transaction was cash and carry—no credit cards. Cash in American dollars was preferred. Euros were acceptable. Gold coin, highly prized, made the impossible possible.

Shortly after arriving at the semi-functional Tripoli International Airport, where Gaddafi's personal Airbus 340 was a smoldering ruin on the tarmac, Dory Eastwood shelled out several thousand dollars in gold Krugerrands for an adequate vehicle and a competent, English-speaking driver to get himself and his two-man video crew to the site of the American Ambassador's demise. Upon leaving Tripoli, the film crew shot some surreptitious video of several black flags, with an occasional green one, flying over high-walled compounds. Eastwood knew the black flags meant al-Qaeda or an affiliate, while the green flags strongly suggested the Muslim Brotherhood. No one knew for sure but for the three Americans in the Toyota pickup, neither were good signs.

The driver, Khalid al-Awalaki, initially agitated and skittish, rued the moment he agreed to the terms and conditions of his hire. However, once they were far from the compounds and flags of the terror organizations, and on the open road, he calmed down. The gold in his pocket had a way of making the passengers and the trip to Benghazi bearable.

After ten hours of driving over fairly flat desert, Eastwood and his crew arrived at the eastern Libyan city of Benghazi. While consulting commercial satellite imagery and a GPS for directions was often helpful, Khalid proved his utility and resourcefulness by stopping to ask directions. Within thirty minutes of entering the city, the Americans found the burned-out hulk of the U.S. Consulate.

Eastwood noticed that as they neared the site of the attack, the surrounding compounds and neighborhood appeared abandoned. There were no vehicles or locals on the road. The last living human beings they had seen were several minutes behind them, and those had droll expressions. The area was sterile, still, and spooky.

Unlike his usual hyperkinetic self, Eastwood cautiously crept from the truck, thinking they might be attacked any moment and would have to retreat at the first sign of trouble. Press credentials and a Libyan driver weren't going to be enough to keep them safe.

They came a long way, though, and he shook off the feeling of impending doom. "Let's get this done," he told the cameramen, who quickly extricated themselves from the back of the HiLux and began shooting video of the remains of the consulate.

Eastwood stepped inside the compound wall and was struck by how quiet the abandoned facility and the entire area were. He looked around, surveying the damage inside the gate and the threat outside. No people or vehicles were on the roads and no one was outside of the consulate. The consulate's high walls were strung with thick concertina wire and were consistent with other compounds' security measures in the area.

The crew noticed that, unlike other areas of Benghazi, the neighborhood was home for well-to-do Libyans. Individual compounds were as large as a block.

Eastwood tentatively peered around the stacked-stone stanchion that once supported the gate, then peered inside the compound. The remains of a custom home were hidden by an overabundance of palms, yucca, and tall grasses. The consulate lay open and exposed, but filled with the stench of old death.

What happened to the house was hard to comprehend. Half the structure looked like an unspoiled 1960's home of Frank Sinatra in Palm Springs. The left half was marked by scorched windows with a burned-out car in the charred carport. The rectangular house was trimmed in stacked stone, sloping to the right for forty feet, with the remains of windows every ten feet. The unscorched stucco looked freshly painted, unpitted or spalled by weather. The flat tile roof was undamaged. As the two cameramen neared the entrance, they saw the front double doors were wide open. Fist-sized holes marked where the handles once attached.

One cameraman followed Eastwood and panned his camera left and right, recording their approach to the house. He anticipated finding the televised smeared blood on the walls. As they reached the edge of the carport, both men stopped and stared at the iconic stains that were broadcast around the world. The streaks, appearing now more like rust than blood, showed the demarcation of destruction.

Eastwood and the videographer forced dozens of foot-long green lizards to scurry away, as they entered the house. Burned walls and the remains of furniture littered the nearly empty house. Anything of value had been removed. Every piece of glass was missing from the window frames. Tiles had been pried from the kitchen, while appliances and cabinets were torn from the walls. The interior doors were removed. Even the hinges were missing.

The building was completely gutted; it was like every other structure in a civil war, a ruined shell with the smell of death. Eastwood froze when he saw a hideous blood splatter against a white wall, the telltale sign of a brain exploding from a bullet.

Through the opening that was once the house's rear kitchen door, he spied another building. He and the cameraman hurried out to the structure, which was the size of a two-car garage. As they entered, they saw that it too, was gutted and ransacked. Papers littered the floor. Eastwood recognized the telltale red security header and footer on one paper with the word *SECRET.* Many others were similarly stamped.

How is it possible that dozens of secret documents are lying around? Didn't anyone from the embassy come to secure this place? What the hell's going on here?

Picking up the papers, he stuffed them into a cargo pants pocket. He went out the door with the cameraman racing behind.

He stopped suddenly, and one cameraman almost collided with him. He noticed something he hadn't seen before—a bright-green flag draped over a compound wall.

"Get a picture of that," he whispered.

It was green, the color of Islam. Centered were two crossed swords bracketing a Qur'an. Along the bottom in white script were Arabic letters. Eastwood couldn't read Arabic but he knew what the words meant. *Strike terror into the enemies of Allah!*

It wasn't the flag of the al-Qaeda. It was the flag of the Muslim Brotherhood.

"Shit," Eastwood said. "Pack your trash. Let's get out of here."

CHAPTER SIXTEEN

0430 September 18, 2012
Cristobal Airport, Panama

Duncan Hunter lined up for the final pass of the night. Exhausted, he fought the controls at every turn. The YO-3A's seventy-five feet of wing provided plenty of lift, and the nighttime air should have offered smooth flying, but unseasonably high winds and thermals bounced him all over the sky for seven straight nights. Without his backseat partner to share flying duties, Hunter overextended himself. He recognized and obsessed over the signs of exhaustion. His heart pounded, and he saw intermittent phosphenes with every heartbeat.

That's when you know you've overdone it, he told himself. *You're so tired, you see stars.*

He'd been working like a madman in the cockpit for six hours, concentrating on completing his mission. With every pass, he checked the GPS to ensure he was lined up on the area to be treated for a *Weedbusters* application. Before executing the run, he checked the FLIR to ensure no humans were in the path of the multi-head laser system. If someone on the ground had his eyes damaged from the operation, Hunter's cover would be blown. The idea of using a silent airplane with an unseen laser was a tremendous drug war fighting capability as long as he left no traces. If poppy, cannabis, or coca farmers suddenly started complaining of a temporary blinding condition known as welder's flash, that would arouse the suspicion of the drug cartels.

The secret to the *Wraith's* success as the ultimate drug crop eradication tool was that it left no fingerprints. No human could detect the aircraft aurally, and the *Weedbusters* system didn't leave any residue. Animals and people rarely looked up when they were engaged with something on the ground. If the international press reported drug crops affected by an unknown blight or disease, it was the only hint that Hunter had been there with his secret airplane.

With the development of *Weedbusters* came concomitant newspaper and newscast comments. Lynche playfully accused Hunter of being a disease, a carrier. "Those plants have a bad case of Hunter's Disease," he said.

The quiet aircraft, with its powerful four-headed laser, was the perfect combination to super-irradiate alkaloid-producing plants. It didn't kill them, shred them, or set them on fire. It just made them sick. The difference between a plant that became sick and died was calculated in dwell time measured in seconds of radiation. He altered their DNA to the point where individual plants couldn't repair the damage from high levels of ultraviolet and the lengthy dwell times of the four laser beams, even when slightly diffused by the atmosphere. Then he moved on to the next hundred or thousand plants.

Weedbusters was his own invention, and it was the perfect aerial eradication solution. The idea wasn't conceived as another method to kill drug crops with herbicides, sprayed from the belly of crop dusters. The *Weedbusters* laser system used UV light—electromagnetic radiation—to make the plants sick. In some high-intensity applications, it killed the plants. The difference between killing plants and making them sick was an engineering equation of distance, power, and dwell.

Each drug plant was different biologically and structurally, and each killing solution was different for opium poppy, cannabis, and coca. The optimum combination of distance, power, and dwell that sickened Afghanistan's poppies and cannabis wouldn't make a dent in coca. Dead coca and cannabis was a good thing in the drug-crop-eradication business. The benchmark of success for interrupting the growing cycle of opium poppy was to make the plants just sick enough to prevent the poppy bulb from which the opium sap was derived from forming. No poppy stalk, no poppy bulb. No poppy bulb, no poppy sap from which to make opium—and no poppy seeds.

For cannabis and coca, the goal was to kill as many plants as possible. After a UV application, the treated plants looked as if all the moisture was sucked from them. Killing coca required Hunter to fly 007 as slowly as possible, right on the edge of stall, while the four laser heads spun, scanned, and saturated the plants with beams of UV. It crushed plants like an invisible foot stomping a cigar butt.

During a very narrow window of opportunity, Hunter had to fly at the lowest possible speed and altitude, with the highest possible laser power and longest dwell time to kill or sicken a plant without leaving a trace. It worked if he could fly the aircraft at the edge of controlled flight. If he flew too fast, the plant wouldn't receive the required dwell time to sicken or kill it. Too slow, and the airplane would fall from the sky.

The narrow window between controlled and uncontrolled flight was two knots. He knew that was the same window between flying and crashing the U-2, Lockheed's super high-flying jet glider. Lockheed helped the U-2 pilot manage his airspeed with an oversized airspeed indicator. Installing such an indicator in the YO-3A instrument panel was the other trade secret for *Weedbusters* missions. The only other limiting factor of the laser system was that it couldn't be made "eye safe" for direct or indirect viewing.

Hunter's old partner, Greg Lynche, while flying the *Wraith* solo, demonstrated the surprising power of the *Weedbusters* system when he caused devastating eye damage to a sniper who was about to kill Hunter. At first Lynche thought the laser would just dazzle him, give the man a temporary case of welder's flash and distract him enough for Hunter to escape. Lynche hadn't anticipated what the system was capable of. He and Hunter never discussed using it for anything other than maiming or killing plants.

When it looked like the sniper was ready to blow Hunter's brains out, Lynche focused all four lasers on the sniper's eyes. At a very low altitude, with less than half a second of dwell time—at full power and intensity—in an area less than the size of a deck of cards, the concentrated laser beams shredded the man's corneas, irises, sclera, and eyelids in an instant, as if a hundred razor blades raced across his face at the speed of light. Vitreous media burst from both eyes simultaneously with the release of pressure, gushing onto the man's cheeks. *Weedbusters* wasn't a toy.

During Afghanistan missions, as the snows retreated into the mountains, and poppy farmers awoke to tend their fields, they and their Taliban masters were at a loss to explain the stench of hundreds of dying or dead poppies. Some plants were lifeless and discolored, but they were still dying. Every morning, they found the stench of rotten plants. There were patches of healthy ones right beside sick ones. What was most disconcerting was that thousands of sick plants were sometimes intermingled with healthy plants. It made no sense.

The Taliban initially thought the Americans were using crop dusters at night to spray the fields with herbicides, as the Russians did thirty years earlier, but no one reported hearing aircraft. Farmers never found any telltale residue on their plants, either. With over 500,000 hectares of poppy in Helmand Province, there were many targets of opportunity.

Every time Duncan Hunter visited Afghanistan, opium production decreased significantly. When he visited South America, coca production decreased significantly. Press reports highlighted the mysteries, stating that for some inexplicable reason, an unknown disease was killing off much of the affected crops.

The physical and mental effort to manage all the variables of airspeed, altitude, power, and dwell were exhausting, even with the supersized airspeed indicator. Hunter was a world-class athlete, but seven days of intense night flying using night vision goggles left him completely drained.

He pitched away from his last run on the last night of killing coca in the Colombian mountains and set a heading for Panama. He engaged the autopilot, flipped his ANVIS-9 night-vision goggles up away from his eyes, and turned the air vent up to Full.

For the first time in a long time, he was afraid he wouldn't reach the airport. He wasn't ill, just fatigued. He feared falling asleep and not waking. The work was demanding when there were two men in the cockpit, when he and Lynche shared flying duties. It was lunacy to think he could remove the back seat and replace it with more capabilities without being adversely affected. Military pilots were sometimes accused of having *get-home-itis* after being away from home for extended periods. Pushing themselves, they ignored obvious maintenance or human-factors problems. Many died from *get-home-itis*, and Hunter was near that category. After a week of incredibly stressful flying, he pushed his personal envelope too far. He shouldn't have removed the back seat. It was obvious that Greg Lynche *was* irreplaceable. Hunter hoped his stupidity wouldn't kill him.

He was task-saturated during the final *Weedbusters* flight, and he was too proud and arrogant to admit he had limits and couldn't keep up the pace while managing all the disparate elements required for his mission. He needed help.

He dismissed some of the unintended consequences when there was no longer a division of labor, and all the work had to be done by him, creating a single point of failure. He should have known better.

Between hard yawns, he excoriated himself. His flight suit was completely drenched in sweat. Fiddling with the air vents, he directed as much cool night air as he could toward his face, hoping it would prevent him from nodding off.

When his head snapped up from a micro-sleep, Hunter was surprised to hear one of the Bobs trying to call him on the radio. He had overflown the airport and was heading toward the Pacific. The shock of falling asleep scared him. The adrenalin jolted him awake, and he turned toward the airport, landing without incident.

As Bob and Bob raced to disassemble the YO-3A and slip 007 into her shipping container, Hunter vowed to find a replacement sensor operator to share the workload, at least on *Weedbusters* missions.

Maybe I could get Lynche back into the cockpit just for these missions, he thought.

He was embarrassed at being so stupid that he almost killed himself. He could have easily flown into the water or a mountain. It wasn't like him to push the envelope.

Yes, it is, he told himself. *Who am I kidding?*

What had been one of his greatest strengths—never giving up—was one of his major weaknesses.

Bob and Bob, recognizing the signs that Hunter wasn't well, helped him into their truck. He immediately fell asleep in the back seat.

After 007 was safely inside her container, the tall Bob drove Hunter to the hotel. He staggered out and continually focused on one coherent thought. He had almost killed himself with his own stupidity.

Duncan Hunter dragged himself to his hotel room in shame and disgust. *What an idiot! Sometimes, Hunter, you prove you're just too stupid to live.*

CHAPTER SEVENTEEN

0755 September 22, 2012
U.S. Embassy
Algiers, Algeria

Nazy Cunningham stood in the window of her third-floor office and watched the U.S. Marine Security Guards in the courtyard below. Three men in tight khaki shirts, red stripes bright against dark-blue trouser legs and topped with crisp white covers marched to the embassy flagpole. The Marine in the middle cradled a folded American flag—a blue triangle of white stars—and held it close against his chest; the apex pointed toward his chin. Upon reaching the flagpole, the men marched in place until all were in position.

In sync, their heels came together and stopped, then each Marine faced the flagpole. One faced west, the other east, the third, north. They stood at rigid attention until the Marine in the middle nodded slightly and slowly lowered the cradled flag. He affixed the hoist ends to the halyard's swivel snaps; the topmost swivel was first and firmly connected to the canton.

The opposite Marine grasped the other side of the halyard. The center Marine waited. At the sound of the National Anthem, the hoisting Marine raised the flag, hand over hand, steady without rushing. The carry Marine allowed the flag to unfold from his arms as it rose. Once it was completely unfurled, he snapped to a smart salute, joining the center Marine, who was already saluting.

As the Anthem's final note sounded, all Marines completed their salute, and their hands snapped down to their sides. The halyard was tied off to the flagpole. The Marines executed facing movements toward the main building and marched off.

The flag ceremony Marines stirred several emotions in Nazy. Only when she worked at an embassy did she witness Marines doing their duty. Seeing the flag raised made her proud to be an American. Then there were the other embassy Marines; bright, cheerful, young but professional. Nazy admired, respected, and thanked them for their service and for protecting the people working at the embassy.

And, then there was Duncan Hunter. Seeing Marines made her think of him. He had been a Marine for a long time; he was an officer and he flew jets. He even showed her "his jet" at the Smithsonian Museum near the Dulles Airport, with *MARINES* on the side of the ancient F-4 Phantom. She knew he had to be someone special to fly such a brutish aircraft with its bent wings and powerful engines.

Everything about my old Marine is special! She turned from the window to sit at her desk and deliberately pushed thoughts of Duncan from her mind. She had work to do. She'd been running nonstop from dawn to dusk since she arrived. She didn't anticipate fully the job of Chief of Station or Station Chief, known within the embassy as the *Trade Attaché,* and appreciated her time with the real Chief of Station, the very pregnant Angie Lazar.

Morning, noon, and night, Cunningham shadowed Lazar in the performance of her duties. CIA officers on overseas postings needed to leave their embassies and collect intelligence, meeting other intelligence officers under their official job as trade attaché or political officer. When Lazar's pregnancy began interfering with her official functions, she could no longer receive and process materials officially provided by foreign governments. She couldn't attend high-level meetings at the Ministry of Defense or the Foreign Ministry.

Being pregnant in an Islamic country introduced problems. Muslim men oftentimes refused to work with the pregnant chief. CIA bureaucrats knew the station chief's condition would lead to problems when her baby bump showed. To continue to nurture personal relationships with the Algerian leadership, the solution was to replace the Arabic-speaking chief with an up-and-coming, brilliant, Arabic-speaking surrogate in the interim.

Nazy was everything Angie Lazar wasn't. Cunningham was

striking, articulate, and poised, all of which illuminated her talent. It was also no secret within the CIA that Nazy Cunningham found Osama bin Laden through hard intelligence analysis. That success placed her in a different category of intelligence executive.

Emaciated, plain, with frizzy dark hair, Angie Lazar was the opposite. She was often distracted and stumbled through briefings, seemingly unable to speak in coherent sentences. The information would eventually be conveyed, but it was painful for all at a conference table to watch the woman struggle to string words together. Impromptu speaking wasn't her forte although she read well from notes. Where Cunningham was structured, organized, and precise, Lazar was barely adequate.

Nazy found Angie struggled with meetings. There was no structure or agenda. No action was taken or directed. The files in the SCIF would never pass a security-compliance inspection.

Once Chief of Station Angie Lazar was safely delivered to the airport and was on an airliner headed home, Acting Station Chief Cunningham got to work.

Her first meeting was with the other CIA officers. She received a threat assessment and status of ongoing operations in the country. Al-Qaeda and the Muslim Brotherhood were growing in influence; nearby mosques seemed to fall under one of the terrorist group's influence. Several times over the years, demonstrators were able to get over the embassy walls before being chased off by Algerian forces. Surprised that little occurred locally, on the 9/11 anniversary, several sources indicated another round of demonstrations was being planned and would occur soon.

Upgrades to the U.S. Embassy made it more difficult for random or spontaneous acts of unrest to get out of hand. It would take a great deal of effort for the usual roustabouts to scale one of the walls and threaten the embassy's occupants. In the past, if the physical security could be breached, the protestors usually focused on one mission—take down the American flag. If they were successful, demonstrators vigorously shredded, stomped, and burned it, preferably in front of a lathered up camera crew.

Cunningham stressed she would pick up the responsibilities of the COS and meet with the country's intelligence officials. The plan to return to the standard of developing the relationship between the intelligence agencies was roundly applauded.

Her second meeting was more important than the first. Maintenance of classified files had been completely ignored. Historical files were stuffed in the back of safes. Files scheduled to be destroyed were simply stacked in the safes. Both shredders were out of oil and had burned up. No one bothered to request new shredders or get the special lubricants or order the spare parts to fix the out-of-service machines. Cunningham also found that the necessary burn procedures weren't being followed when the massive shredders were out of action.

Other security measures had also been ignored or dismissed due to a *laissez-faire* attitude toward security. The combination of an indifferent security chief and a distracted, out-of-touch station chief resulted in a significant material breach of Agency responsibilities. The immediate priority was to fix the files and request a security-compliance inspection from CIA headquarters when that was done. The problems at the embassy would also mean Angie Lazar would never return to Algiers.

After a week of reading old files and assessing their disposition—burn, shred, or file—Nazy came across a pair of old "closed" special access programs that had been scheduled for destruction years earlier. For some reason, they escaped the burn bag and shredder. The accountability forms on the covers of the files were heavily annotated, with dates and names of former station chiefs as the only official to ever open the file.

How can they be called 'closed' when they're opened every year?

Closed files either went into the archives or were destroyed. Open files could be accessed or consulted or have other documents added. That both closed files had been opened at the same time each year made no sense.

Alone in the vault of the SCIF, Nazy opened the first closed file folder to find several copies of cables transmitted from Embassy Algiers to CIA HQ. Documents were placed loosely, newest ones on top. She flipped the file to see the last document in the stack, which should have been the source document initiating the cable. Ignoring the header and footer, she focused on the quote in the center of the cable.

Failure to release my brothers and transport them to Algiers within 48 hours will result in a U.S. American airliner shot down every 48 hours.

She unconsciously raised her hand to her mouth in horror. Her eyes flew to the date and time of the transmission. She struggled with the information in the papers before her that something very bad happened on or near July 15, 1996. She slowly flipped through the next cable and the next. After reading every scrap of paper in the file, she closed it very slowly and deliberately. Looking at the accountability record for the file, she focused on the title of the Special Access Program, *Piper I.*

Stunned, she sat motionless for several excruciating seconds before exchanging files. *Piper I* slid under the other old file, labeled *Piper II.* She spread the manila folder open and shuffled the papers to find the initiating document. She couldn't believe what she read and immediately checked the custody routing sheet on both files. She nearly dropped the folder when she read the name of the chief of station of the initiating *Piper I.* She trembled as she read another quote in the middle of the cable, just as before.

Failure to transport one hundred million dollars in gold coin to Algiers within 48 hours will result in several packages released into your postal system. Several other packages will be released every 48 hours until these demands are met.

Subsequent cables in the *Piper II* file, similar to those in *Piper I,* outlined the frantic inability of the U.S. government to identify the author of the ransom notes or to engage in negotiations. In each case, the initial presidential decision was to dismiss the threat.

In the case of *Piper I,* an airliner was shot down forty-eight hours after receipt of the ransom note at U.S. Embassy Algiers. In the case of *Piper II,* several letters containing weapons-grade anthrax were delivered to members of Congress and other random Americans.

Other cables in each file outlined how the communiqués were transmitted. They were always delivered by a small boy wearing a blue *kufi.* The remaining cables acknowledged that the requisite deliveries were made as directed and on time to the Algiers International Airport.

Cunningham worked to control her breathing. Her heart threatened to pound itself out of her chest. She exhaled in ragged spurts. Her stomach churned. Though she knew she was alone in the SCIF and the vault, she looked around, anyway, following the rule, *Trust but verify.*

Having enough for one day, she felt hot and had to leave. Nazy glanced at the ragged manila folders in her hands, where her knuckles were white from gripping them so tightly. She stood, placed the *Piper* files back in the top drawer of the five-drawer safe, spun the dial, and flipped the magnetic sign to read *Closed.* She moved full burn bags into the vault, closed it, and flipped that sign, too.

The uneasiness in her stomach increased. She couldn't leave the SCIF fast enough and get to the women's restroom near the elevators. She thought she might be ill. She never vomited, but she instinctively knew she needed to be near a commode. Nazy banged open a stall door and barely got into position before she broke into a sweat and emptied her stomach into the toilet. The second time she filled the bowl, she thought she might have pulled a muscle.

She struggled with the toilet paper roll to wipe her mouth and nose, and then flushed the toilet as the smell of bile and undigested food assaulted her senses anew. She wept and retched several more times, but her stomach was empty. Finally, she slid to the floor with her legs splayed unnaturally to the left and right. She hoped no one saw her like that. Thoughts of being found and embarrassed again galvanized her to get up and clean herself.

Looking in the mirror, she saw she was a wreck. She hadn't looked that bad since the last time her husband beat her. After rinsing her mouth and washing her hands and face, she removed her heels and walked unsteadily from the washroom and down the hall to her office.

She still felt sick and miserable. Though she may have looked that way before, she never felt like it. Taking her chair behind the COS' desk, she placed her head in her hands and calmed herself, occasionally sipping from a water bottle. Chilled air from the air conditioning helped to cool her face.

After several minutes, she felt markedly better. She raised her head and thought, *So that's what that was all about!*

Nazy moved her leather-covered, CIA-embossed notebook from the middle of the desk to uncover the oversized calendar beneath it. She counted with her finger—five days. She closed her eyes; her temples pounded with every heartbeat. *It's ... true!*

Before taking the assignment to Algeria, Nazy was read in on a unique special access program. She didn't need to know the SAP's full scope, only a very discrete component requiring a modicum of personal effort. A trusted agent would personally observe the landing of a Gulfstream business jet. The aircrew would deplane, lock the aircraft, and would give the keys to the agent, who would then give the pilot and copilot a ride to the commercial terminal and return to the embassy.

Before entering the embassy, at a designated location and time, the trusted agent would pass the airplane's keys to a little boy who approached the car wearing a bright-blue *kufi*. The agent would then return to the embassy and cable the DCI, mission complete.

Nazy slowly lifted her head from her hands. In five days, she would oversee the transaction phase of the executive special access program, *Piper I.* She remembered as she was being read on that she assumed the requirements were silly. It all sounded like someone trying to play spy. Maybe someone at the National Clandestine Service was running an exercise or simulation for another operation. Even with the DCI's presence, the formality of the security officer and unique access to the executive SCIF, it was hard to take the brief seriously, because what they asked her to do was ridiculous.

She agreed to take the mission just to get away from the DCI. She could play the game. It was a free trip to Algeria. All she had to do was drive the pilots to the airport.

After the exercise, she wouldn't think anything of it. Another side of her thought that the subdued histrionics of being read on a program where success was marked by delivering a set of keys to a boy with a blue hat had to be a practical joke or some weird concoction by the DCI to get her into bed. It was all crazy.

Abu Manu. The name leaped from the *Piper* files. Nazy saw where several recent cables highlighted some MASINT, measurement and signal intelligence, and HUMINT, human intelligence collection successes. Scraps of intel came together. It was threshold material, not substantive. Individually, the analysis was insufficient to indict. However, once the intelligence was appropriately displayed and conveyed, there were enough pieces of the pictures to make an informed decision. In the intelligence and espionage world, no one could "buy a vowel" to complete or solve a puzzle. Over the years, a picture of the man emerged.

The intel had obviously reached a tipping point, but the *Piper* files didn't reflect any analysis. That was done at HQ. The *Piper* files strongly suggested that the rarely seen, largely nocturnal man tentatively identified as Abu Manu was likely behind some of the most-noteworthy terrorist actions against America; terrorist actions that had been attributed to others.

When Cunningham was assigned to consolidate names for the disposition matrix for the DCI, the name Abu Man hadn't come from any of her sources. There was an Abu Manu file, but it was restricted—*DCI EYES ONLY.* She didn't question his placing Abu Manu's name on the disposition matrix. The less time she spent with the DCI, the better.

While she had her own work to do, the creation of the listings was a small additional duty. It would have been difficult to refuse for something so administratively trivial. She racked, stacked, and consolidated terrorists and funders of terrorism and placed them on a single spreadsheet. The DCI could prioritize, add, or delete entries. It was his program; a bizarre social register, a blue book of killers.

Only in the *Piper I* files was there a hint of a possible, not probable, causal relationship between the man identified as Abu Manu and several aircraft brought down around the world by unexplained crashes or secretly attributed to anti-aircraft missiles. As terrorist groups rushed to take credit for an unexpected airline accident, governments rushed to squash any hint of terrorist involvement for fear of a collapse of their aviation industry.

The usual suspects took credit for the incidents, but the intelligence community analysts made it immediately clear if the terrorist groups either had the resources or wherewithal to execute such an action, or they did not. If al-Qaeda had a supply of anti-aircraft missiles, the accepted rationale was they wouldn't be able to contain themselves and would use them against their enemies all across the world. They would immediately threaten the international aviation industry and would likely succeed in shutting down all aviation commerce. There was significant evidence that since al-Qaeda couldn't acquire missiles, easily or at all, they resorted to less sophisticated terrorism efforts—bombing airplanes or hijacking them to fly them into buildings.

If a terrorist acquiring anti-aircraft missiles was an improbable situation, acquiring and dispersing weapons-grade anthrax should have been impossible. The *Piper II* file suggested there was more than a tenuous thread connecting the man responsible for shooting down commercial aircraft and the anthrax attacks in the U.S. It was the same *modus operandi;* the same stationery was used and the same kid in the blue *kufi* delivered the ransom demands.

CIA analysts had some information and pieced together a fuzzy picture. As the U.S. threatened to invade Kuwait and push Iraq out of the country, a long-forgotten, former bioweapons expert made almost daily trips between Baghdad and Amman under a Libyan flag carrier before he bolted for freedom, and became lost to the intelligence community.

When the eerily similar ransom letter was delivered to U.S. Embassy Algiers, and anthrax-tainted letters were found in the U.S. postal system, every suspected and former bioweapons expert on the planet immediately jumped to the head of the list of usual suspects. Through years of analysis, piecing tiny shards and fragments of information together, a picture developed. The CIA believed they got a break and were able tentatively to identify a man of many talents who might be the new kingpin of international terrorism—Abu Manu; a mysterious and sometimes confidant of Muammar Gaddafi.

Before Nazy left on her assignment, the DCI added a name and moved the new candidate, Abu Manu, to the top of the disposition matrix. She knew intuitively that Hunter would soon go after the next name on the DCI's list. He told her he was going to Colombia or someplace in South America, but he would return to Texas soon.

Another ransom payment would be made in five days. Abu Manu was most likely behind the ransom letters. He showed no compunction about injecting anthrax-laced letters into the U.S. postal system; he showed no fear in shooting down airplanes.

Duncan will probably fly to Algiers in a few days. To find and kill a man who shoots down airplanes.

Nazy reached for the small trashcan near her desk. She felt violently ill again.

CHAPTER EIGHTEEN

1635 September 20, 2012
CIA Headquarters
McLean, Virginia

"In five days, we believe we'll have an intercept window," the DCI said, briefing the next target. "Like Mali, this one is time-sensitive. We may not get another opportunity for another year."

Hunter wasn't impressed, though he was curious. Although still sluggish and thick-headed from the exhaustive flying of the previous week, he wondered why the DCI had all but demanded Hunter's presence at HQ. Rothwell barked at him in the encrypted email, expecting Hunter to be in his office at 1630.

Hunter hoped the DCI or his secretary ensured he had his access clearance at the security gate. The man was losing it and apparently didn't handle pressure very well. He assumed there was substantial fallout from the death of the Ambassador to Libya a couple weeks earlier, reportedly by a spontaneous mob, if the press and the State Department's reports could be believed.

He thought anything that came from the media or the socialist-run State Department had to be a lie or diversion. Hunter couldn't imagine how an ambassador could be killed in the line of duty; embassies and consulates were heavily protected. He intuited there was some moronic reason why, but the excuse of a spontaneous mob was obviously a lie and doubted the American public would ever be told the truth. Dead ambassadors weren't his responsibility. He had other things to think about. The fiasco in Libya became one of the furthest things from his mind.

More likely, the DCI was feeling heat from Congress, as the FBI investigation surrounding him and his girlfriends progressively moved from the back page of the *Washington Post* toward the front of the *New York Times*. Hunter followed the DCI's troubles as best he could, even from the English newspapers in Panama. It wasn't yet front-page news in the U.S., but stories about the DCI were creeping around the globe. Every day, a new leak from the FBI pushed the newspaper editors to move the story to the front page.

The CIA public affairs office struggled to keep the DCI's personal life out of the news. No one was calling for his resignation yet, but it was just a matter of time. If Rothwell resigned, Hunter knew *Noble Savage* would cease or go inactive, at least until a new DCI could be named.

He could have used a shower, but the long plane ride from Panama City to the District of Colombia helped restore some of his energy. His Brooks Brothers suit looked like it had been slept in, which it had. He fell asleep within moments of buckling his seat belt, kicking off his shoes, and turning on noise-canceling headphones with a sleep mask over his eyes. His last thought before falling asleep: *Thank God for American Airlines' first class seats.*

"Director Rothwell, I'm not sure it's possible on such short notice," Hunter said. "I just finished a drug-eradication mission, and *the airplane* is still in Panama. We've been using low profile container ships to move the airplane into and out of the country. The only way I can see to do this mission is if we were able to get the Air Force down there immediately and bring her back. Then we need to transfer *Wraith* onto a C-130."

Director Rothwell jumped up from his seat at the conference table, dashed to the door, and yanked it open. "Mayo! I need the Air Force Chief of Staff on the phone, *now!*" He spun around and closed the door. Before sitting down, he asked, "What else do you need?"

Hunter was suddenly at full alert. He never saw a government executive in such a state of anxiety. Either the DCI's world was collapsing, or it was a *seriously* important mission.

"We'll need the latest satellite overheads for launch and recovery sites," Hunter said, "I'll need the target location. If we use your crew, I can go over the mission and abort procedures while we're en route. What am I looking for? There's no file on this guy. I need intel on where and when he's expected to be in the optimum intercept window."

Unlike the other targets on the disposition matrix, Hunter's interest in that particular target was piqued. He waited stonily, as the DCI processed the information. The man was clearly struggling to choose his words carefully.

"What he's done in the past is supervise the unloading of a business jet. It's on the same day every year, at roughly the same time in the evening."

"Sir, that sounds like a job for a Predator."

"We don't…can't use Predators in Algeria. The airstrip is too far from the beach and too protected to use SEALs or Special Activities Group."

Algeria? Nazy's in Algeria…. Duncan sucked air and responded, "Then it sounds like a job tailor made for me."

"I think it's perfect. We just have to get you into position. I'm sure you'll do the rest."

"We're talking about an airstrip. Is this a commercial airport or a private runway?"

"We believe it's the target's villa. There's a house overlooking the Med that's very near the airstrip. There are a few buildings at the…. It's a private airstrip. There's also a hangar and small refueling tank. The runway was repaved several years ago and can handle large business jets. I understand it was a remote airport for Nazi fighters when Rommel was driving all over North Africa."

"So no traffic, per se, to worry about. Will the aircraft be there, or will it land and be offloaded?"

"In the past, a business jet has flown out of Algiers to the villa's runway along the Algerian coast and offloaded. Our target usually leaves his villa to meet the jet. There are no known pictures of him, but what grainy video we have shows he's the commanding presence during offloading. Approximately thirty containers are removed from the aircraft and carried into the hangar. After all the boxes are offloaded, the jet takes off and heads to Abu Dhabi. Our target departs the hangar usually within an hour of takeoff."

Boxes? Containers? "Same time and place?" Duncan asked.

"Always has been. Usually about 0100 local."

The intercom buzzed and Rothwell leaped from the small conference table to squelch it and answer.

"General Alhelm, Norm, thank you for responding so quickly. I need a favor. Let me put you on speaker, so we can convey exactly what we need." He punched a button on the polycom and hung up the receiver, nodding to Hunter to come closer and speak.

"Sir," Hunter said, "we need to recover a standard ten-by-ten, forty-foot shipping container at the Cristobal Airport in Panama, tonight or tomorrow, if at all possible. The container has an airplane and a barrel of avgas aboard. The fuel cell is double-walled and shouldn't give anyone any trouble. We can't let anyone inspect the contents of the container. There are two older gentlemen traveling with the container. I need the container and the gentlemen delivered to Andrews."

"Confirm Cristobal."

"Roger, Cristobal: Charlie Romeo India Sierra Oscar Bravo Alpha Lima. It's on the Atlantic side of the Panama Canal."

"Roger. Is that it? Anything else?" the general asked.

Hunter both nodded and shook his head. Rothwell said, "Yes, Sir. Norm, this is time-sensitive and very important."

"Can do easy. Do I need a point of contact, a phone number?"

Hunter provided his private cell number, and the general rang off. The DCI smiled at Hunter, and then looked away.

Duncan, thinking the meeting was probably over, said, "I thought that shit happened only in the movies."

"I thought so, too. Looked to me like it was the only solution."

"If you want this one done, that was. They just have to get a C-17 or C-130 down there and deliver; we'll likely need a C-130 to execute."

Director Rothwell stood and tapped his ubiquitous cheap pen in his hand against the thin file Hunter hadn't been allowed to peruse. Hunter took a slip of paper from his notebook and offered it to the DCI. It contained challenges and responses for coded email transmissions, as well as a list of actions needed by ground agents in Spain, the Azores, and Algiers.

The DCI looked up from the document and nodded. "This one's very special Duncan. I can't stress how important it is to execute this mission flawlessly. You do this, and you'll be a hero. I'll walk you to the elevator."

The meeting was over.

Hunter wordlessly followed the DCI out of the office. He winked and waved to an overburdened Miss Mayo, with the phone pressed against her ear by one shoulder and her hands full of FedEx envelopes.

As Rothwell reached the elevators, he hit the *Down* button and waited. Hunter looked back at the flailing secretary before turning to Rothwell to ask, "What did he do?"

Rothwell glanced back at Penny Mayo. The distance was sufficient to say a few well-chosen, classified words, as the elevator doors opened, and Hunter stepped inside.

Rothwell held the door open with one hand. "Besides suspected funding and facilitating terrorist acts against the United States, Russia, Great Britain, and France?" He released the door. "He shot down commercial airliners, usually for ransom."

The door closed, and the elevator sped down. Hunter closed his eyes and shook his head. *This is going to be bad.*

CHAPTER NINETEEN

1630 September 20, 2012
Algiers, Algeria

The man sat alone in the small courtyard, the sun strong against his face. He gazed over the city, contemplating his next move. Life had been easy, then hard, then very good. It now had come full circle. It was very bad. Exposure was long the *bête noire* of his business. He screwed up and overexposed himself, or at least, he thought he had. Was it enough to get him killed? Would the Americans find and kill him this time?

He thought his plan was unadulterated genius, like the first time.

He thought he had the benefit of experience, maturity, and hindsight, so he dispatched his team. The American President would ignore the letter, of course, just like the first time. *America doesn't negotiate with terrorists.* A smile crept across his heavily lined face.

The new President would act like the previous one. Make him an offer he dare not refuse; but they always refused, like the first time. They learned quickly and didn't refuse the second time. And they continued to pay.

He removed dark sunglasses and toweled his forehead before replacing them. His confidence was shattered. He hadn't heeded the signs. He assumed Gaddafi would always rule Libya. That assumption almost cost him his life. By ignoring the growing threat, he allowed things at home to get out of hand, and he barely escaped with his life and family. He should have done more, but fear of exposure prevented him from action. He nearly lost everything.

As men were sometimes wont to do when their lives crumbled around them, the man reflected on how he came to that point in his existence. He had an idea; a plan. It was audacious and brilliant. And, it only had to work once.

He closed his eyes, envisioning the missile streaking up and away to find the airliner. He remembered the pictures of the aftermath, the debris on the ocean, with America mourning.

Opening his eyes, he blocked the sun with his hand. Even with dark shades, it was penetrating. He moved his chair into shade.

The American President blamed the airplane and paid the gold. The man chuckled and smiled.

Then there was the second time. Unlike the first, the American President was dealing with a crisis. Jets crashed into buildings. The plan had been in the works for years, waiting for the most-opportune moment. He never anticipated al-Qaeda would use jets to attack America. It was a sign, a gift from Allah. Opportunity coupled with coincidence; and the sign from Allah was to change the message, which he did.

On that day, the same day that al-Qaeda struck the all-powerful Americans; the man discussed his change of plans with the team and moved up the mission's timeline. He correctly assumed the Americans would be in disarray and would be unprepared for another attack—a different *kind* of attack.

The two-man team departed Algiers for Brussels and then Montreal. With Algerian passports, the men drove rental cars into the U.S., deposited freshly printed letters into mailboxes and hotel mail chutes, crushing the tiny ampoules within right before they were released into blue boxes. Americans were so trusting.

The anthrax was released, and the team escaped unharmed as planned. America was attacked again. They might suspect al-Qaeda or even the Muslim Brotherhood, but they would never really know. The American President would blame someone else.

One week after the September 11 attacks, letters containing anthrax were received in newspaper offices run by liberal news media. Two Democratic Senators received them, too.

He smiled at the thought of inciting American intraparty strife and terror.

One week after 9/11, he heard the first reports of a biological weapons attack in America. People began dying of anthrax. There was no excuse. People were warned to take penicillin.

He shook his head as he'd done a thousand times. It was a gamble, and it paid off. One week after the bioweapons attack became world news, as new letters were discovered in the postal system, $100,000,000 in gold coin was delivered to the Algiers airport. Like the first time. Gold arrived on the same day, every year thereafter.

He accomplished the impossible—threaten America and win. With the chaos in Libya, he felt threatened and exposed. He had little anthrax left and lost nearly all his missiles. The American President was sending unmanned airplanes to kill Muslims in Pakistan, Afghanistan, Iraq, and Yemen. What about Africa? Would he send a little airplane to Algeria? Though there were hints, he never saw any aircraft.

He sighed in despair. The next shipment was due in five days. Would there be another? Would they find him this time? If they did, would they let him live? The American President found and killed Osama bin Laden. All Muslims took notice. Anyone involved in the business of fighting America saw the ease with which bin Laden was discovered, hunted down, trapped, and killed. The Americans even made it into theater, lionizing the Muslim American President and the warriors who found and killed bin Laden.

The Muslim President began to foment unrest in Muslim lands, encouraging the dictators of Tunisia, Libya, Egypt, and Syria to step aside and allow the rebels ... "democracy." Words like "democracy" plunged the countries into chaos. Strict Islam and "democracy" are incompatible. Of course chaos ensued.

The Muslim President wasn't all that smart, either. He was overthrown and went into hiding, fearful of the island called Cuba and that place called Guantanamo Bay, or "Gitmo" as some Americans called it.

The new American President wasn't a Muslim or a friendly Democrat. He quietly unleashed special operations people around the world and more unmanned planes—with many more missiles.

The man in the dark sunglasses came full circle. Though he normally didn't show emotion, the stress of the last few weeks took its toll. He was afraid.

Abu Manu hid in the center of town, surrounded by his family. While he feared the new American President, he feared the old al-Qaeda and Muslim Brotherhood the most; they would torture him for his gold and inventory. The Americans wouldn't torture him, but he was convinced, if they ever had the opportunity to find him they would kill him with an unmanned airplane, or a missile. The next shipment, in five days, would be a decoy, a way to lure him into the open. With the new hardline President, Abu Manu felt his time had come.

For several years, he believed the American Presidents would send unmanned airplanes with missiles to kill him in Libya, Tunisia, or Algeria. Every year, he sensed they were getting closer, but every year, the Americans provided the gold and the jet. They were punctual and professional; they were always on time and always surrendered the correct amount. No tracking devices were ever found on the aircraft and he never saw nor heard manned airplanes in the sky.

The new President terrified him. All American Republican Presidents had concerned him. Special operations men could be sent to find and capture him, but there were no special operations warriors in Algeria. There never would be without his knowing it.

Abu Manu pushed aside his paranoia. He refused to become another Carlos the Jackal, an Abu Abbas, or worse, another Abu Nidal. He implemented safeguards. He would be very cautious and would take delivery of this, the last shipment.

Carlos the Jackal never killed anyone for money, just for the liberation of Palestine. Abu Abbas and Abu Nidal killed indiscriminately. The latter became increasingly paranoid and mercurial in his efforts to liberate Palestine. Those three always needed help and recruited bright, fanatical members from Morocco to Syria. Some recruits weren't good, while others were too good to be true Muslims dedicated to the cause. For them, the price of admission to the organization was the threat of or actual torture at the hands of their very small-minded followers. Some were poor spies who left their organizations; some might have made good spies.

Once recruited, members weren't allowed to leave, and they lived under the constant suspicion of being double agents. Constantly under the whip, the weakest minds confessed to betrayal and disloyalty. Some of those that stayed, stayed out of trouble but only because they were uncommonly compliant. Those with education and degrees were sent to Libya or Iraq to learn hard skills about biological or chemical weapons or both. Those with more than half a brain received something more than basic weapons training. The really smart ones got out before one of Abu Nidal's many mass purges, a frenzied cornucopia of torture and beheadings.

As one of Abu Nidal's finest recruits, Muhammad Ali Shazzami al-Bakaar played the survival game and flourished. A member of the fledgling Muslim Brotherhood in Libya, he was caught up in the movement and sought action to liberate Palestine. He soon saw that his leader, the infamous Abu Nidal, was nothing more than a hothead with many supporters that freely gave him encouragement and money. With Abu Nidal and money, smart, compliant supporters could go far.

Shazzami al-Bakaar was smart, educated, and degreed in the United States with Master's degrees in biology and chemistry. Also compliant, he was pushed into the secret chemical and bioweapons laboratories near Baghdad. The young man fell under the spell of the brilliant Islamic scholar, Sayyid Qutb, the father of the Muslim Brotherhood. Soon thereafter, Shazzami al-Bakaar fell away, far from the mystique and money of Abu Nidal. By comparison to Qutb, Nidal was an idiot.

What had been a reasonably good life came crashing down when a jealous contemporary accused Shazzami al-Bakaar of being a traitor. Terrified of being tortured or losing his head, al-Bakaar barely escaped one of Abu Nidal's spontaneous purges.

Abu Nidal was furious. Another traitor had breached his defenses. Al-Bakaar was immediately *persona non grata* with a price on his head.

Abu Nidal fantasized about having al-Bakaar's severed head on a pike.

Shazzami al-Bakaar's escape and banishment from the Abu Nidal Organization drove him home and into the arms of Muammar Gaddafi. Al-Bakaar's home was in Libya, in Benghazi, east of Tripoli. There he took the name Abu Manu and presented his credentials to a heavily medaled military man in his hometown. Within a week, Gaddafi was informed. Intrigued, he called to see the Iraqi-trained former Abu Nidal Organization bioweapons expert. Gaddafi found Abu Manu obsequious, well-organized, and highly motivated to serve. Enamored of the power of biological and chemical weapons, Gaddafi quietly harbored desires to conduct "special activities" against the West. Another bioweapons expert might make enough critical mass of expertise for Libya to finally build sufficient biological and chemical weapons. However, Muammar Gaddafi was enthralled with Abu Manu's ideas on how to attack and punish America.

As a member of the Abu Nidal Organization and being exposed to Saddam Hussein's Republican Guard, the man called Abu Manu became very interested in the activities of the so-called elite soldiers and mercenaries. He was certain no one in the ANO could have been considered an elite warrior. Little to nothing was invested in the ANO to make a warrior be considered good. They were low-cost, technically acceptable, disposable warriors.

On the other hand, Abu Manu was a scientist, physically weak but mentally smart. He was a high-cost, technically acceptable warrior who was served best in a laboratory, not shooting at tanks in the streets of Israel with an AK-47.

Abu Manu was fascinated by the specially vetted men of the American, British, and French elite Special Operations Forces. He read everything he could about Lieutenant Commander Ian Fleming's 30 Commando Unit, any and all elements of the U.S. Special Operations Command, and the French Foreign Legion. He was influenced by the exploits of the *Abwehrkommando,* the Nazi clandestine special forces that operated in disguise, usually wearing Allied or neutral country uniforms. Training costs were astronomical for any element of Special

Forces, and the men were trained to be expert in every possible weapon and situation.

Individual training was intense, embracing the full panoply of combat skills, including language proficiency, parachuting, explosives, underwater demotions, various forms of martial arts, lock picking, safecracking, booby traps, and skiing. The Muslim world had nothing like them. Only the American, British, and French Special Forces conducted special activities—unusual, very sensitive missions, usually under cover of darkness.

Abu Manu suggested if Gaddafi wanted to conduct special activities against the West, Libya needed its own Special Forces. "Your Excellency, I could build you a cadre of Libyan special operations forces to conduct special activities. My benchmark for success would be the U.S. Navy SEAL."

Gaddafi lamented that as smart as his lickspittles thought it would be to plant bombs on aircraft, those who designed the bombs and carried out the missions were little more than sycophantic idiots. He was disgusted with his "intelligence agents." After eight failed aircraft bombing attempts, the only success was the PanAm aircraft.

To his great dismay, the CIA quickly found the components of the PanAm bomb and traced it back to Libya within days. Gaddafi knew there would be retaliation. He wandered his tent aimlessly for days, lambasting himself over how he could have been so stupid as to allow himself to be used like that. His intelligence people weren't intelligent at all. He needed a better, smarter bomber.

When Abu Manu suggested Americans used specially trained men to execute their most closely held, top-secret missions, Gaddafi was intrigued. He heard about the Green Berets and Navy SEALs but dismissed them as American hyperbole. Abu Manu suggested the British, French, and American elite soldiers were smarter, better bombers.

Gaddafi encouraged more information. He came to realize that highly skilled, trained, dedicated Muslims with very specialized training could be useful for many projects he had in mind.

Muammar Gaddafi made up his mind. Although another scientist in his bioweapons laboratories might be helpful, a seed was planted. He had other ideas. He would use the smart scientist, trained by Abu Nidal and Saddam Hussein, to train his own stealthy brand of mercenaries. Gaddafi approved the recruiting and training to develop Muslim SEALs to conduct special activities against the Americans and the West. He could send them all around the globe to strike fear into the Americans anytime, anywhere. His Muslim SEALs could instigate unrest with his neighbors or harass and kill his detractors.

To Abu Manu's surprise, Gaddafi conscripted him to lead the program, and Abu Manu jumped at the chance to please Gaddafi. He targeted lively, intelligent students for the new organization. He kept Gaddafi informed at all times. He preferred strong, young people from refugee camps, not slothful ones from the Libyan army. His recruits would do anything to escape their situation. He could shape their hearts and minds, and backs. Those who worked hard and didn't complain made the best soldiers. Promises of good pay and help with their education encouraged many to jump from the despair of poverty to a path of prosperity or martyrdom.

Abu Manu didn't take just anyone. Twenty of the first 100 applicants survived the initial screening. Five of the twenty completed their training. Abu Manu suggested they be called FAHD, the Panthers; killers of the night. They were modeled after America's best. They would strike a blow against America from within on behalf of the Arab nation and for Libya.

After some meager successes with the early FAHD, Gaddafi was excited and encouraged. He rewarded Abu Manu with a large tract of land for a training camp and a home in Benghazi. For his students and graduates, the Libyan government provided passports, scholarships for studying languages overseas, and a large stipend to live on.

Gaddafi was impressed with Abu Manu's foresight and acumen when he learned that the students always trained at night. He was most excited by Abu Manu's building an underground training camp far from the eyes of the American satellites. Brilliantly conceived, the base was hidden in plain sight.

After a tour of the underground facilities, Gaddafi knew he had in Abu Manu the right combination of intelligence, dedication, and loyalty, and he committed to fund whatever the man needed. He first provided Abu Manu with 10,000 Libyan dinars a month for his small, special-activities army. That eventually grew to 100,000 dinars a month, more than enough to train a handful of special-purpose warriors.

Along with being provided assault rifles, handguns, and other direct assault weapons from around the world, trainees learned the art of bomb making, hand-to-hand combat, scuba diving, parachuting, and English, just like their American counterparts. Abu Manu asked for and received Russian anti-aircraft and antitank weapons from Gaddafi's inventories for advanced weapons training. The more he asked, the more Abu Manu received.

He and Gaddafi became friends, but Abu Manu always knew his place. He complemented Gaddafi on his wisdom, support, and generosity. Gaddafi returned the compliment by saying Abu Manu was a nightmare for America. He was a spirit who moved only at night, creating nightmares. Armed with his FAHD, Gaddafi believed he was a man of destiny and would do great things for the Arab world...and punish the Americans.

In four years, Abu Manu had a steady sponsor, and his graduates could conduct operations in the sea, on land, and from the air, all under cover of darkness. He wasn't certain they were as good as Navy SEALs, but they were the first generation and the finest Muslim special operations forces in all of Islam. Weight and martial arts training were expanded. Skinny recruits became motivated bodybuilders. Improvements always were substantial and trended upward.

Two years later, Gaddafi had his FAHD. Two dozen specially trained mercenaries were on call for any special operation his Libyan intelligence department couldn't carry out. They continued improving their skills and lethality, practicing in Libya and the Sudan. They were given a license to kill.

At the end of their training, Abu Manu issued the graduates a "get out of jail free card" signed by "His Excellency Colonel Muammar Gaddafi." In bold script, the cards ordered, *The bearer of this card will not be interfered with in the performance of his duty by the Military Police or by any other military organization.*

Carlos the Jackal had been a petty but ruthless murderer, killing targets of opportunity under the guise of what was necessary for the liberation of Palestine. The Abu Nidal Organization, led by the inept Abu Nidal and aided by the Russians and Saddam Hussein, provided the concept of Muslim special operations training led by the former Muhammad Ali Shazzami al-Bakaar.

Suddenly, the most-lethal and clandestine terrorist leader was someone no one ever heard of. Abu Manu developed and provided the finest stealthy Muslim commandos in Africa and the Middle East for Muammar Gaddafi. He also kept a few for himself.

When Abu Manu began receiving shipments of American, Russian, British, and French anti-aircraft and antitank weapons for training, he cautiously diverted some to sell on the black market. He was in Benghazi, while Gaddafi was in Tripoli. Gaddafi would kill him if he found out, but he had his own FAHD to keep him safe. If he had to escape, he had his little airplanes at the airport.

Gaddafi would never know Abu Manu trafficked in man-portable air-defense systems, MANPADS, for almost twenty years. He would never know Abu Manu could fly small planes. Abu Manu's FAHD, the instructor cadre of his special operations forces, was perfectly loyal to him. He trained them to be assassins and world-class warriors. He brought his Panthers out of poverty and they lived well in Benghazi. They would do anything for him in exchange for the training he provided, the money he paid, and for caring for their families. Abu Manu was a smart, gifted leader as well as a businessman and pilot.

The American intelligence community was always the last to know when anti-aircraft and antitank missiles popped up for sale on the black market. Abu Manu's small group of FAHDs facilitated the purchase of the missiles, but more often, his FAHD would overpower the sellers and steal them. His FAHD stole Russian, British, and French MANPADS before the CIA began providing American-made *Stingers* to the mujahidin in Afghanistan.

His stockpile of MANPADS grew each year, cleverly hidden in plain sight in his hometown of Benghazi at the family business. That the family was an importer and exporter, with a large fleet of trucks, made them the perfect front company to move MANPADS across the Middle East when needed. Gold coin was the currency. The U.S. was paying him in gold coin not to shoot down any more airliners and not to send more anthrax to American shores.

The organization he so carefully constructed was on a path to destruction. He didn't interpret the signs that were more obvious each day. The idiot Muslim President encouraged al-Qaeda and the Muslim Brotherhood, under the guise of democracy, to replace the leadership from Morocco to Egypt. His speeches sealed Gaddafi's fate. The black flag of al-Qaeda and the green flag of the Muslim Brotherhood began to sprout in the Benghazi neighborhood. It wasn't until it reached a tipping point, when large groups of al-Qaeda and the Brotherhood oozed from compounds all across North Africa, that Benghazi became too unstable for his family, so he moved them to Algeria. There was no time to move his huge inventory. As Gaddafi was chased from his palace Abu Manu barely got his family out of Libya safely. Some loyalists of his FAHD, their pockets heavy from Abu Manu's gold reserves, remained behind to protect their homes and Abu Manu's compound, as well as his inventory of MANPADS.

He completely misread the strength of the rebel forces' commitment to overthrow Gaddafi. He couldn't envision Libya without his benefactor. After Gaddafi fell, Americans and British intelligence agents moved into Tripoli and other cities, including his hometown, establishing consulates and encouraging business. His FAHD reported the American Consulate was established near his family compound. Abu Manu missed his opportunity to move his inventory to a safe location, but he suddenly faced a greater dilemma. He couldn't afford to let his 1,000 MANPADS fall into the hands of al-Qaeda or the Muslim Brotherhood.

It was time to liquidate. The Americans would buy. They always paid in bullion or gold coin. His loyal FAHD would oversee the transaction.

Chased out of Iraq, then Libya, he had unfinished business in Algiers. Algeria was stable for the moment. In addition to the apartment complex in the middle of Algiers, high on a hill overlooking the bay, he had a great house several dozen miles away overlooking the Mediterranean Sea.

He was getting too old to manage properly his three wives and four children, all defective. It was obvious he was the defective one. The women were beautiful, the best money could buy, but for heirs, they were the worst, and money couldn't save them. His wives grew tired of caring for a house full of crippled adult children. The best he could do was make his shattered children comfortable. Every wife shunned him, as if he carried plague. It was heartbreaking.

Abu Manu ignored al-Qaeda and the Muslim Brotherhood competing for and dominating local politics. Al-Qaeda was brash, while the Brotherhood was subtle but untrustworthy. Both organizations, seeking to fill a spiritual vacuum, expanded across North Africa, primarily from the hotbeds of Egypt. It was clear to him that Tunisia would be the next to fall under the black or green flag of the extremists. The only other place to run to and survive was in Algeria.

The apartment in Algiers was the perfect place for his family, close to hospitals, with a strong government that didn't tolerate rebels crossing the border. His family would live in Algiers, and he would be nearby, either languishing in the little courtyard in Algiers or enjoying his villa by the sea. Unfortunately, he couldn't always enjoy the house on the shore for fear of U.S. Navy SEALs finding him and dragging him across the beach and drowning him in the Mediterranean Sea.

He cupped his head in his hands, his sunglasses fell off. He lamented the al-Qaeda and the Muslim Brotherhood had gotten out of control. They were run by weak-minded, pedestrian leaders whose only apparent goal was to create chaos and decimate other Muslims.

The Muslim Brotherhood used to have the greatest leaders and thinkers like Sayyid Qutb, an author, educator, poet, and the leading member of the Egyptian Muslim Brotherhood. Osama bin Laden and the al-Qaeda artfully brought America to its knees.

It wasn't like the days when the cream rose to the top. The top had become dominated and diluted by idiots. Qutb wouldn't recognize the Muslim Brotherhood anymore, and Abu Manu had long abandoned their murderous change in philosophy and refused to be associated with such an unprofessional radical and corrupt organization. Bin Laden was dead, and hundreds of others died with him, killed by SEALs and unmanned airplanes.

Even America proved it was possible to elect simpletons to the highest level, but not the fighter-pilot President. He invaded Afghanistan and Iraq and scared Gaddafi into surrendering his programs to produce weapons of mass destruction. Instead, he quickly made peace with the U.S. Had he not, Gaddafi knew he was next to be eliminated by the unmanned airplanes with missiles.

Then the Muslim President undid it all, embracing the roustabouts of al-Qaeda and the radicals of the Muslim Brotherhood. He unleashed them to spread hate and terror across Africa. With imbeciles in charge of al-Qaeda and the Muslim Brotherhood, they couldn't be trusted with leverage weapons like anti-aircraft missiles. They would be unrestrained, out of control, and indiscriminate; they would shoot down Islamic countries' aircraft as well as American and British airliners. Abu Manu could never allow that to occur.

He'd never been much of a hand wringer, but Abu Manu had gotten old. There were times when he hadn't looked back and didn't second-guess decisions made in real time even when he had imperfect information. Given time, he could always think through the challenges and logistics of a problem. He sensed when the time was right for one of his special operations. As he grew older, he found himself failing in ways small and large, and he couldn't resist self-recriminations.

He sat in the sun, away from the wives who hated him and the cripples who didn't know him. He awaited the hours to pass when he would leave for the coast to get away, await the shipment, and tempt fate.

He brightened, as he committed himself to fly his airplane. It might be the last time he'd be able to experience the freedom, the rumbling humming, of the big nine-cylinder radial engine. There was the joy and rush of acceleration and the challenge of airmanship.

Another thought came to him. Maybe he'd be kidnapped by American SEALs—and maybe he wouldn't. Maybe he'd be targeted by America's funny little unmanned airplanes—and maybe he wouldn't. If they tried, they'd ride a ball of flame to Hell.

CHAPTER TWENTY

2200 September 20, 2012
U.S. Embassy
Tripoli, Libya

After five days of protestors shouting, "Death to America!" and "God is Great!" among other things in Arabic, the *Chargé d'Affaires* reluctantly determined it was time to evacuate again. The embassy had been open only for a year before being evacuated the previous year. Then it was closed for almost a year. One month of grueling security work followed, as twelve experts inspected the buildings and grounds for booby traps or mines. Inside, they checked for listening and surveillance devices.

With the death of Muammar Gaddafi, and rebel groups vying for control of the former kingdom, Libyan security and stability were in a state of flux. Terrorist groups rushed into the major cities to fill the leadership vacuum, seeking a place at the table as they noisily obtruded their position. The country's security and stability continued to deteriorate with the black flags of al-Qaeda or the green flags of the Muslim Brotherhood metastasizing around the broken country. Each group competed for followers.

With the recent killing of the Ambassador to Libya, waves of daily protests at the embassy gate, and more-aggressive activities, including some carrying AK-47s and rocket-propelled grenades, the State Department capitulated and ordered the noncombatant evacuation operation for embassy personnel.

That was well and good, except the NEO encompassed only actual embassy personnel. Contractors working for the State Department or the CIA weren't invited to depart but were "reprogrammed" and given new taskings.

Bill McGee and his SEALs thought they were seeing a replay. When the first wave of protestors marched toward the U.S. Embassy, the local Libyan security personnel abandoned their weapons and posts, and ran. For the former SEALs, such a response by the local constabulary presaged an attack. The local Libyans knew they were about to be overrun or attacked and got out while they could. Or they were part of it. Just like Benghazi.

With few other security resources available, McGee and his team broke out several high-capacity magazines for their black M-4s, night vision scopes, and several grenades. The bald, corpulent pantywaist of a *Chargé d'Affaires,* fearing an overreaction, strenuously voiced his concern urging restraint and calm.

"The situation isn't that dire," he exclaimed to the heavily muscled men who arrived from Benghazi.

McGee jammed a huge, banana-shaped magazine into the decked-out M-4 assault rifle and said, "Your amazing lack of security resulted in a dead ambassador and foreign service officer. You obviously don't understand;these guys play for keeps. I'm not asking permission. I am shooting the first asshole who comes over the wall."

The little fat effeminate diplomat nearly fainted.

McGee didn't have an opportunity to shoot the first asshole who tried to come over the wall, because no one did. Maybe the Muslim Brotherhood masquerading as security officers told their friends there were some very bad men on the embassy grounds, for within minutes, the protesters dispersed and were gone. The grounds were quiet as well as the road in front of the embassy.

The former SEALs continued to walk the grounds of the once-magnificent chancery, constantly checking the perimeter inside the wall and out. They used cover and concealment, and checked for movement and listened for aural clues.

It was quiet. At times, it was *too* quiet. The good news was they were back in their element, working at night, locked and loaded for serious ass-kicking. Their presence and confidence calmed the anxiety of most of the embassy personnel. Feeling the security situation was stable for the first time in months, the men and women relaxed. Some slept, while others packed to depart in the morning.

The bad news was intelligence sources confirmed there would be several demonstrations at the embassy beginning at sunrise.

The plan for the morning, before daybreak, as everyone quietly departed the embassy, was that the U.S. State Department would announce it was temporarily removing its staff for security reasons. Two aircraft would evacuate the embassy's noncombatant personnel as well as the support contractors. Embassy staff would take a jet to Germany. McGee and his SEALs would board the old gray Gooney Bird, the Basler, for Algeria.

McGee looked up toward the embassy windows. No light leaked from them. Special blinds kept light from escaping. Prying eyes with telescopes couldn't monitor the activity in the offices. He knew CIA officers were working overtime to shred files, destroy computers, and ruin sensitive communication equipment. He envisioned the huge, heavy contraptions called disintegrators and industrial-sized shredders turning paper, plastic, and metal to pulp. Anything fed in was chopped into unrecognizable fragments. The shredders ran nonstop, sucking slick shredder oil from gallon jugs to lubricate the spinning blades, turning reams of paper into a million chads in seconds.

As he and his SEALs patrolled the embassy grounds, and as CIA officers destroyed anything with a classification, fresh intel came to the *Chargé d-Affaires* office to suggest the morning would be a different story from the one they planned.

CHAPTER TWENTY-ONE

2200 September 20, 2012
U.S. Embassy
Algiers, Algeria

Nazy Cunningham left her office and locked the door behind her. Still feeling the effects of her bouts of nausea from the morning, she took the elevator to the ground floor instead of the stairs. While waiting for the lift to reach her floor, she glanced at the big metal door and checked that the SCIF was locked. It was. A dull chime signaled the arrival of the lift, and she stepped inside, taking a slow ride down to the main floor.

She waved to the Marine behind the thick bulletproof glass, as she left the main building for her quarters. She inhaled the fresh Algerian coastal air; the cool night air felt good on her face and arms. The compound was fairly well lit, and she cautiously walked across the uneven flagstones to the apartments for the senior civil servants. Technically, she was the second senior person at the embassy, after the U.S. Ambassador. As the trade attaché, she was just another of several run-of-the-mill GS-15s at the embassy on an overseas assignment.

She swiped her electronic key to open the lobby door of the apartment complex and stepped inside. The long walk down the hall to the end apartment momentarily reminded her of Duncan's building and room at the Naval War College. He had a magnificent view of Narragansett Bay through a large picture window. Her room had small frosted windows, reinforced with iron bars, which would have looked over the parking lot if it were possible to open the window. It snowed the entire time she was in Newport with Duncan. It hadn't rained since she arrived in Algiers.

She didn't have to rummage through her purse. She knew exactly where to put her hand as she reached in and withdrew the antique rhombus key tag with the number 7 hammered into the brass plate. Like she had for the previous several weeks, she wrestled with the stout, stainless key until the heavy lock acquiesced.

Nazy flipped the light switch and walked inside, tossing her purse onto the small dining table as the heavy door closed silently behind her. She slid the deadbolt closed and smelled the stale air inside. The air-conditioning near the ceiling was turned on with a remote control. She was home.

As if some Pavlovian response was triggered upon entering the apartment, she immediately stepped forward to look at the countertop where a BlackBerry personal communication device lay, plugged into its charger, and saw a blinking red light.

Texts from Duncan! Keying through the screens to reach the messages from her lover and best friend, they instantly made her feel better.

The little *billets-doux* from Hunter were always just short, sweet lines of love or lust, written in BlackBerry-ese in a short agglomeration of letters and symbols to convey a message in the least possible number of strokes. Sometimes just three letters—IMU—would have her pining for him.

Rarely were their BlackBerries used for anything but an exchange of private thoughts. The little black cellular telephones used special data-network authentication with an unbreakable encryption key. The software successfully passed the highly advanced security tests conducted by the Israeli Ministry of Defense and the CIA's Science and Technology Directorate. Any conversation would be secure and should avoid the scrutiny of the NSA's ECHELON computers, which could break any encrypted voice or data transmission. Voice communications could be intercepted.

After debating with herself all day and reading the half-dozen lines of coded love and sensual suggestions, Nazy turned serious and contemplated sending him a message, a warning. They never had a reason to exchange classified information for fear of losing their clearances and livelihood. After years of being entrusted with some of the government's most-sensitive secrets, a breach at their level would mean not only losing their jobs but losing their freedom. Could she say anything that would warn him not to come to Algeria?

In the end, she took a deep breath, and cradled the device in both hands. For a moment, she wavered, and then her thumbs raced over the kcys.

CHAPTER TWENTY-TWO

0100 September 21, 2012
San Antonio International Airport, Texas

Hunter returned his BlackBerry to its holster as he departed the jetway and spilled out onto the American Airlines concourse. Tired from traveling all day, he felt distracted. He dwelled on Nazy's text message, rolling it around in his mind like tumbleweeds in high winds. He succumbed to the distraction; he tripped and nearly tumbled down the escalator leading to passenger pickup. Even bush-tired, his mongoose-like reflexes saved him from major injury and major embarrassment after he stepped where there wasn't anything under his foot.

After composing and admonishing himself, he hurried through baggage claim. A pair of automatic glass doors separated at his approach. The San Antonio heat assaulted him, as he stepped outside and looked for his ride. He saw the top of the truck moving through traffic a hundred yards away and raised his free hand as Carlos Yazzie flashed the headlights to acknowledge.

Seconds later, the immaculate black Hummer2 pulled to the curb, and Hunter waited until the massive, armor-protected door stopped moving before he jumped in.

He shook Carlos' hand and set his briefcase on the back seat. Hunter ignored the seat belt.

"Welcome home, Boss."

Hunter tried to stifle a yawn but failed. Yazzie waited for an opening in traffic before pulling out.

"Sorry for being late, Carlos," Hunter said. "We were late leaving Dallas. The jet broke down. We know what that's like. For a while, I thought I'd have to drive home from DFW."

"I would've come to get you."

"I know, but no factor. They fixed whatever was wrong, so I made it."

"You look beat, Boss."

"I am tired. I worked all week and flew all day. If I fall asleep, it's because I'm bushed, not a reflection on your sparkling conversation." He slowly buckled up while grinning at the ruddy, fit Apache with a high and tight haircut. Yazzie continued to wear his hair short after he retired from the Marine Corps, like many former Jarheads. "How's Theresa?"

"As feisty as ever. Now that we have Miss Horne visiting, she's excited about cooking a wider variety of meals."

"I'm wounded, crushed even. Is that her way of saying I'm picky?"

"Oh, no. Theresa found out Miss Horne loves Mexican food, so they make a little bit of this and a little bit of that—even hand-made tortillas. Miss Horne loves guacamole, chips, and your favorite salsa."

"Your bride sure can cook."

Without taking his eyes off the road, Yazzie slapped his belly. "Don't I know it!"

They shared a laugh, and then the cabin fell quiet. Hunter leaned his head back and was asleep in seconds.

Yazzie pulled out of the airport and headed north on Interstate 10 toward Fredericksburg. The seventy-mile trip passed in silence except for Hunter's moderate snoring.

When they arrived at the ranch house, Carlos eased the big black Hummer to a stop at the front door. As if on cue, Hunter awoke, stretched, and slapped Yazzie's back. He opened the heavy door and slid to the ground.

"Thank you, Carlos. Please tell Theresa no breakfast for me in the morning. I'll be sleeping in."

"Wilco, Boss. Get some sleep."

"I will. Good night. See you in the morning."

The naps on the plane and truck provided sufficient rest for Hunter to bypass the bedroom and head to his office. Dozens of racquetball trophies and large airplane models filled dozens of shelves.

Racquetball plagues, photographs, and lithographs of airplanes he flew competed for space on the walls. An ancient propeller from a Fokker Dr1, the aircraft made famous by the Bloody Red Baron, Manfred von Richthofen, hung over the door. In a corner sat a banged-up ejection seat from the F-4 Phantom from which Hunter once ejected. His old flying helmet and oxygen mask sat on the seat cushion, icons of his former life.

An eight-foot-wide triangle of smooth canyon onyx wedged into the opposite corner served as a desktop. At one end of the polished slab rested a shiny black model of a YO-3A impaled on a carved mahogany base. His old Marine Corps leather flight jacket draped over the back of his desk chair. The black nametag sported Naval aviator's gold wings and read *Maverick*.

He moved to the center of the desk and awoke the multi-touch desktop computer with a shake of the mouse, typed in several log-ins and passwords, and sat in the chair. His hands flew over the three-foot-wide touchscreen, tapping computer icons and opening programs and web sites that provided email, world news, and international weather. Since he wouldn't have the services of a combat weather forecaster, he had to brief the weather himself. His priorities were the forecasts for Algeria and Southern Spain, which looked reasonable for the next ten days.

He turned to his heavily encrypted email. Bob and Bob confirmed they were picked up by a USAF C-17. They and the *Wraith* were en route to Andrews Air Force Base.

Director Rothwell confirmed the plan was a go. Hunter received the President's authorization to cross the Algerian border. Rothwell indicated he would have recent satellite imagery of the mission target area before takeoff.

Another Rothwell email confirmed an Agency asset would depart Andrews AFB the evening of the 23rd. Hunter checked the time at the corner of the monitor and calculated he had roughly forty hours before they would leave.

Hunter logged off the classified network, switched to an

unclassified email system, and read a string of email from nearly every one of his students. He sent them a blanket message to announce that class for the week would be canceled and provided a list of reading and written assignments for the following week's class. He carefully worded his closing line to say he'd be *out of pocket* for at least a week.

He replied to Kelly Horne that he'd be available for dinner on the 21st, either in Del Rio or Fredericksburg or somewhere between, signing it *Dad*.

Several emails from Greg Lynche provided the status of the YO-3A auction. Lynche looked forward to flying to Washington State to ensure Hunter won the auction. With the only flyable copy outside of NASA's YO-3A, a second Yo-Yo would double their capacity.

We just need another pilot. He jammed fingers in his eyes and rubbed vigorously. He sang, "You picked a fine time to leave me Greg Lynche...." *I need a sensor operator, actually.* He returned to the keyboard, tapping his foot.

He replied that once they won the aircraft, Greg needed to ship it to Fredericksburg. With the Schweizer Aircraft Company closed, Hunter would have to overhaul and update the aircraft himself. He already talked with Saul Ferrier and received assurances he would contact some of his old employees. They were confident a new Yo-Yo could be rebuilt in 007's image.

The next set of email he opened and considered were from his general manager of HAVCO Technologies, Hunter's aviation manufacturing and restoration company. Most of the messages consisted of status reports of the quiet aircraft in production for the Nigerian Air Force. One message was intriguing, but Hunter didn't want to deal with the issue of naming the aircraft, though he had to call them something. The GM, Cory Duarte, suggested calling them the *Hunter*.

Hunter typed a quick reply.

Hunter's already taken—some Army UAVs. I lean toward Harpo, short for Harpocrates, the Greek god of silence. Recall Harpo Marx was the quiet one in Marx Brothers films. The Greek god of chaos, Eris, is also the Daughter of the Night. I think Daughter of the Night is a better fit. What do you think?

Most of the remaining emails were from his scientists at Quiet Aero Systems, and they could wait. He'd see them in the morning.

Hunter closed out all the programs and put the computer to sleep. He extracted his BlackBerry and read Nazy's message again.

I think I'm pregnant.

CHAPTER TWENTY-THREE

0500 September 21, 2012
U.S. Embassy
Tripoli, Libya

Roads in Libya weren't the best and traffic was the worst. Accustomed to jetting from location to location, Eastwood was accustomed to the rigors of road travel in Africa and the Middle East. In Europe and North America, the countryside flew by while driving at high speed on miles of smooth concrete or asphalt expressways. Potholes, while infrequent, were typically small and easily avoidable. In Libya, most towns were connected by two-lane roads of remarkably poor condition, interspersed with traffic-slowing obstacles. Some would call the obstacles "bomb craters," but they could have been made by improvised explosive devices or a bomb dropped from an airplane, but most likely, they came from artillery.

The deep road obstacles grew in length, width, and depth, because there were no repair crews in the country to stop erosion and destruction. Vehicles lumbered into the abyss, breaking off more and more of the roadbed and substrate, carrying off fragments of the road with every passing vehicle.

Even within the washed-out areas of roadbed there were significant holes and bumps. Demetrius Eastwood's English-speaking guide and driver, Khalid al-Awalaki, fought the steering wheel and brake to negotiate one of the most-substantial stretches of holes in the road. He couldn't move forward until the vehicle ahead moved, and that one couldn't move until the one in front of it moved, and so on. Speed was measured in inches per minute when flopping around in the belly of a twenty-foot wide, ten-foot deep ditch. When drivers were able to amble over one of the bumpy edges, they drove as fast as they could to make up for lost time, again closing the gap between vehicles and getting in line while maintaining their interval. Eastwood thought Khalid drove too close to the vehicle ahead, and the man honked his horn incessantly. A comment wouldn't calm his concerns. That was how people drove in Libya and rural Africa under those conditions.

Before they set off to return to the capital, they learned all Tripoli-bound traffic had been diverted to alternate roads because of banditry and bombs. What had been a passable, four-lane highway just hours before, was no longer and forced Khalid to detour to the north. The four men traveled hundreds of miles over three days, going through the seaside towns of Ajdabiya, Sirte, Mistrata, and Homs before reaching Tripoli. They were continually stuck behind trucks and buses belching thick, gritty exhaust. The four-door Toyota had no air-conditioning to help them escape asphyxiation.

Khalid passed such obstacles whenever he could, only to get stuck behind taxicabs that looked as if they were refugees from a demolition derby. Most of the taxis had windshields, all had a working horn, and their drivers used them constantly. With the exception of a few private cars and pickups, every vehicle on the road was overloaded with people. A tiny Nissan taxi sometimes carried eight adults. A truck might have twenty or thirty. A bus had one hundred, with forty bodies hanging on the roof or off the back. The strain broke the undercarriage of many of those vehicles, as the remnants of hundreds of cars littering the sides of the highway showed. All were stripped of any usable spare parts. The horn was the first thing cannibalized from an abandoned vehicle.

Gaddafi's overthrow and subsequent civil war left the infrastructure and transportation systems in ruin. Fuel was scarce. Electrical power was nonexistent unless someone owned a generator. There were places to find food but few beds. Bandits staked out checkpoints, as did the new government. It was hard to tell who was official and who was an opportunistic crook.

Khalid was a man of many driving talents, one of which was sensing trouble and being able to steer around it. The trip to and from Benghazi had been trouble-free except when their Toyota HiLux got a flat tire when they avoided an impromptu checkpoint set up by a black-flag-waving al-Qaeda affiliate.

With no flag to signify if the men were al-Qaeda or the Muslim Brotherhood or the new Libyan government—if that was even possible—they left the roadbed and cautiously drove around the checkpoint. With four-wheel drive, it was best to consider them all bandits and take the road less traveled.

When they couldn't detour and were forced to queue and submit their travel documents, Khalid was able to convince those at the checkpoints that his friends were world-famous journalists who had to reach Benghazi to report on the attacks there. Stopping at checkpoints allowed al-Awalaki to smoke, share a cigarette with the guard, and obtain information. Some of the stubborn bandits at the checkpoints wouldn't let them proceed until there were gifts and fares offered. The philosophy was, *No pinch, no pass.*

On one occasion, a simpleminded oaf with an AK-47 demanded to know if the white men were Americans or Europeans. Khalid puffed himself up and became indignant, railing at the man.

"Who are you looking for? These are not the people you're looking for! Famous journalists from Europe! Let us pass!"

He ridiculed the guard for detaining them, uttering passages from the Qur'an and challenging the man with the gun to finish the verse of the *sura.* When the dullard couldn't, he felt ashamed, and Khalid continued his vituperation and verbally abused the man, at the end of his diatribe calling him an imbecile.

"It's apostasy, a profound insult to God! *You don't know the Qur'an?*! How can anyone let an idiot have a weapon and man a checkpoint?"

Eastwood and his crew grew increasingly nervous at Khalid's antics. Not knowing what he was saying, they wished he would tone it down. To a man, they waited for the Libyan with the machine gun to rack the charging handle and shoot them all.

When the ashamed man turned away and directed them to pass, Eastwood breathed easier. He'd been to the Middle East countless times and felt confident he knew the price of admission, the "pinch," a tribute, was required to facilitate passage.

At every checkpoint, he handed Khalid a half-ounce gold Krugerrand to expedite their departure. Eastwood decided Khalid may not have fully understood what the gold was for. In every case, he challenged the checkpoint personnel. After securing passage, Khalid kept the coins until he had six gold coins in his shirt pocket following six checkpoint encounters.

Khalid was a motivated and thorough driver and guide. He always found wonderful places to eat with great food and service, and he bought fuel at the best prices. He secured adequate overnight accommodations for his passengers in walled compounds in Misrata and Sirte. Khalid slept in the truck, fearing it might be pilfered or stolen.

When they entered Benghazi, Khalid pulled over several times to ask locals what happened or was about to happen in the city, more so, on the return to Tripoli. Those conversations with the residents were invaluable, and as Khalid translated Eastwood took furious notes. Khalid was a treasure trove of information.

After leaving the burned-out consulate, Khalid negotiated several potholes, some of which would completely hide their four-wheel-drive truck, as well as several makeshift checkpoints, where downed palm trees or decrepit, disassembled vehicles functioned as barriers. Some vehicles flew black flags, marking al-Qaeda or an affiliate or a supporter.

At the outskirts of Benghazi, Khalid found another small shop, what would be considered in the U.S. a storage space with a heavy, galvanized, roll-up door. A pair of skinned, gutted carcasses hung from the opening. Eastwood thought they could be the remains of a cat or small dog.

Excited, Khalid stopped for food and drinks. As he did throughout the journey, he struck up a conversation with the merchant. Eastwood and his crew, taking seats near the opening, demanded Khalid ensure the critters for lunch were goat or sheep, not puppies or kittens.

After a lengthy discussion, where both men flailed their arms in supplication several times, Khalid returned to the table where his passengers sat. Eastwood, slightly agitated, stared at the driver, then glanced at the dried, skinned animals.

"Goat," Khalid said.

Eastwood was visibly relieved, but he noticed Khalid's demeanor changed significantly after speaking with the shop owner.

Looking around to ensure he wasn't overheard, Khalid said, "Everyone is afraid. Muslim Brotherhood is growing but also moving west. So is al-Qaeda."

"How are they traveling?" Eastwood asked. "By truck or bus?"

Khalid shook his head in confusion. "No provide good answer. He say they move west but no one leaves homes or mosque. No one explain. Very strange."

"If no one has left Benghazi, why do they say they moved?" Eastwood knew vehicles and fuel were scarce, but the highways overflowed with trucks, buses, and cars. Anything could be had if one were willing to pay enough.

"Maybe I confuse word. Maybe not move, but...." He paused in thought. Removing the gold coins from his pocket, he stacked them on the table. The three men focused on the short stack of new Krugerrands, as Khalid placed his hand on the stack and spread them out uniformly. He looked at Eastwood for confirmation.

"Spread?" Eastwood asked.

Khalid smiled and nodded. "Yes. That's it. Brotherhood and al-Qaeda spread ... west." He returned the coins to his pocket. "When we get food, we leave."

Six hours after leaving the sleepy waterfront town of Homs, the slowly stifling traffic suddenly dissipated, as the road doubled the number of available driving lanes. Khalid soon passed overstressed trucks and buses, dodging overfilled taxis and private motorcars, until he drove into a quiet, nearly deserted Tripoli.

Khalid and Eastwood yawned and repositioned their asses in their seats, as if their butts knew the trip was almost over. Eastwood remained in the passenger seat, keeping Khalid engaged in conversation, worried the man might fall asleep and swerve into oncoming traffic and kill them all. Eastwood had no desire to die in Libya.

When they left the inappropriately described "high-speed road" it was easy to relax and lower their guard. Without other vehicles on the road that serviced several embassies, Eastwood directed Khalid to a hotel close to the U.S. Embassy. He looked forward to going to the embassy in the morning and, if possible, interview the *Chargé d-Affaires* for his story.

Khalid knew the way. After several turns and negotiating a pair of roundabouts, he took the access road leading to the U.S. Embassy. With half a mile to go, he braked hard, almost coming to a full stop.

Eastwood was almost asleep when Khalid said, "Something wrong."

Eastwood and the others came instantly awake.

"What?" Eastwood asked.

Khalid killed the headlights, pulled over to the side of the road, and stopped. He pointed ahead.

At the far end of the boulevard, part of the U.S. Embassy was brightly lit. "Lamps out," he explained. "Many.... All lamps out."

Eastwood noticed the pitch-black space ahead. The only bright lights that were seen illuminated the high, white embassy walls in the distance. There was about half a mile of empty blackness ahead; side roads had an occasional lighted streetlamp.

Before Eastwood could ask why they were sitting in the middle of the road, Khalid looked left and right, shifted into reverse, and backed up.

Eastwood and his crew held on to steady themselves, concerned by Khalid's sudden behavior. Adrenalin spiked in all of the men, making their bodies tingle. The three Americans looked at the driver, who was past being concerned and approached being afraid.

"What do you see, Khalid?"

Nearly whispering, pointing with one hand, he said, "Many men leaving mosques...there and there. Peoples should be asleep. Mosque not open. No prayers at this time. Lights out only this place. Very bad."

Eastwood and his crew became the lookouts, searching right, left and behind for threats. Convinced the action was directly ahead, Eastwood whispered over his shoulder, "Marty, I don't know what we're seeing, but can you get it on camera?"

"I'm doing it. I can see it. Something is definitely up." Cameraman Marty Marceau extricated his video recorder from its case. The silence in the truck was broken by the sound of fasteners being unlatched, switches thrown, and buttons pushed. LEDs glowed in the rear of the truck, as the video camera powered up.

The other man in the back seat retrieved a handheld, low-light TV camera from a bag on the floor. As it energized, he rolled down the window and monitored the activity coming from the side roads.

"They're spilling out of the mosques, there's one on the left and one on the right. *Crap!* Some have AKs and RPGs. They're trying to hide them, but most seem to be carrying something. Looks like at least one has a grappling hook. *Look!*" He handed the device over the front seat to Eastwood's shoulder.

"What?" He snatched the LLTV camera from the man's hand and peered through the viewfinder. "Shit. This is bad." His head snapped up, and he whispered, "They're going after the embassy; is this what they did in Benghazi?"

He watched men with weapons bunch up at the corners of the roads on the left and right.

"I think they're waiting for a signal to start the attack. Marty, you getting this?"

As the cameraman stepped outside his heart pounded with the onrush of fear. He moved to the truck's hood to steady his camera lest his filming was a jumbled shaken mess.

No one noticed a film crew 100 yards away recording the prefrontal assault on the U.S. Embassy, still bright in the distance.

Eastwood checked his watch. It was 0500. When he looked up again, the lights flooding the embassy wall suddenly went out. Half a mile of road was plunged into darkness.

"Shit, shit, shit! They're sitting ducks!" He re-looked into the LLTV eyepiece and scanned the awaiting crowds to find them suddenly agitated and probably ready move toward the embassy; he then panned the device down the road toward the embassy. "Wait. Vehicles are leaving the embassy. Shit, I hope they don't come this way. It's going to be an ambush if they do."

Leaning on the hood, still filming, Mary said, "They're moving. Bad guys moving. Something started them moving."

Eastwood returned to the night-vision device. "They aren't coming this way. They're going the opposite direction. Shit, that's good. They must be evacuating the embassy. That's eight cars and trucks. There's even someone's closing and locking the gate."

"The crowd knows they're late," Marty said from the hood. "They watched them leave. They're running down the road now. Show's over, I think."

He crawled off the hood and returned to the rear of the vehicle, opened his door, and replaced the camera in its bag before sitting behind Khalid. He patted his chest to slow his heart down.

Khalid, ready to leave, looked at Eastwood for instructions. Eastwood handed the LLTV to the outstretched hand from the back seat. "You get all that?"

"Yep."

"They evacuated," Eastwood said to himself. "The embassy knew they were coming, or they were lucky and got out just in time. OK. Evacuations. They must be heading to the airport. Khalid, to the airport? But let's not go that way."

CHAPTER TWENTY-FOUR

0530 September 21, 2012
Tripoli International Airport

The intelligence received over the previous twenty-four hours was damning and correct. The Chief of Station, a twenty-year career CIA intelligence officer, received a call from one of his sources that the embassy would be attacked, just like Benghazi, at five o'clock that morning. He informed the *Chargé d'Affaires* and CIA Langley and started the daunting task of shredding files and destroying sensitive communication equipment ahead of schedule. He had experience evacuating and returning to the Tripoli Embassy. Two years earlier, as well-armed rebels attacked Gaddafi's strongholds, the embassy was repeatedly assaulted by groups of poorly armed rebels. Post-Gaddafi Tripoli was in chaos without a working head of government and no local constabulary to provide protection under international treaty.

On that day, U.S. Marine helicopters dispatched from U.S. Navy carriers landed inside the embassy compound and evacuated the staff and their contracted security details. State Department and CIA personnel waited in Virginia and Germany for nine months before returning.

Once American boots were back on the ground in Tripoli, it was another two months before the embassy was back in shape before the Ambassador, the Chief of Station, and the State Department crew could return to a functional building and a safe complex. Specialized teams of carpenters, welders, plumbers, and electricians swooped into the compound and worked 24/7 to repair the damage done by the rebels. Security teams sniffed out electronic surveillance devices and booby traps, covering every inch of the chancery, the other buildings, and finally the entire grounds. Heavily armed personal security details protected the working men who wore body armor with their hard hats and utility belts.

Intelligence suggested it wasn't rebels that attacked an unprotected embassy. It was most likely al-Qaeda, one of its affiliates, or the Muslim Brotherhood. Whatever group organized the attacks wasn't important. What was paramount was knowledge—intelligence on the enemy regarding the timing of the assault if embassy personnel were to be evacuated safely. The timing could be delayed if the attackers brought high-powered weapons. In such a case, rescue helicopters from a nearby aircraft carrier couldn't risk coming into the compound for fear of being shot down. Being trapped like rats on a sinking ship wasn't an option; memories of the U.S. Embassy being overrun in Iran were always in the back of the minds of State Department executives.

It was better to leave before the bad guys arrived and let them have the building. The U.S. might return or it might not. Such decisions were above the Chief of Station's pay grade. Ten months after moving back in, he was packing his "trash" and heading out again. He thought that had to be a record.

What little intelligence they had was disturbing. Over the past few months, scores of Libyans seeking visas to travel to the U.S. were authorized to enter the embassy to process their applications and discuss travel requirements to the U.S. Most were legitimate travelers looking to escape Libya or visit family in America. However, there were always some, under the pretext of securing a visa, that came to observe the layout of the buildings, the times when security personnel changed shifts, or where or when security guards patrolled the grounds. No bit of information was insignificant. Any and all scraps were useful for the imams at the local mosques as they reconstructed the layout and understood the operational workings of the embassy.

There were secondary indications that something would soon occur at or near the embassy, too. Many Libyans hired locally to perform janitorial and landscaping services failed to come to work the day before the attack. Foot traffic in front of or across the street dropped to nothing. It was clear the neighborhood inhabitants knew an attack was coming, but it required an insider to alert the Chief of Station when the assault would begin.

Tertiary indications suggested the assault would proceed as planned by the informant. Bill McGee and his men monitored the comings and goings of twenty people congregating a third of a mile away. Men congregating late at night weren't noteworthy, but when they congregated near two mosques known for their anti-American imams, during a time when most Muslims were heading to bed, that was "proof enough" of the start of an imminent attack.

The pieces of the puzzle fit together rapidly. The show would begin on time, so the Americans planned to be long gone before they were trapped inside the embassy. The new Libyan government couldn't be counted on to protect embassy personnel, so the prudent thing to do was to evacuate. There would be another day to play diplomat.

Bill McGee was on the last vehicle to leave the embassy. Tonka closed the gate and secured it with a heavy chain and lock. It was a totally useless move, but it was required. As the four-door Toyota pickup left the embassy gate behind, with McGee and Tonka in the bed, McGee saw a horde, backlit from street lamps from the far end of the road, moving toward the embassy.

"Tonka, five minutes later, and we might've had a firefight," he said. "Look! Head's up; they may try to pop off an RPG!"

Tonka turned his head and saw the shadow of dozens of people moving toward the embassy, some carrying weapons. "We might not be out of the woods yet. Timing is everything, Bullfrog."

The string of embassy vehicles took a circuitous route to the airport, arriving ten minutes after they fled the embassy. McGee repositioned himself in the truck bed to watch several men leave their vehicles and run into the executive terminal. He turned as the sound of a truck approached from behind. McGee and Tonka positioned their M-4s to engage if the truck continued its trajectory toward the row of vehicles waiting to enter the airport gate.

"They aren't one of us," Tonka said, concern in his voice, as he raised his weapon. "They are at ramming speed...."

"No ... they're slowing." McGee raised his decked-out M-4 to a firing position, just in case the driver was a suicide bomber.

The truck quick-stopped when the two men aimed their weapons at the vehicle. A tall man in cargo pants and a denim shirt jumped from the Toyota and raced the forty yards to the trailing vehicle. McGee and Tonka lowered their M-4s slightly. Eastwood immediately knew his approach would be seen as threatening in the new world of suicide bombers. Stopping ten yards short, he raised his hands and shouted, "I'm American and unarmed!"

McGee recognized the tall, gray-haired man from his exposé broadcasts on the military. He and Tonka lowered their weapons. McGee jumped from the truck as the man approached.

"Colonel Demetrius Eastwood," McGee called, "what are you doing in Libya?"

Eastwood jogged forward with a smile. He recognized the huge black man, though he struggled to recall the name. The man was the most-decorated SEAL in the history of Special Operations Command, but the name momentarily escaped him. Was it Mac... Mick...Mc...Gill?

When he reached the side of the truck, he held out his hand. "Captain William McGee, I presume?"

McGee smiled and the two warriors shook hands vigorously. "Bill."

The other SEAL in the truck offered his hand, too. "Tonka. You do good work, Sir."

"Thank you. We try. What are you guys doing? We came back from Benghazi and were driving to the embassy. We watched you evacuate. You got out of there as forty unfriendlies with AKs and RPGs were moving toward you."

"Nonattribution?"

"Always!"

"NEO for the embassy personnel. We're heading to Algiers."

"Can I ask what you're doing in Libya?"

"You can't." McGee smiled.

Eastwood understood that McGee was on an operation, and he

knew it could be newsworthy. His curiosity was piqued. "Got it. What are you planning to do in Algeria?"

"Not real sure. Probably augment security there. Half of my crew's headed for Tunis. There may be another uprising. The Ambassador getting killed may have sparked more unrest across North Africa."

"That's why I'm here. Any comment on what happened with the Ambassador?"

"No, Sir. It was a surprise to me." McGee had the passing thought he shouldn't tell Eastwood anything. He was under orders to remain covert, even though his mission was scrubbed.

Eastwood quickly looked over his shoulder. "The word on the street is al-Qaeda or the Muslim Brotherhood is trying to spread and accelerate their influence over the region."

From the corner of his eye, Eastwood saw men run from the executive terminal. McGee and Tonka glanced over their shoulders. The access gate to the airport tarmac was opening, and vehicles at the front of the line began moving. McGee's truck shook, as the driver put it in gear and closed the interval with the truck ahead. They were about to leave.

"Gotta go, Colonel," McGee said. "I can probably get you aboard a plane to Germany. It might not be safe here."

Eastwood considered the offer. "I haven't been to Algeria. What are the chances my crew and I could go with you?"

"Not going to happen. We never had that conversation. You going to Germany?" McGee crawled back into the truck.

"Understand, Sir." Eastwood reached into the pickup bed to shake hands again. "Captain, Tonka. It's been a pleasure. I think there's another story that's related to the U.S. Ambassador getting killed. What we saw at the embassy was the start of an organized attack. We watched them come from a couple mosques. I can't shake the idea that what happened to the Ambassador would be replicated at the embassy. It was too well organized. They moved from Benghazi to Tripoli. I'm not sure who to blame, a rising al-Qaeda or the Muslim Brotherhood."

McGee's vehicle pulled away. Tonka braced himself from falling.

McGee steadied himself and called, "Don't look too hard, Colonel. You might not like what you find. Be safe."

"Maybe I'll see you in Algiers!" He waved as he shouted, then he watched the line of vehicles quickly pass through the access gate.

Eastwood stood in the roadbed until McGee's truck disappeared. He stared down at the ground, arms on his hips; lost in thought. His reverie interrupted when the sliding gate slowly closed. Suddenly feeling alone, he wondered if he made the right decision.

He walked back to the Toyota. When he climbed in, the crew looked at him with incredulity.

"Well?" they asked.

"Khalid, can you take us to Tunisia?"

"Yes. I can do."

Eastwood turned to face his two cameramen in the back seat. "I'm afraid the Tunis Embassy will also be attacked." Under his breath, he added, "If it hasn't been already."

CHAPTER TWENTY-FIVE

0730 September 21, 2012
Fredericksburg, Texas

After Duncan Hunter finished his third set of sit-ups, he jumped onto the pull-up bar and slowly pounded out as many pull-ups as he could when he heard the door slam; he knew Theresa Yazzie had walked out of the ranch house. He knew what was coming next.

"You no like my breakfast? I make *huevos rancheros* just for you! *Cold* Julio's, just how you like it."

"Theresa, of course I love your *huevos rancheros.* I have two miles to go. I'll eat when I'm back in twelve minutes or so." He released the bar and ran down the access road of the ranch.

Theresa shook her head and dashed back into the house. That was their routine. Hunter said he didn't want breakfast, and she poked at him and said he must not like her fried eggs smothered in rich Mexican salsa. He would finish his workout, and, if the weather was good, she would serve breakfast on the terrace. It was a race to see who reached the table first.

Hunter always made the two-mile trip in fourteen minutes, no longer able to run six-minute miles, but that was their little secret. Theresa would be waiting for him with a plate fresh from the oven and a jar of chilled chunky salsa. Hunter always lost their undeclared race, but he won a winning breakfast.

Running suited him when he wasn't playing racquetball. Running was a solitary pursuit, something he could do between racquetball competitions, which were becoming fewer and fewer, as they conflicted with his daily routine, his work, his passion.

After running what was essentially two Marine Corps Physical Fitness Tests back to back, he wolfed down the hot, spicy egg dish and washed it down with a concoction of Fresca and orange juice.

After a shower and shave, he headed for the office, but not until he visited the ranch house's safe room to extract some specialized weapons for the mission. From the walk-in closet in his bedroom, Hunter raised the hidden, folded T-handle from under a flap of carpet and lifted the door leading to the storm-safe room below. The composition of the door, reinforced with sheets of steel, Kevlar, and bullet-resistant Fiberglas, saved his life when a group of Arabs attacked his house in Del Rio shortly after 9/11.

Hunter designed and built the underground warren of rooms, which could sleep ten and were provisioned with months of survival meals and water. Like his old house's safe room, it was designed to withstand tornados and the occasional direct assault by a hostile group.

He flicked on the lights and bounded down the steps into an expansive, armored chamber. He opened one of three tall weapons vaults and extracted his favorite match-grade Colt Python .357 Magnum revolver, a model 1911 Kimber .45 ACP, and a handful of magazines and speed loaders. He bypassed the lensatic compass on the top shelf, locked the weapons vault again, departed the safe room, and left the house.

It was a typical Texas day, with high clouds, calm winds, and the temperature rising toward a high of ninety. Nice weather meant another thing. Carlos pulled the Aston Martin from the garage and parked it in front of the house. Foul weather was a Hummer day. Yazzie took a California duster to the car to keep dust from settling on the gleaming black beauty and playfully saluted Hunter, as he bounded from the house with a brown leather Gladstone in one hand and a black aluminum Zero Halliburton in the other—papers and guns. Under his arm was a large manila envelope.

Yazzie opened the driver's door. Hunter placed the two cases on the passenger seat, handed the envelope to Carlos, and patted his back. "Thank you, Carlos. Can you drop this off at the lawyer's office?"

"Sure, Boss. They won't open until ten or so."

"That's OK."

"Class tonight?"

"It's Friday. Yes, class. I'll be very late."

"Miss Horne?"

"I should see her. I might stay in Del Rio overnight. I didn't tell you I'm off on an adventure tomorrow. I shouldn't be away more than a week."

"One week?"

"Give or take. What's on your agenda?"

"I need to take this to the lawyer, then I'll replace the rear tires on the DB9 when you're gone. If you're going to be gone a week, I can finish that. They need replacing soon."

Every year, Carlos removed the rear wheels of the Aston Martin and took them into San Antonio to a specialty tire and wheel business to have the very wide, very low-profile tires replaced due to Hunter's heavy foot on the accelerator.

Hunter slid behind the steering wheel and smirked. "Is that your way of telling me I have a difficult time controlling the throttle?"

"Oh, no. It's just time to replace the tires." He smiled back.

"You're starting to sound like a politician, Carlos. Don't wait up."

Carlos waved, as Hunter closed the door, depressed the *Start* button, and lightly spun the tires as he left. Both men smiled like kids at their first drag strip, watching top fuel dragster burnouts.

Fifteen minutes later, Hunter pulled into his space in the garage of the old bank building and shut down the engine. He swiped his access card in the card reader, and the door locks unbolted free. As he bounded up the stairs to his office, he found a line of scientists and managers waiting for him in the hallway.

"Is this an insurrection?" Hunter asked, feeling like he forgot something important.

"Staff meeting?" two men asked simultaneously.

Embarrassed, Hunter asked, "Do we need one?"

The materials research scientist, Dr. LaBrake said, "Duncan, we have a couple of proposals ready to submit next week and need final step reviews. There are several RFPs that are interesting, and we need to talk about them to see if we're interested. We also have a couple of white papers for your approval and a couple product demos. That's all."

"Well, that's not all," Dr. Aguirre said. "I need to show you what we've done with the swarm, but that can wait if you don't have the time."

"Everyone here?"

"Just waiting on you," Dr. LaBrake said.

"Then let's get 'em done." He led the troupe into the conference room and didn't emerge until all the management reviews were complete on the proposals that were ready to submit to the government for consideration. Two scientists briefed three requests for proposals for technical services for manned and unmanned aircraft. Hunter approved the bid and proposal money to chase and to capture the work.

Two other scientists passed out PowerPoint slides to discuss a pair of white papers to submit to the DOD on their next generation of camouflage materials. Two managers brought Hunter up-to-date on the progress of the Nigerian quiet aircraft contract and the restoration efforts of two rare airplanes and several old race cars.

Lunch was catered, and the men and women around the table continuously left and returned to the meeting to attend to other calls or bathroom breaks. At the five-hour mark, Dr. LaBrake indicated he had to take a customer call and stood to leave.

Hunter couldn't take his eyes off the documents in front of him. "Brian, do you have enough material for me to have a sheet?"

LaBrake was nonplussed. He'd never been asked for demo materials before. "Sure. How much to you need, Boss?"

"I'm thinking something a little bigger than an airline blanket but not as big as a full bed sheet."

"Uh…I might have enough for that. I'll bring it up. Do you want some of the anti-thermal material, too?" His curiosity was aroused. It wasn't like Duncan to ask for classified or prototype materials, apparently for personal reasons. Their classified materials and aircraft were normally not seen by outside eyes until a contract was in place, but Hunter was the boss.

"No, just what you showed me." He finished the document review, checked his chronograph, and returned to the remaining men and women around the conference table.

"That was a great effort," Hunter said. "Maybe we should do staff meetings weekly."

Several groans sounded from behind closed fists. Smiling, he continued.

"I'll be out of town starting tomorrow," he said. "I expect to be back in a week, give or take. No staff meeting next week. Questions? OK. Nice job all around. Thank you all. See you when I'm back."

Two hours after leaving Quiet Aero Systems he stood in class, trying hard not to look at his daughter in the back of the room, where she normally sat. Between the two, they conducted themselves professionally, collegially, friendly. None of Kelly Horne's classmates would have suspected that the professor behind the lectern was her father.

Hunter picked up where he left off once the students returned from a break.

"You have an obligation to tell the truth," he said. "Report your findings fully and accurately. If you find yourself on an aircraft accident board, you'll find out very quickly that it's very easy to slip into a protective mode. You want to be helpful. You'll start making judgments on how or what you'll report. It's extremely understandable not to be the guy who jams a spear into the heart of a fellow pilot who ejected from a jet. Accident investigations should be a business transaction or a police report. As Sergeant Joe Friday used to say, 'Just the facts, Ma'am.'"

The students' quizzical expressions forced him to reply.

"Don't look at me that way and tell me you don't know who Joe Friday is? I'm getting too old for this. OK. There was an old TV show called *Dragnet* that featured two detectives. One was a hardnosed, no-nonsense 'Just the facts, Ma'am,' guy named Sergeant Joe Friday, played by Jack Webb. His partner was Bill Gannon, played by Harry Morgan of Colonel Potter of *MASH* fame. You do know *MASH*?"

Embarrassed, the students nodded.

"Governments and the media lie. Do you do it? No! Got it? Questions? OK. You're in for a treat, as that's all I have for tonight. If you don't say anything to the center director, we can leave class early, but here's the rest of the deal. I won't make it to class next week, and a sub just won't do. I have a reading assignment and a small writing assignment for next week. The week after that are Finals. Your term paper is due, and I'm sure you can use the time to buff and polish your papers. If you haven't started them...." Hunter shook his head and shuddered at the thought and continued, "Share your papers with your buddies to critique them and make them better. Any and all criticism is non-attribution. Do we have a deal?"

They smiled and nodded. No one had any questions, so class was dismissed. Kelly was the last to leave. Duncan gave her a huge smile.

"So you're leaving me again?" She feigned hurt and sorrow.

Hunter returned his teaching materials to the leather briefcase as he spoke, barely taking his eyes from his daughter's face. "I'll be gone a week, maybe a couple days more. I don't know."

"May I ask what you're doing and where you're going?"

"How's your Latin? *Si ego certiorem faciam mihi tu delendus eris.* Which roughly translates to, 'I could tell you, but then I'd have to kill you.'"

"Dad, are you working for the CIA?" She wanted to ask that question for weeks and finally had the nerve, but he avoided a direct answer. His non-answer, though, was an emphatic yes.

"That's what I want to talk to you about. Can we go to your room or go get some dinner? I haven't had anything since lunch."

"Sure. We can go to town. Take your car?"

Lieutenant Kelly Horne and Professor Duncan Hunter walked side-by-side out of Anderson Hall and across Liberty Avenue to the acres of parking lot, making small talk.

"Do you want to drive the DB9?" he asked.

Her smile screamed, "Hell, yes!"

They placed their bags behind the seats and got in.

As they departed the parking lot, he told her how he had worked at the Air Force Base and drove a yellow Corvette convertible. Hunter pointed to a parking space near a building adjacent to the large, concrete-colored five-bay fire station. "That was where I parked the 'Vette. It wasn't that long ago that you could still see that yellow car in that spot from the overhead…. I'm sorry…from satellite pictures. When we leave the base, there's that sweeping, climbing left turn to merge into traffic.

"Whenever I left the base and headed for town, I always took that corner as fast as I could. My mechanic always wondered how I was able to trash the right rear wheel bearing every year. The answer, of course, was I was a frustrated race car driver at heart and had too much fun with that car. I looked for fun things to do, and taking hard corners fast and right on the edge of losing control was exhilarating.

"The Aston's like that, too, only the luxury is off the chart. By comparison, the 'Vette was like riding in a lawn chair."

"So are you going to kill me for asking if you work for the Agency? I'm driving. We'd both get hurt."

He grinned. "What I can tell is that you have to swear you can't breathe a word of this relationship to anyone. Trust me. If you let out even a hint that I'm your father, your life would be in grave danger. I cannot emphasize that enough. Though it's been several years since someone took a shot at me, the less you know, the better. Do you still want to know?"

"You're scaring me, Dad."

"It's my life, Kelly. It's what I do when I'm not playing with cars and airplanes." Faintly illuminated by the instrument cluster, she saw that his expression was dead serious.

"I do some work for what I call 'Greg's old place.' My best friend and mentor, Greg Lynche, spent thirty-five years with the CIA and was their Chief of Air Branch. After he retired, he and I did some flying work for his old place. I've been doing jobs for them for the last fifteen years."

She blurted out the first flying job that came to mind. "Like renditions?" She felt shocked and slightly uncomfortable that her father transported terrorists from the battlefield to secret prisons or Guantanamo Bay.

"Nothing like that. ISR work. Mostly."

"I thought that was done by unmanned aerial vehicles or C-12s."

"Some of the work can be done only by special-purpose aircraft." He pointed to the Pizza Hut sign in the distance. "Pizza?"

"You mean like an AC-130?"

"That's kind of a yes and no answer. Yes, the AC-130 is specially configured to do several special missions, launch mortars and cannon and machine guns and all that fun stuff. No, in that the AC-130 isn't available anytime, it's supported by a cast of hundreds. I'm talking about a very special aircraft that's used when all other aircraft have been tried and failed. Are you familiar with Red Adair, the famous oil well firefighter?"

"A little."

"There were lots of oil well firefighters across the planet, putting out the fires that popped up from time-to-time. When there was a really bad or complicated fire, Red was called when all other options were exhausted, or he had the only equipment to do the job. John Wayne made an incredible Red Adair."

"So you fly the only airplane that can do a job no one else can do? Is that the little black airplane I saw at the end of your desk? When I saw it, I thought it was so cool, but I have no idea what it is."

She pulled into the nearly deserted parking lot. Hunter guided her to park far from the other cars. When she shut off the engine, he said, "That about sums it up."

The two ordered soft drinks and shared a pizza. The dining area was empty. Horne continued to ask questions. Hunter, reverting to instructor mode, outlined the history of quiet aircraft, from the early Rube Goldberg experimentals to the small production run of Lockheed YO-3As to the Schweizer RG-8s.

"NASA has a YO-3A. They're affectionately called Yo-Yos. That one is number zero-one-zero. Of the eleven produced, 010 is the only copy still known to be flyable."

Kelly sat back in the booth; her fingers intertwined on the table, staring at Hunter, her thin lips forming a hint of a smile. Her mind raced to fit additional pieces of the puzzle that made up her father. He told her several pieces for her to turn over, to fit the spoken knowns and the unspoken unknowns to develop a picture she could start to recognize.

Hunter, amused, watched her flip and tumble through a series of mental gymnastics. He told her more than he should, but she was a smart girl. Like Nazy, Kelly had the gift of making leaps in logic and was able to articulate her findings quickly and succinctly.

She felt she solved it. She *knew* she solved it. Horne leaned forward and whispered, "Father, *you* have a YO-3A. It was probably number seven off the assembly line. Probably serial number double-O seven. It's black and you only fly at night. You work for the CIA and drive a black Aston Martin. Dad, you're James Bond with an airplane."

He grinned, and then he broke into a coughing laughing fit. "No one ever accused me of that before, but you're probably a little on target, except I have only two women in my life, you and Nazy."

Kelly beamed.

Their meat-lover's pizza arrived, with every type of meat on the menu with extra sauce and cheese, the way both of them liked it. Kelly bowed her head, taking her father's hands and leading them in a short blessing.

They talked about her assignment, teaching flight students and how several of the students tried to kill her when she least expected it. She was definitely not like that when she went through the program. Then they discussed her follow-on training. Being an Air Force T-38 flight instructor right out of flight school was the ticket for the next step. Kelly thought she couldn't wait to fly the big, powerful fighters, but, finding her father nearby, she acknowledged she was excited by the direction and trajectory of her career and being in his life.

Several times during their meal, Horne looked over Hunter's

shoulder and stared for a few seconds. Sometimes, he brought her back to the present with a comment, gesture, or sound. Once, she caught herself whiling away whimsically.

She finished her slice and wiped her fingers with her napkin, thinking of her next questions for her dad.

Something was obviously buzzing around in her cranium, and Hunter knew it. *If she figured that out, can she figure out the rest?*

"Dad, how long do you plan to do that? I take it you fly solo. Do you ever need a copilot?'

His BlackBerry buzzed against his hip. "Excuse me for a second, Kelly." Keying in his password, he pressed a few buttons to reach the email screen. He was surprised to find he had several unopened messages. An email from Bob confirmed they were safe in Maryland and the package was delivered. The *Wraith* was loaded aboard the Agency C-130 and Bob had the documentation.

Another email was from Director Rothwell confirming all requested products were delivered to Andrews Air Force Base. Greg Lynche was on his way, likely in his Cessna Skymaster, to Washington State to bid on the other YO-3A.

Nothing new from Nazy. Earlier in the morning, after his run and Theresa's *huevos rancheros,* Hunter had replied to Nazy's message. *Even the hint that you could be a mother fills me with great joy and excitement. I'm so excited for you and me. I love you, Baby.*

He constantly debated whether he should tell Nazy he had a daughter, but putting information like that in an impersonal email or text message wasn't the right thing to do. It was one thing to drop little love notes in a text message, but announcing he found a long-lost daughter raised scores of questions that shouldn't be answered over the Internet.

He resolved the issue by deciding to introduce them, but that had to wait for the right moment. He lifted his head from the little screen and looked at Kelly, drawing a blank. What had they been talking about?

Kelly sensed he was distracted enough to forget her last questions, so she offered to bail him out. "Everything OK?"

Hunter nodded, remnants of Nazy's condition drifting back and forth in his mind, while he had a real, live daughter sitting across from him. *One day I have no kids,* he thought, *and the next, I have one, then two. Maybe three. Only you, Hunter!* "I'm sorry. It's been a very long week. Just confirmation that my trip is set. Where were we?"

"I asked how long do you think you're going to do ... what you do. I also asked if you fly solo and would there ever be a time when you needed a copilot?" She felt she'd be begging for an answer soon.

"I don't know how much longer I can do it. It might be a better question of how long I *want* to do it. My bud, Greg, flew until he was seventy-two. I think, using him as a gauge, I have quite a few years left. The real issue is if I can keep my contract. Unmanned technology is continually improving, but I don't think anyone can replicate what I have any time soon. As for flying solo, I am. There are times when I need, not a copilot, but a sensor operator."

"Is that something I could do?"

The question triggered a wave of emotion in Hunter. He froze, reliving the time when he and Lynche barely escaped a surface-to-air missile, and the Yo-Yo was severely damaged. The idea of putting his daughter in harm's way was abhorrent. He just found her and didn't want to do or say something stupid that would put her in a situation where she could be killed.

A wave of reality crashed over him, and he broke through the surface with insight and resignation. He acknowledged she'd be a fighter pilot someday, and she would train in conditions that would place her well in harm's way, in environments where there could be dozens of surface-to-air radar missiles targeting her. He'd been through the fighter pilot training program; he knew what was in store for her. She could be shot down, taken prisoner, or worse.

And there's nothing you can do or say to change that, he told himself. *Quit being an idiotic protective father. She's a big girl. Maybe she's just inquiring if it's something she could do, not that she wants to. No one would give up the chance to fly some of the world's greatest airplanes just to sit in the back seat of a relic and play with electronic sensors.*

Sucking in air, he tried not to look worried. "Being a sensor operator isn't that big a deal. You're a future fighter pilot. I just don't see…."

"You'd be worried about me. Is that it?"

"That's some of it. I just found you. It's one thing if I put myself in harm's way. It's another to put my daughter there with me."

She sat impassively, thinking that he was being honest and rational. At least he hadn't said, "No."

Duncan mumbled, "I'm not sure I could get you cleared. You'd have to resign from the Air Force and become an intel officer. I'm not sure of the process, but I couldn't just bring you into the program. I'd lose my clearance, and then there'd be no work. There's also the state of the technology. Someone somewhere will figure out low-flying aircraft is the missing link to conduct supersensitive ISR work. Someone will build a new plane or modify an unmanned system."

She reached across the table to take his hand and squeeze it. "I became a pilot because my mother was a pilot. I wanted to be like her. I did that. I found you, and I think you're the most-exciting man I'll ever meet. I ... find myself ... thinking I want to be like you, to be with you. At this moment, that's all I want. It would be awesome to work and fly with you. Anyone can train students. I think what you do is incredible and exciting. I'll do whatever it takes, Dad. However long it takes. I'm serious."

Their waitress broke the conversation by clearing the table and presenting the bill. Kelly insisted on paying, while Duncan smiled. She was just like her mother.

They sat quietly, smiling at each other. Taking sips of water. Thinking. Hunter broke the impasse.

"It's probably a waste of time trying to talk you out of this," he said. "OK. I'll see what I can do, but no promises."

He pulled out his BlackBerry and keyed in his password, so he could scroll to one of the email he just read. He punched buttons, he asked for Kelly's Social Security number. When he finished, he returned the device to its holster.

"What did you just do?" she asked pensively.

"I asked the Director of Central Intelligence if he would transfer you to the CIA and put you in the intelligence officer's course. I said I found a new back seater."

CHAPTER TWENTY-SIX

0830 September 21, 2012
U.S. Embassy
Algiers, Algeria

The flight out of Tripoli was an uneventful success, however, the leg to Algiers took much longer than the aircrew expected. Fuel wasn't the problem. Having to land and take off during daylight was to be avoided as much as possible. Night extractions and insertions were preferable to avoid casual and professional "tail watchers," liberal busybodies who hung out at major airports and made it their goal in life to identify and report on U.S. aircraft operating overseas. Tail watchers used telescopes and binoculars from any available oversight location they could find to read the "N number" that signified the aircraft was registered in the U.S.

All aircraft sported their country's aircraft registration number, usually in big, bold letters and numbers, on each side of the aircraft. Once a tail watcher identified an N number had landed or taken off, the information was broadcast to chat rooms and other uber-communist or terrorist web sites around the world. Hoping to find the CIA in action overseas, many tail watchers were supplied with computers, cameras, and telescopes to help identify passengers and their aircraft when arriving or departing. Some tail watchers were paid very well for their information.

N numbers dumped into search engines were quickly identified to be corporate, or, if they had little or a questionable history, they were probably covert aircraft. In the post-9/11 environment, more than 100 covert intelligence officers and dozens of aircraft had their cover blown from tail watchers using powerful telephoto lenses on cameras taking photographs of the intelligence officer or the aircraft and splashing them across the Internet.

Tail watchers also monitored airport and air traffic radio transmissions. They anticipated when certain N numbers were due in or when they departed to capture the aircraft's call sign. Agency and contracted aircrews changed their call signs while in flight to avoid overflight reporting and confuse a tail watcher's ability to follow a flight across the globe. Most of the time, a unique call sign was sufficiently unusual to give a tail watcher more cause to scrutinize the aircraft. The international cat-and-mouse game that was played out every night, near the larger commercial airports, to thwart tail watchers and other intelligence agencies from locating and identifying CIA and State Department contracted air carriers moved to a different level, like moving a rook from the lower level to the upper deck in three-dimensional chess. Agency flight following personnel raced to acquire new landing clearances from the foreign civil aviation authorities while the aircraft was inbound to the airport.

The Basler Turbo 67 aircrew flew out over the Mediterranean Sea, first toward Palermo, then made an easy westerly turn toward Palma de Mallorca before receiving their new landing clearances and calls signs into Algiers' international airport.

Instead of flying directly from Tripoli to Algiers, a normal three-hour flight, which would have meant crossing the Tunisian border and making several position calls, thus alerting tail watchers, the Basler was forced into a circuitous route around Tunisia with an approach from Spain. The delay assisted the U.S. Embassy in Algiers to obtain landing permission through civil aviation authority and Ministry of Defense channels.

To evacuate U.S. Embassy personnel with a few hours' notice is a Herculean task in logistics. Finding an available aircraft with a cleared aircrew in Europe was, at best, challenging and often impossible. Getting a handful of aircraft and crews on contract for short-notice evacuations at locations where there was a reasonable expectation of civil unrest, such as North Africa and the Middle East, required skill and foresight from State Department planners and schedulers. Several

American aviation companies were placed on contract, pre-positioned at small airports throughout Europe, and were told to be ready to respond at a moment's notice to a State Department evacuation announcement. The U.S. military had quick reaction forces, QRFs, to aid and assist in embassy or consulate attacks or evacuations in unstable regions, but they were oftentimes overlooked or dismissed because of an ambassador's political party. Liberal ambassadors hated calling DOD to rescue them and would rather wait for another option.

Someone dropped the ball in Benghazi, Libya. No assistance was requested or sent to the besieged Ambassador to Libya and his staff. The State Department completely screwed up its response, forcing an internal review of procedures and policies. In the meantime, the CIA's transportation planning and scheduling resources were stretched to the breaking point, as one terrorist situation flared up after another, moving across North Africa, demanding lightning-fast decisions and even putting aircraft into the air to fly the length of the Mediterranean Sea for immediate contingency evacuations. The *U.S.S Eisenhower* left its deep-water port in Naples after a lengthy port call and could be called upon for direct embassy evacuations if embassy personnel couldn't reach their local airport safely. An ambassador just had to call.

The twin turboprops on the Basler provided a steady hum and smooth ride, putting McGee and his crew asleep shortly after takeoff. All three exhausted men had been up all night, protecting the embassy grounds. They found seats, got comfortable, and exercised an old Special Operations Forces axiom: *When given the opportunity to sleep, sleep. You don't know when you'll get another chance.*

The noise of three men snoring like roaring water buffaloes in heat was drowned out by noise from the propellers and wind screaming over the airframe. Earplugs helped, too.

Intelligence from several sources indicated the U.S. Embassy in Tripoli would most likely be subject to another wave of protestors. One source suggested it was just a pretense, that the *Chargé d-Affaires* was personally targeted for kidnap. The source also indicated there would be other attacks in the region, targeting the Ambassador, the *Chargé d-*

Affaires and/or the Chief of Station.

That intel put the State Department and the CIA on red alert. Cables were exchanged with the embassies in Tunis, Algiers, and Rabat, Morocco. Embassy security restricted the movement of key personnel, primarily keeping them within embassy grounds and in the chanceries. Only those who had mission-essential travel were allowed off embassy property. With the death of the U.S. Ambassador to Libya, no one was willing to risk another diplomat falling into the hands of protestors disguised as al-Qaeda or the Muslim Brotherhood.

McGee and his SEALs stepped off the converted DC-3 wearing heavy backpacks and dark sunglasses while carrying long, round nylon bags. Like all Special Operations Forces and embassy personnel operating under cover, dark shades helped mask their identities from tail watchers or hostile intelligence services that would definitely notice three heavily muscled men.

The wind off the Mediterranean, kept the dust to a minimum around Algiers, and provided mostly clear, haze-free blue skies. Sunglasses were essential to keep eyeballs from being fried from the exceedingly bright sunlight. The men's diplomatic passports expedited their passage through customs. Once inside the executive terminal, they boarded an embassy van and were whisked away.

A pair of tail watchers noticed the plane land and the men who arrived and reported the information to an online web site.

McGee, Tonka, and the short-but-solid Kyle Drumm, called "Spanky" in SEAL circles, were visibly impressed by Algiers. Like most places in the Middle East, nearly all the buildings were white, covered with whitewash, white tile, white stucco, or white granite. Cars and trucks were matte white—no reds, yellows, blues, or bright greens. What few women they saw wore chadors. Children wore knitted skullcaps. The protocol seemed to be white, matching their white shirts and trousers.

Spanky asked the driver if there was anywhere to get a dark beer before they reached the embassy, but he was more interested in hearing the man's voice than getting a drink. The driver tried to hide his high, nasal voice when the men offloaded their backpacks into the van. All were startled at how the driver sounded. He took immediate offense and struggled to say there was beer in the cafeteria, adding that alcohol was frowned on in Algeria.

A hard look from McGee warned Spanky to knock it off.

They arrived at the U.S. Embassy in Algiers, and, as all new arrivals did, the three men reported to the security office for their badges, to register their weapons, and to receive a security brief. Tonka removed their weapons from the long, round diplomatic bags and placed them on the counter. The security officer noted the make, model, and serial number onto a clipboard and immediately started a lengthy security brief.

The tall security officer had long, dark hair and sallow features. She reminded McGee of a stockier, heavier Morticia Addams, the matriarch of the *Addams Family.* Facing the three men at her counter, she began her brief.

"Algeria is Muslim, at peace with its neighbors, but has difficulty dealing with outside forces like al-Qaeda and the Muslim Brotherhood. The embassy has been evacuated several times before, while assaults, masked by the actions of protestors, were repelled by the local constabularies. Since 9/11 of this year, we've seen an uptick in the number and tone of protests. The death of the Ambassador to Libya energized opposition forces, and the Algerian military and intelligence services are fully engaged and have responded immediately to several recent, albeit small, organized protests. If you have laptops, they can't be connected to our system until they've been tested by the IT office down the hall."

Five minutes later, Morticia defined the required OPSEC, threats known and unknown, and the emergency procedures for the facility. The men needed to go down the hall to the housekeeping office to get their lodging arranged.

After having rooms assigned and keys issued from a sullen older woman with long, gray braided hair and a matching attitude, they received badges from the polite, professional Marine security guard and passed through the chancery's heavily armored doors. They casually walked toward the apartments across the compound to secure their gear, shower, and head to the cafeteria for food and maybe even a beer.

That was when they saw her.

After the dour Morticia and drab housekeeping shrew, the woman walking across the parking lot toward the apartment shocked all three men mute and dumb. Stunning and breathtaking, she moved with the confidence of a leopard in the jungle. They hadn't seen anything like her in months, and she was totally unexpected in a Muslim country.

McGee looked at Tonka and Spanky, and passed telepathic directions. The three men leaned toward the apartments. In seconds, like boys chasing a baby cottontail in a yard, they raced toward the building, trying to reach the door before she did. Backpacks and bags bounced in their hands, as they closed the gap in an undeclared race to overtake their prey.

In seconds, they caught up with the woman and found her just as striking in person. Tonka, who won the footrace, offered to open the door.

"Here. Let me get that for you." He was annoyed when he yanked on the handle and found it locked.

"Hello," Spanky said. "We're hoping this is where we're staying. Are these the only apartments on the compound?"

The three men surrounded her and smiled like excited teens peeking inside their first *Playboy.*

"You're new." She smiled, her voice silky and sensual, with a touch of a British accent.

"We're in from Tripoli," McGee said, "to augment the security. I'm Bill McGee. This is Tony Parker, or Tonka to his friends, and Kyle Drumm, but he responds to Spanky."

The men could barely contain their excitement and glee. They struggled to keep their eyes on hers and not undress her mentally.

She offered her hand to Bill first, then Tonka and Spanky. The name Bill McGee sparked a faint memory. She heard that name before. Although she had a tremendous memory, she couldn't immediately place it, but it would come.

"Glad to meet you, Bill, Tonka, and Spanky. Nazy Cunningham. I'm the trade attaché. Welcome to Algiers."

CHAPTER TWENTY-SEVEN

1030 September 21, 2012
U.S. Embassy
Algiers, Algeria

Like cowboys lined up for their first square dance and being introduced to their partners, Spanky and Tonka said in unison, "Glad to meet you, Miss Cunningham."

Bill, however, was stunned. It normally took a small earthquake to get any emotion from him. Her name reverberated in his head. He knew this woman. Rather, he knew *of* her. Like him, that name was once disembodied and a possible target for assassination. He didn't have to remember. Her unusual name was the focal point on whether the sniper who'd been killing Navy SEALs after the death of Osama bin Laden would target Bill or her.

He recalled Duncan contacting someone named Nazy Cunningham and encouraging her to seek refuge at CIA headquarters until the episode blew over or she was killed. *That* Nazy Cunningham found the CIA file on the former President. *That* Nazy Cunningham located and interrogated Osama bin Laden.

He was flooded with powerful memories and emotions from that chapter in his life, where he called his friend from the Naval War College for help. He struggled to push those thoughts aside and say something intelligent and coherent to get confirmation.

Meekly and slowly, he asked, "You're Duncan Hunter's Nazy Cunningham?"

Spanky and Tonka's heads snapped toward him, while Nazy's eyes widened, and her jaw slacked. Not expecting to hear Duncan's name, she was taken aback. Her reaction told McGee she was *that* Nazy Cunningham.

The question startled her. No one at the CIA knew she and Duncan were involved. She thought no one anywhere knew. Except for Greg Lynche and his wife, she didn't believe anyone knew she and Duncan were engaged.

She could barely voice a reply, and her British accent nearly vanished. But this man obviously knew Duncan and knew him well enough to know she was Duncan's. "Why, yes. Duncan is…my fiancé."

She stared quizzically into the black man's dark-brown eyes, seeking answers to the questions racing in her mind while she ignored the other two men.

Then she remembered there was a man who, with Greg Lynche, saved Duncan from the sniper who'd been targeting a Bill McGee. She had flashbacks of three hideous black-and-blue welts, each the size of a grapefruit, with a one-inch circular raised white dot that showed the impact point of the .9mm pistol the sniper used on Duncan. Body armor saved his life.

She relived the moment when she shouted at Hunter, "You were shot! When were you going to tell me you were shot?"

The response and subsequent quiescence from Nazy crushed Tonka and Spanky. They looked at her wrist and saw a solid gold Rolex, and on her hand, a huge diamond ring, then they sighed, shrugged, turned to the door and used a card to swipe the card reader and unlock the door.

They left McGee and Cunningham staring at each other, standing uncomfortably on the concrete step. It was incongruous but obvious the man and woman shared a secret about someone named Duncan Hunter. The two former SEALs retreated from the discussion.

McGee was momentarily at a loss for words and slightly embarrassed by chasing down the beautiful woman, only to learn she was the one who found and interrogated Osama bin Laden and found the CIA file on the former President that forced him to resign and flee the country. Captain Bill McGee commanded dozens of secret operations, leading Navy SEALs into mayhem and danger, but those were team events. He took credit when the missions went well and blame when they didn't.

He wasn't standing in the presence of one of those rear-echelon pansies who did little to advance the mission or support the operation. *This* Nazy Cunningham was obviously different. Not only was she incredibly stunning to look at, she was at the top of her game. She *found* bin Laden and the President's file, and she actually *interrogated* bin Laden. The woman standing before him was a quiet patriot, a single point of light and truth during one of the darkest periods of American history.

Duncan Hunter's girlfriend, as McGee called her. *Now his bride-to-be?*

McGee slowly recovered from his shock. *She's so far up the intelligence food chain. What the hell is she doing in Algiers?*

Nazy searched for words and offered an apology with a sense of urgency, as her belly rumbled. "I'm sorry, Bill. We have to talk about Duncan later. I have a meeting I need to get to, and I'm probably going to be late. Can we meet for dinner at the cafeteria this evening, say seven-ish?" She swiped her access card to unlock the door.

McGee grabbed the handle to open it for her. "That will work. Glad to finally meet you, Nazy. Wow. I never expected this."

"Thank you, Bill. I look forward to it. See you tonight." She hustled down the hall, leaving Bill to admire the shapely woman jogging away in high heels. When she disappeared into her room, he started up the stairs, shaking his head in amazement.

After showers and several hours' sleep, McGee, Spanky, and Tonka found the well-provisioned cafeteria in the chancery basement. They wolfed down burgers and fries and finally sat around the table nursing longneck bottles of Casablanca Beer, anticipating the arrival of the leggy, long-haired brunette while intermittently watching the large monitor suspended from the wall, as some CNN newscaster lamented about yet another green energy company going bankrupt.

McGee turned to his charges and explained that the woman was engaged to one of his close friends from the Naval War College, circa 2002. They listened to the scratchy voice emanating from the monitor, what McGee referred to as "the info-babe" on the Communist News Network.

They kept their eyes peeled for the trade attaché while glancing at the TV. McGee checked his huge Seiko dive watch frequently. She was late, but they had CNN, Moroccan beer, and German pretzels to keep them company.

Nazy changed into jeans, trainers, and a billowy white long-sleeved shirt with a tiny pink polo pony embroidered over her breast. She hadn't felt ill for several hours and had an appetite for the first time in a couple of days.

Walking quickly across the yard from the apartments to the chancery, she found the cafeteria busy. Nazy, making eye contact with Bill, went through the grill line and salad bar. With a tray of food and bottled water, she approached the table. All three men stood. Spanky held the lone available chair for her, and she placed her tray among bags of pretzels and beer and soda bottles, as she sat directly across from Bill.

"I'm sorry I'm late," she said. "I understand you gentlemen had quite an adventure."

They grinned as if they'd been caught in the girl's locker room and didn't know how to reply. Beautiful women had a way of turning men into babbling idiots. Tonka and Spanky were rarely in the presence of women who looked like supermodels, so they overreacted to anything she said. Bill, amused by the younger men's ingratiating expressions, was more interested in learning about the woman who found and interrogated bin Laden, as well as how she won the heart of his friend, Duncan Hunter. He doubted she would broach either of those subjects with Tonka and Spanky present.

McGee, not letting her beauty intimidate him, asked, "What have you heard?"

"Well, the President was furious with the new Libyan government for being totally unresponsive and not coming to the aid of the embassy. I understand the embassy had to evacuate, and you're here to help augment our security. That's all." She also knew they had top secret security clearances with SCI and had been polygraphed many times. In a way, they were family in the intelligence community.

"Oh, and the Secretary of State resigned," she added. "I'm not sure if she was forced to because of the Benghazi debacle, or if it was just her time."

The Secretary of State, a rabidly partisan Democrat woman, had been notoriously missing in action from the beginning of the Ambassador's death. She'd been traveling to the Far East and was recalled by the President to come to Washington and be on hand when the Ambassador's body arrived at Andrews Air Force Base for a memorial. It was apparent to all but the most diehard liberals that her appointment by the former President was a strategic move, not because of her leadership abilities but because she had been considered a threat during the election and the President needed to keep his enemies close, if you were to believe the papers.

The new President didn't ask for her resignation when she was sworn in, thinking she would leave voluntarily, unable to work for a conservative Republican President. However, when the security lapses at U.S. Consulates and Embassies became known in the Middle East and North African countries, President Hernandez had no other choice but to ask for her resignation in the wake of the abject leadership failures in the State Department.

Tonka, very much a Gradgrind in political matters, was immediately interested to hear of the resignation. "I know there's more you can't say, but it's about time somebody shit-canned her. She was totally worthless from day one as Sec State."

"That's a start," Spanky said. "I thought it would take years to chase her and her commie friends out of Foggy Bottom, but it only took one dead Ambassador to get her out. The man didn't need to die. Good riddance."

Bill looked left and right, then said in his radio-announcer voice, "Not meaning to be a spoilsport, but could I have a few minutes with Miss Cunningham, privately?"

More confused than wounded, the two men left their seats, beers in hand.

"No problem, Bullfrog," Spanky said. "Good night, Miss Cunningham."

Nazy was amused and shocked by the sudden turn of events.

When the two men departed, McGee was apologetic and embarrassed. He looked around the cafeteria before speaking freely. "Sorry about that, Nazy. That's not really what I wanted to say, but it worked. I've been dying to talk to you all day. I never expected to find in Algiers the woman who found and *interviewed* bin Laden. Duncan didn't tell me much, and he never said he had a fiancée. He's an amazing, lucky man."

Nazy recovered from the brusque departure of the two SEALs, who moved to another table and snatched another round of Casablanca beer. She panned her ponytailed head from side-to-side. "Thank you, Bill. That was a very dynamic time, and I always thought I was the lucky one."

"I don't know how much you know. I'm still shocked that Duncan pulled it off. It was incredible. I think the only one who knows the complete story is Duncan."

"You're probably right. Everything we do here and at HQ is so compartmentalized. I don't know all of it, either. Duncan thought that was best."

Nazy and Bill talked for two hours. He drank Coca Cola; she drank water from a bottle. She explained how she met Duncan, a story Duncan had never fully revealed to McGee. McGee knew his friend was something of a ladies' man at the Naval War College, especially around single female officers. Hunter never told him or hinted about Nazy, though, so McGee was thoroughly intrigued.

She related her story to the point where Hunter confronted her about trying to spy on him. A Boston imam coerced her into finding out as much as possible about a William "MaGayhee" and Duncan.

"He said, 'I sense you're in trouble in some way. I won't hurt you or embarrass you. We're just two friends having dinner and a good time.

If your friends are watching us, they'll see us having a good time.' I told him they weren't my friends. For the first time I could remember, I found myself almost free. Duncan was there to help."

"I'm not sure I'm following you."

"You know when you have a bird and it's been in a cage all its life? When you open the cage door, at first, it doesn't want to leave. It doesn't know any other life. It was that moment. That was when Duncan said he could help. A few days later, well, let's say I was on my way to Virginia."

"And, you're the *trade attaché.*" He grinned widely, revealing a full set of white teeth. He knew the title was code for Chief of Station.

"Actually, the *acting trade attaché.*" Nazy knew he had served with the CIA as a senior military officer. SEALs often worked closely with the CIA. When they passed through embassies, their knowledge of embassy operations and the different offices was total.

They changed topics, as a cafeteria patron passed. Once the person was out of earshot, McGee gave her the rest of the bin Laden story, saying that one of his friends emailed to him, "Got your buddy. Any ideas what to do with him?"

Nazy knew from Hunter that the SEAL Team Six Commander who led the raid into Pakistan was Danny Cox, a senior Navy officer she met and tangentially worked with in the Near East Division at the CIA. That Captain Cox defied a Presidential order to kill bin Laden wasn't news. Duncan already told her.

The real news was that the former Vice President, the first openly homosexual man to serve as the VP, hadn't committed suicide.

She sat quietly, as McGee indicated the VP was likely punished for his role in killing several of his former SEAL shipmates. Cold and impassioned, Bill spoke matter-of-factly about the former sniper and former Vice President. She wouldn't tell him that the former vice president had an even darker past. Hunter may have told McGee the former VP's sordid history at some point during their friendship, but the former VP was dead, while the man sitting across from her rose in stature and earned her esteem as two patriots who learned they fought the same war and were on the same team.

The two discussed the current situation in Algiers. Nazy indicated that the intelligence was fairly accurate that after the attack on the U.S. Embassy and Consulate in Libya, the U.S. Embassy in Tunis would be next, then the embassy in Algiers. Intelligence analysts were at a loss to explain the westerly march and why organizations were singling out and attacking U.S. Embassies across North Africa using al-Qaeda and Muslim Brotherhood elements. Were they acting separately or together? Was there a struggle for dominance between the two organizations in North Africa, or was it something else?

"Then there's that movie," McGee said with energy. "That was all about you." He pointed at her playfully.

"I'm glad they had a nice, cheerful woman play that role. I insisted to the director it wouldn't be appropriate to let it become known that a former Muslim woman found bin Laden by tracking his harem of wives and children from Saudi Arabia into Pakistan. It wasn't that it wasn't exciting enough; it was more an issue that it wouldn't be prudent. The truth was definitely not Hollywood enough."

They laughed.

"As for *interviewing* him, it was a case of the right time and right place. After I taped Duncan's back and chest—it's hard for me to get those three bruises from my mind—I don't want to know how close I came to losing him. He was in pain and had a sense of urgency. I understood you and Greg and Duncan stopped the killer of your friends. I also understood Danny Cox somehow got bin Laden out of Pakistan under everyone's noses. Bin Laden needed to be interrogated, which was the whole purpose of the raid.

"In his mind, Duncan struggled with how to find an interrogator. Maybe the pain from the bullets clouded his senses. He knew I trained as an interrogator for some of the difficult cases at Guantanamo Bay, and I spoke fluent Arabic and Farsi. Somehow, he couldn't seem to ask me. In the end, it all worked out."

"Duncan really made it happen. I'm still astounded he pulled it off. You found the President's file. The political right knew there was something wrong with that guy. The left turned itself into origami pretzels trying to protect him." Smiling, he shook his gray head in amazement and reverence.

"I have to tell you, Nazy, I never expected Duncan to find ... happiness. I never thought he'd find someone like you. He kind of saved me at the War College. I think I was almost chronically depressed for not finding bin Laden. The Navy basically fired me for that and sent me to that school to retire. I met Duncan, and it's been an amazing adventure ever since."

"He saved me, too. I was sent to spy on him. Actually, I was supposed to find out about both of you. He knew right away. He helped free me from a horrible imam and Islam, and Greg Lynche set up the interviews for me to work. Duncan saved me at a time when I was drowning in fear and despair. I owe him my life…and my love."

McGee raised his soda bottle, and she lifted her bottled water.

"Here's to you and Duncan," he said. "May you live a long and prosperous life together!"

"Thank you, Bill. Bullfrog! *Bullfrog?*" She set down the water bottle and raised her hands in a query.

McGee grinned. "I once commanded the Navy Parachute Team. They're known as the Leap Frogs. As the head frog and the biggest, blackest frog in the pond, I was called Bullfrog. I couldn't give it up."

"And, your voice is so…."

"There's that, too. I've been told I have a face and voice for radio. I can't dispute it."

Laughing, she clapped her hands and brought a hand to her mouth to hide her embarrassment. The two paused, as he glanced at his dive watch and took a long pull to finish the soda pop. Nazy had a great time talking to the muscular man, and McGee sensed their mutual connection to Duncan was complete. She was part of the team. There was nothing he wouldn't do for her, or for Duncan.

Their long pause highlighted the fact that there was nothing left to say, and it was time to go their separate ways.

"Well, Bill, I had a wonderful time." Nazy sighed. "I have an early one tomorrow. I probably should get to bed. I have a big day ahead of me."

"And, we're working tonight. I hope the intel's wrong, and things are quiet."

"Amen."

Nazy and McGee stood to shake hands, with a firmness to solidify their new fondness and mutual respect. She walked away, her ponytail bouncing and swaying out of sync with each step.

Tonka and Spanky stood from their chairs, while McGee waited for them to join him.

"You look like you had a good time,"Tonka said.

McGee nodded. "I did. You notice anything wrong with this place? They're expecting trouble, too."

"Shit. Well, besides their having the best-looking trade attaché on the planet. No. Why?" Spanky's eyes darted from man to man in search of an answer.

McGee took the lead and said, "There's more to this embassy than meets the eye. Miss Cunningham is more than good-looking. She's a rock star at Langley, and her being here isn't normal ops at all. That's not what we're being paid for, though."

The two men eyed McGee quizzically. He couldn't shake the notion that more trouble than they expected was coming, but probably not that night. Maybe it would come the following day.

McGee swept away those discordant thoughts with a sigh. "That's enough bullshit. Not as bad as Libya, but this place has some problems and we need to keep our heads on a swivel. Let's go. We've got work to do."

CHAPTER TWENTY-EIGHT

1000 September 22, 2012
Mostaganem, Algeria

The call from Hakimi was ambiguous yet specific and informative. For twenty years a FAHD instructor for Abu Manu, Hakimi and his fellow Panthers were steeped in the special operations tradecraft of intelligence collection, espionage, and secret communication. A simple telephone call anywhere in Africa or the Middle East was monitored —always. If it was necessary to make electronic contact, conversations were in code—always. One never knew who might be listening to the conversation or if the cellular devices were being triangulated for location and position information. Encrypted text messages were the preferred media, because they were impossible to affix a location to the burst transmission.

The downside was that text messages had a disconcerting way of being hung up, ostensibly in cyberspace but more likely being analyzed by the local intelligence-gathering agency. If the message seemed innocuous enough, it would be allowed to pass electronic eavesdropping software.

Abu Manu relaxed, knowing the phrase *safe at home* meant his weapons cache of MANPADS was still undiscovered in Benghazi and was safe from al-Qaeda and Muslim Brotherhood elements. The phrase *Talal wasn't feeling well* meant the capitol city of Tunis would likely be the next focal point of demonstrations and protests, led by either al-Qaeda or the Muslim Brotherhood. *Difficulties with medicine* meant Haimi was still unable to discover the rationale or source behind the terrorists' plans. The only thing certain was that the U.S. Embassies and Consulates were being targeted. It wasn't the British Embassy or any other, just the Americans.

Abu Manu suspected the attack on the consulate in Libya was a botched kidnapping. His loyal, trusted FAHD heard several times during the civil war leading to Gaddafi's ouster that al-Qaeda sought to punish the Americans for killing Osama bin Laden and its leaders. As the calendar ticked toward the anniversary of 9/11, the terrorist groups orchestrated protests and demonstrations against American Embassies. Since the U.S. government wouldn't adequately defend its compounds in North Africa, the al-Qaeda knew they could overrun the facilities and retaliate with the capture and killing of American Embassy leaders.

For the Muslim Brotherhood, however, protests and demonstrations against embassies and other government facilities were just a precursor to a greater prize—the overthrow of the state government. Having extirpated Egyptian president Hosni Mubarak from office, they set their sights on Gaddafi and Tunisia's Ben Ali.

And, they were very successful. Mubarak was captured, Gaddafi was killed, and Ben Ali fled to Saudi Arabia. With Brotherhood successes in Egypt, Libya, and Tunisia, the Algerian and Moroccan leadership were suddenly in the crosshairs of both terrorist organizations. Abu Manu wanted no part of either of them and thought he would have to flee again if the Brotherhood succeeded in Algeria. He could buy protection from the brutish al-Qaeda elements, but not from the zealots in the Brotherhood.

The civil war decimated the FAHD that protected Gaddafi and Abu Manu. Only a handful remained alive, and those who volunteered to stay in Benghazi were either recovering from wounds or didn't have families. Abu Manu's FAHD never asked where the money came from to expedite or facilitate their travel. They owed him everything, including their undying trust.

The others, including Abu Manu, moved their wives and children west, out of harm's way, to Tunisia, Algiers, or Rabat. Worthless Libyan dinars couldn't be used for anything but the most-basic comestibles. Gold coin quietly bought goods and services—and a merchant's silence.

Abu Manu couldn't stand being near his wives and crippled children, but they served a larger purpose. His wives knew when he came to Algiers, it was to conduct business and spend obligatory time with the children. And to bring money. When he came to their home in Algiers, he rarely talked to any of them. He had long since stopped caring for them directly and openly, but now, after Gaddafi's fall, they provided other reasons for him to appear as a doting father and responsible husband. It was a good investment to make their lives comfortable in Algiers. As a businessman and father, it was a good cover story that enabled Abu Manu to travel wherever and whenever he needed.

The apartment complex, furnished in white granite panels and silver-painted wrought-iron accoutrements, was specifically constructed to meet his wives' wishes and his children's needs. There were high walls for security, underground parking for vehicles, and a large but shallow swimming pool for therapy. Large elevators, capable of moving hospital beds and wheelchairs, serviced every floor. It was close to the hospital when the children, technically adults but with infantile minds, required round-the-clock nursing and medical care. Each wife and her children occupied a single floor. When he visited, he slept alone on the top level.

All throughout Libya, and especially in Benghazi, Abu Manu was a virtual recluse who conducted business in the shadows or at night. If not for his five trusted FAHD—Hakimi, Malik, Habib, Hamed, and Hedi—he wouldn't have ventured into town. If he moved, it was at night. Flights to Tripoli to see Gaddafi were always done at night.

In Algiers, Abu Manu was a different person. Usually under the watchful eyes of Malik and Habib, he imbibed in *shisha* at a local hookah bar. He learned of the politics of the day and the pulse of the government, where he cultivated several spies at the highest levels. When he came to Algiers, he would receive friends and people who worked at the U.S. and British Embassies. Slipping them gold coins or bills, he thanked them for their service. Days of boisterous camaraderie, leaving him satiated with the latest news and tobacco, were followed by a drive to the coast and his farm with Malik at the wheel and Habib for security.

Abu Manu was the absentee landlord of a 300-acre operating olive farm. His wives didn't know of the property or any of his real-estate holdings in Algeria. When he left the city, he escaped the chains of being a father and husband for a growing interest in olive husbandry. The farm and its relatively remote location from the major road or other cities satisfied several needs.

The original farmhouse was commandeered by the Nazi Luftwaffe during the early years of the Great War. Nazi architects and Muslim labor built a wooden parking apron and a level 5,000-foot grass runway for their Messerschmitt Bf-109s and Focke-Wulf Fw-190s to interdict Allied fliers sneaking through the Strait of Gibraltar, into the Mediterranean Sea.

The small farmhouse was greatly expanded and enhanced in the style of a Bavarian lodge to support the Luftwaffe operations and an occasional *Kriegsmarine* operation in the Atlantic and British waters. A long pier jutting into the sea could service a U-boat in an emergency. A maintenance hangar was built adjacent to the runway, as were several Quonset-type bunkers, covered in desert sand, to hide the small German fighters inside.

Abu Manu replaced the decrepit wooden hangar with a metal structure with folding doors and completely refurbished the farmhouse. He paved the old grass and clay runway with a mixture of concrete and asphalt. When workers started to remove the interlocking wooden railroad ties that served as the parking apron before the hangar, they found a huge subterranean work area, complete with lights, storage, and furniture. Abu Manu and his FAHD refurbished and upgraded the nine rooms of underground maintenance spaces to become the repository for cases of gold coins and American-made *Stingers.*

His other love was flying. In Algeria he could get out during the day and when he was able to get away from Libya and his family, he slipped into one of his airplanes and escaped for a couple hours before returning to the farm. His FAHD left him at the hangar. Once he was airborne, they went to the farmhouse overlooking the coast and enjoyed the swimming pool.

Three aircraft filled the metal hangar. His aircraft of choice was a Beech Staggerwing. Trimmed in mouse's back on old mauve, the antique American biplane was a stunning example of atypical negative stagger, where the lower wing was farther forward than the upper.

The other aircraft were a completely disassembled de Havilland DH.88 Comet and a flight-worthy Cessna 206 that he used when the Beechcraft was out of service. His FAHD used the Cessna to fly to and from Libya as well as maintain their flight proficiency. After an hour of preflight, greasing fittings, hooking up the battery, and draining the water that pooled at the bottom of the fuel tanks, Abu Manu pulled the Staggerwing out into the sun and started the radial engine. Minutes later, he was airborne, reconnoitering the coast for ships, submarines, or anything else the U.S. Navy might be using near Algeria.

He was wary of Navy SEALs attacking his beachfront villa, but more than anything else, he believed unmanned aircraft would fly off the coast day and night. He had it on good authority that the Americans were out there. He would fly every day and look for a hint of them until the jet arrived.

CHAPTER TWENTY-NINE

1130 September 22, 2012
U.S. Embassy
Algiers, Algeria

Nazy rolled out of bed and ran for the toilet, her morning sickness confirmed, at least in her mind. The day prior, the staff doctor ran a battery of tests to determine if she was pregnant or if something else could be making her ill. She avoided food during the day. By evening, her nausea became an unsettled memory, and the smell of food from the cafeteria fueled her hunger.

She felt ambivalent as she left the clinic clutching a little amber bottle of Zofran. The doctor said she was, indeed, pregnant and in good health and the pills would help control her nausea.

Riding the elevator to the top floor of the chancery made her a little queasy, but she walked steadily toward her office. Opening the door to the trade attaché's office was enough of a distraction for her to set aside the news and prescription on the desk while she focused on her daily routine and the morning's requirements.

The most-recent intelligence, gathered by the subordinate intel officers or delivered to the embassy, suggested not a wave but more of a breeze was brewing in organized terrorism circles. Leading to the anniversary of 9/11, protests and strong demonstrations occurred at U.S. Embassies, while widespread denunciations of America occurred in several venues in Cairo.

When protests, demonstrations, and denunciations erupted at the Libyan Embassy and its consulate—not wholly unexpected on the anniversary of 9/11—it was noteworthy that other U.S. Embassies avoided the backlash. That the U.S. Consulate and Ambassador's residence were overrun, the Ambassador captured and killed, suggested the event may have been more accidental than careful terrorist coordination and planning.

As more evidence arrived to suggest embassy Tunis would be subject to similar hostile actions, new protests and denunciations of America were in full force outside the compound walls. The demonstrations hadn't gotten violent, but with the aftermath of the consulate in Libya as a backdrop, the U.S. Embassy in Tunisia wasn't taking chances and was in full lockdown and on full alert.

One source indicated it was almost as if the mobs were demonstrating and protesting to keep the embassy staff confined within the compound and were just awaiting a signal. Tripoli was still in the throes of the aftermath of Gaddafi's death, with opposition groups fighting the nascent government. Any intel from any source was suspect, but no one at the embassy had ever suspected the consulate would be overrun, with the Annex and embassy subjected to a coordinated attack.

On the surface, that was a problem. It was the anniversary of 9/11, and a reasonable person in the State Department and the U.S. Embassy should have expected some kind of protest or hostile action, especially in a country roiling in anarchy after Gaddafi's demise. With the Muslim Brotherhood's activity in Egypt serving as more of a distraction than bellwether, it was difficult for analysts within the intelligence community to craft a reasonable picture of the situation slowly gripping North Africa. Protests were on the edge of turning violent and expanded to oil field operations. The picture that developed gave analysts more than a hint that Embassy Algiers would be targeted after Embassy Tunis.

Astoundingly, neither al-Qaeda nor the Muslim Brotherhood claimed success or failure in the attack on the U.S. Consulate or the death of the U.S. Ambassador to Libya. Claiming credit for a successful attack was a significant resume enhancer for any apprentice terrorist or terrorist affiliate. The dearth of comments from the two organizations was curious.

Punctually at nine o'clock, wearing a black pantsuit with white silk blouse, Nazy stepped into the conference room to brief the U.S. Ambassador and key leaders at the morning meeting. Her feet hurt as she stood to speak. She willed her stomach to behave and settle down. Nazy hurried her delivery, and almost everyone noticed the unsettled urgency in her voice.

"What information we're receiving is poor at best," she said. "It seems al-Qaeda and/or the Muslim Brotherhood have learned basic operational security. No one is talking. That, in itself, is highly unusual. Our usual sources have had their ears tuned for any suggestion of protests or demonstrations here or Embassy Tunis, but so far, nothing from them. However, a spontaneous demonstration occurred at a large oil drilling facility between Tunis and Algiers.

"We expect Embassy Tunis to be subjected to an increased barrage of protests, demonstrations, and denunciations similar to those that preceded the attacks on the embassy and consulate in Libya. As expected, these are beginning and are small in number at the moment.

"Despite the lack of evidence or local intel, I recommend we raise our threat condition from yellow to orange and review the sheltering and evacuation plans. We might contact the constabulary for greater presence and possibly erect barriers at both ends of our road for a start. That is a minimum.

"I also suggest the embassy raise its threat condition to red if Embassy Tunis comes under greater pressure in the next few days."

Sitting down gingerly, she wobbled slightly in her chair.

At the end of her brief, the Ambassador and Security Officer were interested in Nazy's assessment of when an attack could or would be expected. She took notes from the multiple questions asked by those around the table. She didn't stand to respond.

"We don't have a good sense of when to expect hostile action," she said. "What we have is the start of a trend. After a couple of days of small, intermittent protests, the conditions and dynamics are ripe for escalation. What we saw in Egypt and Libya was exactly that. They had a couple of days of protests, then antagonistic, vocal demonstrations, followed by armed attacks. The protests at the oil facility are worrisome.

"The protests and demonstrations, although intermittent, occurred in Tripoli about one week after those in Egypt. What was expected was something volatile and aggressive associated with the 9/11 anniversary; there was no other known rationale for the attacks.

"Protests and demonstrations are ramping up in Tunis, but they haven't escalated into something more aggressive. Whether there's a break in the action at Embassy Tripoli or it was just coincidental, they exercised a NEO, and all vehicles were clear of the embassy grounds just as armed attackers with AK-47s and RPGs came from several sources a few blocks away.

"Embassy Tripoli didn't have the resources we do. The preliminary report is the Ambassador was ambushed, and his local personal security ran off. There wasn't good intel at Tripoli. I lean to the view that they were very lucky to evacuate when they did. We have three contractors augmenting the security from Embassy Tripoli, and they were tangentially involved in the Benghazi attack. They suggest the security at the embassy was extremely poor, and they were fortunate to leave Tripoli when they did."

The room became quiet. People became pensive as they wrestled with the information. The Security Officer nodded to Nazy, who smiled in return. Finally, the Ambassador spoke.

"Nice brief, Miss C. Thank you. I think the prudent thing to do is at least raise the threat condition level to orange. We can still do our jobs with that added level of security. Can we get the chancery provisioned for a long duration occupation if we have to endure protestors for a few days? I don't want to evacuate unless it's absolutely necessary. Algiers has been at peace for several years. We haven't seen the number of demonstrations as Cairo has with Mubarak's fall. Libyan rebels are still trying to come down from the sugar high of overthrowing Gaddafi. If anything happens to Tunis, we must consider that we're next. Have we heard anything from Morocco?"

Nazy shook her head.

The Ambassador said, "Well, if we see some action, then maybe

Rabat will be next. OK. If there are no other questions, let's get back to work. Keep alert and be careful."

Her latest bout of nausea wasn't as bad as the others. Nazy sat very still at her desk, begging the disgusting feeling to leave her body. She looked at the small prescription bottle filled with a wonder drug to make her feel better. She would no longer have to endure the noxious feeling or run to hug a commode. The foul sensation slowly passed, before the next bout arrived, she took out a single oblong pill and washed the medicine down.

She noticed that when she was still or sitting, the nausea was worse, but, when she moved, it was almost unnoticeable. She hoped she didn't have to take the pills for long, though the doctor said they were especially helpful and wouldn't harm the baby. Unconsciously, she placed a hand on her belly. She had to take care of herself *and* the baby —Duncan's baby.

She remained standing with her notebook and began writing a few notes as one-word memory triggers. *Files* meant to segregate certain files for safekeeping, the others for destruction. Some could be done before the bad guys arrived. *Computer* meant to destroy her hard drive. She would have to unplug it and drop it into the disintegrator in the SCIF. *Reports* had to be drafted and submitted in advance of an expected NEO or embassy attack. *Bug out* was for packing and positioning a "go bag" of essentials. She had to ensure the anti-nausea pills were always nearby.

Six years earlier, when Nazy received an assignment to Saudi Arabia as Deputy Chief of Station, Duncan helped her pack a go bag of essential items to take in an emergency, such as an evacuation. *Text* meant to send Duncan a message: *Definitely going to have your baby!*

Her final entry was *25*. Three days to go before she could execute the special access program *Piper.*

She completed her list before she wandered to the window facing the flagpole and the access road to the embassy. She observed vehicle traffic on the access road was light, and pedestrian traffic was nil. The American flag sagged in the still air.

Some Marines in civilian clothes walked toward the apartments. She thought she was feeling a bit better, and the pill was suppressing her running bouts of nausea. If there was a chance the embassy had to evacuate, she had a thousand things to do.

With a heavy sigh, she turned and walked down the hall to the SCIF to help her people shred files and documents and prepare them to destroy communications and computer equipment.

CHAPTER THIRTY

1200 September 22, 2012
Baltimore-Washington International Airport

Duncan Hunter stepped down the air stairs of Quiet Aero Systems' Gulfstream IVSP, set a helmet bag and backpack onto the tarmac, turned, and lifted and locked the aircraft's door. Dark sunglasses protected his eyes from the bright noon sun. He tossed the backpack over his shoulder, his flight boots padded silently across the hot tarmac.

On the other side of the executive terminal, a black Lincoln Town Car waited for him. Sliding into the soft leather seat, he said, "Misty Black," to the chauffeur.

"Good afternoon, Sir." Through the small sliding glass opening between the seats the driver handed Hunter a manila envelope, taped and double-wrapped, the standard protocol for transporting classified documents. He slipped it into the helmet bag.

Hunter wasn't interested in the package at the moment, nor did he want to banter with the CIA driver, an elderly black man with thick black glasses who'd been a pool driver for the CIA for over thirty years. He transported thousands of sensitive documents and packages and hundreds of the highest-ranking intelligence officers in the CIA. No one talked shop in the vehicles. Rarely did anyone speak to him. Accustomed to the quiet, he liked it that way. Due to heavy congestion on the Beltway, the thirty-five-mile journey to Andrews Air Force base took an hour.

Hunter focused on reading his messages and email on his BlackBerry. First, he replied to Nazy's text. *You need to come home. Algiers is no place for a mom to be. Have something to tell you.* He didn't mention he would be traveling to North Africa or would be very close to where she was working.

He was annoyed by the email response, more of a scolding, from the DCI. Hunter was surprised Dr. Rothwell even read his classified email account. Rothwell said he would forward the request to HR, but to refrain from any others. *Email to the director isn't generally how potential officers are recruited.*

Hunter studied the passing traffic outside and shook his head in mock disgust. He said to himself, "I'd like to see Kelly in the system before you resign, dumb ass."

He worked with his BlackBerry, answering email from students and making two phone calls. He called the taller Bob and asked if there would be anything other than box lunches on the flight. Hearing an unsatisfactory answer, Hunter ordered ten pizzas from a pizzeria near the sprawling Air Force Base's main gate.

He called Greg Lynche, got no answer, and left a detailed voice mail. In coded language, he told Greg he'd call him back when he could and bid him good luck bidding on the YO-3A.

The driver stopped at the pizza parlor, the main gate, and Base Operations. Hunter tipped the man fifty dollars, astounding him into politely trying to refuse. He jumped from the vehicle and helped the shorter Bob carry boxes of pizza into the flight operations complex.

Hunter passed his helmet bag through the X-ray machine and walked through the magnetometer. Once he was on the other side of the security station, he took half the load of pizza boxes from the counter, as he and Bob slid into a golf cart on the air side of the building.

"Works every time," he said as they drove off.

Bob winked, the two men sharing their little secret.

Less than seven minutes later, all aircrew, passengers, and pizzas were aboard the Agency's cargo airplane. As Hunter buckled in, the crew chief stood outside with a long cord, monitoring the engines, as the pilot started the inboards first, then the outboards. Once all the Allison T56 turboprops were turning, the crew chief climbed in, and the loadmaster closed the cargo doors.

Hunter, Bob, and Bob tackled the fourth pizza brought aboard. From the bottom box, Hunter withdrew his Colt Python .357 Magnum and Model 1911 Kimber Special wrapped in plastic, and returned the weapons to his backpack.

It was very noisy inside the belly of one of Lockheed's greatest achievements. For almost 100 years, the Lockheed Aircraft Corporation built some of the world's most-dynamic aircraft. Some designs were a fusion of art and function. Others were a fusion of beauty and lethality or muscle. Lockheed created the indomitable P-38 Lightning; the elegant Super Constellation; the stubby-winged F-104; the high-flying U-2; the fastest aircraft on the planet, the SR-71; the first generation F-117 stealth fighter; its replacement, the F-22 Raptor; and the C-5 Galaxy, one of the largest cargo aircraft ever built. Most of those aircraft flew to the end of their life cycles and ended up in bone yards or were recycled into Coke cans. Some were still flying, quietly operational like the Raptor, the Galaxy, and the secretive U-2.

For almost sixty years, Lockheed's crown jewel of multi-functionality, the venerable C-130 Hercules, was still in production and flying the most diverse missions anywhere—search and rescue, electronic warfare, with skis for Antarctica operations, with cannon and machine guns as an attack platform. The basic cargo aircraft was the Swiss Army knife of the aviation world. It could do nearly anything, anytime, and go almost any place from Antarctica to deserts, from jungles to mountaintops.

The CIA's C-130s, actually L-100s, built and registered as the civilian version of the Hercules, were procured by the former Chief Air Branch, the ever capable Greg Lynche, to transport sensitive materials or people to and from remote places where unimproved landing surfaces were the norm. The aircraft were lovingly maintained and deftly flown by the most-experienced pilots and crew the military could train and the CIA could hire.

Between bites of pepperoni pizza and his ubiquitous iced Diet Mountain Dew, Hunter reviewed the overheads of the private airstrips in Spain and Algeria. Several eight-by-ten glossies of the target area were included in the double-wrapped envelope. The sharp resolution of the photographs, astounding for satellite imagery, always amazed him. A rendering of the man believed to be the target was highlighted in shades of black and white, as if the man was imaged by a forward-looking infrared camera.

Hunter set the FLIR rendering atop a pizza box to study carefully, committing the nuances of the man's eyes, chin, and forehead to memory. He recalled the DCI saying, "There are no known pictures of him, but what grainy video we have shows he's the commanding presence during the offload." The FLIR's pixilated rendering must have been taken at a significant altitude and slant angle, and not from a satellite.

Hunter saw enough and returned the photographs to their envelope. The airplane leveled off at its cruising altitude. Bob and Bob moved in the background. After finishing their meals, they crawled into sleeping bags for the fourteen-hour flight. Hunter replaced his sound suppressors with earplugs, slipped into his sleeping bag, and placed a sleep mask over his eyes. The vibration of the turboprops wasn't felt across the troop seats and the three civilians were asleep in minutes.

CHAPTER THIRTY-ONE

0400 September 23, 2012
U.S. Embassy
Tunis, Tunisia

Demetrius Eastwood should have known the road to Tunis would be paved with trouble. He was in Africa and when you're in Africa nothing goes according to plan. After speeding down the four-lane road—full of two-way traffic—from Tripoli to Zuwarah—they were stopped. Eastwood and his driver stared at a roadblock, an expedient slapdashed barrier. Khalid al-Awalaki stepped from the Toyota to read the makeshift sign. When he returned, he reported the road to Ben Gardane was impassible. He had heard Gaddafi supporters made the road from Tunis to Tripoli impassable, fearing Tunisian irregulars would join the fight against Gaddafi. He said the detour south through Nalut would add several hundred miles and a few days to their trip.

After giving his report, Khalid waited for a decision from Eastwood.

The truck idled, burning precious fuel. Eastwood stared over the hood and makeshift roadblock, feeling tired and close to defeated. He tried to shoo away the thought he made a bad decision, though hopefully not a terminal one. Those crossed scraps of wood barricading the roadbed didn't signify *Do Not Enter,* but he regretted the decision to refuse the offer of aircraft and stay in Libya pursuing the thinnest of leads to a completely undeveloped story.

The situation surrounding the ambassador's killing made no sense. Al-Qaeda and the Muslim Brotherhood didn't collaborate on operations, but in Benghazi, it looked like they had. With the number of black flags of al-Qaeda flying in that city, it was astounding to find the green flag of the Muslim Brotherhood victoriously flapping in the breeze inside the consulate compound.

In Tripoli, two separate groups of protestors, pouring from opposite sides of the road from different mosques, suggested collaboration. Was al-Qaeda on one side and the Brotherhood on the other, or were they working together?

The road on the other side of the barrier was littered with the carcasses of automobiles and trucks. They didn't look like they'd been hit with roadside bombs or RPGs.

"What do you think, Boss?" Marty Marceau asked.

"I think after we've come this far, going several hundred miles out of our way won't get us to Tunis as soon as I'd like. I say we have a four-wheel drive and let's give it a go." He looked over his shoulder at the two men in the back seat, who grimaced but nodded.

Eastwood offered Khalid another gold coin, which the man pocketed.

"We should get more provisions," Khalid said.

He bought chicken and pastries, bottled water, a bicycle pump, and an additional jerry can. He filled the truck's tank and the extra fuel cans.

Twenty miles past the roadblock, they encountered their first obstacle. The asphalt roadbed had been obliterated for a thousand yards, and the bridge over a shallow *wadi* was destroyed. Traces of tire tracks indicated a workaround, and Khalid followed a bit too fast, bouncing everyone against the roof when he hit something deep and hard. They all heard air escaping from a tire when they flopped back into their seats.

The four men crawled out. A sharp metal fragment hidden in the soft sand cut into the sidewall of the front tire. The four leaped into action, removing and replacing the bad tire and mounting the spare in ten minutes. Marty, noticing the spare was soft, raced around the back of the SUV and retrieved the bicycle pump. While he pumped, Eastwood supervised. Khalid heaved the flat tire and wheel onto the roof rack. When the replacement tire was inflated, they got back in the truck and were on their way.

Ten minutes on the other side of the washed-out riverbed, Khalid complained of hard steering. He stopped the truck. He and Eastwood got out to see the spare tire partially deflated. Marty retrieved the pump and gave the tire a hundred strokes. They got back in and raced along the rutted sand road.

Every few miles, they took turns to pump up the tire. Eastwood again admonished himself for going past the roadblock. They drove five miles and spent five minutes pumping the tire. Without tools to repair the tire, they were committed to tag-teaming, pumping and driving.

Up ahead lay a long stretch of asphalt, and the leaking tire was due to be pumped again. Khalid attempted to drive onto the hardpan and hit a pothole, bouncing everyone from his seat. Again they heard air rush from a tire.

Dejected, they got out and were immediately pissed off when they saw the tire bead had separated from the rim. Khalid muttered in Arabic, while the film crew cursed and kicked sand. Eastwood, with arms akimbo, squinted at the wheel, thinking. After a few seconds he said aloud, "Marty, you and Karl remove the tire. Khalid, get me one of the gas cans."

The three men stared with mouths agape, as Eastwood returned to the truck without speaking. Marty, shrugging, went to get the jack. Khalid stood alone, looked at the tire for a moment, and continued to lament Eastwood's decision as he shook his head. *Americans are bold but crazy!*

Eastwood came from the truck wielding a Leatherman multi-tool and flipped open the knife blade. "Khalid, some gasoline, please."

The old colonel walked to the back of the truck, stood on the rear bumper, and cut strips of rubber from the shredded tire on the roof. Marty and Karl exchanged a look. *What's he doing?*

Thoroughly confused by Eastwood's actions, Khalid moved to the back of the truck and extracted a jerry can, wondering what the crazy American was up to.

With the tire off the truck and away from the wheel rim, Eastwood reached inside and cautiously felt for something that might have caused the slow leak. In seconds, he stopped and studied the outside of the tire where his hand touched. The three men watched in fascination.

Eastwood unfolded the handles of his multi-tool until he had a pair of pliers, then he probed the tread and squeezed the handles together to extract a piece of metal. He held up an inch-long pull tab from a zipper in the teeth of the pliers.

"That's what's been giving us the leak. I don't feel anything else. Karl, I hope you still have superglue in your kit." Kneeling in the soft sand, he extracted two three-inch strips of thin rubber from the tire. He collapsed his pliers and extracted a screwdriver blade, setting it on the tire.

"I do." Karl Mann disappeared into the back seat and returned with a small pinch tube of cyanoacrylate.

"OK. Let's saturate these with glue."

The other men watched in amusement, their arms crossed. Though Eastwood might fix the leak, they didn't see how he could reseat the tire bead back against the wheel rim. As Marty squeezed the little metal tube, clear noxious glue oozed out, as Eastwood rolled the rubber strips around and around until they were saturated. He placed the wet strips against the tread. With the screwdriver blade, he pushed the rubber into the slit left by the zipper tab then he reached inside the tire to confirm the rubber strips had gone all the way through.

He closed the screwdriver blade and flicked open the knife blade to cut away the remaining rubber strips, ensuring they were even with the tread.

Satisfied, he said, "Now comes the fun part." They stared as Eastwood unscrewed the jerry can's cap and poured a small amount of gasoline inside the tire. He replaced the cap and lifted the tire, and swished the fuel around the inside.

Eastwood stood and reached into Khalid's pocket to take out his pack of matches. "Stand back."

The three men quickly stepped back from the madman, who lit a match and tossed it into the space between the tire and rim. The vapor ignited with a *woomph!* The explosion expanded the tire so suddenly, even Eastwood was startled. The tire jumped a foot off the ground, and the tire bead violently and loudly snapped against the rim. The three watchers were dumbfounded.

Eastwood checked the tire pressure, feeling it warm and hard. He thumped it, surprised to find the tire fully inflated. He cocked his head in pleasure; he stood, returned the matches to Khalid, and winked at the shocked man.

As Eastwood returned to the Toyota, he said, "It's pumped up. Let's get it on the truck and get the hell out of here."

The patch held. They reached the border on a good road without having to pump the tire again. The three were still discussing Eastwood's creativity when they saw a small fire in the distance that could have been a campfire. It was just twilight, and the road signs indicated they were near the Tunisian border. GPS confirmed they were close.

Khalid suggested what they saw might be a checkpoint at the Libyan border with Tunisia.

Eastwood didn't like the ambiance. They were in the middle of the desert; an unexpected campfire at the border. There was a reason no one came that way. The hair on his neck rose.

As the truck neared the campfire, what had been small flames erupted into a huge conflagration, illuminating three men with *keffiyehs* wrapped around their faces, startled by the approaching vehicle.

"Back up!" Eastwood shouted. *"Back up! Back up! Back up!"*

One man in a dark *keffiyeh* raised an RPG and aimed at them. Khalid was confused. He successfully negotiated the other checkpoints; this was just one more.

"Stop! Stop! Back up! Back up!" Eastwood shouted.

Khalid couldn't resolve the dichotomy between what Eastwood shouted and what his eyes told him, but he allowed the truck to slow. Eastwood, seeing the confusion on the man's face, didn't hesitate. He threw his leg across the gear shift lever and stepped on the brake.

Startled, Khalid tried to speak, but Eastwood mashed the clutch and shifted the transmission into reverse, grabbed the steering wheel, and then stomped on Khalid's foot still resting on the gas pedal.

The vehicle backed quickly and increased speed. Eastwood looked over his shoulder out the back window as he drove. Marty and Karl, riveted to their seats, leaned toward the doors to give Eastwood a clear view to the rear as they stared down the gun sight of a rocket-propelled grenade launcher.

Eastwood glanced to the front, fully expecting the RPG to be launched, but it didn't come. They raced away from the danger in reverse, and Eastwood sensed they were safe and released Khalid's crushed foot, letting the truck coast to a stop.

At three hundred yards from the campfire, Eastwood refrained from shouting at their driver. Khalid was in shock. The two men in the back seat wered dazed. The boss never acted so decisively and dramatically before, but they knew he probably saved their lives. No one had ever pointed an RPG at them before.

He returned his leg to his side of the footwell and found himself breathing hard from adrenalin, as if he sprinted for his life and crossed the finish line to safety.

Between gulps of air, he said, "Those were bandits. We wouldn't have been allowed to pass. They would have robbed us and killed us. We need to find a way around them. Lights off."

Khalid, nodding, rubbed his sandaled foot and took his guide from a light in the distance well south of the campfire. They soon found an unpaved road leading to the highway and began driving north to Tunis. GPS guided them, and they reached the bustling, sprawling city just before four o'clock in the morning.

Tunis was quietly alive. Under brilliant, clear skies and a waxing gibbous moon, small drab cars and dirty overloaded trucks vied for position on the roads and roundabouts. Eastwood directed Khalid to drive directly to the embassy, taking the frontage road to see if the situation was quiet and normal, or if there were demonstrators or worse.

"After we drive past," he explained, "we'll can spend the night at one of the hotels." They saw several hotels in the distance, many stories tall and well-lit with colorful marquees.

Khalid followed the GPS.

As they approached the brightly lit façade of the U.S. Embassy, an exhausted Eastwood could not believe what he saw. *"Shit! Not again!"*

CHAPTER THIRTY-TWO

0800 September 23, 2012
Lajes Field, Azores

As the Hercules landed, Hunter's BlackBerry began to vibrate and ring. While the big cargo plane rolled down the runway he read the text message: *The final chapter of your book was received and is ready for publication.*

The DCI confirmed the airstrip in Spain was physically inspected, there were no impediments on the runway.

The bad news was that their aircraft suffered a mechanical malfunction three hours from the air base, and the four-engined turboprop landed with only three engines running. After parking on the transient alert ramp, the aircrew's two mechanics isolated the discrepancy to a bad component and were hard at work borrowing a work stand to change the suspected bad tachometer generator. If that didn't fix the problem, the mission would be scrubbed. No one wanted that, so the mechanics hurried to troubleshoot and repair the engine.

While they worked, a U.S. Air Force driver took the crew of the white Hercules to the billeting office. The flight engineer raced into the Mid Atlantic Lodge to check in the flight. Prior to dispatch from the U.S., he secured rooms for everyone on the plane—standard procedure on *Noble Savage* missions—so there were limited records of who registered at the on-base lodging facilities. The former Marine reserved eight rooms for all eight men and handed keys to everyone in the base operations van. Hunter, the mission commander, should have been accorded distinguished visitor privileges, but the missions were to be as low profile as possible. While not five-star Marriott accommodations, the suites overlooking the Atlantic provided breathtaking views and were fully equipped with beverages, snacks, and movies. They were more than adequate for a twenty-four-hour layover.

Located on the easternmost part of the island of Terceira, Lajes Field was regularly used by NATO and non-NATO fighter and transport planes while DOD aircraft movements were at an all-time low. With more and more airplanes relying on aerial refueling, the Air Force support component at Lajes was downsized. The DOD ramp was typically deserted except for an occasional transient C-130 or KC-135. Those aircrews that spent the night were treated to great rooms overlooking the ocean. The food and service in town were better than the American flyboys expected, making a layover in Lajes one of the best-kept secrets in DOD.

Duncan walked along the covered porch, found his room, and quietly entered. He tossed his backpack into a chair and went to the refrigerator, removing a tall carton of juice with a picture of an orange and Arabic writing. Sipping the drink, he stopped in front of the large picture window and admired the dark-blue ocean 100 yards away. Although he appeared relaxed, he was anything but. Something about the mission unnerved him, and he couldn't put his finger on it.

The mechanical challenges weren't the issue. It was something else, something the DCI had said and what he didn't say. Again, Hunter went over every aspect of the mission, replaying each expected event in his mind. The actual mission of flying from Spain across the Med to Algiers was the easy part of the calculations.

He struggled to ascertain what was different about this mission and the others he flew. Granted, there were few opportunities to get into position to eliminate the target. He began to see a pattern. One thing about the mission that was different from all his other targets was that they were known figures of some repute, but this one had nothing. No history. No nothing.

Hunter found it curious and almost insulting that he wasn't allowed to review the file. He was given unfettered access to the files of all the other targets; he got to read the intelligence collected on the men and he got to know them. From the file the men Hunter was after were very bad, wicked, men. But with this target, he didn't even have a photograph of the man. How was it possible, with all of the CIA's assets, including NRO satellites and Agency unmanned aircraft, that they had no actual pictures of the man? The FLIR image in shades of gray was pathetic.

The only hint of the man's importance came from the DCI's cryptic remark, "He shot down commercial airliners, usually for ransom."

That statement gave Hunter pause several times during the week. A self-described expert in aviation history, he was unaware of any commercial aircraft, certainly none belonging to the U.S., had been shot down. How? Was it a surface-to-air missile? Bullets couldn't do it. It had to be a SAM.

What's the rest of the story?

Something else gnawed at him. The DCI's actions during their last meeting were a little odd. The man was always a bit odd, but there was something subtler going on with him. It was like the way the press projected only the story they wished to convey, while the rest of the story was ignored, hidden, or obscured.

Hunter was so focused on the mystery that he didn't immediately hear the knock at the door. Once he did, he quickly went to open it.

The shorter Bob smiled. "The plane's fixed. I thought you wanted to know."

"Tach gen?"

"Yep. Ops checked good."

"Thanks. What are you doing now?"

"What's on your mind? You have that look."

He shot down commercial airliners. The phrase ricocheted in Hunter's brain like a BB in a boxcar. The dead time between Bob's question and Hunter's response confused and concerned Bob. Normally, Hunter's responses were immediate, terse, and pithy.

Finally, Hunter nodded and said, "Come inside."

Hunter concluded if the target downed commercial airliners, ostensibly with a *Stinger* or another MANPADS, Hunter could be at risk to a shoulder-fired missile, too. *Why didn't the DCI say something?*

If there was any chance the target had or could use MANPADS, Hunter had to protect himself. The YO-3A carried a countermeasures capability but never used them. They never had to, because the aircraft was picked up by radar only once. Otherwise, it hadn't been discovered in fifteen years of flying at night under the best radar systems.

"Bob, we need to load flares in the cans."

One bushy eyebrow went up. Bob's concern and interest were piqued. They *never* had to load flares in the flare dispensers when Hunter flew an operation. He asked, "Chaff?"

"Flares *and* chaff. Yes, Sir." Hunter continued to consider why the DCI didn't say anything.

"The Yo-Yo doesn't have much of a thermal signature, Boss. It never did, especially if you're in a left turn, masking the exhaust."

"For this one, Bob, I'd feel a lot safer if I had flares aboard. Do we still have some in the safe?"

"We have enough to fill a single can, thirty flares. I can load half chaff and half flares in both cans. I never expected us to use those cans. We won't be able to test them to see if they whistle. We haven't had to. Think this one's hostile?" Bob paused to let his comment air out like nasty gym socks long forgotten in gym locker.

Bob Jones was old-school Army. Every single YO-3A that ever flew over Vietnam had never been shot at or detected. For the fifteen years he and Bob spent maintaining the aircraft for Hunter and Lynche, they never needed to load the heavy M-206 infrared decoys in the dispenser system in the tail of the aircraft.

"Could be. I'll feel better knowing they're back there. I should be far enough away that it won't matter if there's a little whistling. Half the flares on each side, and load the chaff, too." Hunter recalled a photograph of a Special Operations AC-130 dispensing flares at night, illuminating the aircraft as the magnesium burned and fell away from the fuselage. If he had to dispense flares to decoy an infrared-seeking missile away from the Yo-Yo, the mission would be a failure.

"OK, Duncan," Bob said. "Bob and I will go down and ops check the system. We haven't done that, ever. If you think you might need them, we'll make sure the cans work as advertised."

"Thanks."

"Duncan, there may be a problem."

"What's that?"

"I'm sure the flares we have in the safe have long expired. They have a shelf life. There's no guarantee they'll work properly."

"Well Bob, if old flares are all we have then they'll have to do."

After the old mechanic left, Hunter resumed playing in his mind the mission. He returned to thoughts of flares and chaff of flare dispensers, and war-gaming the operation with the cans full. He expected full dispensers would be heavy, dragging on the tail. Landing could be an issue, but nothing the elevator trim and his thick biceps couldn't overcome. Old flares shouldn't be an issue operationally either. *No one ever looks up at the sky!*

Hunter soon returned to a recurring theme as it roiled in his mind. *He shot down commercial airliners, usually for ransom.* No other target Lynche and Hunter encountered were known to possess or be equipped with MANPADS. They rarely flew missions where air defense systems were present or active, but this target was obviously different.

Is this a ransom delivery? Hunter reflected on the scenario the DCI portrayed during the mission brief. *He said approximately thirty containers are removed from the aircraft and are carried into the hangar. Why did he tell me that? How would he know that?*

He paused, recalling a thin thread of something he'd been mulling over earlier.

A thin smile spread over his face, as he closed his eyes and stretched his neck. He admonished himself for missing the obvious. There *had* been a commercial aircraft shot down. He chuckled softly. Officially, it was a fuel-tank explosion. The FBI never interviewed the witnesses who said it was a missile, and so did a couple of Congressmen. They knew the truth. *Apparently so does the CIA!*

Congress held closed-door hearings. When the FBI was pulled from the case, the press jumped aboard the fuel cell explosion lie that the old Democratic administration touted.

The lie collapsed on itself when Hunter was startled by the realization that it was true; his mind released and unburdened by the classified contents of some obscure top secret CIA file. The paradigm was broken. Truths tumbled from his thoughts.

Flight 800 was shot down by a surface-to-air missile.

The government paid ransom to stop other airplanes from being blown from the sky.

Congress tried to put countermeasures on commercial aircraft and failed.

America is still paying ransom.

This is the only opportunity to stop him.

The target was different from all the rest. Duncan Hunter had a final thought before fury overcame him.

Does he know I'm coming for him?

CHAPTER THIRTY-THREE

1700 September 23, 2012
Mostaganem, Algeria

Abu Manu turned the roaring Staggerwing to the east, putting the sun at his back and Algiers, just on the horizon, on the nose. The Wright 1820 radial turned smoothly, and the engine's gentle vibration was pleasing to his back. The only traffic was the occasional jumbo, its contrail streaming five miles overhead on a north-south route. The weather was perfect for flying, with a few cirrostratus and altostratus marking the dark-blue sky. He marveled at the clear weather above, east, west, and north. Over Africa, to the south, stood a wall of suspended sand and dust from the Sahara all the way up to where big jets raced, and disappeared into the dust, as they serviced Africa and Europe.

He pulled the throttle back to idle and allowed the biplane to decelerate for his approach to the runway. He buzzed the farmhouse in a right turn. His FAHD, Malik and Habib, raised their hands in acknowledgement and rushed to the SUV in the courtyard. They would meet him at the hangar.

Abu Manu brushed the outskirts of Mostaganem and the old ruins without seeing any vehicles on the road leading to his property. He continued his right turn to line up for the runway and expertly set the aircraft down on its heavily springed mains before allowing the tail wheel to touch the ground gently.

As he rolled to the hangar, the silver Mercedes SUV approached from the north with his FAHD. He was proud of them. They were the greatest thing he ever did.

He couldn't make normal, healthy children. Wives who were once beautiful and fertile bore him cripples and disgust, offering more pain and suffering than he could endure. In stark contrast, his FAHD were perfect specimens of Arabic intelligence, conditioning, and training.

He was the one who made them. All that they were and would be was because of him. He made them, trained them, and challenged them. They were the finest fighting force the Muslim world ever knew. They trained like American SEALs, with all types of weapons in all possible scenarios.

Like SEALs, his FAHD were master parachutists and competent aviators, able to fly small Cessnas and helicopters and almost anything in between. Navy SEALs were masters on and under water, trained to board ships at sea and leave them undetected; so were his FAHD. It was his favorites, Malik and Habib, who slipped over the side of the small container ship *Al Minya* as it steered toward Long Island. They were the ones who extracted the rubber Zodiac from a shipping container and shot the American jet from the sky, making Abu Manu a billionaire.

That was a long time ago. Abu Manu refocused on the job at hand and slowed the aircraft to a crawl, depressed the rudder pedal, and spun the aircraft 270° in front of the hangar before shutting down the Beechcraft's big engine.

He turned off the battery and checked the Hobbs meter and clock on the instrument panel before dutifully logging his time in his logbook. When he opened the door and stepped out, Malik and Habib greeted him with smiles and helped guide the dark, two-toned airplane into the hangar.

"Anything?" Malik asked.

"Nothing."

"That's good," said Habib.

"Yes, very good. We'll see what tomorrow brings."

CHAPTER THIRTY-FOUR

1700 September 23, 2012
Sheraton Tunis Hotel, Tunisia

Demetrius "Dory" Eastwood, his film crew, and their driver, Khalid al-Awalaki, met in the hotel lounge for food and drinks. Having virtually slept in the Toyota and their clothes for almost a week, the men were ecstatic to have a room, a shower, and a laundry to scrub the road grime from their bodies and sleep on clean sheets. Khalid, never experiencing such luxury and amenities in Libya, pocketed extra bottles of shampoo, conditioner, and bars of soap for when he said good-bye to the Americans. He reflected on his relationship with Eastwood and the men called "the film crew."

He saw movies and TV during his short visit with his father in Texas. Khalid reminisced fondly of traveling with his father, a civil engineer employed by the U.S. Air Force at the Wheelus Air Force Base near Tripoli, Libya. Khalid caddied for Air Force pilots at the base's golf course and quickly learned English and American mannerisms.

His world turned upside down with the Gaddafi coup. His father was hunted and killed as a traitor for working so closely with the Americans. With his father dead and the Americans expelled from Libya, Khalid was alone and isolated from the radicals in power.

Innate survival strategies kicked in, and he found work as a messenger boy, then a taxi driver. He recalled telling Eastwood that Libya was a hateful Muslim country, run by competing clans of crazy people, with mosques led by bad men who distorted the Prophet's message.

"They are in charge," he said, "and you cannot escape. I found ways of getting along, or I would be killed. Get noticed and you're a dead man. Best to be quiet and not bring attention, then you live."

Khalid raced downstairs for his next adventure with the Americans.

After filming a large group of demonstrators approaching the U.S. Embassy in Tunis, Eastwood and his crew turned the camera toward a smaller group—the real attackers—who crouched down and tried to hide their weapons, as they walked behind the large wave of protestors.

Like the group they filmed in Tripoli, a similar-sized group in Tunis brandished several dozen AK-47s and half a dozen RPGs as they marched. The armed attackers were furious to find the building deserted. With no one there, some of the men with weapons fired a few rounds into the compound before they returned to their mosques.

Khalid suddenly made an offer to go with the men from the mosque. "I can find things."

Eastwood considered that, then he offered another gold coin to see if Khalid could integrate with the demonstrators and find out what they were doing and who sent them. Khalid, pleased with himself, felt energized to help. He came to know the three men and was curious, eager to help as the story played out. He was surprised Eastwood offered him the Krugerrand.

Forty-five minutes after leaving the truck, Khalid returned and told Eastwood what he learned. Most of the demonstrators received thirty Tunisian dinars to protest against America and their presence in Muslim lands. When the group carrying weapons began their attack, the protestors were supposed to run. However, when they found the embassy gate open and the compound empty, the protestors turned on the men with weapons, worried they wouldn't be paid their thirty dinars for a night's work.

"Like the Tripoli Embassy," Eastwood said, "they left before they could be attacked."

"Yes, yes," Khalid said. "Like."

"Where are the locals? Marty, Karl, why aren't there any local constabularies? It's as if they knew something, either that the embassy personnel would run or that the attackers were coming, so they called in sick. Something isn't right with all this."

Filming despondent, vociferous protestors walking away from an abandoned embassy didn't make for good copy. The exhausted men drove to the hotel. Eastwood and his crew, standing in the lobby and asking for rooms, brought security officers converging on the check-in and concierge desks.

Eastwood, dirty and tired, felt slightly miffed that no one behind the counter would serve him and his men. It was only when an American Airlines flight crew was departing the hotel for the airport that the pilot recognized Demetrius Eastwood from his shows on the news network and walked over to speak with him and his crew.

A self-professed big fan, the pilot told the clerks behind the counter, "This man is very famous. You need to give them good rooms."

The burly, gray-haired man with four gold stripes on his sleeve turned his back to the staff and asked, "When all they watch is Al-Jazeera, what do you expect?" The airline captain shook every man's hand, including Khalid's.

After securing a room and getting six hours' sleep, Eastwood called his producer in New York. Surprised to find Eastwood in Tunis, not Libya, the angry woman wanted answers. She debated with Eastwood about his next assignment.

She argued that Demetrius completed his real mission of investigating and reporting on the killing of the U.S. Ambassador to Libya. She wanted him to head to Lagos, Nigeria, to investigate a militant jihadist group in the northern part of the country.

Eastwood was in no mood for that assignment. He knew of the growing threat of Boko Haram after they fomented extreme sectarian violence in northern Nigeria, having killed over 1,000 people. Another spinoff Islamist movement, it was a full-service terrorist organization that indiscriminately attacked Muslims and Christians. When they didn't kidnap young girls, Boko Haram machine-gunned children and their teachers in classrooms as a way of sowing fear.

Eastwood wasn't ready to abandon the current investigation. He complained that they hadn't really completed their mission, but they turned up a strange movement and apparent collaboration between terrorist groups, which led them to Tunis. If the scuttlebutt in the hotel was correct, the demonstrators that chased the U.S. Embassy staff from their compound in Tunis were heading west to Algiers and possibly Rabat. He beseeched her for a half an hour until they negotiated a truce. The producer and Eastwood agreed he would investigate the al-Qaeda and the Muslim Brotherhood affiliates if they moved to Algiers. If there was no activity, he and his crew would head to Nigeria for the Boko Haram job.

After agreeing, Eastwood lamented aloud he needed more gold coins if he and the crew planned to go to Nigeria.

Before Eastwood joined the others in the lounge, Khalid, his pocket heavy with gold coins and his bag heavy with bars of soap was resigned that he would soon be leaving the Americans. Maybe he would take them to the airport. He was having the adventure of his life, and he didn't want it to end. He anticipating returning to Tripoli as Eastwood approached the group.

Eastwood held out his hand as Americans did when they met or left. When he pressed another gold coin into Khalid's palm, the Libyan was overjoyed.

"Algiers?" he asked.

"If you're up for it, Khalid."

"Yes, Sir. Yes, Sir!"

Eastwood looked at Marty and Karl, as they finished their drinks. "Giddy-up, Cowboys."

CHAPTER THIRTY-FIVE

1600 September 24, 2012
U.S. Embassy
Algiers, Algeria

The U.S. Ambassador listened intently as the deputy prime minister spoke in halting English. The Algerian intelligence service had new information on the terrorist groups marching across North Africa, attacking U.S. Embassies and Consulates. The little man apologetically lowered his head and eyes as he spoke. It was difficult for him to deliver bad news. It upset him greatly, and his hands trembled slightly, as if he had Parkinson's.

The two men couldn't have been more opposite and incongruous. The Ambassador was tall and thin, with a full head of mottled gray-and-black hair, an aristocratic nose, and full command of his hands. The Algerian minister had remnants of wispy black hair on an oversized head mounted atop a bowling-pin frame. His tremors grew in amplitude and duration the longer he was on the hot seat. The *Chargé d'Affaires* and Trade Attaché took notes without apparent emotion.

The three Americans waited for the Algerian to start again. He notified the Ambassador and his staff that they expected the embassy to be attacked and overrun like the American Embassies in Egypt, Libya, and Tunisia.

"His Excellency, the President," the man said, "regrets to inform Your Eminence that his judgment is ... the American Embassy staff should quietly leave Algeria ... for a short period."

The Ambassador already anticipated the suggestion. "Are you saying, Deputy Prime Minister, that the Algerian government will not provide security for the embassy per international accords?"

The Algerian lowered his head again to marshal his thoughts. His hands shook anew. "Your Eminence, it is more complicated than that. Our sources.... Our sources suggest Your Eminence is at great risk. His Excellency...is very concerned.... For your safety. How do you say? Ah, the Brotherhood wishes to take.... How do you say...?"

"Kidnap?" Nazy offered.

The Deputy Prime Minister tried not to look at the woman who spoke. She should know her place and when to speak to members of the diplomatic corps.

"Yes, that's correct. They wish to kidnap Your Eminence—and the *Chargé* and the Trade Attaché."

The *Chargé d'Affaires* and Nazy's eyes snapped up from their notebooks and they glanced at each other momentarily.

"Deputy Prime Minister," the Ambassador said, "you have extensive information from these radical elements. Is there more? Is there a reason these elements want to kidnap American diplomats?"

Nazy thought the rotund man was ready to fall apart before them. He struggled to reply.

"Your Eminence, they are very angry. They want the Ambassador, the *Chargé,* and the Trade Attaché...to torture them as punishment for killing Sheik bin Laden, to punish the leaders who support America."

The Ambassador cautiously thought over what the terrified man said. "So, His Excellency's position is that for our safety, we should evacuate the embassy? I just want to make sure, Deputy Prime Minister, Sir, that there is no disambiguation on our part."

The Deputy Prime Minister, blinking in confusion, wished the American would use smaller words.

"You believe the Muslim Brotherhood will attack this embassy, as they have attacked Embassies Tripoli and Tunis...."

"With al-Qaeda!"

All three Americans showed concern in their eyes at having their information confirmed.

"Deputy Prime Minister, you believe al-Qaeda elements will also be part of the assault?"

"Yes, Your Eminence. Yes. Most dangerous to stay in Algiers."

The Ambassador paused to think, while the portly man rubbed his shaking hands. "Do you know when this attack will occur?"

"In four nights."

"Deputy Prime Minister," Nazy asked, "how comfortable are you with that time period? Is your source certain?"

The little man detected much arrogance from the Muslima he didn't know. They locked eyes momentarily before he looked away. He chose his words carefully to avoid offending the Ambassador and spoke directly to him, not the woman.

"Yes. Certain. That's the purpose of my mission, to inform Your Eminence of the danger. They are very angry. Their movement is growing. In four nights."

The Ambassador stood abruptly, offering his thin hand. "Thank you, Deputy Prime Minister. You've been most helpful. Please convey my warmest appreciation, admiration, and best wishes to his Excellency."

The little man offered his hand to the *Chargé* but not to Nazy, who was content to smile at him, as she said, "Good night, Deputy Prime Minister. *Ma'assalama.*"

The *Chargé* led the Algerian from the office and downstairs to his car, where the driver waited to receive him and take him away.

"Does that track with what you're hearing, Nazy?" the Ambassador asked.

"Yes, Mr. Ambassador, it does. He left out their vision of collecting an ambassador on the anniversary of 9/11 and tossing him in prison to abuse and humiliate. I'm a little concerned the intel is a definitive four days. Our cohorts in Tripoli and Tunis, I understand, had little notice to evacuate. Both times, they left the compound just as a mob approached the embassy. A specific four days suggests disinformation to ensure we're here when they attack."

"Your professional advice would be that if we go, we leave sooner?"

"Mr. Ambassador, I don't trust Muslim men. The Deputy Prime Minister is probably repeating the intel word for word and is probably an honest broker. The planners in those cells must know someone will leak the attack. It's all disinformation."

"I understand."

"There is more corroborating evidence that something is afoot. We've had a spike in the number of visa applicants over the last two weeks. Security found some of them wandering the compound, claiming they were lost. Our sources tell us there were several phony visa applicants who gained entry to the embassy and reported back to their mosques what they saw. I understand there is a basic model of the embassy buildings and grounds in at least one mosque near here."

"You're suggesting we should leave earlier?"

"Mr. Ambassador, that's your call. I don't have any specific intel other than that which was just confirmed by the Deputy Prime Minister. I'm preparing my team to be ready to leave tomorrow at the earliest. Sir, on your order, my team will be ready to go."

She was definitely more professional, articulate, and attractive than the permanent Chief of Station, and the Ambassador admired and respected her for those qualities. He also appreciated some of her other qualities and looked for opportunities to have meetings and discussions with her. She always brightened those meetings and made the Algerian men squirm. They couldn't keep their eyes off her, and he also fought the urge to stare at her bosom. It was a blessing and a curse she dressed conservatively.

He smiled, allowing himself a sneak peak before spinning away from her, his head down, as he walked toward his desk. Safely behind his chair, he could hide anything that might be misconstrued as arousal.

"OK. Let's plan a NEO for late tomorrow night. I'll call the acting

Secretary of State to get an aircraft here. Normal operations tomorrow until close of business, then we prepare for NEO. You have your reports?"

"Yes, Mr. Ambassador. I'll notify headquarters of the plan. We'll be busy. We have much to shred." She smiled and walked from the office.

"Thank you, Nazy." He pressed his groin against the back of his chair. His eyes never left her derriere as she walked away.

CHAPTER THIRTY-SIX

1700 September 24, 2012
Algiers, Algeria

Abu Manu cut the fuel to the engine, and the propeller chugged to a stop, moments later. Closing his side window, he turned off the battery. Malik and Habib stepped from the Mercedes just as he stepped down from the airplane. He bantered with them, as the men pushed the plane into the hangar. Abu Manu pushed on the horizontal stabilizer, while the others pushed the leading edge of the lower wing.

The well-balanced, dark little airplane's tail wheel pivoted 180°, as they guided it straight in along a painted line on the hangar floor. The main wheels stopped rolling when they met blocks of wood precisely positioned to stop the aircraft. As the wheels hit the chocks, the trailing edge of the rudder was exactly four inches from the rear hangar wall.

The men knew their duties. Abu Manu disconnected the battery, while Malik placed a large aluminum drip pan under the engine drain tubes, and Habib fetched a ladder and accepted a fueling nozzle from Abu Manu. As Malik wiped down the aircraft from cowling to rudder with spray cleaner, Habib refueled both wing tanks from the gravity-fed fuel tank.

Abu Manu checked the fuel level, confirming he needed to refill his main storage tank soon. There was little aviation gasoline in Africa, so it had to be smuggled in from Europe in barrels.

Malik and Habib helped close the hangar doors. Abu Manu fastened a heavy Master lock to the hasp. They drove their leader to Algiers in silence.

Abu Manu checked his watch. *Thirty hours to go.*

Once they entered the city, Habib drove to the Algiers Hilton. Abu Manu and Malik bid Habib *Ma'assalama* as he left them at the entrance of the magnificent, opulent hotel. Malik retrieved their bags from the vehicle and got their keys from the check-in counter. Abu Manu waited patiently in the lobby before following his FAHD. The two men rode the elevator together.

Malik got out on the fifth floor and said, *"Shukran,"* to Abu Manu, who nodded his appreciation as the doors closed. Abu Manu rode to the executive suites on the top floor.

There were twenty-seven hours left, and he had much to do. He would shower and squeeze into a business suit with an open collar, very informal. He would meet the pilots, from Dubai, for dinner. They would take the Gulfstream and sell it to a minor Saudi prince after delivering Malik and the gold to the villa.

He smiled at the thought of being an aircraft broker. He didn't want to deal with the arrogant, disgusting Saudi princes directly, where their wealth was no longer measured by the number of camels they possessed but the size of their aircraft. The pilots would test fly it and confirm the aircraft and engines were new and all log books were correct. Abu Manu always negotiated a good deal.

Abu Manu stepped from the shower and toweled his head while letting the rest of his hair dry naturally. He perfumed his body in the traditional way. As he dressed, he reflected that in the sixteen years of receiving America's tribute, he rarely touched their gold, though he always spent the money and gold from the sale of two jets—about $80 million—every year.

He always smiled at that point in his memories. He almost let the Americans get away, but Allah wouldn't allow it. *Inshallah!*

Gaddafi constantly complained about the Americans and their crimes and wished to punish them, to kill the unbelievers. Americans were proud and arrogant about their airplanes, especially the large jets they called "jumbos." Abu Manu suggested a test of Gaddafi's FAHD.

He had the greatest-trained commandos in the Muslim world. They could do what his intelligence service couldn't; blow up an American airplane undetected.

Though intrigued, Gaddafi had his own ideas on how to punish the Americans. He sought any opportunity to kill Americans after the arrogant Republican movie star president bombed his tent, so he sent three of his FAHD to bomb a building in the middle of America. He got what he wanted. *You bomb my tent. I bomb your building. In the middle of America.*

Abu Manu lamented Gaddafi's lack of vision.

After helping a useful idiot American blow up the building, three of Gaddafi's four FAHD were caught trying to leave the country. They were taken to a secret prison in Cuba.

Abu Manu pored over American newspapers for information on the three missing FAHD. It was as if the Americans didn't want to tell the world Muslim terrorists helped the Army man explode a bomb near the building in middle America.

Abu Manu believed if he didn't know where they were, rescuing his FAHD was impossible. Gaddafi sent them on an impossible mission, squandering all that training for what, to blow up one building?

Abu Manu, narrowed his lips, shook his head. That was the day he broke with Gaddafi. He had dozens of MANPADS, but he was so isolated that his FAHD couldn't adequately launch the shoulder-fired weapons from Benghazi or Tripoli. American jets were embargoed from flying into Libya. Abu Manu had to find a way to go to America and rescue his three loyal FADH. The longer he thought about his missing men, the more depressed he became.

How do I get the FAHD out of prison? He struggled with the question. He had nothing to bargain with. He wasn't a religious man, but he sought spiritual guidance. *What would Mohammad do?*

Disgusted with Gaddafi, Abu Manu left his office and walked to the little pastry shop several blocks from the underground FAHD training compound. The stroll calmed him, helped clear his head of the poisonous thoughts. He sat in the sun, sipping tea and nibbling on sweet, sticky, pistachio-covered treats. He watched dirty cars race up and down the highway, when several tractors with different trailers, what the Americans called "eighteen wheelers," drove by. He hadn't seen the big trucks in a long time on the road, and seeing a string of several, all in a row, was momentarily interesting. At least their growling, rattling, diesel engines broke up the monotony of the whiny dirty cars speeding by.

Abu Manu noticed most of the trailers were rusty shipping containers being carried atop trailer chassis.

Shipping containers?

He smiled as a thought occurred. *Would it be possible to transport the missiles in a shipping container?*

"Millions of containers must transit America every day," he said softly. "They can't all be inspected."

Then the beginning of a thread of an idea struck. *Mohammad would threaten them and intimidate them.*

He tugged on the thread, taking up the slack until he felt tension. *I could threaten Americans with missiles.*

As the tension of the thought became focused and taut, Abu Manu reached a tipping point.

Would Americans be willing to pay for not having their jets shot out of the sky? Would they be interested in a prisoner exchange—my FAHD for not shooting down their airplanes?

He felt it was divine intervention. *Inshallah! God provides!*

It would be very difficult and risky, but his FAHD were the right men to do it. *Inshallah! Inshallah!*

He smiled anew at the moment when he changed the letter to the Ambassador. It was a beautiful, masterful piece of work. Allah's hand was still on him.

Abu Manu always had good handwriting. He was proud of himself. *Inshallah!*

To the U.S. Ambassador Extraordinary and Plenipotentiary
Extremely Urgent

Failure to release my brothers and transport them to Algiers within 48 hours will result in one American airliner shot down every 48 hours.

Also, failure to provide $100,000,000 in gold coins, this year and every year on this date, will result in one American Airliner shot down every 48 hours. I will graciously accept a new Gulfstream jet, this year and every year on this date, in addition to the gold coins.

Please deliver the aircraft and your tribute to the executive terminal of Houari Boumediene International Airport. Do this and no further harm will come to your aircrafts.

Abu Manu buttoned his shirt from the top down, slipped on his loafers, and looked in the mirror. He wanted to hurt America for Gaddafi. He wanted to tell Gaddafi he sent only two FAHD, who did what Gaddafi's intelligence officers couldn't, but he knew that would be suicidal. Muammar Gaddafi would not allow himself to be upstaged by a subordinate.

Abu Manu walked to the large picture window overlooking the city. Algiers was another colorless Muslim city, whitewashed structures and minarets everywhere. Dark cranes suspended rigidly over the vestiges of new buildings were few, a sign of starvation. It depressed him. He didn't want to leave Benghazi. He thought the al-Qaeda or the Muslim Brotherhood would come after him if they knew he had the missiles. The Americans would come after him for the same reason, but he outwitted them all.

As he rode the elevator to the lobby, he wondered again if the Americans would try to find and kill him. He never saw any sign of American Navy ships or their wonderful lethal SEALs. Would the new Republican President bother trying to find him? The Democrat President experienced no pain in paying tribute all those years. Neither the President nor Congress would pay for the gold and airplanes directly.

He read American newspapers, looking for clues. Oftentimes, such answers were available. Abu Manu discovered when it came to the American press that it wasn't a case of what was written in the papers but what was not.

He chuckled, as he walked toward the lounge. *No! They levied a tax to pay for the gold and the airplanes. They called it a passenger service fee. You can't hurt America with threats and ransom. American passengers will pay for the gold and the airplane. American politicians are corrupt. I should have demanded $250 million, not $100!*

Once in the lounge, he ordered a drink. The pilots would arrive soon. Thoughts that Habib was preparing his son for tomorrow's operation pleased him. Malik would hand the jet's keys to the pilots, who would fly to the farm with Malik aboard.

Abu Manu was free of Gaddafi and Libya, free of his wives and sons. He would live as a free man on his farm and grow olives while he grew old flying his airplane.

Abu Manu glanced at his watch. *Twenty-six hours.*

CHAPTER THIRTY-SEVEN

1900 September 24, 2012
U.S. Embassy
Algiers, Algeria

"You have to admit that after Mubarak left, so did the security police. Since then, these attacks have gotten more brazen and violent. You also have to admit the Brotherhood found a great deal of political support from our former President, and they continue to think they have a righteous wind at their back."

Bill McGee reached for his soda, as Spanky and Tonka raised theirs. Three bottles touched the men's lips as if they were mechanically synchronized. They went up at the same time, and every bottle tipped at a 45° angle, at the same time.

Nazy Cunningham, walking into the cafeteria, was immediately impressed by the synchronicity of the men sipping their brews. The men were surprised to see her standing there. Three bottles uncoupled from their mouths and hit the table simultaneously.

"Hello, Bill, Tonka, Spanky. Have you eaten yet?"

Tonka and Spanky unconsciously wiped their mouths with their sleeves.

Bill stood. "Not yet. We were waiting for you."

The other two men sprang to their feet.

"Let's go. I'm famished."

McGee signaled her to lead the way. The three men admired the view of jeans and a white, long-sleeved shirt. After picking up trays of food and drink, the huge men with thick necks surrounded the dainty woman and waited for her to take a chair.

"I'm sorry I interrupted your discussion," Nazy said.

The men, caught off guard, couldn't remember what they were

talking about until McGee came to the rescue and pointed at the TV monitor on the far wall.

"There's a story on TV about what happened to the Ambassador to Libya. We were talking about what really happened and the obvious rise of the Muslim Brotherhood and what they appear to be doing by attacking our embassies in North Africa."

"I know you've heard we're leaving before they can organize and attack this embassy," Nazy said. "The Ambassador's very frustrated. The Algerians are asking us to go…."

"They won't provide security?" McGee asked, unconsciously patting his sidearm, a .45 caliber Model 1911, strapped to his leg.

Nazy nodded. "The embassy has just barely reopened after a year. A previous demonstration got out of control, and the staff barely escaped with their lives. The Algerians don't want another episode like that and asked us to go home until things calm down. The Ambassador, rightfully so, isn't happy with them and is taking it very hard."

"I suppose that's to be expected. Does anyone have a clue what's going on? Like I said earlier, I'm certain it was the Brotherhood that attacked us in Benghazi, but there could have been some al-Qaeda in the mix. The Brotherhood tries to overrun an embassy; al Qaeda just blows them up." McGee spoke softly, hoping his radio-announcer voice didn't carry beyond the table.

Nazy debated whether to add anything. She filled her mouth with salad and let the men talk.

"It was highly unusual for any of them to kill the Ambassador at the consulate," Tonka said. "Take him, threaten him, torture him, and hide him—that's perfectly understandable for the Brotherhood. Having him die at the consulate makes absolutely no sense. These guys always need a breathing diplomat to humiliate and torture."

Nazy winced at the comment.

"But there were al-Qaeda flags everywhere," Spanky told Tonka. "Why do you think it was the Brotherhood?"

"They kidnap diplomats; it's their M.O.," McGee said. "Had to be.

Organizing mobs is the hallmark of the Muslim Brotherhood. AQ is a hit-and-run group, suicide bombers. They inflict as much damage as possible in the shortest amount of time. They want retribution for bin Laden. If it was just al-Qaeda, they would have just blown him up with mortars, RPGs, or bombs—whatever they had on hand that was convenient."

"They may be working together this time," Nazy said.

All three looked at her with interest and concern.

"That's not good if true," McGee said. "They aren't supposed to get along."

"I thought they hated each other." Tonka rolled his soda bottle in circles. "How could so similar groups be so different?"

Two of the three men heard words as Nazy responded and explained but they didn't listen. Tonka and Spanky glanced at the TV monitor for anything new, as their half-empty bottles returned to the table; they were surprised Nazy had finished speaking.

Nazy watched the interaction of the three former SEALs with fascination. She found Spanky a bit immature, cautious, shy, and slightly indecisive. He was definitely a follower but was probably lethal when he had to be. Tonka was different. He gave all the appearance of a human tank, invulnerable and impregnable. From what she knew of Navy SEALs, she believed Tonka—muscular, powerful, and indefatigable—epitomized the breed of warriors who were the finest America could produce.

Then there was Bill McGee. She never met an African American like him, someone who was probably equally comfortable in battle fatigues or a tuxedo. Quiet, but thoughtful, he carried himself with poise and confidence. His tiny, round glasses gave him the air of a scholar. It was obvious to her he was a gifted athlete, soldier, and leader. And he listened intently to what she said.

He was also a gentleman and a conservative, as Hunter explained. Hunter said conservatives were polite, considerate, and had manners, while some of the more vocal liberals were rude, crude with few manners, and wouldn't give their seat to a pregnant lady or an old woman if the bus were on fire. She understood why Duncan would be friends with such a man, and that McGee would call Hunter his close friend. Duncan called him "Bullfrog." She didn't fully understand call signs, but after meeting Bill McGee, the call sign "Bullfrog" made perfect sense.

"That's why we're evacuating," she said. "They could be working together to achieve a particular goal."

"If they're working together," McGee said, "it seems they're on a kidnap mission of some kind. They screwed up Benghazi and Tripoli and are probably working their way west."

"American diplomats." Nazy sighed and lowered her head.

Not just the Ambassador, thought Tonka. *I'll bet you're targeted, too, Miss Cunningham.*

Nazy smiled at the three men. "I hate to be a spoilsport, but I have a big day tomorrow."

Bill stood, and Tonka and Spanky followed.

Nazy lifted her tray. "I'll sleep well knowing you're protecting us."

"Just a couple of average guys trying to do an above-average job," Spanky offered with a suppressed lascivious grin.

"I doubt there's anything average about you. Good night, Gentlemen. I'll see you tomorrow."

She turned gracefully and walked away toward the kitchen to return her tray and dishes, completely oblivious to her double entendre. Spanky leered and Tonka grinned. McGee frowned at both.

They watched Nazy disappear from view. McGee checked his watch and finished his drink. "It'll soon be time to earn our keep."

Tonka and Spanky hurried to the kitchen to deposit their trays, while McGee followed. He reflected on some of the things Nazy said and some she didn't, though her body language told the story.

It shouldn't have been wholly unexpected for the Algerian government to refuse to protect the American Embassy. There was an element of soft bigotry in the low expectations of Muslim men in power—when they were in power, they governed one way or another. They could be complete savages and follow the Saddam Hussein or

Muammar Gaddafi model, or they could be abject cowards like the Algerian government.

In the middle of those two extremes lay some egregious groups with both characteristics, such as the Muslim Brotherhood. They demonstrated savagery and cowardice during the fall of the Egyptian Mubarak uprising, viciously gang-raping liberal women reporters as an insensate mass of thugs.

McGee stepped from the chancery into the cool night, heading for his room to mount up for his and his team's security watch. He couldn't shake the thought of the incompatible philosophies, where Western men put women on pedestals, while Islamists stood on their throats. He had two girls and couldn't imagine a father not protecting or cherishing his daughters and wife. He had heard some Muslim fathers and sons killed daughters and sisters under the excuse of "honor killings." The culture seemed to be moving backward or falling under the influence of Islamist hardliners.

The great tragedy in the Muslim world was that the vast majority of attacks on women weren't reported. Widespread sexual harassment and sexual assault was commonplace but the dirty little secret was if a woman tried to report it, she would be blamed and her attackers would be uncharged, exonerated. It was another extension of bizarre liberal thought that if a woman was raped, the woman deserved it. Because they were out alone or with another man, the Muslim Brotherhood or their ilk would say, "They brought it on themselves. They dressed too provocatively." Avoiding their international obligations to protect an embassy and its personnel was more cowardice and the soft savagery of, "They brought it on themselves."

As he entered his apartment, McGee muttered, "That's progress under radical Islamists."

CHAPTER THIRTY-EIGHT

2100 September 24, 2012
Lajes Field, Azores

The text message ten hours earlier from the DCI infuriated Duncan. Unlike any previous surveillance or other special-purpose missions during the time he and Greg Lynche performed for the Agency, the director had involved the Navy *and* the Air Force. What was supposed to be a completely covert operation—neatly compartmentalized within the CIA—had all the hallmarks of turning into a special operations goat rope. Hunter fumed that the mission would leave fingerprints all over the DOD. The only place worse for keeping secrets than the CIA was the Pentagon. Rothwell's dirty deed was already in motion. Hunter was directed to meet with a pair of senior Naval and Air Force officers before the execution phase of the *Noble Savage* mission. Directors direct and contractors comply.

He was livid. Pretentious, clueless intelligence guys of any grade or rank pissed him off. Adding more people to a top secret program at the last stage made Duncan apoplectic.

Still stunned and angry at the director's treachery, Hunter jumped at a knock on his bungalow door.

"Dr. Livingston, I presume?" asked one of the men, repeating the challenge phrase in Rothwell's text message.

Hunter invited the men in and closed the door. They introduced themselves as "Air Force" and "Navy." Hunter introduced himself as "Maverick."

The men stood just inside the suite as if in a hurry to leave. Pleasant but serious, the Air Force officer, bedecked in a bright-red Tommy Bahama shirt and black shorts, informed Hunter his crew would provide flight following during his phase of flight into Spain,

Algeria, and back.

Hunter, as mission commander, was in disbelief at the thought of an early warning and control aircraft, an E-3, would provide traffic information. "Air Force" indicated the AWACS was necessary to mask the L-100's entry into European airspace if there was any chance of mission success. No one wanted European air defense systems to light up and have the Spanish Air Force launch interdiction fighters to intercept an unresponsive Hercules at the worst possible moment, or find a small aircraft flying under their radar.

Air Force wasn't condescending but pragmatic. Hunter immediately realized the AWACS was a very smart move on someone's part, but he wasn't about to give the director credit. The DCI wasn't that smart. There had to be a knowledgeable Air Force officer providing the DCI guidance. Hunter thought that might be the U.S. Air Force Chief of Staff who was so helpful getting the *Wraith* out of Panama.

"Navy" waited for his turn to speak. He wore khakis, a blue Polo shirt, and deck shoes. He sweated in all the right manly places, as if he'd been dragged off the golf course to give a brief. He stood, slightly nervous, waiting to get out of the building.

"Navy" explained distress procedures and handed Hunter a scrap of paper with discrete frequencies to memorize if his aircraft went down in the Mediterranean. He indicated the U.S.S *Eisenhower* would provide search and rescue.

"Navy" knew nothing of the mission's flight corridor, and Hunter offered that if he had to bail out, he'd have an AN/PRQ-7 handheld radio in his LPU. "Navy" said a naval helicopter could be a few hours away to rescue him if required.

Hunter traded fury for calm, agreeing upon the frequencies, call sign, and code word while he traversed the 200 miles of open sea and confirmed any mayday calls and countless safety procedures hadn't changed since he last flew off a carrier deck. He knew what to do and say if he were in distress.

At the end of the five-minute brief, the two men smiled broadly, offering their hands.

"Good luck, Sir."

They departed as if both were racing back to the golf course and their tee time.

As the sun set and the temperature dropped, the Hercules and the Yo-Yo crews rendezvoused at the transient ramp. The cargo airplane's aircrew fired up the auxiliary power plant and turned the lights on in the cabin, while the flight engineer lowered the cargo door. The first and second mechanics hung a dark curtain to cover the aft of the plane to prevent anyone from looking inside while allowing a cross breeze to pass through and dissipate the strong stench of jet fuel. Once the curtain was up, they began to preflight the big white cargo aircraft.

Bob and Bob opened the YO-3A's container doors and began preparing the little observation plane for flight. Inside 007's container, the canopy couldn't be fully raised, and Hunter couldn't crawl into the cockpit but was able to check off each item methodically on the inch-thick checklist.

"Hot," he called, before checking voltage, and then he cycled the battery switch off.

The taller Bob checked the air in the tires, while the shorter Bob inspected the prop for damage, slowly running his fingers over the leading and trailing edges to feel for any crack or the beginning of delamination of the secret, specially-built wooden propeller. Bob checked the engine and reduction gearbox oil levels before inspecting the brake disks and giving a shot of grease into the grease fittings on the landing gear.

"I have the clevis pins," the shorter Bob announced.

"You have the clevis pins," the tall one replied.

Bob would carry and place each wing's fore and aft wing clevis pins into the freezer in his room. Those pins were of two different sizes to ensure there was no mix-up during insertion when Bob and a mechanic raced to hang the wings on the fuselage. Bob would guide the largest tang into the fuselage clevis openings first and drop the frozen pin into the holes, while the mechanic held the other end of the wing. Freezing the clevis pins shrank them enough to slide into the frame and wing clevis openings without having to hammer them in place. They would just drop in, and Bob would insert a retaining clip at the bottom to ensure the pin didn't back from the fitting.

The taller Bob cut long strips of black duct tape and placed them strategically on each side of the airframe. After the wings were installed, and the flight-control cables were hooked up with their own small clevis pins and retaining clips, Bob would place tape over the seam between the wing and fuselage to ensure no part of the exposed aircraft could whistle during flight. Other pieces of tape would be quickly applied to the fuel tank access doors atop the wings.

The other Bob hurried back inside the container and extracted two long pieces of U-channel extruded aluminum and mounted them on the floor and cargo ramp of the L-100, screwing them into the floor with an electric drill. The tail wheel channel would ensure the YO-3A tracked from the container straight out of the Hercules without any other assistance. Once Bob and Bob pushed the YO-3A from its container, and it began rolling, it would roll straight, all the way out of the L-100. When free of the cargo door, Hunter would stop the forward motion by an ingenious external brake affixed to the main landing gear. After the aircraft stopped moving, Hunter would raise the canopy, get in, apply the brakes, and turn on the battery.

Immediately after landing and as the Hercules decelerated to a stop, two mechanics would lower the three ramps on the trailing edge of the cargo door, one for each Yo-Yo tire for its expeditious roll out of the L-100. Once 007 was out of its container, a flight mechanic and Bob would run inside and carry a wing out to install on the YO-3A.

When both wings were hung, and Bob and Bob secured the clevis pins for the wings and flight controls on either side of 007, each Bob would connect the fuel lines from the wings to the fuselage. The two mechanics would race back inside the Hercules and the container and return with two seven-gallon cans for over-the-wing refueling. Large-bore nozzles and relief valves allowed the fuel to fill the wings in seconds, like a NASCAR racecar being refueled with a huge, wide-mouth, gravity-fed hose.

Fuel pumps moved fuel from the tanks to the engine fuel control. Bob and Bob would secure the fuel caps and tape over the fuel doors with black duct tape, as Hunter engaged the starter and powered away from the idling Hercules. The men could routinely install wings, pins, clips, fuel lines, electrical connections, and fuel the aircraft within three-and-a-half minutes.

After an hour of preparing both aircraft for flight, the two crews closed up the aircraft and drove into town for a late dinner. The pizza shop in an old bucolic and rustic house, across the road from the decrepit whale processing factory, made the best pizza on the island. They ate together as a team and didn't discuss the mission, swapping war stories. By ten o'clock they were in their rooms.

As Hunter settled into his suite, he responded to several emails from Kelly Horne and some of his students from his BlackBerry. There was nothing new from the DCI, but Hunter sent a coded text message that he received his briefs.

His last message was to Nazy, saying he was jealous that Bill McGee got to spend time with her.

They exchanged several messages until she signed off with *BE CAREFUL. ILY.*

He typed back, *ILY2 Baby. CU soon.*

CHAPTER THIRTY-NINE

0730 September 25, 2012
U.S. Embassy
Algiers, Algeria

Nazy Cunningham awoke feeling well for the first time in many days. The little white pills apparently made her morning sickness a bad memory. She stepped from the shower with a towel wrapped atop her head and applied lotion from her neck to her toes. Leaning over the sink on tiptoes, she applied lavender eye shade and black eyeliner, making her platinum-green eyes more striking than usual. Normally, she wore little makeup, but today, she would wear the veil and traditional white *haik* of Algiers. Knowing she would be required to go into town from time-to-time, she learned that in Algeria, wearing the veil was different in various parts of the country. The black *melaya* was preferred in the east and a printed version of the *haik* was found in the south. If a woman wore a veil, it would be white if she was going to or lived in the big city of Algiers.

The few times she'd been off the embassy grounds, she saw that, like her native Jordan, Algerian women wore the veil differently according to age, social status, or ideology. Even the *chador,* though less present, was common. Few *burkas,* a dress imported from Iran and Afghanistan, were seen, largely because young Algerians mercilessly teased the wearers as "crows" or "black bags," referring to the trash bags used everywhere in Algeria.

Nazy made a striking presence in the cafeteria when she sat with Bill McGee for breakfast. They looked like a salt-and-pepper set in their "work uniform," with Nazy in white from head to toe while McGee wore a black, long-sleeved, form-fitting T-shirt and black cargo pants and boots. They laughed at each other.

Between bites and coffee, McGee discussed his and Hunter's escapades at the Naval War College. Nazy was fascinated by Duncan's life, and the chapter involving his time at the war college was one of the least understood. McGee had learned how Nazy was sent to spy on Hunter and not how he spirited her away from an evil imam in Boston and turned her into one of the CIA's best.

McGee was amused, not surprised, that Duncan took her to the Red Parrot restaurant in downtown Newport in an ancient white Rolls Royce. He recalled how he teased Hunter for his interest in rare old cars and beautiful women. He was in full receive mode, however, when Nazy related the story of how she renounced Islam after they returned to the Navy base. Hunter called Greg Lynche, the former CIA Chief of Air Branch, to see if his old place could use a native Arabic speaker, while the Pentagon raced into Iraq during the early stages of the war.

She understood, Lynche was very persuasive and the Agency transferred Nazy to Virginia. McGee wasn't too surprised to learn that U.S. Marshals took Nazy away in a corporate jet.

Nazy lamented how it seemed such a long time ago that a group from Langley had polygraphed her constantly while Duncan was at school. Even Greg Lynche had trouble meeting her. When she was hired as an analyst, she was also given a new identity. Lynche and his wife helped her settle in her new house in Bethesda.

"I seriously thought the government bought me a house and car, but that vision was immediately crushed," she said. "Somehow, my red Mercedes sports car from Newport was sitting in the driveway with Virginia license plates. I knew then that Duncan had somehow acquired the house and the car. I've learned he works in strange and mysterious ways." Nodding and smiling, the two laughed long and hard.

McGee talked about his wife and two daughters. His girls were so impressed watching Duncan play racquetball that they wanted to learn the sport, too, so he enrolled them in classes at the Newport Racquet Club. He confided, "I was certain my daughters would get inside the court and hit a few balls, then drop the sport, because it was too hard to do or something equally defeating. I couldn't have been more wrong. They loved that game!"

His girls, athletically gifted like their father, were so good that soon, they played in and won local tournaments. He was amazed and proud of their capacity and commitment to play the fast game with the little blue ball. A typical pavonine father, he proudly said his oldest daughter might even win a scholarship to play racquetball.

"Hunter provided the spark. I'm proud of those girls. I miss my wife, but she's busy caring for her sick mother so I could take this contract and earn a little extra money. My girls will be heading to college soon."

"How about your life as a SEAL?"

His hand dropped to the sidearm lashed to his leg, as he leaned back in his chair, while his free hand hooked onto a belt loop. "Do you mean, have I any regrets? Some, but that's life. I had a great career. SEALs were my life for almost thirty-five years. It consumes you. I loved being a warrior and a leader of warriors. I loved organizing and executing improbable missions no one would ever hear about. The missions, well.... If I told you, I'd have to kill you." He struggled to keep from laughing.

She leaned closer. "I've heard that before. It's the CIA's unofficial motto." She broke out in a broad smile.

"I was in the company of the best-trained, most-dedicated men, and there was little we couldn't do when we focused on a mission. We were the best of the best, and we trained to be even better, striving for perfection. We weren't just good. We were... magnificent. That's not bragging. It's the truth; if you watch a SEAL at work.... I'd say that if you watch Duncan play racquetball at his level, he plays with such grace, purpose, and perfection, he's...."

"...magnificent."

"Yes, he is."

"I suppose SEALs are like that too."

McGee nodded, "They work so hard to be so good."

"That's a very rare quality. I know what you mean. Duncan's a very rare man."

"He is and he's a very *lucky* man, Nazy. You two will make a *magnificent* couple.

Nazy beamed. McGee finished with a toothy smile. Checking the time, he indicated he should leave.

As they left the cafeteria, the big burly black man in black combat clothes headed for his room to sleep while the slender woman covered in the white *haik* of Algiers walked toward the embassy parking lot.

More than one cafeteria patron watched them go and said, "You never know what you'll see at a U.S. Embassy."

The drive to the international airport in eastern Algiers gave Nazy time to reflect on the mission, but she was unable to focus, distracted by the vehicle she drove. She didn't like the embassy's Chevy Volt. It was too big a vehicle on the road with the smaller cars and trucks, and she was painfully aware she stood out in the unique automobile. In the intelligence community; the first rule of spycraft was to be inconspicuous. *How can you be inconspicuous when some idiot acquired electric cars for the embassy?*

Everyone who passed her on the highway glared at her. She ignored the looks and gestures and made good time. She checked the signs closely for the executive terminal and made the proper turns, staying a few kilometers below the speed limit. She was aghast to find the pilots already on the ground, waiting for her. They walked straight to the Volt as she stopped.

Both tall and handsome, the men hid their eyes behind dark aviator sunglasses, their hair stuffed under professional airline captain hats.

The pilot with four gold braids on his epaulettes leaned into the car and said, "I'd like directions to Corky's BBQ."

Nazy replied, "You can only get that in Memphis."

He tapped the door sill twice with his hand and both men entered the back seat. He handed her a set of titanium keys over the seat. "These are for you."

"Right to the departure level?"

"Yes, please. Thanks for the lift. It's too hot to walk."

For the four minutes it took to drive from the executive terminal to the commercial terminal, the pilot and Nazy engaged in inane pleasantries of flying to Algeria and talk of the weather. The copilot was silent. Unlike the vivacious, loquacious captain, he seemed unapproachable and of limited ability, with a fiercely protective ego. Maybe he was just afraid of Muslim women in traditional garb.

She stopped at the departure gate for British Airways and the two men got out. The captain bid her adieu. The copilot meekly waved good-bye with a flick of the wrist.

Step two was easy and complete. She now faced the penultimate requirement. The drive back to the embassy under the white *haik* began to make her overly hot. With the air-conditioning running at maximum, Nazy was surprised to find herself a little nauseous. She ignored her stomach's rumblings as she referenced the maps she printed of how to make the return trip and mission rendezvous.

Nazy expertly followed the map, negotiating all the turns and a roundabout saturated with cars and trucks inching along, miraculously avoiding a collision and trading paint before she found the well-marked exit. She drove a circuitous route through town. After checking her watch, she turned down Chemin Chekh Avenue, passing in front of the U.S. Embassy before turning onto Rue de Brazza Colonne Voirole. Per the instructions in the file, she slowed at the first possible corner, which was a slight dogleg turn, and rolled to a stop.

She was surprised that no cars or houses could be seen, just tall, thick bamboo lining both sides of the road. She took the vehicle out of gear and looked around to inventory her surroundings. A young boy, no more than eight or nine, wearing white from neck to ankle with a bright blue *kufi,* appeared out of the bamboo and walked straight to the car. His face showed no emotion and he quickly closed the distance.

She rolled down her window as he approached. When he held out his hand, she hesitated for a moment before dropping the silver keys in his palm. He nodded, turned left, and ran back up the road before turning right to disappear into the bushes.

Nazy checked her rearview mirror and closed the window. She placed the transmission into *Drive,* stepped on the accelerator, and the electric car silently moved forward.

She drove through the embassy gate and parked the vehicle in its assigned charging spot. She stepped from the car in a sweat and pulled off the white *haik,* revealing a white, long-sleeved blouse, blue jeans, and gray trainers. She rolled the *haik* into a ball that she stuffed under her arm before walking toward the chancery.

She cabled headquarters, highlighted the dispatch was *Personal For* the DCI and typed two letters—*MC.* Mission complete.

CHAPTER FORTY

1000 September 25, 2012
Ronald Reagan Washington National Airport

Two men stood side-by-side of the thirteenth floor apartment window, overlooking the executive terminal. They looked like a modern-day Abbott and Costello team. One was tall and distinguished, while the other was short and wide with a Howdy Doody face only a prostitute could love.

The tall one handed the binoculars to his companion and said, "I think that's Bruce Rothwell." He stepped to a more powerful telescope on a tripod and focused on the scene below.

"Are you kidding?"

"I'm not."

"Hey, you're right! The Director of Central Intelligence ... going on a trip."

"I think that's a new tail number. I'm also thinking that's a new jet."

The short man pulled the binoculars from his face. He clearly couldn't look and talk simultaneously. "What do you mean it's a new jet?"

The other man continued to glass the DCI, as the CIA man disappeared through the door of the plane. "It's a new jet and a new tail number. It's not on the spreadsheet. We haven't seen it before. But that *was* Rothwell!"

"I think you're right. It *is* a new tail. Yes. Hold it! What's that? Douglass, is that a G-five? I think it's a five." The short man returned the binoculars to his chest, frowning with concentration. He crossed his arms on his expansive chest, tucking his hands under his armpits.

Douglass stood ramrod erect and still, scrutinizing the jet. "Close,

Carlton. I think that's the Agency's new G550. There were rumors on the web the DCI ordered two jets to keep us off guard. Definitely not a rendition airplane if the good doctor is going for a ride, but having a new ride is news!"

"Who's going to report it? One of us needs to get the credit. Do you want to be the hero?"

The tall man turned and bowed gracefully. "I am most appreciative of your generosity. I'll do this one and you can do the next one." As the man named Douglass input the tail number into the web site database and indicated the DCI was on his way somewhere, he commented, "That's the easiest five hundred dollars we've made—and it's not even noon!"

"You saw him first."

"It was my turn to watch, but we share. This is a team event. We are a team."

The two men grinned broadly at each other, sharing the conspiracy.

The short one asked, "I wonder where he's going?"

"We'll never know, but that would be worth two hundred more. We'll have to settle for being the first to ID the DCI's new jet, and that he's on the move."

The short man, frowning, stared at the floor. "I wish we knew where he's going."

"One of these days, Carlton, we might. But not today."

CHAPTER FORTY-ONE

1030 September 25, 2012
Medea, Algeria

Marty Marceau set up a tripod and affixed the video camera atop, as his cohort set up the portable satellite dish out of sight at the rear of the Toyota. Karl Mann's electronic equipment scanned the sky, looking for a friendly satellite. After thirty seconds of searching, the red light indicated the circuitry was interrogating satellites and responded with codes and keys, but it had yet to establish a data link.

Karl was about to terminate the attempted transmission when the green light on the instrument's face confirmed they had one-way communications. He nodded in a panic to Eastwood and Marty. They were exposed in the middle of nowhere, with a camera aimed at a bus full of *jihadis* en route to Algiers.

Both men were obviously nervous, brought on by Eastwood's decision to stop behind the decrepit bus overloaded with protestors, as it picked up even more men. He moved quickly yet cautiously behind the viewfinder, as Eastwood stepped in front of the camera.

Marty signaled they were ready with a thumbs-up, and he began to record and transmit the live feed.

"This is Demetrius Eastwood, reporting from outside Medea, Algeria. We've been following a story that began with the death of an American Ambassador and subsequent coordinated attacks on American Embassies in Tripoli and Tunis.

"What you see behind me is a bus laden with *jihadis* heading to Algiers. Most are members of the Muslim Brotherhood, while some claim to be al-Qaeda in Africa. What we're witnessing is the early orchestration and collaboration of an impending attack on the U.S. Embassy in Algiers."

All three men glanced back at the bus, as the motor raced. Grinding gears signaled the bus was departing. The cameramen's anxiety was replaced by disbelief that they had once again escaped the potential wrath of 100 disgruntled men jammed into and on top of an overcrowded bus. Eastwood remained composed and resolute.

Eastwood turned back toward the camera. "What we've observed in Tripoli and Tunis is that groups of men like these arrive at mosques near the U.S. Embassy before their early morning assault on what should have been a sleeping embassy compound. My earlier report showed how mobs formed, how they poured from mosques, and how they coalesced into a teeming, angry group of protestors.

"As we reported, at the Tripoli and Tunis Embassies, the staff evacuated just as the hundred-man mob raced to intercept the departing vehicles, exposing dozens of armed men who followed closely behind. Those so-called protestors carried AK-47s and RPGs behind their backs until the mob broke ranks and tried to close the distance between themselves and the fleeing embassy personnel."

Eastwood glanced over his shoulder, as the bus trundled out of sight. He faced the camera again. Marty waved his hand, encouraging Eastwood to hurry.

"We think embassy Algiers is next. If this group is consistent with what we've observed over the past week, the men on that bus will either act as protesters, masking armed men, or they'll be the attackers armed with assault weapons and rocket propelled grenades. We're reporting roughly ninety kilometers south of Algiers. I hope Embassy Algiers is prepared for what's coming. This is Demetrius Eastwood, signing off."

CHAPTER FORTY-TWO

1030 September 25, 2012
Algiers, Algeria

Abu Manu stepped confidently from the hotel and into the waiting Mercedes SUV. Habib drove slowly from under the hotel's expansive overhang into brilliant sunshine. Abu Manu screwed his face, quickly donning dark, aviator-style mirrored sunglasses.

"Do we need to stop at the apartment?" Habib asked.

Abu Manu shook his head.

The trip to the villa was made in near silence.

Malik, Habib, and Abu Manu met downstairs in the Hilton's dining area for what was called a Western-style breakfast. The expansive, elegant dining area had fifty tables covered with pressed white tablecloths, with a phalanx of obsequious waiters eager to fulfill their every need. The hostess, a pretty young woman in a skirt and a plain white blouse, her hair free-flowing and straight, unencumbered by a head scarf, greeted the men and escorted them to a corner table away from other patrons.

The men kept one waiter completely occupied retrieving fresh-squeezed orange juice from a machine that pulverized the smallish, green-orange fruit to yield its nectar. Behind a tall glass counter, a chef made omelets to order, while another prepared eggs, French toast, and pancakes.

The men indulged in the usual Western fare and easily overate, stuffing themselves with warm orange juice, cheese omelets, and deli meats. At the end of the meal Habib handed the keys to the jet across the table to Abu Manu who handed the keys to Malik.

"We will see you shortly," Abu Manu said.

"Inshallah."

Abu Manu and Habib pulled the Staggerwing from the hangar and positioned it for engine start. Habib was dismissed, so he returned to the villa, while Abu Manu watched the Mercedes disappear over the hill toward the farmhouse. He stood on the ramp, casually glancing around his property, not expecting to see anyone, but as a precaution. He always took extra security measures when he accessed the underground work spaces under the hangar floor.

The door was cleverly hidden at the back of the hangar. Where the floor was made with excess railroad ties harvested from an abandoned railroad bed that ran between Algiers and the old Roman city of Mostaganem, it was impossible to discern the seams where the twelve-inch-square hewn timbers ended and the inch-thick laminates of the door began. Stepping on the front of the concealed door depressed a latch. A simple counterbalance allowed one person to open and close the door easily.

Abu Manu took one of several flashlights resting on a step and flicked it on. The stairs were also made from railroad ties; a bright beam of light vanished into the space below.

He found what he wanted in the first room and removed a pair of long, green containers from a stack of similar six-foot long Fiberglas boxes. Taking his time, he cautiously pushed the long containers up the stairs until he could lower them to the hangar floor, then he dragged them by their handles to the front of the hangar where he stacked them.

He returned downstairs to the first room, shone the flashlight on the small box safe with a key dangling from its lock in the center of the thick top. The safe was fireproof, the size of an old breadbox, and it held just one item.

Abu Manu lifted the lid and shone the light inside the safe to illuminate a small round glass container with a black cap. Inside, a tiny vial rested on a bed of cotton. He extracted the glass tube and slipped it into his shirt pocket before pausing to look at the safe's lid.

He turned without closing it and replaced the flashlight on the step on his way out of the underground space. The trap door was lowered, but it wasn't latched into place.

He unbuckled the four latches of the topmost container and opened the box, revealing a shoulder-launched *Stinger* missile and three battery coolant units. He stared wistfully at the missile and reviewed the procedures to activate the *Stinger*—insert a charged BCU into the hand guard, aim, and fire.

He placed the glass tube from his pocket within the space holding the BCUs, closed the MANPADS storage container, and closed the hangar door.

Abu Manu rotated the propeller two full turns before he crawled into the cockpit of the Beech Staggerwing. He started the engine. As manifold pressure rose and the oil pressure stabilized, he checked his watch.

Twelve hours.

CHAPTER FORTY-THREE

1200 September 25, 2012
U.S. Embassy
Algiers, Algeria

Tonka and Spanky intently focused on the TV monitor and the attractive newswoman on a sofa surrounded by two men in suits. Bill McGee's booming voice shattered their reverie.

"I finally got through to that little turd of a program manager. Ricky's not happy, but who gives a shit?"

"So they know we're being evacuated?" Spanky desperately tried to pull his gaze away from the former Miss America with the long crossed legs on the screen.

"Uh-huh. I told him I was done. When we return, I'm leaving the program. He whined that he had to find someone new." McGee shook his head in disgust.

"He'll get over it, Boss. You have to admit it was interesting back in Benghazi. That opportunity is long gone, and the government won't pay us to guard their embassy at our rates. They can buy lots of guys with nightsticks. Don't worry about us. We'll find other work. Supposedly we're in high demand!" Tonka smiled at the big man, as he sat down and looked at the TV.

"Ricky hadn't been told we're evacuating," McGee added. "He was apoplectic when I told him. All he could do was complain and tell me we wouldn't get any of the pay differentials once we were airborne. What a douche bag. Were you waiting for me?"

"Yes, Sir," said Spanky.

"OK. Let's eat."

The three men worked their way through several lines in the cafeteria. Tonka and Spanky got burgers and fries, while McGee's plate filled up with a mixture of cheeses and vegetables on a head of lettuce. They lined up at the cashier, and then returned to the round table facing the huge TV monitor.

When McGee heard a familiar voice come from the TV, he looked up before setting down his tray. Tonka and Spanky looked at him inquisitively, then they turned in unison to see what he was looking at. Through intermittent distortion of the video feed, they recognized the internationally renowned war correspondent dominating the center of the screen. He was dirty, disheveled, and clearly nervous, but he talked steadily while glancing over his shoulder and back to the camera. In the background, an ancient bus teemed with men like ants ravaging a discarded pastry. A small green flag waved from a bus window.

The three former SEALs were transfixed, as the man stepped forward until his image filled the screen.

"We think Embassy Algiers is next. If this group is consistent with what we've observed over the past week, the men on that bus will either act as protestors, masking armed men, or they'll be the attackers.

"We're reporting roughly ninety kilometers south of Algiers. I hope Embassy Algiers is prepared for what's coming. This is Demetrius Eastwood, signing off."

The three ex-SEALs glanced at each other.

"I doubt anyone here knows what we just saw," McGee said. "If they watch anything, it's the Communist News Network. I'll run upstairs and see if I can get in touch with Miss Cunningham or the security officer. We need to let someone know. If I were the security officer and saw that, I'd be concerned the bad guys have moved up their timeline."

Tonka and Spanky nodded and set down their trays. McGee was taken aback by their lack of concern. Something else was on their minds, or they simply felt comfortable with McGee leading.

"You won't be long?" asked Spanky.

"Don't eat my food. I'll be back. Besides, I spit in it."

"So did I," said Tonka.

All three grinned, as McGee jogged away.

He returned several minutes later and sat down before his tray, pulling his chair toward the table. "They heard from State. It seems someone at the network called the State Department and the Pentagon, and they got a copy of the video before it was broadcast. Security seems to think they'll try something around zero four or five hundred, but, by then, we'll be on a jet headed for Germany. Looks like a zero one hundred departure."

"So we're outta here in twelve hours?" Spanky suddenly smiled.

"Give or take."

Tonka clapped his hands and shouted, "Hallelujah! About frickin' time."

The three ravenous men wolfed down their food, their eyes rarely leaving the blonde woman on the monitor.

CHAPTER FORTY-FOUR

1400 September 25, 2012
Lajes Field, Azores

The white L-100 taxied to the hold-short line of the runway and stopped. The pilot, copilot, and flight engineer scanned the engine instruments and system indicators for any sign of trouble. With engines running, propellers turning, and no caution or advisory lights illuminated on the instrument panel, the pilot ran through the take-off checklist with his co-pilot.

"Safety belt and shoulder harness, fastened and locked. Trim tabs—set. Flaps—set, fifty."

"Confirmed fifty percent for takeoff," the copilot said.

The pilot pulled and pushed the yoke all the way to the stops, then rotated it right and left, as he moved the rudder pedals full throw with his feet on the brake pedals. "Flight controls—checked and free. Hydraulic pressures—three checked good in the green. IFF/Transponder—on and set. Ready to go?"

"All set," the copilot said.

The flight engineer double-clicked his microphone switch.

The pilot's thumb depressed the radio button on the yoke, and he spoke into his boom microphone. "Lajes Tower, Carson triple seven, holding short runway 33, ready for takeoff with Sierra."

"Carson triple seven, Lajes Tower. You're cleared for takeoff runway 33. Contact Departure Control three four zero point three, squawk four five eight eight."

The pilot released the brakes, and programmed the condition levers forward to get the aircraft moving. He checked right and left through the windows and said, "Roger, Lajes Tower. Cleared for takeoff, runway 33; copy freqs and squawks. Thank you, Sir, and good day."

He steered the nose wheel, as the bulky cargo airplane lumbered onto the runway, straddling the center line stripe, and stopped.

"Set takeoff power," the copilot said.

The pilot programmed the condition levers to MAX.

"All instruments in the green," the flight engineer called out.

The Hercules roared as the four Allison T56 turboprops clawed the air and shook the aircraft, and strained to be released.

"Feet off the brakes," the pilot said. "We're going flying!"

After an uneventful takeoff and departure, the aircraft leveled off at 15,000 feet, and the Hercules cruised at 300 knots with a slight tailwind. The copilot checked in with the E-3 AWACS 1,500 miles away.

"How are our guests doing?" the pilot asked the flight engineer.

"They're in their bags asleep, of course."

"They sleep a lot," the copilot said smugly with a grin.

The pilot returned the look and keyed the microphone. "They're old. What do you expect?"

The flight engineer offered, "What is wrong with this picture? A bunch of young studs are taking the old dudes for a ride and all they want to do is sleep. They're as bad as my grandfather...."

The copilot interjected, "Well, you wouldn't drop your granddad off in the middle of nowhere and hoped he could find his way back. Maybe they're just resting."

The pilot nodded as the flight engineer said, "ETA five hours."

CHAPTER FORTY-FIVE

1600 September 25, 2012
U.S. Embassy
Algiers, Algeria

The Toyota HiLux slowed and pulled to the side of the street as a Brobdingnagian white mosque with four towering blue-spired minarets filled the windshield, and the conveyance they'd been following all morning suddenly slowed to a crawl. The bus approached a patch of ruts and deep potholes in the unimproved road and wobbled dangerously, rocking side-to-side, tossing some roof riders off their precarious perch.

Eastwood, Khalid, and the men in the back of the truck were startled when the old bus rocked back and forth violently. Because it was overloaded inside and on top, the effect was exaggerated, like a dog shaking water from its coat. With every heave of the carriage, it shed men left and right, flicking people off the roof as if they weighed nothing. Those who remained on top desperately tried to find something substantial to hold onto, as the driver cautiously negotiated each hole and washboard rut before the bus regained purchase on level ground and continued down the road more slowly before stopping in front of the mosque.

Most of the men who'd been tossed off, staggered after the vehicle, as it waddled toward the big white-and-blue structure. Some remained on the ground, injured from their fall and writhed in pain. No one came to their aid or seemed to care.

Khalid and Eastwood scanned the narrow crossroads to the left and right before returning their gaze to the huge edifice. With a hundred road-weary young men slipping out of or down from the forty-foot ancient transport, only danger lay ahead.

They had followed the dingy pale-blue bus for hours. Few of the dark-haired, bearded men inside and on the roof carried bags, as they left the door or crawled off the top. They watched a withered old man with a wiry white beard, dressed in a traditional *dishdasha* welcome the exhausted travelers.

Eastwood saw enough. “Khalid, let’s go to the embassy. According to the GPS, it’s to the left and down this road about a mile.”

Marty and Karl glanced at each other, and began organizing their cameras and belongings into backpacks. By the time they zippered their bags, Eastwood was opening the truck door and stepping toward the embassy guard shack.

Khalid al-Awalaki watched in fascination as Eastwood spoke to a man behind the thick glass and held up his passport. A polished brass pass-through emerged under the glass, and he placed his passport into the opening. A second later, the device closed and retracted into the shack.

Eastwood was animated and cheerful, as he spoke to the U.S. Marine Security Guard behind the heavy bulletproof window. From the truck, it appeared the Marine saluted Eastwood, who informally returned it and walked back to the Toyota. He came to the driver’s side and said, “Khalid, this is where we get off.”

Marty and Karl stepped from the truck at the sound of Eastwood’s voice, and walked to the rear of the vehicle to extract bags and equipment cases. Khalid, taken aback by Eastwood’s sudden announcement, struggled to get out of his seat. He stood toe-to-toe with Eastwood, becoming more despondent by the second.

“I don’t know how to say ‘thank you’ any more. Khalid, you were terrific getting us here in one piece. It was an adventure and pleasure to ride with you this past week across Libya, Tunisia, and Algeria. We plan to stay here and see what happens.”

Khalid began to tremble as he fought his emotions and burst into tears. He muttered something incomprehensible in Arabic and English as he pumped Eastwood’s hand in gratitude and friendship. Eastwood took whatever Khalid said as positive, knowing the man was probably a bit sentimental and wasn't ready for the adventure and excitement to end. He reached deep into one of his cargo pockets and extracted a fistful of gold coins. Taking Khalid's hand, he counted out six one-ounce gold Krugerrands.

"There's a bonus for all your trouble. I will remember you, Khalid. You're a good man."

"*Sahib* Eastwood, you are most generous!" He dared to look into his palm, then his eyes widened. He closed his hand and brought his fist to his chest.

"You deserve it, Khalid. Thank you. We have to go now."

Marty and Karl came around the truck and said good-bye to the driver, as Eastwood tossed his backpack over his shoulder. The cameramen walked to the guard shack, leaving Eastwood alone with Khalid one last time.

"Safe travels, Khalid. Be careful!"

"Inshallah."

"Thank you again." Shaking the Libyan's hand, Eastwood moved toward his men at the gate.

The Marine buzzed them in, and each one gave Khalid a final good-bye wave before disappearing into the embassy.

Khalid gaped at the road for several moments. Taking several deep breaths, he looked at the handful of gold coin, nodded to himself, slowly slid behind the seat of the Toyota, and drove off.

The Marine behind the glass watched the truck leave and noted its departure in his logbook. Just as he finished, he pressed a selector switch to open one side of the double gate for an embassy car to depart. Bill McGee and Tonka drove off in one of the embassy's pool vehicles.

Eastwood and his camera crew met another Marine Security Guard, who escorted them to the chancery and checked them in at another glass-protected Marine with a Model 1911 semiautomatic pistol. The men exchanged their passports for visitor badges and clipped them on their shirts above the waists as directed.

Lieutenant Colonel Demetrius Eastwood engaged the two

Marines in professional badinage. He asked where they were from, how their folks were doing, and said their parents were proud of them. He told them he was. They were given a unique opportunity to "make the Marine Corps look glorious" and to do outstanding work for America.

"You're a cut above your fellow Marines," he said. "You've been entrusted with something special, representing your nation abroad. You're the first person someone sees when he comes to the embassy. You'll have dozens of opportunities to screw it up royally, but I know you're well-trained and dedicated. You won't let your Commandant down. Ooh-rah!"

The Marine behind the glass called the other Marines, who rushed to the chancery to meet the world-famous Lieutenant Colonel, former presidential candidate, war correspondent and author of history books. In less than two minutes, ten young Marines descended on the reception area to meet the famous Marine Corps officer.

Eastwood signed autographs while he reiterated for them to do great things, "but don't be like me, an old grunt who has a hard time staying out of trouble."

The reception area erupted into laugher and a chorus of "Ooh-rahs!" of approval.

The cameramen were mesmerized by the rock-star reception their boss received from men young enough to be his grandchildren. Everywhere he went, Marines loved him and he returned that love with admiration, encouragement, and pride.

Nazy finished shredding files and dumped her laptop into the disintegrator when an announcement came over the SCIF intercom that her presence was requested, Code one, in the Blue Room. The Ambassador used that code only on the premises, so she closed and locked the empty safes and hurried from the SCIF.

She went downstairs to the small conference room, festooned with blue carpet and curtains, used for official visitors. Aggravated by the interruption, she had much to do before the evacuation.

She smelled the newcomers before she saw them. She rounded the corner and stepped into a wide-open conference room to find the Ambassador, the Security Officer, and the *Charge d-Affaires* sitting across the table from three dusty, dirty men, one of whom looked vaguely familiar.

When she entered the room, every man stood. The Ambassador provided introductions and introduced "Miss C."

Eastwood knew instantly that the stunning woman was CIA. He hadn't seen such a remarkable beauty at the Agency when he visited there working from the White House in what he affectionately called a previous life. During that time, he had an attractive redhead for a secretary. He recalled how difficult it was to work with beauty and brains in close quarters, especially where wives were concerned. He assessed Miss C quickly, determining she was another beauty with brains, but there was something else that wasn't easy to discern. It would bother him for hours.

Nazy shook hands all around and sat at the seat at the far end of the table, hopefully downwind of the visitors. The Ambassador looked directly at her and said, "It was Lieutenant Colonel Eastwood's report that suggested an attack on the embassy was probably in the making."

The Ambassador gestured to Eastwood to continue. "Could you pick up where we left off?"

"Yes, Sir, Mr. Ambassador. As I said, we filmed groups of men poised to attack the embassies in Tripoli and Tunis. We found ourselves behind a bus full of *jihadis*, and our driver was able to mingle with them when we stopped for gas. He reported they were Muslim Brotherhood supporters heading to Algeria to protest the U.S. Embassy.

"Sir, what we saw at Tripoli and Tunis—and filmed—was that the protestors would go first, almost locking arms they were so tight, to create a wall of unarmed men—a human shield if you will, while a number of men carrying AK-47s and several RPGs, followed. It was a highly organized, coordinated operation, but it fell apart instantly when the lead group watched embassy vehicles speed away from the compound."

"Was your driver able to determine the purpose or goal of these protests or attacks?" Nazy asked.

"No, Ma'am, he didn't. We tried to find out when we were in Benghazi and Tripoli. It was hard to get anyone to talk to him, but we looked at the evidence of the consulate, where black flags of al-Qaeda flew over some of the outlying compounds, while a huge green flag of the Muslim Brotherhood dominated one wall of the consulate. No news service broadcast that image. They had no problem transmitting bloody handprints on white stucco but stopped short of transmitting the Brotherhood's calling card. I'm on record that the media transmits what it wants when it supports their agenda."

"What do *you* think happened?" the Ambassador asked.

Eastwood paused to make eye contact with everyone in the room. "I have no proof, but I think what we saw at Benghazi was a botched kidnapping attempt. The Brotherhood kidnaps and holds for ransom; al-Qaeda just blows stuff up. Benghazi had all the hallmarks of a Brotherhood plan gone wrong.

"In essence, the same thing occurred in Tripoli and Tunis but with different outcomes. A wall of protestors fronted men armed with AK-47s and RPGs, only to have the embassy evacuate before they could reach the gates. It looked like they couldn't get enough locals to participate and had to bus in reserves.

"Mr. Ambassador, I was concerned you were next. When we stopped for fuel, I risked filing my report. I hoped my network would pass along the information. I guess it worked."

"It did. That was a very brave thing you did, Colonel Eastwood."

"There's more, Mr. Ambassador. My initial thoughts were that the Muslim Brotherhood wouldn't or couldn't possibly team up with al-Qaeda. The way these guys normally work is that the Brotherhood spends time fending off its rival or what we thought were al-Qaeda affiliates.

"I'm convinced, in this particular case, my early assessment was wrong. While we saw the black flags of al-Qaeda in places like Benghazi and Tripoli, what got our attention were the many green flags of the Brotherhood. We saw their flags from the time we left Benghazi to the time the bus stopped at the mosque a mile down the embassy's frontage road. They've taken over the Egyptian government and are vying for power in Libya and Tunis. I think the Muslim Brotherhood and al-Qaeda wants American diplomats for hostages, and they have some common goals. I suspect Algeria is next on their agenda. Some will work together to attack the embassy while the local Brotherhood chapter moves in to destabilize the government."

The Ambassador brought his hands together as if in prayer. "Thank you for that firsthand account." He nodded to Nazy. "That's excellent information that'll give our analysts something to mull over during the next few weeks. In part because of your warning, and by direction of the State Department, we'll be evacuating Embassy Algiers early in the morning. Please accept my invitation to come along. There should be plenty of seats. I trust you'll be accompanying us?"

The people around the table envisioned the embassy under assault. Islamists seizing the embassy would be dramatic and popular with many Algerians and would be viewed as a Muslim triumph. Having escaped the possible wrath of two groups of pissed-off armed protestors, Eastwood wasn't about to press his luck. As the American Consulate in Libya proved, overrunning an embassy or consulate sometimes had bad, unforeseen consequences. The Ambassador looked Eastwood in the eye and waited for his response.

Marty and Karl shot Eastwood a look.

"We're in, Sir," Eastwood replied.

"Good. That's settled. Any questions?"

It was quiet for a moment, as the men thought, and Nazy analyzed. Eastwood debated whether to ask if Bill McGee was also in Algiers, but with his crew dirty, grimy, and worn out from chasing 100 terrorists across North Africa, he asked, "If we're leaving in the morning, what are the chances of a shower and clean clothes?"

The meeting broke up with the Security Officer and the *Chargé d'Affaires* escorting Eastwood and his film crew to Security and Housekeeping for processing and room assignments in small apartments on the compound. The Ambassador was predisposed to making hand gestures for emphasis and direction, and Nazy barely caught the subtle momentary wave of his hand and his serious expression asking her to remain.

Once the others were gone, she moved closer to the Ambassador, who was seemingly lost in deep thought.

"What do you think?" he asked at last.

"Mr. Ambassador, Colonel Eastwood added the data point that this apparently well-organized band of terrorists are a mile away and could attack at any time. Coupled with the report that the Algerian military has stopped patrolling Chemin Cheikh Avenue an hour ago, it strongly suggests Algerian intelligence knows this group is in town, and they haven't given you a courtesy call.

"I'd say we're on our own, and we'll be attacked sooner rather than later. And given Colonel Eastwood's broadcast report, they know we know what's imminent. They know we evacuate. They know we leave in the early morning. Just as we push up our timetable, they may act immediately. Also, I don't have an updated status of the aircraft. I've been busy finishing up closing down the SCIF."

"I've been assured a jet's coming. I haven't been called, and I tried this afternoon to speak with the Deputy Prime Minister. He and the Prime Minister are out of town."

"Cowards." Her expression didn't change.

"That might be a little indelicate, Miss Cunningham, but maybe there's a ring of truth to it." He smiled to ensure his comment was taken as banter, not criticism, displaying a mouth of perfect incisors and canines, the work of many years of orthodontia.

Nazy smiled to indicate she hadn't taken offense, though she quickly returned to her professional persona. "The last status update I heard was that the State Department's having trouble getting a NEO aircraft here before three o'clock in the morning. It was supposed to be on its way from the States." She paused. "We have a two hour window where we're exposed. Do we have a backup plan?"

"What do you mean?"

"Mr. Ambassador, one of the findings that came from the preliminary investigation into the death of our Ambassador to Libya was that the U.S. military wasn't called to provide support. They have quick response teams in Europe to provide the kind of help we seem… the kind we *will* need to escape.

"Am I correct in assuming that the plan is to shelter in place until the aircraft arrives? The bad guys are a mile down the road. It seems that when the Algerians refused to provide the protection expected under international protocol, we may not get protection if we're sitting at the airport; I think we should ask for military help. Even at this hour, it might be too late."

He was taken aback by her serious, cogent argument. It made sense. All data points and new information pointed toward one conclusion—the embassy was ill-prepared if the *jihadis* planned an early attack. He was guided by the misplaced belief that any protest would lead to a demonstration, and the demonstrators would just want to get over the wall to tear down the American flag, hoping to shred it, burn it, and piss on it. That was standard when Muslim demonstrators captured a flag.

The embassy staff would hunker down in the well-protected chancery until the Algerian media came to film the demonstration. Before it got out of control, the embassy would evacuate in peace and dignity, but still with its tail between its legs.

"Nazy, we don't want to lose control of events and overreact, which would allow the NEO to be disrupted. I'm certain that part of the Algerian's intel is correct, and we'll be able to evacuate peacefully on our schedule."

"I understand, Mr. Ambassador." She fought to contain her

disappointment. All signs pointed to an early attack.

Not about to give up, she suppressed the desire to rail at the man who was ignoring the obvious, even when his ignorance would probably kill or hurt people on his staff. Once she had her emotions under control, she worked to find the right mixture of words and tone.

"Mr. Ambassador, on the chance that the embassy does come under attack earlier than expected, please tell me you'll reconsider requesting military help."

He took a deep breath and nodded. He was past worrying about the embarrassment of having to evacuate his embassy. He had something else on his mind, and his opportunity to articulate those thoughts was becoming fewer. "For you, Nazy, I'll do that."

"Thank you, Sir." She felt momentarily buoyed, but she heard an element of something else in his response. She turned to leave when he surprised her by touching her arm to stop her.

"Nazy, there's something else I wanted to ask. There's no time like the present. When we get out of this and are back in Washington, would you consider having dinner with me?"

Air filled her lungs, and her bosom heaved, drawing the Ambassador's eyes from her face to her chest. "Mr. Ambassador, I'm flattered, but…."

"Nazy, I hope I didn't say anything inappropriate."

"…but I don't think my fiancée would understand. I do appreciate the thought."

"Oh. I didn't know you were engaged. I'm sorry."

"Mr. Ambassador, as my fiancée would say, 'No harm, no foul.' I'm flattered."

"Thank you. I suppose the next time I see you, we'll be on a plane heading home.'

"Let's hope!" She lowered her head and walked away, trying to marshal her thoughts on the seriousness of the situation at the embassy. Instead, her mind kept returning to, *Duncan was right again about liberals. They can be so clueless.*

Waiting for the elevator to take her to her office on the third floor, she imperceptibly shook her head in disbelief at the idea that the Ambassador asked her for a date.

The office was bare and stark. All the personal effects of the Chief of Station had been taken down, removed from the desk, boxed and mailed to her. Nazy checked the burn bag a final time to ensure nothing was left to burn. Any classified paper in the Chief of Station's office and the SCIF had been removed, shredded or pulped.

Locking the door behind her, she walked to the communications vault to file her final report to Langley on one of the last remaining computers. After inputting several log-ins and passwords to the classified system, she confirmed some files had been dispatched to HQ via courier—primarily the *Piper* files—all others were destroyed, the SCIF had been disestablished and closed, and she and her team were awaiting transportation. She wasn't expecting a response or read receipt, so she signed off. All that was left was to drop the computer into the disintegrator and change into something casual, pack her personal belongings, and get a bite to eat, assuming the cafeteria hadn't closed.

The embassy officially closed for business under Threat Condition Red, and the last of the visa applicants departed the premises just as Bill and Tonka returned from reconnoitering the area around the embassy.

Tonka parked the car in its charging space. He and McGee tried to locate the groundskeeper who managed the fleet of embassy cars.

"We'll see him at dinner and give him the keys," Tonka said.

They returned to the apartment building to retrieve their gear and stash it in advance of the evacuation. A corner of the "Blue Room" was filling up fast with suitcases, backpacks, and diplomatic bags and the former SEALs contributed theirs to the growing pile.

Bill stopped before they entered the building. "I wish we'd gotten back there to take a look." He pointed to the brick and concrete wall adjacent to the apartments.

"Bullfrog, that's a driveway. We drove by it when we first left. I'm certain we looked it over. I've been up there and looked around. That area's well lit. It demarks a short driveway for the house on the corner."

"Yeah, I think you're right. OK. See you in a couple hours for dinner?"

"Roger."

CHAPTER FORTY-SIX

1830 September 25, 2012
West of Cartagena, Spain

Dull red lights illuminated the full length of the cabin, as the L-100 crew signaled the hard turn left toward the coast of Spain. The men in the cabin sprang into action, while the pilot and copilot donned helmets and night vision goggles for the ingress to the unprepared landing strip. The cockpit was completely dark, but the instruments and controls were fully readable and illuminated to the aircrew by their night vision devices.

Under the red lights in the cargo area, aircraft mechanics and the flight engineer watched intently as Hunter changed into a black NOMEX flight suit, while Bob and Bob opened the doors of the *Wraith's* container, locking them in place. It was show time.

The former Marines were a bit intrigued, as Duncan extracted a black leather holster and huge black revolver from his helmet bag, inserting his arm through the shoulder holster's opening and letting the weapon hang under his left arm. Hunter donned an LPU—life preserver unit—for his trip over the water.

Over the last few years of flying support for the super-secret YO-3A missions, the Agency's aircrew was always mesmerized by Hunter's preflight ritual. They were entranced as he removed the heavy black revolver, a six-inch Colt Python, and opened the cylinder to verify that five rounds were loaded in the six-shooter. Hunter meticulously closed the cylinder to ensure the open chamber was at the twelve o'clock position, protection that the hammer and firing pin couldn't strike a cartridge's primer during a hard landing or sudden impact which could blow a hole in his lung or worse.

The men learned from Duncan that it was a Marine Corps combat helicopter pilot trick. They never flew with the hammer of a revolver positioned over a live cartridge, and they always carried the biggest damn pistol they could get their hands on. Uncle Sam's .38 Specials didn't have the stopping power when someone needed to defend himself. That was why Hunter chose the .357 Magnum with hollow-point ammo. When a man was hit with a magnum load, he stayed down.

The aircrew in the cabin were cued to take their places with the sounds of the hydraulic system lowering the flaps; the three mechanics moved toward the rear of the airplane. The flight engineer activated the control valve which lowered the cargo ramp and raised the cargo door. The six men at the back of the plane looked out the opening, as the Hercules crossed the Spanish coast, no longer "feet wet" but "feet dry." Six men checked their watches. It was two minutes to touchdown.

Thirty minutes earlier, the taller Bob squeezed into 007's container and unlocked the safe, where the cartridge-activated devices and the hybrid propellant bullets were safely kept while in flight. Between turbulence and calm winds, the two Bobs loaded flares and chaff cartridges into the left and right countermeasures dispensers at the back of the black airplane.

After filling the dispenser can, the taller Bob reached into the safe and extracted a red rectangular plastic case. He removed the contents and reached over the empennage to hand Hunter the twenty-pound, ten-round clip of laser-designated .70-caliber ammunition. Hunter depressed two fasteners on the port side of the YO-3A to open the sensor access panel and loaded the airplane's gun. He made sure the rounds were fully seated into the breach before closing and taping over the seams on the panel.

Hunter and the L-100 aircrew then keyed on the sound of the hydraulic system lowering the landing gear as the flaps programmed to full down, changing the pitch of the L-100 to a more nose down orientation. The six men moved into the final phase of the "landing checklist." The flight engineer returned to the cargo ramp controls, and the two mechanics moved to the hinge of the ramp and floor. Bob and Bob worked their way to the rear of the YO-3A container, as they felt the additional drag on the L-100 when the Hercules' tires and wheels were lowered into the airstream. The aircraft slowed perceptibly, and the Hercules bounced around in the turbulent night air near the coast.

The red cabin lights flashed three times—sixty seconds to touchdown. In less than five minutes, Hunter would be airborne.

Landing any aircraft at a remote airfield under night vision goggles was challenging, and it was more so for the L-100, the largest aircraft outfitted with night vision goggle-capable cockpits. The devices were fantastic visual aids in wide open areas, but in the landing phase, they greatly limited the pilot's ability to judge properly the aircraft's rate of descent. With no depth perception available through NVGs, sometimes landings could be considered good, bad, or "colorful."

The landing was textbook perfect, with no "soft shoeing" of the landing gear and no bouncing to find *terra firma*. As the pilot set the nose wheels down smoothly, the copilot reversed the pitch of the propellers. The big cargo plane decelerated quickly, making the six men in back lean heavily toward the front, obeying Isaac Newton's law.

The flight engineer timed the lowering of the ramp perfectly. It touched the ground just as the Hercules stopped and rocked gently. The two mechanics stepped to the trailing edge of the ramp and lowered three small wedges to the ground. They moved outboard to get out of the way and verified that the YO-3A was rolling out of its container and through the cargo opening of the Hercules and onto the ground.

007's main landing gear rolled across the precision-placed ramps attached to the cargo ramp. The tail wheel rolled neatly in the aluminum channel, guiding the YO-3A straight and true, out of the back of the L-100 and onto the grass strip.

The two mechanics allowed the Yo-Yo to pass them, then raced into the container and each helped lift one wing from its cradle. Duncan tracked along with the fuselage of the YO-3A, gently depressing the footbrake to control the matte black airplane's speed down the cargo ramp and modulated its deceleration with varying foot pressure.

When the YO-3A was clear of the Hercules' tail, Hunter stepped hard on the brake. He unfastened the footbrake and raced back to the cargo ramp to place it there for one of the Bobs to retrieve, just as the two men and the mechanics brought out 007's wings.

Hunter ran back to Lockheed's little spy plane and opened the canopy, scrambled up, and stepped in. He pulled on his helmet and turned on the battery switch. As the electrical systems powered up, he fastened his seat belt and shoulder harness across his parachute before connecting his helmet to the aircraft's interphone system.

With one Bob at the far end of the container, they waited until their mechanic returned to lift the small tip of the wing. The old men lifted the heavy end. Once it was free of its cradle, the men walked purposely out of the container to the 007, with the young men taking the long route to spread the wings, as each Bob rotated the wing 90° until it was flat, parallel to the ground, and expertly guided the tang of the wing into the aircraft's open clevis mount. Each Bob slipped a frozen clevis pin into each of the two fore and aft wing mounts.

With the wing "hung," each Bob inserted a safety pin into the openings at the bottom of each clevis pin and connected the electrical and fuel-line fittings with a twist of their wrists. As the two wings fit tightly into their mounts, Agency mechanics raced back into the container for jugs of aviation gasoline. On each wing, Bob connected the aileron control cables to the airplane's cabling and secured the access doors, as the first of the two fuel cans were dumped into the left and right wing tanks.

Hunter monitored the assembly of the wings and the over-the-wing fueling before engaging the fuel pumps. When each Bob removed their hands from the flight-control cables, each man raised a thumbs-up signal to show their hands were free and for Hunter to check the operation of the ailerons.

He looked over to the edge of the wing, night vision goggles over his eyes, and rocked the control stick left to right, then raised two thumbs-up to verify the controls responded properly.

Hunter returned his gaze to the cockpit to complete the items from the memorized start, taxi, and takeoff check lists. With fueling complete, Bob and Bob and the two mechanics ripped cut tape from the side of the airframe and the wing, taping all exposed joints and fuel-access doors, as Hunter pressed the engine starter.

The high-performance, six-bladed propeller spun three times before the engine started. Duncan allowed oil pressure to rise and stabilize for a second before powering away into the night. The five men watched as the little airplane disappeared from view. Neither the YO-3A's propeller nor the engine exhaust could be heard over the L-100's four idling Allisons.

The two exhausted septuagenarians dragged themselves up the cargo ramp, each carrying an empty fuel jug in each hand, as the mechanics lifted the three small ramps from the ground. The flight engineer spoke into his microphone, as he pressed the selector valve to raise the large cargo ramp and lower the overhead cargo door. "All clear."

Sixty seconds later, the Hercules was airborne and heading toward the coast.

High overhead somewhere, an AWACS E-3 established the encrypted data link to 007. On Hunter's multifunction panel, he read the bullet phrase narratives that he was in the clear, and his playmate was feet wet again.

CHAPTER FORTY-SEVEN

1900 September 25, 2012
U.S. Embassy
Algiers, Algeria

Bill McGee was astonished to see Lieutenant Colonel Demetrius Eastwood leaving the entrance of the apartment building. He should have known better. He'd been around long enough to know he should expect the unexpected. Eastwood said he might see McGee in Algiers, and there he was, presumably with his film crew.

Since leaving the man at the airport in Tripoli, McGee hadn't thought about Eastwood until he saw him on TV earlier that morning. If Eastwood was at the embassy that meant the bus he followed reached Algiers, and the bad guys were nearby.

McGee knew Eastwood had a story to tell, and he wanted to hear it. He and Tonka diverted their path to intercept the retired Marine and his men.

"Look what the cat drug in!" McGee shouted.

Once Eastwood recognized the beefy man with tiny glasses, he accelerated to a jog to meet him with a smile and a handshake. "Captain McGee, good to see you again! I wondered if our paths would cross in Algiers."

"So they did. Nice work on that report. It looks like you got the State Department off its ass finally, and we might get out of here—if the bad guys don't surprise us and knock down the door early."

"Well, Sir, they're about one mile, that way."

"I'm sorry...."

"Please call me Dory."

"William or Bill?"

"Bill or Bullfrog."

Eastwood made introductions, and McGee indicated there was one more with him.

"Spanky will show up later," McGee said.

"We're heading to get some chow."

"Same here. It's pretty good, good selection. The price is right."

"And the scenery is incredible," Tonka added.

Eastwood got his drift. "It can't get any better than the Miss C we met when we talked with the Ambassador."

Tonka looked around the area as if hurt. "Well, that's the extent of the good-looking women here. She's it. She'll probably join us for dinner." He gave McGee a mischievous look. "Her and Bullfrog are friendly."

McGee frowned and gave a stinging rejoinder. "She's the fiancée of one of my closest friends. Anybody's better to talk to than Numb Nuts here."

"She's obviously CIA. I suppose I can't say anything?"

"She might tell you, but I'm certain she won't want to talk on the record. I expect...I *know* she can't afford to be interviewed or photographed." He nodded toward Eastwood's cameramen.

The tone of the conversation became more concerned. "She knows I'm a correspondent. If we see her, nothing's on the record. I suppose we'll talk benign stuff."

The five men in the circle nodded, then McGee broke ranks.

He and Eastwood walked side-by-side down the walkway to the chancery. The other men followed.

Once in the cafeteria, the preferred purlieu of newcomers and beer drinkers, Eastwood and McGee took a couple Coca Colas from the cooler and found a table, while the other men worked the food lines and grabbed a diminishing number of bottled beers.

McGee was curious about what Eastwood observed in Benghazi and Tripoli, and how he concluded that the men on the bus were wannabe *jihadis* headed for Algeria. Eastwood explained his driver, a Libyan named Khalid, was absolutely fearless and had a journalist's sense of curiosity. He entered the belly of the beast.

Eastwood explained that when they stopped for fuel, Khalid jumped in the middle of the men riding the bus and asked what they were doing. He guessed they were going to work in the Algerian oil fields, but they corrected him and said they were on a mission from Allah to punish Americans wherever they were. Their group would demonstrate at the embassies, while another was going to protest the big American oil companies.

"We never saw a bus full of men like the one we followed. They probably didn't need that many to disrupt oil-field operations," Eastwood said. "What about you, Bill? Something interesting and special had to pry you away from the war college."

"I wish I could tell you. It's an incredibly bad situation. People I worked with basically up and left. I have no clue where they went. Because we were still on contract with State, we were sent to Algiers to provide additional security. There's no one left in Libya to do what we were sent to do."

"Bad?"

"The worst. You can't imagine how bad." McGee wanted to find someone, *anyone*, who could make the decision to remove the MANPADS in Libya. The Ambassador wasn't the right guy, and neither was the acting Chief of Station. No one had a need to know, and they weren't read in on the special access program.

Every day those weapons weren't neutralized was another day closer to having terrorists like al-Qaeda getting their hands on them. If they or the Muslim Brotherhood ever found them or bought them, the worldwide destruction and terrorism would be unimaginable. They could dispatch missiles anywhere in the world and shoot down any plane they wished. It was the worst-possible situation, with no apparent solution on the horizon.

He toyed with the idea of telling Eastwood something, giving him enough hints and a broad brush of the situation he left in Benghazi, but he signed a nondisclosure agreement that he would take *any* classified information he was given to his grave. *Still....*

Eastwood, breaking the impasse, started talking about the *jihadis.*

There was something he couldn't resolve. "It seems like these mosques are wired together and are mutually supporting. I'm locked into a paradigm that churches are independent, standalone affairs, and that mosques act the same way. I'm assuming that's how they operate, but from what I've seen this past week, I think my assumptions are way off base."

"You know what they say when you assume something…." McGee grinned.

"Yes, Sir. It makes an ass out of you and me. I've been an ass to think like that."

"Dory, let me tell you a story. I was in the same boat last year. I haven't shared this with anyone else. Please keep it close."

"Absolutely."

"You're probably unaware that after bin Laden was taken ... *out*, a number of SEALs were targeted and killed. The former President ran around patting himself on the back, telling everyone how great he was and that he was the guy who got bin Laden."

"I saw his stupid little act. It was disgusting. But I don't remember hearing about any SEALs getting killed."

"I think you were in Afghanistan, embedded with some Marines."

"I usually am and probably was."

"I determined that the shooter, a Muslim sniper, received his targeting information from local mosques. He received detailed info from email he got on a notebook computer. I couldn't resolve the fact that there was a network, that somehow, those mosques in the U.S. were connected virtually.

"That didn't click at the time, but now it does. For the few days I was in Benghazi, we were given a crash course on all the players in Libya. I discovered something that may or may not be important, but if you look at their published charters, nearly every mosque in Libya was an extension of the Muslim Brotherhood. Our driver essentially articulated there is a connection. They *are* connected. They're a network of mosques run by radical imams who are connected by the Web and the Qur'an.

"I've done a little research for a war college course, and I found these guys are, by and large, liberal or radical but definitely fascist in nature and structure. Contrast that with the good, moderate Muslims, who are conservative and democratic. They just want to work, raise their families, and don't go radical or postal when they don't get their way. The sad news is, like all those with a conservative bent, there are too few of them, and they don't fight these guys hard enough, so they let them walk all over them until they finally have enough. That's usually when their backs are against the wall, but by then it's usually too late to do anything about it."

"You won't get an argument from me," Eastwood said.

"Liberals take advantage of conservatives' good nature and fill the power vacuum with the dumbest, most-odious, obnoxious leaders on the planet. They do it at home, and they do it in the Muslim world, where we'd better not call them radicals, or, worse, Islamists."

Eastwood laughed so loud, the other patrons noticed. He composed himself, as McGee took a swig from his soda. "What's the real deal with Miss C? When I look around this place, it's pretty apparent that she's…."

"Different?"

"You don't find women of that caliber, beauty, and brains in federal service."

"As I recall, you had quite a looker for a secretary."

"*Touché.* Point taken, but she was different. In that short time we spent with the Ambassador, you could tell she was cut from a different grade of cloth. There must be an interesting story there."

"I don't know if there's a story or not. I know she's just filling in for the trade attaché. She's the fiancée of a very close friend. She's probably the real reason everyone waits and hangs out in the cafeteria. When she leaves, so does everyone else."

"She's a magnet. I'll bet even lesbians lust after her. But I'll bet there aren't many of them here, but at the State Department...well, it's not called liberalville central for nothing."

They smirked at the comment regarding the Department of State's natural leftist political leanings and the derisive moniker worn well at Foggy Bottom in the heart of Washington, DC.

They stopped laughing long enough for another drink of their soda. A murmur swept across the tables from one side of the cafeteria to the other. McGee checked the monitor on the wall, sensing it was a newsworthy item that got tongues wagging, but there was nothing to see but some termagant on the TV.

When Nazy Cunningham strode into the room, all hubbub ceased. Heads and eyes snapped toward the entrance, as she appeared in jeans and a shirt, her hair pulled back in a long dark ponytail.

"It's just Nazy." McGee chuckled and stood.

Eastwood, who didn't see her coming, was slow to rise. When he turned and saw it was Miss C, he was embarrassed and then grateful she chose to sit with him and McGee.

"I hope I'm not interrupting anything." She pulled out a chair, sat and artfully slid it to the table.

"Nope," McGee said. "Just waiting for you."

"So what have you been talking about?"

"Would you believe we were talking about 'but nots'?" offered Eastwood.

"But nots?" She was instantly suspicious. She just met the man and didn't know him, so she sensed a trap.

"Sure. Democracy is promoted in the Middle East, *but not* if it brings the Muslim Brotherhood to power. Nuclear proliferation is bad for Iran *but not* for Israel. Human rights are demanded for China *but not* for Saudi Arabia."

"You can negotiate with anyone," McGee added seriously, "*but not* with terrorists."

Nazy lowered her eyes. "You can try to fool some of the people all the time, *but not* me."

Their table erupted in laughter and short applause. The other people in the cafeteria knew the woman and two men were having way too much fun. The other patrons wished they were having as much fun during such a somber and gloomy time.

"Mr. Eastwood, I must tell you my fiancée is a big fan of yours," Nazy said. "He's a retired Marine. He flew jets."

"What's his name?"

"Duncan Hunter."

Eastwood snapped his fingers and pointed at her. "I know Duncan Hunter. Prior enlisted, captain, flew F-4s, a great American and a great patriot."

Nazy, startled, almost choked up, but she acknowledged by nodding. Two men in Algeria who knew Duncan. *It was a small world.*

"Wow," she said. "That's impressive. How do you know him?"

"It's a long, old story, but I think I can remember all of it. It kinda goes like this. I was working out of the White House, and someone from Langley asked if I knew anyone who played racquetball. I said I kinda did. There was this Marine pilot who flew in from the west coast with his general—he must've been the general's aide—and they played racquetball at the POAC, the Pentagon Officer's Athletic Club. Hour after hour, they beat the snot out of everyone. Anyone could see it was the captain who was the superstar, not the general.

"After a couple phone calls, I had his name, Captain Duncan Hunter, F-4 pilot and multiple All-Marine racquetball champ. The guys across the river heard Pablo Escobar, the cocaine drug lord, loved to play racquetball, and they wanted to see if they could somehow get a tracking device on Escobar.

"A couple weeks passed, and the next thing I knew, Escobar was found and killed. I heard through my contact that Pablo met Hunter, and they played racquetball and had a good time. Pablo was so impressed by Hunter; he supposedly bought everything in Hunter's racquetball bag or some such story.

"The tracking devices were in the bag or a ball or racquet. I don't know for sure. It was something the S&T dudes came up with. Anyway, the next thing I knew, Escobar was found and killed. I have to tell you, I *know* Duncan Hunter, but I haven't met him."

"I haven't heard that story." She felt confused and proud.

"I have," McGee said.

"I found out more about Captain Hunter," Eastwood continued. "What I heard was unbelievable. He's quite a talent, and he's your fiancé? Marine flyboy and trade attaché? There has to be a story there."

"I'm afraid not, Mr. Eastwood," she demurred. "I met Duncan when he was a civilian at the Naval War College. There really isn't anything else to it. I really need to get something to eat. I understand it's going to be a long flight tonight. What about you?"

"We thought we were going to drink all the beer," McGee said.

Eastwood continued, "We didn't want any of it going to waste. But as you see, it's all gone. We have Coke. Evacuations go better with Coke."

McGee admired how easily Nazy redirected the surreptitious interview request. If she didn't want to elaborate on her relationship with Hunter, that was her prerogative. He would have been very surprised if she had. She wasn't about to blow Duncan's cover...or hers.

Nazy ambled to where Tonka, Spanky, and the two cameramen sat. She chatted with them for a few minutes, while McGee and Eastwood retrieved two more bottles of Coke and finally got in line for dinner. Nazy joined them, bringing up the rear. They felt uncomfortable having the raven-haired beauty behind them and insisted she move in front. They fought to keep their eyes on the food choices, and not her.

Eastwood attempted to tell a "there I was" story, but it fell flat. McGee was distracted by the TV and not the *laissez-faire* attitude of the local diplomats and embassy at large. Nazy's mind ran down mental checklists, trying to convince herself she took care of every requirement in advance of the NEO. Since all three were preoccupied with different priorities in their minds, they ate in subdued silence.

The cafeteria was very quiet. The stress of the impending evacuation was uppermost in everyone's thoughts. Nearly every eye was focused on the TV monitor for the latest news. There were no press releases about the threat level at the U.S. Embassy in Algiers or its impending evacuation. Nothing was said about the evacuated embassies in advance of the coordinated Muslim Brotherhood protests and attacks in North Africa. No one cared about baseball scores or the weather in the Great Lakes. The natural disparate smells of a cafeteria didn't register, as anxiety permeated the room.

Nazy finished, said her good-byes, and left the men to their drinks and tell war stories. She waved at the men at the other table and acknowledged others in the cafeteria with a wave and smile. In jeans and her trademark white, long-sleeved shirt, she walked out with every eye on her.

Seconds after she disappeared from view, Eastwood screwed up his face in mock pain, showing how much it hurt to see the beautiful Miss C walk away. Bill, more composed, smiled and offered to tap the neck of his Coke bottle with Eastwood's in a manly telepathic ritual.

The men's eyes slowly returned to the overhead monitor, as they drained their drinks. As McGee's bottle returned to the table, the windows lining the cafeteria blew out, and a powerful pressure wave from an explosion sent glass and debris flying everywhere.

CHAPTER FORTY-EIGHT

2000 September 25, 2012
Houari Boumediene International Airport
Algeria

The driver of the hotel limousine departed when the three men were safely inside the executive terminal. The short, demure Emirati with four gold braids on his shoulders sauntered into the flight-planning area, his corpulent copilot joining him after a stop at the men's room. The FAHD called Malik watched them split up to prepare for their long flight.

He walked to the reception desk and he leaned against the elegant, stainless-steel counter, and spoke softly to the pair of uniformed young ladies behind the counter. Their wide, bright eyes shone under tight matching white veils, suggesting they were eagerly ready and willing to help. The only men who came through the executive terminal were either very rich or very powerful or the aircrew for the rich and powerful.

Malik dressed the part in black silk suit and tan oxfords with an Islamic green tie; his hair pomaded and raked straight back. He carried Abu Manu's belting leather briefcase, primarily to conceal the Russian 9mm Makarov inside. He requested the final bill for the fuel and ground handling services for the white and blue Gulfstream parked on the ramp.

In seconds, the bill was presented, and he offered an American Express card. In ten minutes, the pilots filed their flight plan, and the three men stepped outside the terminal for their first look at the aircraft.

It was difficult to take their eyes off it. Under the ramp's floodlights, the new Gulfstream radiated beauty and elegance, the pinnacle of American aircraft manufacturing. The white paint was flawless, and the dark-blue trim was razor-sharp and unmarred by hours of high-speed flying. The Gulfstream 550 was breathtaking; an amalgamation of art and engineering, and it would soon be sold to the highest bidder in Dubai.

"It's a beautiful night for flying, *Sahib,*" the man with four gold braids said. "I'll return you to your master in short order."

Abu Manu's man bowed slightly and said, "*Inshallah.*"

Malik handed the keys to the captain, who said, "*Shukran.*" *Thank you.*

The pudgy copilot quietly kicked the chocks from the wheels and preflighted the aircraft as best he could from the ground. He wasn't the kind to expend the extra effort to find a maintenance stand and check the oil or any of the fluids. He walked around the plane, visually looking for anything out of the ordinary; he assumed the aircraft was properly serviced. His main contribution to the preflight was gently kicking the tires, and he seemed satisfied by their hardness.

The pilot inserted the key into the door lock and lowered the air stairs. Malik waited for the captain to board and monitored the progress of the fat little copilot. As the copilot waddled along the underside of the starboard wing, the pilot started the auxiliary power plant and turned on the external lights.

The high-pitched whine of the tiny jet engine was too much for Malik's ears, and he ascended the airstairs followed by the copilot, who closed and locked the door behind him before scurrying into the narrow opening to the cockpit like a rat squeezing through a sewer pipe.

Malik stood in the galley, watching the two aviators go through their checklists, as they prepared the aircraft for flight. Four multifunction displays and dozens of indicator lamps flooded the cockpit in differently colored and sized lights, as the men's hands moved handles, depressed buttons, and twisted knobs on the instrument console and overhead panels. Switches activated myriad systems, pumps, and igniters. One engine was started, then the other.

Malik saw that cockpit choreography many times, but he was always enthralled with the pilots' activities every time Abu Manu called for a lift. He turned toward the cabin to assess the accommodations. Six luxurious, overstuffed white leather chairs, three on each side, filled the front half of the jet. The back half held dozens of twenty-four-inch cubes with silver buckles and handles. The glossy black Fiberglas containers were spread and stacked evenly down the aisle, their weight centered and disbursed over the main spar of the wings.

Malik placed the briefcase in the seat of the first row of chairs and took the opposite, and then he leaned heavily on an armrest to watch the pilots work.

CHAPTER FORTY-NINE

2000 September 25, 2012
U.S. Embassy
Algiers, Algeria

The instinctive response to the explosion and windows shattering overhead was duck and cover. The blast pulverized the heavy glass panels into tiny cubes, like debris from a shattered windshield in a car crash, sending shards and metal framing flying over the heads of the seated patrons. Nearly everyone, momentarily stunned, was unable to move. Their brains struggled to comprehend what just happened, and their ears rang from the blast.

Immediately after the blast wave rocked the cafeteria, the four exceptions were the three former SEALs and the Marine, who raced out of the room. There was no hesitation or debate. The sound and effects of rocket propelled grenades galvanized the old warriors, who reacted and moved.

Cafeteria patrons reacted differently. Those who started making sense of their newly shattered world screamed and trembled, some cowered in abject fear.

McGee, Spanky, and Tonka drew their Model 1911 Colt Automatic Pistols, as they raced down the hall, racking the slides to chamber a round. They were loaded, locked, and cocked with safeties off. The four men flew up the half-flight of stairs in one giant leap, one after the other. In a line, McGee, Eastwood, Spanky, and Tonka blew past the bewildered Marine Security Guard behind the thick glass and pounded the embassy door's crash bar to get outside the chancery.

McGee tucked and rolled onto the lawn, the .45 held in both hands in an aiming position. He looked for someone to shoot, while he wondered, *Where's Nazy?*

After dinner, Nazy turned to the apartments and was midway between the chancery and the apartment building when the embassy wall was blown out. The pressure wave of multiple RPGs and debris from the disintegrated wall knocked her off the sidewalk, smacking her down. She was unconscious when she hit the ground, bleeding from shrapnel. Half of her blouse was shredded, the buttons torn away. Her bra strap was cut and scraped, as were her jeans. One tennis shoe was blown off. The side of her body nearest the explosion took the brunt of the damage. Her face, arm, and leg were riddled with dozens of tiny cuts, as shards of concrete punctured soft tissue and bone. Fresh blood oozed from each wound.

Armed men poured through the dust in the breach in the wall. The hole was as wide as a dump truck. Two RPGs had obliterated the section of cinder block wall. The first three men through the gap saw a woman crumpled on the ground. One man raced to Nazy and lifted her head by her hair like a trophy hunter raising an animal's head for a photograph. He smiled like a wild man.

"See ah!" he shouted. *"See ah!"*

They recognized her from surveillance as a key member of the embassy, the trade attaché and suspected CIA, or *see ah.* A medium-built man picked Nazy up, while another man helped toss her over his shoulders. He struggled against the additional weight to hurry from the compound against the flow of men who poured into the embassy grounds.

As McGee and Tonka spilled out of the door, they immediately saw two men a few yards away raising RPGs to firing position. With one knee firmly on the ground and his shooting eye lined up with the front and rear sights, McGee shouted, "Right!" and shot the man on the right, blowing off the top of his head. Tonka shot the bearded man on the left in the face. Both RPGs fell from the dead men's hands, and clattered on the driveway.

It was teamwork, like they practiced a thousand times on active duty. Some skills were nonperishable, like riding a bicycle and killing terrorists with a single bullet to the head.

After engaging the RPG shooter, McGee lined up his .45 for another target only to see a man with someone draped over his shoulders maneuver through the sea of onrushing people and disappear through a massive, dusty gap in the embassy's east wall. The bloody white shirt and long black hair still in its ponytail meant it could be only one person.

McGee quickly did the mental math in an instant, war gaming the situation to resolve the probability that the man was, in all likelihood, carrying Nazy Cunningham. From the time she left the cafeteria until the explosion meant she couldn't have reached her apartment safely and was caught in the open. There wasn't anyone else like her at the embassy. Based on the proximity and timing of when she left the cafeteria, she would have been injured in the blast.

They've got her!

McGee was in a stupor until Spanky killed another jihadi with a weapon and he snapped out of his trance. Tonka shot everyone coming through the wall who carried a weapon. Men without guns saw their comrades' heads erupting in sprays of blood, bone, and brain and immediately reversed course to run back the way they came.

"Marines are engaging those coming through the breach!" Eastwood yelled. "From the rooftop!"

McGee recovered and shouted at Tonka, "We have to go after her!"

Both men knew that going through the hole in the wall with only a .45 was a bad idea.

Tonka ran toward the parking lot. "I have the keys to the pool car!"

McGee and Eastwood followed at a run.

As he ran, McGee shouted to Spanky, "Don't shoot us when we come back with Nazy!"

As they neared the vehicles in the parking lot, Tonka double-pressed the unlock button on the key fob. The headlights flashed, and the three men got into the white Chevy Volt. Tonka hesitated; he flipped around in the seat to verify that the embassy gate was closed and locked, and there was no way anyone would open it with armed men on the other side.

"Through the breach!" McGee shouted, pointing.

Tonka stomped on the pedal and flipped his .45 over the seat to Eastwood, sitting in the back. The electric car's wheels spun momentarily before gaining traction and moving across the embassy's lawn and sidewalks. The vehicle's electric recharging handle snapped from its receptacle.

Tonka steered wildly to hit three men who passed through the gap only to find themselves in the crosshairs of a quiet car bearing down on them. One man crumpled at the impact and bounced off. Tonka didn't slow as the Volt silently ran over the human speed bumps.

In seconds, they were out of the compound. New protestors ricocheted off the fenders. As they shot through the gap, Tonka had to slow and swerve away from the fence of the adjacent property. Regaining control, he hit several more protestors, kicking them to the side of the road in crumpled heaps of crushed flesh and bone.

Eastwood suddenly raised the gun and shot a man who tried to aim an AK-47 at the car. The shot inside the closed vehicle nearly deafened all three men.

"I won't do that again!" he shouted over the ringing in his ears.

Tonka kept his foot on the accelerator and skidded onto the main embassy road just as McGee pointed ahead.

"I think that's her!" McGee said.

The embassy went into full lockdown mode. Marines streamed into and out of the armory, racing to their defensive posts. Spanky and several Marines fanned out onto the roof of the embassy to shoot anyone coming through the breach. The compound was littered with bodies. Some men writhed in agony from Tonka's circuitous route over whoever was in his way, driving over arms, legs, and the occasional torso.

The *Chargé d'Affaires* ran from the shard-covered cafeteria, reaching the safe room, where he repeatedly muttered, "We need to be evacuated now!" to anyone willing to make eye contact.

The U.S. Ambassador was on the phone, screaming at a low-level functionary at the foreign ministry for help and protection. When his frustration level exceeded his capacity for reason, he slammed down the phone and shouted, "Why are they shooting at them?"

The Security Officer calmly replied, "Mr. Ambassador, they've shot RPGs to blow a hole in the embassy wall, and they tried to blow down the main door, but those contractors stopped them. My guess is they were coming for you."

Color drained from the Ambassador's lips. Nonplussed, he shut up. As other gunfire chattered outside, he slowly recovered, and understanding settled in. He hung his head as Marines in full battle gear hurried into and out of the safe room.

He surveyed the protected space. With all the noise and confusion erupting over the last few minutes, he scanned the faces of his staff and realized something wasn't right. The noise and excitement made it impossible to focus. It took another round of shooting outside for him to compose himself and take mental inventory of his people.

Some were missing, and he ticked names off with his fingers. When he came to Chief of Station, he double-checked, pursed his lips, and asked no one in particular, "Do we know where Nazy is?"

CHAPTER FIFTY

2030 September 25, 2012
Mostaganem, Algeria

Duncan Hunter skimmed the Mediterranean Sea at 500 feet and 200 knots. He was thirty minutes to feet dry. Crystal clear skies over the water, away from any light pollution, allowed the Milky Way to fill his canopy. Hunter was rarely able to enjoy the celestial majesty of the heavens when he was airborne.

When he flew with his partner, Greg Lynche, the men talked and bantered during ingress and egress of target areas, mostly for stress relief. Like the men they surveilled, they rarely looked up to the skies.

With Lynche off the program and out of the cockpit, the time that would have been eaten up with Lynche's drivel and Hunter's bullshit was replaced by the vibration of the engine and propeller and radio silence. Not even the AWACS talked to him. He was alone over the water, heading toward a terrorist who had a propensity for shooting down airplanes.

Hunter forced himself to change the topic in his mind. He waited for the next data load from the E-3. He looked up but didn't see a single jet racing across the sky. At his low altitude, it was impossible to pick up any lights on land, either. He really was alone.

Bringing his eyes back to the cockpit, he scanned the instrument panel, allowing a thin stream of consciousness to guide his thoughts. His little airplane was a marvel of engineering for special-purpose missions. Hunter was aware of and impressed by the parallels and opposite extremes of the other Lockheed marvel, its first jet-powered glider, the U-2. That plane was specially built for ultrahigh flight. It could fly so high, it was invisible to the naked eye even when it retained its aluminum finish. The long-winged YO-3A was at home going low and slow, aurally invisible to the most-sensitive ear. It was painted black to blend into the night sky and moved as noiselessly as its code name, *Wraith.*

Thoughts of the high-flying U-2s quickly led to images of Francis Gary Powers getting shot down over the Soviet Union. His capture forever changed the way the CIA regarded manned flights over sensitive areas. Never wanting to be embarrassed again, Langley dumped millions of dollars to develop unmanned aircraft and expand their capabilities. Money was no object. Classified contracts flowed to giant defense contractors.

As unmanned technology improved, a significant, unintended consequence arose. The logistical footprint for an unmanned aerial system increased three to ten-fold over that of a manned system. For a covert operation, having a cast of hundreds, including external pilots, remote pilots, specialized mechanics, and electronics technicians, wandering near a base of operations was unworkable.

Then there was the problem of attrition. For every unmanned system brought on line, it was soon involved in a crash, destroying hardware and software at an alarming rate. The Agency would contract for ten aircraft. By the time the last one rolled off the assembly line, the first seven had been destroyed in mishaps of some kind.

When the retired Chief of Air Branch approached the DCI with an old-time alternative—something extremely reliable and actually covert, with a low operating cost and miniscule logistical footprint—the DCI asked, "Where do I sign?"

With no alternate capability and increasing requirements, the Agency was desperate for a workable solution that didn't crash and roll itself into a flaming aluminum ball at the slightest malfunction. The DCI was forced to choose between an immature program and hope the unmanned systems stopped crashing faster than they could be built, or try a stopgap measure.

Caught between a very bad situation and one that still wasn't ideal, the DCI awarded Greg Lynche a contract for surveillance work using a manned special purpose aircraft. For fifteen years, Lynche and his rock-star pilot, Duncan Hunter, flew 100 missions from a single aircraft at relatively low cost and with a tiny support footprint. The work was incredibly dangerous and stressful, and highly lucrative.

As defense contractors strained to find solutions to their little unmanned aircraft crashing constantly, the Lynche-Hunter solution was the only reliable show in town. Supply and demand dictated the answer. The available number of low-noise profile aircraft was one, with a very high demand. As long as the unmanned systems crashed or "went stupid" at the most-inappropriate times and locations, Greg Lynche was able to negotiate great contracts.

The YO-3A wasn't a revolutionary airplane but an *evolutionary* one. Number seven off the assembly line, 007 reached its shelf life before Greg Lynche saved it from the bone yard, museum, or scrap heap. Like the first U-2s, the prototype YO-3A weren't built for long-term use. None of the Lockheed spy planes were manufactured for heavy or dramatic maneuvers. Both contracts were signed to get an aircraft built in the least amount of time and into the hands of a small band of specially trained pilots. Both aircraft were lightweight, tricky to fly, and didn't come with ejection seats. Gary Powers' spy plane was shot out of the sky and he almost died struggling to bail from his crippled U-2.

Like the CIA of old, the new CIA didn't want to discuss what would happen to a pilot if he bailed out. There was Survival, Escape, Resistance, and Evasion training, with heavy emphasis on evasion. For the old U-2 pilots and Duncan, they carried gold coins—universal currency—in their seat pans, along with a weapon. In the case of the Cold War *Overflight* pilots, it was probably assumed the .22 caliber silenced pistol Gary Powers carried wasn't for protection but as a means to avoid being captured.

Hunter carried what was widely regarded as the most-beautiful handgun ever built, a .357 Magnum Colt Python with laser sights. He also had dozens of rounds in speed loaders. If he went down, he convinced himself he wasn't going to be captured without a fight.

He patted the gun in its holster as new data appeared on his multifunction panel, and lights appeared on the horizon. He disconnected the autopilot and grasped the flight controls. It was time to go to work.

The AWACS indicated a Gulfstream departed Algiers International, heading toward the target area at low altitude. That information was also relayed to the White House and CIA Headquarters. Any clandestine incursion of a CIA asset into another country required Presidential approval, and the operation was monitored from the Situation Room. Unlike the U-2 overflights, where the White House approved each mission based on the available intelligence of Soviet ICBM tests, the *Noble Savage* missions were based on precise intel derived from myriad air and ground sources.

Agency ground intelligence officers knew who would be where and when, and Hunter just had to be at the appointed place and time to complete the intercept. With the intercept point dead ahead, Hunter retarded the throttle to reduce power and configured the aircraft for its quiet mission profile.

He tightened his seat belt, deployed the speed brakes, and deployed the FLIR. The aircraft decelerated significantly with the added drag of the large FLIR ball slipping into the airstream. Then Hunter deployed the gun and armed the system after it fully locked into place.

He slewed his head to the right and aimed the gun toward the Rock of Gibraltar before pulling the trigger. The propellant-assisted projectile traced a bright white arc in the FLIR until it splashed into the sea. The gun check was complete.

AWACS announced bird inbound at ten o'clock.

"Tally ho!" Hunter said to himself, visually identifying the aircraft by its position lights. He checked the GPS, ensuring he was on the correct track and approaching the villa at the correct angle from the east.

The target aircraft was higher than Hunter but descending and closing the distance between them. Hunter was impressed by the quality and specificity of the intel and the AWACS coordination. He had plenty of time. It would take the Gulfstream several minutes to make its approach.

Hunter checked his instruments closely. He didn't need any surprises at that stage of his flight.

He slewed the forward-looking infrared to a position slightly off the nose, trying to locate the airstrip and hangar. He saw the villa in the FLIR at his two o'clock, just as the Gulfstream was in a gentle, descending, right turn. After the jet passed him, Hunter zoomed to 800 feet above sea level, expecting to see a runway over the hill.

The runway lights surprised him. Hunter didn't expect to see them on the private strip, because they never showed in the satellite images. Their heat burned brightly in the FLIR display, as did the Gulfstream's engines. The jet would eat up that mile-long runway in a few seconds, and Hunter knew where it was headed.

The point of interest was the hangar. He turned the FLIR toward the building and zoomed in on an image stepping out of a sport utility vehicle. The Tri-Star embedded in the grill indicated it was a Mercedes. He spent several seconds scrutinizing the image of the man before turning the FLIR ball back to the runway just as the jet flared for a landing.

Hunter watched the tires disappear in a burst of thermal white energy, as the landing gear touched down. The man who stepped from the Mercedes was stocky and carried the arms of a body builder, but he didn't command any special presence.

Two miles from the runway, Hunter set up for a gentle left turn. He was anxious about reflections and being seen with the runway lights burning so brightly. The YO-3A's matte-black paint shouldn't have reflected any spurious light, but it was still a momentary concern.

A stray thought came to him about one of the main lessons learned from Gary Powers' U-2 flight over Russia—avoid anti-aircraft missile batteries. Hunter hoped he wasn't violating that simple rule of thumb, but, for the current mission, he assumed the worst. If his target was successful in shooting down a commercial airliner, the man could easily bring down an unarmed surveillance aircraft. Since he was running without lights and couldn't be heard, the advantage was Hunter's to exploit.

Hunter reassessed his new altitude to monitor the target and confirmed he was on his planned track. Based on his view of the available, most-probable threat sources, the main threat would likely come from the hangar. Although the YO-3A's muffler system dissipated hot gasses and exhaust sounds, the engine generated a significant heat signature for a heat-seeking missile to lock onto. The top-secret exhaust system was designed to kill the sound of the exhaust, not diffuse the thermal signature.

He reminded himself that left turns would mask the exhaust system from anyone on the ground listening, but the engine-bay heat would still instantly attract a heat-seeking missile. Taking a deep breath, he sensed his scan was missing something to do with missiles and exhaust.

Dread spread through him, as he closed the gap to the hangar. *What am I missing?*

His anxiety spiked when he realized he hadn't armed the flare and chaff dispenser. Years of flying without checklists and never arming the countermeasures made him complacent. He quickly flipped the switches to activate the warning systems and armed the dispensing system. The oversight startled him and he worked to control his hard breathing. He wasn't close to hyperventilating and it wasn't time to pat himself on the back for remembering at the last minute.

He scanned his instruments again and the FLIR, then he focused on the hangar and the jet. Hunter realized the jet was taking too much time taxiing down the runway after landing. He pulled into a hard right turn and headed away from the hangar. He would reverse course when the jet stopped. It would take a few moments for the jet's door to be lowered and the occupants to disembark.

He programmed the FLIR and gun barrel toward the hangar and waited for the jet to stop and disgorge its passengers. Though he felt relieved that he caught his mistake, and his situational awareness had returned, he didn't have his confidence back.

What else will go wrong?

CHAPTER FIFTY-ONE

2030 September 25, 2012
Algiers, Algeria

Tony "Tonka" Parker steered into three more protesters before turning right on Chemin Cheikh Avenue. Two men stopped running toward the embassy and stared in disbelief at the oncoming car. They saw it moving toward them, but they didn't understand why it didn't make any sound. Any other car in Algeria would at least make sputtering engine noises. During their wonderment, they failed to realize that the driver of the noiseless car was steering right at them.

When they finally realized they were in danger and tried to jump aside, Tonka timed it right and hit both men with the passenger side fender. Their bodies suddenly and grotesquely distorted. The third man, behind the other two, tried to jump out of the way and was run over at 40 mph. The sound of his head shattering on the asphalt thudded inside the Volt, as the car bounced on top of the man, pinning him underneath.

Tonka pushed the pedal to the floor, and drive wheels torqued against the pavement, overcoming the friction of the man's carcass and grinding layers of meat and bone before leaving a wide, vivid red smear for a quarter-mile until his remains tumbled out from under the car between the rear wheels.

Eastwood looked out the back window and saw the red skid mark disappear from sight. McGee and Tonka exchanged glances; McGee's disapproval was negated by Tonka's impish grin.

Once clear of the obstruction, Tonka asked, "OK. Where are we going?"

"I've been looking for that getaway vehicle," Eastwood said from the back seat, "but I haven't located it. It has to be close."

"I had it, then I lost it when you whacked those dudes. It's doubtful they took her anywhere close. They wanted to kidnap diplomats, so they had to have a getaway vehicle, maybe several, to take away the prisoners."

"So we're looking for…?" Tonka began.

A few hundred feet ahead, a white four-door Toyota HiLux turned hard and skidded onto Chemin Cheikh Avenue, its tires smoking as it violently rounded the corner from the Due de Brazza.

"A speeding truck!" McGee shouted. "That has to be them! Go, go, go!"

The quiet car was in hot pursuit. McGee repeated, "That has to be them. Don't lose them."

Without any other evidence besides erratic driving to suggest the truck ahead carried Nazy Cunningham, McGee hoped he was right.

All three men silently focused on the white truck ahead, as it suddenly swerved right and entered a highway that looked like it led from the city. Tonka, matching its acceleration and speed, maintained a good interval.

"Do we have a plan?" Eastwood asked.

"I'm not sure what we can do," McGee said. "I'm afraid if we get too close, they'll see our American faces and will do something ugly, like toss her out so they can escape. At this speed, that'll kill her if she isn't already dead from the RPG blast."

"How about we try to take them down when they stop?" Tonka asked. "They have to stop sometime."

Reaching into his cargo pants, Tonka pulled out several full magazines for his weapon and handed them to Eastwood. "Sir, you may need these if we bail out and try to rescue her. I have to drive."

"Thanks, uh…."

"Tony Parker, Sir. Call me Tonka."

""Glad to meet you, Tonka. Demetrius Eastwood. You can call me Dory."

"Yes, Sir. You do a great job reporting on the troops."

"Thank you." Eastwood smiled and reflected how absolutely

normal it was for complete American strangers to race into the face of uncertainty and possible death when one of their own was in trouble. That was the hallmark of a warrior.

Then, with a lull in the action, they would politely introduce themselves as if it were perfectly understandable why they were there. They would share, with absolute conviction, the belief that they would succeed.

He allowed another stereotype to form: Given the same set of circumstances, liberals would run and hide and worry about themselves. If two liberals ran from a lion, one would try to trip the other, so he would become lion food, and the other could escape.

Eastwood inhaled and said, "Let's see if we can get closer."

After a few minutes of driving away from city lights, McGee concurred, "Let's get a little closer." He was dying to see if Nazy was really in that vehicle.

Street lights became fewer up ahead, and the road disappeared into darkness. Few houses and fewer mosques sat along the stretch of road.

Tonka nodded and accelerated, cautiously closing the gap.

Three things happened simultaneously. The inside of the car suddenly filled with the smell of burning electrical insulation. The instrument panel immediately showed a dozen red lights. As the Volt closed the interval between it and the truck, the white Toyota suddenly slowed and turned onto a dirt road.

As the Volt overshot and passed the pickup, it was illuminated by a lone weak streetlight, and McGee watched helplessly as someone in the back seat flailed their arms, and a man used his fists to subdue the person.

Smoke filled the interior of the car. Two seconds later, the instrument panel of the Chevy Volt died, and Tonka steered to the side of the road. McGee stared at the Toyota truck at his four-o'clock position, as it climbed a small rise and turned left to travel in front of widely-spaced, multi-story houses that paralleled and overlooked the highway. As the Volt finally stopped, so did the Toyota. In front of the third house along the road, the pickup immediately entered the compound and disappeared behind a sliding gate.

"That's got to be them." McGee continued staring at the house.

"We gotta get out of here," Tonka said. "I'm afraid this thing is about to blow up."

McGee seemed oblivious to the smoke, as he stepped out and walked back toward the intersection they just passed. Eastwood already opened his door to get some fresh air.

Tonka and Eastwood ran to catch up to McGee, who pointed and said, "Safe house."

The underside of the Chevy Volt burst into flames.

"I think I killed it," Tonka said sarcastically, stepping farther away.

'That's what happens to all electric cars," Eastwood said. "That's why they stopped building them 100 years ago."

"We gotta move," McGee said, leaving the roadbed with his pistol down at his side, guided by the gate that swallowed the Toyota.

They jogged in a column with McGee leading and Tonka providing rear cover. McGee established a direct path to the leftmost house. His powerful legs churned soft sand, which chirped underfoot with every step.

The only sounds were from an occasional vehicle rumbling down the highway and the thick sand squeaking with each step. Though it annoyed McGee, he never took his eyes off the house.

When they were within 50 yards, he raised his hand, and all three crouched in a circle. McGee planned and assessed the target. It was a perfect safe house—remote, innocuous, with good visibility all around. Like the other houses along the road, it was three stories tall with large windows. Every house on the lane featured high walls for protection and a sturdy metal gate. While the other houses had lights on in their upper floors, the third house didn't.

Tonka scrutinized the compound. "Looks like glass on top of these walls," he whispered.

McGee nodded, and Eastwood looked again, seeing the faint glint of light reflecting off what he assumed were the remains of broken bottles. He nodded and thought that was a good catch. If they tried to scale the wall without protection, their hands would be cut to ribbons.

"Gate," McGee said. "I'll need a boost."

Eastwood tossed Tonka's pistol into the air, spinning it 180° and catching the muzzle before he offered the .45 back to Tonka. "I can do that. Tonka, you'll need this more than me."

Tonka quietly racked the slide to check there was a round in the chamber. McGee did the same and both men checked to ensure their weapons were unsafetied and ready to fire.

Eastwood and Tonka waited for Bill to lead. McGee, unfocused, felt livid that he came too late. Nazy was a great lady and was Duncan's girl. McGee chastised himself. He should have walked her to her apartment, but he wanted to share a manly moment with the Marine. While he often felt heroic, now he felt stupid and ashamed. But it was no time for recriminations.

Tonka, seeing the scorn in McGee's face, prayed that they chased the right vehicle.

Eastwood wondered where was a camera crew when he needed one?

McGee took a deep breath and nodded. The men raced across the dirt road in a crouch until they were at the corner of the third house. McGee sidled up to the gate and saw it had to be scaled.

He waved the others closer and gestured "up" with his thumb. Eastwood braced himself, interlocking his fingers into a step while he leaned against the metal gate. McGee placed his foot into Eastwood's hands and bounced twice on his other foot, generating momentum, then he jumped. Eastwood lifted simultaneously.

McGee silently reached the top of the gate and looked around before waving his pistol for Tonka to follow. McGee disappeared over the top. Eastwood repeated the procedure and lifted the heavier man up, pushing against his foot until he was safely on top of the gate. A moment later, Tonka vanished, too. Knowing it wasn't safe to be seen at the front of the house, Eastwood moved to the side of the wall and hid in the shadows.

McGee was astounded there was no lookout or security, which

could be good or bad. He slid beside a dirty white Toyota HiLux and felt the hood, which was still hot. They had the right truck. Inside, the keys dangled from the ignition. He and Tonka peered over the hood, assessing every detail of the front of the house—door, walkway, stairs, and windows.

Then they heard chanting. McGee glanced at Tonka in concern, his eyes squinting behind his small spectacles.

A sharp, muffled scream startled the two SEALs. They padded silently across the driveway. Tonka stopped at the door, his pistol raised and ready, as McGee moved to the side of the far window with his pistol up, too. The window was backlit, indicating a greater probability that someone was inside. Light leaked around the sides.

McGee glanced at Tonka, then back to the slit of light. He saw movement through the quarter-inch crack between the window frame and shades, but it was impossible to discern anything else other than noting the chanting was louder there. He moved his head slightly to see if the space between the frame and the shade on the other side offered a better view. He eased down, slipped across, and was pleased to find the space was a full inch wider. He cautiously leaned over so his eye was in front of the gap.

Bill McGee had been a SEAL for thirty-five years and saw the horrors of war. He had seen the bodies of friends and enemies torn apart by bullets and explosives. It was part of the job, the ugly part of being a warrior in the service of his country. He'd stitched up dozens of his friends, set broken bones, and once reached inside the body of a fellow SEAL to find a torn artery.

Every time a SEAL went in harm's way, he was expected to be prepared for any emergency and contingency, but McGee wasn't prepared for what he saw. A bloody, naked Nazy was being slapped while four men held her down and another man raped her.

McGee focused on another man in the room, one who held a knife. He was wild-eyed, and he held the tip of Nazy's breast with his fingertips and stretched it, shaking it while waving the stiletto menacingly toward it.

CHAPTER FIFTY-TWO

2100 September 25, 2012
Mostaganem, Algeria

The Gulfstream 550 rolled in front of the hangar and turned 180º, so the aircraft door faced the open door in the structure. As the engines shut down, the runway lights turned off. Abu Manu took his hand off the electrical power box and emerged from the hangar to approach the jet cautiously. This was the most-critical time of the transfer.

Hunter was surprised when another man appeared seemingly from nowhere inside the hangar. He quickly resolved the dichotomy. Something had masked the man's heat signature while he was in the hangar. He was behind or under something when Hunter first scanned the building, and he must be the one responsible for turning off the runway lights. The man carried himself as if he were in charge.

He must be the target! Tally ho! Game on!

The auxiliary power plant was running at the back of the jet. It continually streamed hot exhaust gas and in the FLIR showed as rippled shades of white and gray heat signatures. The engines couldn't be recognized due to their immense thermal signature plume in the FLIR, but Hunter knew the aircraft and expected that part of the image would wash out his cockpit display.

The beefy guy from the Mercedes helped lower the aircraft door and raced up the airstairs. He and another man carried a box down the stairs and placed it just inside the hangar. The presumed target cautiously walked out of the hangar but wasn't focused on the aircraft or the men racing up and down the airstairs or the containers they carried. Hunter expected his target to meet and greet the occupants as they deplaned, and he noted the man's curious behavior. He rotated the thumb wheel on the cyclic stick to zoom the FLIR image of the man. At full zoom Hunter was momentarily confused as the man appeared to scan the sky from left to right.

When he stopped and looked right at Hunter, the FLIR display first filled with the man's gaze, then his sudden incredulity. Both the target and Duncan recoiled in astonishment.

He saw me! He sees me! How is that possible?

He immediately aligned the crosshairs of the targeting system on the man's chest as the computer software slewed the gun barrel toward the hangar. The laser rangefinder and designator dot rested on the man's chest for less than a split-second, just as the man bolted inside the hangar.

Hunter tracked him into the hangar, where he immediately disappeared, masked by the unknown screen. Duncan lifted his head from the display, quickly checked his altitude and attitude, then returned his gaze back to the hangar as two men stepped onto the ramp from the aircraft.

He refused to believe he was discovered. His pulse increased dramatically with a rush of adrenalin. With his target out of sight, he sensed he was in great danger. The hair on the back of his neck stood up, as he made a decision.

In the periphery of the FLIR scope, images of a thin and heavyset aircrew, epaulettes on their shirts, came into view. They emerged from the aircraft after the other man ran up the stairs and disappeared. The two pilots stepped down casually onto the ramp. Their body languages and head gestures suggested they expected someone to greet them. They looked around, but whoever was supposed to meet them wasn't visible in the FLIR. There was no sense of urgency in the men's demeanor, and they stood in place, at the foot of the jet's stairs, as if waiting for a bus.

Hunter moved the laser designator to the back of the pilot and pulled the trigger on the cyclic stick. The gun aiming system took half a second before launching the first .70 caliber round downrange.

One-and-a-half seconds later, the bullet impacted the thin image, slightly high and to the right of the aiming point. In the FLIR, a white flash of thermal energy erupted from the man's back. The copilot was instantly stunned, taken aback by the sight and sound of the captain's chest blowing out in a spray of blood and organs.

Hunter moved the LD to the fat little man and pulled the trigger again. The copilot was blown forward from the impact and was dead before his body hit the ground. After the bullet passed through him, it ricocheted off the ground and spun a white-hot arc far from the hangar.

As the white-hot bullet shot away, the target reappeared in the FLIR display. He carried a shoulder-launched anti-aircraft missile and aimed it directly at Hunter.

After Abu Manu cut the power to the runway lights at the control box in the rear corner of the hangar, he was pleased to see the jet in all her beauty. The G550 was spectacular in starlight and the small amount of light escaping from the open aircraft door. He watched the first of the containers being carried off the aircraft.

Taking his eyes off the airplane, he walked out of the shelter of the hangar to search the skies, not expecting anything but knowing it was necessary. He didn't trust the infidel Americans not to follow the jet or do something brazen like send one of their unmanned aircraft to spy on him.

After almost completing a 180° sweep of the skies, he recoiled in disbelief when he saw something moving along the horizon, momentarily masking and unmasking the stars in the background. He barely made out the basic shape of an airplane with unusually long wings. As the specter moved from right to left in a slight left bank, he discerned it would be able to watch most of the offloading operation. He never saw the red dot of the laser designator appear on his chest, as he exploded into action, running toward the boxes of *Stingers* just as the pilot and copilot sauntered down the aircraft stairs.

Abu Manu tore open a container on the floor and jammed a battery pack into the launcher's pistol grip to power up the electronics. Ten seconds later, green lights signaled the battery had activated the gyroscopes and circuitry inside, as a shot of gas was routed into position to fire off the solid rocket booster of the anti-aircraft missile.

The first crack of a bullet tearing through the pilot's body startled him so severely, he almost dropped the launcher. His head snapped up as he saw, in the distance, a small white flash accompanied by another loud crack of a bullet blowing out the copilot's chest

Abu Manu nervously stepped from behind the stack of *Stinger* containers, trying to acquire the stealthy airplane in the viewfinder. The suddenness of the aural tone made him jump. The missile instantly locked onto the heat source of the aircraft's engine, and he depressed the trigger.

Duncan was momentarily stunned as the FLIR display exploded in a flash of white-hot energy, as a missile was launched toward him. The danger shocked him into action.

The missile launch warning system lit up the cockpit in bright red lights. He mashed the countermeasures button on the control stick. Immediately, the sky behind him was illuminated by the phosphorous and magnesium flares being ejected from the flare dispensers. It was an automatic reflex to depress the little red button if he detected a missile launch.

Flares jettisoned from the rear of the airplane completely illuminated the YO-3A. The black profile of the glider became visible, its long wings distinct and unmistakable in the backlit illumination. Abu Manu lowered the *Stinger* launcher in awe as the anti-aircraft missile arced toward it, only to follow a white-hot flare aft of the airplane and into oblivion well behind it.

After a dozen flares were ejected, the little black powered glider flew out of the light and was invisible again, completely unharmed. He never saw anything remotely like the unique airplane melting into the night sky, masking and unmasking stars as it escaped to the west.

Habib and Malik started to descend the stairs with another container when they heard the unmistakable crack of a large-caliber bullet pass nearby. They set the heavy box on the floor, as Habib peeked around the corner of the aircraft door in time to see the copilot shudder from the bullet's impact and crumple, while the distinctive sound of a ricochet was audible over the high-pitched whine of the small gas turbine.

He explained what happened and added, "We're under attack."

Malik couldn't believe it and pushed Habib out of the way to look for himself. The bodies of the two crewmen leaked fluids onto the ramp. He watched intently as Abu Manu moved from the shadows of the hangar and launched a *Stinger* into the sky.

"You're correct, my brother," Malik said. "I shouldn't have doubted you. We *are* under attack."

They looked at each other and realized it wasn't safe yet to be outside the aircraft.

Abu Manu struggled to compose himself after the missile's failure. He never anticipated countermeasures. The American infidels were smart and had taken the offensive. He hurried to the stack of containers and retrieved another *Stinger,* pausing for a moment to reflect on the tiny vial lying with the batteries.

He slipped the glass tube into his shirt pocket, then jammed a battery pack into another launcher. His eyes darted left and right across the sky, up and down. He expected the airplane to have continued its left-handed trajectory to the west and parallel the coast, but, as he searched that part of the sky, he became anxious, unable to locate the glider again.

Hunter bellowed, as a fiery missile streaked behind him and followed a flare away from the YO-3A and down to the sea. He anticipated another launch, but he knew enough about MANPADS to know he had a few seconds to improve his position.

As the man disappeared from his FLIR, Duncan countered by turning hard right with a four-G pull and snap rolled the wings level to reduce the platform from view. With his long wings covering and uncovering a large number of stars, it probably wasn't that hard for someone to find him if they looked up and scanned hard enough.

He blinked wildly as a thought came through his mind. *Was he alerted about me? It sure looked like he knew exactly where to look.*

At night, few adversaries looked up at the sky when they worked. The North Vietnamese never did as they toiled to build tunnels and bridges and moved troops at night, while YO-3As flew overhead, taking pictures and relaying real-time intelligence.

As Hunter scanned the hangar with the FLIR, he blamed himself for the failure. The target was still alive and probably readying another missile for him. He shook his head to banish the thought. He knew what he needed to do. He had to find the target and kill him before he got off another missile. He would probably pop into view, acquire Hunter's plane, and fire another missile at him.

He didn't have any additional time to allow the target to gain the advantage. While he could be located visually, Hunter gambled that the next time the target would use the thermal seeker head of the MANPADS to find him. His engine generated enough heat for a missile to guide itself to the YO-3A.

With enough flares for another engagement, he was grateful even the old ones did the expected—eject the hottest possible heat source away from his aircraft.

Hunter scanned the hangar without detecting heat sources or movement. He slewed the gun barrel toward the hangar opening, waiting while the suspense and his frustration grew.

"Come on, Asshole. I know you're in there."

Abu Manu was in shock and his hand trembled. He fought with the missile launcher. In fits and jerks, he gradually placed it on the topmost *Stinger* container. The aircraft out there had to be equipped with forward-looking infrared, FLIR, and those systems could pick up the minutest sliver of thermal energy. He had to be careful not to expose any part of his body.

He was certain the aircraft was unmanned, armed with a high-powered rifle to kill at long range. He never heard of one, just like he hadn't heard of a black glider, but the Americans were crafty and resourceful.

With the missile launcher armed, it should be able to find the airplane's heat signature—if only he could stop shaking.

While it was possible to hide a person's thermal image, it was virtually impossible to hide an airplane's heat source from a similar heat-sensitive detector. Both men were the hunted and the quarry, using the best-available technology to locate and kill the other. Abu Manu had the second missile fully charged and armed, and he used the containers and launcher to hide his body and thermal signature, hoping the missile's heat-seeking head would find the stealthy black airplane and alert him with its trademark growl when the target was acquired.

Duncan had his large-bore rifle aimed at the hangar with the FLIR's sensitivity at max. Someone had to make a mistake. The winner would live, the loser would die.

Hunter's movement across the sky changed the aspect of the sight picture on the ground in the FLIR. He scanned the inside of the hangar and recognized a MANPADS launcher on top of what appeared to be shipping crates, probably MANPADS shipping crates. His target had to be behind those crates.

A tiny flash of white flared in the FLIR. Hunter guessed that was the man's finger on the trigger of the launcher. He selected the targeting system and aimed a fraction lower than the area where the small heat source leaked out from under the launcher.

Abu Manu's patience was rewarded when he heard the increasing low growl of the *Stinger's* heat-seeking head pointed in the general direction of the aircraft. He moved the launcher slowly to the right, and the tone intensified. Satisfied that he had acquired the little airplane, he pulled the trigger, and the *Stinger* shot from its tube.

Again the FLIR flared, signaling a missile launch. Hunter reacted by simultaneously pulling the gun trigger and crushing the little red button to disperse flares. The bullet tore through the launcher as flares leaped from the dispenser one at a time at one-millisecond intervals. He was so excited he unconsciously mashed a rudder pedal.

His aircraft became awash in the light of burning metal and chemicals when one flare didn't spit out and away. Instead, it shot out of its ejector tube like a bottle rocket and was caught in turbulence from Hunter's cross-controlling the rudder pedals. The flare erupted and flew ahead of the YO-3A, hitting the front canopy. Hunter was monitoring the fiery progress of the MANPADS trajectory toward his airplane when the flare bounced on his canopy and shot past over the wing. The white-hot magnesium flare seared his eyes, blinding him instantly.

He instinctively jerked his head away from the light and rolled the airplane on its side. The missile guided on the itinerant flare and struck the high wing, igniting the fuel tank.

CHAPTER FIFTY-THREE

2200 September 25, 2012
Algiers, Algeria

Bill McGee decided he had to move fast. Running to where Tonka stood, he whispered, "I'm going in. I have the left."

"I have the right."

McGee watched in amazement, as Tonka depressed the door handle, and it opened. The fools from the Toyota were so excited to have captured the American, they threw all security to the wind once they got her where they thought they were safe. He and Tonka stepped inside the doorway and rushed into the room filled with chanting men and a bloody mess. Every man in the room froze, their eyes focused on the dull gray American pistols.

In less than one second, Bill put a bullet through the head of the man with the bloody knife, then he killed the man standing between Nazy's legs. The first bullet punctured a hole in the knifeman's forehead and excited the back of his head in a burst of hair, bone, and bloody brains. The second entered just above the tumescent man's ear and blew a square channel across his skull. Both men fell backward.

Tonka took two steps into the room, leaning left, and shot the two men on the left half of the room holding Nazy's arm and leg. At near point-blank range for the .45 caliber, the men's heads exploded in a shower of bone and gray matter. Nazy's limbs fell to the floor. Cordite filled the room, and the echo of spent brass casings reverberated in the enclosed space.

The other two men holding Nazy's other arm and leg tried to run, but their hearts and minds weren't in it. McGee shot the man holding Nazy's leg in the eye. Tonka killed the man who tried to release her arm and get away. The .45 bullet entered his temple and didn't exit the cranium, so Tonka shot him again. The back of the man's head exploded in a gray, pulpy torrent.

"Clear the house," McGee shouted. "I'll take care of Nazy."

Tonka glanced at the woman's naked, unmoving bloody body and changed magazines, and then he darted into every room of the house, his .45 ready with both hands on the grips.

McGee stepped over one dead man and knelt to check her pulse and breathing. He took quick inventory of her wounds. The one in her breast was significantly deep and would need dozens of stitches to close. Her face was bloodied and bruised. He recognized the wounds from explosive blasts. She had pieces of concrete lodged under her skin, but her eyes, ears, and face were largely undamaged.

He looked at the beautiful, unconscious woman with shame, not lust. He hadn't arrived in time to save her. He never saved a damsel in distress. Like all SEALs, he was an expert at killing America's enemies and blowing shit up, but saving women was rarely a mission parameter. There would be no ticker-tape parade or crush of press for saving the day. He couldn't find and kill Osama bin Laden, and he couldn't rescue the stunning Nazy Cunningham from being violated by a group of Islamic thugs. He hung his head momentarily, hoping Hunter would forgive him. He had to save her and get them out of the house.

Tonka reentered the room carrying bed sheets. He and McGee gently placed Nazy into the sheets and wrapped her tightly. McGee deadlifted her with an arm under her neck and legs. As he stood, he said, "Burn it," and carried her outside.

Tonka drove the confiscated Toyota HiLux, as Eastwood rode shotgun. The three men drove past the Chevy Volt, completely consumed in fire. Behind them, the third house on the right was also engulfed in flames.

In the back seat, McGee broke out the first-aid kit all SEALs carry in their ubiquitous cargo pockets and worked furiously to stem the light bleeding from the hideous attempt to remove one of Nazy's breasts.

He gave up trying to find the bleeders in her breast and continued to apply as much pressure as he dared for fear he'd break a rib or two. After several minutes of mashing the open wound with his hand to stop the bleeding, McGee determined that whatever had been bleeding freely had stopped. He cleaned Nazy's wound with the remainder of his dry gauze pads and began tying off twenty ugly stitches. He cleaned and bandaged her wound under the fold of her breast. He scanned her body and realized she was also bleeding from the rape. With no idea what to do, he stuffed the remainder of the bandages he had between her legs. Taking final stock of his work, he wrapped her in the sheet, and slipped into the seat.

With Nazy's head resting in his lap, he began treating her face. Tonka asked if he had enough bandages and handed over his own kit. Bill cleaned her bloodied face with antiseptic towelettes, as hard fragments flaked from some of the open punctures.

"You did good, Boss," Tonka said, unable to look back at McGee.

"You, too. We could've been a little earlier, though."

"What happened back there?" Eastwood asked.

McGee was too emotional to speak, and Tonka knew it, so he said, "Bullfrog was able to peek into a window in time to see some thugs raping her, with one asshole trying to cut off her boob. We went in and stopped them. Oh, I set fire to their little safe house. By now, they're nothing but barbecued bandits."

They drove in silence for several minutes. The lights of Algiers lay at the end of the highway, becoming more numerous and brighter with each minute. The men wouldn't talk about what might be waiting for them back at the embassy. With no radio or cell phones, they were isolated and couldn't talk with the embassy's communication room.

Eastwood, restless, itched to say something. Finally, he said, "For the last ten years, tromping through this part of the world, I've been told several times some variation of, 'You must view the world through the lens of Islam to see the logic of these things.' After tonight, I don't think any sane person can see the logic. There is no excuse, rhyme, or reason for any of this. Extremists do a lot of nutty things, but Islamic extremists are just evil. The only way to deal with them is to kill them."

"You won't get any argument from me," McGee said softly.

Tonka moved to look at McGee in the rearview mirror. McGee softly stroked Nazy's hair, his eyes and thoughts elsewhere.

"Or me," Tonka said.

"Bill, what's the plan?" Eastwood asked.

McGee sighed and raised his head. "I'll tell you what I'm thinking. Nazy needs a doctor and surgery. The embassy should be evacuating soon, if that's still possible, and I'm very reluctant to take her to a local hospital. There's no telling what would happen to her or us if we stay. From what I can tell, her bleeding has stopped, but I don't know if she has internal injuries from the blast. We need to get her to a good hospital."

"The best ones are across the Med in Italy or Germany," Eastwood offered.

"Maybe we just need to go to the airport and wait for the NEO aircraft," Tonka said. "I can find an airplane in the sky and follow it. The airport has to be close by."

McGee stroked Nazy's hair and said, "As much as I hate to say this, I think we need to get back to the embassy and see what's going on. We need to join up with them. If the place is occupied, we'll go to the airport."

Tonka and Eastwood nodded. As Tonka drove, Eastwood tried to help navigate back to the embassy.

McGee stroked Nazy's hair and thought of his wife and children, the women who were important to him. It was a terrifying ordeal for

Nazy, and her nightmares had yet to begin. Driven by a senseless hatred of anything American, the unprovoked kidnapping, rape, and mutilation carried out by a band of thugs was a crime of the first order. He finally rescued a damsel in distress, but he was late, and she might die.

It wasn't supposed to end like this. And it's not going to.

CHAPTER FIFTY-FOUR

2200 September 25, 2012
Mostaganem, Algeria

Duncan Hunter was painfully blinded by the light from the magnesium flare on his right and the *Stinger* impacting his wing and igniting ten gallons of high-octane aviation gasoline on his left. Even with his eyes closed, the light was so intense it burned through his eyelids, saturating his optic nerve.

007 was uncontrollably on fire. At such a low altitude, he had to bail out immediately if he were to have any chance of survival. His eyes were completely useless and unresponsive, as if he'd been looking directly at the sun. In a way, he had.

As he was lightly pressed into the seat, he felt the aircraft climbing slightly but knew intuitively that was only temporary. The aircraft was continuing on a ballistic arc. In a few heartbeats, gravity and drag would win the tug of war, and the Yo-Yo would flip onto its back. Then the heavy nose would drop toward the ground.

While everything was moving in slow motion, Hunter had to ignore the blindness and move. Death was certain if he didn't. He raced against the aircraft tumbling out of control, trapping him inside.

He struggled to see. Even totally blind, he knew every switch, handle, knob, button, thumb wheel and coolie hat in the airplane. All military pilots practiced cockpit switch location with their eyes closed. Hunter maintained that life-saving practice over the years. With hours of muscle memory to guide him, he reached with his right hand and found the canopy jettison handle, racking it backward with a jerk. The twisted shear wire broke free, and the clamshell canopy instantly departed. At seventy knots, the canopy was up and over the tail in a tenth of a second.

When the wing departed the YO-3A, the down wing leveraged all its lift and helped upright the craft out of its turn. With no attitude indication reference to guide him, the blind Hunter felt the rotation of his aircraft in his ass as it passed from 90° down and momentarily rolled the wings level.

At the first hint of zero G, he unbuckled his lap belt and reached for his helmet bag at the right side of his seat. Just as the wing passed through 135° of roll, he pushed up from the canopy rails and dived from the cockpit into the slipstream, rolling over the side of the dying airplane.

When he was clear, the wing with all the lift flipped the Yo-Yo onto its back, and the nose fell until it pointed straight down. Its propeller turning, it slowly corkscrewed all the way to the ground.

Clear of the aircraft, Hunter automatically located and pulled the D ring on his chest. The parachute deployed, snapping him severely when it fully inflated. He instinctively looked up to ensure he had a good parachute and the canopy didn't have any suspension lines crossed, but all he could see was bright-white light, as if his face were jammed inside a giant snowball.

Hunter didn't have time to reflect on losing the YO-3A or escaping it. He was falling blind. He recalled he'd been at 800 feet above ground and knew he would smack down in seconds. Air rattled through the center cells of the black nylon rectangular parachute. Cool wind buffeted his face and slipped under his helmet, tugging against his chin strap and distracting him from the next phase of survival—executing a perfect parachute landing fall.

Anxiety dominated every moment. Falling blind was easy. It was the sudden stop that would hurt. Hunter grabbed the risers and immediately lifted his legs to 45° and bent his knees slightly. The balls of his feet would touch down first, and the landing fall should come in one continuous, smooth motion.

Straining his eyes to see without success, he sensed he was about to touch down, so he pulled hard on the risers to slow his descent when he struck the ground. The balls of his feet hit first. He relaxed his body to absorb the shock, as he rolled on the side of his momentum—calf, upper leg, rear end, and finally his side. He tucked his elbows in close and rolled onto his side. When he stopped moving, there were no sharp pains or broken bones.

He was safe on the ground for the moment. His silent cry of elation was trumped when the still-inflated parachute jerked him, caught a gust of wind, and began dragging him across the desert. Hunter knew he was in the desert, because he was being bounced on his chest and face, he tasted sand with each bump on the ground.

Old survival training kicked in. He reached up to locate one of the risers, gripped, and pulled hard. The action shifted his weight substantially, flipping him onto his back, where the relief from banging his face in the sand and his chest being thumped on small dunes was instantaneous.

Being dragged on his butt was a temporary respite, just like he remembered it when they practiced in the primary phase of flight training. He was still moving over uneven terrain and spitting sand, as he reached up to disconnect the parachute harness' upper release fittings to stop the wild ride. The uncoupling was immediate. The sudden stop slammed his head down into the sand and his brain rattled around in his helmet.

Oh, man.... I don't remember that part. Ouch! I'm getting too old for this shit.

He lay on the desert in disbelief. His chest heaved. He was alive but still blind. All he could see was white, but the pain in his eyes and degree of blindness were slowly subsiding.

He was exhausted, breathing hard, and his heart slammed in his chest. Hunter lay still to calm down and take inventory of his situation before planning his next move. He needed to survive. He reflected that he faced the man who shot airplanes out of the sky for sport or money. Instead, he failed, shot out of the sky by a missile.

A sense of urgency flooded his senses. He didn't know if he succeeded in killing the terrorist, and there was at least one other man inside the Gulfstream. He had to assume the worst—he might have landed near the Gulfstream. They were alive, and they knew he bailed out of his shattered airplane. They would be looking for him. His next move was to escape capture, only then could he escape Algeria.

Hunter parachuted blind and lived to tell about it, only to find himself a hunted man. Visions of being hounded by pissed-off men with guns and dogs filled his head. He had to get away. His paramount goal was survival.

Hunter blinked wildly to encourage his eyes to recover; he rolled to his knees and pushed himself up. Not knowing which way to go, he removed his helmet and skull cap and strained his ears for any clue which way *not* to go.

Two distinct sounds, one close, the other distant, gave hints that his airplane was burning nearby, while a jet engine, probably the Gulfstream APU, was running in the distance. He turned his head to sense where the jet noise came from, then he picked a direction and ran the opposite.

Straining his eyes, he willed them to clear faster. They were improving, but they were still useless. After a dozen steps, he stumbled when his boot caught on a tiny sandbar with a sprig of grass sprouting from it. Hunter went down in a heap but never lost his helmet. In the race of his life, he tripped every few steps.

After several episodes of running and falling, he realized he had to change his strategy. He dropped his helmet in the sand and took a few more steps removing things from the helmet bag hanging at his elbow. After a few more paces, he discarded the empty nylon bag.

He had a plan. If his luck worked for him while his vision recovered, he might live to see another day. He just had to avoid being found and captured.

CHAPTER FIFTY-FIVE

2230 September 25, 2012
Somewhere over the Mediterranean Sea

The weapons controller shouted, "Shit!" as a tiny streak of energy raced toward the tiny radar icon on her scope. She jumped forward in her seat, mouth open in abject disbelief, waiting for the next set of radar returns to update the screen.

There was no doubt. A missile had just been fired at her low-flying aircraft that recently penetrated Algerian airspace.

Something interesting happened on Master Sergeant Michelle Bowman's screen. The lieutenant colonel Air Battle Manager standing behind her crushed his coffee cup, gushing hot coffee all over his hand at her outburst. Days earlier, the ABM had briefed an "older gentleman" at Lajes Field in the Azores, and somewhat cavalierly indicated he would provide traffic and flight-following information, as well as keep the Spanish Air Force in the dark when the Agency's Hercules popped in and out of Spanish airspace. Master Sergeant Bowman never expected anti-aircraft missiles to be part of the flight-following, nor did the scalded lieutenant colonel.

Aboard the AWACS, the sudden outburst galvanized the other twelve combat-hardened weapons controllers to jump from their positions and race to her console. *Action*! *Finally!*

E-3 controllers normally monitored their assigned area of a battlefield, detecting, identifying, and tracking airborne enemy forces far from the boundaries of NATO countries. It was another dull, boring, egregiously quiet night over southwestern Europe. The Russians weren't invading the Crimea or playing any war games or moving unusual numbers of military aircraft on their side of the border. The Russians hadn't moved any military aircraft on their side of the border for months.

With the fall of the Berlin Wall and the demise of the Soviet Union, peace broke out in fits and starts in Eastern Europe. The quietest area of all was near the cliffs of Gibraltar. With a reconstituting Russia, the life of U.S. Air Force weapons controllers aboard their airborne early warning and control aircraft was relegated to monitoring commercial and military air traffic and watching African borders for any signs of unusual military movement. Missiles fired from within Algeria were highly unusual. It never happened anywhere in the Med.

"Talk to me, Bowman!" the lieutenant colonel shouted, while controllers gathered around the woman's radar scope. He jumped around, flicking scalding liquid off his hand, and trying to regain his composure while butting his way closer to the woman's station.

The ABM frowned. The mission was supposed to be circumspect, not a circus. It wasn't good.

"Missile launched at our playmate," she replied. "Seems he's still airborne, and the missile fell into the sea."

Murmurs and looks from the other controllers raced around the console. They hadn't known there was an operation in progress. Once they heard and huddled around Bowman, it would be impossible to send them back to their stations. It was the most exciting event they had in six months, and they weren't leaving.

For those struggling to see her screen, Master Sergeant Bowman provided running commentary. "Playmate has reversed course. Backtracking. Definitely not a jet to make that maneuver."

The other controllers nodded. They shared questioning glances.

"Playmate maintaining 800 feet AGL, seventy knots. Very slight left turn."

The controllers began to think the mission was just an exercise. *What airplane flew at seventy knots?* Several noticed the flight strip for the aircraft was incomplete. There was no call sign, no aircraft type, no clearance, no flight plan. Only airspeed, vector, and altitude information was shown in the colored box on the radar scope.

Convinced the excitement was generated for an undeclared exercise, several weapons controllers drifted back to their terminals.

"Missile!" Bowman shouted, echoed by several other controllers.

The ones who wandered away ran back. Every eye was glued to the screen, as they waited for the radar to refresh.

"Missile impact. Playmate's been hit. Zero air speed. Negative vertical velocity increasing. He's going down."

The twelve weapons controllers inhaled simultaneously. No one moved, their eyes focused on the screen.

The tiny square data tag, with symbology and flight strip information, disappeared. Master Sergeant Bowman struggled to say, "Playmate's down."

She never witnessed an aircraft killed by a surface-to-air missile strike and refused to look up from her screen. The other controllers looked to the Air Battle Manager for answers. If it was just an exercise, he'd better announce it soon. The controllers knew when the data tag and flight strip disappeared from the screen, the lost icon represented an actual aircraft, not an exercise tool.

"Nothing to see here," the ABM said. "Back to your stations, Airmen."

He monitored the scope, as the other weapons controllers silently walked to their terminals. He hunched over and looked at Bowman, who knew what he wanted.

"He's gone, Sir," she said quietly. "No radio call, no beacon. Nothing. I'll continue to monitor the area. I'm sorry, Sir."

The lieutenant colonel patted her back and leaned over to whisper, "Michelle, yes, please. Monitor for any movement or radio transmissions. I want to know if anything moves or pops up on the net."

"Wilco."

The ABM walked to the front of the E-3 and entered one of three small offices. He inserted a crypto PC card into the front slot of what appeared to be an ordinary high-end office desk telephone. Lifting the receiver of the remote Secure Terminal Equipment, he dialed the first of two special numbers. The pilot of the CIA's white L-100 Hercules answered the secure satellite telephone and set course to return to base in the Azores, per the contingency plan.

The second encrypted call bounced off an NSA satellite, connecting in seconds to ring one of several telephones in the White House Situation Room.

A woman answered on the first ring and said, "Proceed."

"*Noble Savage* is down. No further information available at this time."

"Carry on."

CHAPTER FIFTY-SIX

2230 September 25, 2012
Mostaganem, Algeria

For the moment, the two FAHD, Habib and Malik, felt safe inside the cabin of the business jet. Standing in the doorway, they peered around the corner to gain a better understanding of the situation unfolding from their narrow view of the world. Without warning, they witnessed their *sahib* race back into the hangar and extract a missile launcher from a stack of containers. He fired a shoulder-launched missile into the night.

Confusion reigned supreme, as their sense of urgency to help Abu Manu was overshadowed by his direction telling them to stay in the airplane. Even under fire, their master protected them. They couldn't see what he aimed at, and the damage inflicted on the aircrew was more consistent with heavy bullets used by American sniper teams.

Abu Manu had shot at something in the sky, and the picture Habib and Malik tried to interpret was incongruous. Snipers couldn't shoot from a moving vehicle with any accuracy. It wasn't impossible to shoot from an airplane, but being accurate was.

The U.S. Air Force solved the inaccuracy problem by mounting a six-barrel Gatling gun in a C-130 to deliver thousands of bullets a minute, placing each one in every square foot of a mile-long swatch. The men looked at each other with concern and fear, as Abu Manu launched a missile into the sky. Was it now possible to shoot from the sky? They traded glances at Abu Manu and each other, trying to answer questions they couldn't comprehend.

Within milliseconds of the second missile launch, the two men in the jet heard a third round slam into the missile launcher Abu Manu held, instantly shattering it as the bullet tumbled and split, spewing fragments of metal and molten plastic that scattered into the hangar in a small vapor cloud.

Abu Manu spun away violently in the throes of someone who'd been hit. Habib and Malik had to decide whether to stay on the aircraft until the threat passed or take the risk of tending to their wounded master and benefactor.

They assessed their chances, first glancing at the lifeless bodies of the pilot and copilot, dropped where they stood, their blood glistening in the poor moonlight. Then they looked at each other.

Without a word, Habib bolted down the stairs of the Gulfstream and ran across the ramp to find Abu Manu alive but seriously wounded. The slower, heavier-set Malik, following ten paces behind, took shelter behind the stack of missile containers. Bright movement caught his eye, and he peered over the containers to locate the threat and saw flaming, tumbling wreckage fall from the sky several hundred yards north. He assumed Abu Manu succeeded in shooting down the aircraft. As the falling inferno hit the ground near the horizon, Malik joined his master and friend.

Abu Manu lay wounded and bleeding on the old wooden hangar floor. His ears rang like alarm bells, and he seemed concussed. No longer shaking, he tried to get up to see if his missile found its mark. He moved jerkily, like a man in shock, wobbling unsteadily as if he'd been cold-cocked with a skillet.

Ignoring the pain in his head and hand, he focused on the airborne target, certain it wasn't an unmanned airplane but a manned aircraft. Habib tried to comfort Abu Manu, but the injured man broke free. After a few unsteady steps, he fell hard against the hangar floor. He sat upright, remaining still.

He was dazed and astonished when he saw his FAHD, Malik and Habib, come into view. Their familiar faces didn't register immediately. He was so focused on the black airplane, he was slow to realize he'd been severely wounded.

He struggled to ask, "Did I kill the infidel?"

"Yes, *Sahib,*" Malik said. "The airplane is in flames. No more."

"Find him! Go. Find him and bring him to me!"

Habib and Malik exchanged glances. Only Malik saw the aircraft fall in flames. They knew how their master feared unmanned aircraft. If the flaming aircraft had a pilot, no man could have survived the fire and crash. They resolved that Abu Manu was concussed and confused, severely injured and impaired. All three shared the thought from many intelligence briefings and training sessions: *Americans no longer fly manned surveillance aircraft.*

The jet's APU continued to ululate in the background. Cabin light spilled from the aircraft door onto the ramp, tossing scraps of light on the dead bodies of the air crew. Boxes of gold coin remained on the jet and the ramp. The flames from the crashed airplane less than half a mile to the north lit the horizon.

An unstable Abu Manu was missing fingers and a thumb, and he bled from his head and face. Habib and Malik conferred. Their first priority was to get Abu Manu to a hospital.

They helped their injured *sahib* to his feet, while he again demanded to see if his adversary had escaped. While Habib and Malik took positions on either side of their master and lifted him to his feet, Abu Manu wasn't ready to leave. Acting like a man possessed, he demanded answers.

Abu Manu searched the sky with jerks and tremors until he spotted the burning wreckage. Although it took several seconds to comprehend the sight, he became wide-eyed and energized, almost falling from the men's arms, in shock. What had driven him suddenly depleted him. He stared with the eyes of a victor, realizing he vanquished his tormentor.

Habib and Malik regripped Abu Manu's arms, as he suddenly relaxed. They encouraged each other to lift him and move him to the vehicle.

After taking a moment to rest his eyes as he was moved, Abu Manu opened them again and turned toward the flames, feeling joyful at seeing the bright conflagration in the distance.

Then he froze, as if rigor mortis set in. The two FAHD stopped when he stiffened, looking at Abu Manu for a clue to what happened. Abu Manu trembled and blinked uncontrollably. He couldn't believe his eyes when he saw a man momentarily silhouetted against the distant flames, and then he was gone.

He stopped shaking, his eyes wide. It wasn't possible. He shook his head violently, trying to speak, but all he managed was a guttural, "Nooo!" at seeing his enemy escape.

Overcoming the shock of seeing the man running, Abu Manu tried to jump from his men's arms. He would find and kill the man himself.

"Leave me!" he shouted when they wouldn't let go. "Kill the pilot!"

The two men looked cautiously toward the fiery heap but didn't see anyone. They shared a quiet glance and continued moving their boss to the Mercedes SUV. Malik opened the truck's rear hatch and positioned the delirious Abu Manu inside, forcing him to lie down. Habib turned on the overhead light, as the two gave Abu Manu first aid. Habib got out the emergency kit and opened the metal box. The lamps inside the vehicle gave them details not seen in the subdued, extraneous light of the aircraft or the moon. Whatever projectile hit the missile launcher shattered it. The shrapnel tore off Abu Manu's ear and ripped his scalp from temple to nape, exposing bone in places.

Habib lifted his eyes from the first-aid kit and recoiled at seeing Abu Manu's condition; the man wobbled from side-to-side and strained to sit upright. As if he were exhausted, he gave up and plopped down on his back. When Abu Manu held up his right hand and arm, he couldn't feel anything. Malik stared at the bloody stump, while Abu Manu struggled to comprehend how he lost four fingers and a thumb from his right hand.

Habib, horrified at the severity of Abu Manu's bloody injuries, barked at Malik, insisting they take him to a hospital. Malik reluctantly agreed and helped make Abu Manu comfortable in the back of the vehicle. Habib drove away from the hangar and was going south toward the main highway when Abu Manu suddenly erupted and refused to go any farther.

"*Stop! Stop! I kill you! Stop*!" he shouted.

Habib stopped the vehicle, and the two FAHD raced to the back. Abu Manu slurred his words slightly, frightening them.

"No! No! No! You must get him! Find the infidel!" Though nearly incoherent, he was very insistent.

The men capitulated, but they wouldn't leave Abu Manu until they rebandaged his wounds and made him more comfortable. After several worried minutes, they stabilized their boss and bandaged his head and hand. Habib lifted the rear hatch open, and Malik left Abu Manu resting in the SUV.

The two men met at the front of the Mercedes to consider their options. Neither was convinced there was an infidel on the run. Both felt Abu Manu was so badly injured he was hallucinating.

"He is rarely wrong about anything," Habib said. "If he's right, and we let this man escape, we will never be forgiven for doubting him."

"I can look for the man while you take Abu Manu to the hospital. I don't know how long he'll survive if he doesn't receive medical help soon."

They stared at each other in an impasse, their mouths closed and lips mashed together. Without a word, Habib suddenly didn't trust Malik being left alone. With the gold and the airplanes in the hangar, Malik could disappear as a very wealthy man.

"Let's both find the man," Habib said. "If we search for a few minutes and are convinced there isn't a man, we can return together and drive Abu Manu to Algiers."

"Agreed."

"Shukran."

Before they set off, they shed their shoes and pulled on boots, donned body armor, and armed themselves with flashlights and AK-47s from the Mercedes. They ran north as quickly as they could in the soft sand toward the burning wreckage, ignoring the sand squeaking underfoot with each step.

Malik and Habib jogged in silence, as if it were just another nighttime FAHD training run. Their flashlights swept from side-to-side, looking for evidence of a pilot. The skill to track a man over the ground, "cutting sign," was one of the first lessons to becoming a FAHD.

After ten minutes of slogging in the soft sand, Malik pressed his hand against Habib's chest and stopped him. He pointed down at footprints in the sand leading east.

Habib rapidly waved his arm toward the ground and whispered, "Get down!" He cursed that the fire would silhouette them, and they'd been too complacent. They hadn't believed their master, and they were caught in the open, close enough to the flames to be seen. It might be too late, but they were finally on full alert. Both men depressed the safeties on their AK-47s, making the assault weapons hot.

Malik dropped to the sand and cursed himself for doubting Abu Manu. The two FAHD switched from lackadaisical Doubting Thomases to ultimate trained Muslim night warriors. They began using hand and arm signals to communicate silently, standard protocol when in attack mode.

They tried to make sense of the eastbound tracks. From what they saw in the dwindling firelight, the tracks arced one way and another, as if they traveled in a wide circle. Malik crawled forward on his elbows to study the footprints. One could learn much from tracks left in any media, including whether it was a person or animal, how big or tall the person was by the spacing of the footprints, and if he was running.

The tracks suggested someone running. He flicked off his flashlight and returned it to a pocket.

More to himself than Habib, Malik muttered, "You can run, infidel, but you'll die tired."

With a forward motion of his hand, Malik got up to crouch and walk cautiously abeam of the tracks. Habib followed. After ten minutes of cutting sign and slow, careful tracking, their flashlight beams revealed ahead a military pilot's helmet, complete with night-vision goggles. Farther up in the splayed sand was a nylon bag with flimsy nylon handles.

Habib sensed a booby trap. Malik, scoffing at the notion, scrutinized the equipment before picking up the helmet, and, a few paces later, the helmet bag. He considered the two disparate items for several seconds before sliding the helmet into the bag, pleased that they went together. They would be his souvenirs, as would the head of the infidel.

Americans think of everything except dying, thought Habib.

A minute later, they reached a point in the sand where the footprints stopped. Smooth, undisturbed sand lay forward and to the sides without any additional tracks of covered footprints.

Malik took out his flashlight and shone the weak beam of light forward and to either side of the trail. There was nothing but unmolested sand. He turned to Habib.

"He must have doubled back."

"Not possible."

The two FAHD again swept their flashlights forward and to the sides. Finally, they knelt closely to scrutinize the sand for secondary signs. There were no indications of sweeping brush marks to show their quarry tried to continue on the path and hide his tracks.

The two men, confused and aggravated, investigated the area more intently to ensure the infidel pilot wasn't there, careful to remain on their walkway. After a minute, they quietly conferred and agreed the man had tricked them and somehow doubled back.

They reversed course and slowly moved west, retracing their footprints and starting the process of cutting sign in reverse. Their flashlight beams swept in giant arcs to either side of the trail, looking for any minute disturbance in the sand.

CHAPTER FIFTY-SEVEN

2300 September 25, 2012
U.S. Embassy
Algiers, Algeria

Tonka steered the smelly HiLux onto Chemin Cheikh Avenue, one of the many Algerian streets lined with embassies. The three men expected to see protesters and demonstrators ahead in the throes of defeating and embarrassing America at its embassy.

Tonka stopped and looked at Eastwood and McGee. Emergency vehicles of various sizes and purposes, their overhead blue strobe lights flashing, blocked the road directly in front of the embassy. Floodlights illuminated the signage, gate, and white-tiled wall. There wasn't a single protester in sight.

"No fire trucks," Eastwood said. "That's a good sign. Right down that road at that mosque was where we followed that bus. Maybe they retreated."

McGee glanced down the road at the well-lit, supersized mosque, then back to the embassy. "Let's go. We have to get Nazy to a doctor."

"Aye-aye, my captain," Tonka said.

They approached a cordon of white and blue BMW police SUVs and green military vehicles. Several police officers approached the Toyota with hands raised, the international sign to stop. Tonka complied, as Eastwood got out and saw his cameramen, Marty Marceau and Karl Mann, filming the security operation from the curb. He also saw the familiar shape and clothing of Khalid al-Awalaki.

"I don't think you need me anymore," he told the two in the truck. "Thank you for a wonderful evening. I'll see you guys later."

After Eastwood walked away, Tonka asked, "Did we need him?" He glanced in the rearview mirror for a response.

McGee wasn't in the mood for cheap humor. "Tell them we're Americans and have an injured woman. We need to get her medical help now."

"Roger." Tonka unbuckled his sidearm and slid it under the seat, got out, and walked toward the policemen and military who converged on him. He was immediately engaged in several conversations. He and the other men gesticulated toward the embassy and the HiLux.

With an Arabic-looking man hovering nearby, Eastwood and his crew converged on the scene, keeping Tonka's back to the camera. Soon, the policemen and Tonka nodded. There were more arm gestures, and then both men stood with arms akimbo.

"He's a good man, but there's no telling what he's telling them," McGee said, lowering his gaze to study Nazy's bloody, pocked face. Gritting his teeth, he sighed. "I'm sorry, Nazy. I'm so very sorry."

A distant, familiar sound caught his attention. When he looked up, he saw a broadly smiling Tonka walking briskly toward the truck. Right before he opened the door, he made eye contact with McGee and pointed up. From his peripheral vision, McGee also saw Eastwood, the Arab, and the film crew pointing their fingers and camera to the sky.

McGee felt thumping rotor blades beating the air. Helos were inbound. The cavalry had arrived. McGee pinched his lips and stroked Nazy's hair from her face one last time, praying there were medical staff aboard.

Without the need to drive into the embassy, McGee kicked open his door and stepped out with Nazy in his arms. The big man walked confidently, as if he could carry the injured woman 100 miles. Tonka, recovering his weapon, left the truck idling on the road and jogged to catch up with McGee, as Algerian police and military men opened a path for them.

Eastwood turned to Khalid, who was happily animated. "What are you doing here?"

Khalid al-Awalaki held out his fist and dropped all the gold coins he had into Eastwood's hands. "Mr. Dory, I want to go with you. I can be helpful. I want to go to America. I can pay."

Eastwood smiled and wondered how a man like Khalid could leave family and life behind. He nodded, returned the coins to Khalid's shirt pocket, and held out his hand. Khalid shook it vigorously.

"OK. Stick close with me and act like you're part of the crew. I agree you might be helpful."

Tears welled in Khalid's joyful eyes, as Eastwood and Karl moved into position to watch the developing scene. Marty raised the camera toward the man with the woman, wrapped in a sheet, in his arms.

McGee, sensing he was being filmed, glared at the cameraman. Eastwood put his hand up to the camera and gently pushed it away from Marty's eye.

Khalid and Karl were confused.

"You can't take that picture, Marty," Eastwood said. "I know it would be a great picture, and it's a great story, but you can't film that man—*ever.*"

Marty frowned in disappointment then turned the camera toward the gray helicopter making its approach to the road before the embassy.

The dull rattle of helicopter rotor blades became progressively louder. McGee and Tonka disappeared through the embassy gate and were met by the Ambassador and the *Chargé d'Affaires.* The U.S. Ambassador, shocked to see Nazy's bloodied, bruised face, stepped toward McGee, trying to find meaningful words.

Anticipating the man's concern, McGee said, "She needs to be on the first helo. She needs a doctor and surgery."

"Of course. She's the priority now. What happened to her?"

McGee ignored the question and glanced at the approaching helicopter, holding Nazy as if she were weightless. "I didn't think the locals would show up."

The Ambassador sighed in irritation. "President Hernandez called the Algerian President. A few minutes later, the constabulary and the military arrived. As you can see, the Navy's here, too. Our President, apparently, was very persuasive."

"Republicans, generally, aren't cowards." McGee stared at the helicopter.

The Ambassador, knowing a backhanded insult when he heard one, walked away to get in line to board the helicopter. The *Chargé d'Affaires* followed closely behind. McGee was certain that if the Ambassador stopped suddenly, the *Chargé* would break his nose.

The pilot of the gray HH-60 flew a slow, coordinated approach to the landing spot. Former SEAL Kyle "Spanky" Drumm was in front of the landing area, giving hand and arm signals to the pilot, guiding him in. Hurricane-force winds buffeted the police cars and trucks, violently shaking palm trees on either side of the road.

Khalid never saw an American helicopter before and was frightened and excited at the prospect of climbing inside the incredibly noisy machine.

McGee and Tonka watched intently. To ensure he was heard over the din of the turbines and rotors, Tonka leaned close to McGee's ear and shouted, "Probably the easiest landing he'll make in months. The ground isn't pitching and rolling."

McGee almost grinned for the first time in hours.

The pilot landed softly, tail wheel first, then the mains. When he programmed the collective stick full down to set neutral pitch of the main rotor, the winds disappeared, but not the engine and rotor noise. The crew chief stepped off the aircraft, motioning the first evacuees to board.

McGee stepped off and winked at Tonka, who shouted, "Take care of her. See you on the boat, Sir."

When Spanky saw McGee carrying the woman with long black hair toward the helicopter, he raced from the front of the helicopter to the embassy.

Demetrius Eastwood watched the scene unfold in silence. His crew begged him to film the man carrying the injured woman. Their Pulitzer material vaporized when McGee vanished from view.

"Now you're cleared in hot, Marty." Eastwood beamed broadly.

The exasperated cameraman tossed the video camera onto his

shoulder and filmed ten healthy people walking to the helicopter, bent at the waist, apparently afraid the rotors would droop and lop off their heads. Khalid would make sure he bent over when his turn came.

Once inside the HH-60, McGee was relieved to find a doctor and corpsman aboard. Nametags on their flight suits were the first hint, a pair of huge medical bags was the second, but the stethoscopes draped around their necks and rubber gloves on their hands gave them away.

McGee slid along a troop seat to the far side of the helicopter and held the sheet-bound Nazy close to him. The three men conversed for a moment, as McGee summarized her injuries. The doctor and a corpsman gently took Nazy from McGee and positioned her on a stretcher, leaving McGee with no option but to observe.

The doctor gently unwrapped the bloody sheet from her body, as the corpsman ripped open both medical bags and pulled out fluids, needles, bandages, and sundry medical items. They worked as a trauma team. The corpsman immediately started an IV in the back of one of Nazy's hands, while the doctor started a unit of plasma dripping into the other. The corpsman placed a blood pressure cuff on one arm to check her vital signs.

McGee noticed the helicopter had somehow become filled with people who couldn't take their eyes off the doctor and corpsman working furiously on the woman they knew as the trade attaché. McGee saw a backpack being handed toward him, and Spanky's face materialized at the door. He pointed to the bag, then to Nazy.

McGee nodded and transferred custody of Nazy's bag from one SEAL to another. McGee noticed the Ambassador and *Chargé d'Affaires* staring at his arms. He looked down and saw he was covered in fresh blood. Nazy had been through hell and back and was fighting for her life. Maybe he should have taken her to a local hospital. Maybe he was too late to save her. She was in the doctor's hands now.

I did all I could. Don't die, Nazy!

CHAPTER FIFTY-EIGHT

2330 September 25, 2012
Mostaganem, Algeria

Conscious of the desert sounds, the jet turbine, and the dying flames of 007 snapping in the distance, Hunter walked away, not toward them. His feet chirped with each step in the sand. It wasn't a loud squeak, but it would be enough to alert a nearby pursuer. Since he couldn't see well enough to aim a weapon accurately, his only chance of survival was to target his pursuers from the sound of their own footsteps in the sand. Time finally ran out. He couldn't increase the interval between him and them. He was sure he was probably wobbling all over the desert and would soon be tracked down and caught. The thought of a shootout, or, worse, having his head cut off by an angry Islamist, didn't appeal to him.

His sight improved marginally and slowly. He needed time for his eyes to recover from the super-saturation of light on his optic nerve. Phosphenes, spasms of blood vessels in the brain, replaced the pure-white snowball before his eyes. He would make a stand and hope to avoid capture.

Hunter subscribed to the big-sky-little-airplane theory, that the millions of miles of open sky generally precluded two aircraft from finding each other to swap paint or cause a serious mishap. He wondered if the big-desert-little-dude theory applied, too. He was the luckiest guy he knew, and it was time to test his theory.

Duncan sprinted as fast as he could for a half-dozen steps, just like he was racing for a ball on the racquetball court, then he changed course and jumped at a 45° angle from his original direction. He dived and tucked like an Olympic tumbler. When his hands touched sand, he rolled into a ball and rotated four times before stopping. The burst of energy after laboring in the desert made his chest heave for air.

He oriented himself as best he could, and faced where he surmised his last footsteps would be visible in the sand. He was breathing loudly for a quiet desert night. If he could hear it, so could someone else. Calming himself, he got his heart and breathing under control.

Rolling onto his butt, he pulled out the sheet of light-bending camouflage material from his flight suit. Unfolding and spreading out the slick cloth by feel, he was ecstatic to realize it was double-bed size, not bath-size. Glassy side up, he spread it fully and turned over onto his elbows, feeling the edges to assure himself he was completely covered.

Operational combat testing, he thought. *It has to work.*

He unclipped and withdrew the Colt Python from his shoulder holster. Once it was cocked and had the safety off, he switched on the laser sight, his finger rested on the trigger. He strained to see the red dot of the targeting laser on the material over him, but he still couldn't see details and tried to convince himself that he wasn't just imaging the little red dot. He lay still and listened.

Using the experimental camouflage, he no longer had to contend with the bright white light in his eyes. The whiteness had definitely turned more gray, his vision was transitioning from white to incrementally darker shades of white. His breathing was almost back to normal. For the first time in several minutes, whether it was shattered nerves or growing confidence, he grinned. He could make out a hint of the image of the red laser sight.

The out-of-control flare, burning magnesium and phosphorus, came so close to his canopy; the light saturated his optic nerve with something as bright as the sun, like getting welder's blindness. That had happened to him before, getting "his eyes burned out," as he called it. Hunter recalled the worst part of flying in formation in a fighter jet was trying to maintain his wingman position on his flight lead when turning into the sun. Even through the ultra-dark helmet visor, the sun's energy was so bright, it burned through. It was as if someone jammed a stick into his eye, as he tried to maintain position through deft touch on the control stick and with enough G and power to maintain the tight Blue Angel formation, to fly close and steady with enough step down to be safe.

Looking into the sun, he found the light so painful that a pilot's normal response was to turn away his head. If he did, he would lose sight and bump into his lead flight or worse. A pilot was stuck with no choice, you burned out your eyeballs when the two jets were at their closest and avoid making the tiniest wrong control stick movement which could result in disaster. Jet pilots sucked it up; vision would return to normal.

A pilot never passed up an opportunity to look good coming back to the field or the carrier. Otherwise, he never heard the end of it. Hunter's vision always recovered, so he bet it would happen again—if he could just evade detection and capture.

His reverie was broken by the familiar *squeak, squeak* of footsteps in the sand. He froze, doubting what he just heard. He didn't know if it was real or imaginary, like taking a hearing test when someone had a mild case of tinnitus and it was difficult to differentiate between the actual electrically-generated tone and the one constantly in one's head.

At fifteen feet away, he heard the sand squeaking from at least two men, and then he caught their distinct huffing and puffing. They stopped and he imagined their concern and confusion.

Can they see where I tucked and rolled? Adrenaline flooded his body. His heart was getting a workout, and he was close to shaking with fear. *The glassy side is out. Is the camo working?*

A terrifying minute passed before he heard someone speak in Arabic, then the other. Hunter fine-tuned their direction from their voices and aimed the Colt that way. Their tone suggested confusion and incredulity. If he understood Arabic, he would have heard them say the infidel must have doubled back. At least, that was what he hoped they said.

His heart and temples pounded. His hearing became more acute. He opened his eyes and saw a wide, fuzzy red blotch from his laser pointer on the camo material. He blinked wildly and confirmed he saw well enough to identify a red patch up close.

It was quiet for a dozen seconds before he heard the men step away, their boots squeaking with each step. He slipped the material off his head and thought he saw two indistinct silhouettes barely illuminated by the distant fire walking side-by-side. He would recall later that he aimed at and fired on a mere "shade differential."

He aimed at the first silhouette two-handed, seeing a diffused red spot vaguely in the middle of the shade differential near its center of mass. He squeezed the trigger, and the gun recoiled. Hunter let it drop and slipped the red dot in the middle of the other silhouette and fired again.

He blinked and strained his improving eyes to see anything else—a shadow or a silhouette—but couldn't. Confident he hit both men, he wanted to get up and finish them, but he decided to wait. He closed his eyes, as fewer phosphenes exploded and gave way to better clarity. Slipping the camo material back over his head, he hunkered down to wait and listen.

He assumed the men wore body armor. Good body armor would stop a .357 Magnum round, but the wearer would be out of action for days with broken ribs and internal injuries. Designed to stop a bullet from entering a body, the Kevlar-matrix material would dissipate a bullet's energy without puncturing or fracturing. Body armor allowed most men to live to fight another day.

It was hard thinking about anything but survival. He reverted to his two-decades-old high-level SERE course. Survival Evasion, Resistance, and Escape training was given to military aircrew and special operations personnel considered to be at high risk of capture. If captured, the game changed dramatically, and Hunter had no compunction about using his Colt on himself to avoid being taken prisoner.

A pilot captured in Muslim lands would be unlike anything other downed pilots experienced or endured. Gary Powers' capture over the Soviet Union was a mere business transaction. Confused peasants and farmers handed him over to their local policemen, who handed him over to the KGB.

Pilots shot down over North Vietnam were beaten by their captors, then imprisoned and interrogated for days. The men who checked into the Hanoi Hilton were beaten and tortured sometimes around the clock. Torture was a widely subjective term. What some State Department weenie or liberal Congressman considered torture was just normal SERE training or general living conditions for a Marine or a SEAL.

Torture in a Muslim land was a blood orgy. For 1,000 years, knives and swords were the tools of the Islamic torturer. Political torturers using rubber hoses designed to avoid detection under the Geneva Convention generally meant prisoners would be held until they were no longer politically useful. They would eventually be released, though sometimes broken and shattered in body, mind, and spirit if they lived. If Islamic torturers didn't immediately saw off a prisoner's head, they would take their time and slice off body parts, turning torture into a horrific art form.

Hunter doubted if he were captured that he'd be allowed to live very long. No one would give him lectures about the wonderfulness of Islam. He wouldn't be interrogated under bright lights, subjected to loud music, made to stand for long periods, or be continually beaten with hoses or steel rods until the jailer grew tired. If he were captured, he would be interrogated under the knife, then his head would be cut off. For shooting Muslims in Muslim lands, the punishment was death, if not immediate, then long and painful.

If caught, he knew his Muslim captors would be unlikely to ask about his airplane and its capabilities. When the Soviets held Gary Powers, they demanded to know what his U-2 plane was capable of. What was its range, but more importantly, what was its maximum altitude? Was it 60,000 feet, 70,000, or 80,000?

With the old, venerable YO-3A and a jet engine in the background, Hunter could have flown directly over their heads. The wind from his quiet airplane would have been enough to blow their hair around or knock a *keffiyeh* from their heads. He had no intention of being captured, but he had no intention of being blinded before his airplane was shot from the sky, either. Such were the vicissitudes of war.

Five long minutes passed. Hunter still didn't hear anything. There were no cries of pain or squeaking of footsteps, no voices, nothing. It was decision time. Hunter slipped out from under the camouflage material and checked his vision.

The remains of his plane still burned on the horizon. The blurry image was unrecognizable. He guessed it was the only recent plane crash in Africa, an oblique reference to the horrendous accident rate on the continent. He scanned toward where he shot the two men.

He crawled low in that direction, the revolver in one hand, hoping his vector took him toward where they fell. The desert sand was uneven, but that didn't impede his speed. Hunter crept forward, pushing sand for propulsion, until he crested a two-foot dune and saw two fairly distinct, man-shaped shadows spread-eagled face down and unmoving. A flashlight lay in the sand, its fuzzy beam shining into infinity. The nearest man held Hunter's helmet bag.

The only sound was his own breathing and the buzz of the little jet engine in the distance. He continued crawling toward the two men, Colt ready, until he reached them and pressed the muzzle of the Python into the temple of the closest one and pulled the trigger. He scurried to his knees, aimed a blurry red dot, and shot the other man in the head. If he had any doubts about his pursuers' viability, those two bullets ended them.

Hunter crawled to one body to recover the flashlight before he stood and shone the light on the two men's backs. Although his vision was improving, it was noticeably better when he was close to what he viewed. There was something unusual about those bodies.

Hunter felt the men's arms and necks and stared at the shapes for a few moments until he finally figured it out. His eyes still couldn't render a sharp image, but the two men were the biggest, most powerfully built men he ever saw in Africa. They were huge and muscular, like men who spent five hours a day in a gym. Like weightlifters; like SEALs.

They're as big as Bill McGee! He reluctantly holstered and safetied his big Colt. Hunter was still not certain he was out of danger.

Moving closer, as if shortening the distance to one inch would make his vision more acute and give him the granularity he sought, he strained his eyes and fingers to determine how the big men died. He patted their backs, feeling the familiar material and thickness of top-of-the-line body armor. He knew it would have stopped even his Magnum rounds, but he wasn't sure what could have knocked them down permanently.

He finally felt the point of impact, dead center in the man's back. He must have a shattered spinal column. Without time to investigate the second man's demise and no real desire to know if it was mechanics or blind luck behind his semi-blind shooting, Hunter stood and placed his hand over the top of the flashlight.

Hunter peeled the helmet bag from the dead man's fingers and started slogging toward the faint jet noise. The Gulfstream's APU was still running. Though blurred, he was able to recognize a short, horizontal row of fuzzy lights that must be the jet's portholes. Blinking several times, he looked up. Instead of stars, he saw soft, fuzzy points of light. After several steps, he remembered he forgot something and reversed course.

It took more effort to return to where he hid to retrieve the camouflage material. He spent several minutes looking for the invisible sheet before giving up. Pulling on his helmet, he turned on the NVGs and was amused to see the camouflage material was well defined even with his degraded eyesight. It lay on the sand only a few feet away. He stumbled around without seeing it, because for a partially blind man, it looked like amorphous sand. He retrieved the material, folded it, and slipped the sheet and his helmet into the nylon bag. The camouflage helped him avoid capture once. It might prove useful again.

As he labored against the soft sand, he fished his AN/PRQ-7 emergency radio from his black flight suit. He depressed the *ON* button, but, when he brought it near his face, he couldn't read anything on the backlit crystal display. Although his vision was better, it would need to be a whole lot better for him to read the display and call for the Navy's search-and-rescue helicopter.

Until then, he shut it down and replaced it in his pocket, as he trudged toward the turbine sound. Again, he heard his feet chirping in the sand with each step. As he walked, several conflicting ideas dominated his thoughts.

That has to be all of them except my target. The target's operation has all the hallmarks of being cover and "lone wolf." What I saw from the air screamed that his business was hiding in plain sight.

Duncan stopped walking to clip his helmet bag to his flight suit. He pulled on his helmet and set the NVGs in place over his improving eyes. He unholstered the Colt Python and cocked the hammer, and set out again for the airplane.

Four down, one to go. I definitely won't be taken alive.

CHAPTER FIFTY-NINE

0030 September 26, 2012
U.S.S. Dwight D. Eisenhower
Mediterranean Sea

The gray HH-60 was cleared to land on Spot 1. An LSE, Landing Signal Enlisted, guided the helicopter to the flight deck, his lighted coveralls and illuminated wands marked his location. The bright-white lights embedded in the coverall's material formed an X on the otherwise darkened ship. The Sikorsky pilot flew a slow, coordinated, angled approach to the landing spot. The LSE signaled "come forward" and "move to the right" over the landing zone.

As the helicopter crept forward, the pilot applied differential pressure on the rudder pedals to center the aircraft over the flight deck. The LSE crossed his wands to signal, "Stop your forward motion."

The helicopter hovered five feet off the deck, the pilot deftly maintaining his position and heading with thirty-five knots of wind racing down the flight deck. In a single motion, the LSE brought the crossed wands to his knees, signaling "land here."

The pilot programmed the collective stick lower and lower and centered the cyclic stick until the tail wheel touched down, then the main landing gear. The LSE well in front of the helicopter, saw the rotor blade tip lights outlining the rotor disc.

With the parking brake set and the aircraft barely touching the ship, the pilot programmed the collective stick the rest of the way down to set neutral pitch on the main rotor. Safe aboard the aircraft carrier, the crew chief stepped off the chopper as four blue-shirted aircraft handlers lugging heavy chains raced up to attach the chains to the aircraft. Once it was lashed to the boat, the helicopter and ship rocked and pitched with the waves as one.

The LSE motioned with one hand for the passengers to depart. Eleven people were directed to an open door in the Island, the superstructure located starboard on the aircraft carrier. In seconds, all passengers but one had disembarked.

Four "white shirts" with red crosses on their jerseys and white sound suppressors over their ears raced toward the helicopter. Two of the white shirts grabbed one end of a stretcher and pulled it from the helicopter cabin. The others grabbed the other ends and walked away perpendicular to the helicopter fuselage, where the turning rotor blades were programmed at their highest during full down collective.

Once clear of the rotor, the four white shirts turned left 90º toward the bow and the door of a twin-engine turboprop airplane 100 feet away. The doctor and corpsman who tended Nazy followed alongside, carrying IV and plasma bags.

From the Island hatch, Bill McGee watched the Navy medical corps securely transfer Nazy onto a Carrier Onboard Delivery aircraft, a gray C-2 Greyhound. The four white shirts maneuvered the stretcher through the door, deftly entering the airplane one at a time until all six medical men were aboard. After three minutes, the four white shirts spilled out and walked back to the Island.

Someone wearing a yellow jersey, signifying he was part of flight deck control, came to McGee and encouraged him to get off the fight deck and get below. McGee acquiesced, and stepped inside the Island. Several other members from the embassy waited impatiently to ease themselves and their belongings down the steep metal stairs the Navy called "a ladder."

As he waited his turn to descend the ladder, McGee replayed what he heard as the trauma doctor relayed his patient's condition to the helicopter pilot requesting she be immediately transferred to the Naval Hospital at Naval Air Station Sigonella, Italy.

"Tell them she requires life-saving and reconstructive surgery." The words still reverberated in McGee's ears.

CHAPTER SIXTY

0030 September 26, 2012
Mostaganem, Algeria

Abu Manu slipped his good hand into his shirt pocket. His fingers trembled slightly as he verified the glass tube hadn't been crushed. It was a mistake to carry the special vial so carelessly, but *Inshallah,* it was safe and unbroken. He relaxed after feeling the smooth glass under his fingers and returned to rest in the back of the vehicle. His bandaged stump was soaked in blood as he it leaned against the vehicle's side. Somehow, through the pain, he knew it needed to be elevated to help control the bleeding.

His FAHD had been gone a very long time. He was tired and felt cold. He moved the blood-dripping, bandaged stump and tried to move fingers that weren't there. Pain streaked all the way to his shoulder. *Allah's punishment for stealing!*

He returned his damaged hand to its elevated position, turning his head and leaking tears in shame and frustration.

He snapped out of his self-pity when he heard two shots in rapid succession. He tried to sit up, but his bad hand throbbed when he lowered it, blood rushing to the missing digits, making him wince with a muffled scream. He returned to his quiet position in the vehicle, his arm held high. After a minute, the powerful throbbing in his hand subsided greatly.

Satisfied the pain wouldn't return, he focused on his FAHD and their success, and a thin smile marred his bloody face. They accomplished what he started. They killed the American infidel. It was two shots to the head, what the American Special Operations Forces called a "double tap." Hate replaced glee, as his emotions swung between extremes. Anxiety and fury weaved through his consciousness.

Returning to the present, he wondered where Habib and Malik were. Their mission done, he was ready to go to the hospital. He screamed with hate, "The Americans will pay for their treachery!"

Periods of lucid ratiocination were interrupted by rambling. "Sending an airplane … to kill me … was … clever." He felt colder, and his body was getting stiffer.

"Where are they?" He coughed. Minutes later, he thought of the American. "An assassin, an airborne assassin," he raved, and shuddering before screeching, "Bring him to me!"

The burst of energy prompted a coughing fit. That, coupled with the intense pain of his injured hand, nearly made him faint. In a low voice, he said, "I want to ... punish the infidel ... for what he did to me."

With nearly all his energy reserves spent, Abu Manu closed his eyes and rested, and waited for his men to return.

Five quiet minutes later, he heard two more shots in quick succession like the first time. His eyelids opened, but he was unemotional. The gun sounded different than the crack of an AK-47. Why would his FAHD shoot two bullets? His breathing came in ragged spurts, followed by short coughing spells.

As seconds passed, he became more concerned and more anxious. Struggling with rational, coherent thoughts, he slipped in and out of paranoia. *What if Malik killed Habib for the gold? No, no, no! Habib would never allow Malik to kill me, not for gold.*

Abu Manu lay on his back, his hand elevated, his eyes closed. The loss of blood impaired his judgment and sense of reality with every drop that ran down his arm.

Then his eyes flew open. *Two shots? Muslims never shoot two bullets. My FAHD shoot many bullets!*

Somewhere in his blood-starved brain, leaked a lucid thought. *Oh, God, the infidel's alive!*

Fear galvanized him. He ignored the pain in his maimed hand. He had to leave the truck and hide. Abu Manu struggled to move from the back of the Mercedes. He trembled from cold earlier, but now it was from fear. He unsteadily slipped from the SUV, almost falling while protecting his damaged hand. He tried to ignore the pulsing pain in his stump. Terror grew with each passing minute.

Protect me from the infidel!

He stood, wobbling at the corner of the truck, then used the door to steady himself. His thoughts were a mélange of the sane and insane.

I'll look for Malik and Habib. Where could they be? I have no weapon! My FAHD carry weapons. Protect me!

He rocked back and forth at the edge of the vehicle when another rational thought drilled through the fog of unreasonableness. With his bad hand held high and away, he frantically searched the vehicle, stripping away the plastic cover hiding the spare tire from its mountings and clumsily throwing it from the SUV. He clawed inefficiently at the carpet and spare tire, struggling with his one good hand.

He had been right-handed, and the strain of relying on his left for even simple tasks was frustrating. He nearly burst into tears as he swung between mental states and was almost overcome with joy when he located the goal of his search. Once he had the spare tire out of its well, he held up the tire wrench like a victorious gladiator.

A wild look replaced his pained expression, as he wobbled away from the Mercedes. If his FAHD couldn't be found, he would kill the infidel American.

Cautiously sweeping his surroundings, the NVGs highlighted nothing but open desert to the east and west. To the south, in varying shades of green, was the airplane hangar and jet on the runway.

Duncan walked north toward the YO-3A's crash site and approached the fire, turning off the NVGs to save battery power before he flipped them up and locked them in place. His vision improved with every heartbeat. The flames cast enough light around the area to show several interesting items. First, the cockpit was crushed but untouched by flames. The propeller was missing, and the engine broke free of its mounts.

He stared at the bare firewall for a second, scanning the crash site. The accident investigator in him surmised the remaining wing broke off at impact and caught fire. Aviation gasoline burned in the sand. The second noticeable item was that it appeared he parachuted to the sand only a few feet from where the wing lay folded and burning. A couple feet farther north, and he would have landed on top of the broken Yo-Yo and into an inferno.

I'm still the luckiest guy on the planet.

There was no time to be maudlin. He reached into his helmet bag and withdrew a hefty Leatherman multi-tool and selected a screwdriver blade, locking it in place. He walked to the other side of the crumpled airframe to get what he wanted. He'd been foolish enough to leave the original Lockheed data plate on the aircraft. He undid the four mounting screws and looked at the two-by-three-inch metal plate, barely able to make out the words *Serial number 007.*

He slipped the tool and data plate into the helmet bag and walked toward the jet, its APU still running in the distance. He pulled the AN/PRQ-7 handheld radio from his flight suit pocket and handled it for a second before returning it. He wasn't ready to claim failure yet and have the Navy rescue him when he hadn't completed his mission. Once away from the fire, he put the NVGs over his eyes again and set his course for the jet and hangar.

Once Hunter was away from the crash site, he realized he had a splitting headache. He'd been too fired up to know his head hurt. Scanning the area, he looked up. Stars filled the oculars. The light amplification device flooded the scopes with ten times more stars than could be seen with the naked eye.

Where's the target? He has to be out there somewhere.

He walked southwest toward the hangar and jet. From his vantage point, he saw the partial roof outline of a sport-utility vehicle down the road, farther south past the hangar. Hunter recalled seeing one during his two passes and noted it had moved away from the hangar. *Why didn't they drive it closer to the crash site?*

As his eyesight improved, he felt more confident. He stopped to check his surroundings again. Hunter glanced back at the scattered flames and thought if he had parachuted between the crash site and the hangar, he was probably visible to the men. They cut across the desert to intercept him. That was why they found him so quickly. They didn't have NVGs, but they didn't need them when they carried flashlights and he left tracks in the sand.

He stopped and knelt, turning off the laser pointer to conserve the battery. Hunter uncocked the Colt and unlocked the cylinder. He mashed the cartridge-eject cylinder to dump all rounds from the cylinder. From his lower flight-suit pocket, he pulled out a full speed loader and inserted six hollow-point rounds into the Colt with the press of a button. He safetied the gun, then continued his approach to the hangar and jet.

Duncan was within 100 feet of the aircraft when he paused to view the area. He moved closer, each time advancing twenty-five feet and stopped to review and reassess. His head swiveled, constantly scanning forward and side-to-side. When he stopped, he scanned his six o'clock in case someone tried to sneak up from behind.

At twenty-five feet from the blaring jet engine, he recognized the shapes of two men lying on the far side, most likely the aircrew he shot. Still on one bent knee, he looked at the jet, lit from inside and ready for departure. He debated whether he should take the jet and escape, but the inescapable thought won. If he hadn't killed his target, what was to prevent the man from shooting him down again?

His anxiety went up a notch. He repositioned the heavy Colt in his hand and scanned the hangar and area. He was sure he was missing one terrorist. There was plenty of detail in the NVGs to assure him there were plenty of opportunities to stumble into a trap. He couldn't leave until he was certain.

He shot at the man, but he wasn't sure the bullet found its mark. Hunter focused on several containers stacked atop each other. That's where the man hid. Those containers masked his position, they could do it again.

Hunter assessed the layout of the hangar, the aircraft inside, and where and how the containers were situated. His brows furrowed, as he again thought, *Did he know I was coming? Why would anyone position those containers like that? That's just not normal.*

He shook the strange thoughts from his mind and bolted for the airplane, running under the jet until he was behind a main landing gear strut and wheel. He slowly panned right to left, searching for anything in his NVGs. Nothing in his green sight picture changed but its size.

Where's the target? He has to be here somewhere. It's the moment of truth, Big Boy.

He flicked on the laser pointer and unsafetied the weapon and dashed, hunched over, to the closest corner of the hangar, both hands on the Colt in front of his body, clearing the area left and right. He saw no one on the outside. There was only the SUV down the road. He peered inside and saw two airplanes and several shipping boxes—MANPADS containers. He moved quickly from those to the parked airplanes, seeking a body hidden along the back wall or in the aircraft without finding anyone.

No one in the hangar. Check. No one in the aircraft. Check.

He raced back to the MANPADS containers and scrutinized the area. Flipping up the NVGs, he removed the flashlight and saw blood. Debris littered the hidden side of the shipping boxes. He moved the torch light up toward the rear of the hangar and found the shattered *Stinger* launcher. When the torch beam moved a little farther toward the back of the hangar, he saw the bloody remains of fingers and what was probably a thumb.

Hunter lamented. There wasn't enough blood. He had hurt the shooter, but the fingerless target wasn't here. He was certain the guys he shot had all their fingers.

"There's one more," he decided.

He had enough of the jet's APU. He checked the blood spoor again, but no blood trail led toward the Gulfstream. Instead, blood drops led away from the hangar.

This might be crazy. He raced toward the Gulfstream, entered the cockpit, and with the knowledge of a seasoned Gulfstream pilot, he knew exactly where the switches were located and shut down the APU and turned off the battery.

He was back inside the hangar in less than thirty seconds. Within a minute, total silence dominated the hangar. Without light from the jet cabin, the surrounding area was completely dark. He turned on the NVGs.

Advantage, me!

Abu Manu jerked awake when the APU suddenly quit running. Terror froze him. The infidel was in the hangar.

Hunter took inventory of his surroundings behind the *Stinger* shipping containers. In shades of green, he stared at the iconic Beechcraft Staggerwing dominating the middle of the hangar. He never saw one up close, only in photographs. To his trained eye, the biplane looked well-maintained and was probably airworthy, as was the other aircraft, a Cessna.

The tires of the two airplanes were obviously fully inflated. He knew high pressure aircraft tires go flat quickly when not used. A clean drip pan under the Beechcraft and three barrels of AVGAS with a fuel nozzle along the back wall of the hangar signaled the two airplanes were operational. To the right of the barrels sat several major airplane parts—wings, fuselage, horizontal stabilizer—of a disassembled aircraft, leaning against the wall. He struggled to identify it. It was definitely British, and those aircraft weren't his forte, especially when they were in pieces.

And, you call yourself an aviation expert. Come on. Ah, yes. I think that's a de Havilland Comet.

He returned his gaze to the Staggerwing, running his NVGs over the complete aircraft.

There used to be general aviation aircraft all over Africa, but with little aviation gasoline and virtually no spare parts anywhere on the continent, small private aircraft were largely knocked out of commission by attrition and lack of aviation gasoline. Virtually every airport in Africa featured piles of aircraft carcasses, oftentimes with dozens of Russian cargo and passenger airplanes that were towed to one end of an airport as scrap. Small, out-of-service general aviation aircraft were just tossed onto the heap, usually occupying a sheltered place under the big aircraft's decaying wings. Above and below the equator, the dry desert conditions preserved the more-delicate, small personal aircraft.

The target has good taste in rare airplanes.

He continued searching his surroundings. His vision and acuity were nearly back to normal, but wearing the NVGs for so long made his eyes and head ache. He always gave his eyes some rest after wearing the goggles for long periods and shut down the NVGs. His hand returned to the Colt, as he listened. Even wearing his helmet, the dull tinkle of the jet's turbine blades clicking into place as the engines wind-milled in a light breeze was crisp and clear.

Inside and out, the world was pitch black. With the exception of the jet engines wind-milling, the area was quiet. Hunter shifted position, from a crouch to a kneel, trying to reposition his knees for more comfort, but his lug-soled boots snagged on the roughhewn wood of the hangar floor.

Eventually, he succeeded in moving his feet but not before he noticed the unusual composition of the hangar deck. Such floors were usually smooth, white, and polished in Hunter's world, but not this one. He reached down to confirm it was old wood impregnated with creosote. Testing it with his heel, he wondered, why there were railroad ties for a hangar floor?

He pursed his lips. He never saw anything like it before and certainly never heard of such a thing.

He flipped the NVGs back on and checked his surroundings again.

The area was still clear as far as he could see. Hunter turned his attention to one of the two small containers on the wooden floor; he tried to drag it closer to the stack of boxes where he hunkered down.

The weight surprised him. It wouldn't move. He estimated the box weight a couple hundred pounds, making it more of a challenge to drag it across the rough-hewn wood floor than he could handle. Ensuring his surroundings were clear, he shut down the NVGs again. With the Colt in one hand, he flipped open the four buckles and lifted the container's lid.

Duncan wasn't shocked but confused. He lifted one of the long plastic tubes and guessed they contained, based on weight, gold coins. He returned the roll to the box and the Colt to its holster. Flicking on the flashlight and hooding the light, he checked the open end of the tube. It was filled with newly minted $50 American Gold Eagles. He guessed there were 100 to a roll, shrink wrapped in a tube, and probably fifty tubes to a container.

He tossed the roll in his hand and thought, *Ransom delivery, as I thought.*

He tossed the heavy roll back and forth until it slipped. He tried to catch it in the dark, but he missed. It fell and landed with a substantial *thwack.* The noise immediately shook him, because it gave away his position.

He clicked the NVGs on and drew the Colt Python. A quick scan of the hangar and ramp showed all was clear and quiet.

Through the NVGs, he studied the roll of coins pensively. Even though his helmet, they made an odd sound when they hit the floor. The coins didn't move in the heavy plastic wrap, so it was something else.

He resolved the dichotomy when he realized he expected to hear a thud. Instead, he heard a thwack. There was an element of resonance where there shouldn't have been.

The floor should be solid, but...it's not!

He returned the Colt to its holster and the roll of coins to its container while scrutinizing the floor for a clue. He smiled when he saw the clear seams of each railroad tie running the width of the hangar. Each uniform railroad tie abutted another. They weren't staggered like a regular wood floor but formed perfect lines, suggesting there were support beams underneath. With the weird sound the coins made when they hit the beam, Hunter thought there might be a hollow space under them. If so, there had to be a way in.

Maybe that's where my target is.

He popped his head up over the *Stinger* shipping containers and scanned the outlying area. Again, he saw nothing unusual. He returned his NVGs to scan the hangar to continue his search. During a rapid scan left and right, he didn't see anything out of the ordinary. When he slowed, he noticed small circles shimmering in the night-vision device. There were many dozens of those spots in the NVGs that he could have missed.

He reached down and touched one of the largest ones. It was still wet and sticky, which surprised him. It was still reasonably fresh in the warm autumn night. The trail of dots went out the hangar door, turned right, and headed east.

Hunter looked around, aggravated by the lack of depth perception. He flipped the NVGs up to give his eyes a break and used the flashlight beam behind him to study the shattered missile launcher, which was covered in blood. The remains of fingers rested against a railroad tie that was elevated about an inch.

Hunter grimaced and drew his Colt, releasing the safety. He moved the NVGs back over his eyes and shoved the missile launcher away from the partially opened door with his toe. The door pivoted up with little effort.

Everything told him not to go down in there, but there was no blood. There was blood on the launcher but there was no blood trail. Hunter gambled his target hadn't gone underground. Instead, he left the hangar and took the SUV. He had to check the cellar. The man was injured, missing fingers and a thumb. He wouldn't hide in the subterranean space when he needed a doctor. *There's no blood!*

It was a crazy and high risk. Adrenalin rushed into every capillary. There was no way to calm himself. Chance and the evidence were on his side. He stepped down the stairs illuminated by the NVGs, his big Colt led the way.

Abu Manu staggered against soft sand toward the hangar, holding his injured arm up, his triceps parallel to the ground. He carried the tire iron at his side during the times when he hadn't dropped it. He lost the heavy lug wrench several times already, as he weaved unsteadily and favored one leg. His FAHD had let him down.

Where are they? The infidel killed my FAHD. The American is coming!

Thirty feet from the hangar, Abu Manu dropped the tire iron again and strained to retrieve it, his sense of balance greatly diminished. Hatred propelled him, as he wobbled toward the hangar.

He struggled to raise the lug wrench over his head before losing his grip yet again. It tumbled in front of him.

I ... kill you!

Duncan Hunter peered down the stairs, blinking wildly to encourage his eyes to improve that last little bit to being normal. He couldn't see the bottom step no matter how many times he blinked or squinted. There wasn't enough ambient light down there, meaning he'd be blind again, but this time, from total darkness.

NVGs allow images to be produced at levels of light approaching total darkness, but moving from an area with some ambient light to total darkness meant the image-intensification technology would fail. With no photons to capture and amplify, NVGs were useless.

It was the scariest thing he ever did. His breathing came in spurts, and his brain refused to move his feet. He lowered the Colt and selected the switch on the laser pointer; the explosion of photons from the laser completely illuminated the darkness below. The intensifier tubes brightened the image of steps and partial views of stacked shipping containers.

He calmed immeasurably. With no blood spoor, he doubted there were any booby traps, and he flew down the stairs.

When he was at the base of the steps, he swept the Colt from side-to-side and saw several thick parallel support beams of old, treated timbers. There were several rooms, right and left, apparently made of the same railroad ties as above.

He raced to clear each room, the Colt leading the way, and found hundreds of small containers like the two he left on the hangar floor, stacked to the ceiling, many rows deep. Spinning, he checked the last room and saw it was filled with MANPADS shipping containers and crude wooden furniture.

On top of a decrepit table rested a small trapdoor safe, the kind of small fireproof safe to protect important documents. Open and empty, it meant nothing to him.

Anxiety drove him to finish and get the hell out. He sped up the railroad-tie steps and back into the hangar. In a crouch, he swept the area again, the Colt jerking left-right-left. Hyperventilation was a real possibility, and he demanded his senses, heart, and breathing slow before he became lightheaded or fell over in a faint.

One minute of self-induced terror, followed by thirty seconds of peace and harmony, left him chilled. Hunter broke into a sweat and thanked God he hadn't pissed all over himself. As his breathing calmed, he thought, *The Algerian chapter of Fort Knox. Every one of those containers must be filled with gold coins.*

He'd been on the ground for over an hour and hadn't called for the cavalry to come to his aid. Not using his radio was probably a mistake. He could see well enough to read the LCD display, but he still hadn't found his target. If he didn't neutralize the target, what would prevent him from shooting down a rescue helicopter?

Gritting his teeth, Hunter pushed himself to complete his mission—find the target, kill him, and get the hell off the continent. His window of opportunity to radio and escape was narrowing, and it would probably close at dawn.

The dots of blood leading from the hangar beckoned. Increasing dread and growing panic pushed him to finish and escape before the door closed.

"That leaves the truck," he whispered.

CHAPTER SIXTY-ONE

0045 September 26, 2012
U.S.S. Dwight D. Eisenhower
Mediterranean Sea

Twelve men stepped from the last helicopter and followed the direction of sailors wearing yellow turtleneck jerseys. Jet engines and rotor blades spinning overhead made it impossible to hear anything. The men in yellow were especially adept at hand and arm signals, and used multiple versions to control the movements of the evacuees. The last of the men from the U.S. Embassy in Algiers walked to the red light spilling from the hatch at the base of the Eisenhower's Island.

Bill McGee was on hand in the Island to welcome Spanky, Tonka, Eastwood, and his film crew to their new home for a few days. When the C-2 Greyhound returned from its mercy mission transporting Nazy to the Naval hospital in Italy, most if not all of the evacuees would experience the adventure of being catapulted off the deck of an aircraft carrier. Virtually all SEALs got to experience that ride at some point in their careers, but it wasn't something civilians and Marine ground officers got to do. Eastwood and his crew would appreciate the ride of a lifetime.

Eastwood recognized that he and his crew had little to show for their time in Algiers. With a Naval helicopter on the flight deck and another airplane roaring at the front of the 1,100-foot-long ship, Eastwood yelled in Marty's ear, "Take pictures!"

The video camera was on Marty's shoulder in seconds, and he shot video of the helicopter they just left and the propeller-driven aircraft a few hundred yards away.

While the news correspondents took pictures of Naval flight operations, Tonka turned to McGee's ear and asked where Nazy was.

McGee pointed to the C-2 Greyhound on the catapult in preparation for launching from the flight deck and said, "They're taking her to Sig's Naval hospital."

"She going to be OK?"

McGee's pinched lips and eyes said solemnly, *I don't know.*

The helicopter shut down its engines, and the rotor stopped turning. Eastwood and Marty tried to creep along the Island to film the aircraft on the catapult, its turboprops straining against the holdback, as the jet-blast deflectors raised. When the massive metal plates were lifted hydraulically behind the long, thin, twin-engine airplane, Marty looked away from the eyepiece. The JBDs obscured what little view they had of the aircraft on the "cat."

Eastwood also recognized they couldn't see from that angle. He and Marty tried to race down the flight deck for a better view only to be stopped by a big black man in a yellow turtleneck, matching yellow helmet, and wearing old-time flight goggles. He frowned and pointed for them to go back to the Island, and the two men complied, just as the Greyhound shot off the bow of the carrier.

What had once been a hubbub of activity and continuous 100+ decibels generated from jet engines, helicopter rotors, and turboprops was suddenly eerily quiet. The only sound was the wind racing across the flight deck and through the antenna farm high above on the Island.

The yellow shirt hurried Eastwood and Marty off the flight deck toward the open hatch of the Island. As the correspondents neared McGee, Tonka, and Spanky, McGee said, "You're lucky that dude didn't throw you over the side of the ship!"

The other SEALs looked on incredulously.

Though embarrassed, Eastwood smirked. "That probably wasn't one of my finer moments."

Heads nodded.

"Nazy was on that plane," McGee said.

Amusement instantly replaced seriousness. The huge black man in the yellow shirt stepped inside the Island and looked at the motley group from the embassy. In a deep, rumbling voice, he said, "Follow me." No one spoke as they descended the ladder.

The men wound down through six flights of stairs and walked along a long passageway. The yellow shirt stopped at a hatch and offered the men to step inside. "Welcome to the Snake Pit. Sheets, blankets, and pillows are on each rack. The head is down the passageway. Good night, Gentlemen. We'll see you in the morning for breakfast. Don't be late, or you won't get fed."

He turned and walked away, his massive shoulders filling the hallway.

A voice erupted from the intercom and reverberated down the hallway. "Secure from flight quarters. Secure from flight quarters."

Tonka faced McGee with a squint. Something was on his mind, and McGee guessed what it was. McGee, a retired Navy captain, deserved better accommodations than open squad bay facilities and the enlisted man in Tonka wasn't happy about his captain being overlooked and dishonored.

"Tonka, I know what you're thinking," McGee said. "Please know I appreciate it. We've had a hell of a day. All I want right now is a shower; some sleep, and be on time for breakfast, *capice?*"

"You're the boss, Bullfrog." With a grin, he added, "Aye, aye, Captain."

CHAPTER SIXTY-TWO

0045 September 26, 2012
Mostaganem, Algeria

Hunter followed the blood trail. He moved cautiously to the corner of the hangar. Helmet and NVGs on, both hands gripped the Colt Python, the laser sight aimed toward Andromeda in Orion's Belt. His vision was near-normal and getting sharper by the minute, with far fewer phosphenes bursting each second, the kind of stars boxers saw after being hit by Mike Tyson.

He didn't see the blow, but something dull and hard smashed into his helmet, knocking him face-first into the ground. In a microsecond, his NVGs were swept from his face, and the helmet was knocked from his head.

Whatever hit him also knocked the Colt from his hand. Instinctively, Hunter rolled away from the direction of the assault, away from the lee and dark side of the hangar. Adrenalin flooded his bloodstream, and he moved with the speed of a mongoose in full retreat.

When he stopped rolling, he heard slurred, ragged English. *"I kill you, Infidel!"*

Whether it was adrenaline or the glancing blow to his helmet, Hunter saw infinitely more stars than a second before. Slightly dazed, he scrambled to his feet, trying to acquire the target and his Colt when the shape of a man holding the long end of a lug wrench stepped from the dark side of the hangar. In the poor moonlight, the shadow of a man labored to raise a tire iron and moved with the speed and grace of Karloff's Mummy. The target was clearly out of breath and labored to move toward Hunter.

"I kill you, Infidel!" he sneered again.

Hunter couldn't make out the man's age or infirmity in the available light, but his movements suggested he wasn't the Paul Bunyan type who could ring the bell at a county fair. The man staggered like a drunk orangutan or a very damaged terrorist. He dropped the tire iron and held up his hand, his bandage wrappings flitting in the breeze. He was obviously the shooter, Duncan's target. The man was severely injured and struggled to retain his balance.

Just as he did thousands of times on a racquetball court, Duncan Hunter sensed and verified his opponent's weakness and exploited it. He lunged at the man's chest and bowled him over. Hunter caromed off the thick man, tucked, and rolled once.

Once on his feet in his new position, he looked for his revolver. The target wobbled on his back in the sand, as Hunter saw the red laser emanating from the gun, pointing south. He scrambled to retrieve it from the sand and cocked it. He raced against some imaginary clock.

Finish it and get out of here!

He walked toward the man in the desert and found him laughing between coughing fits. Duncan leaped astride the terrorist's body and jammed the Colt under his chin.

"You don't know you're dead...American...*infidel.*"

Unimpressed by the arrogant man's response, Hunter pulled the trigger. The powerful Colt bucked, and the bullet exited the top of the man's head. The old man went limp, as if a balloon burst.

"Well, *you're* definitely dead, asshole."

He slid his gun and arm off the dead man, and reached into his flight suit to retrieve the flashlight he took from one of the other men. Surprised it still worked; he shone the beam in the man's face. "Who are you?"

The man was plump, with thinning, straight hair that hung limply around his broad, bloody forehead. Several deep, long cuts showed on one side of his face. Sand covered an open wound where an ear had been attached, probably collateral damage from shrapnel when the *Stinger* launcher was destroyed.

He wasn't interested in the exit wound, but he did notice white powder against the man's dark-blue shirt, as if a tiny flour bag burst inside his pocket. He stared at the residue for several seconds and stopped breathing.

He understood the man's cryptic message. "Fuck me." *I've been exposed to anthrax, and I haven't had the shots. Shit. What do I know about anthrax? I know I have cipro tabs and atropine in my bag. If that shit is anthrax, I'll need help fast.*

He overrode the temptation to shoot the man again. Instead, he holstered his Colt and stood. He panned the flashlight to find his helmet and crushed NVGs. With them in one hand and the flashlight in the other, he solemnly walked back into the hangar and dumped them onto the stack of *Stinger* shipping containers. He reached back to unclip his helmet bag from his flight suit, tossed it onto the makeshift table top, and rummaged through one of the pockets.

A plastic bag the size and thickness of a paperback novel was illuminated by the weak light. Hunter opened the field first-aid kit and rifled through the contents before he found the package of Ciprofloxacin. Punching the pills from the foil-backed card, he swallowed them.

Atropine for nerve gas, he thought. *Ciproflaxin for anthrax. Check. Tell Kelly pilots can get anthrax ... I don't think so!*

He zip-locked shut the first-aid kit and all of its little goodies and tossed it inside his flight bag.

For the first time in an hour, he felt calm, but he was also a man possessed. There was no time to reflect on the men he killed or his possible anthrax poisoning. Confident all the terrorists were dead, he felt he had some housekeeping to attend to before he left Algeria.

With his flashlight, he located several feet of rope and the five-gallon can of fuel he saw earlier at the rear of the hangar and hauled them to the front edge of the structure. He cut a wide swath around the dead man and jogged to the truck 100 yards to the south.

Not surprised to find the keys in the ignition, he drove it back to the hangar, where he loaded the heavy gas can into the back of the SUV. He lassoed one end of the rope to the dead man's legs and the other to the Mercedes' bumper. In a minute, he dragged his prime target to the Yo-Yo crash site, which was almost completely burned out, though small fires remained in a few places. He crashed the SUV into the plane's fuselage, splashed the pungent aviation gasoline all over the Mercedes, the airplane, his target, and the anthrax, and set them on fire.

Back at the hangar, arms akimbo, Hunter stared at the jet—the immediate fast ride off the continent. He looked over his shoulder at the Staggerwing. It was one or the other.

He made his decision and walked toward the aircraft.

After all this, this may actually kill me.

CHAPTER SIXTY-THREE

0100 September 26, 2012
Somewhere over the Mediterranean Sea

Something totally unexpected happened on Master Sergeant Michelle Bowman's radar screen. A small icon appeared on the weapons controller's scope out of nowhere, exactly where the mission aircraft went down hours earlier. She stared at the lone icon and empty data tag. The AWACS' giant radar disc picked up the plane during its takeoff roll, and one of the Cray-sized computers in the big jet displayed what information it could analyze and crunch—altitude, airspeed, and heading. Radar symbology suggested the blip was a small aircraft and not the heavy corporate jet that landed earlier.

Bowman frowned and crossed her arms on the console. She leaned closer to the scope, wondering if the computer software was malfunctioning. The previous images confirmed the mission aircraft was shot down by a surface-to-air missile, and now it appeared the mission aircraft somehow regenerated and took off from the remote field.

She looked around the cabin of the modified Boeing 707, but her lieutenant colonel wasn't in sight. With a toggle of her microphone switch, she spoke into the intercom, requesting his presence.

When the man in the flight suit sauntered over to her station, she looked up with a frown. Confusion showed on her expressive face. "I don't know how he did it, but it's him. He's back in the air and just radioed *Eisenhower.* At his present speed, he'll be there in an hour."

"Are you certain?"

She looked up, spread her arms wide, and nodded before returning her eyes to the scope.

"That's incredible." The lanky Air Battle Manager watched the radar trace an arc over the water on a vector to the aircraft carrier. "Stay on top of him. Nice job, Michelle." He patted her shoulder.

Shaking his head in disbelief, he walked to the front of the big jet to deliver some good news. *Somebody at the White House will be happy.*

CHAPTER SIXTY-FOUR

0100 September 26, 2012
Somewhere over the Mediterranean Sea

Takeoff in the Beechcraft was exhilarating and cathartic. After torching his smashed airplane and his target, Duncan Hunter sprinted to the hangar and prepared the Staggerwing for flight. Using the nearly dead flashlight for vision, he kicked the wood block from the front of the main landing gear, opened the door, and checked the cockpit for the battery switch. Once he found it, he toggled the switch to power the electrical system, but nothing happened.

Not surprised, he backed from the cockpit and shone the dull light over the fuselage until he found the battery-access panel. He attached the quick-disconnect fitting to the battery. It checked good and the fuel tanks were full. He crawled under each wing and used a screwdriver blade from his Leatherman to depress the wing tank poppet valves to drain the fuel tanks of any water.

Hunter hustled to get into the airplane and get airborne. In his rush to escape Algeria, he decided to take the antique airplane, not the jet. Although he could have flown the jet easily, he couldn't take it and fly somewhere without blowing his cover, and he couldn't land it on the aircraft carrier. He knew the Agency L-100 and his support crew were over halfway to the Azores by then, and the most-logical solution to finding a safe haven with medical care for an anthrax infection meant flying to the carrier. If they'd let him land was a question he'd have to ask once he was airborne. All he had to do was start the Staggerwing. He could take care of the rest.

The last time he flew a radial engine aircraft was thirty years earlier. Those were North American T-28s out of Naval Air Station Whiting Field north of Pensacola, Florida. The venerable T-28

Trojans were being replaced by another Beechcraft product, the T-34Cs, and new incoming flight students were being shunted to the new turboprop. Upon arriving at Pensacola for flight school, Hunter politicked to go to the last operational T-28 training squadron, even though it was reportedly "closed" for new students.

A friendly racquetball match with the student control officer in charge of squadron assignments proved too much for the senior naval aviator, and the last T-28 flight student to enter the program was Second Lieutenant Duncan Hunter, USMC.

The trick to doing well and flying the T-28 was; first of all, don't blow off the exhaust stacks during engine start. Second of all, don't blow off the exhaust stacks if it didn't start the first time.

The Staggerwing was still in the hangar when Hunter rotated the big Hamilton Standard propeller through several times to break the seal of any oil that might have drained and been trapped in the lower cylinders since it was last flown. He settled into the left seat behind the only set of rudder pedals. Without a checklist, he reached back into his prodigious memory and found the ancient cockpit similar to the old T-28. He turned the fuel selector to the main tank, cracked the throttle open, and wobbled the hand pump exactly five times to prime the engine.

He switched on the *MASTER*, set magnetos to *BOTH*, and the big radial fired immediately to life. With a careful hand on the throttle, he managed to avoid blowing an exhaust stack on the huge nine-cylinder radial.

In the confines of the hangar, the sound was deafening, and Hunter shouted, "Yeah!" as he adjusted the throttle and checked the manifold pressure.

The structure filled with white, oily smoke and deafening noise from the engine exhaust. Once the smoke cleared, he programmed the throttle to get the plane moving from the hangar, flipped on the landing light, caged the gyro, and checked that the flight controls were free and unobstructed. He taxied around the Gulfstream.

I forgot how loud these things can be.

Hunter applied power smoothly to thirty-seven inches manifold pressure, which provided 2,300 RPM, enough to get airborne. Sixty seconds later, he retarded the prop to 2,200 RPM and tried to raise the landing gear, but he couldn't find the handle. He didn't know much about Staggerwings and without an obvious landing gear handle, he resolved that it might have fixed gear. He smiled at himself for not noticing whether it was a fixed-gear model or retractable, as he turned the aircraft north toward the sea.

He settled into the flying rhythm of an airplane he never flew before. The excitement of not killing himself during takeoff and learning a new airplane, especially one as rare and iconic as the Staggerwing, distracted him for a while, but he quickly settled down. In his rush to get off the ground as fast as possible, he bypassed all the normal checklist items and didn't preflight the aircraft. He had no technical knowledge of the Staggerwing and wouldn't have known where to check the oil level or where to add a quart if needed. He gambled his life that the owner of the Beechcraft was as diligent about maintaining his airplane as Hunter was with his. When he leveled off at 3,000 feet, it appeared the gamble paid off. All the engine instruments read in their operating ranges.

Hunter felt around the sides of the seat for the seat belt parts and snapped them in place. Once he was feet wet, he removed his handheld radio from his LPU and paused to consider his words, but the words didn't form in his mind or spill from his lips. The strain of the previous hour on the ground released a short, uncontrolled burst of tears and tremors. Salty drops spilled over his cheeks. He had survived and escaped. He expected such a reaction. A man could go only so long under great stress before it released, whether he was ready or not.

His last big stressful flight had been many years earlier, flying TA-4Js out of Kingsville, Texas, when an oil line broke and sprayed hot, black fluid all over the underside of his jet. He nursed the jet back to the field sixty miles away, his instructor following in close formation, ready to assist in case Hunter had to eject. Six miles from the field, the vibration from the engine trying to shake itself apart was so severe,

Hunter couldn't read the instrument panel.

At three miles, his instructor on his wing realized his student had to eject, because the jet started trailing white smoke. Hunter lowered the gear and arresting hook and shut down the engine as he crossed the runway threshold to take the short-field arrestment. His squadron mates called him a hero for his coolness and professionalism for such a long-duration emergency and for bringing the jet back to base in one piece.

When it came time to write up the discrepancy; he didn't have to worry anymore. His hands shook so severely, he couldn't hold a pen.

Hunter was safe and back in his element, flying an airplane. Embarrassed at being so emotional, he took some deep breaths, trying to refocus on the task at hand. He wasn't finished yet.

With the controls trimmed nicely for straight and level flight, and the engine running smoothly and coolly, he composed himself and initiated distress procedures. He smiled at the clarity of the radio screen. His 20/20 eyesight was back. He selected the emergency frequency in his AN/PRQ-7 handheld and keyed the microphone.

"Navy Control, Red Bull four one, over."

The response was immediate. "Red Bull four one, Navy Control. Go ahead."

"Good evening, Navy Control. Red Bull four one is feet wet at 3,000 heading 045. Request a vector and a line to your air boss or skipper, over."

"Red Bull four one, squawk 0528. Standby on your request."

"Navy Control, Red Bull four one, unable to squawk."

"Roger Red Bull four one. Turn thirty degrees north for ident. Altimeter two niner niner niner."

"Roger, Navy Control. Thirty degrees north for ident. Niner niner."

"Red Bull four one, radar contact, 120 miles. Turn 055, maintain this freq."

"Roger, Navy Control. Heading 055."

Hunter relaxed and scanned the instruments. Everything inside the Staggerwing was running smoothly. It was a beautiful night for flying.

There were no thermals, just smooth, cool air. He continually trimmed the controls and was impressed with the plane's flight characteristics, not unlike the YO-3A.

As he waited for the *Eisenhower's* captain or air boss to come to the radio, he practiced what he would say. *Such a deal I have for you. You don't have to provide any Search and Rescue, but could you let me land aboard your nice, big carrier. Oh, and by the way, I'm pretty sure I've been exposed to anthrax. Will that make a difference?*

"Red Bull four one, Ramrod." The ship's captain clearly wasn't impressed with the late night, early morning antics of some dumbass Agency pilot.

Hunter paused for a moment and shook his head once. There was something familiar in the radio voice. "Ramrod, Red Bull four one. Sir, permission to come aboard. I have an emergency."

Seconds ticked away. The pause in the radio transmission meant massive amounts of trouble. Hunter envisioned the Navy captain erupting with a fount of spittle and invective.

Instead, what Hunter heard was, "Maverick? Sarge."

Hunter's jaw dropped. After two seconds, he recovered his composure enough to say, "My God. Sarge! Congratulations, Sir. I had no idea."

"Well, you never write, but neither do I. What's going on, Mav?" Captain Mike Zacker, call sign "Sarge," more for his earthy, bucolic looks than a reflection of the time he spent in the enlisted ranks, was one of Duncan's classmates at the Naval War College, class of 2003. Zacker was an F-18 pilot, drove a very rare red BMW M6, and collected other red-hot Beemers. When Hunter wasn't playing racquetball tournaments or racing his Corvette on weekends, he and Sarge drove all over New England searching for nice, collectable M-series Beemers.

"Sir, I can tell you some of it when I see you."

"Why not? It's been a hell of a night. Reopening flight ops means you'll have to buy a boatload of beer for about a thousand sailors. If you can handle that, then permission granted."

"Thank you, Sir. Sarge, be advised I think I've been exposed to anthrax. I haven't had the regimen but took some cipro I carry for emergencies. Over."

"Mav...."

"Sarge, I was thinking as soon as I land, I'd push this plane over the side and strip on the fantail. I was hoping a decon team could scrub me down. Maybe the doc can shoot me up with antibiotics."

"I'll be there with a wire brush, a *long* wire brush. I'll see you soon, Mav. Be safe, and I'll turn you back over to approach. What are you flying?"

"Would you believe a beautiful Beech Staggerwing?"

"I never know what to expect with you. I suppose you're still at it?"

"Yes, Sir. Sarge, you can call Langley Command Center and tell them you have *Noble Savage,* emergency code *Diablo.*"

Yawning into the microphone, Sarge said, "Great. Do not, I repeat, do not push that airplane into the sea. I'll take care of it."

"Aye, aye, Captain. Thank you, Sarge. Looking forward to seeing you, Sir."

Hunter set the handheld radio down in the seat and broke into a broad grin. "Hunter, if ever there was a doubt, that just proves you *are* the luckiest shit on the planet."

CHAPTER SIXTY-FIVE

0200 September 26, 2012
Somewhere over the Atlantic

The aide for the Director of Central Intelligence unplugged the satellite phone from the airplane's RJ-11 connection jack. Data transferred from the SATPHONE to the Director's electronic notebook was complete. He exhaled forcefully. The FLASH message and *Noble Savage* status report changed the dynamic of the download.

Two hours earlier, the Command Center forwarded the information that *Noble Savage* went missing from radar scopes, likely shot down in Algeria. Dr. Bruce Rothwell went to his private suite at the rear of the Agency's Gulfstream G-550. As he got into bed, he said, "I won't lose any sleep over that great loss."

The aide knocked on the suite door an hour later. There was a new download and new dispatch. Rothwell awoke to learn the U.S. Embassy Algiers had been evacuated by U.S. Navy helicopters, and the acting COS was the only injured. Turning off the electronic notebook, he pulled the blanket over his shoulder before returning to sleep and muttered, "Now *that* wasn't supposed to happen."

An hour later, Rothwell barked at his aide when the man again rapped on the private suite's door. "This better be important!"

The aide rolled his eyes, wondering if the DCI was serious or just cranky. The door flew open. The aide handed him the notebook, and the door slammed shut in his face.

Rothwell powered up the notebook and scanned the new FLASH dispatches. Two caught his attention. Nazy Cunningham was en route to the Naval Hospital in Italy for surgery, and Duncan Hunter had reported in and activated the emergency code.

As the information sank in, Bruce Rothwell nearly dropped the small computer tablet. He exhaled his disappointment, "Fuck me." He turned over and tried to sleep, but there would be no more sleep that night.

CHAPTER SIXTY-SIX

0200 September 26, 2012
U.S.S. Dwight D. Eisenhower
Mediterranean Sea

Insomnia was rampant in the Snake Pit. The excitement of evacuating from Algiers was traumatic for some of the embassy staff, while others weren't affected. Groups of State Department men, in twos and threes, huddled together in the dull red light to check on and reassure each other. Some were weepy and maudlin, while others would need therapy. On the other side of the berthing area, all ten U.S. Marine Security Guards were fast asleep and snoring.

Bill McGee and Demetrius Eastwood couldn't sleep for other reasons. When McGee quietly suggested they try to find Officer Country and get coffee at the Officer's Mess, Eastwood gave the old SEAL a thumbs-up to avoid waking anyone nearby.

Eastwood had never been aboard an aircraft carrier when he was on active duty. As a correspondent, he had visited every carrier in the Navy. McGee's experience was dated, but he remembered enough to ask the first person they met for directions. After climbing several ladders and passing through dozens of hatches, the crusty old "greybeards" wandered the halls of the gigantic ship before passing under the sign "Officer Country" and entered the O-Mess. Twenty officers in flight suits and khakis looked up at the two gray-headed retirees in civies who entered their Mess.

Pandemonium replaced the quiet in the room, as many patrons recognized the war correspondent and former Presidential candidate. Shouts of "Colonel Eastwood!" and "Ooh-rah," the Marine Corps' unique greeting, reverberated around the room, as men and women gathered to meet and greet the former Marine officer. Eastwood basked in the spontaneous adulation, while McGee crossed his arms, grinned, and enjoyed the show. Men and women elbowed their way in to shake Eastwood's hand.

As Bill headed toward the twin aluminum towers filled with coffee, Eastwood quickly turned the tables. "Ladies and Gentlemen, thank you for that welcome. You're great Americans and patriots, and you can't know how proud I am of you. I'm no hero, though, but that man with the coffee cup is Captain Bill McGee. He's a true American hero. You may not know it, but he's the most-decorated SEAL ever to wear the uniform."

The Officer's Mess went stone-cold silent, as the men and women of the U.S.S *Eisenhower* left Eastwood and lined up to shake the other man's hand. Where the officers had been boisterous and rowdy with Eastwood, they were reverent and respectful in the presence of Captain Bill McGee, the quiet Navy icon largely unknown outside Special Operations Command. It was Eastwood's turn to cross his arms, grin, enjoy the show, and wish once again he had a video camera. Then he remembered he couldn't photograph McGee.

The quiet of the Mess was shattered when the *Eisenhower's* Captain stormed through the door and found a covey of his officers surrounding a big, African American man who had his back to him. The junior officers who saw the Captain enter the Mess froze as if caught passing cheat sheets during finals.

Captain Mike Zacker would never become accustomed to his sailors stopping all activity when he entered a room—especially the Mess—but when he was a junior officer, he did the same thing. It was a natural response, but something interesting was going on in Officer Country, and he wanted to find out what the hell it was.

His gaze fell on the lone man observing the horde and instantly recognized him from his TV shows as Lieutenant Colonel Demetrius Eastwood. As the Captain came to grips with having the retired Marine and sometime war correspondent on his ship, his eyes went to the big man who slowly turned to face him.

Holy shit! Captain Zacker thought. *That's Bill McGee ... Captain*

Bill McGee from SEAL Team Six. My Naval War College class president. How come no one told me these two were on the evacuation helicopters? Someone's going to pay!

The eagles on Captain Zacker's collars and the gold wings on his chest sparkled in the overhead lights as he walked up to McGee and the young officers and offered his hand deferentially. "Captain McGee, welcome aboard, Sir."

The junior officers surrounding McGee knew the party was over and dispersed to their tables or left the Mess.

McGee allowed the Captain to come to him. He vaguely recognized him but couldn't place him. They probably met at the Naval War College. Hundreds of students passed through Newport, and he could never meet or remember them all. His eyes went to the man's name tag.

"Thank you, Sir," McGee said. "You have a great ship and some fine officers."

"Thank you, Bill. Newport; class of 2003."

"That's exactly right. You've done well. Congratulations. Not anyone gets to drive one of these."

Eastwood joined the two sailors and exchanged salutations and handshakes. The addition of the Marine changed the dynamic of the conversation, and it returned to business.

Captain Zacker asked, "I take it you and Colonel Eastwood came aboard on the helos?"

"Yes, Sir."

"Where do they have you berthed? Please tell me you're not in the Snake Pit."

The retired officers grinned and laughed softly. After rolling his eyes, Zacker apologized profusely.

"Mike, absolutely no factor," McGee said. "I could've said something."

"Bill, it's my fault. I should have been on deck to welcome everyone, but I had an Ambassador to deal with. As you probably know, they require special handling. I put him to bed in one of the command suites. We notified the State Department he was safely aboard. As for you...we'll get you—both of you—into something better ASAP."

"Really no factor, Sir," Eastwood said. "It's late, and everyone probably should be in bed."

"Well, I'm just getting started." Zacker chuckled. "It must be Newport Reunion Days or something."

McGee and Eastwood didn't understand, and it showed on their faces.

Zacker took a deep breath. "Bill, I don't know if you remember Duncan Hunter from the War College, but he's coming aboard in about an hour."

Eastwood and McGee's demeanor changed dramatically. They quickly exchanged glances, concern showing on their faces. The sudden change in their expressions was remarkable.

Zacker thought their reaction was highly unusual and wondered, *Whiskey Tango Foxtrot, over?*

"The woman medevaced in the Greyhound was Hunter's fiancée," Bill said seriously. "It's been a hell of a night."

"Holy shit. Oh, Man, that's incredible. Does he know?" Captain Zacker asked. "Do I want to know what the hell happened back there in Algeria?"

McGee shook his head to both questions and frowned.

Eastwood waited for the two captains to quit talking and stop waving their arms with painful thoughts. "Sir, excuse me, what do you mean, he's coming aboard in an hour?"

Captain Zacker appreciated the diversion. Pointing to a table, he spoke first to McGee. "You remember everyone thought Duncan was CIA? Even our lone CIA student thought he was, but no one could find out anything on him.

"I just came from Approach Control. Duncan just radioed the ship on a special freq and asked to speak to me. I recognized his voice when he popped a program name and slapped a CIA emergency code word on my ass. It went all the way to the White house. I'm to assist in whatever he needs. He needs to come aboard, so...."

"CIA?" Eastwood asked.

Zacker's mind raced. "Close hold. I have no idea what's going on, but I'm very interested. Hunter claims to be flying a Beech Staggerwing."

"What's that?" McGee asked.

"One of the most-beautiful old aircraft every produced. It was probably the first private or corporate aircraft for business executives. It's a biplane built in the early-to-late forties. The bottom wing is forward, and the upper wing is aft a bit. There's more."

Eastwood's mind churned. "More?"

"That lad's definitely high maintenance. He said he was exposed to anthrax."

"*What?*" Eastwood and McGee asked simultaneously.

Zacker pinched his lips and nodded.

"Let me get this straight," Eastwood said. "You're about to have a retired Marine fighter pilot land a 1940-ish biplane on your ship. He's CIA, has anthrax, and you two know him from the Naval War College?"

"When he wasn't playing racquetball on weekends, he and I drove all over New England looking for rare BMWs," Zacker said.

"My family and I watched him play racquetball tournaments," Bill said. "He's really good. My girls took up the sport because of him." He left out the part where Duncan forced the charlatan in the White House to resign and interrogated Osama bin Laden. "And, he's going to marry the Algerian Embassy's Chief of Station."

Eastwood offered, "I never met him, but I've heard more about him in a few short hours than anyone else I know. Captain Zacker, I'd love to be able to film the Staggerwing landing on your ship, Sir, if that's possible."

"For the moment I don't see any problems. It might not be good to take his picture, though. The Agency, the White House, and the SecDef would have me canned if it ever got out I allowed you to photograph a spook at work."

The comment reminded Eastwood of a similar concern. He leaned closer to McGee. "Bill, I wouldn't let my cameraman film you when you carried Nazy aboard the helicopter."

A serious smile came over the old warrior's face. "I appreciate that."

"You carried her aboard?" Zacker asked. "Oh, God. Now I *have* to know what happened—all of it. Did you use some of that SEAL shit to kill some bad guys? Please tell me you killed dozens of terrorist shitheads and saved the damsel in distress."

McGee nodded painfully. "I had some help."

"I was the lookout and gave them a boost over the gate," Eastwood offered.

"All I do all day is herd kittens. God bless you, Gentlemen."

McGee wrestled with the idea of telling Zacker what he did for the CIA. His NDA with the Agency came to mind and he canceled that idea. There really wasn't anything the captain of the ship could do.

Captain Zacker pushed away from the table and walked to a wall phone to set up the early morning flight operations for the unusual recovery and to awaken medical personnel so they could decontaminate Hunter and pump him full of antibiotics.

Eastwood trailed the Captain with visions of filming a WWII-era biplane landing on one of the Navy's newest aircraft carriers.

McGee, alone in the Mess, sat with his thoughts and nursed his coffee, wondering what the hell he would tell Duncan.

CHAPTER SIXTY-SEVEN

0300 September 26, 2012
U.S.S. Dwight D. Eisenhower
Mediterranean Sea

It could have been mistaken for a dim, steady, fixed star low on the horizon. What started as a tiny light over the sea slowly grew in intensity. To the uninitiated, the single star in the night sky seemed to wander left and right, a function of the eyes' natural pursuit movement, but it was actually steady and growing brighter each second.

As the point of light grew, fifty people crowded the different levels of the Island, waiting in anticipation, their heads fixed toward the fantail. Word spread through the sleeping ship that something that hadn't happened in over seventy years on an American aircraft carrier, was about to make history.

Radar approach control helped guide the pilot through position reports. He was on glide scope and on course. Updates were provided every three seconds. The "meatball," the carrier's Fresnel lens assembly, was also illuminated, helping the pilot gauge his position on the glide scope. Hunter was familiar with the process with over a hundred night "traps" in his old F-4.

The aircraft's radial engine rumbled over the sea, the ancient sound conjuring images of black-and-white films of open-cockpit aircraft crashing while attempting to land on WWII-era carriers. Nearly every observer sucked air as the diminutive, strange-shaped airplane suddenly came into view, punching through the flight deck's dull red flood lights. It was a little higher and slower than expected, but it was reasonably centered over the landing area. The growing crowd, anticipating the worst, elbowed themselves into position for a better finish-line view of the impending carnage.

A ghost from the past roared in slow motion from the fog of night. The dark airplane steadily descended over the landing area, past the number one and two wires. Silence and stillness reigned on the Island, as the pilot struggled to keep the dark Beechcraft Staggerwing level as it steadily flew low over the last two arresting cables. The pilot seemed to chop the throttle as the main landing-gear wheels touched down just past the number-four cable, perfectly centered on the centerline.

After rolling twenty feet, the tail wheel touched down, also on the centerline, and the aircraft stopped, as the propeller wound down and quit moving. The crowd held their breath until the vintage airplane stopped, then they erupted in earsplitting approval, jumping up and down, clapping and pumping their fists.

Captain Zacker exhaled and shook his head. *Amazing job Hunter.*

Four blue shirt aircraft handlers, carrying several tie-down chains, converged on the aircraft at a dead run, as a man in a black flight suit stepped from the strange-looking biplane and walked quickly to the aft of the ship. Six more blue shirts raced to the airplane and pulled or pushed it off the flight deck onto the nearest elevator. Blue shirts with chains lashed it down. The aircraft disappeared from view, as Duncan Hunter stripped off his boots and flight suit and tossed them off the back of the ship.

Six people in full decontamination suits—clear face masks, rubber boots, and gloves, and plastic-coated overalls—waddled onto the fantail, slowly chasing the man until they cornered him on a small patch of flight deck at the edge of the flattop. Two of the amorphous shapes lugged man-portable M13 decontaminating units filled with an astringent decontamination solution. Two decon technicians carried long-handled brushes like samurai swords. One decon tech dragged a water hose, and another carried several towels, a flight suit, boots, and socks from ship's stores.

Duncan was freezing as he stood naked in the thirty-five knot wind. As one tech hosed him down with decontamination solution, another scrubbed every inch of his body with the yard-long brush. When the bristles flayed his skin, Hunter felt decon solution penetrating every pore. His skin burned after each pass of the brush. Rubber gloves moved his genitals to scrub the crack between his legs. Hunter gritted his teeth not just against the assault on his flesh, but his core temperature was dropping rapidly as wind raced down the flight deck, over his body, and out to sea.

They're saving your life, Hunter! Buck up. It'll soon be over. Take it like a man!

After five minutes of spraying and scrubbing, the decon technician with the hose rinsed Hunter from head to toe. Thinking he was done, Hunter reached for a towel, but another member of the decon team shook it's head. The other man-portable decon unit sprayed more green fluid all over Hunter, as well as 007's data plate, a speed loader, and the Colt Python in his hands.

Apply, rinse, repeat, Hunter thought, understanding the drill. He shook like a paint shaker at a hardware store.

He turned around again, as the two technicians with the brushes scrubbed his skin, his cobblestone abs, his ass, and his feet. They tapped his thighs, forcing him to spread his legs again, so they could decontaminate hard-to-reach areas. Hunter squealed like a girl through his chattering, grinding teeth, but the wind carried the sound off the back of the ship.

After all four technicians gave him thumbs-up, the tech with the hose conducted a final rinse, and Hunter was motioned to step forward. When one technician finally offered a towel, a hypothermic Hunter stiffly moved toward the neon-green shape and accepted it. As he dried his face and chest for the first time, he noticed the face behind the transparent faceplate was a very young woman. He immediately tried to cover his nakedness with the towel as he scanned the other faceplates only to find the entire team was female, and all were smiling.

When one of the decon techs finally offered him a flight suit, he graciously accepted it and turned his back to them, slipping his legs in first, then his arms, before slowly zipping it from crotch to chin. The show was over. The seven people turned and walked briskly back to the Island three hundred feet away.

With arms crossed, Captain Mike Zacker waited outside the main flight deck hatch of the Island for the crew and their decontaminated subject to approach. The decon crew removed their hoods and gloves, keeping pace with the barefoot man in the flight suit, who was almost jogging. Duncan wanted to get out of the wind and stop his teeth from chattering. Captain Zacker sensed Hunter was in no mood for jocularity, just self-preservation. Though he'd just been decontaminated, he wasn't out of the woods yet.

As Hunter came within ten feet, he stopped and saluted. "P—P—P—Permishn ta c—c—c—come aboard, Sir?"

"Granted, Maverick. Let's get you down to sickbay."

"Tha…Tha…Thank you, Sir. You are most…most…most gracious." He turned to the decon team as they entered the Island. "Ladies, I very much…much appreciate your help in saving my…my life. That probably wasn't easy for any of us, and I…I…I thank you for your service and your…your professionalism. I'm not sure ... I could have done ... what you did and ... keep a straight face. I hope the experience doesn't ... doesn't give you nightmares."

"It was our pleasure, Sir," one woman said.

All the women smiled at him.

Hunter hurried to slip his bare feet into the new boots. Before he could lace them up, Captain Zacker's impatience was on full display. He frowned and bellowed, "Gangway!" All the onlookers stepped aside.

Hunter nodded and took his cue to follow Zacker and start moving toward sickbay. Once inside the Island, a flight surgeon and a corpsman joined the men.

"Doc, is he contagious?" the Captain asked.

"Skipper, if he's been exposed to anthrax, he's not contagious. He might get pneumonia, but he isn't contagious."

"I don't know. Maybe he needs another decon shower on the fantail. I might be taking a hell of a risk." Zacker's impish grin gave Hunter time for a retort.

"I'd rather be keelhauled than go through that again," Hunter said. "I can't believe you sent those pretty young things out there to scrub down an old man. That has to be some form of sexual harassment."

"I don't know ... they were all volunteers and they did a good job. It was a nice touch. You're very welcome." Zacker turned and winked at the man wearing a light-green lab coat and a stethoscope around his neck.

They went down four sets of ladders with Captain Zacker leading the way to sickbay and opening the door for Hunter, who carried his revolver. The flight doctor behind them directed Hunter to a table.

"Is that thing loaded?" Captain Zacker asked.

All medical personnel, suddenly aware their patient was armed, watched in concern as he waved the gun around with the barrel toward the ceiling.

Hunter opened the cylinder and ejected six cartridges in his lap before handing the Captain the gun. The others noticed the bullets were hollow-point ammunition.

"What's the chance I could get someone to clean this before it starts rusting?" Hunter asked.

"Standby." Captain Zacker went to a phone attached to the bulkhead wall and barked instructions into it.

The doctor asked Hunter dozens of questions and asked him to remove his flight suit. He probed his chest with the Littmann's as a phlebotomist jabbed a needle into Hunter's arm to draw blood. Another corpsman placed a sphygmomanometer on his other arm and squeezed the orange bulb, pumping the cuff to check Hunter's blood pressure.

A sailor in a blue uniform barged into sickbay, saw the Captain, and immediately came to attention. "Someone need a gun cleaned, Sir?" After the Captain nodded, the sailor took the Colt Python and speed loader and raced away.

Duncan related that he believed he was exposed to anthrax, and he wasn't on an anthrax-vaccine regimen. He didn't say how he knew or why he suspected he'd been exposed other than an odorless white powder probably transferred to his flight suit. He added that he took two Ciprofloxacin tablets.

The corpsmen on either side of Hunter listened intently. For the first time, they understood their patient may have been exposed to deadly spores and were silently grateful they were immunized. Knowing that the man landed on the carrier in the middle of the night, in an ancient biplane, had to be decontaminated on the fantail, and carried a big black revolver made it the weirdest evening they could remember.

When Captain Zacker returned, he demanded a prognosis.

"I'd like to give him some fluoroquinolone antibiotics and put him on a *Ciprofloxacin* regimen. We'll check his blood, but I think he'll be fine. We'll watch him."

"He's not contagious?"

"No, Sir. Nothing could have survived what you just did to him."

"Thanks, Doc." He added a conspiratorial grin and sly wink.

"Thanks, Doc, and thank you, Corpsmen," Hunter said, "for your expert work and professionalism." When he offered his hand, all three men shook it without hesitation.

"Put your boots on, and we'll get coffee," Captain Zacker said. "I've got a surprise for you."

"I can hardly wait, Sir."

The medical staff watched in awe as the man who claimed to have been exposed to anthrax nonchalantly pulled on his socks and boots with a smile. There was something unique about him, and no one knew why. It was inconceivable to them that anyone could arrive at three AM without being concerned about his health, then have the Skipper ready to do anything for him. The unnamed pilot was polite and deferential even when shivering.

He had to be someone special to be treated with such familiarity by the Captain. No normal person would ever be shot full of antibiotics as if it were a flu shot, then be escorted by the Captain to get a cup of joe.

As Hunter graciously thanked the doctor and corpsmen again, he hurried after Captain Zacker, leaving the medical men staring at each other, searching for the answers to several bizarre, unasked questions.

Finally, one corpsman asked, "What the hell was that all about?"

The doctor who treated Hunter rubbed his eyes and yawned. "Sometimes, it's best just to nod, do your job, and hit the rack. Let's get out of here. We can still get a few hours' sleep before we have to be back."

The meeting in the Officer's Country Mess was a mare's nest of emotions. Duncan was astounded to find Bill McGee and Demetrius Eastwood on an aircraft carrier in the middle of the Med, and his face lit with recognition and surprise.

Bill dreaded seeing Hunter, knowing he was bearing bad news about Nazy. He couldn't muster enough of a smile to hide his emotions. Hunter, expecting happiness, saw instead severe conflict and concern.

Eastwood, initially impressed by the obviously athletic man in the flight suit, felt his curiosity boil over when he finally met the quietly famous Marine pilot. "What's a Marine like you doing in a place like this?"

Captain Zacker wanted to know how in hell Hunter was connected to the CIA and have the White House as top cover. He was fearful of his ship, and, by extension, his career. He allowed the men to finish their greetings and salutations before he stopped them and demanded answers.

Captain Zacker entered the Mess and snatched the telephone on the wall to growl orders into the receiver in his command voice. Hunter stopped in front of the powerfully built retired SEAL and former Marine infantry officer and shook their hands. Words failed him, though, because he saw dread in his friend's eyes.

McGee motioned Hunter to a seat across the table from him. "Duncan, I have to tell you about Nazy."

The words crushed him for a moment. His voice suddenly felt hoarse. The Mess was silent, and his voice reverberated in the enclosed space. "What about Nazy?"

Bill McGee explained but left out the details of what happened when she was held by her tormentors. He explained the explosion at the embassy, touched on her kidnapping, and glossed over the rescue. He finished with the evacuation of the embassy and that Nazy was taken by plane to NAS Sigonella for surgery.

"I believe she'll be OK," McGee finished.

Hunter sat in disbelief, struggling to comprehend a new set of horrors and the thought of a life without Nazy. He'd been through an emotional roller-coaster all night. Tears filled his eyes, as Eastwood compassionately patted his back. McGee hung his head.

Hunter looked at McGee, who finally raised his head. "You rescued her, didn't you?"

"I did." McGee fought his emotions. "She'll be OK. I promise." He hoped it was a promise he'd be able to keep.

Hunter leaned across the table to shake the big man's hand. Eastwood watched in awe as the two men communicated with their eyes their admiration and respect for each other. What could have been an outburst filled with anger, frustration, and pounding of fists on the table was instead marked by quiet, subtle turbulence, like a rushing subterranean river crashing into boulders. There might be intense action and deafening roaring underneath, but it was calm, cool, and collected on the surface.

Eastwood saw that while in combat in Vietnam. The two men had gone through something that fused them together as Brothers. How a Navy SEAL and an old Marine fighter pilot could ever encounter such a life-threatening situation was beyond his imagination.

With the phone receiver still glued to his ear, Captain Zacker curiously watched Hunter and McGee's intense, spontaneous interaction. He was too preoccupied with running his ship and helping the men at the table to reflect on anything else. Once he received the requested information, he gave a few more commands and waited for the duty officer at the other end of the phone line to quit quaking in his boots.

"Thank you, Sir. I don't know how I'll ever repay you," Duncan said.

"That bill was paid a long time ago, Apex."

Duncan smiled and gritted his teeth at the old name.

"Apex?" Captain Zacker walked to the coffee towers after ending his call. He drew a large cup of coffee and moved toward the others, smiling like a conquering hero.

"All good news, Gentlemen," he announced. "You, too, *Apex*. Your future bride is out of surgery and resting. She'll be fine and will make a full recovery." He pulled out a chair and sat down.

"It looks like the CIA already sent a jet to take her back to Washington when she's ready to travel. What's with this Apex bullshit? You have another call sign? What's this, your CIA call sign?" He had a bemused grin.

McGee raised his fist across the table, and Hunter bumped it with his. They held their fists in position, and the other two men raised fists, too. Momentarily, all four fists touched with energy and hope.

"Thank you, Gents," Hunter said. "Thank you for everything you did for Nazy and me."

Zacker nodded then turned to Hunter and spat, "You're very welcome, *Maverick*. You land a biplane on my ship. I have to decon your ass. Now will someone please tell me what the fuck is going on?" Zacker looked around the table, his eyes demanded answers.

"I was lucky," Hunter said. "It's like riding a bike in the old days. It scared the shit out of me. No LSO, no graded pass. I thought it was OK."

"OK? Seriously? It was barely passable. You landed past the four-wire! *That's a no grade!*" Zacker's smile showed the others he was lying. "But since you didn't have a tailhook, I'd give you a 'fair' at best." Eastwood and McGee were confused but Hunter got the inside joke of the carrier pilot's grading system.

McGee and Eastwood refrained from asking what the two carrier pilots were talking about. Their reluctance to speak was noticed and Captain Zacker wondered if it came from Eastwood's presence and not from the carrier pilot's obscure vernacular.

"Sarge, what will you do with the airplane?" Hunter asked.

"Keep it. Decon it and crane it off. Spoils of war or some BS like that," Zacker said. "Don't avoid the question, *Maverick*."

"I really wanted to film that decon operation," Eastwood said. "It was a thing of beauty." He raised his cup and smiled.

Bill McGee started nodding until his whole body moved. He looked around the Mess to ensure they were alone. "Mike, I watched Duncan beat a professional racquetball player. After a year of watching him in all the intramural sports, I said he was at the top of the athletic food chain and was deadly with a racquet. I learned our friend here was the Military Male Athlete of the Year many moons ago. He's an apex predator. It's my little pet name for a friend who could have, and should have, been a SEAL."

Hunter and McGee smiled at each other as only old friends do. Zacker shook his head in disbelief that no one was going to answer his question. Eastwood remained amused at the conversation and the interaction of the three friends.

McGee decided it was time to tell his story, at least as much as he dared. He instantly changed the subject, immediately getting everyone's attention. "OK. This can't leave this room."

The men questioned each other with their eyes. It was totally quiet in the Mess. The husky radio-announcer voice coming from the big man commanded immediate attention.

"What happened, Bullfrog?" Hunter asked, breaking the silence.

"Long story. The short version is I was contracted to help Langley find and buy MANPADS from a group of Libyans. I don't know if they were part of Gaddafi's stash or what. We made our contacts and were shown the stockpile. There were hundreds of anti-aircraft missiles in a huge underground bunker. My handlers made an offer.

"I know where they are, but then the Ambassador was killed, and every gringo had to evacuate from Benghazi. I have no idea if those missiles are still there, but I'd stake my reputation and clearances that they are. No doubt they'll go to the highest bidder.

"When we arrived in Tripoli, I was reassigned to provide additional embassy security in Algiers. There was some hope we'd return and get those missiles out of there, but the Agency boys weren't going back until things settled down in Libya. The rest of my team when to Tunis, then they were evacuated, too."

Hunter, Zacker, and Eastwood were dumbfounded. Suddenly, Eastwood thought the residual mayhem they encountered with the death of the Ambassador in Benghazi was somehow related or attributed to the CIA's attempt to purchase those shoulder-launched missiles. Only the purblind could ignore that some pieces of the puzzle were being held by the four men sitting at that table.

"I'm unaware of anything dealing with MANPADS," Eastwood said. "We filmed suspected al-Qaeda and Muslim Brotherhood turds spilling out of mosques in advance of the attacks on the embassies in Tripoli, Tunis, and Algiers. I don't know how else to describe it other than they were somehow connected into a network operation of sorts. Groups of protesters fronted scumbags with AKs and RPGs.

"Before we discovered what was going on, I planned to set up for a nightly broadcast immediately in front of the embassy, just outside the gates, hoping to film Libyans and Tunisians and Algerians shouting, 'Death to America,' or *'Allah akbar,'* or some such crap. This wasn't my first rodeo, and I knew that the rhetorical hostility wasn't normally directed at American journalists personally. It was always for show.

"It's the Islamic rage boy turning on fake outrage while foaming at the mouth and screaming into a camera who turned it into an art form. I wanted to show how much phoniness there was behind the protests. You'll never see that story in the liberal news services. They'll show the Islamic rage boy in a continuous loop and nothing else.

"With those guns and RPGs, though, it was clear we were dealing with a new paradigm."

"New sheriff in town," Hunter said. "The Muslim Brotherhood has stepped up their game." He considered what the other Marine said. Something triggered a memory, but he would wait for his turn.

"With the meteoric rise of the Muslim Brotherhood after Mubarak's fall," Eastwood continued, "attacks on Western reporters increased a hundredfold in Cairo. As you know, some women reporters were raped in Tahrir Square, surrounding by thousands of chanting, raging Muslim men waiting their turn."

"Only brain-dead, left-leaning news organizations would be so...so totally clueless, fucking incompetent, and worthless to send women into the heart of a widespread Muslim protest," offered McGee.

Zacker was amused by Hunter's comment and McGee's outburst. However, when Eastwood called it a "network operation of sorts," McGee noticed. The previous year, when he and Hunter tracked down a sniper who was killing former and active-duty SEALs after Osama bin Laden's death, the forensic evidence suggested the sniper received his targeting information from a network of mosques in the United States. McGee couldn't see a direct link, but the hint of a presumed network bothered him. Was it unusual or to be expected? He began searching his memory for a distant thread that held a related piece of the puzzle.

Hunter thought about Nazy and what he heard. The three men looked at him, waiting for his confession. They would wait a long time. He was still tied to an Agency NDA, and the *Noble Savage* program was an Executive Special Access Program not to be disclosed or shared —ever. Rank-and-file CIA officers rarely knew of the existence of an E-SAP. Disclosure meant firing and jail time—if he wasn't killed and his body sent through an Agency disintegrator.

He checked the Mess, left and right, for any other person in the facility and found he was alone with his friends. He drummed his fingers, a new nervous habit, as his mind raced over what he might be able to share. The Mess wasn't a SCIF but it would have to do. Taking a deep breath, he said, "I was shot down by a *Stinger.*"

The electricity around the table sizzled.

Three shocked men leaned forward, scarcely believing what they heard. Captain Zacker pointed an accusing finger at Hunter and said, "You really *are* CIA!"

"Not really. Just a contractor."

"A contractor with access to the White House? Bullshit!"

Eastwood's face wrinkled in confusion. "How were you shot down if you flew aboard a carrier?"

"Gentlemen, it's a long story, one I probably can't fully share." He looked at Eastwood. "I was in another airplane. I took the Staggerwing off the guy who shot me."

"Ah…what kind of…?"

"I can't say any more than that. However, what I can say is this. I think all of this is somehow related, but there are still some missing pieces." He concentrated on drawing links and connections but still came up with dead ends. *Were anti-aircraft missiles in Libya and Algeria a link or a coincidence? Could it be the same guy?*

"Duncan," McGee asked, "what about that network of mosques? You're the one who told me that."

"What are you talking about, Maverick?" Captain Zacker asked, preferring to use his Marine Corps call sign.

Hunter marshaled his thoughts, trying to screen what he could say from what he should. *Screw it. These are my friends.* "Yeah, that's right. There weren't just four aircraft and nineteen hijackers for 9/11. There were over sixty people involved, a handful of who were pre-board screeners. They facilitated the terrorists getting weapons onto planes.

"That info wasn't in the 9/11 Commission report. It never made the blotter, so to speak. In addition to New York City and Boston, where just two contracted pre-board screeners allowed their buddies to get weapons through the X-ray machines, there were over sixty other screeners and terrorist buddies who passed through the airports at Dallas, Denver, Chicago, Miami, Memphis, and LA."

"What?" Eastwood was stunned at the unbelievable news.

Captain Zacker leaned back, confused and concerned. If Hunter was telling the truth, it should have been reported in the press.

"I can tell you it took several hours for FBI field agents to get into those airports and check the concourse security tapes," Hunter continued. "What they found in those tapes weren't only those famous box cutters but knives that passed through the X-ray machines just as Eastern-looking men passed through the magnetometer at the same time as their carry-ons. Not once did any of those X-ray machine operators stop their machines. The cameras showed a Muslim man or woman, some women wearing head scarves, as the operators at the time.

"It was obvious the operators identified their buddies in the security line. After all the Eastern-looking men passed through the magnetometer and retrieved their bags from the X-ray machine, the X-ray operators took off and were never seen again. The FBI knew if they raced into the local mosques to search for them, holy hell would have been raised. They didn't do it, more for sensitivity reasons than security.

"It stood to reason the only way a group could do something like that was to be connected in a network of mosques. They were all connected. It was obvious. Then other mosques were found to be complicit in a half-dozen deaths of SEALs."

"Holy shit," Captain Zacker said, stunned.

The Mess fell silent, as the men digested this information.

"Duncan, why was Nazy in Algeria?" Eastwood asked, breaking the silence. "It seemed to me she was…overqualified to be Chief of Station. When I met her, I wondered why such a high-powered woman was in that position."

Hunter tilted his head toward the Marine, wondering if that was the question of a correspondent or a concerned friend. At first, it seemed like an innocuous query, but the longer Hunter considered the genesis of Nazy's impromptu mission assignment, the more his thoughts raced down another rabbit hole. He didn't like the direction the conversation was going.

"She replaced a pregnant woman who was the regular COS," Hunter said. "I was surprised by the assignment. Back home, Nazy is the Deputy Director for Counter Terrorism. She's SIS. One could make a case there's an obvious disconnect." He didn't add that she may have taken the temporary assignment to escape a lecherous DCI.

McGee whistled. Zacker blinked wildly. Eastwood knew he was onto something huge.

While the other three men mulled over his comments, Hunter thought that Bill just said something interesting and related. He ran it through mental trap lines, looking for snags in the logic.

"Bill, you said you were contracted to help Langley find and buy MANPADS from the Libyans," Hunter said slowly. "What are we talking about? A handful of old MANPADS lying around?"

"No. Hundreds, if not a thousand—British, French, Russian, and American. Many are new in their shipping cases, as if they came from the factory and went straight into an underground bunker."

"Are you shitting me?" Captain Zacker asked incredulously. "Christ!"

Eastwood, realizing his mouth was gaping open, quickly closed it. The men sat back, recoiling in horror at the thought of weapons capable of mass destruction so close to a terrorist's fingers.

"And mere blocks from where the American Consulate was located. There were black flags of al-Qaeda flying here and there."

"And the green flag of the Muslim Brotherhood was draped in the consulate compound," Eastwood added.

The three men looked at Eastwood in astonishment, knowing they just stumbled upon a significant terrorist event, but what it meant had yet to be discerned.

"Can you describe the underground bunker?" Hunter asked.

"What do you mean?" McGee narrowed his brows and frowned.

"Was it a Quonset hut or a Colfax barn covered with dirt?"

McGee shook his head. "No. It was the strangest setup I ever saw. It was huge. I think they drilled holes in the desert floor and inserted uh…paper-wrapped…you know…cylinder-shaped tubes into the ground. I hit one, and it was obviously filled with cement. I think they poured cement over the top of the desert floor, then they carried out the sand. It was rough, primitive, and ingenious. Among other things, they had a full obstacle course down there. It was dark, but it was like they had a small SEAL training facility."

"Come on, you two," Zacker snapped. "What the hell are you thinking?"

Hunter scanned the men's faces. "I think I saw something similar in Algeria—stacks of MANPADS in a makeshift underground bunker. I ran into two dudes as big as you. Un-fuckin' natural for local Muslims. I remember thinking, 'They're as big as Bullfrog.' They acted like they were trained in the arts, including body armor and AK-47s. They knew how to cut sign and almost found me.

"Please know I'm not trained in the arts, but I've been around enough of you guys long enough to know. When you see the difference, it's obvious. I thought they were Muslim SEALs. Weird."

"That can't be a coincidence." McGee's mind raced. There was no such thing as a Muslim SEAL. The idea was ridiculous, impossible… or was it? *I saw some too!*

Curiosity jolted Eastwood. "Muslim SEALs? Duncan, how did you know? I mean, how'd you ID those guys? Where'd you see them?"

"I killed them." He spoke as unemotionally as if he took out the trash or collected the mail.

"Damn," Eastwood and Zacker said.

"Apex predator," McGee said. "What'd I tell you? Duncan, I saw one too—he was one of the sellers. I'm pretty sure that can't be a coincidence."

"I agree." Hunter tapped his fingers on the table before turning to Captain Zacker. "Sarge, we need some help."

"You got me at a good time. I'm hopped up on caffeine and I'm in a helpful mode. What do you need, Maverick?"

"Presidential authority."

Six eyebrows rose. Torn between doing nothing and letting history and circumstances take their course, Hunter resolved that the circumstances were too great to allow the status quo to continue. After his friends promised no disclosure, Hunter vaguely outlined his mission into Algeria, his similar findings in the bunker, and his escape.

"It's imperative to remove those MANPADS and the other containers in Algeria," Hunter finished. "Time is critical. I can draft a Top Secret FLASH message for your release."

The men nodded and Hunter followed Zacker from the Mess.

Captain Zacker and Hunter entered the buzzing communications center, where the Captain snagged a communications specialist petty officer and told him, "Type whatever this gentleman tells you to type."

Hunter spoke in bullets, repeating his mission name and gave the petty officer the emergency code. "If they don't like this, they can cancel my contract," he said.

Bouncing off two National Security Agency satellites, the message was sent to the White House Situation Room and the Director of Central Intelligence in less than three seconds.

Three minutes later, Captain Zacker received a reply from the White House.

Concur with your assessment and plan. Use all available resources necessary to accomplish recommendation ALPHA. CJCS and SECDEF directs 22 MEU to support immediate extraction of materials from BRAVO.

Once he had Presidential approval, Captain Zacker called for flight quarters and sent runners to wake the National Reconnaissance Office and National Security Agency personnel on the ship. He demanded satellite overheads of Benghazi and a discrete channel for the White House Situation Room to receive and relay live aircraft cockpit feeds.

Five F/A-18E crews were briefed, with Bill McGee providing details. Two aircraft were loaded with six 500-pound GBU-54/B Laser Joint Direct Attack Munitions each. Two F/A-18Es were outfitted with four canisters of napalm with guided bomb unit components. One F/A-18E would act as primary laser designator. Two HH-60s, with six SEALs, would launch as a flight of two well in advance of the F/A-18Es on a vector to Mostaganem, Algeria. The lead HH-60 would carry one additional passenger.

CHAPTER SIXTY-EIGHT

0530 September 26, 2012
U.S.S. Dwight D. Eisenhower
Mediterranean Sea

The Commanding Officer and Captain William McGee, Retired, dominated the bridge of the U.S.S. *Dwight D. Eisenhower,* overlooking the flight deck. From the stately leather chair, surrounded by computer screens, Zacker gave McGee a tour. McGee appreciated the refresher, as Captain Zacker explained he directed the helmsman, who, in turn steered the carrier, while the lee helmsman directed the engine room to control the ship's speed.

Zacker introduced the Quartermaster of the Watch, who was responsible for navigation. The others on the bridge served as lookouts and provided a range and depth of support, such as getting the skipper a cup of coffee or delivering a personal message.

As the commanding officer stepped onto the bridge, the Officer of the Deck transferred responsibility of the "Con" to Zacker and stepped aside. The helmsman repeated the Officer of the Deck's direction, "The Captain has the Con, aye!"

One level down in Primary Flight Control, or Pri-Fly, the Air Boss was busy directing aircraft activity on the flight deck, positioning two helicopters for immediate takeoff and preparing five F/A-18Es with full combat loads—bombs, missiles, flares, and chaff.

"Let's go, Ladies," the Air Boss said into his radio. "I thought you'd be off already!"

A pair of yellow shirts stood in front of the two helicopters, ready to give them the start-engine signal. The lead yellow shirt waved a tall man in a green shirt to approach the lead helicopter. The green shirt surrendered a freshly cleaned and oiled custom revolver to an older man in a green flight suit; he put six bullets in the man's hand. Seconds later, the engines of the Sikorskys started, and the rotors slowly turned until they were up to flight idle speeds.

Two minutes after being barked at by the Air Boss, two HH-60 Sea Hawks lifted into a hover, slipped to port over the deck, and turned toward Africa.

The moment the helicopters disappeared from view, the pilots of five F/A-18Es, with ordnance loaded and armed, lowered their canopies and waited to be positioned. The Air Boss monitored the five aircraft as they moved on the flight deck, pulled by a diminutive-yet-powerful tug into position for start, taxi, and takeoff.

Demetrius Eastwood and his cameraman, Marty Marceau, fought the wind blowing over the flight deck, as each F/A-18E was started and taxied into position. Marty struggled to keep the camera still while each jet took its position at the rear of the catapult, directed by a yellow shirt using hand and arm signals. The pilot responded to the precise commands, as the jet slowly taxied over the catapult shuttle. A closed fist meant stop, and a sweeping motion directed the pilot to lower the nose wheel tow bar to the shuttle.

Another set of commands, and the jet blast deflectors rose behind the twin-engine jet, as the yellow shirt checked the connection of the holdback device and jumped into the pilot's view. The man spun two fingers to signal the pilot to run up the engines to military power and engage the afterburners. The pilot saluted the yellow shirt, as the man looked up and down the catapult lane, touched his knee to the deck. When he touched his fingers to the deck and pointed toward the front of the ship, he signaled the catapult to be released.

When the jet was in afterburner, the temperature on the flight deck went up 100° F, and the front third of the carrier was illuminated by the cherry-red flames of the twin engines burning eight gallons of JP-5 every second. Once released, the jet streaked down the catapult, and its speed increased to 170 knots in three seconds.

One-by-one, the jets were slung off the bow and flew to rendezvous altitude to await the rest of the flight. Darkness again enveloped the men and women on the flight deck, as the JBDs retracted, and the next jet was positioned for takeoff. In less than four minutes, five jets were airborne.

Flight operations on an aircraft carrier were the most-exiting thing Eastwood and Marty ever saw. They were ecstatic and bounced around the flight deck like four-year-olds in an air-filled funhouse.

On the bridge, McGee was awed by the men and women who moved the aircraft, loaded ordnance, and launched from the carrier on a mission of national importance. Watching one F/A-18E after the other being catapulted into the inky blackness, all he could say was, "Wow!"

The strike package of five jets screamed over the Mediterranean Sea at 1,000 feet MSL. Twenty miles from the target, the number-five pilot jammed the throttles into afterburner and climbed to mission altitude. He slammed his throttles back to idle to acquire and lased the target. The pair of F/A-18Es with JDAMs went to military power and split from the formation, racing ahead of their playmates. They spread out into attack profile, one mile apart. The other jets, equipped with laser-guided napalm canisters, maintained altitude and airspeed in close echelon.

"Target Hot; Spot on," someone said over the encrypted radio, as the JDAM-equipped F/A-18Es pulled up at a thirty-degree angle, rolled over onto their backs, and pulled the stick to acquire and center the laser spot in their HUD before rolling the wings level again. The pilot put the target in the middle of his heads-up display—targeting symbology cued him to make corrections for a perfect release. Bomb sight and flight information filled the HUD. The seeker head on each bomb nose acquired the laser-designated target, the compound containing hundreds of MANPADS south of Benghazi.

The first aircraft's computer released the six 500-pound GBU-54/B bombs, rippling them off one at a time. The tiny fins on each bomb moved and deflected to keep the bomb's trajectory on course and target to where the laser designator was the brightest.

The second JDAM-equipped F/A-18E pulled six Gs to offset his flight lead and repeated the process with a 30° pop-up, invert, pull, roll level, drop, and egress.

The bombs punctured the bunker's concrete shell and exploded underground, destroying the MANPADS in the compound; secondary detonations of the underground missiles burst white-hot. The napalm-equipped F/A-18Es followed the same flight track as their teammates in ten-second intervals. The sticky, flammable mixture of fatty acids and gasoline splashed liquid fire into every remaining space in the crumpled, burning underground compound. What hadn't been obliterated by the 500-pound bombs was incinerated by the napalm that spread throughout the remaining underground spaces.

Two minutes later, five F/A-18Es were feet wet, joined up, supersonic, and headed back to the *Eisenhower*. Satellite photos three hours later in the morning daylight showed that the bomb and napalm deliveries were so precise, the compound walls remained undamaged.

As the Navy F/A-18Es crossed the Libyan beach, the twin HH-60s overflew the helicopter carrier U.S.S. *Iwo Jima.* Several Marine Corps Amphibious Assault Vehicles spewed from the ship's well deck and headed toward the Algerian coast, officially conducting rescue operations of American oil-field workers. In response to the initial threat to the U.S. Embassy in Algiers prior to the evacuation, the Ambassador had issued a warning for all American citizens in Algeria to leave the country or seek appropriate shelter. When terrorists overran an oil refinery and killed eighty men of all faiths, U.S. Marines from the 22nd Marine Expeditionary Unit were dispatched to rescue the remaining countrymen and protect other petroleum workers from the Islamic terrorists.

Duncan Hunter patted the pilot's shoulder, as he stepped from the helicopter. He directed the six heavily weaponized SEALs from his helicopter to move toward the hangar. The SEALs from the other helicopter joined them, as ten SEALs set up a defensive perimeter around the hangar and airstrip.

The two HH-60s lifted off, one after the other, and flew toward the *Ike*. When the wind and noise from the rotor wash died down, Hunter led the SEAL team commander into the underground part of the hangar.

"All containers need to be removed from this facility," Duncan said.

The commander instantly recognized *Stinger* shipping containers in his powerful flashlight beam and was surprised by the number of boxes and the lot numbers. Leaning closer to verify the date of manufacture, he was surprised see they were only a few years old.

"The small containers are very heavy," Hunter added. "They'll need special handling. I don't know how many there are, but all need to go."

"Can do easy, Sir."

Hunter and the SEAL emerged from the hangar floor, as Marine green-tracked vehicles clattered on the horizon, their headlights poking through increasingly thickening ground fog and kicked up dust.

Duncan looked skyward and north before facing the SEAL. "Lieutenant, off in the distance there is the remains of an airplane and an SUV. It would probably make Uncle Sam very happy that the gun bolted to that airplane disappears. I can envision a Marine AAV chaining the carcass and haul the plane and the gun into the Med." Hunter looked at the man with a curious smile.

"I think we can make that happen," said the SEAL. "You have to love a good conspiracy."

"Thank you. Also, please make sure the Marines don't overload their AAVs with those containers. I don't want anyone having to come back here because someone thought he could carry more than was safe."

"Well, they *are* Marines, Sir." The SEAL grinned at the older civilian. He knew Hunter was a Marine, and there was nothing like a little inter-service rivalry among friends, especially when there were bodies on the ramp and a couple more in the desert, courtesy of an old, retired Marine. The lieutenant was impressed that the old dude with the revolver knew how to take care of business.

Hunter reciprocated and shook the man's hand. "Thank you."

As Hunter stepped toward the Gulfstream 550, the SEAL commander asked, "Hey, Maverick! Do you know what's in these boxes?"

"Probably a few billion dollars' worth of American taxpayers' money," said Hunter over his shoulder.

The SEAL yelled, "In that case, wouldn't it be a good idea to get a hand receipt?"

Hunter lowered the door of the jet and barked, "If you can't trust a SEAL, who can you trust?"

CHAPTER SIXTY-NINE

0430 September 26, 2012
Somewhere over the Mediterranean Sea

The lights of the Gulfstream cabin were nearly off, with the rheostat set somewhere between where the occupants could sleep in the dark and still provide enough light to move around without disturbing a snoring neighbor. The DCI's security team and private aide were asleep in the oversized captain's chairs.

In the suite at the rear of the jet, the DCI had been awake for hours. The news from HQ that Duncan Hunter was still alive would have relieved any other DCI, but Dr. Bruce Rothwell was furious.

He sat up and threw his stockinged feet over the side of the bed. Faint opaque lamps along the floor provided sufficient light for him to see his surroundings. Closing his eyes, he held his head in his hands, cursing the man. He had long felt the hand of Fate closing around him. The crazy irate women who came forward, accusing him of sexual misconduct or harassment were mere irritants. At some point, they would stop coming out of the woodwork. The number kept mounting, and there were already calls from someone in Congress asking for his resignation. He knew that was coming, but he still had work to do. While the women were figuratively killing him, Duncan Hunter would actually be the death of him.

When Dr. Rothwell finished rubbing his eyes, he turned his focus back to the electronic notebook on the small desk in the suite. He depressed the *On* button to reenergize the screen. The device immediately illuminated with the latest string of classified messages received from CIA HQ communications center.

The last message from the White House was wholly unexpected and incredible. *How did he know? I definitely underestimated you,*

Duncan Hunter. You completely hosed me!

All Rothwell could do was shake his head in wonder.

Fate, it is said, determines the span of each man's life. The DCI was convinced that Duncan had just shortened his. A prickle of fear pushed him to draft two messages for immediate release and direct the aircrew to change course.

The first message went to two handpicked professionals from the National Clandestine Service: *The Marines have landed.* They would understand the significance of the dispatch and would stand down. It meant others were on the scene, and the mission was aborted. They had to leave Algeria.

Rothwell referenced an earlier message from HQ that read, *Nazy C out of surgery. Resting. Expect full recovery.* He replied to the communication center, attention Director of National Intelligence, *Plan to recover N Cunningham and return her to GWMA as soon as she's fit to travel.*

That should buy him some time. No matter what, the situation wouldn't end well.

Rothwell checked his watch and anticipated the aircraft would be descending soon. He frowned and sighed heavily, then slammed his fist against his thigh. *Hunter, you were supposed to die!*

CHAPTER SEVENTY

September 27, 2012
New York Times

Americans Evacuated from Algeria

UPI. The Department of State issued a press release that U.S. Embassy Algiers was evacuated during the early morning hours in response to expected armed demonstrations. The action follows embassy evacuations in Libya and Tunisia over the previous week, resulting from a wave of anti-US demonstrations in North Africa, from Egypt to Algeria, which followed the death of the U.S. Ambassador in Libya on September 11.

Americans throughout Algeria were advised to leave the country after eighty men (including 10 Americans) were killed at an Algerian oil refinery. Over thirty oil field workers from two remote oil refinery installations were also evacuated by U.S. Marines from the U.S.S. *Iwo Jima.* Helicopters from the U.S.S. *Eisenhower's* Battle Group provided round-the-clock airlift support.

CHAPTER SEVENTY-ONE

2200 September 28, 2012
Anderson Hall, Laughlin Air Force Base
Del Rio, Texas

Duncan Hunter rubbed his eyes and couldn't stifle a yawn, as his students wandered back into the classroom. His black herringbone suit maintained its freshly pressed seams, a flashy red-ribbed tie in a reverse four-in-hand knot closed the classic collar, and gold coin cufflinks punctured his French cuffed shirt. Before he fell down from exhaustion, he leaned across the lectern and pushed to finish the last hour of his class.

Hunter's students exchanged nervous glances. Their instructor was operating on a narrow edge of his personal envelope.

"OK," Hunter said. "Before I fall down in a heap, let's wrap this up and call it a night. Preview for my next class, which I believe is on the schedule for next semester, is Aircraft and Spacecraft Development. It should be a fun class. I'll ask you to buy and read the book *Skunk Works* before the first night. With the development of the F-117 and our textbook, you'll have a good start on what it takes to conceive an aircraft, get a contract to build it, and then learn all the pain and suffering it takes in developing, building, and delivering a state-of-the-art radical design.

"You'll learn one of my favorite axioms—if it looks good, it'll fly good. There is a corollary—if it looks cool and sexy, it'll sell. Boeing had no chance of ever selling their X-32 joint strike fighter. It's probably the most-hideous airplane ever built and is the Aztek, Smart Car, and Prius mistakes of the jet world, all rolled into one."

Most students laughed heartily at his disparaging assessment of losing aircraft and automobile designs. He grinned back and said,

"Don't put that on my critique, please."

That brought another round of laughter from the men and women in flight suits. Kelly Horne, sitting in the back of the room, shook her head in admiration. He looked ready to have his eyelids slam shut and fall asleep at the lectern, but he pressed forward.

Hunter extracted loose papers from his Gladstone. "I have one last thing to hand out, an FBI report on Flight 800. I suppose enough time has passed that the FBI had their guard down when my lawyer submitted the Freedom of Information Act request.

"In my view, the FBI's redacted report was the smoking gun that it was a missile. It's pretty obvious the USG never told the truth. Here's your copy of the un-redacted report. Please pass them around. I'll give you a few minutes to read the report." Hunter yawned and watched the second hand make two laps on his Rolex.

After a dozen heads popped up from their reading assignment, Hunter offered, "Some final thoughts. Why would the FBI missile team spend so much time and effort looking for shoulder-fired missile evidence if Flight 800 was out of range and they were sure it wasn't hit by a missile? The answer, of course, is they knew it was in range of a *Stinger.* Someone in the Administration made the decision to dismiss any discussion of a missile. They had their reasons; they didn't want the public to know. That's politics.

"So that's it. Please turn your instructor critiques over to Major Cooper, who has graciously volunteered to deliver them to the center director. Ladies and gents, please know it's been a pleasure. I hope you had a great time—I sure did. You guys were great. I don't know the Air Force equivalent of the nautical blessing, 'Fair winds and following seas.' May the roads rise with you and the wind be always at your back —except on takeoff and landing.

"In any case, keep it on the centerline and always have enough lift under your wings. Keep the dirty side down. May your landings equal the number of your takeoffs. Safe travels. Good night."

The students gave a polite but genuine round of applause and slowly departed the classroom, their five minutes of shaking hands and friendly banter energized Hunter. Strong, firm grips and slaps on the back helped pump him up. He smiled and nodded to Kelly Horne, as they silently left the classroom and building.

She felt he was genuinely saddened the class was over, but he was hiding something. He looked good in his professor's uniform, but she winced at his demeanor, as if he wasn't just exhausted but had lost weight since she last saw him. She ascertained he was severely jet lagged and was fighting his body's natural desire to return to its own biorhythm and sleep cycle. As they walked down the ten-foot-wide staircase, she debated scolding him for doing too much. She reasoned, *That's what daughters do!*

When they walked through the glass double doors, Kelly saw a crowd at the edge of the curb surrounding a vehicle. It was most of Hunter's late-night students, and the vehicle was a stunning 1974 Jaguar XKE. The hump on the roadster's bonnet and the chrome V12 badge on the boot indicated it was a very rare convertible. Kelly forgot what she was going to say to her father when he apparently thought twice about placing his leather briefcase in the dark red passenger seat and set it on the curb.

In the streetlight, Hunter opened the boot and bonnet for his awed students to see the vehicle's inner workings. After ten minutes of questions and answers, the group dispersed, leaving Hunter and Horne standing in the street.

Duncan smiled broadly and handed a pair of small keys to his daughter. "There are some things you just don't miss. Happy Birthday Kelly."

She dropped her backpack, her hands flew to her face in surprise. Her mother's gold Rolex popped out from under the sleeve of her flight suit. Her reaction was more than Hunter could have asked for.

CHAPTER SEVENTY-TWO

September 30, 2012
The Washington Post

CIA Director Resigns

Associated Press. In a surprise announcement yesterday, the Director of Central Intelligence, Dr. Bruce Rothwell, submitted his resignation to the President, citing health concerns. The President accepted the DCI's resignation with sorrow and said, "A career intelligence officer, Dr. Rothwell led the CIA through challenging times. I'll miss his wise counsel."

Dr. Rothwell's resignation did not come as a surprise, as many members of Congress called him to step down after several women accused him of sexual misconduct and sexual harassment. The DCI may have been forced to resign after an international website dedicated to tracking U.S. government aircraft used in the commission of extraordinary renditions filmed the usually reclusive Dr. Rothwell personally supervising the transfer of medical personnel and an individual on a stretcher onto the director's aircraft. The President will nominate a replacement DCI in the coming days.

CHAPTER SEVENTY-THREE

0800 September 30, 2012
Walter Reed National Military Medical Center

Duncan Hunter nearly dropped a fistful of flowers when he found the Director of Central Intelligence in Nazy's room. His eyes fell to Nazy—no makeup, one side of her face dotted with round, tan bandages, her mouth closed, looking as beautiful as ever—then to a very surprised DCI. The room was strangely quiet and unlit. Only ambient light spilled into the room from half-open window blinds.

Tiny lights from myriad equipment indicated the machines were active, while a single display flashed pulse and temperature data onto the monitor over her bed. A thick gray wiring harness was connected to her, as was a single IV attached to the back of her hand.

Nazy slept, as a very confused Dr. Rothwell nodded for Hunter to follow him out of the room. Hunter placed the bouquet on the sink and left, one step behind Rothwell.

Hunter read in the *Washington Times* that morning that Rothwell may have been forced to resign as DCI. The Web was abuzz with accusations that he took an agency jet to meet one of his many girlfriends in Europe but was forced to divert the aircraft to pick up a terrorist. With a new bimbo erupting onto the political scene almost every week, giving salacious details of their relationships with the roué Dr. Rothwell, the cry for his resignation from members of Congress was nearly unanimous.

The President, as reported on various talk radio stations, officially and reluctantly accepted the resignation. Unsurprisingly, Rothwell was in hiding, unavailable for comment. As Hunter digested the details of the article, his contempt for the news media was complete when he heard their portrayal of the disgraced DCI as warm-hearted, compassionate, and easygoing. The tone was altogether *sympathique*, nothing like the real man, who could be cold, arrogant, scheming, and a contemptible tyrant.

As Duncan drove to the hospital, he engaged in a little *schadenfreude* and was glad the DCI would be gone from the Agency and no longer hovering around or hounding Nazy. Then Duncan found him in her room, longing for her as she slept. He was relieved to find her safe and resting, but Duncan wanted the despicable dirtball Rothwell away from her before he did something he would regret.

Seeing Rothwell in Nazy's room changed several assumptions in Hunter's view of the world. He assumed the CIA sent a special jet to retrieve her from the naval hospital, but with Rothwell in the area, it was more likely he diverted his own jet to bring her to the States and not a terrorist.

Until Duncan walked into the room, Rothwell hadn't made the connection that Nazy and Duncan knew each other, were close, or might be a couple. The only people who could know Nazy had returned to the U.S. were Connie Lynche, the emergency point of contact listed on her personnel data card, and the operations duty officer. Seeing Duncan in the doorway, with his escape and escapades in Algeria—still a crushing blow to his plans—in the back of his mind, Rothwell suddenly realized that a large piece of the amorphous puzzle he had been wrestling with had fallen into place. Without a security detail to protect him. Dr. Bruce Rothwell immediately feared for his life.

Hunter checked his anger at the door, because he needed time to think. He was polite but direct, his voice almost an octave lower than usual. "I take it you brought her back from…Italy?"

Rothwell heard the voice of an inquisitor before he served judgment. "Hello…Duncan…Hunter. What a surprise to see you… here." Diluvial adrenalin shot into every extremity. The tiny hairs on the back of his shaved neck vibrated in warning. The Norman Bates quality of Duncan's voice frightened Rothwell. He fought the urge to void his bladder. He had to get away from the man who'd been shot down and left to die in Algeria.

"Thank you for bringing her home, Dr. Rothwell."

"They wouldn't let her travel…unless she had a flight nurse accompany her. She's…she's doing very well. I'm surprised she's still asleep." He leaned aside, hoping to get away, but his feet refused to move.

"Again, thank you, Dr. Rothwell. I thought we'd be able to debrief, but I hear you've resigned."

"You don't need to tell me what happened. I understand you completed the mission. You're a hero." He felt trapped, like he'd stepped on the trip wire for a Claymore mine and realized he was in the fragmentation pattern if he moved. His eyes darted, looking for an escape route.

Hunter crossed his arms. "I think I know why you're here, but you don't know why I'm here. Nazy and I are engaged. We have been for quite some time."

"I…I…I didn't know that. Con…congratulations, Duncan." Now he knew Nazy had told Duncan about his advances. Being face-to-face with a jealous boyfriend who was a killer was the ultimate terror. Rothwell felt Hunter wouldn't hurt him in the hospital, but he didn't want to risk it and sought an excuse to leave.

Hunter worked to contain his growing fury. His fingers unconsciously dug into his arms, as he glared at the man. "What I didn't know at the time was how my target knew I was coming. I'm having a difficult time believing you didn't have something to do with my getting shot at and shot down. I'll find out the truth, Rothwell. One of these days, I'll find out, but for now, you need to leave."

Rothwell's eyelids fluttered. Somehow, Hunter knew. He might not know all of it, but he discerned part of it. Dr. Rothwell lowered his eyes in submission, forcing his stiff legs to move. He jerkily slipped away.

Hunter watched the man turn and walk off. Rothwell took the closest opportunity to leave the floor, ducking into the stairwell and raced down the stairs.

A nurse walked past, breaking Hunter's trance, as she entered

Nazy's room. He followed her through the door and expected Nazy to be in narcosis, but she was awake. In the subdued lighting, she sported two black eyes. The two lovers immediately brightened in mutual surprise, though her reaction was heavily delayed by sedation.

Hunter was shocked at her condition. He hurried to her bedside and leaned over gently to kiss her lips. His heart raced when he pulled back to look at her in all her beauty. He couldn't take his eyes off her. Her face was a mélange of yellows, blues, greens, and reds. Still sedated, she closed her eyes for a moment, evidently in pain. A dozen small circular bandages dotted the right side of her face.

"I haven't brushed my teeth," she protested, when he kissed her again.

"Baby, I got here as soon as I could." He held the hand without the IV. Pangs of guilt struck him.

"I haven't been here long. I arrived last night. Did Rothwell leave? I pretended I was asleep when he came in." Though she slurred her words slightly, her voice and accent was steady.

"That's my girl. He did." He hovered over her, his arm braced on the opposite rail, smiling like a lovesick fool fighting to hold back his emotions. He had been warned but never imagined her external condition to be so extreme.

"Do you know…what happened?"

"I know some of it, Baby. I understand there was an explosion at the embassy, and you were caught outside. I counted thirteen of these." He pointed at the round bandages and grinned.

She struggled with long sentences. "The doctor told me they removed…. My whole side had shrapnel. I was told they got most of it…them. The doctor said some will pop out of my skin when I least expect it."

Hunter feigned pain. "Hurt?"

"My whole side hurts. I ache all over. My belly and face hurt. If it wasn't for the painkillers, I'd probably be wailing like an old Muslim woman." She tried to lean forward, though the effort was feeble. She hadn't realized how tired she was.

Hunter forced a smile. It pained him to see her like that. "You're an animal. You need to rest, Baby. Take it easy." He squeezed her hand while staring into her platinum-green eyes, ignoring the hematomas.

He fought to remain composed. "I also know Bill McGee rescued you. I'm pretty sure he saved your life, but you know how old SEALs are. They never tell you the whole story, and they're humble to a fault."

Nazy's slowly moving expression was questioning. She tried to move her facial muscles, but it hurt and distracted her, so she stopped. She wasn't sure she remembered Bill McGee. The blast affected part of her memory. "Who…where did you see him?"

Hunter shifted his eyes to the nurse, then back to Nazy. With a fuzzy but growing memory of McGee, she was glad to change the subject. They could discuss him later.

She had to tell Duncan about the baby. Suddenly, she was very afraid, and she closed her eyes and turned her head away. She didn't know how he would react. Would he be happy or sad? Would he be crushed or would he be angry?

When she finally opened her eyes, Nazy focused at the foot of the bed and considered her options.

The nurse injected a syringe of clear liquid into an access port on the IV tubing. "This is to make you sleep."

Nazy and Hunter's eyes followed the nurse as she worked. After she checked Nazy's bandages and monitor connections, she left.

Nazy smiled with heavy eyelids and yawned at Duncan. "Excuse me." The medication made her British accent more pronounced and slurred.

Hunter was ready to tell her he knew. It would be difficult for her to say she lost the baby, *his* baby. He expected the worst for Nazy after learning she'd been pulverized during the embassy bombing. When he arrived at the intensive-care ward, Hunter stopped at the nurse's station to ask which room was hers. The four nurses stopped to regard him, looking at each other as if mentally drawing straws for who had to tell him the most-horrible news of all. Their reactions stunned him. He hadn't been prepared.

"Are you Duncan Hunter?" asked an attractive Hispanic woman in baggy turquoise scrubs.

He hadn't expected to hear his name dropped so casually by an unknown woman. Blinking, he tipped his head, searching for an answer to, *How could she possibly know who I am?*

The nurse read his astonishment. "May I see some ID, Mr. Hunter?"

After racking his brain, he slowly removed his wallet and produced his retired military ID card. The woman, who had the name *Dr. Blanca Ortega* embroidered on her tunic, stepped from behind the long, white granite counter and directed Hunter to follow her to an adjacent office. The name on the door informed him she was a Commander in the U.S. Navy Medical Corps.

Duncan looked around the office, mentally recording the desk in the middle of the room, two chairs in front of it, dark thick glass in the windows, the bookcase filled with scores of medical books and pamphlets and two framed pictures. One showed a dark-haired woman with two stripes on her sleeve, suggesting she was a flight attendant for an unknown airline. The other eight-by-ten portrait was of a swarthy man wearing the uniform and insignia of a Navy Captain.

"Thank you, Mr. Hunter. Please have a seat."

Hunter took the chair farthest from the window, his mind racing. He expected the worst. "Dr. Ortega, Miss Cunningham is my fiancée."

"Yes, Sir. I understand that, but that's not why I'm here. I need to tell you that Miss Cunningham is a special interest patient. Her status and condition are reported to the White House every six hours. Her CIA emergency data card didn't list you as the emergency contact. We got that information from Mr...."

"Greg Lynche. Yes ma'am. He contacted me and told me Nazy left Italy and would be transferred to Bethesda." He spoke warily, waiting for bad news. The doctor was too businesslike, which presaged pain and suffering.

"I spoke to the President and he let me know to look out for you, that you'd be here probably sometime this morning. That's not what I wanted to talk about with you, Sir."

Commander Ortega offered a slim file with the word *CONFIDENTIAL* stamped on the front. "This is Miss Cunningham's medical record of her injuries and the steps that were taken in Italy to treat her."

"Why don't you give me the bottom line?"

She pressed her lips together and opened the file. "The bottom line, I'm afraid, isn't that simple, Mr. Hunter. Patient Cunningham was evacuated from Algeria and medevaced from the U.S.S. *Eisenhower.* Upon admission, she presented severe internal hemorrhaging that required immediate surgery."

She looked up at him over her reading glasses. "She suffered from multiple physical injuries consistent with a close proximity detonation of high explosives. She was admitted with a ruptured right eardrum and shrapnel punctures and lacerations from her right temple to her right calf. None were life-threatening. Patient Cunningham suffered multiple contusions and other external frontal injuries consistent with severe physical abuse—dual preorbital hematoma, no broken facial bones indicated."

She again looked up from the file. "Miss Cunningham had two black eyes, but no damage to the corneas or ocular hypertension. Her eyes are undamaged."

Tears welled in his eyes. His temples bulged with every heartbeat, and his hands unconsciously formed fists.

"Patient Cunningham suffered from injuries consistent with violent rape. The uterus was significantly torn. Naval Hospital Sigonella removed the damaged uterus, a non-viable fetus, and repaired the internal vaginal structure during hysterectomy. Her ovaries were undamaged and were not removed. They also repaired a large laceration under the left breast, essentially reattaching it. The field surgeon achieved hemostasis; essentially, he applied enough pressure and compression to stop the internal bleeding, and closed the wound, probably saving her life, and, at minimum, her breast."

Hunter closed his eyes as tears leaked from the corners. He was quiet, though his breathing was ragged. When he opened his eyes, Dr. Ortega continued.

"The attending physician noted her physical conditioning was exceptional and likely contributed to her ability to withstand the extent and severity of her injuries. Her prognosis for a full recovery is good, with a few *caveats.*

"Mr. Hunter, due to the internal damage to the female organs, your fiancée will most likely be unable to enjoy a normal physical relationship. Miss Cunningham, like most of our war injured, will require substantial physical and psychological rehabilitation. We can expect a significant level of Post-Traumatic Stress Disorder, PTSD, associated with her injuries."

Duncan broke eye contact, lowered his head into his hands, and wept. *Nazy was raped? She was blown up and raped? What do they mean, they essentially reattached her breast? Oh, God, Nazy. What happened to you?*

"I'm sorry, Mr. Hunter." Commander Ortega offered tissues from a large box. While she waited for him to compose himself, she wondered if she could have handled the situation better. The President suggested the man could be considered one of the special operations types. Even if the news was bad, such men rarely wanted it sugarcoated or drawn out. Duncan asked, "What's the bottom line?"

She set down the file and walked to the door, planning to give Duncan time to grieve in private. She was surprised when he stood and followed her out with dry eyes, though he had the look of a dazed, dangerous man.

"Are you OK, Mr. Hunter?"

He nodded. "I am. Thank you, Commander. I know that must have been hard. I didn't know. I really didn't know, but I'll take care of her. Thank you, Ma'am."

"She's been through hell and back. When you see her, please know that from a medical standpoint, she looks great and is responding very well to treatment. You'll see her facial inju…her shiners are dissipating, but we're keeping her sedated to mitigate the pain. We awakened her so you can have a few minutes with her, then I want her back asleep."

Hunter pinched his lips and nodded. "How much does she know?"

"Shortly after she came in, I understand she asked about the baby. When I arrived this morning, I had to tell her. I don't know if she knows she was raped or assumed she miscarried due to the explosion. My guess, based on her reactions, is that I'd be very surprised if she knew. She didn't respond as if she'd been raped. Not knowing is probably the best outcome."

"She's a smart woman, Doc." He begged for good news.

"Then she knows or suspects. Women's intuition and all that. It won't be helpful if you bring it up. If and when she wants to talk about it...."

"Got it." He closed his eyes to comprehend the hideous news and its implications. Several seconds later, he opened them and said, "I don't envy you, Doctor, but I thank you for all your help."

"Mr. Hunter, I see good things for Nazy. She'll be OK, but it will take time for her life to return to something approaching what was once called normal. We get blast victims here all too frequently, but rarely is it a woman. I've seen good, bad, and ugly. I'm confident she will fully recover, but it will take time. It'll never be like it was, but, with love and care, it can get close."

Hunter reached for her hand to thank her. He glanced at it to ensure a firm grasp and was taken aback to see Ortega's hands were heavily scarred from burns and corrective surgeries. She looked down but didn't pull away from him.

Without missing a beat, she re-gripped his hand and said, "I know what she's going to go through. In 2004, I was in a café in the Green Zone in Iraq when a suicide bomber walked in and blew himself up. My clothes were burned off my body. There was much shrapnel. I've had seventy surgeries. It took a long time to recover, to adjust to the new normal. Now I dedicate myself to helping others who were injured in war, mostly women. Good luck, Mr. Hunter."

She released his grip, allowing her gaze to fall to the floor as she returned to the nurse's station.

Duncan surrounded Nazy's hand in his and leaned over to kiss her fingertips, pinching tears from his eyes. When he looked up to tell her, she was already asleep. Her jaw was slack, mouth open, looking very unladylike. She was still the most beautiful woman he'd ever seen.

Stifling a wave of emotion, he released his grip, wiping away tears on his sleeve. *Oh, Nazy. That's how you really sleep.* He stood quietly and smiled. *God, you're an amazing woman. I won't let you down, Baby.*

CHAPTER SEVENTY-FOUR

0930 September 30, 2012
Washington, DC

Duncan waited impatiently at the traffic light. Traffic was unexpectedly heavy for a Sunday, and he tried to analyze if any of the usual suspects—weather, accident, or construction—were responsible. His emotions flipped between sorrow and happiness. He was ecstatic that Nazy was doing well but was shocked and depressed to learn the extent of her physical injuries and the unknowns of dealing with her psychological issues. Dr. Ortega indicated Nazy would be strong enough to come home within ten days, possibly by the end of the week. The nurse's cautions reverberated in his mind.

"She'll need some personal attention for several weeks. She won't be allowed to lift anything for a good long while. And she'll need to be in therapy."

As was the case with patients who experienced horrific injuries, what shook Hunter to his core and continued to echo in his ears was what the doctor told him just as he left the ward.

"You can thank the field surgeon who sewed her up for saving her life."

Over and over, Duncan's thoughts returned to his friend Bill McGee who was more of a hero than the old SEAL ever let on.

Once free of the labyrinth of concrete barriers for force-protection measures at the Walter Reed National Military Medical Center, he shot through the security gate and headed for the Beltway. As he entered Wisconsin Avenue, his BlackBerry vibrated and rang loudly.

Violating all the Maryland laws regarding texting and driving, Hunter one-handed the little black device, punching in a password of letters and numbers until he reached his in-box. It wasn't every day he received an email from the middle of the Mediterranean Sea from Captain Mike Zacker. The subject line read *Thank you.*

"Thank you?" he said aloud. "Sarge, I should be thanking you. What the hell did you send me?'

A press of the *Track* button and the email appeared in tiny letters.

Maverick, have to thank you for the awesome gift you gave to the men and women of the U.S.S. *Eisenhower.* Seems you know how to leave an impression, and not just on the distaff side of the ship.

I'll bet you had no clue you found *the* long lost A17FS Staggerwing. You probably didn't notice the wheel covers or the Wright 1820 radial or that the nose cowling was different from all other Staggerwings.

A little research found your gift was built for the 12K mile race in 1934, which was won by a twin-engine de Havilland DH-88 Comet—also curiously lost to history. (You don't have that squirreled away, do you?)

Put one of our anthrax detectors in the cockpit for two days and got absolutely no hits, so the airplane is clean, and, by extension, so were you. All the antibiotics probably cleared you of any clap you picked up in your worldwide travels. You have to be the luckiest $h!t on the planet

Be safe, Mav. Good luck with your little lady, and thank you again for an amazing four hours. Probably make admiral because of you. Make some time for my wet down.

Semper Fi,

Sarge

Hunter slipped the device into his shirt pocket and said, "And I was going to shove it over the side. I guess God does smile on fools and drunks. He can add idiots to the list."

He turned toward the interstate with a torrent of emotion and boisterous laughter. Midway down the on ramp, he had an epiphany and realized the disassembled aircraft in the target's hangar in Algeria could have been a de Havilland DH-88 Comet. *What are the chances of that?*

Laughter turned to seriousness as he wrestled with the dichotomy of an Islamic terrorist with two rare aircraft—American and British built, no less—that had been lost from history.

I may never know the answer to that. Now how the hell will I get that other airplane?

CHAPTER SEVENTY-FIVE

1030 September 30, 2012
Annapolis Yacht Club

The Highway 50 exit for Annapolis and the Naval Academy triggered a touch of melancholy and wonder for Duncan Hunter. With entry aptitude scores off the chart, the Marine Corp recruit was asked by a sneering, frothing drill instructor if he was interested in attending the United States Naval Academy. For seventeen-year-old Marine Recruit Private Hunter, if he were given the opportunity to attend, he swore he would have made the best of it.

After ten weeks of boot camp, nothing more was ever mentioned about attending the Academy and Hunter had orders to go to another school as an aviation electronics technician. Once he passed under the supersized green sign suspended over the highway, he forgot about old failures and what-ifs and looked forward to meeting his mentor and best friend, Greg Lynche.

The former CIA Chief of Air Branch was enjoying retirement, living on the golf course, flying his Cessna Skymaster when the weather was good, and sailing his forty-eight-foot sailboat whenever he liked.

Hunter's former business partner and sensor operator for the YO-3A didn't miss the stress of flying surveillance missions, especially after the CIA changed the dynamics of the missions from less ISR to an increasing amount of direct action while serving as a low-altitude laser designator for high-flying drones armed with missiles to kill high-value terrorists. A low-flying Yo-Yo could see things the high-altitude robots couldn't. The change in an active mission profile assaulted Lynche's liberal leanings, and he looked for an excuse to quit flying when there was the potential of killing directly or indirectly.

It was difficult to quit working completely when, for fifteen years, Hunter's mission planning and execution, coupled with Lynche's mission selection and contract-negotiation skills, launched the fortunes of the two men into the stratosphere. Greg, known as the "Grinch," wasn't totally out of the business and did work for Hunter from time-to-time, primarily when Duncan was out of the country on a mission or business trip.

When Hunter's schedule prevented him from going to Washington State to bid on a YO-3A a museum had up for auction, Hunter begged Greg to go in his place and bid whatever it took to buy it. Hunter was excited by the prospect of acquiring a second Yo-Yo, now a replacement airplane, since he lost the one Lynche gave him.

The two men simultaneously pulled into the parking lot of the Annapolis Yacht Club, one behind the other and parked nose-to-nose in the graveled parking lot. Lynche shut off his burgundy Mercedes SL560 and looked up only to realize the driver of the non-descript rental car was none other than his old partner.

He gave his hearty, infectious smile and showed that even at the age of seventy-three, he was the epitome of the buoyant professional. There was a reason he'd been the personal aide to two DCIs—he was an outgoing, vivacious genius, who knew the intelligence business and knew how to keep secrets.

Hunter waited for the six-foot-two Lynche to unfold his lanky legs from the two-seater and stand up before he hugged him, which was an unusual response, Lynche noted. Conservative and liberal, former business partners and best of friends, the two men walked up the wide staircase continually chatting about Connie's new knee, new tennis racquet, and new tennis pro before stepping onto the observation deck for lunch. They sat in a far corner so they could look out over Chesapeake Bay and talk privately.

"How's Nazy?" Greg asked.

"Improving. I didn't know how bad it was, Greg. She was hurt worse than I could have imagined, but the doctor says she's doing well. I might be able to bring her home in a week to ten days."

"That's fantastic, Mav. Scared Connie to death when my old place called. What have you been up to? Nothing good, I hope."

"You know—if I told you, I'd have to kill you, or some such BS. You know the drill." He interrupted his smile to flip Lynche a $50 American Gold Eagle.

Lynche had good reflexes for an old, wrinkled, sunburned guy and caught the well-tossed coin. Hunter waited for the questions he knew would come.

Lynche turned it over repeatedly, brows furrowing and running questions in his mind, as if he never saw an American gold coin. Then again, Hunter remembered that the sometimes uppity Greg Lynche didn't know what Chic-fil-A was, either.

"What's this?" Greg asked.

"Technically, it's a $50 American Gold Eagle. Point 999 percent pure gold, graded fine, one ounce, worth about $1,500 on the open market at today's prices."

"Where'd you get it?" He fingered the shiny, heavy gold coin. He was amused and curious.

"Took possession of an abandoned airplane and found it onboard."

Lynche's expression changed from confused and questioning to incredulous and sardonic. "I really don't want to know, do I?"

"That's right."

"Ah. I think I created a monster."

"Wow. That's a first. A liberal actually accepting responsibility for his actions? I think we have *movement!*"

Lynche rubbed an eye with his middle finger in feigned indifference. He returned his eyes to the coin with newfound respect.

"That's yours. Check this out." He removed 007's data plate from his shirt pocket and tossed it across the small table.

Lynche recognized it instantly. "Now I'm worried what else you'll pull out of your…pocket."

"Now, Greg, you know I'm not that kind of guy. I'm pretty sure it's *your* guys who expose themselves to children, shit on cop cars during a protest…."

"Yeah, yeah, yeah."

"OK. You know what that means?"

"It means you finally took some of my advice and removed the data plate so the Yo-Yo can't be traced back to me."

"Well, good sir, what it really means is that this is all that's left of 007."

Greg Lynche was the epitome of crestfallen. Hunter explained the particulars of the *Noble Savage* mission up to the point where he met the disgraced DCI in Nazy's room at Walter Reed. He stopped talking when the waitress returned with fresh drinks and waited to take their order.

The two men ordered the house special, rib eye steak sandwiches. Hunter drained his glass of water, as Greg stopped sipping wine and sat dumbfounded at the turn of events in Algeria. Hunter checked his Rolex and wondered about the YO-3A Lynche was sent to buy at auction.

"Well?"

"Well what?"

"Yo-Yo?"

"Oh, that what. I bought it. In fact, I bought two of them."

"Two? Wha.... You can't be serious!" Hunter was shocked and incredulous. His eyebrows rose until they met his hairline. A pair of YO-3As was the best news he heard in days.

"I ran into a guy at the auction who looked like he was going to bid on the airplane when he saw me bidding. He came over, introduced himself, and wanted to chat. I didn't need thirty-five years of CIA training to know when someone was pumping me for information. This guy was worse than a rabid Agency polygrapher.

"He was hyper-curious about my interest in the airplane. I asked him a few questions, more for entertainment value than anything else, and he said he's interested in doing some government work—presumably DOD—he hoped to do some surrogate UAV work. He then said something I completely forgot about. The bird for sale *had been operational* after they left the Army. He knew, because the cockpits had been updated with multifunction displays and glass cockpits."

"Oh, crap!" Hunter grinned like a Cheshire and snickered.

"I know! Remember when you suggested to SOCOM to use the museum Yo-Yos for work in Afghanistan, and they pulled them out of museums? Well, they put glass cockpits in them and never put the old, original steam gauge cockpits back in. This guy noticed and started nosing around. It seems all the birds on display, from Pima to Rucker, still have new cockpits."

"The Army never removed the old cockpits? You've got to be shitting me! I forgot all about that. Out of sight , out of mind and all that." Feeling concerned, Hunter ran some what-if scenarios in his head. If someone got the whiff of the story behind the upgraded YO-3A cockpits, who knew how many others would start nosing around and inquiring about the whereabouts of the remaining Lockheed spy planes? How did the 1960-vintage airplanes acquire cockpits that looked remarkably like those from an F/A-18 that just rolled off the assembly line?

"So did I. Probably, so did Ferrier. So that guy was prowling around like a detective. When I won the auction, another gentleman came up and asked if I wanted another one, right in front of Jack Friday."

"No shit?"

Lynche nodded and grinned broadly. "He was one of the private owners and was getting up in years. He said he flew them in Vietnam and became a PanAm pilot and bought a Yo-Yo when one came up for sale. He got it airworthy and flew it at air shows. Seems the word's out on those guys and what they did in country with the YO-3As. They even have a web site. Biennial conventions and all that. The quiet airplane shit's no longer secret."

Hunter was concerned, but that didn't register. No one would ever believe a small group of men had been flying a highly modified YO-3A for the CIA. He was more interested in the second aircraft and its condition.

"So you bought the other airplane?"

"I did. He said he was there to sell his plane to the losing bidder. I told him I'd buy it, too, at the same price as the other. I knew you wouldn't hesitate on getting a second one, even if it was just for spares. They're both being shipped to Texas. They should arrive in a week or so. I love spending other people's money."

"Spoken like a true liberal!" Hunter clapped in joy and offered a hand to shake. As they shook, he said, "Two Yo-Yos! Nice job, Sir!"

"Numbers two and three. One's from Washington, the other from California."

"It'll take months to get another airplane anywhere near 007's configuration, but we do have all the engineering drawings for quick-changing the wings and the composite panels. You outdid yourself, Greg."

"Wait until you get my bill."

"You need to keep a running tab. I have another request."

"This will be expensive. I just know it."

"I have some news."

"You and Nazy set a date?"

"I have a daughter."

"Nazy had a baby?"

"That's actually a yes-and-no answer. For now, no. I had a long relationship with a woman during my early days flying F-4s."

"The redheaded Air Force pilot?"

"You knew that, too?"

The old spook smiled wistfully. "I knew everything." Before his assignment as Chief of Air Branch, Greg ran a CIA program to identify unusually talented men and women for recruitment into the CIA. Hunter made the list based on his unusual skills and experiences, and had been tracked for twelve years when the Agency terminated the program.

Hunter lowered his eyes and sighed. "You didn't know she passed away giving birth. My daughter found me, and we've been seeing each other for about a month. Your mouth is open, Greg. It's not very manly."

Lynche snapped his jaw shut and frowned, then he tossed the gold coin back to Duncan. "So you have a daughter. That's great, or is it a problem? What does Nazy say?"

"I haven't had the opportunity. Nazy got blown up. She told me she was pregnant when she was in Algeria, and the doc said she lost the baby. We haven't had that discussion, and I have no clue how she'll react. I need a favor."

The waitress brought their food and sashayed away.

"A favor? What do you need from me?"

"I'd like to get Kelly into the program, maybe in the clandestine service. I asked the DCI, and he blew me off. Then he resigned, so I think it went nowhere."

"Uhhh, wow. OK. I'll see what I can do, but no promises. My contacts are more than a little dated."

"You always know what to do and say. You might be out of the inner circle, but you're still connected. If you can, you know I'd appreciate it."

"What's next?"

"I debrief POTUS in a couple hours."

"Sounds like fun."

"I have to head to your old place to get a ride to the White House. One of these days, I'll get to ride in a limo, not the back of a bread truck."

"But that's where all Marines ride! Besides, you should be grateful to get a ride at all."

Hunter finished a bite of his sandwich and looked at Greg. "You have a point. I *am* grateful—very grateful that you picked me from a lineup and let me fly your plane, grateful we flew together for fifteen years, which were some of the most-exciting times of my life, and I'm grateful you didn't kick my ass off the program."

"You saved mine a couple times. We're square."

"That goes both ways, Sir."

They ate their sandwiches and admired the scenery. Chesapeake Bay was full of boats large and small, with engines or powered by sail. Beautiful, sleek sailboats suited Greg, while loud, powerful Corvette race cars suited Duncan. Lynche was a liberal, and Hunter was a conservative. The two men were very different, but they were joined at the hip when it came to airplanes, clearances, and special access programs. They were the closest of friends. No thoughts were off limits. It might take one of them awhile to bring up something personal, but, when it happened, the other listened seriously.

"I guess I'm at a crossroads," Hunter said slowly. "My girl was blown up, and she'll need a lot of TLC for who knows how long. I have a daughter who I thought would be a great replacement for you at some point in the future, but, if that's to happen, she'll need training. She can fly but she'll need to know all that spook shit. I learned the hard way you're a tough person to replace, Greg Lynche. I nearly killed myself a couple times trying to do it all myself. I'm very lucky I wasn't injured when I jumped from 007. I didn't mention I was blind for several minutes.

"I always said I'm the luckiest guy I know, but it might be time to stop doing crazy shit and settle down, run my businesses, and let someone else do this job."

Lynche looked at the bill and signed the chit. "Nice try, Maverick. Settling down isn't in your DNA. What you need is a business manager so he or she can run the business while you play with quiet airplanes. I can go to Texas for a couple weeks if you and Nazy need to get away for her to recuperate."

"You're a god, Lynche, but there are no friggin' lakes near Fredericksburg." The oblique reference that Lynche wouldn't be able to go sailing in Texas drew a smirk from the older man.

"Yeah, yeah, yeah. What's the plan?"

"I don't know. Maybe I'll take her home to Texas, where Theresa and I can wait on her hand and foot. Maybe she wants to stay at her place."

"You have to be the one to tell Connie if you want me to go to Texas. She can't refuse you, you know."

"Coward!" Hunter 's banter was easily dismissed as fluff.

"As you would say, Maverick, spoken like a true liberal."

"*Touché.* I'll know more in a week or so. There'll be time for us to talk about it."

"Let me know." Lynche held up two fingers. Hunter got the hint. Greg Lynche wasn't coward but someone who could make the impossible happen.

"Nice getting the two Yo-Yos, Grinch, and thanks for lunch. Give Connie a hug for mc."

"Get your own damn hug!"

CHAPTER SEVENTY-SIX

1100 September 30, 2012
Ronald Reagan Washington National Airport

"The Agency's new jet just taxied in," cooed the tall, distinguished-looking man with a starched, high-collar Joseph A. Bank shirt and cuffed trousers. Douglass pulled his eye away from the telescope. "Want to watch?" He offered the monocular to the shorter portly man in bright suspenders and loafers who waddled over to look.

"It won't be Rothwell. He quit. That's what you get when you play with girls." He looked up and smirked at his partner.

The tall man patted the shoulder of the obese one, as the Lou Costello clone resumed his scrutiny of the Gulfstream G550. It pulled to a stop, and the airstairs immediately came down.

"Douglass, they're doing a quick turn! Start the camera! Get your binoculars! Move!"

Thirteen stories up, with a provocatively narrow view overlooking the Ronald Reagan Airport executive terminal, the apartment was the perfect location to observe the comings and goings of corporate and business jets cycling through the downtown Washington, DC airport. There was so much interest in apartment number 1313; it had to be auctioned to the highest bidder. The realty company believed the unusual interest in the 1,300-square-foot condo and subsequent bidding war was between competing triskaidekaphobes, who felt that owning such a unique address would help tenants face their fears.

The realtor would never comprehend that the fight over the property was actually between professional tail watchers and a handful of amateurs. The number of professional tail watchers was growing worldwide. The key to success in monitoring the lifts of the rich and famous—and certain government officials—was location, location,

location. Quietly funded by extreme liberal and communist organizations, the number of teams was growing worldwide, and some were getting rich. Such was the winner who secured the perfect location for the Washington, DC market.

"You don't have to bark at me, Carlton. I got it." The tall man flipped switches and pressed buttons on a stack of electronic and video-recording equipment. "There you go. We're recording and live."

The little fat man couldn't take his eye from the powerful telescope's eyepiece. "That's the Agency's new jet again; the same one Rothwell took last week. Oh! Oh! Douglass, there's movement!"

The tall and debonair man hurried to the window and scrutinized the executive terminal with a stout pair of binoculars with a long body and wide objective lenses.

When the recently-resigned Director of Central Intelligence, Dr. Bruce Rothwell, raced up the airstairs, the two men were stunned speechless. They couldn't believe it and didn't know how to resolve the dichotomy. Why would the disgraced DCI still use an Agency jet?

"Did you see who that was?"

"That was Rothwell!"

"I know. It makes no sense, but hey, we have to…report it."

Douglass repeated the words as if he refused to believe what he saw. "That was Rothwell."

"Hard to believe, I know. But if we're going to get paid, we have to report it. I believe it is your turn."

The tall man snapped from his bewilderment, turned, and bowed deeply. "You're generous to a fault."

"But no one is going to believe it."

"But we have the video! I'll input the tail number and indicate the former DCI is flying somewhere. That should be worth a few hundred dollars."

"That's most curious," the short man said. "Where do you think he's going? Where does a resigned DCI go, anyway?"

"We'll probably never know, but it's money in the bank, if they believe us. I really don't give a hoot where he's going." He patted the little fat man on the butt again, as he went to the computer terminal, his thin, bony fingers flew across the keyboard.

The short man shook his head and then looked through the telescope eyepiece again. “He’s probably going to Hell.”

The tall man behind the computer monitor broke into a huge smile and called over his shoulder, “Only if he’s Republican.”

CHAPTER SEVENTY-SEVEN

1600 September 30, 2012
Capitol Building
Senate Select Committee on Intelligence

Demetrius Eastwood sat alone at the long table, waiting to be sworn in and read his statement into the record. Many years before, dozens of strobe lights from power-winding cameras flooded the hearing room when he was asked to stand and raise his right hand, swearing that he would tell the truth, the whole truth, and nothing but the truth. That was the last time he testified before Congress. That wasn't a good day for Lieutenant Colonel Demetrius Eastwood, United States Marine Corps, because on that day, he had something to hide. He was a National Security Council staff member involved in a major scandal concerning the release of U.S. hostages held by Islamist radicals; before the Islamists found that they could be more effective if they organized.

Today, there were no observers in the balcony or anywhere else. No cameras, strobe lights, or reporters lined the witness table when Eastwood stood to be sworn in. It was just him, a microphone, and a bottle of water at the witness table. Today, he had something to tell. He would have welcomed an audience, but the Committee Chairman said otherwise.

The Closed Door hearing had been hastily called at the request of the Committee Chairman who saw the Eastwood video from Algeria, warning the U.S. Embassy personnel in Algiers of an impending attack. The Chairman threatened to subpoena Eastwood and compel him to appear before the Select Committee on Intelligence. The man was dumbfounded when Eastwood said, that wasn't the real story and agreed to testify behind closed doors, away from cameras, reporters, and the press. After the Committee Chairman thanked Eastwood for coming he indicated Eastwood could proceed.

Demetrius Eastwood took a drink of water and turned on the microphone before him. "I have a prepared statement. Thank you, Mr. Chairman and members of the Committee, for the opportunity to share what I recently learned during my investigation of the death of our Ambassador to Libya. I went to Libya with several preconceived notions, such as the Ambassador's death was an accident or the result of a mob that got out of hand. It was difficult for me to believe that one of the major terrorist networks, al-Qaeda or the Muslim Brotherhood—didn't have some role in the Ambassador's death. I assumed they didn't have sufficient presence in Libya to play a role. The previous administration wanted us to believe, al-Qaeda was on the run, decimated and losing influence in the Muslim world.

"What we found, surprisingly, was that there was more to the story than we thought. What we found, and filmed, was that not only al-Qaeda but other radicals were being quietly supported—being given material and intelligence support—by a network of mosques. We found mosques in Libya, Tunis, and Algeria are more connected than anyone in the intelligence community could possibly or want to imagine, and there was great danger dismissing or ignoring radical Islamists, just because they aren't limited to groups with names such as al-Qaeda.

"What was originally thought to be a loose confederation of tribes, they are now being organized. These organized groups are working together in an interconnected web—a network. A network of mosques."

He described the mosque network was reminiscent of the Iranian national networks of mosques that waited patiently for the period where Islam would eventually rise up and smite the infidels. He described a gentleman from Libya, his fearless driver, sitting outside the hearing room, who gained entry into the mosque network and could tell the panel how radical imams see their mosques as useful meeting places to rally public displays or investigate private or sensitive matters, such as watching people deemed of interest to the movement.

The most important thing Eastwood's driver found was that the mosques served as bases of operations for intelligence gathering or special activities.

"I thought al-Qaeda didn't have the organizational skills to build a clandestine network across Africa or throughout the United States, as it pursued its strategic goals of restoring the caliphate and ending the Western presence in Islamic lands. I was wrong. They have succeeded. After my latest research and experiences, it's clear to me—primarily the Muslim Brotherhood but also al-Qaeda to a lesser extent—there is a clandestine network in the United States, and it is up and running. It should not be a surprise there are community centers which are deep sleeper cells. This committee knows full well the FBI was investigating individual mosques before they were unilaterally pulled off the case. Now they're waiting for the right time or signal. I believe today they could be activated at any time in the future to destabilize the U.S. government through spectacular operations, such as 9/11.

"My film crew and I were sent to Libya to investigate and report on the death of our Ambassador in Benghazi. It wasn't until we were being evacuated from Algeria when the gentleman outside this hearing brought a pamphlet from a local mosque in Algeria. It was a recruiting poster, a cry for help to target American embassies and their Ambassadors and other key personnel for abduction. The pamphlet encouraged others to help take high-value American prisoners. In discussions with an imam, they would be exchanged for their brothers held at Guantanamo Bay.

"I initially thought the action against our Ambassador to Libya was a random act of violence of the kind seen daily in the Muslim world, a target of opportunity. We didn't expect to find that the Muslim Brotherhood had established a core network in Libya, Tunisia, and Algeria, and that the network remains clandestine and refrains from using the Brotherhood name. The same could be said of al-Qaeda.

"During several interviews with local merchants and people in the town of Benghazi, their viewpoint was that al-Qaeda sought to take advantage of the Libyan revolution to recruit militants and reinforce their operational capabilities. The overthrow of Gaddafi was a tremendous opportunity for al-Qaeda to create a safe haven in Libya and extend their area of operations.

"However, the network had already been established. It wasn't overt. While al-Qaeda's network is technically clandestine, they quietly rally affiliates and shadow groups to their black flag. Like zombies attracted to fresh meat, these groups feel the pull of gravity toward the black flag of al-Qaeda. Everyone in this room should know the black flag has come to symbolize al-Qaeda. It is their recruiting poster and where it flies is their rallying point.

"Some here may know the green flag has come to symbolize the Muslim Brotherhood. It doesn't have the same cachet as the al-Qaeda black flag. When we entered the consulate in Benghazi, we found a large green flag of the Muslim Brotherhood on the wall of the compound. When we saw that, we thought the worst, that the Brotherhood had changed their MO and became more active and kinetic. That they had learned a few things from al-Qaeda."

Eastwood looked up at the panel. The liberal congressmen fiddling with their BlackBerries set them down to listen intently to the man at the table. After sipping from his water Eastwood continued.

"Immediately after our evacuation from Algeria, I learned of the actions of a few mosques in the United States. Some of you may know of the correct number of Muslims—excuse me, Eastern-looking men and women—who were involved in eight, not two, airports on 9/11. Some of you may know that the correct number of Muslim conspirators on 9/11 wasn't just nineteen hijackers on four airplanes. There were over sixty men and women, with a total of ten aircraft planned for hijacking, but if not for the FAA grounding every airplane that day, we will never know how many more lives were saved.

"I doubt few of you know that several of these same mosques—in the same cities as the other six unsuccessful 9/11 airports—provided information for a sniper to kill several of our brave Navy SEALs after the death of Osama bin Laden. It's obvious to me that the evidence strongly suggests that al-Qaeda is not only alive and well in America, but they are on the march. Like the Muslim Brotherhood, they have formed sleeper cells in mosques in the United States, and they are likely connected to an al-Qaeda underground network that encompasses North Africa and the Middle East.

"These clandestine networks are certainly *jihadist* groups, committed to their objective of eradicating Western influence in the Muslim world and spread Muslim influence into the Western world. These terrorist organizations continue to prize secrecy. What is needed is more effort to better penetrate The Brotherhood and al-Qaeda's clandestine networks, at home and abroad.

"I'm now a correspondent and very familiar with the significant number of liberal politicians and commentators who downplay the risk of radical Islamist-led insurgencies. That is a very dangerous view. After a week of chasing rebels who attacked our embassies, I've determined these clandestine networks are in an expansion phase.

"They have shifted strategies. They've moved from bombing airplanes and buildings to individual *jihadists* building bombs and going on killing sprees. If you pick up the *Post* or the *Times,* you might find an article about a lone wolf who massacred several Americans with bombs or bullets. As these groups expand their sphere of influence, we'll see U.S. mosques running training camps and recruitment campaigns on social-media platforms. They're already doing it, and it's doubtful the FBI is aware. They've been systematically pulled off long-standing surveillance programs, courtesy of civil-liberty organizations.

"Upon arriving back in America, I found the clandestine networks were alive and well in North America. The gentleman sitting outside visited several mosques here in the Greater Washington Metropolitan Area. Like their North African counterparts, they publicly display a peaceful, gentle religious program of tolerance and peace, but, when the doors close, they revert to their true mandate and espouse a Taliban-like religious orientation and their devotion to Sharia law. They call for strict adherence to Islam. In America, these imams knew and boasted that their brothers sought to kidnap our ambassadors, diplomats, and chiefs of station in Tripoli, Tunis, and Algiers and exchange them for their brothers in Gitmo. The al-Qaeda-types continue to seek weapons of mass destruction.

"I'll host a special in the near future where these militant imams and their sympathizers publicly walk the walk and talk the talk. They're fairly open about what they're doing and why. "While some of these leaders openly distanced themselves from these groups, my television special will demonstrate these same men say one thing and do something different. They work clandestinely, in the shadows, and work to expand the terrorist networks in the U.S. with the ultimate goal of overthrowing the U.S. government.

"I was once sworn, just as you Committee members were, to uphold and defend the Constitution of the United States of America against all enemies foreign and domestic. Al-Qaeda and the Muslim Brotherhood intend to infringe on the First Amendment rights and impose a state religion. It is time for us to recognize our sworn duty to defend our Constitution.

"As a good friend of mine is fond of saying, there's a war on Christianity, not just from liberal elites here at home but worldwide, and ignoring it won't make it go away.

"That completes my prepared remarks. I'm ready to take your questions."

CHAPTER SEVENTY-EIGHT

1600 September 30. 2012
The White House

Entry into CIA Headquarters was smooth and efficient, although Duncan Hunter drove a rental car. Black uniformed security men with black M-4s, black boots, and black hats gave the car extra scrutiny. They didn't like rental cars at the CIA. It was too easy to hide something in one, which made them dangerous.

Once he was cleared to enter the facility, Hunter took the long route around the acres of parking to pass near the black titanium A-12 up on concrete blocks at the back of the new headquarters building.

Arriving at the transportation center, Hunter found a vehicle idling and waiting for him. Astonished and unable to believe his good fortune, he slid into the soft leather seat of the black Lincoln Town Car.

"Good afternoon, Sir." The driver closed the door behind him.

Duncan settled into the plush seats, yawned, and closed his eyes. It had been a hectic ninety-six hours. If he were allowed to rest for two minutes, he knew he'd fall asleep.

After flying the ransom Gulfstream 550 directly to Texas, Hunter taxied the jet to his hangar. With the corporate Quiet Aero Systems Gulfstream on the ramp in Baltimore, he towed the 550 into the Quiet Aero Systems corporate air-conditioned hangar and closed the door. Carlos Yazzic picked him up and drove Duncan to the house.

After a few hours' sleep, Hunter showered, shaved, and headed to Del Rio to teach his class at Laughlin Air Force Base and personally delivered the keys and the Jaguar to his daughter.

When you're a father, there are some things you don't miss, like your daughter's birthday.

With a very late night return to the ranch in Kelly's old rattletrap Fiero the following morning, Hunter enjoyed his first real meal in days —*huevo rancheros*—after a slow, painful six-mile run. He conducted staff meetings at Quiet Aero Systems and HAVCO Technologies and tossed to a bewildered scientist a dusty and sandy sheet. "The camouflage material you invented has been operationally checked, and I think it works very well." Hunter did not say the nanotechnology matrix had saved his life.

At the end of the day, he had dinner with the owner of a classic Jaguar. Kelly understood and supported the decision when Duncan said he'd be away from Texas awhile as Nazy recovered from surgery, and that he'd be with her morning, noon, and night.

The elegant and polite driver had driven hundreds of the highest-ranking intelligence officers in the CIA, in and around the Greater Washington Metropolitan Area, but never on Sunday. He wondered what the CIA was coming to, chauffeuring *a contractor* to the White House, but his job was to drive, not to judge.

When the only vehicle in the lot was the Town Car, Hunter knew there had to be a mistake. He was a ride-in-the-back-of-a-bakery-truck kind of guy, but he wasn't about to complain or ask questions. That was one ride he would enjoy.

The snappily dressed driver greeted and addressed Hunter by name as he held the door. After passing through the main security gate at the CIA, Duncan tried to engage the driver in a little conversation and light banter, but the diminutive man focused on driving safely and not entertaining his bored passenger. Hunter fought fatigue during the twelve-mile, thirty-minute journey to the White House. Before arriving, he woke himself several times by snorting.

After hours at the White House meant no personal secretary to avoid, no kitchen staff to sequester, and no closet to hide in. Hunter almost felt like a real executive in his Brooks Brothers suit meeting the country's head of state. In his role, he wasn't a high-powered business executive but a contract pilot with a Level-One Yankee White clearance and an ancient tangential relationship with a former Congressman, now the President of the United States.

The drive onto the White House grounds was expeditiously handled by the Secret Service security guards, and the limousine pulled to a stop near a side door. The President wanted a quiet, personal debrief.

No skullduggery through the odiferous kitchen this time! Hunter told himself. *You're moving up in the world.*

President Javier Hernandez appeared at the double doors, where a single six-foot-eight United States Marine stood guard. Hunter bounded from the car and across the portico as the President offered his hand.

The President, in navy-blue Polo, chinos, and deck shoes, led Hunter into the Oval Office and closed the door. He motioned Hunter to sit on the sofa and broke into a toothy smile.

"Duncan, it seems like every time I see you, it's to give you an award for something unusually meritorious. I'm not sure what we can do this time, although the circumstances warrant something more substantial than a slab of pot metal in a wooden presentation case. I'll think of something while you tell me what you know and what happened in Algeria. I especially want to know how you got aboard the *Eisenhower* and how you came to know of the weapons in Libya. First, tell me how Miss Cunningham's doing."

"Mr. President, Sir, she's doing well. I appreciate all the help and support she's receiving. I understand Nazy is a special interest patient."

"Duncan, Blanca Ortega is my niece. I asked her to look after her personally. She's the head of Internal Medicine. I don't think she told you she almost died in Iraq from a suicide bomber. She knows more than anyone what it's like to bounce back from devastating injuries.

Please know Miss Cunningham's in great hands."

Duncan remembered the doctor's severely scarred hands and nodded. "Again, thank you, Mr. President. I could tell she was a great, strong lady. As for some of the finer points of the mission, I regret to say I'm not sure I'll be much help, as there's a lot I still don't know. Somehow, all the connections converged on the last man from your disposition matrix. This man—the DCI never provided his name—I think was the trigger puller, the financier, or the facilitator of the shoot down of Flight 800, the TWA 747 that was lost shortly after takeoff in July, 1996.

"The DCI indicated the unnamed man quote, 'shot down commercial aircraft, usually for ransom.' I got into position to survey the situation, and I hadn't been on scene more than a few minutes when the man launched a *Stinger* at me."

"*A... Stinger?* Did it hit you?"

"The first one didn't, but the second one did. It blew off the end of my right wing. I bailed out." He vividly related the events leading up to the errant countermeasures flare and missile blast as if they were high-definition video, when everything went white. He was blinded by the flare only inches from his face, which shut down his optic nerves. He decided not to embellish with too many details unless requested by the President.

"My God."

"I was forced to protect myself and completed the mission the best way I knew how. Before neutralizing the target and his team on the ground, I discovered a trove of shipping containers in an underground bunker whose roof served as the floor of an aircraft hangar. In addition to other MANPADS, there were hundreds of cases of what I determined to be filled with gold coins. I took one of the target's private airplanes to escape from the facility. With my emergency radio, I called the carrier on station in the Med to lend assistance and requested permission to land.

"The carrier's captain approved my landing. I told him I suspected I'd been exposed to anthrax. With my CIA emergency code, he allowed me to land and had a decontamination team waiting. They scrubbed me down and shot me full of antibiotics. The skipper, Captain Mike Zacker, and I went to the Officer's Mess to help warm me up." Hunter didn't discuss being naked on the fantail of the carrier, freezing his tail off while exposed to a bevy of young sailors. That was too much information.

"I ran into two gentlemen, Bill McGee and Demetrius Eastwood, who were evacuated from Embassy Algiers. Sir, McGee, Zacker, and I were all that the Naval War College in 2002-2003."

"A fortuitous connection."

"Yes Sir. The President of the War College said we wouldn't believe where or when we'd run into NWC alumni. Zacker was an F-18 pilot. We were both prior enlisted guys, but he was always Navy, and he made captain, like McGee. McGee's a thirty-five-year retired SEAL, also a former enlisted man, and now a faculty member of the school.

"I learned McGee had been contracted by Langley to help locate and identify caches of MANPADS, ostensibly Gaddafi's, which were in an underground storage facility in Benghazi. The fact that there were MANDPADS in both locations, and both had similar makeshift underground storage facilities, was too much of a coincidence for me. I had seen similar structures used by drug smugglers when I was with the Border Patrol.

"That's amazing, Duncan."

"Ingenious. Sir, when the target said something to the effect that I was already dead, right after I saw white powder on his shirt, I realized it burst from his shirt pocket. It was totally unexpected. It appeared the guy wasn't only responsible for the attack on the TWA jet and maybe other unsolved commercial airliners crashes but may have been the real belly button responsible for the anthrax attack after 9/11. I'm certain some CIA file would have the details and the truth. I admit I was pretty excited and anxious about getting away and completing the mission, but what happened in the desert made it clear to me that the target probably had access, at least at one time, to a large cache of anthrax. Sir, no disrespect, but I assumed you knew all this when you approved the man on the disposition matrix."

President Hernandez chose his words carefully. Multiple topics he wanted to discuss were crowding his thoughts. "Duncan, Rothwell indicated he had a fast-moving opportunity, so I approved the operation without receiving the usual brief from the DCI. There wasn't a rogue bioweapons scientist?"

"Doesn't look like it, Sir. You could get a full debrief, obviously... unless Rothwell destroyed the file...."

"What are you thinking?"

Hunter shook his head. "Mr. President, at the time, I didn't think anything of it, but Nazy had been read-in on a special access program and went to Algeria under the auspices of temporarily replacing the Chief of Station, who was pregnant."

The President's eyes narrowed, and he cocked his head, thinking hard. "Go on."

"Sir, Nazy was the sole casualty, as I understand, from the Algerian embassy evacuation. Bill McGee and I are still unsure how or why she was singled out for being kidnapped. I understand our SEALs took out several gate crashers—protesters with AKs and RPGs—before they blew a hole in the chancery to do who-knows-what. Maybe Nazy was a target of opportunity. Captain McGee was able to follow the kidnappers and recovered Nazy, then brought her back to the embassy where they were evacuated to the *Eisenhower*. She was transferred to Naval Air Station Sigonella and underwent surgery.

"I assumed the Agency sent a jet to recover her when she was fit to travel, but, when I found the DCI in Nazy's room at Walter Reed, he confirmed he was the one who brought her back from Italy."

"Duncan, I had no idea. How'd the protesters get to her? Did they know she was acting station chief? Do we know anything?

"Mr. President, I don't have those answers. From the guys on the ground, they were fairly certain the embassy had been cased. Maybe during an investigation—I'm assuming there will be one—they'll find out or get a better understanding of why. Bill McGee or one of his fellow SEALs, someone, witnessed a couple of Algerians who were there to ostensibly get a visa, but they wandered away from their handler, as if it was all a mistake. The SEALs knew it was a crude ruse so they could case the compound.

"After the wall was blown open, Bill couldn't come up with any other reason why Nazy was immediately spirited from the embassy other than someone knew who she was and targeted her, or she was a target of opportunity. Once he had time to reflect, he thought some of the protesters had to know who to look for. The SEALs indicated Nazy definitely stood out of the crowd as one of the few women stationed at the embassy. McGee surmised whoever first came through the wall stumbled across her and carried her from the embassy. She was injured in the blast and was probably unconscious when they carried her off."

"And she's recovering well, I hope. I've asked for updates on her condition."

"Yes, Sir. Thank you. Nazy's still heavily sedated. Commander Ortega indicated she might be able to come home in a week or ten days."

"That's marvelous, Duncan."

Hunter nodded and continued. "The other man in this story is probably just as important. I learned a lot from Colonel Eastwood when we were on the *Ike*. These weren't your run-of-the-mill vanilla protesters wanting to crawl over an embassy wall just to capture the American flag and burn it or piss on it to make a statement and demand the U.S. get the hell out of their country. They rushed people with RPGs and AK-47s into the compound immediately after it was breeched. Our SEALs stopped them from entering the chancery.

"Lieutenant Colonel Eastwood was in Algeria and filmed the group that eventually assaulted the embassy. I understand he saw the aftermath of the consulate in Libya, with the green flag of the Muslim Brotherhood still hanging inside the compound almost a week after our Ambassador was killed."

"I didn't know that."

"I don't know if that's the press' omission or commission to keep their mouths shut. Eastwood has it on film, and he watched and filmed these guys rolling in on the embassies in Tripoli and Tunis with some coordination—excuse me, apparent collaboration—of the local mosques. He found it odd that the mosques appeared to be connected or tied together somehow. Eastwood thought what he saw was a stealthy network. They're all connected, as if they're sleeper cells waiting for the call to action.

"His driver, a Libyan, I understand, was able to meld in with the groups who attacked the embassy. He entered their mosques and found a highly organized operation. There was nothing spontaneous or passive. They had an agenda to kidnap the Ambassadors, Station Chiefs, and others, presumably to exchange them for prisoners being held at Gitmo."

"That's an absolutely frightening thought."

"There's more, Sir. Eastwood's driver found those imams wanted the ambassadors, diplomats, and chiefs of station to torture them as punishment for taking out Osama bin Laden and for supporting Muslim leaders who oppose al-Qaeda or the Muslim Brotherhood. The imams had a vision of collecting our diplomats, putting them in a prison, and abusing and humiliating them. They planned to do all the things the left accused the previous Republican administration of doing to the detainees at Guantanamo Bay."

"My God. I haven't heard any of that in my PDB, my daily brief from the Agency."

Duncan Hunter related his discoveries and theories that related to the actual number of Muslims involved in the 9/11 attacks. He outlined the methods used to smuggle weapons through X-ray machines at a number of airports, not just Boston and JFK, and how the suspected Muslim screeners left the airports and were never heard from again. Then he told the story how Navy SEALs had been systematically killed after the death of bin Laden, that a sniper got his info from the same local mosques in the same towns where those SEALs were killed.

"When we had McGee, Eastwood, and me at the same table—

three guys with different pieces of the puzzle—we saw an obvious conspiracy. It was huge. The common denominator was the quiet, peaceful mosques. They were the focal point for organizing the airport screeners, providing the sniper information on his targets, and the embassy attacks. They're somehow connected and obviously talk to each other. It's ... clearly a clandestine network.

"They can portray themselves as peaceful and upstanding in the community, but their actions, like cops putting clues on a board to discern trends and links to a crime, indicate they're the focal point of these events. We agreed there had to be a sleeper cell in every one. It was the only thing that made sense. You wouldn't think they had anything to do with this, but, when you put all the pieces on the table, it starts to form a picture."

President Hernandez felt like he swam through a whirlpool of information. He finally popped up after being overwhelmed by succeeding waves of new information delivered in rapid-fire, excited bursts. "That picture shows we have a problem. Duncan, what do you need from me? Any recommendations?"

"Mr. President, I don't know if anyone from the FBI is looking into any part of this. Colonel Eastwood is on the Hill testifying as to what I just told you. I don't know what else we can do, but...if I had the power to do something, I'd put those mosques from which information was provided when the SEALs were killed on some kind of terrorist watch list. I'd probably do the same for the mosques that supported and hid those screeners and failed hijackers. They need something to highlight them so they can be investigated.

"It's probably not practical or politically viable—the civil liberties wonks will go crazy—but something needs to be done. In my view, those are our enemies, foreign and domestic. If they don't actively support terrorist activities, they're at least giving cover to sleeper cells until someone needs them and activates them."

"They will scream bloody murder. I can imagine blood squirting from their eyes."

"They already have been. I read something last year about how the

FBI set up a sting operation at a few mosques to see if anyone was interested in blowing up Americans. The program required high-level approval from a special sensitive operations review committee, and it worked. They disrupted *jihadist* terror plants at nearly every mosque the FBI entered.

"Somehow, the program got exposure. Groups sued the FBI for allegedly violating the Muslims' civil rights. Now mosques are 'hands off' to FBI surveillance or undercover sting operations.

"Anyway, whether these limitations were set up from political pressure by Islamic groups or it was another area of the Department of Justice where the previous President interfered enough to protect his buddies, I don't know. Your predecessor ensured the NSA could track our every phone call and keystroke under the guise of stopping terrorists, but he wouldn't authorize any action in mosques, where we've got actual terrorists."

The President shook his head in defeated agreement. "There are no easy answers. It's amazing the damage he caused." He sat stoically, assimilating the information and wrestling with its implications.

"Circumstantial evidence points to their involvement," Duncan said. "One more thing, Sir, an observation. It's not *conservative* Muslims who are the problem. If you look at those guys critically, they're hardworking and industrious. They do great things and are family men and women. They want to be left alone and are, by and large, some of the best law-abiding citizens anywhere. They remind me of the men and women of the Royal Jordanian Air Force. Peaceful, professional, proud, and patriotic.

"On the other hand, it seems to me it's the political liberal side of the Muslim world that's the problem. That ten-to-fifteen percent. They're arm-in-arm with their socialist liberal cousins—presidential assassins, anarchists, mass murderers, and heads of radical movements. There's a critical mass of extremists, and it's growing. Islamofascists will always be at war with Muslim nations and ... us. We have to be forever vigilant. They'll attack our planes, buildings, and even civilians in a mall or running a marathon.

"I think the reason conservative Muslims don't dare say anything against their murderous liberal cousins is that not only have they been intimidated by them for so long, conservative Muslims have never had the right to protect themselves. In one way, since there's no such thing in the Muslim world as the Second Amendment, conservative Muslims react like they're whipped dogs. They do whatever it takes to get along. If they don't, they or their families can be killed.

"Rdical Muslims, like our crazy liberals, are out of control. I know we have to find ways to work with our liberal cousins, but when they're actively trying to destroy the country and the Constitution, it's hard to lock arms and sing *Kumbaya* with them."

"That's as good an analysis as anything I've heard," the President replied. "One could make the case that the reason liberals attack the Second Amendment is because it's the only thing keeping them in check. A very interesting set of observations, Duncan."

The President tapped his fingers on the back of the sofa, nodded in syncopation to unheard music. He stood and walked to the resolute desk. After shuffling some papers, he returned with a notepad and sat down, referencing his notes as he talked.

"Confirmation from the ground," he began. "We had a man check, and they are assured all the MANPADS in Benghazi were destroyed. There was evidence of a massive weapons cache. The compound was completely incinerated. The Marines from the 22nd Marine Expeditionary Unit recovered another twenty missiles from the underground bunker in Algeria, but the real prize was nearly every gold coin the U.S. paid as ransom since 1996 was recovered, over three billion dollars.

"That you, Duncan Hunter, found and facilitated its recovery is most noteworthy. It was an unexpected bonus. The United States needs to find a way to properly reward you."

"Sir, I believe I've been sufficiently rewarded." He smiled.

"Hold that thought. I have to tell you, what Paul Harvey would say, is the rest of the story."

"Sir?"

"All hell's breaking loose, Duncan. There's one scandal after another from the previous administration. Whistleblowers are coming out to tell their stories or dump classified documents online. I'm not sure it'll become a scandal, but it should. I understand there's a new film coming out about Flight 800. Some whistleblowers got up enough courage to tell how they were told to keep their mouths shut during the accident investigation."

"That's amazing, Mr. President. We knew that airplane was knocked down by a missile, but that administration did everything it could *not* to call it terrorism."

"Indeed. When you related how you thought the target was the man responsible somehow for the shoot down of Flight 800, I debated whether to tell you that my family was impacted by that act of terror. Duncan, my sister was on that flight. She was a head flight attendant and had been with TWA forever. She was one of their few Hispanic stewardesses. Blanca is her daughter, my niece.

"You eliminated from this Earth the vermin who did that. Please accept that is one of the greatest gifts you could have given me and my family. Celeste's killer received his due justice." He squeezed Duncan's shoulder as both men's eyes welled. The two men were quiet for a moment. "Thank you, Duncan Hunter."

"Sir, you're welcome; it has been an honor to be able to serve and make a difference. I'm glad I had the opportunity. This program works."

President Hernandez stifled a smile. "You see, when I said it was an unexpected bonus, it really was. It allows us to move on. Still, as I said, I need a way to reward you properly."

With a conspiratorial grin, Hunter playfully said, "Well, Mr. President, you might find this hard to believe, but I found an abandoned Gulfstream jet in Algeria. I was going to try to acquire it legally as salvage. All the ownership paperwork was on the jet. All anyone has to do is fill in his name on the title. I'm certain there's someone in government who'd like it back. I'd like to keep it and avoid any difficulties or challenges to claiming it as salvage."

"Duncan, instead of a percentage of the recovered amount, I'll authorize its transfer. The U.S. government owes you a huge debt of gratitude. It may not be as nice as another medal, but a salvaged aircraft, well, if that satisfies you, we'll call it even."

The President offered his hand, and Hunter shook it to seal the deal. Several seconds passed before the President asked, "What are your plans with Miss Cunningham?"

"Sir, when she's released, we'll go to my ranch and take it easy while she recovers. When I saw her earlier today, she was tired but doing well. Doc Ortega said she'd make a full recovery, though it won't be easy."

"Good. That's good to know." The President exhaled loudly and rocked back and forth. "It's been a hell of a week."

"Yes, it has. You probably have better things to do than have me mess up your weekend. I should get going, Mr. President."

"Duncan, you may not believe it, but talking with you is probably the best thing that happened to me this week. We've had to evacuate an embassy and some oil fields, because Americans were killed by Islamic terrorists during a refinery attack in Algeria. Over eighty from a dozen Islamic countries were killed altogether. Of course, the DCI resigned, and I have to find a replacement. I thought he would be a good one. He came up from the ranks and had an impressive résumé."

"Sir, there might be one more thing you could do for…us."

"What's that, Duncan?"

Duncan paused and considered his next words. There was an ominous tone in his voice. "Mr. President, when you said the DCI resigned, it reminded me of something I've been mulling over. I don't know how, but somehow I'm positive Rothwell had a part in this Algerian mess. I'll go to my grave suspecting my last target knew I was coming, and he knew where to look in the sky to find and target me. He may have been paranoid or just lucky, but if it wasn't the former and it wasn't luck, then the only person who could have provided that bit of information was Rothwell. When he saw me today, he looked like he'd seen a ghost, and he couldn't get away from me fast enough."

The President allowed his thoughts to wander, not sure what Hunter was intimating. There were rumors about Rothwell that troubled him, but it was only after Rothwell assumed the DCI position that other things came out. They were never discussed openly and rarely mentioned behind closed doors.

The one item not found on any résumé and never considered during his confirmation hearings, because he was such a highly decorated, accomplished intelligence officer, was that several years earlier, shortly after the 9/11 attacks, a rumor surfaced that Dr. Rothwell converted to Islam. It made a compelling story. To know the enemy, one had to understand him, and Rothwell studied the Qur'an and worked in the National Clandestine Service, where he lived in the Middle East as an undercover agent.

Converting to Islam supposedly gave him an advantage, especially when the CIA struggled to gain any advantage in trying to infiltrate al-Qaeda or other terrorist organizations. It was a terrific story when Rothwell relayed it to the President during a personal interview.

However, once the President became aware, he didn't want to think he would have withdrawn Rothwell's nomination to the DCI just because he was Muslim convert. The man was largely an American hero which few knew anything about. In light of events of the past week, that nomination proved a gross mistake.

President Hernandez returned his attention to Hunter's soliloquy.

"...the DCI just happened to be in the immediate area, with all the atmospherics surrounding him in Washington, it was just too coincidental for my sense of...proportion. There's something there. It wasn't just another pissed-off girlfriend. I was supposed to whack a terrorist when he popped out of a hole, and the DCI is magically in the area where they're going to offload the gold? Why he was there at that time makes no sense. It can't be coincidence."

"Duncan, what you've said is troubling. It may be doubly so when I tell you that Dr. Rothwell converted to Islam sometime before 9/11. I don't know how or why it would make a difference."

"Now *that* is very interesting, Mr. President. I understood his conversion to be a rumor. It's another piece of this very difficult puzzle." His gaze went to his lap, as his mind processed data and made calculations that would have given an IBM Big Blue supercomputer a hernia.

The President was taken aback when Hunter seemed to slip into a trance for a few moments. When Duncan slowly raised his head, a devious smile spread across his face.

"Sir, if the President asked for an investigation of Dr. Rothwell, it might prove very interesting to know if there were other Agency personnel on the ground in and around that area in Algeria where the gold was found and recovered. Maybe check his email or text messaging account. I'm pretty sure the NSA does that shit all the time. There has to be more people involved than just Rothwell."

President Hernandez showed surprise, then he became animated. "Wow. That's incredible, Duncan. I don't know where that came from, but when you framed it like that, I begin to see what others may not see."

"Mr. President, if you need a good name for a replacement DCI, I have a candidate. He won't screw you or the country over."

The President, amused by the offer, asked who the person was and why. Hunter explained his choice and rationale.

"It wouldn't be unprecedented," President Hernandez said, stroking his chin in thought. "I'd need someone to clean house."

"Sir, there are too many closet radicals and liberals on the payroll. The CIA needs an enema."

President Hernandez laughed so hard he began coughing and choking. Hunter worried that if the President didn't recover quickly, he might have to perform the Heimlich maneuver on him or have the Secret Service haul him away for killing the President with a bad joke.

When the President finally stopped coughing, he wiped tears from his cheeks and waved a thick finger at Hunter. "Oh, that was funny. Woo-hoo! Duncan, that was a good one."

"Sorry, Sir. He's a liberal, but he's not rabid. I'll bet he would sail through the Democratic Senate confirmation hearings."

"I'll think about it." Squeezing tears from his eyes, he checked his watch. After taking a deep breath, he smiled.

The meeting was over. The men stood and shook hands. President Hernandez reminded him that the CEO of British Airways granted Hunter a lifetime pair of first class ticket to anywhere for saving his jet and crew.

"Without a quiet airplane, what are your plans?"

"Sir, I have acquired another YO-3 but it needs to be overhauled and modified. Several months' worth of work. While that is going on, when she's up to it, I'd like to take Nazy to a faraway corner of the planet to recuperate. I'm thinking Fiji."

"I'd go to Tahiti if I had the chance."

"Tahiti or Bora Bora would be nice this time of year. Thank you again, Mr. President."

"Thank you, Duncan Hunter. You're a great American. Thank you for all you've done and will do to help protect these United States."

CHAPTER SEVENTY-NINE

1955 September 30, 2012
New York City, New York

The attractive TV reporter, blonde and blue-eyed in a black suit with dozens of sparkling diamonds dangling from her earlobes, stared directly into the camera without blinking and read the teleprompter.

"Immediately following this broadcast, we'll present a special report hosted by our correspondent, Demetrius Eastwood, entitled *Is Your Neighborhood Mosque a Sleeper Cell?* Just watch us tonight at eight o'clock Eastern and learn how al-Qaeda and the Muslim Brotherhood infiltrated the U.S. government with help from the former President and how these terrorist groups are on the march, growing in North Africa and the Middle East. That's tonight, following these messages from our sponsors."

CHAPTER EIGHTY

2000 September 30, 2012
Walter Reed National Military Medical Center
Bethesda, Maryland

Nazy Cunningham slept. Duncan's chin rested on his chest, as he snored beside her bed, his fingers intertwined with hers. Nazy's full-throated, open-mouth snoring competed with Duncan's deep rumbling until the nurse on her rounds crashed through the door and upset the delicate, harmonious, phlegmatic noisemakers. Hunter awoke, Nazy stirred. A yawn prefaced a stretch, and Nazy's eyes strained to open.

She felt the nurse poking, prodding, checking, and was surprised to find her fingers trapped. She opened her eyes to investigate what constrained her hand before she returned to blissful sleep.

"Duncan...," came from her lips, her British accent thick and sticky.

"Hey, Baby," he said in a deep husky voice, trying to be quiet. He wasn't trying to sound sexy.

In a sultry voice she hadn't used in months, she replied, "When you talk ... like that ... it makes me ... all melty."

Hunter looked up and saw the nurse stifle a grin. "I'm sure the nurse needed to hear that, Miss Cunningham."

The nurse's grin broadened. "It seems our patient feels *much* better."

Nazy rolled her head toward the voice and said, "I *am* feeling better, just tired." She rolled back and looked at Duncan with fuzzy wide eyes, as if to say, *"Oops!"*

The nurse checked the monitor connections before looking at Nazy's IV and the bandage on her breast. She pulled the sheet and blanket back to Nazy's chin, then rescanned the room to ensure everything was in place and operating.

Six vases with jasmine, orchids, roses, and carnations filled all available flat spaces in the room save for the tray hovering over Nazy's feet. Satisfied the myriad flowers wouldn't interfere with the patient's sink or window, the nurse pumped more fluid into the IV port and checked the multisystem monitor one last time.

Without looking at Hunter, she said as she left, "Visiting hours are over."

Hunter ignored her. He squeezed Nazy's hand gently and gazed into her eyes. Nazy's expression remained the same—resigned to telling Duncan the news. She was still worried what he would think and say. "Duncan, I have to tell you I'm not…I was…pregnant."

"I know, Baby. I'm so sorry. I love you, and I'm glad you're OK, safe, and getting better. Right now, that's all that matters."

"How did you know?"

"Dr. Ortega told me. Are you OK?"

"I am. I was worried about you. I was afraid what you thought." She yawned, and Duncan knew time was running out. He needed to go, but he needed to tell her about Kelly.

"I'm sorry, Baby," he said. "All that matters is I have you back, you're safe, and I can't wait to take you home."

When she squeezed his hand, he stood and kissed her, willing her to be strong. It was his turn, but he delayed, trying to find the right words.

"I was so afraid, Duncan. I was afraid I'd lose you. I was so happy when I saw you this morning." She held his hand tighter, lighting the room with her smile.

Duncan stroked her unmarked cheek with the back of his hand and wondered what she was talking about. The turn of the conversation was a little odd. Was she still under the influence of the drug that made her sleep? Was she babbling or impaired? She seemed lucid, but her words didn't make sense. Why would she be afraid for him? She yawned, stretched, and relaxed; she settled down for more drug-induced sleep.

Her focus on him, not the baby, surprised him. He expected a bigger emotional reaction, but, with the trauma she'd been through, maybe her reaction wasn't so unusual. "Baby, why would you be afraid for me?" He wanted to tell her about Kelly before the nurses threw him out, but his curiosity was spiked with concern.

"Rothwell.... I don't trust...Rothwell. He's was...." She was going limp, in preparation for sleep.

Hunter sensed he was too late to tell her about Kelly, but the mention of Rothwell immediately piqued his interest. *Of course she doesn't trust Rothwell. Who would? Why does it matter?*

"What about Rothwell, Baby?"

She quickly slipped into the stage of progressively diminishing responses to his question, and he had even more to ask. She was in the nebulous stage bridging the gap between wakefulness and sleep. If she didn't respond quickly before entering light sleep, she'd leap across a chasm of drug-induced sleep and wouldn't hear anything for hours.

"Bad. He's bad, Duncan. I was afraid he'd hurt...you. He was ...Algiers station...chief. ...afraid he'd kill you...." She stopped speaking. Only the shallow rise and fall of her blanket-covered bosom showed she was still breathing.

Duncan gripped her hand and shook it gently, insisting she stay awake a little longer. "Baby, stay with me. What do you mean he was station chief? Why would you be afraid he'd kill me?"

"Man on ...the lissst. Rothwell...met...him...."

"Please, Nazy. One more." Hunter hovered over her, almost crushing her hand, as she slipped away. Whatever was shot into her IV was very strong and very fast.

"Uh...huh...," she said sleepily. With her next breath, she snored gently in rhythmic, noisy breaths so softly it was easy to ignore.

Hunter jammed his tongue against his cheek in exasperation. He kissed her lips before her jaw fell slack, and she began serious, unladylike snoring.

His mind raced through the data. He would talk to her again in the morning.

CHAPTER EIGHTY-ONE

2130 September 30, 2012
JW Marriott Presidential Suite
Washington, DC

Duncan hadn't spoken a word since leaving Nazy's room. He drove from the hospital into downtown on autopilot and checked into the hotel by flipping his American Express card on the granite countertop. When he received his electronic keys, he turned from the reservation desk without even acknowledging the courteous service of the receptionist behind the counter.

He had one question on his mind, and he couldn't answer it. He needed help that wasn't in Washington or at the bottom of a bottle. He was afraid the guy who might be able to answer the question ricocheting around in his brain, splintering into one dead-end possibility after another, was asleep several states removed from the People's Republic of Maryland, as he often called the egregiously liberal state.

He rode the elevator to the top floor while pressing keys on his BlackBerry. Crappy signal strength prevented him from immediately sending the terse text message.

As he slipped into his room, he checked the device again and pressed *Send.*

Bullfrog, are you home or are you asleep?

Hunter walked to the toilet. By the time he zipped his pants, his BlackBerry rang.

Home.

Do you have ten minutes for a vet? Can be in Newport in a couple hours.

See you at airport 2330.

On my way.

CHAPTER EIGHTY-TWO

2330 September 30, 2012
Newport State Regional Airport

The late-night arrival of the Gulfstream IV Special-Purpose business jet didn't raise any eyebrows. The rich and famous continually flew in and out of the airport at the most-ungodly hours, while a small group of dedicated tail watchers monitored the comings and goings of the corporate or business aircraft. Hunter made the job of professional and hobby tail watchers as difficult as possible. If tail watchers tried to identify the Gulfstream through an Internet search of the aircraft's N number in the FAA registry, they would have found it assigned to a jet from an oil-drilling company in New Mexico and wouldn't be able to trace it to Quiet Aero Systems of Fredericksburg, Texas. Duncan taxied to the front of the terminal after promising Ground Control he would be on the ground for less than thirty minutes.

Bill McGee stepped from the executive terminal and onto the tarmac as the big, white jet shut down its engines. The auxiliary power unit still ran, providing power to the aircraft's internal and external electrical systems. The floodlights that normally illuminated the tail and engine cowlings were off, making it impossible to see the N number. Green and red position lights, as well as a tiny white tail bulb, were on, as were the cabin lights. Hunter lowered the stairs, and Bill raced up inside the G-IVSP.

After salutations, family inquiries, and an update on Nazy's condition, Duncan got to the point. The two men sat in the cabin's huge tan leather captain's chairs, facing each other. Hunter took the lead and related what he knew Nazy went through—the blast, the rape, the attempted mutilation, and couldn't thank McGee enough for rescuing her, patching her up, and saving her life.

"As I said," McGee replied, "that debt was paid long ago, *Amigo.* What's on your mind, Apex? There's more, and it must be pretty important for you to bring a jet at this late hour."

"I don't know if it is or not. You know the DCI recently resigned?"

"Yeah. He had trouble keeping his dick in his pants."

"I prefer to call it a series of unrestrained bimbo eruptions that he couldn't handle. Anyway, this morning I found Rothwell in Nazy's room, and I also learned he's the one who picked her up in Italy and brought her to the States. She's at Walter Reed."

"Don't you mean Bethesda?"

"Yes, Sir. I suppose it'll always be Bethesda for Marines and Sailors. He wasn't expecting me to waltz through the door. Nazy and I kept our relationship secret for several reasons. I thought the turd would piss himself when he saw me, and he got out of there as fast as he could.

"A few hours later, I debriefed with the President and talked to Nazy a little before they knocked her out to sleep through the night. Something both the President and Nazy said bothered me. Before they kicked me off her floor, what Nazy said got me to thinking there's more to that guy than meets the eye. I'm certain he's gone to ground. My question is how do I find a guy like Rothwell if he's bolted?"

Bill pressed his lips together and squinted, forming a massive frown on the man's heavily lined face. He took his time to respond, because he wasn't sure what Duncan was leading up to. "There are dozens of ways…if you're the FBI, NSA, or CIA. Otherwise, you have to play by the rules and look for him in unconventional ways."

"You mean like Google?"

McGee shook his massive head. "He wouldn't pop up in a search engine like that. He's a pro and knows all the tricks. If he went to ground, he's hiding and knows how to stay off the grid. It could be very difficult and maybe impossible.

"But ... there are other ways. Sometimes a little money and a little luck can find…ah, where he's been. If he doesn't want to be found.... It's nearly impossible to find the location of a trained spook when he's running in the black or in deep cover. They're too well trained. They practice all the time. What are you thinking?"

"I want to ask him a few questions."

"I'll bet you do." He spoke matter-of-factly in his radio-announcer voice.

"Bill, how'd you track down that sniper? I thought if you could do that, maybe you could do some of that special SEAL magic and…."

"…point you in the right direction?"

"Something like that. Let me tell you what I think I'm dealing with. Rothwell resigns and the President tells me he converted to Islam…."

McGee jerked upright. Suddenly, the night was getting interesting, but it always did when Duncan was in town.

"Rothwell was in the area when I was getting shot down," Duncan continued. "I'm fairly certain my number-one girl told me Rothwell met the guy who shot me down. I think she also suggested Rothwell was station chief in Algiers when the whole ransom thing started."

"What ransom thing? You never mentioned anything like that when we were on the *Ike.* You only mentioned or told us about a network of mosques."

"I couldn't. What I couldn't and shouldn't say is the guy who shot me down somehow used his cache of *Stingers* or other MANPADS to shoot down a TWA 747 in 1996. The jet was probably random. It just happened to be in the sky at the wrong place and time. The previous Democratic administration covered it up. They said it was a center wing fuel cell problem when several eyewitnesses were adamant they saw a missile fired from a boat or submarine. The FBI slow-rolled the investigation and never talked to any of the eyewitnesses. I think it was the same guy who shot me down. Rothwell basically told me as much."

"OK. Why were you there? Just taking pictures?"

"Would you believe I was in my YO-3A to kill him? I flew from Spain across the Med for the mission. Rothwell knew he'd be there at that time and place."

"Kill him? *From an airplane?*"

"I had a gun mounted—rotated out from the fuselage—so I could shoot up to two miles away with laser-guided bullets. They were seventy-caliber, rocket-propelled. I thought it's probably old newfangled SEAL shit, but I got it from the Science and Technology labs. That sucker works good."

"You *are* an apex predator, a one-man killing machine. You kill 'em on the ground and from the air. Welcome to the big leagues, GI Dog!"

Hunter grinned at the compliment. "I think he was holding the U.S. government hostage in some way. I tried to reverse engineer it and apply what I learned as aircraft accident investigator. Either he or one of his minions shot down the TWA jet and probably threatened to shoot down more if the U.S. didn't pay—in gold coins."

"Gold coins?"

"Remember I told you, Zacker, and Eastwood there was a bunker with MANPADS in Algeria? What I didn't say, because of Eastwood and Zacker, who don't have need to know, was that in the same underground bunker were hundreds of small containers. When I opened one, it was full of $50 U.S. Gold Eagles; rolls of gold coins. They weighed 200-250 pounds per container, and there were hundreds of those high-density plastic containers down in that bunker."

"Just like in Benghazi with all the MANPADS."

Hunter nodded. "I sent—Zacker sent—a message from the ship to the White House. They approved their recovery along with taking out the MANPADS you found."

"Duncan.... How'd you know to go to Algeria?"

"Executive Special Access Program. POTUS and the DCI had a list of shitheads who needed terminating. Think about it. If we had killed bin Laden when he was thirty, we would have changed history and saved 3,000 lives. It's culling the herd of radicals and Islamofascists before they get too out of control."

"And you killed Osama."

"No. Actually, I let rats eat him. He's now a hundred pounds of rat turds in Africa. Back to Rothwell—he's a rat, too, and I want to find him."

"Turn him into rat turds?"

"Be still my beating heart."

"Apex, I'll find him. I have some resources and some of my old connections. Do we have time?"

"I think so. He can run but he can't hide for too long."

"Nazy could find him. She found bin Laden and al-Zawahiri."

"I know, but I don't think she'll be looking for shitheads any time soon. It'll take more than a little while for her to recover before she's ready to return to work, at least, according to her doc."

"Well, if I had a real special airplane...."

"If I had an airplane, POTUS might put the Islamic-converted Rothwell at the top of his disposition matrix, and I'd go after him."

"Disposition matrix? That has a nice ring to it. What do you mean, if you could?"

"If I had an airplane—which I do, but it'll be months before we get it reworked to function like the original 007—I'd still be limited to remote or denied areas. I couldn't find him or shoot him if he was in downtown Cairo, for example. Too much light from the city."

McGee turned to look out the Gulfstream's window, then faced Duncan Hunter. "Sounds like you need a ground guy."

"It does. Know one?"

CHAPTER EIGHTY-THREE

October 5, 2012
The Washington Post

President Nominates New DCI

UPI. President Hernandez nominated a retired career CIA executive, Greg Lynche, as the next Director of the Central Intelligence Agency. In Lynche, Hernandez said, the CIA "will have the leadership of one of our nation's most-skilled and respected intelligence professionals. I hope that the Senate will act on this confirmation promptly."

Lynche is largely unknown since retiring from the Agency in the 1990s. He said he would make it his mission to ensure that the CIA has all the necessary tools it requires to keep our nation safe, and that the Agency's work will always reflect the liberties, freedoms, and values that Americans hold so dear.

The Senior Senator from Arizona said he had many questions and concerns about Lynche's nomination, "Especially what role he played in the so-called enhanced interrogation programs" but withdrew his comments when it was learned Lynche had been retired from the Agency for six years before 9/11 and could not have played any role during the Agency's post 9/11 enhanced interrogation efforts.

CHAPTER EIGHTY-FOUR

0600 October 10, 2010
Yellow Corvette Ranch
Fredericksburg, Texas

The BlackBerry vibrated on the nightstand, waking the dozing Duncan Hunter fully. Nazy Cunningham didn't move from his side, as he quickly silenced the smartphone.

Confident Nazy's sleep hadn't been interrupted; Hunter pressed several keys with his thumbs to get past the password and into the text message system.

Found him. What do you want to do?

Duncan stared at the diminutive rectangular screen and the eight words transmitted from Bill McGee. *Indeed!* Duncan replied, pressing buttons rapidly.

Where?
Amman, replied McGee.
Will call soon.

McGee didn't respond and Hunter didn't expect a reply. He hadn't said Middle East or Jordan, just Amman.

The last ten days had been a maelstrom of activity with the discharge of Nazy from Walter Reed National Military Medical Center. Before Hunter flew Nazy to Texas to recover from her wounds, he had to deal with a spitting-mad Greg Lynche who "just knew" Hunter was behind his nomination as Director of the CIA. Hunter smirked at the invective and vitriol hurled at him from his best friend and mentor.

Lynche railed and flapped his arms like a dodo, shouting, "I'm retired! I don't want to work! I did my time over there! I can't believe you did this to me!"

Connie Lynche stood to one side, arms crossed, watching the two main men in her life go at each other in her kitchen. She knew Hunter was playing dumb when he insisted he didn't know what Lynche was talking about. She also knew the best man for the job was the one standing in her kitchen, even if there was spittle flying as Lynche lambasted his best friend. Lynche hadn't been able to refuse when the leader of the free world asked him to come to the Oval Office and offered him the top intelligence job in America.

"Greg, I don't know why you're ranting at me. I didn't twist your arm. You could have said, 'No.' I'm surprised you're not honored," Hunter offered meekly to the usually Ciceronian man.

Having run out of vituperative nerf balls, the invigorated Lynche finally agreed it would be an honor and a privilege to lead his old place. After a minute, he calmed down but his mind was still in overdrive. There were things he wasn't going to like about the top position. But there could be some advantages to being the DCI.

Connie and Duncan rolled their eyes as the obvious situation unfolded; Greg Lynche would become the next Director of Central Intelligence. A twisted smile appeared on his face as he pointed his finger menacingly at Duncan. "Remember this asshole; you'll be working for me again! Payback's a bitch!" Hunter howled.

Extracting a weak, recovering Nazy from the hospital was more challenging than Hunter imagined. She was dependent on the painkillers and sleeping solution injected into her IV. She didn't want to leave the building, let alone her room. It was safe, and she felt secure there.

Dr. Ortega warned Hunter that Nazy would be very fragile and would respond in unexpected ways. Two days after being officially discharged, he pushed a wheelchair with a mildly sedated Nazy Cunningham from Walter Reed. Greg and Connie Lynche helped transfer Nazy onto the Gulfstream. She slept on the jet while Hunter flew them to Texas.

Theresa welcomed home an impaired Nazy and tended to her needs with the utmost concern and care. After three days, when Nazy indicated she was doing well and didn't need round-the-clock support, she quietly asked Duncan if she could sleep in his bed. She appeared to be moving back toward her old self, but Hunter was wary of little things that provoked an emotional outburst he might be unprepared to handle.

Any discussion of his long-lost daughter, Kelly Horne, was held in abeyance for another day. Plans for taking the bus on the road to restore the vitality of the formerly ebullient, dynamic woman would also have to wait until she felt well enough to travel.

The two Yo-Yos Lynche bought were waiting Hunter's instructions and directions. Duncan was crushed when he saw the sorry state of the two airplanes. He hoped at least one quiet airplane would be able to be put back into the air and made airworthy quickly, but neither one was anywhere close. The two Bobs estimated it would be months before an aircraft was ready for a test flight.

Contributing to the challenge of shortening the overhaul time of a single YO-3A was the near-total loss of corporate knowledge on the last flyable YO-3A. The Schweizer Aircraft factory closed due to a merger and acquisition. The men and women with top secret security clearances, who modified, repaired, overhauled, and worked on 007 occasionally for almost fifteen years had scattered to the winds; retired or had moved to other companies. It would be more work to find them and see if they could be enticed to come to Texas for a period, to help out with another quiet airplane project.

On top of concerns for Nazy, the time to modify the replacement YO-3A compounded Hunter's defeat. Ignoring the financial health of the old glider company, he assumed the status quo. If he couldn't get one of his replacement aircraft up and running soon, the CIA would find another contract to do the airborne counterterrorism work, even with Lynche at the helm. That would mean the end of Hunter's clearance and the Special Access Program.

Nazy slept fitfully. Duncan rolled out of bed and pulled on sweat pants and a Corvette racing jersey, slipping his BlackBerry into a pocket. Theresa Yazzie pulled a hot plate of *huevos rancheros* from the oven and followed Duncan outside to the patio table setting. She patted his shoulder as she walked away.

Hunter returned to McGee's message: *Found him. What do you want to do?*

What do I want to do? The thought upset the priorities of Nazy's recuperation and the remanufacture of his two nearly decrepit airplanes. At some point, he still had to tell Nazy about Kelly.

What do I want to do? Nazy needs me. She's the priority. What could I do? It's not like the President would send a hit squad after Rothwell. The former POTUS might have sent a drone up his ass, but I've got a life now, a daughter and a bride-to-be. That's enough. Like Lynche said, I did my time. It's someone else's turn! You have to face it Hunter. You're in the intelligence community and doing counterterrorism work; and like all addictive drugs, it's hard to walk away from the IC and get off of the CT stuff.

He saturated his eggs with more chilled salsa and wolfed down everything on the plate before washing it down with OJ.

What do I want to do? That's a damn fine question, McGee. What the hell would you do? What the hell is Rothwell doing in Amman? That's a strange place for a former DCI to run to.

"Why there?" *Hmmm. Maybe not such a bad place if you're a disgraced DCI. You could sell what's in your head to the highest bidder. That would be easy ... if you ... were a practicing Muslim. Oh, shit.*

Bill answered on the first ring. "What kept ya?"

"Do you know what he's doing there?"

"Consorting with the enemy, I think. Friends are watching him."

"How…?"

"Someone spotted him getting on a jet in DC and getting off in Amman. It's an obscure tail-watcher group run out of France and probably funded by some of their little commie friends who crushed Napoleon. One of my old guys recognized him walking through the lobby of the Sheraton in a *dishdasha.* He's trying to grow a beard."

"Seriously?"

"I couldn't make this shit up. So what do you want to do?"

"I don't know. My best girl needs me more than ever."

"That she does."

"I have to tell you I passed up a little work in Amman, because the conditions weren't right. Very high risk of being seen, if you get my drift, so I had to punt. It was obvious doing the work needed a ground crew. I thought Greg's old place would handle the job, handle the work internally."

McGee's crushed-velvet radio-announcer voice oozed, "I'm your ground crew."

Hunter froze in shock. "I can't ask you to do that, GI Dog. My problem."

"Foreign and domestic. Brothers. Semper Fi and all that."

"You're crazy."

"You can't *Apex.* I can. Call back later if you have a better idea."

A disconnect click sounded in Hunter's ear. Dazed by the conversation with McGee, he wasn't conscious of Theresa clearing his empty plate from the table or hearing her ask, "Was that enough, Señor Duncan?"

She had to repeat the question before he replied in a whisper, "Yes. Thank you, Theresa. That was great."

She walked away slowly looking over at her boss, who was deep in thought. She scolded herself for bothering him when he was thinking. *Señor Duncan had much on his mind, with worrying about Miss Nazy and all.*

When Theresa turned to enter the house, she nearly collided with

Nazy, still in silk pajamas and slippers, heading toward the patio where Duncan sat. The sound of the two women apologizing to each other startled him. He stood and rushed over to her and took her hand. Nazy had been taking her meals in her room, so being out and about for the first time could be troublesome—or maybe not.

Nazy politely asked for one of Theresa's special breakfasts, and an energetic, smiling Theresa raced off to the kitchen to comply. Hunter took Nazy's hand, and they walked to the patio table. He held her chair, like he always did, until she sat.

They held hands again. Nazy was initially pensive, but she assured Duncan she was fine and was feeling stronger and better every day. The glazed look in her eyes was gone.

"I'm glad," he said. "I can see it." That was true. He could see it in her pupils and face and feel it in her hands. She lost a little weight, which was totally expected.

Hunter was glad her appetite returned. "You keep this up, and you'll want to go jogging soon."

He tried to solicit a smile, but she remained serious.

"Maybe, Duncan, but you need to get back to work. I have Theresa or Carlos if I need anything. I'll be all right. I'm serious. *Really.*"

As if on cue, Theresa burst through the double doors with a steaming Belgian waffle on a plate. Coffee, orange juice, and ice water filled the table. Nazy weakly winked at the woman, who ran back into the house.

For the first time since she returned to Texas, Nazy smiled.

"Baby, work can wait." Duncan waited for a happier response, but Nazy seemed remorseful and introspective. He wasn't going anywhere.

She stared at her food. Something was clearly on her mind, and she wouldn't look at him. He lived with her menopausal mood swings for a week while she was in the hospital. He was warned, and whatever she did, he was along for the ride.

Hunter was about to speak when she said softly, "I think I was out of it for a while. I don't know what happened to me. I have fragments of memories of being at the embassy, going through files, and meeting

Algerians. Last week, I could remember little else. I don't think it's all back. There were Marines carrying the flag, my morning daily brief, morning sickness, pills, tests, my mission…."

"Your mission?"

"Uh-huh."

"Can you share?"

Nazy nodded. "I was afraid—for you."

"Nazy, you said that before. Why would you be afraid for me?"

She took a tiny bite of waffle, then looked up from the table and told him. Confidence filled her clipped voice. An element of catharsis rode on her British accent.

"I was briefed on an Executive Special Access Program. I didn't even know what it was. Presidential directive—POTUS and DCI eyes only. I know that's what you're doing now. It all makes sense."

Hunter's eyes scanned the house and begged Theresa not come and interrupt the spilling of national secrets.

"Rothwell was the program manager of record for *Piper I* and *Piper II*. Aircraft and their cargo were delivered in response to a message delivered to the embassy. Airliners would be shot down, and anthrax would be injected into the postal system—pay in gold or suffer the consequences."

Hunter was shocked by the revelation and sat transfixed; he hung onto Nazy's hand and her every word.

"Rothwell converted to Islam to try to penetrate the organization. All of this was in dispatches. It was still in the files. Abu Manu was the man at the top of the listing I developed for the DCI. He was in the *Piper* files, a suspected mastermind who shot down airplanes.

"After you went to Mali, I knew you would be going after him. The mission was in progress, and I couldn't say anything. I couldn't get a message to you. Even if I told you, you would have still executed your mission, so I hoped and prayed you'd be OK…." She squeezed his hand and smiled faintly. "And you are."

Duncan hadn't told her he had been shot out of the sky. As she was recovering, she didn't have a need to know. Now Duncan was glad he hadn't said anything about his traumatic experience in Algeria.

She lowered her head and slowly drank water. She felt ashamed and guilty, and waited for the hangman's verdict. She had again been on the wrong end of a top secret file that had could have gotten her best friend and lover killed. Both times she said nothing and both times Duncan escaped being killed.

Duncan realized the obvious; in addition to the trauma sustained at the hands of Islamic thugs Nazy would beat herself up thinking she hadn't warned him and she would have felt responsible for Duncan being killed. He again squeezed her hand and said, "Wow, Baby. Yes, I'm OK. Hey, look at me. You did the right thing and I'm Ok. There's nothing to worry about; nothing to be ashamed about."

Nazy looked at him with baleful despondent eyes, then put her head in her trembling hands and wept.

She sometimes woke screaming. She tensed as if racked by spasms, followed by low growls, her body struggling to shout or run, but she was trapped. When her screams came, it was as if part of her died inside.

When she took something to help her sleep, the nightmares didn't come. When she slid into bed, they slept apart. Duncan tried to comfort her as she tossed and turned, trying to escape the gruesome and horrific evil in her mind. First, he tried placing a comforting arm on her hip or shoulder, but she couldn't be touched or held. She wouldn't allow it even after they fell asleep. She woke up, recoiling from the horrors. She didn't want to talk about them.

Duncan squeezed her hand to show her he was still there, that he still loved her, and he would always be there for her. She struggled to compose herself and gripped his hand in a death grip. Finally, after a week, Nazy allowed Duncan into her hell.

She raised her eyes to his and steadied herself. She whispered, "I'm having nightmares. It's the same dream. I'm being held down and … raped. You've been killed. There's no one to protect me, and I'm caught, held down, and raped."

"Oh, Baby…."

"Very vivid and intense. I try to get away, but they hold me, punish me. When a man comes at me with a knife, I scream. That's when I wake up. I almost vomit."

She lowered her head as if in shame. As she struggled to talk, Hunter saw the effects of her Post-Traumatic Stress Disorder taking its emotional toll on her mind. Urgency crept into her body language and her voice cracked when she found the strength to speak.

"I think ... that's what happened to me. I thought it was just bad dreams, but I think I'm reliving what happened. Muslim men raped me!" She raised her head, tears streamed down her cheeks as she locked eyes with him. Her voice was full of pity and sorrow; it crackled with every syllable. "Is that what happened to me, Duncan?"

He was terrified. He had to choose his words carefully and coax her away from a cliff edge. She'd know if he lied. He was mortified what her response might be if he said, "Yes." Would she collapse into a heap of emotional rubble, her mind destroyed by the recurring images that would surely come? Would she attempt suicide, knowing that another man defiled her and killed her baby? As a mental timer ticked down seconds, Hunter felt as if he were trying to defuse a bomb while riding a unicycle.

Their relationship was at a crossroad. After being released from the hospital, they hadn't been close. During periods when she was lucid, she intimated at being intimate. As time passed at the hospital, Nazy became more withdrawn. She didn't respond when Hunter kissed her. He treated her with the utmost care and concern but she wanted to be left alone.

Nazy demanded silk pajamas, ostensibly to hide her scars and bruises. She couldn't sleep on her favored side due to her injuries. She progressed in baby steps, asking to move into Duncan's bedroom, and he moved to the other side of the bed so he could hold her. It turned out holding her was too much, too soon. Suddenly Hunter had a red-star cluster indication why she remained distant.

He stepped around the table and knelt at her chair. He didn't let go of her hand when he whispered, "Yes, Nazy."

When the tremors returned, he took her gently into his arms. He held her tight as he whispered into her ear, "It wasn't your fault, Baby. It wasn't your fault! You got caught in the bomb blast and men carried you away from the embassy."

She wailed and buried her face against his shoulder.

"Bill McGee went after you and…rescued you. He found you and saved you. He brought you back to the embassy, and you were evacuated to Italy. You didn't know you'd be blown up. It wasn't your fault. You didn't know you'd be kidnapped. Bill McGee saved you. He saved you for me. *It wasn't your fault!*"

Hunter cried with her. She was nearly hysterical when he stopped talking. Hunter held her tightly, not about to let her go.

After several minutes, Nazy collapsed, her trembling and sobbing subsided. Theresa stood in the doorway with tears streaming down her face, embarrassed to be caught watching them yet still caught up in the emotion of the moment.

Hunter's shirt was drenched with Nazy's tears, as she strained to compose herself. She stopped hyperventilating and slowly calmed, as Hunter stroked her hair and held her close.

"Bill…Bill *saved* me?"

"Yes, Baby. I think that is why he was there. I'll forever be in his debt for going after you and bringing you back to me. He was in the middle of a combat zone, and he went after you for you…and for me. It wasn't your fault. None of it was your fault."

"It wasn't my fault, Duncan. *It wasn't my fault!*" A new round of pitiful crying ensued, as she pounded his chest with her fists repeatedly.

"No, no, no! It wasn't your fault, Baby. It was completely out of your control. Nothing you did.... I love you, Baby, always and forever!"

She pushed away from him. "How can you do that?" she pleaded. Again, she wailed, *"How can you do that?"*

"Because it doesn't matter. Look at me. Anything you think or say, it doesn't matter. I'm not a Muslim man. If I were, I might be conditioned to think it matters, but I'm not like that, and you aren't like that anymore, either. It's our little secret. I know you can't push it aside or down a hole. It wasn't your fault. I'd love it if we could dump it into a safe, drop the file anywhere, slam the drawer closed and forget the combo, burn the burn bag, but the only thing that matters is that you're safe with me, and I'm going to love you."

After several minutes, Nazy's intense tremulations subsided and she relaxed against his chest and Duncan held her very tight. Theresa stepped inside the house, a napkin pressed against her mouth to hide her emotions. Nazy's hands were balled into fists with her arms between herself and Hunter. His ancient bony knees were killing him for kneeling for so long on the hard, wooden deck.

Nazy returned her head to his chest and slowly relaxed the tension in her arms and hands. Her arms transitioned from barriers against him to wrapping around his back slowly. "I don't know, Duncan."

He stroked her hair, speaking softly against it. "We have to do this together, Baby. I won't go away. When you're not at therapy, I'm your therapy and medicine. I'll always be here for you."

Her limp arms slowly tightened, and he reciprocated. They embraced for several moments until she pulled away. Hunter, anxious, confused, and alert for another round of raw spontaneous emotions, was concerned that a dynamic had shifted, and he was completely out of ideas.

"Baby, do you want to go for a walk, a ride, or something?"

Her response was terse and emotionless. "No," came in a hint of a whisper. Her mind raced. She looked down, avoiding eye contact.

Duncan tried to read her body language and assumed he pushed too hard. He must have said something stupid and wrong. *This is what it's going to be like,* he thought, *as Dr. Ortega said. It will be a long, painful recovery. Nothing will move quickly. Her psychologist said she was very fragile and to expect wild emotional swings and outbursts.*

He felt as if he were at the top of a rollercoaster, ready to crash.

"I need ... a shower," Nazy whispered.

Hunter unconsciously recoiled at the forceful interruption to his thoughts. Nazy shifted in her chair and leaned toward the doors, leaving Duncan on his knees, feeling dejected. One hand gripped his fingers as she stood, moving away from the table.

She tugged at him with a hint of compulsion, as if he had to walk with her. Confused and curious, he got to his feet and followed.

Nazy solemnly led him through the kitchen, down the hall, into his sprawling bathroom. Floor-to-ceiling earth-toned tiles dominated walls and floor, save for the shower, which featured intricate, turquoise cut-tile mosaics behind a large, clear glass door.

Nazy stopped short of the shower stall and released his hand. She slowly unbuttoned her pajama top and said to the floor, "I need ... you ... to *clean* me." There was no hint of anything but work.

It was direction, not desire or a suggestion. It didn't invite discussion or questions. Her somber tone indicated it wasn't something negotiable or the prelude to something more—something more ceremonial than practical?

Duncan pinched his lips, closed the bathroom door, and started the water running in the shower, as Nazy slipped from her pajamas. He quickly shed his sweat pants and jersey and entered the stall to set the water temperature.

It was the first time he had seen her naked in months. Her bruises were nearly gone, but dozens, of small, light scars dotted one side of her leg and torso. Her legs hadn't been shaved. She looked a mess as she stepped into the four-by-eight-foot shower and stood in the center of the stall, her eyes closed in trepidation.

She spread her arms until her fingers touched the walls and braced herself. Duncan didn't say a word and began by washing her hair, using a spray wand to soak and shampoo her long, black mane. She gave no feedback about whether he did a poor or a good job. Though she made no sound, her body language suggested she was screaming on the inside.

Duncan took his time, not yet realizing his actions were more cleansing than a simple, freshening shower. He gently scrubbed her face with a soapy washcloth and was surprised at the lack of makeup around her eyes; Nazy always wore shadow of some kind. The bruises around her eyes were almost completely gone.

He moved to her back, the only area not damaged by shrapnel or stiletto. Hot water cascaded down his own back as he worked up loads of lather and gently scrubbed her shoulders and back. Dozens of bright red scars dotted her hips and buttocks.

Wordlessly, she spread her feet, inviting him to wash there, too. He moved to face her and saw she was crying. He didn't think he hurt her, but he wasn't about to wash her damaged breast. After much *angst*, he retrieved his razor and bar of soap to sit on the shower floor and deftly soaped her good, unmarked leg.

Filtered sunlight cast shadows into the shower. Steam clouds gathered to hover along the ceiling, fogging the tops of the mirrors over the sinks and windows. Hunter was in virgin territory. He never shaved her legs before and was afraid he might nick her with a clumsy flick of the multi-blade razor, startling her and upsetting the delicate balance of what was becoming a cleansing ritual.

He gained confidence with every long, deliberate stroke of the gleaming metal razor. Too fast would not be acceptable under any conditions, and too slow, like cutting his beard, would tug and pull, making it painful. He found a moderate speed and pressure didn't draw blood or make Nazy flinch.

Still braced against the walls, she let him lift her leg and shave her bent knee. He delicately trimmed the tiny hairs around her ankle. He pressed the button of the hand wand to rinse her butt and legs. When he looked up, Nazy was no longer crying. He braced himself for the challenge of shaving her bumpy, heavily scarred leg.

Nazy never moved. Her steady breathing didn't belie any concern or fear. With loads of soap in preparation, Duncan, still sitting on the shower floor, deftly scraped thick and thin hair off while avoiding the sensitive scars on her damaged leg. He was so afraid of nicking her, he almost gasped in relief when it was time for a gentle rinse.

He started to replace the razor in one of the shower's triangular trays, but she anticipated him and pushed his hand away from the shelf. She re-braced herself and half-stepped toward him, so his nose was aligned with her bikini line.

Duncan blinked wildly, as she cried softly, her bosom heaving as she again braced herself against the shower walls. If Hunter had been afraid of shaving and nicking her legs, he was horrified at the idea of scraping away the last vestiges of Algeria. There were no flat surfaces, just curves and rolling hills. It was multiple engineering equations. Too fast was impossible. Even medium speed would be too fast for conditions. It would require slow, deliberate work.

After several tense minutes, Hunter was done, but he had little time to admire his work. Nazy's pendulous breasts remained—one good, the other with stitches recently removed. What had been in other settings a playful, erotic event was a moment where he treaded slowly and stood up.

He ran a hand down over his tingling, numb ass. Hundreds of indentations from the mosaic tile floor left their imprint. Nazy had stopped crying, but she looked as if she dreaded the finale.

Hunter lathered a washcloth and gently scrubbed her left breast, underarm, and her flat belly. He shaved one armpit, then the other. He looked at her stony face for a clue if it was safe to proceed. Without a washcloth, he washed the healthy-looking but discolored breast with extraordinary care as if it were a priceless Ming vase.

Then it was over. Hunter was buoyant. He negotiated all the potential land mines without triggering an explosion or worse. His nerves were as worn as if he flew a *Weedbusters* mission solo.

He rinsed her from neck to toes with the wand set for a final warm spray, grateful he accomplished what heretofore had seemed impossible —entering and leaving a shower with Nazy without an erection.

He stood with water cascading down his back from the

showerhead. Nazy didn't move or cry, nor did she give him any hint what was running through her mind, but she sensed he was done and was ready to shut off the water and leave.

Mission accomplished, he thought.

Steam and condensate billowed over the shower door, filling the bathroom with moisture and leaving everything in the room with a thin veneer of water.

Duncan turned to twist the water control valve when Nazy shattered the solemnity of the cleansing by whispering above the torrent of water, "No. Again."

Hunter, taken aback, gently recoiled, wondering why. She opened her eyes, momentarily pleading with him to continue and finish what wasn't yet complete.

Hunter nodded. As she closed her eyes again, he immediately realized he wasn't done and couldn't be. He assumed he was, but all decontamination washes required at least one main wash to purge the majority of poisons from the body, then a second decontamination ensured no trace of poison remained.

The epiphany rocked him. *What an idiot I am,* he thought, remembering the young women in their decontamination suits who trundled out into the wind of the carrier deck to save his life. They weren't done until they scrubbed him twice, and all traces of anthrax were eliminated and neutralized. After being violated by anthrax spores Duncan was saved and given a new lease on life on the fantail of the U.S.S. *Eisenhower.*

Nazy's mental health was still extremely fragile, and a curative path had yet to be found, but somehow, she saw her way through the incredible pain, trauma, and knowledge of the assault. Somehow, perhaps with women's intuition, she knew what needed to be done to find a way ahead. Mostly, she wanted Duncan to prove to her it didn't matter to him what happened. Only thoughtful, caring, loving hands could begin the process of ridding her of the poisons from Algeria by scraping and washing them away.

Duncan had been a dunce the first time around, but he finally understood.

He shampooed her hair again slowly. It would be done when it was done. There was no urgency. He left kisses where he had been. He washed, rinsed, and kissed her shoulders and neck. He thought when he kissed her neck and ear, there was a slight reaction. That was a good sign, a start. Soapy hands massaged her back and buttocks, slowly and thoroughly.

He returned to the floor and washed her legs, feet, and toes one-by-one. Nazy took a deep breath and repositioned her legs slightly. He washed there, too, then her belly. A hint of a thin smile showed on her face. Hunter became more animated and active, excited but not aroused.

When his floor work was done, he stood. He was in no hurry and quietly thanked some salesman for encouraging him to buy the largest hot water heater in stock. Duncan soaped her arms and hands, then her delicately thin, wrinkly fingers one-by-one. As he did previously, he carefully, gingerly soaped her breasts. Any other time, he would have moved behind her to knead soapy, hard nipples and nuzzle her neck, but it wasn't an erotic shower.

Another spray from the hand wand, and the last soapy remnants slid down her body to swirl down the drain. Hunter was prepared for another go, but Nazy released her hands from the wall and motioned to leave the shower. She dragged the back of her fingers across his cheek as she stepped out, opened the bathroom door, and strolled from the drenched bathroom without a word and without a towel.

Duncan went to the porch and nursed a large glass of juice and Fresca, hoping Nazy would join him. He had no idea what to expect if or when she emerged from her room.

Bill McGee's words returned. *What do you want to do?* Fury metastasized in him with the suspicion that the cowardly Bruce Rothwell set up Hunter for termination by *Stinger* missile. Whatever his reason for drafting Nazy into the executive black program in Algiers, at an absolute minimum as an unintended consequence, it nearly got her killed.

What do I want to do?

When she made her entrance onto the wooden deck, in jeans and a white, long-sleeved shirt, she looked like the Nazy of old, poised and confident. She took the time and effort to make up her face and lacquer her nails. No residuals from the last time they were on the patio. *PTSD was like that,* Duncan thought. *One moment they're OK and functional, and the next, they are ... not.* She had come a long way since she walked naked out of the shower, through Hunter's bedroom, to the guest room.

Theresa raced from the kitchen to bring drinks to the table. Duncan stood and squeezed Nazy's hand, and gently kissed her lips. He helped her into her chair at the small patio table overlooking hundreds of acres of free-range Southwest Texas. Bright green eyes and dashes of makeup and nail polish brought a thick smile to Hunter's face. It had been an hour since Nazy emerged from the guest room after they emptied the hot water tank.

As Nazy sat quietly and stared out across the landscape, not as radiant or sensual as she'd been in the past but nonetheless still stunning and striking. She turned to him and smiled. Hunter smiled back, not too forcefully and not suggestively. A smile of gratitude. An imperceptible nod prefaced his decision.

I know what I must do.

He welcomed her hand and lips. He relished the missed passion but was under no illusions that Nazy was cured or healed. He expected mood swings good and bad, but, for the moment, he was ecstatic to see the woman he grew to love, admire, and worship, up and about, like the Nazy of old. Even if this respite was only for a few minutes, Hunter was in and committed.

They intermittently and playfully rubbed their legs under the tables like new lovers, telegraphing their feelings without being too obvious. After a long break between leg rubs, he saw a change in her body language. She wanted to speak. Hunter was afraid it was the PTSD rearing its ugly head again. He positioned himself to catch her if she fell.

"I want to go somewhere," Nazy said. "Get away."

Surprised and intrigued, Hunter asked, "Where to?"

"Nowhere special." The words were melancholy yet wishful.

"Well, I've *always* wanted to go *there*." The playful Hunter of old couldn't help himself to be a bit teasing and tantalizing.

"Where?" Nazy looked at him with fascination in her eyes.

"Nowhere special. Anyplace with you will be special."

"Where would we go?" She smiled and turned away, and then dove deep in thought. *There are so many places...where would we go?*

"How about the Northeast? The leaves are changing color, and it's beautiful this time of year." An idea crept into his mind.

Nazy rocked slightly and started another round of leg rubs. "I like that. We haven't been there since ... Newport."

"Then, that's what we'll do."

"I don't want to fly."

"I thought of taking the bus. I need to stock it and get it ready. Maybe we could go through Newport."

Her leg stopped moving, and she searched his eyes. "Would you want to see ... Bill McGee?"

"We wouldn't have to. We can go anywhere or nowhere. We'll go where you want or where the bus takes us."

"But you'd want to." She stroked his leg again and looked pensive.

"If we were in the area, I would, Nazy. He saved your life, and I'm forever in his debt. Show him you're doing better. It would be almost a crime to be so close and not stop to say hi, even if it was just for a few minutes. I know his girls are grown up and understand they've become little racquetball champions. They promised to beat me up if I ever came to Newport."

"That would be fun. What's his wife's name? I forgot."

"Angela."

"I haven't seen you play in a very long time. Do you play girls?"

"Not very often. They can be mean! It might be good to see Bill. I've always wanted to drive through Maine, maybe see some moose."

She stopped rubbing her leg against his and leaned across the table to coo, "When can we go?"

Duncan leaned forward until they were almost nose-to-nose. When he inhaled, he smelled faint cinnamon. "Carlos and I can go to town and get the bus. Maybe we could be on the road in a couple hours."

"You don't think I'm crazy and impetuous?"

"I think you're wonderful."

"I feel much better." She gently brushed noses with him and closed her eyes. When she reopened them, she saw Duncan grinning broadly. She said, "Thank you, Baby. You get the bus, and I'll pack."

CHAPTER EIGHTY-FIVE

1900 October 15, 2012
Newport Athletic Club
Middletown, Rhode Island

Nostalgia filled the interior of the motor coach, as Hunter crossed the apex of Claiborne Pell Bridge spanning Narragansett Bay on their way to Newport. He and Nazy pointed at the Naval War College at their nine-o'clock position and talked of dinner at the Red Parrot. It was their first night together, where an ugly, old life ended and a new one began.

Nazy drifted into warm thoughts of Duncan's home away from home and the place where he taught her how to make love to the Moody Blues' *The Other Side of the Life.*

"I think I remember how to get to the club. I'm certain there's no place to park all forty-three feet of this thing," he lamented playfully, shattering her little daydream. "We should be a little early, but with traffic and finding a parking place, we may have to hoof it to the club or take a cab."

Nazy nodded, smiled, and returned to her earlier thoughts, contemplating what she would say to Bill McGee, her savior in Algeria, when they met. *What should I say? What should I do? What will his wife say or do? Maybe this was a bad idea. I'm not sure I'm ready for this!*

She agonized over the future until Duncan announced they arrived at the Newport Athletic Club but they had to walk.

Pulling into an overflow lot, he quickly shut down the bus and helped Nazy down the coach stairs. She didn't need help with stairs, but he didn't want to break contact with her. Her days and nights were better when he held her hand or touched her to reassure her he was there. When he held her as she slept, nightmares no longer invaded their bed. Nazy still remained a bit skittish around other people. The trip from Texas to Rhode Island was made with much sightseeing and hiking along remote trails where few others visited. Up to the club they walked hand-in-hand, Hunter's racquetball bag draped across his shoulder.

A horn blasted behind them, and Hunter turned. Bill McGee's white Toyota pickup bore down and passed them, as it approached the incline to the entrance of the fitness club. Hunter slipped his arm around her and pulled her closer, hoping that the diversion wasn't too much, too soon, for Nazy to handle.

The McGee family was waiting for them at the club entrance. Bill was stunned when he saw Nazy. The last time he saw her, she was a bruised, bloody mess with black eyes and IVs in both arms. Angela McGee vaguely remembered the handsome man lugging the huge racquetball bag. Once he stepped from his warm-up clothes, she would remember his chiseled quadriceps and calves.

Nazy and Angela migrated to each other as long-lost friends, hugging, holding hands, and talking close as intimate friends are supposed to do. Hunter and McGee shook hands. Amid greetings and salutations, McGee silently expressed his incredulity at Nazy's condition. Hunter just nodded.

The two daughters, who were built like their father—heavily muscled and ripped—studied their competition with disdain.

As Nazy and Angela disengaged, Bill's radio-announcer voice boomed, "Nazy, I have to say you look incredible. You're a sight for sore eyes."

Nazy looked up at the massive black man, wrapped her arms as far around him as she could, before bursting into tears. Angela and the girls recoiled with surprise. Bill wrapped his thick arms around the diminutive woman, holding her close, embarrassed at having a woman attached to him in front of his family.

Nazy broke down, shuddered, and wept. Angela was mute and agape. The daughters were confused. As Nazy cried, Duncan moved to

Angela's side and offered an explanation.

"Girls, your father saved Nazy's life last month when they were in Algeria. He's a true American hero. You hear that stuff all the time, but in his case, he's the real deal. He chased some bad guys who took Nazy from the embassy. After he rescued her, he performed life-saving first aid and got her to medical facilities. I think Nazy's just saying thank you."

Nazy quickly composed herself and nodded against the man's massive pectorals. Releasing her grip, she looked into his dark-brown eyes. "I do thank you, Bill," she said hoarsely. "I'm OK. I'm sorry."

Angela stepped up to Nazy to comfort her.

"You have nothing to be sorry about, Nazy," Bill said. "You're very welcome."

Nazy wiped her eyes on her sleeve and turned to Angela. "I'm sorry. I don't know what came over me. I'm OK. Let's go…let's go inside. I'll be fine." She glanced at Duncan, who winked and mouthed, *You sure?*

Nazy nodded and held Angela's arm, leaning toward the door to lead everyone into the athletic club.

"You be nice to my girls," Bill demanded in a threatening tone, wagging his finger at Hunter as he and the youngsters walked toward the racquetball court.

Before entering the court, Hunter said, "We're going to play two against one, with you two against me. You get two serves, I get just one. Standard rules apply. Any questions? Oh, yes. I'll give you twelve points. First one to reach fifteen wins."

The teens and their parents thought he was crazy.

"We only have to score three points?" the taller girl asked. "You're in trouble, Old Man."

Nazy, Angela, and Bill laughed and applauded, urging the girls to crush the arrogant Hunter.

With center-court seats and a full glass back wall, the unusual match of two African-American girls and an old, pasty-white man was a sight. A crowd developed as the match wore on. The youngsters hit good shots, while the decrepit man hit better shots and ran up the score.

When they left the court, their faces told the story.

"Old age and treachery will beat youth and skill every time," Duncan said. "They almost did it."

He smiled, but the girls were dejected, crushed that all they gained was one point against him.

"Ladies, you are great players," Hunter said. "I took advantage of you, because you didn't know how to play me, plus you took me for granted. Dad tells me you're national junior champions, and *you know* you should have won.

"Here's how you can beat me. Instead of playing side-to-side, one of you plays front, the other covers back. You need to talk to each other. It's a team effort. You ready to try again? I know you'll play a lot better. You have all the shots. This time we play straight up, zero-zero. Ready? Let's go have some fun."

The embarrassed girls brightened at the chance to redeem themselves in front of their parents, galvanized by the chance to take out the old dude. After a quick conversation, they developed a new strategy and played hard, not taking Duncan for granted again.

In the end, they won. The crowd of thirty onlookers jumped to their feet, as the youngest daughter smashed a passing kill shot just out of reach of Hunter's diving outstretched arm. When he stopped rolling, he was spread-eagled on the floor, chest heaving in exhaustion. The girls jumped up and down in glee.

"Who knew beating up an old man could be so much fun?" Hunter asked, as he emerged from the court. "Now were they great or what?"

The girls beamed, and their proud parents hugged them, as did Nazy.

"I don't understand," Bill said.

The three adults didn't understand how the two games were so dramatically different. The excitement of watching Duncan play overshadowed most of Nazy's anxieties. She acted and responded as she did before being deployed to Algiers.

"First of all, you guys were great," Hunter told the girls. "I mean that sincerely. You're talented and can really play the game. I'm very impressed."

"He wasn't easy. He hit stuff I never saw before."

"Old Man stuff," Hunter suggested, turning to the confused parents and Nazy. "Part of this game, when you reach their level, is that the discriminator becomes attitude and the ability to bounce back. I knew they'd start off by playing side-to-side. Singles. If you play doubles with other youngsters, that's how they do it, and they try to hit the ball as hard as they can. But they are not a team. They didn't think they need to work together. It was easy to get the ball past them. In the second game, they actually played their game—they were a team—and my old legs couldn't keep up. You did good, Mom and Dad."

Bill smiled as only a proud father can. Angela hugged Nazy, while Hunter rummaged in his large tournament bag and pulled out a pair of collared polo shirts.

"The winners of the championship of the free world go to Nicole and Kayla McGee. Congratulations, Ladies. These are from the National Singles Championships. I expect one of these days, you'll be a force to be reckoned with. May these bring you good luck."

"Thank you, Mr. Hunter," the girls said in unison, somewhat surprised at winning something in the undeclared contest. They showed their parents the finely embroidered, colorful shirts.

Nazy smiled and winked at Duncan, proud of the way he comported himself with the girls and how he was constantly at her side. He looked like he had a glorious time on the court, and the side trip to Newport was OK, if not a total, surprising success.

Nazy, Duncan, and the McGees left the high humidity of the athletic club for the higher humidity of a cool Newport night. Hunter mumbled something to Bill as the family said their good-byes and headed toward their pickup truck.

"OK. I'll meet you at your bus," Bill said.

Nazy and Duncan walked arm-in-arm down the middle of the parking lot, surefootedly negotiating the steep decline to the lone motor coach in the auxiliary parking area, as Bill's truck pulled up alongside.

Duncan opened the coach door, and Nazy stepped in. He turned to Bill, who stepped outside his truck. Hunter lifted one of the large panels on the side of the bus and tossed his racquetball bag inside the cavernous undercabin storage area where two shipping containers rested.

Hunter and McGee wrestled out the smaller of the two black fiberglass shipping containers, using the thick metal handles on the sides, to lift—then slide—the 250-pound box into the Toyota's truck bed. The other container, three times bigger yet three times lighter, was easily handled solo by the powerful giant.

Nazy, Angela, and the girls watched the two men embrace and shake hands before they entered their respective vehicles.

One of the girls asked, "What's in the boxes, Daddy?"

"He gave me a little something in appreciation for helping Ms. Nazy. That's all."

Angela cocked her head and studied her husband. She didn't believe a word he said.

CHAPTER EIGHTY-SIX

0300 October 24, 2012
Sheraton Amman Al Nabil Hotel

Eight quadrotors lifted from the base of the elevator. Their thirty-two rotor blades spun at a deafening 4,000 RPM. In the enclosed elevator, they sounded like a billion angry hornets.

The security man, covered in a tan *thobe* and a black and white *keffiyeh,* heard the buzzing and furrowed his eyebrows, wondering what the sound was. The unusual noise grew louder with each second. He placed his hand on the elevator door, trying to sense if the sound came from the car or the elevator shaft, and if it was coming closer. He never heard the bell announcing an approaching elevator on the tenth floor. The high-frequency vibration grew in amplitude, as 130 decibels squelched all indication that mayhem and death arrived.

He recoiled in horror, his *keffiyeh* dislodged from his head, as the doors opened, spilling the sound of millions of venomous bees onto the landing. He was momentarily conflicted, but he was the personal security guard of the *sheikh* and swore a blood allegiance to protect the cleric at any cost. He had his fighting knife and pistol.

He struggled with the urge to run or fight, but the unnatural screaming demons penetrated his brain with their sonic barbed sting, shattering his eardrums. His hands flew to his damaged ears, and he screamed as a pair of quadrotors shot from the elevator, stopped, searched, and located the only guard on the floor. One device pivoted and slewed left and right, as if it were hunting for a target.

The man was terrified and transfixed. He struggled to run and sound the alarm, when a six-inch harpoon shot into his mouth. As he collapsed where he stood, six additional quadrotors filed out of the elevator, two abreast and four feet off the floor. They passed over the guard's twitching body. When all eight tiny multi-rotor helicopters joined in a column of twos, the swarm moved forward and turned left. The deafening sound and vibration from the rotors reverberated down the long hall.

A floor below, in the stairwell, a man in a black *thobe* and black *keffiyeh* touched the split screen of the notebook computer, controlling the direction and speed of the eight tiny rotorcraft, steadying their flight path as they deliberately flew down the hall of the hotel. Their high-pitched buzzing woke everyone asleep on the floor; those that were awake initially dismissed the incessant earsplitting noise, and then wondered what it could be.

Two of the twelve-inch-square aircraft broke from the pack and trundled down the hall to two doors on the left and right; blocks of Semtex, shaped in a V, were suspended under each of the quadrotors.

The man used two fingers to sweep the multi-touch screen, directing two rotorcraft to fly up, pivot ninety degrees, and hit the door. Two taps on the touch screen ignited each of the detonators inserted into the *plastique.*

The simultaneous explosions, on the left and right side of the hall, disintegrated the heavy wooden doors and vaporized the suicidal quadrotors. All debris from the shattered doors was shunted into the two targeted rooms in clouds of dust and splinters and shards of wood.

The men jumped from their beds, pushing concubines off of them. The thrumming sounds and explosions were fearful, and they scurried to their feet and tried to run from the blasts, but in the suite, there were few places to hide. The remaining quadrotors formed a wedge of three and entered the smoky, dusty spaces to chase the naked men to the far end of their rooms, up against the curtains of glass patio doors.

Tiny cameras on the lead quadrotors relayed images to the man with the notebook controller and verified the identities of the two terrified men. Two taps of his fingers transmitted the signal to detonate a pound of the high-velocity *plastique* carried by each quadrotor.

After descending nine flights of stairs to the bottom-most floor, the man pounded the crash bar of the door, and before exiting the building, in one graceful move, he removed the glassy sheet draped over his head and shoulders, and stepped outside into a warm autumn night. As he strolled away from the fire alarms and shrieking men and women, he wrapped the notebook computer with the slick cloth and slipped it under his arm and evacuated the hotel grounds with all the other guests.

CHAPTER EIGHTY-SEVEN

0700 October 24, 2012
Dulles International Airport

Reports of drones killing terrorists at an Amman, Jordan, hotel were met with abject skepticism. Foreign correspondents streamed into Jordan. The bombing of a hotel, limited to two rooms on one floor, suggested a clumsy bomb maker, not the work of precision flying killing machines. No reliable reporter in any press pool suggested it could have been assassination by drones.

It was a good day to catch a flight to Amman. A tall, gray-haired man, camouflaged rucksack in one hand and a Burberry trench coat in the other weaved through the crush of slower, plodding travelers. Lieutenant Colonel Demetrius Eastwood bobbed and weaved through the TSA VIP line and onto the concourse to chase another story. His contact at the FBI suggested the remains of one of the terrorists was on their most-wanted, albeit secret, list.

"If it's the right guy, he purchased tickets for the 9/11 hijackers and provided them with cash when they arrived in the U.S. He was former AMCIT, converted to Islam. He was an Islamist cleric for AQ on the Arabian Peninsula. Very unusual."

Eastwood listened intently to the leaker.

"That isn't the real story. We think the other guy was Bruce Rothwell, former DCI. Quick-stick DNA tests confirm some pieces were what's left of him."

"That doesn't sound like a bomb maker having a bad day. That sounds like a hit."

"Reportedly, there's not much left of either one. The Bureau is trying to send forensics teams to Amman. We're hoping the Jordanians will let us investigate. Right now they're not letting us in. But you shouldn't have any trouble getting in."

Incredulity spread over Eastwood's face. He began to ask an uncomfortable question when the FBI agent read his face and his mind. "I know what you're thinking. The Agency would never admit to a hit. They are adamant it wasn't them."

Eastwood stowed his gear in the overhead bin and slipped into his first-class seat. Flight attendants doted on the handsome war correspondent. He sat quietly, fingers in a teepee, wondering, *What the hell was Rothwell doing with one of the country's most-wanted terrorists?*

CHAPTER EIGHTY-EIGHT

0700 October 29, 2012
Camp Perry, Virginia

Greg Lynche, the new Director of Central Intelligence, was introduced to the students and faculty of the Intelligence Officer's Course. The tall, graying man in the navy Brooks Brothers suit walked across the dais to the lectern.

"Good morning, and welcome to the Farm," he began with a chuckle. "I'm very pleased to see the twenty-seven men and women here who represent some of the finest minds this nation has to offer. I'm reminded of the words of a former Vice President when he was a lone Congressman from Wyoming. He said, 'This may be a small delegation, but it's all quality.'

"That's the hallmark of this particular intelligence officer class. You come from the top echelon of your professions. In a world that depends on American intelligence capabilities and prowess, we'll be counting on all of you. You're the tip of the spear wherever you go worldwide. I don't know where you'll go after you graduate, but I do know that wherever you're posted, you'll arrive with the knowledge, training, and skills to excel and succeed in the performance of your duties.

"The war on terror has influenced our culture. How we prepare for the future will define much of your career. You must learn to understand the nature of the enemy; and you will. They are as brutal and heartless as any we've faced in any war. They plot and plan in secret. They target the defenseless and peaceful. Those who refuse to bow to the tyrants have been brutalized or killed.

"We must stop them before they arm themselves with the tools of mass destruction—chemical, biological, or nuclear weapons. We must take them seriously. Only through a robust intelligence program will we have a chance to oppose them and defeat them. Our existence depends on it. That isn't hyperbole.

"Terrorists and terrorist states don't reveal their intentions. Without intelligence and the hard work of you, our intelligence officers, we won't be able to find, track, and destroy the enemies of the United States. Work hard, study hard, practice well and faithfully. Begin writing your own chapter of excellence and achievement in the CIA.

"That concludes my remarks, but I understand I have a little time for a couple questions. Any brave souls out there have a question? Yes, the young lady in the back row."

"Director Lynche, Kelly Horne. Sir, as you were introduced, I understand you used to be Chief of Air Branch. I'm a former Air Force pilot. How did you, an intelligence officer, steer your career toward that position? Do you think my flying experience and certifications may help me qualify for a flying position somewhere down the road?"

He broke into a broad, toothy smile. *If she only knew!* "I must say, Miss Horne, it certainly won't hurt if you can maintain a high level of flying currency. That's what I did, and I think being a pilot helped, not only to be selected for Air Branch but to carry out the Agency's flying missions. It really takes an aviator to be effective in that position. Learn the arts and crafts of an intelligence officer. Maintain your flying proficiency and good things will likely happen to you."

"Thank you, Sir."

"Any other questions? OK. Well, I'll see you at graduation. Good luck and Godspeed to you all." He made eye contact with Kelly and winked at her. She reciprocated with a wink and a smile, as Lynche left the dais.

CHAPTER EIGHTY-NINE

1000 October 29, 2012
The White House

The President's secretary ushered the woman from the CIA into the Oval Office. Several men and women were gathered on the two opposing sofas to hear the morning's intelligence brief. President Hernandez received the President's Daily Brief as the CIA woman professionally summarized, "Al-Yemini's remains were verified forensically, as were Dr. Rothwell's. Dr. Rothwell's body has not been recovered. It's unknown what he was doing in Amman."

"Conjecture?" the Chief of Staff asked.

"It appears he was in contact with al-Yemini."

The new DCI added, "We're scrubbing all of his Special Access Programs. I regret to say he had access to everything in the intelligence community. The damage to our intelligence network worldwide may be incalculable."

"Or it may be status quo," the President said, thinking if Rothwell was on the wrong side of an explosion, damage could be limited.

"We'll know soon if and when our officers' cover are blown," the Vice President said. "They could have easily taken him into custody and pumped him for information. Any other spook on the planet would have been snatched off the street for interrogation, but not him. Why not? That fact alone tells me he defected. The whole thing stinks."

The President thanked everyone for coming, as they filed from the Oval Office, leaving him alone to make some private telephone calls and check the news on the monitor. First, he had administrative work to do.

From the bottom of the *Resolute Desk*, he withdrew a lengthwise-folded, legal-sized spreadsheet. Unfolding it, the President laid it in the middle of the desk.

As he studied the list, he withdrew a heavy wood pen from his suit pocket and drew lines through two names on the disposition matrix.

CHAPTER NINETY

1200 November 29, 2012
Dallas-Fort Worth International Airport

Duncan Hunter held Nazy Cunningham's hand, as they slipped into the airport lounge and found seats overlooking ramp operations. Clear skies allowed a hazy view of downtown Dallas and the airplanes, coming and going. They had time to kill before boarding their American Airlines jet for Honolulu; their final destination the St. Regis Resort in Bora Bora. Nazy mulled over the exotic destination Duncan recommended they escape to when she felt well enough to fly.

"Why Bora Bora?" she asked.

"To get far enough away from liberals and terrorists, so we don't have to think of them or work. I only want to be distracted by you."

She smiled thinly. He was definitely crazy—and the sanest man she ever met.

Nazy settled into the expansive leather seat of the Admiral's club and relaxed. Duncan furiously pressed keys on his BlackBerry, trying to finish some work before takeoff. She relived some of the finer moments they shared on the bus and on some of Vermont's and Maine's challenging hiking trails, and other places of interest like Ben and Jerry's, where Duncan consumed a pint of coffee ice cream. They never saw a moose.

It was good to take the trip, get away, and be distracted by external stimuli and not introspection. Nazy felt she came to grips with the direction life took her. Work at the Agency was interesting and demanding, even exciting, requiring her best. She missed it and she missed it greatly. She acknowledged tacitly she'd unwittingly stumbled into what was called the war of terror, less as an immigrant but more as someone seeking asylum and committed to doing what she could to help her new country.

She'd been *so* dispirited, *so* disgusted, and *so* disenchanted with life under the veil that she walked away from Islam.

No, she thought, *I ran.* She glanced over her shoulder at Duncan with appreciative, loving eyes, while he studied the screen on his BlackBerry. *I ran away and right into his arms.*

Had she stayed in Jordan, her spirit would have been broken, and she would have been another sad, disenfranchised Muslim woman.

Duncan really did save me from a miserable, forgettable life. I can't return to that life. Like a child who touches a hot stove, I have learned my lesson. I have to be more careful, if I ever return to work or have to work again in the Middle East. I'll always be a target, as a tafkir. *If I were ever caught, they'd be even more brutal, heartless, and evil. They would punish me—again—for renouncing Islam. I won't go back there, ever again.*

Duncan brought his gaze from the handheld device to find Nazy lost in thought so deep it was almost a trance. He anxiously leaned into her to gently break into her train of thought.

"Hey, Baby, what are you thinking about?"

His BlackBerry buzzed and chirped several times—more email and more work.

She immediately brightened and smiled, dragging a finger along his chin. "Would you believe I was thinking how wonderful you are and how lucky I am to have you in my life?"

"That's the right answer!" He leaned over his shoulder to kiss her gently. "No thinking about work, just getting away for the vacation we never took, right?"

Nazy oozed her sexy British accent. "That's right, Duncan, and that means you, too." She pointed at his BlackBerry.

"Ah, well, yes. You're right. I have a few more emails to take care of, and then I'll shut this off. Looks like Colonel Eastwood wants to do an interview. Come to Texas to see the garage and plant."

"That doesn't sound bad. It might be fun."

"I think I can do that. He's a good guy."

"Anything else?"

As Hunter read the little handheld computer, he straightened the front of his meretricious Tommy Bahama shirt and wiggled in his seat to get more comfortable. Leaning on the armrest, he whispered, "I made Bill McGee an offer. I asked if he'd be interested in coming to Texas to join us and maybe run the garage. He might do a little IC work on the side. Captain Bill McGee could do some of the groundwork, and little old Captain Hunter could do air stuff."

"You two working together? That almost sounds, well, dangerous." Her smile was impish and conspiratorial.

Hunter nodded. A thought drew a pensive smile on his face, recalling how he told McGee, *I think he was after the gold.*

He pushed aside thoughts of dead SEALs and dead spooks. He leaned over to Nazy and asked, "Do you know what they call a group of captains? You know, like a flock of birds, a hive of bees, and an exaltation of larks?"

"Darling Duncan, I have no idea what you're talking about."

"A gathering of captains is called a conspiracy of captains."

Nazy giggled and rolled her eyes. "Oh, Baby, you two *captains* would get into so much trouble!"

He smiled slyly. "Don't I know it!" *The good captain slipped in and out of Amman and took care of some unfinished business that I couldn't.*

Nazy tried to complete her train of thought before Duncan interrupted her again. *They are evil. They plot and plan in secret. They target the defenseless and the peaceful. They're tyrants who brutalize and kill, and they will continue doing evil unless someone stops them. I don't want them here, in America.* Duncan started talking again and she was not ungrateful for the diversion.

"I got some good news and some bad news," Hunter added. "The Grinch said it looks like his predecessor was found in Amman, or what's left of him."

Incredulity and confusion overcame her. "*Really?* What do you mean?" She and Duncan grudgingly avoided TV and newspapers while on the road, but it was difficult for the conservative political junkie not to sneak peeks on his BlackBerry. Fighting terrorists and liberals would have to wait.

"It seems that Dr. Rothwell was somehow involved in the Sheraton Amman explosion of last week."

Nazy was slightly taken aback. Concern swept across her pretty face.

"I'll say it. You don't have to. No one knows what happened. They're still investigating." Duncan felt it couldn't have happened to a nicer piece of shit.

"What's the bad?"

"You mean from the new DCI? He wants to know when you're coming back to work. If I read between the lines, a high-ranking al-Qaeda turned himself in. He wants you to debrief him."

Nazy spun in her seat, immediately recoiling. "*Me?* How would he know about me?"

"I should have said Greg wants you to debrief him. The guy was their chief information officer."

"More like their chief disinformation officer." She became quiet and distant. Her eyes fell over the Dallas skyline in the hazy distance.

Hunter knew she was contemplating something.

"Duncan…."

"Yes, Baby?"

"I think I'm ready to go back to work."

"What? Are you serious? I don't think so."

"I am."

"After Bora Bora?"

She shook her head. He was confused.

"Now?" He was incredulous. Where had the change come from? He didn't understand. *That damned Lynche!*

Nazy took his hand and looked at him, seeing hurt and confusion. His concern and strife dissipated quickly, as her platinum-green eyes bored into his soul. "Yes, Duncan."

"But…."

"I know. I'm OK. The doctor said I'm doing well and I feel much better. I'm ready to go back. I'm needed."

"I *need* you, Nazy. The Grinch can wait."

"You need to go back to work, too. You can't worry about me like you have. I really am OK. I need you, too, but I'm ready to get back to work. I hope you'll understand."

Duncan looked crushed, the life drained out of him. Nazy bumped shoulders with him and smiled.

"Baby, what am I going to do with you?" he asked.

Platinum-green eyes thrilled him. Red lips said, "Love me."

"That was the plan. Romantic Bora Bora…." He wiggled in his seat, a crude hula dance.

Nazy whispered into his ear, "We need to go to the Texas Gaylord."

"Seriously?" They hadn't been intimate since her injuries. The change in her attitude was a tectonic shift.

She stroked his chin and cooed. "I'm ready."

They stared at each other for a long while almost nose-to-nose. Duncan acted like a young fool in love, stupid grin notwithstanding. Passengers moved around them, into and out of the airport lounge. Nazy and Duncan didn't talk or move. They certainly didn't look like they were going anywhere.

As the world passed around them, he finally caved in and turned off his BlackBerry before tossing it into his backpack. "Well, I hear the Gaylord is fantastic this time of year."

She said coyly, "Yes ... very fantastic." She gently rubbed her leg against his. Nazy closed her eyes and pushed aside the old painful thoughts. She regaled how salaciously Duncan would caress and lightly stroke the inside of her thighs, and how unexpectedly lascivious and exciting his fingers and mouth would ignite her, thrill her and arouse her; and how enthusiastically wet and messy it all would be. She gently shuddered and stretched her legs in anticipation.

Duncan couldn't take his eyes off her as she raked her tongue across her teeth. He'd seen that look before and thought it had died in Algeria. An eager smile rushed, "OK Baby. Let's blow this popsicle stand."

Nazy smiled, opened her eyes and filled her lungs. She dismissed and ignored the unknown American idiom; she was momentarily surprised to find they were in an airport.... She stood and kissed him.

Everyone in the lounge shifted their eyes to the burst of passion at the slowly kissing couple. Some wag who wasn't impressed by the public display of affection said loudly, "Hey, get a room!"

Nazy's lips slowly uncoupled from Duncan's. She ignored everyone in the lounge and placed loving arms around his neck. His arms encircled her waist. Their eyes locked. They rubbed noses tenderly.

"Did you hear that, Miss Cunningham?"

"I did, Mister Hunter."

"Well, then, I think we should."

She leaned close and whispered into his ear, "I'll need ... a shower."

Duncan gripped Nazy's hand and they ran out of the terminal, all the way to the airport taxi stand.

AFTERWORD

Shoot Down is a work of fiction. Some incidents, such as the circumstances of Flight 800 on July 17, 1996 and the special-purpose airframes cited, reflect historical events to provide the backdrop for the theme of this book. Any implied or specific information attributed to a specific event, location, or person is wholly manufactured by the author. Any location, aircraft, incident, company, corporation, government institution, or facility used in *Shoot Down* is either fictitious or used fictitiously. Any characters mentioned or implied in *Shoot Down,* past or present, are also either fictitious or used fictitiously.

ACRONYMS/ABBREVIATIONS

A - Attack aircraft
ABM - Air Battle Manager
ACP - Automatic Colt Pistol
AK - Automatic Kalashnikov
ANO - Abu Nidal Organization
ANVIS - Aviator Night Vision
APU - Auxiliary Power Unit
AQ - Al-Qaeda
AWACS - Airborne Warning and Control System
BCU - Battery Coolant Unit
C - Cargo aircraft
CAD - Cartridge Activated Devices
CAT - Catapult
CH - Cargo Helicopter
CIA - Central Intelligence Agency
CEO - Chief Executive Officer
CNN - Cable News Network
COS - Chief of Station
CTC - Counter Terrorism Center; short for NCTC
CV - Cargo Vertical; tilt rotor aircraft
C-4 - Composition C-4; a variety of plastic explosive
DC - District of Columbia
DC - Douglas Aircraft Company
DCI - Director of Central Intelligence
DEVGRU - Naval Special Warfare Development Group
DHS - Department of Homeland Security
DIC - Distinguished Intelligence Cross
DNA - Deoxyribonucleic acid
DO - Director of Operations

DOD - Department of Defense
DOS - Secretary of State
E - Electronic Aircraft
ETA - Estimated Time of Arrival
ER - Emergency Room
F - Fighter aircraft
F/A - Fighter/Attack aircraft
FAHD - "The Panthers" Libyan Spccial Operations Commandos
FARC - Fuerzas Armadas Revolucionarias de Colombia; the Revolutionary Armed Forces of Colombia
FBI - Federal Bureau of Investigation
FDR - Franklin Delano Roosevelt
FLIR - Forward Looking Infra-Red
G - Gravity
G - Gulfstream aircraft
GBU - Guided Bomb Unit
G-IVSP - Gulfstream Model 4, Special-purpose
G-550 - Gulfstream Model 550
GI - Government Issue
GPS - Global Positioning System
GS - General Schedule
H - Helicopter
HAVCO - Hunter Aviation Company
HH - Hospital Helicopter
HPB - Hybrid Propellant Bullets
HQ - Headquarters
HR - Human Resources
HUMINT - Human Intelligence
IC - Intelligence Community
ICBM - Intercontinental Ballistic Missile
ID - Identify/Identity/Identification
IED - Improvised Explosive Device
IO - Intelligence Officer
IP - Instructor Pilot

ISR - Intelligence, Surveillance, and Reconnaissance
IT - Information Technology
IV - Intravenous
JBD - Jet Blast Deflector
JDAM - Joint Direct Attack Munitions
JFK - John F. Kennedy International Airport
JP-5 - Jet Propellant, Navy jet fuel
JW - John Willard, for JW Marriott
K - Refueling Aircraft
KC - Refueling-Cargo Aircraft
KGB - Komitet Gosudarstvennoy Bezopasnosti; the foreign intelligence and domestic security agency of the Soviet Union
L - Lockheed Aircraft
L-100 - Lockheed Model 100
LLTV - Low-Light Television
LPU - Life Preserver Unit
LSE - Landing Signal Enlisted
LZ - Landing Zone
MASINT - Measurement and signature intelligence
MFD - Multi-Function Display
MI5 - Military Intelligence, Section 5; the domestic counter-intelligence and security agency of the United Kingdom
MO - Modus Operandi
MPH - Miles per Hour
MSL - Mean Sea Level
M4 - Carbine version of the longer barreled M16
NATO - North Atlantic Treaty Organization
NCS - National Clandestine Service
NCTC - National Counter Terrorism Center
NE - Near East Division
NEO - Noncombatant Evacuation Operation
NOFORN - Not Releasable to Foreign Nationals
NRO - National Reconnaissance Office

NSA - National Security Agency
NSC - National Security Council
NTSB - National Transportation Safety Board
O - Observation aircraft
OBL - Osama bin Laden
OCONUS - Outside the Continental United States
OJ - Orange Juice
OSS - Office of Strategic Services
PC - Printed Circuit
PDB - President's Daily Brief
POAC - Pentagon Officer's Athletic Club
POTUS - President of the United States
POW - Prisoner of War
PTSD - Post-Traumatic Stress Disorder
RPG - Rocket Propelled Grenade
RPM - Revolutions per Minute
RTB - Return to Base
QRF - Quick Reaction Force
QT - Quiet Thruster
S&T - Science and Technology
SAM - Surface to Air Missile
SAP - Special Access Program
SCI - Sensitive Compartmented Information
SCIF - Sensitive Compartmented Information Facility
SEAL - Sea, Air, Land
SECDEF - Secretary of Defense
SERE - Survival, Escape, Resistance, and Evasion
SIS - Senior Intelligence Service
SITREP - Situation report
SOCOM - Special Operations Command
SOF - Special Operations Forces
SR - Surveillance Reconnaissance aircraft; SR-71
SUV - Sport Utility Vehicle
T - Trainer Aircraft

TS - Top Secret
TSA - Transportation Security Administration
TS/SCI - Top Secret/Sensitive Compartmented Information
TV - Television
UAV - Unmanned Aerial Vehicle
U.K. - United Kingdom
UPI - United Press International
U.S. - United States
USS - United States Ship
UV - Ultra Violet
VIP - Very Important Person
VP - Vice President
V12 - V-type engine with twelve cylinders
Wilco - Will Comply
WMD - Weapon(s) of Mass Destruction
Y - Prototype aircraft
YO-3A - Prototype Observation aircraft, model 3, series A
XKE - Jaguar E-Type